SYBIL

BENJAMIN DISRAELI was born in London, in December 1804, into a prosperous Jewish family; his father was the novelist and literary historian Isaac D'Israeli. Baptized into the Church of England in 1817, he would remain an Anglican, though one with a strong sense of the Jewish roots of Christianity. After two years in a solicitor's office, he embarked on a career as a writer, publishing his first novel, *Vivian Grey*, in 1826–7 and following it with nine more novels, a long poem, and a book of political theory before becoming a Tory MP in 1837. His major trilogy of political novels, *Coningsby*, *Sybil*, and *Tancred*, was published between 1844 and 1847 and by the end of the decade he had become the effective Leader of the Opposition, a role he would fill, with brief periods of office, until 1866. He was Prime Minister in 1868 and 1874–80, published two more novels in 1870 and 1880, and was ennobled as the First Earl of Beaconsfield in 1876.

NICHOLAS SHRIMPTON is an Emeritus Fellow of Lady Margaret Hall, Oxford. He is the editor of Trollope's *An Autobiography*, *The Prime Minister*, and *The Warden* for Oxford World's Classics. His other publications include *The Whole Music of Passion: New Essays on Swinburne* (1993), *Matthew Arnold: Selected Poems* (1998), and *Ruskin and 'War'* (2014).

OXFORD WORLD'S CLASSICS

*For over 100 years Oxford World's Classics have brought
readers closer to the world's great literature. Now with over 700
titles—from the 4,000-year-old myths of Mesopotamia to the
twentieth century's greatest novels—the series makes available
lesser-known as well as celebrated writing.*

*The pocket-sized hardbacks of the early years contained
introductions by Virginia Woolf, T. S. Eliot, Graham Greene,
and other literary figures which enriched the experience of reading.
Today the series is recognized for its fine scholarship and
reliability in texts that span world literature, drama and poetry,
religion, philosophy, and politics. Each edition includes perceptive
commentary and essential background information to meet the
changing needs of readers.*

OXFORD WORLD'S CLASSICS

BENJAMIN DISRAELI

Sybil

or

The Two Nations

Edited with an Introduction and Notes by
NICHOLAS SHRIMPTON

OXFORD
UNIVERSITY PRESS

OXFORD

UNIVERSITY PRESS

Great Clarendon Street, Oxford, OX2 6DP
United Kingdom

Oxford University Press is a department of the University of Oxford.
It furthers the University's objective of excellence in research, scholarship,
and education by publishing worldwide. Oxford is a registered trade mark of
Oxford University Press in the UK and in certain other countries

Published in the United States of America by Oxford University Press
198 Madison Avenue, New York, NY 10016, United States of America

British Library Cataloguing in Publication Data

Data available

Library of Congress Control Number: 2016946842

ISBN 978-0-19-875989-8

Printed in Great Britain by
Clays Ltd, St Ives plc

CONTENTS

SYBIL

INTRODUCTION

*[Readers who are unfamiliar with the plot may prefer to treat
the Introduction as an Afterword]*

DISRAELI'S *Sybil; or, the Two Nations* is a novel which has left a
permanent mark on the language of politics. From Vladimir Lenin to
David Cameron and Theresa May, politicians have used its subtitle to
denounce the way in which societies are divided into rich and poor, or
called for a 'One Nation' politics to heal the split. Tony Blair saw his
concept of a 'stakeholder economy' as 'the economic side of the One
Nation society', while the official blog of the Tory Reform Group takes
its name, 'Egremont', from the hero of Disraeli's book.[1] Given this
remarkable political currency, it is easy to forget that *Sibyl* is actually
a love story. Charles Egremont first sees Sybil Gerard in Chapter V of
Book II, manages to meet her nine chapters later, and spends the rest of
the novel struggling to persuade her to like him. He is an Old Etonian
Tory MP and the younger brother of an Earl. She, on the other hand,
is the daughter of a Chartist factory worker and shares her father's radical views. Though he is handsome, kind, clever, brave, and, unlike Jane
Austen's Mr Darcy, never snobbishly condescending, she sees the
'gulf' between them as 'impassable'. *Sybil* is, in large part, a novel about
what it feels like to be in love with someone who disapproves of you.

That relationship is the central string of the plot. But other things
are tied to it for *Sybil* is an entertainingly heterogeneous book. In part
it is a piece of social reportage. In the general preface to the 1870 collected edition of his fiction Disraeli identified the three novels
Coningsby; or, the New Generation (1844), *Sybil; or, the Two Nations*
(1845), and *Tancred; or, the New Crusade* (1847) as 'a real Trilogy'. This
is true, though not in the usual sense that the later books are sequels:
much of the action of *Coningsby* and *Sybil* takes place simultaneously
and it is minor, not major, characters who significantly reappear.[2] A shared
theme, rather than a continuous narrative, is what makes these novels

---

[1] For Lenin see N. K. Krupskaya, *Memories of Lenin* (London: Lawrence & Wishart,
1942), p. 65; for Cameron see <https://www.gov.uk/government/speeches/election-
2015-prime-ministers-speech>; for Blair see *The Times*, 15 January 1996, p. 2; for
Egremont see <http://toryreformgroup.tumblr.com>.

[2] Coningsby, Sybil, and Tancred have dinner together, in *Tancred* Book II, Chapters
XIII–XIV, but this is an exceptional (and odd) event.

a trilogy. That theme is 'the condition of the people of this country', and 'the means by which it might be elevated and improved'. *Coningsby* discusses the nation's political parties, while *Tancred* examines its religion, or the moral grounds on which a better society might be based. *Sybil*'s purpose is to give a 'picture' of the people's current 'moral and physical condition'.[3] The farm labourers of Marney in their tumbledown cottages, the coal miners in their pithead pub, the Black Country metalworkers of Wodgate, and the textile makers of Mowbray are vividly depicted and, in some cases, strikingly characterized. These are the 'conditions' endured by the English working classes in the early years of the 'Hungry Forties'.

The claim in the 1845 'Advertisement' to *Sybil* that the descriptions had been written 'from his own observation' is, however, an exaggeration. Disraeli would certainly have seen the flax mills in Shrewsbury, his parliamentary constituency from 1841 to 1847. Elsewhere, he made a brief visit to the great cotton town of Manchester in 1843 and a slightly longer one in 1844. On the latter occasion he saw 'the miserable dwellings of the hand-loom workers',[4] before going on to stay with friends in Lancashire and Yorkshire. He visited William Standish at Duxbury Hall, Chorley (a cotton-manufacturing centre), Lord Francis Egerton at Worsley Hall (with its coal mines), William Busfeild Ferrand at Harden Grange, Bingley (notable for its woollen mills), and Monckton Milnes's family at Frystone Hall, near Wakefield (another area of mines and mills). At some point he seems also to have visited the cotton manufacturer Henry Ashworth in Bolton.[5] But these trips were country house visits, rather than serious exercises in social investigation, and Disraeli's 'picture' was chiefly drawn from written sources, often in the form of unacknowledged quotation. As one of the novel's first reviewers, W. R. Greg, pointed out, the account of 'the condition, feelings, and wants of the artisan class' was 'derived from published reports'.[6]

The leaking cottages of Marney were taken from Edwin Chadwick's *Report on the Sanitary Condition of the Labouring Population of Great Britain, 1842*. The coal miners and the tommy-shop came from *The First Report from the Midland Mining Commissioners, South Staffs* (1843).

---

[3] Benjamin Disraeli, 'General Preface', *Lothair* (London: Longmans Green, 1870), pp. viii–ix.

[4] Edmund Gosse, 'The Novels of Benjamin Disraeli', *Transactions of the Royal Society of Literature*, 36 (1918), p. 18, citing a conversation with Lord John Manners.

[5] See Rhodes Boyson, *The Ashworth Cotton Enterprise* (Oxford: Clarendon Press, 1970), pp. 257–9.   [6] *Westminster Review*, 44 (September 1845), pp. 141–52.

Wodgate is an amalgam of the descriptions of Willenhall, Sedgley, and Wolverhampton in the *Second Report of the Children's Employment Commissioners: Trades and Manufactures* (1842), while the factory workers of Mowbray and their 'Temple of the Muses' are borrowed from the account of Stockport in William Dodd's book *The Factory System Illustrated in a Series of Letters to Lord Ashley* (1842).[7] Members of Parliament were meant to read the official reports known as 'blue books' and to use their contents in speeches—when we see Charles Egremont at his desk in Book IV, Chapter V, he is surrounded by 'his parliamentary papers, and piles of blue books'. Using them in works of fiction is perhaps another matter and may offend our sense of literary originality. If not quite plagiarism, these sections of the novel are more a collage, or scrapbook, than an individual picture. But they do at least have the virtue of authenticity. With the exception of William Dodd (who was discovered to have been blackmailing manufacturers who wished to avoid adverse comment on their mills), these are the reports of disinterested social investigators and Disraeli makes apt and effective use of them.

His account of the other 'Nation', the rich, is rather different. Popular as a wit and a dandy in the high society of the 1830s, and an MP since 1837, Disraeli was thoroughly at home in the world of the wealthy. As a consequence, his picture of it has the freshness and vivacity of first-hand experience. The novel begins with a brilliant sketch of the young men about town gathered in Crockford's Club on the eve of the 1837 Derby, and follows it with a lively record of the race itself. The conversation at the dinner tables of Marney Abbey and Mowbray Castle is acutely depicted, with a waspish caricature of the campaigner for the rights of baronets, Sir Vavasour Firebrace (based on the real Sir Richard Broun), and a lethal portrait of Lord Marney as a social and intellectual bully. Dickens would have made such a figure a fool or a monster. Disraeli, more subtly, constructs him as a clever and sophisticated man who has been poisoned by privilege. Political society, in Westminster, is caught just as sharply. Ministers, MPs, and their hangers-on are here shown with a vivid verisimilitude which only an insider, like Disraeli, could have hoped to achieve. The fictional action of the novel is, indeed, mapped precisely against the political events of the

---

[7] Conditions in Marney are chiefly based on Chadwick's quotations from W. S. Gilly's book *The Peasantry of the Border: An Appeal on their Behalf* (1841), with some additional material from his own accounts of Truro, Epping, Tiverton, and Cerne; see Louis Cazamian's *The Social Novel in England, 1830–1850* (1903, translated London: Routledge and Kegan Paul, 1973), and the articles by Sheila Smith (1962, 1970) and Martin Fido (1975, 1977) listed in the Select Bibliography.

period: the lingering death of King William IV and accession of Queen Victoria in 1837, the first Kersal Moor Monster Meeting in 1838 (here moved slightly forwards into the spring of 1839), the 'Bedchamber Crisis', the presentation of the first Chartist Petition, the second Kersal Moor Meeting, and the Newport Rising in 1839, the advent of Peel's Conservative government in 1841, the Plug Plot strikes and riots in 1842, and, in the final chapter, the economic recovery of 1844. Even more remarkable is the genealogical detail used in the detective plot, as Baptist Hatton seeks to establish Sybil's aristocratic ancestry. Disraeli could easily have fabricated, or only vaguely suggested, this material. Instead, the medieval history of the Warren, Valence, and Mountchesney families is literal, specific, and remarkably accurate. Did his antiquarian father help with this research, one wonders? Or his diligent and devoted sister, Sarah? Whoever did the spade work, the result is a triumph of meticulous realism.

When Disraeli summed up *Sybil* as a 'picture', however, he was not telling the whole truth. The novel does paint, or assemble, an image of 'the moral and physical condition' of England. But it is also a tendentious, polemical book and, as such, draws on the example of the novelists of his father's generation. When Morris Speare claimed, in 1924, that 'The Political Novel was born in the prismatic mind of Benjamin Disraeli'[8] he overlooked the fact that there had been a flourishing school of political fiction in the 1790s: the 'Jacobin' and 'Anti-Jacobin' novels written by William Godwin, Thomas Holcroft, and Mary Wollstonecraft, or (in the 'Anti-Jacobin' camp) by Charlotte Smith, Elizabeth Hamilton, Henry Pye, and Disraeli's father, Isaac. D'Israeli the elder's *Vaurien: or, Sketches of the Times* (1797) is, indeed, one of the best examples of this Tory, or 'Anti-Jacobin', mode of fiction. These books were, however, more concerned with political theories than with practical problems and, by the 1830s, had been superseded by a new kind of social–protest novel, short on ideas but long on harrowing detail: Dickens's *Oliver Twist* (1837–9) and *Nicholas Nickleby* (1838–9) and Frances Trollope's *Michael Armstrong, The Factory Boy* (1839–40) are the best-known examples. Benjamin Disraeli's innovation was to combine this fashionable mode of indignant reportage with a revival of the ideological fiction of the era of the French Revolution. *Sybil* is both a report on the Condition of England and a provocative contribution to the political debate over what should be done about it.

---

[8] Morris Edmund Speare, *The Political Novel: Its Development in England and America* (New York: Oxford University Press, 1924), p. 1.

Until the early 1840s Disraeli was best known as an author. Born into a prosperous, Jewish, London family in 1804, he had published nine novels between 1826 and 1837 (one of them written jointly with his sister and issued under a pseudonym), together with a work of political theory, a good deal of polemical journalism, several poems (including the three-book *Revolutionary Epick* of 1834), numerous essays and short stories, and at least one play. Though always interested in politics, he was an unsuccessful candidate in five elections before finally winning a seat in 1837, and did not establish a reputation as an effective parliamentary debater for several years. By 1842, however, this strangely literary back bencher was beginning to emerge from the shadows. His stylish speeches were eagerly anticipated and widely reported, especially when they contained criticisms of his own party leaders. As the spokesman for 'Young England', a small but conspicuous group of recently elected Tory MPs, this dissident quality became increasingly pronounced. By May 1845, when *Sybil* was first published, he was in open revolt against the Prime Minister, Sir Robert Peel, and actively defining a distinctive political position.

To understand that distinctive position one needs to de-synonymize two terms often used identically: 'Tory' and 'Conservative'. The Tories were originally the supporters of the Stuart claim to the throne. As such, they disliked the 'Glorious Revolution' of 1688, regretted the arrival of a Hanoverian monarch in 1714, and functioned as an opposition to the dominant Whig party between 1715 and 1760. They re-emerged in the 1780s, under the leadership of William Pitt (as 'Pittites') and went on to be the party of government for more than forty years. By 1820 they were once again starting to be called 'Tories'. But in 1830 an article in the *Quarterly* suggested that 'Conservative' would be a better name.[9] The rapid adoption of the new term meant that the old one became available to identify a body of opinion which, in the 1830s, found itself increasingly at odds with the mainstream party.

The split was initially caused by a Tory government's repeal of the Test Act in 1828 and abolition of Roman Catholic disabilities in 1829: measures which removed the barriers to participation in public life by non-Anglicans. A second shock to the established conception of the British constitution was delivered in 1832 when a Whig government passed the First Reform Act. This gave votes to a new body of urban middle-class men and thereby broke the traditional link between political power and the ownership of land. How should the Tory (or Conservative)

---

[9] 'Internal Policy', *Quarterly Review*, 42 (January 1830), p. 276.

party respond to these developments? Peel's shrewd answer, in his
Tamworth Manifesto of 1834, was to welcome them. Conservatives would
accept the enlarged franchise and shed their exclusive link with Crown,
Church, and Land. The new middle-class electorate created by the
Whigs was something which his party should seek to attract and absorb.

Tories (or Ultra-Tories as they were often called) took a different view.
For them the answer was simply to reject these unwelcome innovations.
Once the party had a parliamentary majority, the Reform Act could be
repealed and the previous constitutional model restored. The Church
of England would regain its unchallenged spiritual and moral authority. The Crown, aristocracy, and landed gentry would reassume their
traditional control over public policy. While the Conservatives were in
opposition, the dispute remained an academic matter. But in 1841 they
won a General Election and formed a government. Slowly but surely
this fundamental disagreement worked its way to the surface of parliamentary debate. In the spring of 1845, while also trying to write the
second half of *Sybil*, Disraeli, in the House of Commons, led the Tory
attack on the Conservative Prime Minister, Sir Robert Peel. In February
he declared that Peel 'had caught the Whigs bathing, and walked away
with their clothes' ('Tory men and Whig measures,' as he had put it in
Coningsby the year before). In March he insisted that 'Conservative', as
distinct from Tory, government was 'an Organised Hypocrisy'. In April
he called Peel the 'great Parliamentary middleman' and called for 'the
salutary check of a constitutional Opposition'. As well as being a love
story and a picture of the condition of England, *Sybil* is an articulation
of this Tory case against the abandonment of the party's traditional
assumptions.

To reinforce his assertion of a distinctly Tory political identity,
Disraeli inserted an idiosyncratic potted history of modern England
into the third chapter of his new novel. Whig historians, with their
claims for 'progress', were entirely wrong (Lord John Manners entertainingly summarized their stock assumptions in his notice of *Sybil* in
the *Oxford and Cambridge Review*: ' "mediaeval darkness," — "Papal
tyranny," — "blessed Reformation," — "unhappy Charles," — "glorious Revolution," — "principles of the House of Brunswick," — "immortal Pitt" ').[10] Instead, Disraeli offered a Tory narrative of decline and
fall. The Whigs were an aristocratic oligarchy which had despoiled the
monasteries, destroyed the benign social system of the Middle Ages,
reduced the monarch to an impotent Venetian Doge, and treated

---

[10] [Lord John Manners], *The Oxford and Cambridge Review*, 1 (July 1845), p. 1.

government as a matter of greedy self-aggrandizement. A few heroic Tory voices had been raised against them: Bolingbroke, John Carteret, Lord Shelburne, and Edmund Burke. But Whigs, Utilitarians, and political economists had prevailed. Returning to the topic in Chapter XIV of Book IV, Disraeli argued that, 'Toryism will yet . . . bring back strength to the Crown, liberty to the Subject, and . . . announce that power has only one duty: to secure the social welfare of the PEOPLE.' This is not the negative, or exclusive, version of 'One Nation' theory which argues that the ideal is to be achieved by the elimination of the privileged classes. Rather, it is a belief in the existence, both in the past and potentially in the future, of a mutually supportive and harmonious social hierarchy.

This dispute involved matters of current social policy as well as historical and constitutional issues. The Whig government of 1830 did not just reform the franchise, it also transformed the welfare system. The Tories were the chief opponents of this 'New Poor Law' of 1834, a measure which took the relief of poverty away from individual parishes and transferred it to impersonal 'Unions' or regional workhouses. Peel's refusal to abolish it after his victory in 1841 ('Peel, in or out, will support the Poor-Law,' the Conservative Lord Marney cheerfully observes in Book II, Chapter I of *Sybil*) was bitterly held against him. More generally, the Tories saw the middle class as selfish and socially irresponsible. Unlike the old landed gentry who, in principle at least, accepted a duty of care towards the people who worked on their estates, the owners of the new mills and factories had no traditionally established responsibility for the well-being of their workforce. As a consequence, it was Tory politicians, like Richard Oastler, Michael Sadler, and Lord Ashley (later Shaftesbury), who led the parliamentary campaigns for factory legislation and protection of the poor. In Oastler's words, in 1841, 'A Tory is one who, believing that the institutions of this country are calculated . . . to secure the prosperity and happiness of every class of society, wishes to maintain them in their original beauty, simplicity and integrity.'[11] Peel wished to draw the new bourgeoisie into the ambit of the Conservative Party. Tories believed that the industrialists' exploitation of their employees, as documented in the blue books, made the case for a return to a parliamentary system which denied them political power and gave it, instead, to a benign monarch and an altruistic landed aristocracy.

[11] *Fleet Papers* 1 (23 January 1841) quoted in John Ward, *W. B. Ferrand: 'The Working Man's Friend'* (East Linton: Tuckwell Press, 2002), p. 219.

Given this, it was a brave step to make the rural poverty of the country town of Marney the first example of 'the condition of the People' in *Sybil*. But here we are moving from parliamentary politics to a deeper, cultural battle. Disraeli knew perfectly well that the actual aristocrats of the period rarely corresponded to his benevolent ideal. This, however, simply meant that the aristocracy required reform, as well as the political system, and in both cases the change involved a return to a previous condition. The constitution needed to revert to its state in 1827, or 1687 if the Whig innovations of the eighteenth century were to be erased. The aristocracy needed to go back still further: to the Christian Middle Ages. *Coningsby*, *Sybil*, and *Tancred* are an expression, not just of Toryism, but of Romantic medievalism.

In its early stages Romanticism had been closely linked to the revolutionary spirit of the 1790s, and in the poetry of Shelley and Byron that radical note continued to be heard. But by the 1830s Romantic culture was increasingly identified with tradition rather than innovation, and with the rediscovery of the medieval past. As early as 1790 Edmund Burke had lamented the way in which 'ten thousand swords' had failed to leap from their scabbards to defend Marie Antoinette from the French revolutionaries, for, alas, 'The age of chivalry is gone,' and, 'that of sophisters, oeconomists, and calculators, has succeeded'.[12] Since then, Chateaubriand's *Génie du christianisme* (1802), Kenelm Henry Digby's *The Broadstone of Honour* (1822), Southey's *Colloquies on the Progress and Prospects of Society* (1829), Victor Hugo's *Notre Dame de Paris* (1831), Carlyle's *Past and Present* (1843), and, above all, the novels and poems of Sir Walter Scott had put an enthusiasm for the art and society of the Middle Ages at the forefront of avant-garde thought.

Disraeli's friends in the 'Young England' group of Tory MPs combined their commitment to the constitution of pre-1688 Stuart England with an equally outspoken medievalism. Lord John Manners published his pamphlet *A Plea for National Holy-Days* in 1843, arguing for the return of 'Maypoles' and the festivals of 'Merry England'. Speaking at Birmingham in August 1844 he regretted the end of 'feudalism' and deplored 'the unhappy separation of the classes which now existed'. Most famously, in his poem 'England's Trust' in 1841 he praised the

---

[12] Edmund Burke, *Reflections on the Revolution in France* (1790), from *The Writings and Speeches of Edmund Burke* (Oxford: Clarendon Press, 9 vols, 1981–2000), Vol. 8, *The French Revolution 1790–1794*, ed. L. G. Mitchell (1989), pp. 126–7.

aristocracy of the era of 'Crecy and Poictiers' (that is, the mid-fourteenth century) and exclaimed:

> Let wealth and commerce, laws and learning die,
> But leave us still our old Nobility![13]

This ideal view of the medieval aristocracy had been encouraged by Digby's *The Broadstone of Honour*, first published in 1822 but enlarged and reissued in four volumes (*Godefridus*, *Tancredus*, *Morus*, and *Orlandus*) between 1826 and 1829. The original subtitle, 'Rules for the Gentlemen of England', suggests the reason for its popularity: it was seen as a handbook for the newly wealthy and socially ambitious upper-middle classes. Its subsequent subtitle, 'The True Sense and Practice of Chivalry', indicates where those rules were to be found: in the behaviour of what Chaucer had called the 'veray parfit gentil' knights of the Middle Ages. Tancredus, for example, after whom the eponymous hero of Disraeli's *Tancred* would be named, was a Norman knight from southern Italy who served in the First Crusade. Using material from the *Gesta Tancredi* of Ralph of Caen, Digby presents him as a figure of 'heroic devotion . . . accompanied with the greatest humanity and moderation'. His contemporary Godfrey de Bouillon (Godefridus) is 'bountiful to the poor, merciful to those who were in fault; distinguished by humility, humanity, soberness, [and] justice'.[14]

In Disraeli's account, the noble families of medieval England had for the most part died out during the Wars of the Roses and the aristocracy created to replace them was merely 'pseudo Norman' (Book III, Chapter X). These men, Tudor functionaries like the Marneys or Nabobs like the Mowbrays, had acquired estates without accepting the feudal obligations which went with them. But a 'New Generation' (the subtitle of *Coningsby*) would soon supplant them and provide the chivalric leadership needed to reunite the nation. Medieval precedents were crucial to Gothic Revival architecture and Pre-Raphaelite painting, the most exciting modern art of the 1840s. In the same way, it seemed, the imitation of medieval models would be the best basis for an effective modern politics.

Important though it is, the medievalist argument of *Sybil* is actually a curious mixture of two different theories. One is the old notion of

[13] See Lord John Manners, MP, *A Plea for National Holy-Days* (London: Painter, 1843), pp. 14–15; *The Times*, 4 September 1844, p. 5; *England's Trust and Other Poems* (London: Rivington, 1841), p. 24.

[14] Kenelm Henry Digby, *The Broad Stone of Honour, The Second Book, Tancredus* (London: Joseph Booker, 1828), pp. 6 and 26.

'The Norman Yoke'. This was the claim that the common people of Anglo-Saxon England had enjoyed political rights which were stolen from them by their Norman conquerors. Used by the Levellers in the 1640s (Disraeli mentions their spokesman John Wildman in Book I, Chapter III), the idea was memorably dramatized by Sir Walter Scott in his novel *Ivanhoe* (1819). Set in the England of the late twelfth century, the book depicts a nation split, socially and linguistically, between Saxon serfs and Norman rulers. In the first chapter two Saxons, Gurth and Wamba, discuss the way in which 'swine' and 'oxen' are referred to by Anglo-Saxon words as long as they are the responsibility of farm-workers but become the French 'pork' (porc) and 'beef' (boeuf) when they arrive on the tables of their Norman landlords. Wamba sums up the issue in a piece of indignant doggerel in Chapter 27:

> Norman saw on English oak,
> On English neck a Norman yoke;
> Norman spoon in English dish,
> And England ruled as Normans wish.[15]

Sybil Gerard and her father are, initially at least, strongly associated with the Saxon, rather than the Norman—so much so that it is easy to assume that they are meant (like Ivanhoe in Scott's novel) to be the living descendants of an Anglo-Saxon family. Walter Gerard takes 'a cup of the drink of Saxon kings' (beer) in Book II, Chapter VIII, and, thirteen chapters later, wishes that 'the battle of Hastings were to be fought over again, and I was going to have a hand in it'. Sybil's dog is called Harold, after the Saxon king killed in that battle, and, when Charles first visits her, she is reading Augustin Thierry's *History of the Conquest of England by the Normans* (1825). The wretched inhabitants of Marney are 'a Saxon peasantry' (Book II, Chapter III), just as the working people championed by the Chartists are identified as a 'Saxon multitude' in Book V, Chapter I. Even the young Queen Victoria is seen, in Book I, Chapter VI, as having 'the blood and beauty of the Saxon'. She will 'inspire troubadours and guerdon knights' to 'break the last links in the chain of Saxon thraldom'.

But the theory of the Norman Yoke was, by the 1840s, beginning to seem old-fashioned. It was associated with calls for the extension of the franchise, and Tories were paternalists not democrats. It had been cast into doubt by recent historical research. Above all, it was incompatible

---

[15] Sir Walter Scott, *Ivanhoe, a Romance* (1819), ed. A. N. Wilson (London: Penguin, 1984), pp. 14–15 and 286.

with the new medievalism which celebrated the High Gothic world of the later Middle Ages. If the Normans had ruined everything, how could the thirteenth and fourteenth centuries have been so wonderful? Accordingly, the suggestion of a Saxon identity for the Gerard family gradually disappears. One of their ancestors had been, in the sixteenth century, the last Abbot of Marney. But that did not mean that he was a Saxon, and when the nineteenth-century Walter Gerard boasts about his ancestry it is to say that 'we were tall men in King John's reign' (that is, in the era of *Ivanhoe*, 130 years after the Conquest) and 'drew a bow at Azincourt' (in 1415). Baptist Hatton's researches into the history of the Gerards suggest that they are actually related to the Valence family, the Norman earls of Pembroke (Book IV, Chapter X).

The symbolic implications of the marriage between Egremont and Sybil are, as a consequence, rather more complicated than critics of the novel have tended to assume. An upper-class man marries the daughter of a Chartist factory worker, thereby suggesting the possible reconciliation of the 'Two Nations'. But she isn't working-class really because she turns out to be an aristocrat. She is not even a Saxon aristocrat but a direct descendant of the invaders. It seems to be a lazy compromise and, as such, has led to the frequent accusation that the novel's argument is inconsistent. Richard Monckton Milnes made this point as early as 1847 in an article in the *Edinburgh Review* ('no better means of amalgamating the alienated classes are discovered, than the alliance of two persons—who turn out both to belong to the upper one')[16] and it became a stock criticism of *Sybil* in the second half of the twentieth century. John Lucas, in 1966, insisted that the discovery of the heroine's noble pedigree means that 'the whole idea of the rich and poor being reunited goes out of the window'.[17] For Patrick Brantlinger, in 1977, the 'symbolic union . . . turns into tommyrot' and the novel as a whole is so 'riddled with irony' that it ends up as 'a skein of contradictions'. Even the subtitle was, in his account, ironic because the 'Two Nations' phrase is spoken, within the book, not by the author but by Stephen Morley, of whom Disraeli disapproved.[18] Catherine Gallagher, in 1985, writing with a deconstructor's enthusiasm for the discovery of

[16] [Richard Monckton Milnes], 'Mr D'Israeli's *Tancred*—the Emancipation of the Jews', *Edinburgh Review* 86 (July 1847), p. 142.

[17] John Lucas, 'Mrs. Gaskell and Brotherhood', in David Howard, John Lucas, and John Goods, eds, *Tradition and Tolerance in Nineteenth-Century Fiction* (London: Routledge and Kegan Paul, 1966), p. 157.

[18] Patrick Brantlinger, *The Spirit of Reform* (Cambridge, Mass.: Harvard University Press, 1977), pp. 96–104.

contradiction, enlarged these points into a claim that the novel was so universally ironic that its arguments dissolved into 'meaninglessness'.[19]

The sense that Disraeli made extensive use of irony was not new: Leslie Stephen had drawn attention to it in 1874, noting that we are sometimes uncertain whether Disraeli is taking himself seriously or not.[20] But 'sometimes' is not the same thing as 'always' and John Holloway gave the most sensible account of the matter in 1953: 'Disraeli's farcical and fantastic touches are a kind of safety-valve; they provide for scepticism because they do not have to be taken in full seriousness . . . they provide for a margin of disagreement within the frame of a general agreement.'[21] The ironies, in other words, are incidental and salutary. As for contradiction, even Gallagher had seen the symbolic marriage as a Coleridgean union of Church and State rather than of rich and poor, while Robert O'Kell suggested that it was of 'secular leadership to the spirit of piety and devotion'.[22] The truth, I think, is a rather more literal version of these claims. The wedding is a union of Saxon and Norman, with the roles unexpectedly reversed. Sybil turns out to be the Norman. Charles Egremont, correspondingly, is really Saxon and the significance of their partnership is not a merging of rich and poor (which Disraeli did not believe in) but an enaction of his Tory views. The High Gothic ideal which had replaced the theory of the 'Norman Yoke' saw a cultural development in the twelfth and thirteenth centuries which was achieved, in the words of the historian Sharon Turner, 'by the Norman graft on its original Saxon stock'.[23] Norman and Saxon had blended, or married, to produce the model society of the later Middle Ages.

Scott had actually begun to suggest this in *Ivanhoe*, where he spelt the idea out in linguistic terms by describing 'the gradual formation of a dialect, compounded betwixt the French and the Anglo-Saxon', from which arose 'the structure of our present English language, in which the speech of the victors and the vanquished have been so happily blended

[19] Catherine Gallagher, *The Industrial Reformation of English Fiction* (Chicago: University of Chicago Press, 1985), pp. 203–7.

[20] Leslie Stephen, 'Mr Disraeli's Novels', *Fortnightly Review*, 22 (October 1874), reprinted in his *Hours in a Library* (London: Smith Elder, 1892), 2.109–10.

[21] John Holloway, *The Victorian Sage* (London: Macmillan, 1953), p. 105.

[22] See Robert O'Kell, *Disraeli: The Romance of Politics* (Toronto: University of Toronto Press, 2013), p. 260, and Gallagher, *The Industrial Reformation*, p. 215.

[23] Sharon Turner, Preface to 6th edition (1836) of his *History of the Anglo-Saxons* (first published 1799–1805; London: Longman, 1836), p. ii. Turner was Disraeli's godfather, when he was baptized in 1817.

together'.[24] Disraeli enacts the concept in the marriage of Sybil and Charles. Jointly they become what Aubrey St Lys, the vicar of Mowbray, already is, 'the Norman tempered by the Saxon' (Book II, Chapter XI), and an embodiment of 'the baronial principle' (Book III, Chapter VIII). Wodgate, with its pagan Saxon name, shows us a 'natural' aristocracy, in a state not yet refined by 'the Norman graft'. Lord Marney and Lord Mowbray are aristocracy in its decadent, post-Christian form. Charles and Sybil, in conjunction, represent the ideal. Tories, Disraeli asserts in his *Vindication of the English Constitution* (1835), 'looked upon the nation as a family'.[25] Just as families are not egalitarian systems but hierarchies led by parents, so, in this social model, the poor should be protected by a benign and enlightened aristocracy.

Ivanhoe's more old-fashioned Norman Yoke material was, nonetheless, important to the invention of Disraeli's subtitle. In itself, the phrase 'two nations' was a commonplace. It occurs again and again in the newspapers and parliamentary debates of the 1840s, usually with reference to Britain and France or England and Ireland. Disraeli's innovation was to apply it, paradoxically, only to England. Scott's portrait of an English society divided, in the late twelfth century, into Saxon and Norman ethnic groups clearly helped with this conception. Warnings about the gulf between rich and poor were also very frequent. Young England often spoke in such terms, as Lord John Manners had done at Birmingham in August 1844. But the most resonant statements came from another branch of the Ultra Tories: the Radical Tories of the north who had been fighting to improve working conditions in factories since Richard Oastler's famous 'Yorkshire Slavery' letter to the *Leeds Mercury* in September 1830. In Parliament the most eloquent of these campaigners was William Busfeild Ferrand, with whom Disraeli stayed at Bingley in October 1844. Busfeild was a Keighley solicitor who in 1839 inherited the estates, and adopted the surname, of his maternal uncle. On a cold morning in the early 1830s he had found 'a little factory slave half-buried in a snow-drift' on its way to work and, 'From that hour . . . became a "Ten Hours Bill" man and the unflinching advocate of "protection to native industry!" '[26] In 1841 he became Tory MP for Knaresborough and on 28 September, in the House of Commons, attacked the New Poor Law. Insisting that 'wealth has its

---

[24] *Ivanhoe* (Harmondsworth: Penguin, 1984), p. 9.

[25] Disraeli the Younger, *Vindication of the English Constitution in a Letter to a Noble and Learned Lord* (London: Sanders and Otley, 1835), p. 24.

[26] Ferrand's public letter to the Duke of Newcastle, January 1852, quoted in Ward, *W. B. Ferrand*, p. 11.

duties, as well as its rights', he went on to denounce the truck system and, standing in the House, tore up a piece of cloth full of what he called 'devil's dust'.²⁷ In December 1843, speaking in Manchester, Ferrand declared that:

We are now divided, as nearly as possible, into two classes—the very rich and the very poor. Search history, and you will learn that no country can long exist in which society is broken into such widely distant divisions.²⁸

The northern Tories were more substantial allies than the little group of 'Young England' enthusiasts, and Disraeli increasingly identified himself with them. In *Sybil* he combined Ferrand's account of division into two economic 'classes' with Scott's description of a split between two ethnic groups to create his memorable phrase 'Two Nations'. This real but unhappy condition was the result of a Whig view of society as a mere aggregation of rationally self-interested individuals. A paternalist policy of benign rule by dutiful aristocrats would, he suggests, reunite the alienated classes into a single national family.

Despite their humane intentions, the Tories were, of course, controversial even in their own day. Trollope, speaking as a Whig, dismissed their agenda as 'tests and qualifications, rotten boroughs, and the divine right of kings'.²⁹ Marx and Engels saw the 'bitter, witty and incisive criticism' produced by Young England writers as a 'Feudal Socialism' hampered by its 'incapacity to comprehend the march of modern history'.³⁰ Though authors like Carlyle and Ruskin would still be recommending such views in the 1870s, Disraeli, as a practical politician, was soon obliged to reconsider his opinions. In May 1846 he would lead the attack on Peel's abolition of the Corn Laws and, a month later, would defeat the government on its Irish Coercion Bill, thereby splitting the Conservative Party and denying it a majority for almost thirty years. By the early 1850s, however, it was clear that the repeal of the Corn Laws had not, in fact, harmed British agriculture and that Oastler's appeal to 'Altar, Throne and Cottage' was no longer a viable political programme. Disraeli's response was, in the eyes of his enemies, a hypocritical adoption of Peelite policies. A more sympathetic view

---

²⁷ Ward, *W. B. Ferrand*, pp. 30–2, quoting *Hansard* and the reminiscences of Alexander Baillie-Cochrane.   ²⁸ Ward, *W. B. Ferrand*, p. 54.

²⁹ Anthony Trollope, *The Prime Minister* (Oxford: Oxford University Press, 2011), p. 252.

³⁰ Karl Marx and Friedrich Engels, *Manifesto of the Communist Party* (London, in German, 1848; translated by Samuel Moore, 1888; New Haven: Yale University Press, 2012, ed. Jeffrey C. Isaac), p. 93.

would be that, once he had recognized their validity, he took on the laborious duty of 'educating the party' to accept them, a task which Peel had neglected when he suddenly changed tack on agricultural protection in 1846.[31] Henceforth Disraeli's Toryism would be, not the Bolingbrokean model of return to a previous state, but the Burkean concept of evolutionary social change. In 1858 a Tory minority government, with Disraeli as its Chancellor of the Exchequer, would pass one of the points of the Charter (the abolition of property qualifications for MPs) into law. In 1867 it would be Disraeli, as the Prime Minister of another minority administration, who carried the Second Reform Bill. In the 1870s, as Prime Minister of the first Conservative majority government since 1846, he would chair a cabinet responsible for a series of major social reforms: two important Trade Union Acts (one of which legalized peaceful picketing), the Artisans Dwellings Act, a Public Health Act, the Agricultural Holdings Act, an Act to safeguard the funds of Friendly Societies, a Sale of Food and Drugs Act, an Elementary Education Act, a Merchant Shipping Act, and the Factory and Workshops Act of 1878 which finally established the 'ten-hour' limit on the working day. Some commentators have seen this as an eventual fulfilment of the dreams of *Sybil*. But Disraeli was old, ill, and no longer interested in detail, and the reforms of 1874–6 can alternatively be seen as measures designed to quieten the working-class discontent that might otherwise have troubled the middle-class supporters whom the party had, at last, acquired.[32]

Sybil is also controversial as a work of art. Its prose can be florid and its manner is sometimes melodramatic or stagy. Trollope, speaking as a novelist, condemned Disraeli's fiction as 'the glory of pasteboard, and . . . a wealth of tinsel'.[33] It would have been a kindness to readers if Disraeli had taken the trouble to invent less similar names than Marney, Mowbray, and Morley for major characters, while the plots have some awkward loose ends. The 'Arabella' who is the wife of Charles Egremont's brother turns out to have been the woman with whom Charles himself had been in love when he was 'four-and-twenty'. But this is not explained at the time and we are given a very slight account

[31] See Norman Gash in Lord Butler, ed., *The Conservatives* (London: George Allen & Unwin, 1977), pp. 102–6.

[32] See Paul Smith, *Disraelian Conservatism and Social Reform* (London: Routledge & Kegan Paul, 1967), pp. 321–3, and Robert Blake, *Disraeli* (London: Eyre & Spottiswoode, 1966), pp. 553–6.

[33] Anthony Trollope, *An Autobiography and Other Writings* (Oxford: Oxford University Press, 2014), p. 161.

of the subsequent relationship between Charles and his sister-in-law. The attempted murder at the end of Book III is another oddly undeveloped narrative motif. As Charles walks to the station, in the fog, a 'dark enemy' tries to throw him over a cliff. Though we assume that this 'mysterious and unseen foe' is the jealous Stephen Morley, the matter is forgotten until Morley's deathbed confession, thirty-eight chapters later.

More seriously, there is a flaw in the inheritance plot by which Sybil inherits the Mowbray estate. Since Baptist Hatton is an antiquary who provides genealogical evidence for peerage cases, we can assume that his argument for Sybil's claim to the Mowbray title (Book IV, Chapter XIII) is sound. Her claim to the Mowbray land is, however, an entirely different matter. The Warrens bought it, apparently in good faith though with what has turned out to be an imperfect legal title, during 'the throes of Lord North's administration' (the early 1780s); the 'deed of '77' (Book IV, Chapter XIII) which indicates a flawed conveyance has subsequently been acquired and hidden in their castle. But since they have occupied the estate for more than twenty years (both before and after the discovery of the deed) the legal doctrine of adverse possession (under the Real Property Limitation Acts 1833) would override the paper title and establish their ownership. The reader is not meant to notice this and it is thematically appropriate that the 'New Generation' of ideal aristocrats should, at the end of the novel, own and control Mowbray. It is, however, an error or, at least, an unacknowledged difficulty. Though Hatton is so convincingly villainous that the brilliant motif of his stroking a 'white Persian cat' would be borrowed for the evil genius of the James Bond movies, his grasp of land law seems to be imperfect.

In other respects, *Sybil* is constructed very skilfully. The town of Mowbray, for example, is an ingenious combination of Yorkshire and Lancashire, blending Bingley and Kersal moors, Ripon and Manchester churches, and woollen and cotton mills to encapsulate the whole of the textile industry which was both the powerhouse and the moral problem of the Early Victorian economy. There are some telling symbolic effects: the mazurka being danced at a Park Lane party while a Polish émigré sleeps rough outside, or the broken statue of Cupid in the melancholy garden behind the house in Smith Square where Charles makes his unsuccessful proposal to Sybil. And the book as a whole is neatly shaped by the clever use of a minor character. Opening with the affected disappointment of Alfred Mountchesney ('one gets so bored with good wine'), it ends with his real disappointment, as the heiress he has married loses her fortune. Disraeli formed his manner as a novelist in the 1820s, ten years before Dickens began *The Pickwick Papers*, and his model was the satirical fiction of Thomas Love Peacock, with its thinly veiled portraits of real people, slight plots, and sprawling dialogue.[34] *Sybil* combines the satirical zest of Peacock with an early version of the stronger narrative and more sophisticated structure which would become customary in the great realist novels of the mid-Victorian period: the works (all later in date than *Sybil*) of the Brontës, Thackeray, the mature Dickens, Trollope, and George Eliot.

The novels with which *Sybil* is most often directly compared are the 'Condition of England' texts of the late 1840s and early 1850s: Elizabeth Gaskell's *Mary Barton* (1848) and *North and South* (1855), Charles Kingsley's *Yeast* (1848) and *Alton Locke* (1850), and Dickens's *Hard Times* (1854). *Sybil* pre-dates these books as well, yet is not liable to one of the key criticisms made of them: that they have no answer to the problems which they indignantly depict.[35] One may not consider Disraeli's Tory view to be the right one—Liberals might invoke the self-healing powers of the market, while many critics would clearly prefer a Socialist solution, either revolutionary or Fabian. It is, however, unquestionably an answer, with a parliamentary programme to back it up.

Sybil is effective in other ways as well. It is both exceptionally well informed and richly informative. The story can be read as a helpful guidebook to the early years of the Chartist movement, with a lively sketch of the Plug Plot riots of 1842 and a good, if unsympathetic, account of the views of an Owenite or Thompsonian socialist. The understanding of trade unionism may be limited and the heroine's conversion from Moral Force Chartism to Ultra Toryism is, perhaps, achieved too easily. But *Sybil* also gives us a provocative alternative to the Whig interpretation of English history, an insider's view of parliamentary life in the earliest years of the Victorian era, and a memorable account of

[34] Disraeli told the older novelist, in 1848, that he saw him as his 'master'. Peacock's response, in a subsequent conversation with John Cam Hobhouse, was, 'I did not know he was my pupil'; see Lord Broughton, *Recollections of a Long Life*, ed. Lady Dorchester (1911), here quoted from James Ogden, *Isaac Disraeli* (Oxford: Oxford University Press, 1969), p. 61.

[35] See, for example, Raymond Williams: 'Sympathy was transformed, not into action, but into withdrawal' (*Culture and Society 1780–1950* (London: Chatto & Windus, 1967), p. 109), though Williams did find a 'solution', albeit a malign one, in *Sybil* where he interpreted the marriage between Sybil and Charles as the Peelite alliance between the industrial and landed classes which the New Left deplored. This, of course, overlooks Disraeli's nineteenth-century assumption that husbands rule wives.

the political medievalism of the 1840s—without ceasing, in the process, to be both a touching love story and an entertaining piece of detective fiction. This is a witty, engrossing, and, above all, intelligent book which shows how argument, narrative, and the expression of controversial opinions can combine to create the successful novel of ideas.

NOTE ON THE TEXT

DISRAELI began work on *Sybil* in August 1844, just three months after the successful publication of *Coningsby*. Though the parliamentary session would not end until 5 September, Thomas Duncombe borrowed a file of Chartist material from Feargus O'Connor for him in early August (probably 3 August 1844; *Letters*, 4.146), and on 15 August George Smythe wrote to ask, 'How are the two Nations?' (*Letters*, 4.144). Disraeli moved from London to Bradenham (his father's house in Buckinghamshire) on 31 August and stayed there until January 1845, except for a visit to his constituency, Shrewsbury, at the end of August, and a trip to Lancashire and Yorkshire in October. On 29 November 1844, he wrote from Bradenham to Lord John Manners to say that:

I get on to my satisfaction; but authors are not the best critics of their own productions; I am more anxious about your opinion than my own. The sustained labor is however very painful: & I am daily more convinced, that there is no *toil* like literature. However once in &c. It is too late to moralize—I want to clear the deck if I can by end of Jany:, for action & speculation will never blend (*Letters*, 4.151).

Disraeli and his wife moved back to their London house, 1 Grosvenor Gate, on 3 January 1845 but he did not manage to 'clear the deck' before the next parliamentary session began on 4 February. On 25 January 1845, indeed, he was still conducting research for *Sybil*, since he wrote then to Lord Lansdowne to ask for information about his father, Lord Shelburne, for 'a work wh[ich] now engages my attention' (*Letters*, 4.155) and Lansdowne's courteous reply on 29 January (*Letters*, 4.155) appears to have influenced the account of Shelburne in Book I, Chapter III. Though Disraeli may here have been checking and correcting a passage drafted earlier, much of the novel would be written in February, March, and April 1845 while he was also heavily involved in controversial parliamentary business. On 6 February 1845 he wrote to his sister Sarah, 'I write a line, very tired . . . I am at p.600 & 300 more will do it well, wh: allowing for chaps &c. makes a short 1000—long eno'' (*Letters*, 4.156–7).

Henry Colburn, Disraeli's publisher, announced *Sybil* as 'In the press' (in an advertisement which included its wrongly attributed epigraph) on 27 March 1845 (*The Times*). It was, however, still 'In the press' a month later (*The Times*, 23 April 1845) and 'Just ready' a week after that (*The Times*, 1 May 1845). Disraeli's letter to his sister Sarah on 1 May 1845 (written from Crockford's gambling club) makes it clear that the delay was his fault:

Sybil was finished yesterday. I thought it never cd. be—the printers were on my heels & have been for the last month—but I don't think it can be published till the middle of the month. I can't send the rough proofs; they would destroy the illusion, & I have no clean sheets, nor do I think there are any yet dry, as we have only commenced striking off within these ten days. I have never been thro' such a four months, & hope never again. What with the House of Commons wh: was itself quite eno' for a man & writing 600 pages, I thought sometimes my head must turn—& this must be my excuse for not having written wh: was clearly impossible. I have never had a day until this that I have felt as it were home for the holidays. (*Letters*, 4.163–4).

Disraeli's belief on 6 February that he could complete the book in '300' pages had clearly proved to be over-optimistic: in practice it had required another '600 pages', all written during the parliamentary session, to bring the novel to a satisfactory conclusion.

Review and presentation copies appear to have been sent out on 9 May 1845: *The Times* printed the first section of its two-part review on 13 May, on which day Colburn advertised the book as 'Now ready'. Though Colburn's accounts record publication on 9 May (*Letters*, 4.164), it would not be until 3 June that he advertised it for sale as 'published this day' (*The Times*). The first edition was of 1,000 copies; the manuscript is at Hughenden Manor (National Trust).

A second edition (of 1,000 copies; *Letters*, 1.164) was advertised as 'Now ready' on 7 July 1845 (*The Times*) and a third on 5 August; this third edition (of 500 copies) was 'published this day' on 15 August (*The Times*). A one-volume English edition ('Sanctioned by the Author for Continental Circulation') was published in Leipzig by Bernhard Tauchnitz Jun., as Volume 83 of his 'Collection of British Authors' series, also in 1845. A three-volume German translation by Dr Fr. Hermann appeared in 1846 (*Sybil oder die bieden Nationen* von B. d'Israeli—Parlamentsmitglied.—Verfasser von *Coningsby*, Grimma Verlags-Comptoir, 1846). The first of the French translations was published in 1847; the version made 'Sous la direction de P. Lorain' was 'Traduit avec l'autorisation de l'auteur' (Paris: Hachette, 1869). A five-reel silent film of *Sybil* would appear in 1921 (directed by Jack Denton, adapted by Colden Lore, and with Evelyn Brent and Cowley Wright as Sybil and Charles); the film is now lost.

A ten-volume Uniform Edition of Disraeli's novels would be published in 1853 by David Bryce (who had worked as Disraeli's private secretary since 1849; *Letters*, 5.184). Textual corrections were made for this edition (nominally by the author, in practice by his sister Sarah), chiefly in order to remove embarrassing material from the early novels *Vivian Grey* (1827) and *The Young Duke* (1831). These revised texts were used for the Longmans Collected Edition of 1870–1 and have been followed in most modern reprints.

This edition of *Sybil* returns to the text of the first edition of 1845. A few changes made in the 1853 edition are adopted, silently when they are corrections of obvious printers' errors or slips of the pen; some substantive changes are recorded in the Explanatory Notes but not adopted. The original punctuation is altered only on the rare occasions when it is likely to mislead or annoy the modern reader. The same policy has been adopted with Disraeli's spelling: 'eat' becomes 'ate', and 'potatoe' becomes 'potato', but for the most part his idiosyncratic usage is retained. In accordance with modern practice, the names of political parties ('tory', 'whig', 'conservative', 'chartist') are given initial capital letters. In other respects, however, this edition prints the text of this topical novel in the form in which it was received by its original readers in the summer of 1845.

SELECT BIBLIOGRAPHY

Life and Letters

Benjamin Disraeli Letters, ed. M. G. Wiebe et al. (Toronto: Toronto University Press, 1982–present).

Blake, Robert, *Disraeli* (London: Eyre & Spottiswoode, 1966).

Jerman, B. R., *The Young Disraeli* (Princeton: Princeton University Press, 1960).

Monypenny, W. F., and Buckle, G. E., *The Life of Benjamin Disraeli, Earl of Beaconsfield* (rev. edn, 2 vols, London: John Murray, 1929).

Ogden, James, *Isaac D'Israeli* (Oxford: Clarendon Press, 1969).

Richmond, Charles, and Smith, Paul, eds, *The Self-Fashioning of Disraeli 1818–51* (Cambridge: Cambridge University Press, 1998).

Historical and Political Background

Berlin, Isaiah, 'Benjamin Disraeli, Karl Marx and the Search for Identity', in his *Against the Current*, ed. Henry Hardy (London: Pimlico, 1997).

Boyson, Rhodes, *The Ashworth Cotton Enterprise: The Rise and Fall of a Family Firm 1818–1880* (Oxford: Clarendon Press, 1970).

Chandler, Alice, *A Dream of Order: The Medieval Ideal in Nineteenth-Century English Literature* (London: Routledge & Kegan Paul, 1970).

Faber, Richard, *Beaconsfield and Bolingbroke* (London: Faber and Faber, 1961).

Faber, Richard, *Young England* (London: Faber and Faber, 1987).

Gash, Norman, *Politics in the Age of Peel: A Study in the Technique of Parliamentary Representation, 1830–1850* (London: Longmans, Green, 1953).

Gash, Norman, *Reaction and Reconstruction in English Politics 1832–1852* (Oxford: Clarendon Press, 1965).

Gash, Norman, 'From the Origins to Sir Robert Peel', in Lord Butler, ed., *The Conservatives: A History from their Origins to 1965* (London: George Allen & Unwin, 1977).

Girouard, Mark, *The Return to Camelot: Chivalry and the English Gentleman* (New Haven: Yale University Press, 1981).

Hawkins, Angus, *Victorian Political Culture: 'Habits of Heart and Mind'* (Oxford: Oxford University Press, 2015).

Hill, Christopher, 'The Norman Yoke', in his *Puritanism and Revolution* (London: Secker & Warburg, 1958).

Morrow, John, ed., *Young England: The New Generation* (London: Leicester University Press, 1999).

Simmons, Clare, *Reversing the Conquest: History and Myth in Nineteenth-Century British Literature* (Brunswick, NJ: Rutgers University Press, 1988).

Smith, Paul, *Disraelian Conservatism and Social Reform* (London: Routledge & Kegan Paul, 1967).

Southgate, Donald, *The Passing of the Whigs 1832–1886* (London: Macmillan, 1962).

Southgate, Donald, 'From Disraeli to Law', in Lord Butler, ed., *The Conservatives: A History from their Origins to 1965* (London: George Allen & Unwin, 1977).

Ward, John Towers, *The Factory Movement 1830–55* (London: Macmillan, 1962).

Ward, John Towers, *W. B. Ferrand 'The Working Man's Friend' 1809–89*, edited and with an introduction by Norman Gash (East Linton: Tuckwell Press, 2002).

Whibley, Charles, *Lord John Manners and his Friends* (2 vols, Edinburgh and London: Blackwood, 1925).

Critical Studies

Blake, Robert, 'The Trilogy 1844–7', in his *Disraeli* (London: Eyre & Spottiswoode, 1966).

Bodenheimer, Rosemarie, 'Looking Back into the Future: *Sybil*', in her *The Politics of Story in Victorian Social Fiction* (Ithaca, NY: Cornell University Press, 1988).

Brantlinger, Patrick, 'Two Responses to Chartism: Dickens and Disraeli', in his *The Spirit of Reform: British Literature and Politics, 1832–67* (Cambridge, Mass.: Harvard University Press, 1977).

Braun, Thom, *Disraeli the Novelist* (London: Allen and Unwin, 1981).

Braun, Thom, 'Mr Disraeli Changes Trees', *Disraeli Newsletter*, 3.1 (1978).

Braun, Thom, '*Sybil*: A Misprint', *Notes and Queries*, 23 (June 1978), 232–3.

Cazamian, Louis, *The Social Novel in England, 1830–1850: Dickens, Disraeli, Mrs Gaskell, Kingsley* (1903; trans. Martin Fido, London: Routledge and Kegan Paul, 1973).

Fido, Martin, 'The Treatment of Rural Distress in Disraeli's *Sybil*', *Yearbook of English Studies*, 5 (1975), 153–63.

Fido, Martin, ' "From his Own Observation": Sources of Working Class Passages in Disraeli's *Sybil*', *Modern Languages Review*, 72 (1977), 268–84.

Flavin, Michael, *Benjamin Disraeli: The Novel as Political Discourse* (Brighton: Sussex Academic Press, 2005).

Gallagher, Catherine, 'The Politics of Irony: Representation by Opposition in Disraeli's *Sybil*', in her *The Industrial Reformation of English Fiction: Social Discourse and Narrative Form, 1832–67* (Chicago: University of Chicago Press, 1985).

Guy, Josephine, *The Victorian Social-Problem Novel: The Market, the Individual and Communal Life* (Basingstoke: Macmillan, 1996).

Handwerk, Gary, 'Behind *Sybil*'s Veil: Disraeli's Mix of Ideological Messages', *Modern Languages Quarterly*, 49 (1988) 321–41.

Holloway, John, 'Disraeli', in his *The Victorian Sage* (London: Macmillan, 1953).

Kettle, Arnold, 'The Early Victorian Social Problem Novel', in Boris Ford, ed., *Dickens to Hardy*, The Pelican Guide to English Literature Vol. 6 (Harmondsworth: Penguin, 1958).

Lucas, John, 'Mrs Gaskell and Brotherhood', in David Howard, John Lucas, and John Goode, eds, *Tradition and Tolerance in Nineteenth-Century Fiction* (London: Routledge and Kegan Paul, 1966).

McCabe, Bernard, 'Disraeli and the "Baronial Principle": Some Versions of Romantic Medievalism', *Victorian Newsletter*, 34 (Fall 1968), 7–13.

[Monckton Milnes, Richard], 'Mr D'Israeli's *Tancred*—The Emancipation of the Jews', *Edinburgh Review*, 86 (July 1847), 138–55.

O'Kell, Robert, '*Sybil*: Two Nations, or One? Disraeli's Allegorical Romance', *Victorian Studies*, 30 (1987), 211–34, reprinted in his *Disraeli: The Romance of Politics* (Toronto: University of Toronto Press, 2013).

Schwarz, Daniel R., *Disraeli's Fiction* (London: Macmillan, 1979).

Smith, Sheila M., *The Other Nation: The Poor in English Novels of the 1840s and 1850s* (Oxford: Clarendon Press, 1980).

Smith, Sheila M., ed., *Mr Disraeli's Readers: Letters Written to Benjamin Disraeli and his Wife by Nineteenth-Century Readers of 'Sybil; or the Two Nations'* (Nottingham: Sisson and Parker for the University of Nottingham, 1966).

Smith, Sheila M., 'Willenhall and Wodgate: Disraeli's Use of Blue Book Evidence', *Review of English Studies*, 13 (1962), 368–84.

Smith, Sheila M., 'Blue Books and Victorian Novelists', *Review of English Studies*, 21 (1970), 23–40.

Speare, Morris Edmund, *The Political Novel: Its Development in England and in America* (New York: Oxford University Press, 1924).

Stephen, Sir Leslie, 'Mr Disraeli's Novels', *Fortnightly Review*, 22 NS 16 (October 1874), 430–50, reprinted in his *Hours in a Library*, 3 vols (London: Smith Elder, 1892), 2.106–40.

Stewart, R. W., ed., *Disraeli's Novels Reviewed 1826–1968* (Metuchen, NJ: Scarecrow Press, 1975).

Stone, Donald, 'Benjamin Disraeli and the Romance of the Will', in his *The Romantic Impulse in Victorian Fiction* (Cambridge, Mass.: Harvard University Press, 1980).

Thackeray, William Makepeace, '"Codlingsby," by B. de Shrewsbury, Esq.', *Punch*, 12 (1847), 166, 198–9, 213–14, 223.

Williams, Raymond, 'The Industrial Novels', in his *Culture and Society 1780–1950* (London: Chatto & Windus, 1967).

A CHRONOLOGY OF BENJAMIN DISRAELI

Life	*Historical and Cultural Background*
1748 Benjamin Israeli (1730–1816) moves from Cento (Italy) to London; changes name to D'Israeli.	End of the War of the Austrian Succession.
1749	Henry St John, Viscount Bolingbroke, *The Idea of a Patriot King*
1753	Jewish Naturalization Act (repealed 1754).
1760	Accession of George III.
1766 Isaac D'Israeli born.	Goldsmith, *The Vicar of Wakefield*
1776 Benjamin D'Israeli (the elder) becomes stockbroker.	American Declaration of Independence. Smith, *The Wealth of Nations*
1783	William Pitt PM (Tory) to 1801.
1789	French Revolution.
1790 Isaac Disraeli, 'A Defence of Poetry'.	Burke, *Reflections on the Revolution in France*
1791 Isaac D'Israeli, *The Curiosities of Literature*; inherits fortune from maternal grandmother.	Burke, *An Appeal from the New to the Old Whigs* Paine, *Rights of Man*
1793	War with France.
1797 Isaac D'Israeli, *Vaurien*.	Holcroft, *Hugh Trevor* (1794–7)
1799 Isaac D'Israeli, *Romances*.	Combination Laws; Income Tax; Sharon Turner, *History of the Anglo-Saxons* (1799–1805) Pye, *The Aristocrat*
1802 Isaac marries Maria Basevi.	Wordsworth, Preface to *Lyrical Ballads*
1804 Benjamin D'Israeli born 21 Dec., London (spells name as Disraeli from *c*.1820).	Napoleon crowned Emperor, 2 Dec.; Pitt PM (to 1806).
1805 Isaac D'Israeli, *Flim-Flams!*	Battles of Trafalgar and Austerlitz. Scott, *Lay of the Last Minstrel*
1811 Isaac D'Israeli, *Despotism, or, The Fall of the Jesuits.*	Prince of Wales becomes Regent. Jane Austen, *Sense and Sensibility*
1812–17 Benjamin at boarding school in Blackheath run by Nonconformist minister.	

Life	*Historical and Cultural Background*
1812 Isaac D'Israeli, *Calamities of Authors*.	Spencer Percival, PM since 1809 (Tory), assassinated; Luddite riots; Lord Liverpool PM (Tory). Byron, *Childe Harold*
1813	Battle of Leipzig; Wellington expels French from Spain. Austen, *Pride and Prejudice* Byron, *The Giaour* Robert Owen, *New View of Society*
1814 Isaac D'Israeli, *Quarrels of Authors*.	Napoleon abdicates and retires to Elba. Austen, *Mansfield Park* Scott, *Waverley*
1815	Napoleon's return from Elba; Battle of Waterloo; Congress of Vienna; Corn Laws. Scott, *Guy Mannering*
1816 Isaac D'Israeli, *The Character of James I*.	Cobbett's *Political Register* (1802–36) adopts cheap format; Income Tax abolished. Austen, *Emma* Byron, *Prisoner of Chillon* Scott, *The Antiquary* Peacock, *Headlong Hall*
1817 D'Israeli and Basevi families leave congregation of Bevis Marks Synagogue; Benjamin and his brothers baptized.	Civil unrest; suspension of Habeas Corpus. Death of Jane Austen. Keats, *Poems* Byron, *Manfred* Coleridge, *Sybilline Leaves* Scott, *Rob Roy* Peacock, *Melincourt*
1817–20 Benjamin at Higham Hill School, Walthamstow, run by Unitarian minister.	
1818 Isaac D'Israeli, *The Literary Character*.	Scott, *The Heart of Midlothian* Mary Shelley, *Frankenstein* Peacock, *Nightmare Abbey*
1819 Isaac D'Israeli collecting the works of William Blake (by 1824 the largest contemporary collection).	Peterloo Massacre; Six Acts to prevent sedition; first Factory Act. Scott, *Ivanhoe* Byron, *Don Juan* Shelley, *The Cenci*
1820–1 Benjamin studies at home.	Accession of Prince Regent as George IV; trial of Queen Caroline.
1821 Nov.: Benjamin articled to firm of City solicitors.	Death of Keats; death of Napoleon. Russell, *Essay on the English Constitution*

Life	*Historical and Cultural Background*
1822 Possibly the author of melodrama *Cherry and Fair Star*, Covent Garden, 8 Apr.	Castlereagh (Foreign Secretary) commits suicide, Canning replaces him; Robert Peel becomes Home Secretary. Kenelm Digby, *The Broad-Stone of Honour* Peacock, *Maid Marian*
1824 Writes novel, 'Aylmer Papillon' (unpublished but developed as *Popanilla*, 1828); tours Belgium and Rhine with father. Nov.: leaves solicitors, reads for the Bar; assistant to the publisher John Murray II; speculates in mining shares.	Combination Laws repealed; death of Byron. Theodore Hook, *Sayings and Doings* Carlyle's translation of Goethe's *Wilhelm Meister's Apprenticeship* Scott, *Redgauntlet* Cobbett, *History of the Protestant 'Reformation'* (1824–6)
1825 Collaborates with Murray on launch of Canningite Tory daily newspaper, the *Representative*; writes pamphlets puffing mining shares; stock market crash in Oct. plunges him into debt.	Commercial crisis; Combination Laws reimposed; George Basevi (Disraeli's cousin) designs Belgrave Square; Stockton to Darlington railway. Robert Plumer Ward, *Tremaine, or the Man of Refinement* Scott, *The Talisman*
1826 *Representative* starts publication Jan., closes July; *Vivian Grey* Part 1 (Apr.); contributions to *The Star Chamber* (satirical weekly, Apr.–June) probably including 'The Dunciad of Today' and a notice of Blake's *Illustrations to the Book of Job*; Murray disowns him; tour of Europe with Benjamin and Sarah Austen.	Scott, *Woodstock* Cooper, *The Last of the Mohicans* Lister, *Granby*
1827 *Vivian Grey* Part 2; nervous breakdown; lives with parents in London and at Bradenham, Buckinghamshire (1827–9).	Hazlitt, 'The Dandy School' (review of *Sayings and Doings* and *Vivian Grey*); Canning PM (Tory) Apr. but dies Aug.; Goderich PM (Tory). Ward, *De Vere* Bulwer-Lytton, *Falkland* Keble, *The Christian Year*
1828 *The Voyage of Captain Popanilla*; Isaac D'Israeli, *The Life and Reign of Charles I* (1828–30).	Wellington PM (Tory); repeal of Test and Corporation Acts; Macaulay, 'Hallam's History' Bulwer-Lytton, *Pelham* Lister, *Herbert Lacy*
1829	Catholic Emancipation; Greek independence. Southey, *Colloquies with Sir Thomas More* Carlyle, 'Signs of the Times'

Life	*Historical and Cultural Background*
1830 Tour of the Mediterranean and Near East: visits Spain, Malta, Albania, Greece, Turkey.	Accession of William IV; Grey PM (Whig); Oastler, 'Yorkshire Slavery'; *Quarterly Review* begins distinction between 'Tory' and 'Conservative'; Liverpool–Manchester railway. Tennyson, *Poems, Chiefly Lyrical*
1831 *The Young Duke* (Apr.); visits Jerusalem (Feb.), Egypt (Mar.); his companion William Meredith dies in Cairo (July).	Reform Bill proposed (Mar.), rejected by Lords (Oct.); Truck Act; Mazzini founds Young Italy ('La Giovine Italia') movement. Peacock, *Crotchet Castle* Elliott, *Corn-Law Rhymes* Hugo, *Notre Dame de Paris*
1832 *Contarini Fleming, a psychological Auto-biography* (May); lodges in Duke Street, Mayfair; affair with Clara Bolton; contests High Wycombe by-election (June) as Radical, and general election (Dec.) as Radical Tory in High Wycombe and Tory Radical in County of Bucks; 'Ixion in Heaven' (*New Monthly Magazine*, Dec. 1832–Feb. 1833); Isaac D'Israeli awarded Oxford DCL.	Revised Reform Bill delayed by Lord Lyndhurst's wrecking amendment (May) but passed (June); Bentham dies; Scott dies. Sadler, *Report on Factory Children's Labour* Lytton, *Eugene Aram* Lister, *Arlington* Tennyson, *Poems* Martineau, *Illustrations of Political Economy* (to 1834, when Part iii will be 'A Manchester Strike')
1833 *The Wondrous Tale of Alroy* and *The Rise of Iskander* (Mar.); contests Marylebone by-election as Radical (Mar.); *What Is He?*; affair with Henrietta, Lady Sykes; 'Walstein, or a Cure for Melancholy' (*Court Magazine*, July); Isaac D'Israeli, *The Genius of Judaism*.	Abolition of Slavery; Factory Act; Education Grant Act; Keble's 'National Apostasy' sermon begins Oxford Movement (July). Carlyle, *Sartor Resartus* (in *Fraser's Magazine*, Nov. 1833–Aug. 1834) Bulwer-Lytton, *England and the English* (partly dedicated to Isaac Disraeli).
1834 *The Revolutionary Epick* (Book 1, Mar., Books 2 and 3, June); *A Year at Hartlebury* (with Sarah Disraeli, Mar.); 'The Infernal Marriage' (*New Monthly Magazine*, July–Oct.); becomes protégé of Lord Lyndhurst; contests High Wycombe in general election as Radical with Tory funding (Dec.–Jan. 1835); *The Crisis Examined* (Dec.).	Melbourne PM (Whig); Tolpuddle Martyrs (Mar.); New Poor Law (Aug.); Houses of Parliament destroyed by fire (Oct.); Whig ministry dismissed by King (Nov.); Peel PM (Tory); Peel, *Tamworth Manifesto* (Dec.); Coleridge dies; Ludolf Wienbarg names 'Young Germany' movement. Bulwer-Lytton, *The Last Days of Pompeii*

Life	*Historical and Cultural Background*
1835 Contests Taunton by-election as Tory (Apr.); public quarrel with O'Connell; 'The Carrier Pigeon' (in *Book of Beauty*); leading articles in *Morning Post* (22 Aug.–7 Sept.); *A Vindication of the English Constitution* (Dec.).	Melbourne PM (Whig; Apr.); George Basevi designs Fitzwilliam Museum, Cambridge. Dickens, *Sketches by Boz* Bulwer-Lytton, *Rienzi*
1836 'The Consul's Daughter' (in *Book of Beauty*); 'Letters of Runnymede' articles in *Times* (Jan.–May); joins Carlton Club; financial troubles; breaks with Henrietta Sykes (Aug.); *Henrietta Temple, a love story* (Dec., dated 1837); 'A New Voyage of Sinbad' (*The Times*, 15 Dec.–10 Feb. 1837).	Barry and Pugin win commission for new Houses of Parliament (built 1840–60) William Lovett founds London Working Men's Association; poor harvests and economic depression (to 1842). Pugin, *Contrasts* Dickens, *Pickwick Papers* (1836–7) Browning, 'Porphyria's Lover' and 'Johannes Agricola' in *Monthly Repository* Talfourd, *Ion*
1837 Isaac pays some of Benjamin's debts; *Venetia, or the Poet's Daughter* (May); wins Maidstone seat as Tory in general election (July); maiden speech in House of Commons (7 Dec.).	Accession of Queen Victoria (20 June); London Working Men's Association draws up six-point Charter; Feargus O'Connor launches *Northern Star* newspaper (Nov.). Macaulay, 'Bacon' Dickens, *Oliver Twist*
1838 Successful speeches in House on Corn Laws (15 Mar.) and Copyright Bill (25 Apr.); 'Old England by Coeur-de-Lion' (*Times* 3–15 Jan.); 'A Syrian Sketch' (*Book of Beauty*); courting Mary Anne Wyndham Lewis.	People's Charter published (May); Anti-Corn Law League (Sept.). Dickens, *Nicholas Nickleby* (1838–9) Lytton, *The Lady of Lyons*
1839 *The Tragedy of Count Alarcos*; speeches on the Education Bill (20 June) and Chartism (12 July); two poems in the *Book of Beauty*; 'Laelius' letters supporting Peel and sonnet 'To the Duke of Wellington' (*The Times*, May–Aug.); marries Mary Anne Wyndham Lewis (Aug.); moves to her house at Grosvenor Gate (now 93 Park Lane).	Whig government majority falls to five and Melbourne resigns (May); Peel declines office when Queen refuses change of courtiers ('Bedchamber Crisis'); Melbourne resumes office; Stanley (later Lord Derby), Graham, and some other Whigs join Peel's Tories; Chartist petition rejected by Parliament (July); Newport Rising; William Lovett imprisoned; Eglington Tournament. Carlyle, *Chartism* Frances Trollope, *Michael Armstrong, the Factory Boy*

Life

Historical and Cultural Background

1840 Speeches expressing sympathy with Chartists; much praised speech on the Parliamentary Papers Act; 'The Valley of Thebes' (*Book of Beauty*); Isaac Disraeli attends opening of London Reformed Synagogue.

Queen Victoria marries Prince Albert; Feargus O'Connor imprisoned. Dickens, *The Old Curiosity Shop*, *Barnaby Rudge* (both 1840–1) Lytton, *Money* Darwin, *Voyage of HMS Beagle*

1841 Elected MP for Shrewsbury (July); unsuccessfully asks Peel for office; 'Munich' in *Book of Beauty*.

Whig government falls (June); Robert Peel PM (Tory); Ferrand, Speech on the New Poor Law (28 Sept.); *Punch* founded. Carlyle, *On Heroes* Newman, *Tract 90* and *The Tamworth Reading Room* Browning, *Pippa Passes* Elizabeth Tonna, *Helen Fleetwood* Pugin, *True Principles* Lord John Manners, *England's Trust*

1842 Feels 'isolated' from the 'men who are in office' (25 Feb.) despite highly praised speech against Palmerston (8 Mar.); begins to lead what would become the 'Young England' group of new Tory MPs (11 Mar.); defends Peel's budget by invoking Lord Shelburne (1737–1805) as a free-trader (May); 'Eden and Lebanon' in *Book of Beauty*; in Paris meeting French politicians (Oct. to Jan.).

Peel's budget reintroduces Income Tax, abolishes duty on 700 items, and lowers barrier to imported corn (Apr.–May); Mines Act; second Chartist petition rejected; Plug Plot riots; Chadwick, *Report on the Sanitary Condition of the Labouring Population*; emergence of the 'Young Ireland' movement. Frances Trollope, *Jessie Phillips* Macaulay, *Lays of Ancient Rome* Tennyson, *Poems* Browning, *Dramatic Lyrics*

1843 Disraeli, Smythe, Baillie-Cochrane, and Manners begin to be known as 'Young England' and vote against the government on Irish issues (July and Aug.); 'labour has its rights as well as its duties' (speech at Shrewsbury, 9 May); Sept. at Deepdene working on *Coningsby*; Oct. trip to Chester, Liverpool, and Manchester; 'The Midland Ocean' in *Book of Beauty*.

O'Connell's 'Monster Meetings' in Ireland; O'Connell arrested; Arms Act; Theatres Act; economic recovery; Poor Law Commissioners' reports on *The Employment of Women and Children in Agriculture*; Ferrand's speech at Manchester Corn Exchange: 'We are now divided . . . into two classes— the very rich and the very poor' (14 Dec.). Carlyle, *Past and Present* Dickens, *A Christmas Carol* Hood, *Song of the Shirt* Lytton, *Last of the Barons* Lord John Manners, *The Monastic and Manufacturing Systems* and *A Plea for National Holy-Days*

Life	*Historical and Cultural Background*
1844 Supports government on Ireland, though famously defines 'the Irish question' as 'a starving population, an absentee aristocracy, an alien church and . . . the weakest executive in the world' (16 Feb.); *Coningsby; or, the New Generation* (May); opposes government on Sugar Duty (June); Duncombe lends him a file of Feargus O'Connor's Chartist correspondence (Aug.?); Young England group speaks at Manchester Athenaeum (Oct.); tour of the North, visiting Worsley Hall, Fryston, and W. B. Ferrand at Bingley. Winter at Bradenham working on *Sybil*.	Factory Act; Bank Charter Act; Rochdale Pioneers found cooperative store; Ashley's Ragged Schools Union. Thackeray, *Barry Lyndon* Dickens, *The Chimes* Elizabeth Barrett, *Poems* Smythe, *Historic Fancies*
1845 Writing *Sybil* (Jan. to 31 Apr.); speeches attacking Graham and Peel, declaring that Peel had 'caught the Whigs bathing, and walked away with their clothes' (28 Feb.), denouncing 'Conservative' [i.e. not Tory] government as 'an Organised Hypocrisy' (17 Mar.), describing Peel as the 'great Parliamentary middleman', and calling for 'the salutary check of a constitutional Opposition' (11 Apr.); Young England group splits over Maynooth; *Sybil; or, the Two Nations* (10 May); Sept. to 16 Jan. in Cassel and Paris.	Peel's second budget reduces import and export duties (Apr.); increased grant to Maynooth College for Irish Catholic clergy (June); Irish Famine begins (to 1849); Russell's 'Edinburgh Letter' (Nov.); Peel resigns (Dec.) but Russell (Whig) refuses to form government, so Peel remains PM (Tory); railway boom; Newman becomes Roman Catholic. Browning, *Dramatic Romances and Lyrics* Stewart, *Rodenhurst* Engels, *The Condition of the Working Class in England* (Leipzig, in German; English translation 1887)
1846 Savage attack on Peel's proposal to repeal the Corn Laws (22 Jan.); coins phrase 'Manchester school' and makes case for a 'territorial constitution' (20 Feb.); three-hour speech on Corn Law Bill (15 May); dishonestly denies soliciting office from Peel (15 May); Disraeli and Bentinck lead defeat of Peel on Coercion Bill (25 June); autumn and winter at	Peel declares for repeal of Corn Laws (Jan.); Corn Bill passes third reading in Commons with Whig support, despite 242 Tory votes against (May); government defeated on Coercion Bill (June); Peel resigns; Russell PM (Whig); Tory party splits into Peelites and Protectionists (led by Stanley in Lords, with Bentinck as Leader of House in Commons). Brontës, *Poems by Currer, Ellis and Acton Bell*

Life	*Historical and Cultural Background*
Bradenham writing *Tancred*; begins negotiations to acquire Hughenden Manor.	Lear, *Book of Nonsense* Lytton, *Lucretia* Dickens, *Dombey and Son* (to 1847)
1847 On front bench for first time, though for Protectionist wing of a split Tory party; adopts more sober dress and manner; *Tancred; or, the New Crusade* (Mar.); elected MP for Buckinghamshire (June); speech supporting Russell's motion to remove Jewish civil disabilities (Dec.).	Factory Act (ten-hour day for women and minors); financial crisis (Sept.); Bank Charter Act suspended (Oct.); Lionel de Rothschild elected but unable to take his seat; Russell's motion to remove Jewish disabilities defeated; Bentinck resigns as Protectionist leader in Commons. Charlotte Brontë, *Jane Eyre* Emily Brontë, *Wuthering Heights* Thackeray, *Vanity Fair* (to 1848)
1848 Death of Isaac D'Israeli (Jan.); 'On the Life and Writings of Mr D'Israeli' prefaced to 14th edn of *Curiosities of Literature*; opposes Public Health Act; speech (Aug.) summing up the session ('the speech which made me leader'); sudden death of Lord George Bentinck (Sept.); meets Peacock and hails him as his 'master'; completes purchase of Hughenden.	Revolutions in Europe; Chartist Meeting on Kennington Common (Apr.); Public Health Act (July); Pre-Raphaelite Brotherhood. Elizabeth Gaskell, *Mary Barton* Kingsley, *Yeast* Bulwer-Lytton, *Harold, The Last of the Saxon Kings* Marx and Engels, *Manifesto of the Communist Party* (published in London but in German; English translation in Chartist magazine *The Red Republican*, 1850) Mill, *Principles of Political Economy*
1849 Trumvirate of Disraeli, Granby, and Herries appointed to lead Tories in Commons (1 Feb.); Disraeli de facto leader in lower House by Mar.; 'uneasy' relations with Stanley; searching for an alternative to Protection as Tory cause; preface added to 5th edition of *Coningsby*.	European revolutions suppressed; cholera pandemic. Charlotte Brontë, *Shirley* Kingsley, *Alton Locke* Arnold, *The Strayed Reveller* Ruskin, *Seven Lamps of Architecture* Dickens, *David Copperfield* (to 1850) Macaulay, *History of England* (to 1861)
1850 Effective 'leader of the Opposition' (letter to his sister, 18 Apr.); opposes Mines Inspection Act (Aug.).	Palmerston's 'Civis Romanum sum' speech (June); death of Peel (July); Public Libraries Act. Carlyle, *Latter-Day Pamphlets* Tennyson, *In Memoriam* Wordsworth, *The Prelude*

Life	*Historical and Cultural Background*
1851 *Lord George Bentinck, A Political Biography* (Dec., dated 1852).	Russell resigns (20 Feb.) but returns immediately because Stanley (Lord Derby from July) is unable to form an administration; Ecclesiastical Titles Act (Aug.); Palmerston resigns as Foreign Secretary (19 Dec.); Great Exhibition Elizabeth Barrett Browning, *Casa Guidi Windows* Ruskin, *Stones of Venice* (to 1853)
1852 Chancellor of the Exchequer in Tory minority government (Feb.); friendship with Henry Lennox; his budget defeated (16 Dec.) and government resigns; returns to opposition.	Russell resigns (23 Feb.) after Palmerston defeats him on Militia Bill; Derby PM; Tory minority government resigns after budget defeat (20 Dec.); Aberdeen PM (Whig/Peelite coalition). Dickens, *Bleak House* (to 1853) Thackeray, *Henry Esmond* Arnold, *Empedocles on Etna*
1853 Founds, and contributes to, the *Press* (1853–66); uniform edition of his novels, with revised texts, published by David Bryce; awarded Oxford DCL.	Preston cotton spinners' strike (Oct. to May 1854). Arnold, *Poems* Charlotte Brontë, *Villette* Elizabeth Gaskell, *Ruth*
1854 Supports government on the 'just but unnecessary' Crimean War.	Crimean War (Mar.); Northcote-Trevelyan Report. Dickens, *Hard Times* Gaskell, *North and South* (to 1855)
1855 Helps defeat government on Roebuck's motion for an enquiry into the conduct of the war (29 Jan.).	Palmerston PM (Whig; Feb.); capture of Sebastopol (Sept.); newspaper tax abolished. Dickens, *Little Dorrit* (to 1857) Trollope, *The Warden* Tennyson, *Maud* Browning, *Men and Women*
1857 Speech on India, opposing Westernization and insisting that we should 'respect their laws, their usages, their customs, and, above all, their religion' (27 July).	General Election (Apr.); Indian Mutiny (May); Matrimonial Causes Act. Trollope, *Barchester Towers* Kingsley, *Two Years Ago* G. A. Lawrence, *Guy Livingstone*
1858 Chancellor of the Exchequer (Feb.); sells the *Press*; appoints Ralph Earle as private secretary; Lytton made Colonial Secretary, so two novelists in cabinet.	Palmerston resigns after defeat on Conspiracy to Murder Bill; Derby PM (Tory minority government; Feb.); abolition of property qualification for MPs (June: first point of the 'Charter' to be adopted); abolition of Jewish disabilities (July). Trollope, *Doctor Thorne* Morris, *Defence of Guenevere*

Life	*Historical and Cultural Background*
1859 Returns to leadership of the Opposition in the Commons (June); *Works of Isaac Disraeli* (7 vols, ed. nominally by Benjamin but actually by Sarah Disraeli); death of his sister Sarah (Dec.).	'Fancy franchises' Reform Bill defeated (Mar.); Derby resigns (June); Whigs, Peelites, and Radicals meet in Willis's Rooms: origin of Liberal party (6 June); Palmerston PM (Whig/Liberal; June); Macaulay dies. Mill, *On Liberty* Darwin, *Origin of Species* Dickens, *A Tale of Two Cities* George Eliot, *Adam Bede* Ruskin, *The Two Paths*
1860 Discontent with his leadership within the Tory party; attack on him in *Quarterly* (Apr.) by Robert Cecil (later Lord Salisbury); offer to resign refused (June); talks out Russell's proposed reform bill.	Derby and Disraeli adopt policy of tacit support for Palmerston ('masterly inactivity'); Lords defeat abolition of duty on paper; Coal Mines Act abolishes truck payment; *Essays and Reviews*; Wilberforce/Huxley debate, Oxford. Dickens, *Great Expectations* (to 1861) Eliot, *Mill on the Floss* Peacock, *Gryll Grange*
1861 The Crown and Church 'insure liberty by securing order' (speech at Aylesbury, Nov.).	Gladstone prevents future Lords interference with financial measures; American Civil War (to 1865); death of Prince Albert. George Eliot, *Silas Marner* Trollope, *Framley Parsonage*
1862 Mocks Gladstone's budget (Apr.); denounces 'bloated armaments' (May); letter to Anne Gilchrist about his family's Blake collection (5 Nov.); Hughenden remodelled by E. B. Lamb (to 1863).	Bismarck president of Prussia. George Eliot, *Romola* (to 1863) Christina Rossetti, *Goblin Market*
1863 Disraeli's debts bought by Andrew Montagu; attends Prince of Wales's wedding; elected Trustee of British Museum on grounds of 'literary eminence'.	Lincoln, 'Gettysburg Address'; Thackeray dies. Huxley, *Man's Place in Nature* Lyell, *Antiquity of Man* Gilchrist, *Life of Blake*
1864 'Is man an ape or an angel? My Lord, I am on the side of the angels' (speech at Oxford, Nov.).	First national Trades Union conference. Trollope, *Can You Forgive Her?* (to 1865) Dickens, *Our Mutual Friend* (to 1865) Browning, *Dramatis Personae* Newman, *Apologia pro vita sua* Derby, *The Iliad of Homer*

Life	*Historical and Cultural Background*
1865	Liberals win General Election (July); Palmerston dies (Oct.); Lord John Russell PM (Liberal).
	Arnold, *Essays in Criticism*
	Carroll, *Alice in Wonderland*
	Swinburne, *Atalanta in Calydon*
1866 Combines with Adullamite Whigs to defeat Gladstone's Reform Bill and brings down government; Chancellor of the Exchequer; elected to Athenaeum Club; appoints Montague Corry as private secretary.	Banking crisis (May); Liberal Reform Bill defeated (June); Derby PM (Tory minority government, July); Hyde Park riots (July); Prussia defeats Austria at Sadowa.
	George Eliot, *Felix Holt*
	Trollope, *Last Chronicle of Barset* (to 1867)
	Swinburne, *Poems and Ballads*
1867 Introduces Tory Reform proposals (Feb.); Reform Bill on household suffrage basis (Mar.); majority on first vote (Apr.); cheered at the Carlton Club ('Here's the man who rode the race . . . and . . . did the trick!'); Reform Act (Aug.): 'we have dished the Whigs'.	Reform Act doubles electorate from one to two million men; Factory Act.
	Carlyle, 'Shooting Niagara'
	Arnold, *New Poems* ('Dover Beach')
	Trollope, *Phineas Finn* (to 1869; 'Mr Daubeny' as a version of Disraeli)
	Bagehot, *The English Constitution*
1868 Lord Derby resigns on health grounds and Disraeli becomes PM (Feb.): 'I have climbed to the top of the greasy pole'; *Tragedy of Count Alarcos* performed at Astley's Theatre Royal; Leader of the Opposition (Dec.); his wife made Viscountess Beaconsfield (he choosing to stay in the Commons).	Disraeli PM (Tory minority government; Feb); Corrupt Practices Act; public executions abolished; first Trades Union Congress; Tories defeated in General Election (November); Gladstone PM (Liberal; Dec); Collins, *The Moonstone*; Trollope, *He Knew He Was Right* (to 1869).
1869 Writing *Lothair*; death of Lord Derby (Oct.); attacked in *Quarterly* by Salisbury as 'a mere political gamester'.	Church of Ireland disestablished; Debtors Act; Municipal Franchise Act.
	Arnold, *Culture and Anarchy* (previously as articles 1867–8)
	Clough, *Poems*
	Mill, *On the Subjection of Women*
	Reade, *Put Yourself in his Place*
1870 *Lothair* (May); ten-volume edition of *Novels and Tales* (Longmans, Nov.) with 'General Preface' identifying *Coningsby*, *Sybil*, and *Tancred* as 'a real Trilogy'; begins *Endymion*.	Franco–Prussian War (to 1871); Irish Land Act; Elementary Education Act; Married Women's Property Act; death of Dickens.
	Dickens, *Edwin Drood* (unfinished)
	Rossetti, *Poems*

Life	*Historical and Cultural Background*
1871 Opens campaign of attacks on the Liberal government, especially on Irish policy and the budget.	Abolition of religious tests for universities; Trades Union Act; Paris Commune. George Eliot, *Middlemarch* (to 1872) Carroll, *Through the Looking Glass*
1872 Speeches at Manchester (Apr.; the cabinet as 'a range of exhausted volcanoes') and Crystal Palace (June: 'proud of belonging to an Imperial country'); death of his wife (Dec.).	Ballot Act (secret voting; second point of the 'Charter' to be adopted); Licensing Act. Hardy, *Under the Greenwood Tree* Tennyson, *Poems* Butler, *Erewhon*
1873 Defeats government on Irish University Bill (Mar.); refuses to form government.	Financial crisis; agricultural depression (to 1884); Judicature Act; Lytton dies; Mill dies. Mill, *Autobiography* Trollope, *Phineas Redux* (to 1874) Hardy, *Pair of Blue Eyes* Pater, *The Renaissance*
1874 Wins General Election and becomes Prime Minister (Feb.); moves to 2 Whitehall Gardens; arranges purchase of paintings by Botticelli and Piero della Francesca for National Gallery; ill health; winter in Bournemouth.	Disraeli PM (Tory); Public Worship Regulation Act; Factory Act. Hardy, *Far from the Madding Crowd* Trollope, *The Way We Live Now* (to 1875) Meredith, *Beauchamp's Career* (to 1875) T. H. Green, Introduction to Hume's *Treatise of Human Nature*
1875 Arranges with Rothschild for purchase of shares in Suez Canal Company; sanctions but does not himself manage his government's social legislation ('He detests detail', Carnarvon); restoration of Hughenden Church by Blomfield.	Employers and Workmen Act; Conspiracy Act; Artisans' Dwellings Act; Factory Act; Public Health Act; Sale of Food and Drugs Act (chiefly the work of Richard Cross, Home Secretary); Hartington replaces Gladstone as Liberal leader. Hardy, *The Hand of Ethelberta* (to 1876) Trollope, *The Prime Minister* (to 1876)
1876 Makes Queen Victoria (at her request) Empress of India (Mar.); 'Fiction must be first-rate or it is nothing' (letter to Lady Bradford, 12 Apr.); last speech in House of Commons (11 Aug.).	Merchant Shipping Act; Education Act; Royal Titles Act. Gladstone, *The Bulgarian Horrors* (Sept.) George Eliot, *Daniel Deronda* James, *Roderick Hudson* Trollope, *The American Senator* (to 1877) Trevelyan, *Life of Macaulay*

Life

Historical and Cultural Background

1877 Becomes leader in the Lords as Earl of Beaconsfield (Feb.); ill health; moves to 10 Downing Street; Queen visits Hughenden (Dec.).

War between Russia and Turkey (May); cabinet secretly agrees on war with Russia should Constantinople be threatened; Russians take Plevna (Dec.). James, *The American* Trollope, *Is He Popenjoy?* (to 1878)

1878 Gives away the bride, Hannah Rothschild, at her wedding to Lord Rosebery (Mar.); attends Congress of Berlin (June); 'Russia accepts the English scheme for the European frontier of . . . the Sultan' (telegram, 22 June); Bismarck: 'Der alte Jude, das ist der Mann'; Treaty of Berlin (July); Order of the Garter; resumes work on *Endymion*.

British fleet sent to Dardanelles (Feb.) and reserves mobilized (Mar.); Treaty of San Stephano (Mar.); Treaty of Berlin (July) establishes autonomous Bulgaria but keeps Constantinople in Turkey; *Ruskin v. Whistler* trial. Hardy, *Return of the Native* Swinburne, *Poems and Ballads* (second series)

1879 Dismisses his previous support for agricultural Protection as 'musty phrases of mine forty years ago' (18 Mar.).

Zulu War: British defeat at Isandlhwana but victory at Ulundi (July); Afghan War: British legation at Kabul murdered (Sept.) but successful invasion (Oct.); Gladstone's Midlothian campaign. Trollope, *The Duke's Children* (to 1880) James, *The Europeans* Meredith, *The Egoist*

1880 Visited at Hughenden by Prince of Wales; decides (Mar.) on early General Election which Tories lose (Apr.); holds last cabinet meeting (21 Apr.); remains Leader of the Opposition; completes *Endymion*; Corry (now Lord Rowton) tells Disraeli, during debate in the Lords, of Longman's offer of £10,000 for copyright; *Endymion* published Nov.; starts work on *Falconet* (unfinished).

Gladstone PM (Liberal); Bradlaugh, atheist MP for Northampton, excluded for refusing to take oath; Lord Randolph Churchill leads 'Fourth Party' of young Tory rebels; Land League disturbances in Ireland; George Eliot dies; Flaubert dies. Hardy, *The Trumpet Major*

1881 Moves to 19 Curzon Street (Jan.); last speech in Lords (15 Mar.); catches chill returning late from a dinner party (22 Mar.); bronchitis and uraemia; Queen offers to visit: 'It is better not. She would only ask me to

Obstruction of Commons business by Irish members during Coercion Bill; Treaty of Pretoria; Tory party jointly led by Lord Salisbury in Lords and Stafford-Northcote in Commons; Irish Land Act; Carlyle dies. James, *Portrait of a Lady*

Life

take a message to Albert'; dies 19
Apr.; Hughenden Edition of the
Novels and Tales (11 volumes,
Longman).

1882 His nephew Coningsby Disraeli
(1867–1936) inherits
Hughenden; library, including
major items from the Blake
collection, sold at Sotheby's.

Historical and Cultural Background

Trollope, *Ayala's Angel*
Rossetti, *Ballads and Sonnets*
Wilde, *Poems*

SYBIL;

OR,

THE TWO NATIONS.

BY

B. DISRAELI, M.P.

AUTHOR OF 'CONINGSBY.'

'The Commonalty murmured, and said, "There never were so many Gentlemen, and so little Gentleness." '—BISHOP LATIMER.*

IN THREE VOLS.

VOL. I.

LONDON:

HENRY COLBURN, PUBLISHER;

GREAT MARLBOROUGH STREET.

1845.

I would inscribe these volumes to one whose noble spirit and gentle nature ever prompt her to sympathise with the suffering; to one whose sweet voice has often encouraged, and whose taste and judgment have ever guided, their pages; the most severe of critics, but—a perfect Wife!*

ADVERTISEMENT.

THE general reader whose attention has not been specially drawn to the subject which these volumes aim to illustrate, the Condition of the People, might suspect that the Writer had been tempted to some exaggeration in the scenes which he has drawn and the impressions which he has wished to convey. He thinks it therefore due to himself to state that he believes there is not a trait in this work for which he has not the authority of his own observation,* or the authentic evidence which has been received by Royal Commissions and Parliamentary Committees. But while he hopes he has alleged nothing which is not true, he has found the absolute necessity of suppressing much that is genuine. For so little do we know of the state of our own country that the air of improbability that the whole truth would inevitably throw over these pages, might deter many from their perusal.

GROSVENOR-GATE,
May-Day, 1845.

VOLUME I

BOOK I.

CHAPTER I.

'I'LL take the odds against Caravan.'

'In poneys?'*

'Done.'

And Lord Milford, a young noble, entered in his book the bet which he had just made with Mr. Latour, a grey-headed member of the Jockey Club.*

It was the eve of the Derby of 1837.* In a vast and golden saloon,* that in its decorations would have become, and in its splendour would not have disgraced, Versailles in the days of the grand monarch,* were assembled many whose hearts beat at the thought of the morrow, and whose brains still laboured to control its fortunes to their advantage.

'They say that Caravan looks puffy,' lisped in a low voice a young man, lounging on the edge of a buhl table that had once belonged to a Mortemart,* and dangling a rich cane with affected indifference in order to conceal his anxiety from all, except the person whom he addressed.

'They are taking seven to two against him freely over the way,' was the reply. 'I believe it's all right.'

'Do you know I dreamed last night something about Mango,' continued the gentleman with the cane, and with a look of uneasy superstition.

His companion shook his head.

'Well,' continued the gentleman with the cane, 'I have no opinion of him. I gave Charles Egremont* the odds against Mango this morning; he goes with us, you know. By the bye, who is our fourth?'

'I thought of Milford,' was the reply in an under tone. 'What say you?'

'Milford is going with St. James and Punch Hughes.'

'Well, let us come into supper, and we shall see some fellow we like.'

So saying, the companions, taking their course through more than one chamber, entered an apartment of less dimensions than the principal saloon, but not less sumptuous in its general appearance. The gleaming lustres poured a flood of soft yet brilliant light over a plateau glittering with gold plate, and fragrant with exotics embedded in vases of rare porcelain. The seats on each side of the table were occupied by persons consuming, with a heedless air, delicacies for which they had no appetite; while the conversation in general consisted of flying phrases referring to the impending event of the great day that had already dawned.

'Come from Lady St. Julian's, Fitz?' said a youth of very tender years, and whose fair visage was as downy and as blooming as the peach from which with a languid air he withdrew his lips to make this inquiry of the gentleman with the cane.

'Yes; why were not you there?'

'I never go anywhere,' replied the melancholy Cupid, 'everything bores me so.'

'Well, will you go to Epsom with us to-morrow, Alfred?' said Lord Fitzheron. 'I take Berners and Charles Egremont, and with you our party will be perfect.'

'I feel so cursed blasé!' exclaimed the boy in a tone of elegant anguish.

'It will give you a fillip, Alfred,' said Mr. Berners; 'do you all the good in the world.'

'Nothing can do me good,' said Alfred, throwing away his almost untasted peach, 'I should be quite content if anything could do me harm. Waiter, bring me a tumbler of Badminton.'*

'And bring me one too,' sighed out Lord Eugene De Vere, who was a year older than Alfred Mountchesney, his companion and brother in listlessness. Both had exhausted life in their teens, and all that remained for them was to mourn, amid the ruins of their reminiscences, over the extinction of excitement.

'Well, Eugene, suppose you come with us,' said Lord Fitzheron.

'I think I shall go down to Hampton Court and play tennis,'* said Lord Eugene. 'As it is the Derby, nobody will be there.'

'And I will go with you, Eugene,' said Alfred Mountchesney, 'and we will dine together afterwards at the Toy.* Anything is better than dining in this infernal London.'

'Well, for my part,' said Mr. Berners, 'I do not like your suburban dinners. You always get something you can't eat, and cursed bad wine.'

'I rather like bad wine,' said Mr. Mountchesney; 'one gets so bored with good wine.'

'Do you want the odds against Hybiscus,* Berners?' said a guardsman looking up from his book, which he had been very intently studying.

'All I want is some supper, and as you are not using your place—'

'You shall have it. Oh! here's Milford, he will give them me.'

And at this moment entered the room the young nobleman whom we have before mentioned, accompanied by an individual who was approaching perhaps the termination of his fifth lustre,* but whose general air rather betokened even a less experienced time of life. Tall, with a well-proportioned figure and a graceful carriage, his countenance touched with a sensibility that at once engages the affections, Charles Egremont was not only admired by that sex, whose approval generally secures men enemies among their fellows, but was at the same time the favourite of his own.

'Ah, Egremont! come and sit here,' exclaimed more than one banqueter.

'I saw you waltzing with the little Bertie,* old fellow,' said Lord Fitzheron, 'and therefore did not stay to speak to you, as I thought we should meet here. I am to call for you, mind.'

'How shall we all feel this time to-morrow?' said Egremont, smiling.

'The happiest fellow at this moment must be Cockie Graves,' said Lord Milford. 'He can have no suspense. I have been looking over his book, and I defy him, whatever happens, not to lose.'

'Poor Cockie,' said Mr. Berners; 'he has asked me to dine with him at the Clarendon* on Saturday.'

'Cockie is a very good Cockie,' said Lord Milford, 'and Caravan is a very good horse; and if any gentleman sportsman present wishes to give seven to two, I will take him to any amount.'

'My book is made up,' said Egremont; 'and I stand or fall by Caravan.'

'And I.'

'And I.'

'And I.'

'Well, mark my words,' said a fourth, rather solemnly, 'Rat-trap wins.'

'There is not a horse except Caravan,' said Lord Milford, 'fit for a borough stake.'

'You used to be all for Phosphorus,* Egremont,' said Lord Eugene de Vere.

'Yes; but fortunately I have got out of that scrape. I owe Phip Dormer a good turn for that. I was the third man who knew he had gone lame.'

'And what are the odds against him now.'

'Oh! nominal; forty to one,—what you please.'

'He won't run,' said Mr. Berners, 'John Day* told me he had refused to
ride him.'

'I believe Cockie Graves might win something if Phosphorus came
in first,' said Lord Milford, laughing.

'How close it is to-night!' said Egremont. 'Waiter, give me some
Seltzer water;* and open another window; open them all.'

At this moment an influx of guests intimated that the assembly at
Lady St. Julian's was broken up. Many at the table rose and yielded
their places, clustering round the chimney-piece, or forming in various
groups, and discussing the great question. Several of those who had
recently entered were votaries of Rat-trap, the favourite, and quite prepared, from all the information that had reached them, to back their
opinions valiantly. The conversation had now become general and animated, or rather there was a medley of voices in which little was distinguished except the names of horses and the amount of odds. In the
midst of all this, waiters glided about handing incomprehensible mixtures
bearing aristocratic names; mystical combinations of French wines and
German waters, flavoured with slices of Portugal fruits, and cooled with
lumps of American ice, compositions which immortalized the creative
genius of some high patrician name.

'By Jove! that's a flash,' exclaimed Lord Milford, as a blaze of lightning seemed to suffuse the chamber, and the beaming lustres turned
white and ghastly in the glare.

The thunder rolled over the building. There was a dead silence. Was
it going to rain? Was it going to pour? Was the storm confined to the
metropolis? Would it reach Epsom? A deluge, and the course would be
a quagmire, and strength might baffle speed.

Another flash, another explosion, the hissing noise of rain. Lord
Milford moved aside, and jealous of the eye of another, read a letter
from Chifney,* and in a few minutes afterwards offered to take the odds
against Pocket Hercules. Mr. Latour walked to the window, surveyed
the heavens, sighed that there was not time to send his tiger* from the
door to Epsom, and get information whether the storm had reached the
Surrey hills, for to-night's operations. It was too late. So he took a rusk
and a glass of lemonade, and retired to rest with a cool head and a cooler
heart.

The storm raged, the incessant flash played as it were round the burnished cornice of the chamber, and threw a lurid hue on the scenes
of Watteau and Boucher that sparkled in the medallions over the lofty
doors. The thunderbolts seemed to descend in clattering confusion
upon the roof. Sometimes there was a moment of dead silence, broken

only by the pattering of the rain in the street without, or the pattering of the dice in a chamber at hand. Then horses were backed, bets made, and there were loud and frequent calls for brimming goblets from hurrying waiters, distracted by the lightning and deafened by the peal. It seemed a scene and a supper where the marble guest of Juan* might have been expected, and had he arrived, he would have found probably hearts as bold and spirits as reckless as he encountered in Andalusia.

CHAPTER II.

'WILL any one do anything about Hybiscus?' sang out a gentleman in the ring at Epsom. It was full of eager groups; round the betting post a swarming cluster, while the magic circle itself was surrounded by a host of horsemen shouting from their saddles the odds they were ready to receive or give, and the names of the horses they were prepared to back or to oppose.

'Will any one do anything about Hybiscus?'

'I'll give you five to one,' said a tall, stiff Saxon peer, in a white great coat.*

'No; I'll take six.'

The tall, stiff peer in the white great coat mused for a moment with his pencil at his lip, and then said, 'Well, I'll give you six. What do you say about Mango?'*

'Eleven to two against Mango,' called out a little humpbacked man in a shrill voice, but with the air of one who was master of his work.

'I should like to do a little business with you, Mr. Chippendale,' said Lord Milford in a coaxing tone, 'but I must have six to one.'

'Eleven to two, and no mistake,' said this keeper of a second-rate gaming-house, who, known by the flattering appellation of Hump Chippendale, now turned with malignant abruptness from the heir apparent of an English earldom.

'You shall have six to one, my Lord,' said Captain Spruce, a debonair personage with a well-turned silk hat arranged a little aside, his coloured cravat tied with precision, his whiskers trimmed like a quickset hedge. Spruce, who had earned his title of Captain on the plains of Newmarket,* which had witnessed for many a year his successful exploits, had a weakness for the aristocracy, who knowing his graceful infirmity patronized him with condescending dexterity, acknowledged his exist-ence in Pall Mall as well as at Tattersalls,* and thus occasionally got a point more than the betting out of him. Hump Chippendale had none

of these gentle failings; he was a democratic leg, who loved to fleece
a noble, and thought all men were born equal—a consoling creed that
was a hedge for his hump.

'Seven to four against the favourite; seven to two against Caravan;
eleven to two against Mango. What about Benedict? Will any one do
anything about Pocket Hercules? Thirty to one against Dardanelles.'*

'Done.'

'Five and thirty ponies to one against Phosphorus,' shouted a little
man vociferously and repeatedly.

'I will give forty,' said Lord Milford. No answer,—nothing done.

'Forty to one!' murmured Egremont who stood against Phosphorus.
A little nervous, he said to the peer in the white great coat, 'Don't you
think that Phosphorus may after all have some chance?'

'I should be cursed sorry to be deep against him,' said the peer.

Egremont with a quivering lip walked away. He consulted his book;
he meditated anxiously. Should he hedge? It was scarcely worth while
to mar the symmetry of his winnings; he stood 'so well' by all the
favourites; and for a horse at forty to one. No; he would trust his star,
he would not hedge.

'Mr. Chippendale,' whispered the peer in the white great coat, 'go
and press Mr. Egremont about Phosphorus. I should not be surprised
if you got a good thing.'

At this moment, a huge, broad-faced, rosy-gilled fellow, with one
of those good-humoured yet cunning countenances that we meet occasionally on the northern side of the Trent, rode up to the ring on a square
cob* and dismounting entered the circle. He was a carcase butcher,
famous in Carnaby market,* and the prime councillor of a distinguished
nobleman for whom privately he betted on commission. His secret service to-day was to bet against his noble employer's own horse, and so he
at once sung out, 'Twenty to one against Man-trap.'*

A young gentleman just launched into the world, and who, proud of
his ancient and spreading acres, was now making his first book, seeing
Man-trap marked eighteen to one on the cards, jumped eagerly at this
bargain, while Lord Fitzheron and Mr. Berners who were at hand and
who in their days had found their names in the book of the carcase
butcher, and grown wise by it, interchanged a smile.

'Mr. Egremont will not take,' said Hump Chippendale to the peer in
the white great coat.

'You must have been too eager,' said his noble friend.

The ring is up; the last odds declared; all gallop away to the Warren.*
A few minutes, only a few minutes, and the event that for twelve months

has been the pivot of so much calculation, of such subtle combinations, of such deep conspiracies, round which the thought and passion of the sporting world have hung like eagles, will be recorded in the fleeting tablets of the past. But what minutes! Count them by sensation and not by calendars, and each moment is a day and the race a life. Hogarth in a coarse and yet animated sketch has painted 'Before' and 'After.'* A creative spirit of a higher vein might develope the simplicity of the idea with sublimer accessories. Pompeius before Pharsalia, Harold before Hastings, Napoleon before Waterloo,* might afford some striking contrasts to the immediate catastrophe of their fortunes. Finer still the inspired mariner who has just discovered a new world; the sage who has revealed a new planet;* and yet the 'Before' and 'After' of a first-rate English race, in the degree of its excitement, and sometimes in the tragic emotions of its close, may vie even with these.

They are saddling the horses; Caravan looks in great condition; and a scornful smile seems to play upon the handsome features of Pavis, as in the becoming colours of his employer,* he gracefully gallops his horse before his admiring supporters. Egremont in the delight of an English patrician scarcely saw Mango, and never even thought of Phosphorus—Phosphorus, who, by the bye, was the first horse that showed, with both his forelegs bandaged.*

They are off!

As soon as they are well away, Chifney makes the running with Pocket Hercules. Up to the Rubbing House* he is leading; this is the only point the eye can select. Higher up the hill, Caravan, Hybiscus, Benedict, Mahometan, Phosphorus, Michel Fell, and Rat-trap are with the grey,* forming a front rank, and at the new ground the pace has told its tale, for half a dozen are already out of the race.

The summit is gained; the tactics alter: here Pavis brings up Caravan, with extraordinary severity,—the pace round Tattenham corner terrific; Caravan leading, then Phosphorus a little above him, Mahometan next, Hybiscus fourth, Rat-trap looking badly, Wisdom, Benedict and another handy. By this time Pocket Hercules has enough, and at the road* the tailing grows at every stride. Here the favourite himself is hors de combat, as well as Dardanelles, and a crowd of lesser celebrities.

There are now but four left in the race, and of these, two, Hybiscus and Mahometan, are some lengths behind. Now it is neck and neck between Caravan and Phosphorus. At the stand Caravan has decidedly the best, but just at the post, Edwards, on Phosphorus, lifts the gallant little horse, and with an extraordinary effort contrives to shove him in by half a length.*

'You look a little low, Charley,' said Lord Fitzheron, as taking their lunch in their drag* he poured the champagne into the glass of Egremont.

'By Jove!' said Lord Milford, 'Only think of Cockie Graves having gone and done it!'

CHAPTER III.

EGREMONT was the younger brother of an English earl, whose nobility being of nearly three centuries' date, ranked him among our high and ancient peers, although its origin was more memorable than illustrious. The founder of the family had been a confidential domestic of one of the favourites of Henry the Eighth, and had contrived to be appointed one of the commissioners for 'visiting and taking the surrenders of divers religious houses.' It came to pass that divers of these religious houses surrendered themselves eventually to the use and benefit of honest Baldwin Greymount. The king was touched with the activity and zeal of his commissioner. Not one of them whose reports were so ample and satisfactory, who could baffle a wily prior with more dexterity, or control a proud abbot with more firmness. Nor were they well-digested reports alone that were transmitted to the sovereign: they came accompanied with many rare and curious articles, grateful to the taste of one who was not only a religious reformer but a dilettante; golden candlesticks and costly chalices; sometimes a jewelled pix; fantastic spoons and patens,* rings for the fingers and the ear; occasionally a fair-written and blazoned manuscript—suitable offering to the royal scholar. Greymount was noticed; sent for; promoted in the household; knighted; might doubtless have been sworn of the council, and in due time have become a minister; but his was a discreet ambition—of an accumulative rather than an aspiring character. He served the king faithfully in all domestic matters that required an unimpassioned, unscrupulous agent; fashioned his creed and conscience according to the royal model in all its freaks; seized the right moment to get sundry grants of abbey lands, and contrived in that dangerous age to save both his head and his estate.

The Greymount family having planted themselves in the land, faithful to the policy of the founder, avoided the public gaze during the troubled period that followed the reformation; and even during the more orderly reign of Elizabeth, rather sought their increase in alliances than in court favour. But at the commencement of the seventeenth century, their abbey lands infinitely advanced in value, and their rental swollen by the prudent accumulation of more than seventy years, a Greymount, who was then a county member, was elevated to the peerage as Baron Marney.* The heralds furnished his pedigree, and assured the world that although the exalted rank and extensive possessions enjoyed at present by the Greymounts had their origin immediately in great territorial revolutions of a recent reign, it was not for a moment to be supposed, that the remote ancestors of the Ecclesiastical Commissioner of 1530 were by any means obscure. On the contrary, it appeared that they were both Norman and baronial, their real name Egremont, which, in their patent of peerage, the family now resumed.

In the civil wars, the Egremonts pricked by their Norman blood, were cavaliers and fought pretty well. But in 1688, alarmed at the prevalent impression that King James intended to insist on the restitution of the church estates to their original purposes, to wit, the education of the people and the maintenance of the poor, the Lord of Marney Abbey became a warm adherent of 'civil and religious liberty,'—the cause for which Hampden had died in the field, and Russell on the scaffold,—and joined the other Whig lords,* and great lay impropriators, in calling over the Prince of Orange and a Dutch army, to vindicate those popular principles which, somehow or other, the people would never support. Profiting by this last pregnant circumstance, the lay Abbot of Marney also in this instance like the other Whig lords, was careful to maintain, while he vindicated the cause of civil and religious liberty, a very loyal and dutiful though secret correspondence with the court of St. Germains.*

The great deliverer King William the Third, to whom Lord Marney was a systematic traitor, made the descendant of the Ecclesiastical Commissioner of Henry the Eighth an English earl; and from that time until the period of our history, though the Marney family had never produced one individual eminent for civil or military abilities, though the country was not indebted to them for a single statesman, orator, successful warrior, great lawyer, learned divine, eminent author, illustrious man of science, they had contrived, if not to engross any great share of public admiration and love, at least to monopolise no contemptible portion of public money and public dignities. During the seventy years of almost unbroken Whig rule, from the accession of the House of Hanover to the fall of Mr. Fox,* Marney Abbey had furnished a never-failing crop of lord privy seals, lord presidents, and lord lieutenants. The family had had their due quota of garters* and governments and bishoprics; admirals without fleets, and generals who fought only in

America.* They had glittered in great embassies with clever secretaries
at their elbow, and had once governed Ireland when to govern Ireland
was only to apportion the public plunder to a corrupt senate.

Notwithstanding however this prolonged enjoyment of undeserved
prosperity, the lay abbots of Marney were not content. Not that it was
satiety that induced dissatisfaction. The Egremonts could feed on. They
wanted something more. Not to be prime ministers or secretaries of
state, for they were a shrewd race who knew the length of their tether,
and notwithstanding the encouraging example of his grace of Newcastle,*
they could not resist the persuasion that some knowledge of the interests and resources of nations, some power of expressing opinions with
propriety, some degree of respect for the public and for himself, were
not altogether indispensable qualifications, even under a Venetian constitution,* in an individual who aspired to a post so eminent and responsible. Satisfied with the stars and mitres and official seals, which were
periodically apportioned to them, the Marney family did not aspire to
the somewhat graceless office of being their distributor. What they aimed
at was promotion in their order; and promotion to the highest class.
They observed that more than one of the other great 'civil and religious liberty' families,—the families who in one century plundered
the church to gain the property of the people, and in another century
changed the dynasty to gain the power of the crown,—had their brows
circled with the strawberry leaf.* And why should not this distinction
be the high lot also of the descendants of the old gentleman usher of
one of King Henry's plundering vicar-generals? Why not? True it is,
that a grateful sovereign in our days has deemed such distinction the
only reward for half a hundred victories.* True it is, that Nelson, after
conquering the Mediterranean, died only a Viscount! But the house of
Marney had risen to high rank; counted themselves ancient nobility;
and turned up their noses at the Pratts and the Smiths, the Jenkinsons
and the Robinsons* of our degenerate days; and never had done anything for the nation or for their honours. And why should they now?
It was unreasonable to expect it. Civil and religious liberty, that had
given them a broad estate and a glittering coronet, to say nothing of
half-a-dozen close seats in parliament, ought clearly to make them dukes.

But the other great Whig families who had obtained this honour, and
who had done something more for it than spoliate their church and
betray their king, set up their backs against this claim of the Egremonts.
The Egremonts had done none of the work of the last hundred years
of political mystification, during which a people without power or education, had been induced to believe themselves the freest and most

enlightened nation in the world, and had submitted to lavish their blood and treasure, to see their industry crippled and their labour mortgaged, in order to maintain an oligarchy, that had neither ancient memories to soften nor present services to justify their unprecedented usurpation.

How had the Egremonts contributed to this prodigious result? Their family had furnished none of those artful orators whose bewildering phrase had fascinated the public intelligence; none of those toilsome patricians whose assiduity in affairs had convinced their unprivileged fellow-subjects that government was a science, and administration an art, which demanded the devotion of a peculiar class in the state for their fulfilment and pursuit. The Egremonts had never said anything that was remembered, or done anything that could be recalled. It was decided by the Great Revolution families,* that they should not be dukes. Infinite was the indignation of the lay Abbot of Marney. He counted his boroughs,* consulted his cousins, and muttered revenge. The opportunity soon offered for the gratification of his passion.

The situation of the Venetian party in the wane of the eighteenth century had become extremely critical. A young king* was making often fruitless, but always energetic, struggles to emancipate his national royalty from the trammels of the factious dogeship. More than sixty years of a government of singular corruption had alienated all hearts from the oligarchy; never indeed much affected by the great body of the people. It could no longer be concealed that by virtue of a plausible phrase power had been transferred from the crown to a parliament, the members of which were appointed by an extremely limited and exclusive class, who owned no responsibility to the country, who debated and voted in secret, and who were regularly paid by the small knot of great families that by this machinery had secured the permanent possession of the king's treasury. Whiggism was putrescent in the nostrils of the nation; we were probably on the eve of a bloodless yet important revolution; when Rockingham,* a virtuous magnifico, alarmed and disgusted, resolved to revive something of the pristine purity and high-toned energy of the old Whig connection; appealed to his 'new generation' from a degenerate age, arrayed under his banner the generous youth of the Whig families, and was fortunate to enlist in the service the supreme genius of Edmund Burke.

Burke effected for the Whigs what Bolingbroke* in a preceding age had done for the Tories: he restored the moral existence of the party. He taught them to recur to the ancient principles of their connection, and suffused those principles with all the delusive splendour of his imagination. He raised the tone of their public discourse; he breathed a high spirit into their public acts. It was in his power to do more for the Whigs than St. John could do for his party. The oligarchy, who had found it convenient to attaint Bolingbroke for being the avowed minister of the English Prince with whom they were always in secret communication, when opinion forced them to consent to his restitution, had tacked to the amnesty a clause as cowardly as it was unconstitutional, and declared his incompetence to sit in the parliament of his country. Burke on the contrary fought the Whig fight with a two-edged weapon: he was a great writer; as an orator he was transcendent. In a dearth of that public talent for the possession of which the Whigs have generally been distinguished, Burke came forward and established them alike in the parliament and the country. And what was his reward? No sooner had a young and dissolute noble, who with some of the aspirations of a Cæsar oftener realised the conduct of a Catiline,* appeared on the stage, and after some inglorious tergiversation adopted their colours, than they transferred to him the command which had been won by wisdom and genius, vindicated by unrivalled knowledge, and adorned by accomplished eloquence. When the hour arrived for the triumph which he had prepared, he was not even admitted into the Cabinet,* virtually presided over by his graceless pupil, and who, in the profuse suggestions of his teeming converse, had found the principles and the information which were among the chief claims to public confidence of Mr. Fox.

Hard necessity made Mr. Burke submit to the yoke, but the humiliation could never be forgotten. Nemesis* favours genius: the inevitable hour at length arrived. A voice like the Apocalypse sounded over England and even echoed in all the courts of Europe. Burke poured forth the vials of his hoarded vengeance into the agitated heart of Christendom; he stimulated the panic of a world by the wild pictures of his inspired imagination; he dashed to the ground the rival who had robbed him of his hard-earned greatness; rended in twain the proud oligarchy* that had dared to use and to insult him; and followed with servility by the haughtiest and the most timid of its members, amid the frantic exultation of his country, he placed his heel upon the neck of the ancient serpent.*

Among the Whig followers of Mr. Burke in this memorable defection, among the Devonshires and the Portlands, the Spencers and the Fitzwilliams, was the Earl of Marney, whom the Whigs would not make a duke.

What was his chance of success from Mr. Pitt?*

If the history of England be ever written by one who has the knowledge and the courage, and both qualities are equally requisite for the undertaking, the world would be more astonished than when reading the Roman annals by Niebuhr. Generally speaking, all the great events have been distorted, most of the important causes concealed, some of the principal characters never appear, and all who figure are so misunderstood and misrepresented, that the result is a complete mystification, and the perusal of the narrative about as profitable to an Englishman as reading the Republic of Plato or the Utopia of More, the pages of Gaudentio di Lucca or the adventures of Peter Wilkins.*

The influence of races in our early ages, of the church in our middle, and of parties in our modern history, are three great moving and modifying powers, that must be pursued and analyzed with an untiring, profound, and unimpassioned spirit, before a guiding ray can be secured. A remarkable feature of our written history is the absence in its pages of some of the most influential personages. Not one man in a thousand for instance has ever heard of Major Wildman:* yet he was the soul of English politics in the most eventful period of this kingdom, and one most interesting to this age, from 1640 to 1688; and seemed more than once to hold the balance which was to decide the permanent form of our government. But he was the leader of an unsuccessful party. Even, comparatively speaking, in our own times, the same mysterious oblivion is sometimes encouraged to creep over personages of great social distinction as well as political importance.

The name of the second Pitt remains, fresh after forty years of great events, a parliamentary beacon. He was the Chatterton of politics; the 'marvellous boy.'* Some have a vague impression that he was mysteriously moulded by his great father; that he inherited the genius, the eloquence, the state craft of Chatham. His genius was of a different bent, his eloquence of a different class, his state craft of a different school. To understand Mr. Pitt, one must understand one of the suppressed characters of English history, and that is Lord Shelburne.*

When the fine genius of the injured Bolingbroke, the only peer of his century who was educated, and proscribed by the oligarchy because they were afraid of his eloquence, 'the glory of his order and the shame,' shut out from Parliament, found vent in those writings which recalled to the English people the inherent blessings of their old free monarchy, and painted in immortal hues his picture of a patriot king, the spirit that he raised at length touched the heart of Carteret born a Whig, yet sceptical of the advantages of that patrician constitution which made the Duke of Newcastle the most incompetent of men, but the chosen leader of the Venetian party, virtually sovereign of England. Lord Carteret had many brilliant qualities: he was undaunted, enterprising, eloquent;

had considerable knowledge of continental politics, was a great linguist, a master of public law; and though he failed in his premature effort to terminate the dogeship of George the Second, he succeeded in maintaining a considerable though secondary position in public life. The young Shelburne married his daughter.* Of him it is singular we know less than of his father-in-law, yet from the scattered traits some idea may be formed of the ablest and most accomplished minister of the eighteenth century. Lord Shelburne, influenced probably by the example and the traditionary precepts of his eminent father-in-law, appears early to have held himself aloof from the patrician connection, and entered public life as the follower of Bute* in the first great effort of George the Third to rescue the sovereignty from what Lord Chatham called 'the Great Revolution families.' He became in time a member of Lord Chatham's last administration; one of the strangest and most unsuccessful efforts to aid the grandson of George the Second in his struggle for political emancipation. Lord Shelburne adopted from the first the Bolingbroke system; a real royalty, in lieu of the chief magistracy; a permanent alliance with France, instead of the Whig scheme of viewing in that power the natural enemy of England; and, above all, a plan of commercial freedom, the germ of which may be found in the long-maligned negotiations of Utrecht,* but which in the instance of Lord Shelburne were soon in time matured by all the economical science of Europe, in which he was a proficient. Lord Shelburne seems to have been of a reserved and somewhat astute disposition: deep and adroit, he was however brave and firm. His knowledge was extensive and even profound. He was a great linguist; he pursued both literary and scientific investigations; his house was frequented by men of letters, especially those distinguished by their political abilities or economical attainments. He maintained the most extensive private correspondence of any public man of his time. The earliest and most authentic information reached him from all courts and quarters of Europe; and it was a common phrase, that the minister of the day sent to him often for the important information which the cabinet could not itself command. Lord Shelburne was the first great minister who comprehended the rising importance of the middle class; and foresaw in its future power a bulwark for the throne against 'the Great Revolution families.' Of his qualities in council we have no record; there is reason to believe that his administrative ability was conspicuous; his speeches prove that, if not supreme, he was eminent, in the art of parliamentary disputation, while they show on all the questions discussed a richness and variety of information with which the speeches of no statesman of that age except Mr. Burke can compare.

Such was the man selected by George the Third as his champion against the Venetian party after the termination of the American war. The prosecution of that war they had violently opposed, though it had originated in their own policy. First minister in the House of Lords, Shelburne entrusted the lead in the House of Commons to his Chancellor of the Exchequer, the youthful Pitt. The administration was brief, but it was not inglorious. It obtained peace, and for the first time since the Revolution introduced into modern debate the legitimate principles on which commerce should be conducted. It fell before the famous Coalition* with which 'the Great Revolution families' commenced their fiercest and their last contention for the patrician government of royal England.

In the heat of that great strife, the king in the second hazardous exercise of his prerogative entrusted the perilous command to Pitt. Why Lord Shelburne on that occasion was set aside will perhaps always remain a mysterious passage of our political history, nor have we space on the present occasion to attempt to penetrate its motives. Perhaps the monarch, with a sense of the rising sympathies of his people, was prescient of the magic power of youth in touching the heart of a nation. Yet it would not be an unprofitable speculation if for a moment we paused to consider what might have been the consequences to our country if Mr. Pitt had been content for a season again to lead the Commons under Lord Shelburne, and have secured for England the unrivalled knowledge and dexterity of that statesman in the conduct of our affairs during the confounding fortunes of the French revolution. Lord Shelburne was the only English minister competent to the task; he was the only public man who had the previous knowledge requisite to form accurate conclusions on such a conjuncture; his remaining speeches on the subject attest the amplitude of his knowledge and the accuracy of his views; and in the rout of Jena, or the agony of Austerlitz, one cannot refrain from picturing the shade of Shelburne haunting the cabinet of Pitt, as the ghost of Canning* is said occasionally to linger about the speaker's chair, and smile sarcastically on the conscientious mediocrities who pilfered his hard-earned honours.

But during the happier years of Mr. Pitt, the influence of the mind of Shelburne may be traced throughout his policy. It was Lansdowne House that made Pitt acquainted with Dr. Price, a dissenting minister, whom Lord Shelburne when at the head of affairs courageously offered to make his private secretary, and who furnished Mr. Pitt, among many other important suggestions, with his original plan of the sinking fund. The commercial treaties of '87 were struck in the same mint, and are notable as the first effort made by the English government to emancipate

the country from the restrictive policy which had been introduced by
the 'glorious revolution;' memorable epoch, that presented England at
the same time with a corn law* and a public debt. But on no subject was
the magnetic influence of the descendant of Sir William Petty* more
decided, than in the resolution of his pupil to curb the power of the
patrician party by an infusion from the middle classes into the government of the country. Hence the origin of Mr. Pitt's famous and long-
misconceived plans of parliamentary reform. Was he sincere, is often
asked by those who neither seek to discover the causes nor are capable
of calculating the effects of public transactions. Sincere! Why, he was
struggling for his existence! And when baffled, first by the Venetian party,
and afterwards by the panic of Jacobinism, he was forced to forego his
direct purpose, he still endeavoured partially to effect it by a circuitous
process. He created a plebeian aristocracy and blended it with the patrician oligarchy. He made peers of second-rate squires and fat graziers. He
caught them in the alleys of Lombard Street, and clutched them from
the counting-houses of Cornhill.* When Mr. Pitt in an age of bank
restriction declared that every man with an estate of ten thousand a-year
had a right to be a peer, he sounded the knell of 'the cause for which
Hampden had died on the field, and Sydney on the scaffold.'*

In ordinary times the pupil of Shelburne would have raised this country to a state of great material prosperity, and removed or avoided many
of those anomalies which now perplex us; but he was not destined for
ordinary times; and though his capacity was vast and his spirit lofty, he
had not that passionate and creative genius required by an age of revolution. The French outbreak was his evil dæmon: he had not the means
of calculating its effects upon Europe. He had but a meagre knowledge
himself of continental politics: he was assisted by a very inefficient diplo-
macy. His mind was lost in a convulsion of which he neither could comprehend the causes nor calculate the consequences; and forced to act,
he acted not only violently, but in exact opposition to the very system
he was called into political existence to combat; he appealed to the fears,
the prejudices, and the passions of a privileged class, revived the old
policy of the oligarchy he had extinguished, and plunged into all the
ruinous excesses of French war and Dutch finance.*

If it be a salutary principle in the investigation of historical transactions to be careful in discriminating the cause from the pretext, there is
scarcely any instance in which the application of this principle is more
fertile in results, than in that of the Dutch invasion* of 1688. The real
cause of this invasion was financial. The Prince of Orange had found
that the resources of Holland, however considerable, were inadequate

to sustain him in his internecine rivalry with the great sovereign of France. In an authentic conversation which has descended to us, held by William at the Hague with one of the prime abettors of the invasion, the prince did not disguise his motives; he said, 'nothing but such a constitution as you have in England can have the credit that is necessary to raise such sums as a great war requires.' The prince came, and used our constitution for his purpose: he introduced into England the system of Dutch finance. The principle of that system was to mortgage industry in order to protect property: abstractedly, nothing can be conceived more unjust; its practice in England has been equally injurious. In Holland, with a small population engaged in the same pursuits, in fact a nation of bankers, the system was adapted to the circumstances which had created it. All shared in the present spoil, and therefore could endure the future burthen. And so to this day Holland is sustained, almost solely sustained, by the vast capital thus created which still lingers amongst its dykes. But applied to a country in which the circumstances were entirely different; to a considerable and rapidly-increasing population; where there was a numerous peasantry, a trading middle class struggling into existence; the system of Dutch finance, pursued more or less for nearly a century and a half, has ended in the degradation of a fettered and burthened multitude. Nor have the demoralizing consequences of the funding system on the more favoured classes been less decided. It has made debt a national habit;* it has made credit the ruling power, not the exceptional auxiliary, of all transactions; it has introduced a loose, inexact, haphazard, and dishonest spirit in the conduct of both public and private life; a spirit dazzling and yet dastardly; reckless of consequences and yet shrinking from responsibility. And in the end, it has so overstimulated the energies of the population to maintain the material engagements of the state, and of society at large, that the moral condition of the people has been entirely lost sight of.

A mortgaged aristocracy, a gambling foreign commerce, a home trade founded on a morbid competition, and a degraded people; these are great evils, but ought perhaps cheerfully to be encountered for the greater blessings of civil and religious liberty. Yet the first would seem in some degree to depend upon our Saxon mode of trial by our peers, upon the stipulations of the great Norman charters, upon the practice and the statute of Habeas Corpus,*—a principle native to our common law, but established by the Stuarts; nor in a careful perusal of the Bill of Rights,* or in an impartial scrutiny of the subsequent legislation of those times, though some diminution of our political franchises must be confessed, is it easy to discover any increase of our civil privileges. To those indeed who believe that the English nation,—at all times a religious and Catholic people, but who even in the days of the Plantagenets were anti-papal,*— were in any danger of again falling under the yoke of the Pope of Rome in the reign of James the Second, religious liberty was perhaps accept-able, though it took the shape of a discipline which at once anathema-tized a great portion of the nation, and virtually establishing Puritanism in Ireland,* laid the foundation of those mischiefs which are now endangering the empire.

That the last of the Stuarts had any other object in his impolitic manœuvres, than an impracticable scheme to blend the two churches, there is now authority to disbelieve. He certainly was guilty of the offence of sending an envoy openly to Rome, who, by the bye, was received by the Pope with great discourtesy; and her Majesty Queen Victoria, whose Protestantism cannot be doubted, for it is one of her chief titles to our homage, has at this time a secret envoy* at the same court; and that is the difference between them: both ministers doubtless working how-ever fruitlessly for the same object; the termination of those terrible misconceptions, political and religious, that have occasioned so many martyrdoms, and so many crimes alike to sovereigns and to subjects.

If James the Second had really attempted to re-establish Popery in this country, the English people, who had no hand in his overthrow, would doubtless soon have stirred and secured their 'Catholic and Apostolic church,' independent of any foreign dictation; the church to which they still regularly profess their adherence; and being a practical people, it is possible that they might have achieved their object and yet retained their native princes; under which circumstances we might have been saved from the triple blessings of Venetian politics, Dutch finance, and French wars: against which, in their happiest days, and with their happiest powers, struggled the three greatest of English statesmen,— Bolingbroke, Shelburne, and lastly the son of Chatham.

We have endeavoured in another work,* not we hope without some-thing of the impartiality of the future, to sketch the character and career of his successors. From his death to 1825, the political history of England is a history of great events and little men. The rise of Mr. Canning, long kept down by the plebeian aristocracy of Mr. Pitt as an adventurer, had shaken parties to their centre. His rapid disappearance from the scene left both Whigs and Tories in a state of disorganization. The distinctive principles of these connexions were now difficult to trace. That period of public languor which intervenes between the breaking up of parties and the formation of factions now transpired in England. An exhausted sensualist* on the throne, who only demanded from his ministers repose, a voluptuous aristocracy, and a listless people, were content, in the absence of all public conviction and national passion, to consign the government of the country to a great man, whose decision relieved the sovereign, whose prejudices pleased the nobles, and whose achievements dazzled the multitude.

The DUKE OF WELLINGTON* brought to the post of first minister immortal fame; a quality of success which would almost seem to include all others. His public knowledge was such as might be expected from one whose conduct already formed an important portion of the history of his country. He had a personal and intimate acquaintance with the sovereigns and chief statesmen of Europe, a kind of information in which English ministers have generally been deficient, but without which the management of our external affairs must at the best be haphazard. He possessed administrative talents of the highest order.

The tone of the age, the temper of the country, the great qualities and the high character of the minister, indicated a long and prosperous administration. The only individual in his cabinet who, from a combination of circumstances rather than from any intellectual supremacy over his colleagues, was competent to be his rival, was content to be his successor. In his most aspiring moments, Mr. Peel* in all probability aimed at no higher reach; and with youth and the leadership of the House of Commons, one has no reason to be surprised at his moderation. The conviction that the duke's government would only cease with the termination of his public career was so general, that the moment he was installed in office, the Whigs smiled on him; political conciliation became the slang of the day, and the fusion of parties the babble of clubs and the tattle of boudoirs.

How comes it then that so great a man, in so great a position, should have so signally failed? Should have broken up his government, wrecked his party,* and so completely annihilated his political position, that, even with his historical reputation to sustain him, he can since only re-appear in the councils of his sovereign in a subordinate, not to say equivocal, character?

With all those great qualities which will secure him a place in our history not perhaps inferior even to Marlborough, the Duke of Wellington has one deficiency which has been the stumbling-block of his civil career. Bishop Burnet, in speculating on the extraordinary influence of Lord Shaftesbury,* and accounting how a statesman, so inconsistent in his conduct and so false to his confederates, should have so powerfully controlled his country, observes, 'HIS STRENGTH LAY IN HIS KNOWLEDGE OF ENGLAND.'

Now that is exactly the kind of knowledge which the Duke of Wellington never possessed.

When the king, finding that in Lord Goderich* he had a minister who, instead of deciding, asked his royal master for advice, sent for the Duke of Wellington to undertake the government, a change in the carriage of his grace was perceived by some who had the opportunity to form an opinion on such a subject. If one might venture to use such a word in reference to such a man, we might remark, that the duke had been somewhat daunted by the selection of Mr. Canning. It disappointed great hopes, it baffled great plans, and dispelled for a season the conviction that, it is believed, had been long maturing in his grace's mind; that he was the man of the age, that his military career had been only a preparation for a civil course not less illustrious; and that it was reserved for him to control for the rest of his life undisputed the destinies of a country, which was indebted to him in no slight degree for its European pre-eminence. The death of Mr. Canning revived, the rout of Lord Goderich restored, these views.

Napoleon, at St. Helena, speculating in conversation on the future career of his conqueror, asked, 'What will Wellington do? After all he has done, he will not be content to be quiet. He will change the dynasty.'

Had the great exile been better acquainted with the real character of our Venetian constitution, he would have known that to govern England in 1820, it was not necessary to change its dynasty. But the Emperor, though wrong in the main, was right by the bye. It was clear that the energies that had twice entered Paris as a conqueror, and had made kings and mediatised princes at Vienna,* would not be content to subside into ermined insignificance. The duke commenced his political tactics early. The cabinet of Lord Liverpool,* especially during its latter term, was the hotbed of many intrigues; but the obstacles were numerous, though the appointing fate, in which his grace believed, removed them. The disappearance of Lord Castlereagh* and Mr. Canning from the scene was alike unexpected. The Duke of Wellington was at length prime minister, and no individual ever occupied that post more conscious of its power, and more determined to exercise it.

This is not the occasion on which we shall attempt to do justice to a theme so instructive as the administration of his grace. Treated with impartiality and sufficient information, it would be an invaluable contribution to the stores of our political knowledge and national experience. Throughout its brief but eccentric and tumultuous annals we see continual proof, how important is that knowledge 'in which lay Lord Shaftesbury's strength.' In twenty-four months we find an aristocracy estranged, without a people being conciliated; while on two several occasions, first, the prejudices, and then the pretensions of the middle class, were alike treated with contumely. The public was astonished at hearing of statesmen of long parliamentary fame, men round whom the intelligence of the nation had gathered for years with confidence, or at least with interest, being expelled from the cabinet in a manner not unworthy of Colonel Joyce,* while their places were filled by second-rate soldiers,* whose very names were unknown to the great body of the people, and who under no circumstances should have aspired beyond the government of a colony. This administration which commenced in arrogance ended in panic. There was an interval of perplexity; when occurred the most ludicrous instance extant of an attempt at coalition; subordinates were promoted, while negotiations were still pending with their chiefs; and these negotiations, undertaken so crudely, were terminated in pique; in a manner which added to political disappointment personal offence. When even his parasites began to look gloomy, the duke had a specific that was to restore all, and having allowed every element of power to escape his grasp, he believed he could balance everything by a beer bill.* The growl of reform was heard but it was not very fierce. There was yet time to save himself. His grace precipitated a revolution* which might have been delayed for half a century, and never need have occurred in so aggravated a form. He rather fled than retired. He commenced his ministry like Brennus, and finished it like the tall Gaul sent to murder the rival of Sylla,* but who dropped his weapon before the undaunted gaze of his intended victim.

Lord Marney was spared the pang of the catastrophe. Promoted to a high office in the household, and still hoping that, by the aid of his party, it was yet destined for him to achieve the hereditary purpose of his family, he died in the full faith of dukism; worshipping the duke and believing that ultimately he should himself become a duke. It was under all the circumstances an euthanasia; he expired leaning as it were on his white wand* and babbling of strawberry leaves.

CHAPTER IV.

'MY dear Charles,' said Lady Marney to Egremont the morning after the Derby, as breakfasting with her in her boudoir he detailed some of the circumstances of the race, 'we must forget your naughty horse. I sent you a little note this morning, because I wished to see you most particularly before you went out. Affairs,' continued Lady Marney, first looking round the chamber to see whether there were any fairy listening to her state secrets, 'affairs are critical.'

'No doubt of that,' thought Egremont, the horrid phantom of settling-day seeming to obtrude itself between his mother and himself; but not knowing precisely at what she was driving, he merely sipped his tea, and innocently replied, 'Why?'

'There will be a dissolution,' said Lady Marney.

'What are we coming in?'

Lady Marney shook her head.

'The present men will not better their majority,' said Egremont.

'I hope not,' said Lady Marney.

'Why you always said, that with another general election we must come in, whoever dissolved.'

'But that was with the court in our favour,' rejoined Lady Marney mournfully.

'What, has the king changed?' said Egremont. 'I thought it was all right.'

'All was right,' said Lady Marney. 'These men would have been turned out again, had he only lived three months more.'

'Lived!' exclaimed Egremont.

'Yes,' said Lady Marney; 'the king is dying.'*

Slowly delivering himself of an ejaculation, Egremont leant back in his chair.

'He may live a month,' said Lady Marney; 'he cannot live two. It is the greatest of secrets; known at this moment only to four individuals, and I communicate it to you, my dear Charles, in that absolute confidence which I hope will always subsist between us, because it is an event that may greatly affect your career.'

'How so, my dear mother?'

'Marbury! I have settled with Mr. Tadpole* that you shall stand for the old borough. With the government in our hands, as I had anticipated at the general election, success I think was certain: under the circumstances which we must encounter, the struggle will be more severe, but I think we shall do it: and it will be a happy day for me to have our own again, and to see you in Parliament, my dear child.'

'Well, my dear mother, I should like very much to be in Parliament, and particularly to sit for the old borough; but I fear the contest will be very expensive,' said Egremont inquiringly.

'Oh! I have no doubt,' said Lady Marney, 'that we shall have some monster of the middle class, some tinker or tailor, or candlestick-maker, with his long purse, preaching reform and practising corruption; exactly as the liberals did under Walpole: bribery was unknown in the time of the Stuarts; but we have a capital registration,* Mr. Tadpole tells me. And a young candidate with the old name will tell,' said Lady Marney, with a smile: 'and I shall go down and canvass, and we must do what we can.'

'I have great faith in your canvassing,' said Egremont; 'but still, at the same time, the powder and shot—'

'Are essential,' said Lady Marney, 'I know it, in these corrupt days; but Marney will of course supply those. It is the least he can do: regaining the family influence, and letting us hold up our heads again. I shall write to him the moment I am justified,' said Lady Marney, 'perhaps you will do so yourself, Charles.'

'Why, considering I have not seen my brother for two years, and we did not part on the best possible terms—'

'But that is all forgotten.'

'By your good offices, dear mother, who are always doing good: and yet,' continued Egremont, after a moment's pause, 'I am not disposed to write to Marney, especially to ask a favour.'

'Well, I will write,' said Lady Marney; 'though I cannot admit it is any favour. Perhaps it would be better that you should see him first. I cannot understand why he keeps so at the Abbey. I am sure I found it a melancholy place enough in my time. I wish you had gone down there, Charles, if it had been only for a few days.'

'Well I did not, my dear mother, and I cannot go now. I shall trust to you. But are you quite sure that the king is going to die?'

'I repeat to you, it is certain,' replied Lady Marney, in a lowered voice, but a decided tone; 'certain, certain, certain. My authority cannot be mistaken: but no consideration in the world must throw you off your guard at this moment; breathe not the shadow of what you know.'

At this moment a servant entered and delivered a note to Lady Marney, who read it with an ironical smile. It was from Lady St. Julians, and ran thus:—

'Most confidential.

'MY DEAREST LADY MARNEY,

'It is a false report: he is ill, but not dangerously; the hay fever; he always has it; nothing more; I will tell my authority when we meet; I dare not write it. It will satisfy you. I am going on with my quadrille.

'Most affectionately yours,

'A. ST. J.'

'Poor woman! she is always wrong,' said Lady Marney throwing the note to Egremont. 'Her quadrille will never take place, which is a pity, as it is to consist only of beauties and eldest sons. I suppose I must send her a line,' and she wrote:

'MY DEAREST LADY ST. JULIANS,

'How good of you to write to me, and send me such cheering news! I have no doubt you are right; you always are. I know he had the hay fever last year. How fortunate for your quadrille, and how charming it will be! Let me know if you hear anything further from your unmentionable quarter.

'Ever your affectionate
'C. M.'

CHAPTER V.

LORD MARNEY left several children; his heir was five years older than the next son Charles who at the period of his father's death was at Christchurch and had just entered the last year of his minority.* Attaining that age, he received the sum of fifteen thousand pounds,* his portion, a third of which amount his expenditure had then already anticipated. Egremont had been brought up in the enjoyment of every comfort and every luxury that refinement could devise and wealth furnish. He was a favourite child. His parents emulated each other in pampering and indulging him. Every freak was pardoned, every whim was gratified. He might ride what horses he liked, and if he broke their knees, what in another would have been deemed a flagrant sin, was in him held only a proof of reckless spirit. If he were not a thoroughly selfish and altogether wilful person, but very much the reverse, it was not the fault of his parents, but rather the operation of a benignant nature that had bestowed on him a generous spirit and a tender heart, though accompanied with a dangerous susceptibility that made him the child and creature of impulse, and seemed to set at defiance even the course of time to engraft on his nature any quality of prudence. The tone of Eton* during the days of Charles Egremont was not of the high character which at present distinguishes that community. It was the unforeseen eve of the great change,* that, whatever was its purpose or have been its immediate results, at least gave the first shock to the pseudo-aristocracy of this country. Then all was blooming; sunshine and odour; not a breeze disturbing the meridian splendour. Then the world was not only made for a few, but a very few. One could almost tell upon one's fingers the happy families who could do anything, and might have everything. A school-boy's ideas of the Church then were fat-livings, and of the State, rotten-boroughs. To do nothing and get something, formed a boy's ideal of a manly career. There was nothing in the lot, little in the temperament, of Charles Egremont, to make him an exception to the multitude. Gaily and securely he floated on the brilliant stream. Popular at school, idolized at home, the present had no cares, and the future secured him a family seat in Parliament the moment he entered life, and the inheritance of a glittering post at court in due time, as its legitimate consequence. Enjoyment, not ambition, seemed the principle of his existence. The contingency of a mitre, the certainty of rich preferment, would not reconcile him to the self-sacrifice which, to a certain degree, was required from a priest, even in those days of rampant Erastianism. He left the colonies as the spoil of his younger brothers; his own ideas of a profession being limited to a barrack in a London park, varied by visits to Windsor.* But there was time enough to think of these things. He had to enjoy Oxford as he had enjoyed Eton. Here his allowance from his father was extravagant, though greatly increased by tithes from his mother's pin-money. While he was pursuing his studies, hunting and boating, driving tandems, riding matches, tempering his energies in the crapulence of boyish banquets, and anticipating life, at the risk of expulsion, in a miserable mimicry of metropolitan dissipation, Dukism,* that was supposed to be eternal, suddenly crashed.

The Reform Act has not placed the administration of our affairs in abler hands than conducted them previously to the passing of the measure, for the most efficient members of the present cabinet with some very few exceptions, and those attended by peculiar circumstances, were ministers before the Reform Act was contemplated. Nor has that memorable statute created a Parliament of a higher reputation for public qualities, such as politic ability, and popular eloquence, and national consideration, than was furnished by the old scheme. On the contrary; one house of Parliament* has been irremediably degraded into the decaying position of a mere court of registry, possessing great privileges, on condition that it never exercises them; while the other chamber that, at the first blush, and to the superficial, exhibits symptoms of almost unnatural vitality, engrossing in its orbit all the business of the country, assumes on a more studious inspection somewhat of the character of a select vestry,* fulfilling municipal rather than imperial offices, and beleaguered by critical and clamorous millions, who cannot comprehend why a privileged and exclusive senate is required to perform functions which immediately concern all, which most personally comprehend, and which many in their civic spheres believe they could accomplish in a manner not less satisfactory, though certainly less ostentatious.

But if it have not furnished us with abler administrators or a more illustrious senate, the Reform Act may have exercised on the country at large a beneficial influence. Has it? Has it elevated the tone of the public mind? Has it cultured the popular sensibilities to noble and ennobling ends? Has it proposed to the people of England a higher test of national respect and confidence than the debasing qualification universally prevalent in this country since the fatal introduction of the system of Dutch finance? Who will pretend it? If a spirit of rapacious covetousness, desecrating all the humanities of life, has been the besetting sin of England for the last century and a half, since the passing of the Reform Act the altar of Mammon has blazed with triple worship. To acquire, to accumulate, to plunder each other by virtue of philosophic phrases, to propose an Utopia to consist only of WEALTH and TOIL,* this has been the breathless business of enfranchised England for the last twelve years, until we are startled from our voracious strife by the wail of intolerable serfage.

Are we then to conclude, that the only effect of the Reform Act has been to create in this country another of those class interests, which we now so loudly accuse as the obstacles to general amelioration? Not exactly that. The indirect influence of the Reform Act has been not inconsiderable, and may eventually lead to vast consequences. It set men a-thinking; it enlarged the horizon of political experience; it led the public mind to ponder somewhat on the circumstances of our national history; to pry into the beginnings of some social anomalies which they found were not so ancient as they had been led to believe, and which had their origin in causes very different to what they had been educated to credit; and insensibly it created and prepared a popular intelligence to which one can appeal, no longer hopelessly, in an attempt to dispel the mysteries with which for nearly three centuries it has been the labour of party writers to involve a national history, and without the dispersion of which no political position can be understood and no social evil remedied.

The events of 1830 did not produce any change in the modes of thought and life of Charles Egremont. He took his political cue from his mother, who was his constant correspondent. Lady Marney was a distinguished 'stateswoman,' as they called Lady Carlisle* in Charles the First's time, a great friend of Lady St. Julians, and one of the most eminent and impassioned votaries of Dukism. Her first impression on the overthrow of her hero was, astonishment at the impertinence of his adversaries, mingled with some lofty pity for their silly ambition and short-lived career. She existed for a week in the delightful expectation of his grace being sent for again, and informed every one in confidence, that 'these people could not form a cabinet.' When the tocsin of peace, reform, and retrenchment sounded, she smiled bitterly; was sorry for poor Lord Grey* of whom she had thought better, and gave them a year, adding with consoling malice, 'that it would be another Canning affair.' At length came the Reform Bill itself, and no one laughed more heartily than Lady Marney; not even the House of Commons to whom it was presented.

The bill was thrown out, and Lady Marney gave a grand ball to celebrate the event, and to compensate the London shopkeepers for the loss of their projected franchise. Lady Marney was preparing to resume her duties at court when to her great surprise the firing of cannon announced the dissolution of Parliament. She turned pale; she was too much in the secrets of Tadpole and Taper* to be deceived as to the consequences; she sank into her chair, and denounced Lord Grey as a traitor to his order.

Lady Marney who for six months had been writing to her son at Oxford the most charming letters, full of fun, quizzing the whole Cabinet, now announced to Egremont that a revolution was inevitable, that all property would be instantly confiscated, the poor deluded king led to the block or sent over to Hanover at the best, and the whole of the nobility and principal gentry, and indeed every one who possessed anything, guillotined without remorse.

Whether his friends were immediately to resume power, or whether their estates ultimately were to be confiscated, the practical conclusion to Charles Egremont appeared to be the same. Carpe diem.* He therefore pursued his career at Oxford unchanged, and entered life in the year 1833, a younger son with extravagant tastes and expensive habits, with a reputation for lively talents though uncultivated,—for his acquisitions at Eton had been quite puerile, and subsequently he had not become a student,—with many manly accomplishments, and with a mien and visage that at once took the fancy and enlisted the affections. Indeed a physiologist would hardly have inferred from the countenance and structure of Egremont the career he had pursued, or the character which attached to him. The general cast and expression of his features when in repose was pensive: an air of refinement distinguished his well moulded brow; his mouth breathed sympathy, and his rich brown eye gleamed with tenderness. The sweetness of his voice in speaking was in harmony with this organization.

Two years passed in the most refined circles of our society exercised a beneficial influence on the general tone of Egremont, and may be said to have finished his education. He had the good sense and the good taste not to permit his predilection for sports to degenerate into slang; he yielded himself to the delicate and profitable authority of woman, and, as ever happens, it softened his manners and brightened his wit. He was fortunate in having a clever mother, and he appreciated this inestimable possession. Lady Marney had great knowledge of society, and some acquaintance with human nature, which she fancied she had fathomed to its centre; she piqued herself upon her tact, and indeed she was very quick, but she was so energetic that her art did not always conceal itself; very worldly, she was nevertheless not devoid of impulse; she was animated and would have been extremely agreeable, if she had not restlessly aspired to wit; and would certainly have exercised much more influence in society, if she had not been so anxious to show it. Nevertheless, still with many personal charms, a frank and yet, if need be, a finished manner, a quick brain, a lively tongue, a buoyant spirit, and a great social position, Lady Marney was universally and extremely popular; and adored by her children, for indeed she was a mother most affectionate and true.

When Egremont was four-and-twenty, he fell in love—a real passion. He had fluttered like others from flower to flower, and like others had often fancied the last perfume the sweetest, and then had flown away. But now he was entirely captivated. The divinity was a new beauty; the whole world raving of her. Egremont also advanced. The Lady Arabella was not only beautiful: she was clever, fascinating. Her presence was inspiration; at least for Egremont. She condescended to be pleased by him; she signalized him by her notice; their names were mentioned together. Egremont indulged in flattering dreams. He regretted he had not pursued a profession; he regretted he had impaired his slender patrimony; thought of love in a cottage, and renting a manor; thought of living a good deal with his mother, and a little with his brother; thought of the law and the church; thought once of New Zealand.* The favourite of nature and of fashion, this was the first time in the life of Egremont, that he had been made conscious that there was something in his position which, with all its superficial brilliancy, might prepare for him, when youth had fled and the blaze of society grown dim, a drear and bitter lot.

He was roused from his reveries by a painful change in the demeanour of his adored. The mother of the Lady Arabella was alarmed. She liked her daughter to be admired even by younger sons when they were distinguished, but only at a distance. Mr. Egremont's name had been mentioned too often. It had appeared coupled with her daughter's, even in a Sunday paper. The most decisive measures were requisite, and they were taken. Still smiling when they met, still kind when they conversed, it seemed, by some magic dexterity which even baffled Egremont, that their meetings every day grew rarer, and their opportunities for conversation less frequent. At the end of the season, the Lady Arabella selected from a crowd of admirers equally qualified, a young peer of great estate, and of the 'old nobility,' a circumstance which, as her grandfather had only been an East India director,* was very gratifying to the bride.

This unfortunate passion of Charles Egremont, and its mortifying circumstances and consequences, was just that earliest shock in one's life which occurs to all of us; which first makes us think. We have all experienced that disheartening catastrophe, when the illusions first vanish; and our balked imagination, or our mortified vanity, first intimates to us that we are neither infallible nor irresistible. Happily 'tis the season of youth for which the first lessons of experience are destined; and bitter and intolerable as is the first blight of our fresh feelings, the sanguine impulse of early life bears us along. Our first scrape generally leads to our first travel. Disappointment requires change of air; desperation change of scene. Egremont quitted his country, never to return to it again; and returned to it after a year and a-half's absence, a much wiser man. Having left England in a serious mood, and having already tasted with tolerable freedom of the pleasures and frivolities of life, he was not in an inapt humour to observe, to enquire, and to reflect. The new objects that surrounded him excited his intelligence; he met, which indeed is the principal advantage of travel, remarkable men, whose conversation opened his mind. His mind was worth opening. Energies began to stir of which he had not been conscious; awakened curiosity led him to investigate and to read; he discovered that, when he imagined his education was completed, it had in fact not commenced; and that, although he had been at a public school and a university, he in fact knew nothing. To be conscious that you are ignorant is a great step to knowledge.* Before an emancipated intellect and an expanding intelligence, the great system of exclusive manners and exclusive feelings in which he had been born and nurtured, began to tremble; the native generosity of his heart recoiled at a recurrence to that arrogant and frigid life, alike devoid of sympathy and real grandeur.

In the early spring of 1837, Egremont re-entered the world, where he had once sparkled, and which he had once conceived to comprise within its circle all that could interest or occupy man. His mother, delighted at finding him again under her roof, had removed some longstanding coolness between him and his elder brother; his former acquaintance greeted him with cordiality, and introduced him to the new heroes who had sprung up during the season of his absence. Apparently Egremont was not disinclined to pursue, though without eagerness, the same career that had originally engaged him. He frequented assemblies, and lingered in clubs; rode in the park, and lounged at the opera. But there was this difference in his existence, before and since his travels: he was now conscious he wanted an object; and was ever musing over action, though as yet ignorant how to act. Perhaps it was this want of being roused, that led him, it may be for distraction, again to the turf. It was a pursuit that seemed to him more real than the life of saloons, full of affectation, perverted ideas, and factitious passions. Whatever might be the impulse Egremont however was certainly not slightly interested in the Derby; and though by no means uninstructed in the mysteries of the turf, had felt such confidence in his information that, with his usual ardour, he had backed to a considerable amount the horse that ought to have won, but which nevertheless only ran a second.

CHAPTER VI.

Notwithstanding the confidence of Lady St. Julians, and her unrivalled information, the health of the king did not improve: but still it was the hay fever, only the hay fever. An admission had been allowed to creep into the Court Circular, that 'his majesty has been slightly indisposed within the last few days;' but then it was soon followed by a very positive assurance, that his majesty's favourite and long-matured resolution to give a state banquet to the knights of the four orders,* was immediately to be carried into effect. Lady St. Julians had the first information of this important circumstance; it confirmed her original conviction; she determined to go on with her quadrille. Egremont, with something interesting at stake himself, was staggered by this announcement, and by Lady St. Julians' unshaken faith. He consulted his mother: Lady Marney shook her head. 'Poor woman!' said Lady Marney, 'she is always wrong. I know,' continued her ladyship, placing her finger to her lip, 'that Prince Esterhazy has been pressing his long-postponed investiture as a Grand Cross,* in order that he may dine at this very banquet; and it has been announced to him that it is impossible, the king's health will not admit of it. When a simple investiture is impossible, a state banquet to the four orders is very probable. No,' said Lady Marney with a sigh; 'it is a great blow for all of us, but it is no use shutting our eyes to the fact. The poor dear king will never show again.'

And about a week after this there appeared the first bulletin. From that instant, though the gullish multitude studied the daily reports with grave interest; their hopes and speculations and arrangements changing with each phrase; for the initiated there was no suspense. All knew that it was over; and Lady St. Julians, giving up her quadrille, began to look about for seats in parliament for her sons.

'What a happiness it is to have a clever mother,' exclaimed Egremont, as he pondered over the returns of his election agent. Lady Marney, duly warned of the impending catastrophe, was experiencing all the advantages of prior information. It delighted her to meet Lady St. Julians driving distractedly about town, calling at clubs, closeted with red tapers,* making ingenious combinations that would not work, by means of which some one of her sons was to stand in coalition with some rich parvenu; to pay none of the expenses and yet to come in first. And all this time, Lady Marney, serene and smiling, had the daily pleasure of assuring Lady St. Julians what a relief it was to her that Charles had fixed on his place. It had been arranged indeed these weeks past; 'but then, you know,' concluded Lady Marney in the sweetest voice and with a blandishing glance, 'I never did believe in that hay fever.'

In the meantime the impending event changed the whole aspect of the political world. The king dying before the new registration was the greatest blow to pseudo-toryism since his majesty, calling for a hackney coach,* went down and dissolved parliament in 1831. It was calculated by the Tadpoles and Tapers that a dissolution by Sir Robert,* after the registration of 1837, would give him a clear majority, not too great a one, but large enough; a manageable majority; some five-and-twenty or thirty men, who with a probable peerage or two dangling in the distance, half-a-dozen positive baronetcies, the Customs for their constituents, and Court balls for their wives, might be induced to save the state. O! England, glorious and ancient realm, the fortunes of thy polity are indeed strange! The wisdom of the Saxons, Norman valour, the statecraft of the Tudors, the national sympathies of the Stuarts, the spirit of the latter Guelphs* struggling against their enslaved sovereignty,—these are the high qualities, that for a thousand years have secured thy national developement. And now all thy memorial dynasties end in the huckstering rule of some thirty unknown and anonymous jobbers! The Thirty at Athens* were at least tyrants. They were marked men. But the obscure majority, who under our present constitution are destined to govern

England, are as secret as a Venetian conclave.* Yet on their dark voices all depends. Would you promote or prevent some great measure that may affect the destinies of unborn millions, and the future character of the people,—take, for example, a system of national education,*—the minister must apportion the plunder to the illiterate clan; the scum that floats on the surface of a party; or hold out the prospect of honours, which are only honourable when in their transmission they impart and receive lustre; when they are the meed of public virtue and public services, and the distinction of worth and of genius. It is impossible that the system of the thirty can long endure in an age of inquiry and agitated spirit like the present. Such a system may suit the balanced interests and the periodical and alternate command of rival oligarchical connections: but it can subsist only by the subordination of the sovereign and the degradation of the multitude; and cannot accord with an age, whose genius will soon confess that Power and the People are both divine.

'He can't last ten days,' said a Whig secretary of the treasury* with a triumphant glance at Mr. Taper as they met in Pall Mall; 'You're out for our lives.'

'Don't you make too sure for yourselves,' rejoined in despair the dismayed Taper. 'It does not follow that because we are out, that you are in.'

'How do you mean?'

'There is such a person as Lord Durham* in the world,' said Mr. Taper very solemnly.

'Pish,' said the secretary.

'You may pish,' said Mr. Taper, 'but if we have a radical government, as I believe and hope, they will not be able to get up the steam as they did in—31; and what with church and corn together, and the Queen Dowager,* we may go to the country with as good a cry as some other persons.'

'I will back Melbourne against the field, now,' said the secretary.

'Lord Durham dined at Kensington* on Thursday,' said Taper, 'and not a Whig present.'

'Ay; Durham talks very fine at dinner,' said the secretary, 'but he has no real go in him. When there is a Prince of Wales, Lord Melbourne means to make Durham governor to the heir apparent, and that will keep him quiet.'

'What do you hear?' said Mr. Tadpole, joining them; 'I am told he has quite rallied.'

'Don't you flatter yourself,' said the secretary.

'Well, we shall hear what they say on the hustings,' said Tadpole looking boldly.

'Who's afraid!' said the secretary. 'No, no, my dear fellow, you are dead beat; the stake is worth playing for, and don't suppose we are such flats as to lose the race for want of jockeying. Your humbugging registration will never do against a new reign. Our great men mean to shell out, I tell you; we have got Croucher; we will denounce the Carlton* and corruption all over the kingdom; and if that won't do, we will swear till we are black in the face, that the King of Hanover* is engaged in a plot to dethrone our young Queen!' and the triumphant secretary wished the worthy pair good morning.

'They certainly have a very good cry,' said Taper mournfully.

'After all, the registration might be better,' said Tadpole, 'but still it is a very good one.'

The daily bulletins became more significant; the crisis was evidently at hand. A dissolution of parliament at any time must occasion great excitement; combined with a new reign, it inflames the passions of every class of the community. Even the poor begin to hope; the old, wholesome superstition still lingers, that the sovereign can exercise power; and the suffering multitude are fain to believe that its remedial character may be about to be revealed in their instance. As for the aristocracy in a new reign, they are all in a flutter. A bewildering vision of coronets, stars, and ribbons; smiles, and places at court; haunts their noontide speculations and their midnight dreams. Then we must not forget the numberless instances in which the coming event is deemed to supply the long-sought opportunity of distinction, or the long-dreaded cause of utter discomfiture; the hundreds, the thousands, who mean to get into parliament, the units who dread getting out. What a crashing change from lounging in St. James's street to sauntering on Boulogne pier; or, after dining at Brookes' and supping at Crockford's, to be saved from destruction by the friendly interposition that sends you in an official capacity to the marsupial sympathies of Sydney or Swan River!*

Now is the time for the men to come forward who have claims; claims for spending their money, which nobody asked them to do, but which of course they only did for the sake of the party. They never wrote for their party, or spoke for their party, or gave their party any other vote than their own; but they urge their claims,—to something; a commissionership of anything, or a consulship anywhere; if no place to be had, they are ready to take it out in dignities. They once looked to the privy council, but would now be content with an hereditary honour; if they can have neither, they will take a clerkship in the Treasury for a younger son. Perhaps they may get that in time; at present they go away growling with a gaugership; or, having with desperate dexterity at length contrived to transform a tidewaiter into a land-waiter.* But there is nothing like asking—except refusing.

Hark! it tolls! All is over. The great bell of the metropolitan cathedral announces the death of the last son of George the Third who probably will ever reign* in England. He was a good man: with feelings and sympathies; deficient in culture rather than ability; with a sense of duty; and with something of the conception of what should be the character of an English monarch. Peace to his manes! We are summoned to a different scene.

In a palace in a garden*—not in a haughty keep, proud with the fame, but dark with the violence of ages; not in a regal pile, bright with the splendour, but soiled with the intrigues, of courts and factions—in a palace in a garden, meet scene for youth, and innocence, and beauty—came the voice that told the maiden she must ascend her throne!

The council of England is summoned for the first time within her bowers. There are assembled the prelates and captains and chief men of her realm; the priests of the religion that consoles, the heroes of the sword that has conquered, the votaries of the craft that has decided the fate of empires; men grey with thought, and fame, and age; who are the stewards of divine mysteries, who have encountered in battle the hosts of Europe, who have toiled in secret cabinets, who have struggled in the less merciful strife of aspiring senates; men too, some of them, lords of a thousand vassals and chief proprietors of provinces, yet not one of them whose heart does not at this moment tremble as he awaits the first presence of the maiden who must now ascend her throne.

A hum of half-suppressed conversation which would attempt to conceal the excitement, which some of the greatest of them have since acknowledged, fills that brilliant assemblage; that sea of plumes, and glittering stars, and gorgeous dresses. Hush! the portals open; She comes! The silence is as deep as that of a noontide forest. Attended for a moment by her royal mother and the ladies of her court, who bow and then retire, VICTORIA ascends her throne; a girl, alone, and for the first time, amid an assemblage of men.

In a sweet and thrilling voice, and with a composed mien which indicates rather the absorbing sense of august duty than an absence of emotion, THE QUEEN announces her accession to the throne of her ancestors, and her humble hope that divine providence will guard over the fulfilment of her lofty trust.

The prelates and captains and chief men of her realm then advance to the throne, and kneeling before her, pledge their troth, and take the sacred oaths of allegiance and supremacy.

Allegiance to one who rules over the land that the great Macedonian could not conquer; and over a continent of which even Columbus* never dreamed: to the Queen of every sea, and of nations in every zone.

It is not of these that I would speak; but of a nation nearer her footstool, and which at this moment looks to her with anxiety, with affection, perhaps with hope. Fair and serene, she has the blood and beauty of the Saxon. Will it be her proud destiny at length to bear relief to suffering millions, and with that soft hand which might inspire troubadours and guerdon knights, break the last links in the chain of Saxon thraldom?*

END OF THE FIRST BOOK.

BOOK II.

CHAPTER I.

THE building which was still called Marney Abbey, though remote from the site of the ancient monastery, was an extensive structure raised at the latter end of the reign of James the First, and in the stately and picturesque style of that age. Placed on a noble elevation in the centre of an extensive and well wooded park, it presented a front with two projecting wings of equal dimensions with the centre, so that the form of the building was that of a quadrangle, less one of its sides. Its ancient lattices had been removed, and the present windows though convenient accorded little with the structure; the old entrance door in the centre of the building however still remained, a wondrous specimen of fantastic carving: Ionic columns of black oak, with a profusion of fruits and flowers, and heads of stags and sylvans.* The whole of the building was crowned with a considerable pediment of what seemed at the first glance fanciful open work, but which examined more nearly offered in gigantic letters the motto of the house of Marney. The portal opened to a hall, such as is now rarely found; with the dais, the screen, the gallery, and the buttery-hatch all perfect, and all of carved black oak. Modern luxury, and the refined taste of the lady of the late lord, had made Marney Abbey as remarkable for its comfort and pleasantness of accommodation as for its ancient state and splendour. The apartments were in general furnished with all the cheerful ease and brilliancy of the modern mansion of a noble, but the grand gallery of the seventeenth century was still preserved, and was used on great occasions as the chief reception-room. You ascended the principal staircase to reach it through a long corridor. It occupied the whole length of one of the wings; was one hundred feet long, and forty-five feet broad, its walls hung with a collection of choice pictures rich in history; while the Axminster carpets, the cabinets, carved tables, and variety of easy chairs, ingeniously grouped, imparted even to this palatian chamber a lively and habitable air.

Lord Marney was several years the senior of Charles Egremont, yet still a young man. He was handsome; there was indeed a general resemblance between the brothers, though the expression of their countenances was entirely different; of the same height and air, and throughout the features a certain family cast; but here the likeness ceased. The countenance of Lord Marney bespoke the character of his mind; cynical, devoid of sentiment, arrogant, literal, hard. He had no imagination, had exhausted his slight native feeling, but he was acute, disputatious, and firm even to obstinacy. Though his early education had been very imperfect, he had subsequently read a good deal, especially in French literature. He had formed his mind by Helvetius,* whose system he deemed irrefutable, and in whom alone he had faith. Armed with the principles of his great master, he believed he could pass through exist-ence in adamantine armour, and always gave you in the business of life the idea of a man who was conscious you were trying to take him in, and rather respected you for it, but the working of whose cold, unkind, eye defied you.

There never had been excessive cordiality between the brothers even in their boyish days, and shortly after Egremont's entrance into life, they had become estranged. They were to meet now for the first time since Egremont's return from the continent. Their mother had arranged their reconciliation. They were to meet as if no misunderstanding had ever existed between them; it was specially stipulated by Lord Marney, that there was to be no 'scene.' Apprised of Egremont's impending arrival, Lord Marney was careful to be detained late that day at petty sessions,* and entered the room only a few minutes before dinner was announced, where he found Egremont not only with the countess and a young lady who was staying with her, but with additional bail against any ebullition of sentiment in the shape of the Vicar of Marney, and a certain Captain Grouse, who was a kind of aide-de-camp of the earl; killed birds and carved them; played billiards with him, and lost; had indeed every accomplishment that could please woman or ease man; could sing, dance, draw, make artificial flies,* break horses, exercise a supervision over stewards and bailiffs, and make every body comfortable by taking everything on his own shoulders.

Lady Marney had received Egremont in a manner which expressed the extreme satisfaction she experienced at finding him once more beneath his brother's roof. When he arrived indeed, he would have pre-ferred to have been shown at once to his rooms, but a message imme-diately delivered expressed the wish of his sister-in-law at once to see him. She received him alone and with great warmth. She was beautiful, and soft as May; a glowing yet delicate face; rich brown hair, and large blue eyes; not yet a mother, but with something of the dignity of the matron blending with the lingering timidity of the girl.

Egremont was glad to join his sister-in-law again in the drawing-room before dinner. He seated himself by her side; and in answer to her enquiries was giving her some narrative of his travels; the Vicar who was very low church, was shaking his head at Lady Marney's young friend, who was enlarging on the excellence of Mr. Paget's tales;* while Captain Grouse, in a very stiff white neck-cloth, very tight pantaloons, to show his very celebrated legs, transparent stockings and polished shoes, was throwing himself into attitudes in the back ground, and with a zeal amounting almost to enthusiasm, teaching Lady Marney's spaniel to beg; when the door opened, and Lord Marney entered, but as if to make security doubly sure, not alone. He was accompanied by a neighbour and brother magistrate, Sir Vavasour Firebrace, a baronet* of the earliest batch, and a gentleman of great family and great estate.

'Well Charles!'

'How are you George?'

And the brothers shook hands.

'Tis the English way; and if they had been inclined to fall into each other's arms, they would not probably have done more.

In a few minutes it was announced that dinner was served, and so, secured from a scene, having a fair appetite, and surrounded by dishes that could agreeably satisfy it, a kind of vague fraternal sentiment began to stir the breast of Lord Marney: he really was glad to see his brother again; remembered the days when they rode their poneys and played cricket; his voice softened, his eyes sparkled, and he at length exclaimed, 'Do you know, old fellow, it makes me quite happy to see you here again. Suppose we take a glass of wine.'

The softer heart and more susceptible spirit of Egremont were well calculated to respond to this ebullition of feeling, however slight; and truly it was for many reasons not without considerable emotion, that he found himself once more at Marney. He sate by the side of his gentle sister-in-law, who seemed pleased by the unwonted cordiality of her husband, and anxious by many kind offices to second every indication of good feeling on his part. Captain Grouse was extremely assiduous; the vicar was of the deferential breed, agreed with Lady Marney on the importance of infant schools, but recalled his opinion when Lord Marney expressed his imperious hope that no infant schools would ever be found in his neighbourhood. Sir Vavasour was more than middle aged, comely, very gentlemanlike, but with an air occasionally of absence which hardly agreed with his frank and somewhat hearty idiosyncracy; his clear brow, florid complexion, and blue eye. But Lord Marney talked a good deal, though chiefly dogmatical or argumentative. It was rather difficult for him to find a sufficient stock of opposition, but he laid in wait and seized every opening with wonderful alacrity. Even Captain Grouse could not escape him; if driven to extremity Lord Marney would even question his principles on fly-making. Captain Grouse gave up, but not too soon; he was well aware that his noble friend's passion for controversy was equal to his love of conquest. As for Lady Marney, it was evident that with no inconsiderable talents, and with an intelligence richly cultivated, the controversial genius of her husband had completely cowed her conversational charms. She never advanced a proposition that he did not immediately bristle up, and she could only evade the encounter by a graceful submission. As for the vicar, a frequent guest, he would fain have taken refuge in silence, but the earl, especially when alone, would what he called 'draw him out,' and the game once unearthed, with so skilled a pack there was but little fear of a bad run. When all were reduced to silence, Lord Marney relinquishing controversy, assumed the positive. He eulogized the new poor law, which he declared would be the salvation of the country, provided it was 'carried out' in the spirit in which it was developed in the Marney Union;* but then he would add that there was no district except their union in which it was properly observed. He was tremendously fierce against allotments,* and analysed the system with merciless sarcasm. Indeed he had no inconsiderable acquaintance with the doctrines of the economists, and was rather inclined to carry them into practice in every instance, except that of the landed proprietary, which he clearly proved 'stood upon different grounds' to that of any other 'interest.' There was nothing he hated so much as a poacher, except a lease; though perhaps in the catalogue of his aversions, we ought to give the preference to his anti-ecclesiastical prejudice: this amounted even to acrimony. Though there was no man breathing who was possessed with such a strong repugnance to subscriptions of any kind, it delighted Lord Marney to see his name among the contributors to all sectarian institutions. The vicar of Marney, who had been presented* by himself, was his model of a priest: he left every body alone. Under the influence of Lady Marney, the worthy vicar had once warmed up into some ebullition of very low church zeal; there was some talk of an evening lecture, the schools were to be remodelled, certain tracts were actually distributed. But Lord Marney soon stopped all this. 'No priestcraft at Marney,' said this gentle proprietor of abbey lands.

'I wanted very much to come and canvass for you,' said Lady Marney to Egremont, 'but George did not like it.'

'The less the family interfered the better,' said Lord Marney; 'and for my part, I was very much alarmed when I heard my mother had gone down.'

'Oh! my mother did wonders,' said Egremont; 'we should have been beat without her. Indeed, to tell the truth, I quite gave up the thing the moment they started their man. Before that we were on velvet; but the instant he appeared everything was changed, and I found some of my warmest supporters, members of his committee.'

'You had a formidable opponent, Lord Marney told me,' said Sir Vavasour. 'Who was he?'

'Oh! a dreadful man! A Scotchman, richer than Crœsus, one McDruggy, fresh from Canton,* with a million of opium in each pocket, denouncing corruption, and bellowing free trade.'

'But they do not care much for free trade in the old borough?' said Lord Marney.

'No, it was a mistake,' said Egremont, 'and the cry was changed the moment my opponent was on the ground. Then all the town was plac-arded with 'Vote for McDruggy and our young Queen,' as if he had coalesced with her Majesty.'

'My mother must have been in despair,' said Lord Marney.

'We issued our placard instantly of 'Vote for our young Queen and Egremont,' which was at least more modest, and turned out more popular.'

'That I am sure was my mother,' said Lord Marney.

'No,' said Egremont; 'it was the effusion of a far more experienced mind. My mother was in hourly communication with head quarters, and Mr. Taper sent down the cry by express.'

'Peel, in or out, will support the Poor Law,'* said Lord Marney, rather audaciously, as he reseated himself after the ladies had retired. 'He must;' and he looked at his brother, whose return had in a great degree been secured by crying that Poor Law down.

'It is impossible,' said Charles, fresh from the hustings, and speaking from the card of Taper, for the condition of the people was a subject of which he knew nothing.

'He will carry it out,' said Lord Marney, 'you'll see, or the land will not support him.'

'I wish,' said Sir Vavasour, 'we could manage some modification about out-door relief.'

'Modification!' said Lord Marney; 'why there has been nothing but modification. What we want is stringency.'

'The people will never bear it,' said Egremont; 'there must be some change.'

'You cannot go back to the abuses of the old system,' said Captain Grouse, making, as he thought, a safe observation.

'Better go back to the old system, than modify the new,' said Lord Marney.

'I wish the people would take to it a little more,' said Sir Vavasour; 'they certainly do not like it in our parish.'

'The people are very contented here, eh Slimsey?' said Lord Marney.

'Very,' said the vicar.

Hereupon a conversation took place, principally sustained by the earl and the baronet, which developed all the resources of the great parochial mind. Dietaries, bastardy, gaol regulations, game laws, were amply discussed; and Lord Marney wound up with a declaration of the means by which the country might be saved, and which seemed principally to consist of high prices and low church.

'If the sovereign could only know her best friends,' said Sir Vavasour, with a sigh.

Lord Marney seemed to get uneasy.

'And avoid the fatal mistakes of her predecessor,' continued the baronet.

'Charles, another glass of claret,' said the earl.

'She might yet rally round the throne a body of men'—

'Then we will go to the ladies,' said the earl, abruptly disturbing his guest.

CHAPTER II.

THERE was music as they re-entered the drawing-room. Sir Vavasour attached himself to Egremont.

'It is a great pleasure for me to see you again, Mr. Egremont;' said the worthy baronet. 'Your father was my earliest and kindest friend. I remember you at Firebrace, a very little boy. Happy to see you again, Sir, in so eminent a position; a legislator—one of our legislators. It gave me a sincere satisfaction to observe your return.'

'You are very kind, Sir Vavasour.'

'But it is a responsible position,' continued the baronet. 'Think you they'll stand?* A majority, I suppose, they have; but, I conclude, in time; Sir Robert will have it in time? We must not be in a hurry; 'the more haste'—you know the rest. The country is decidedly conservative. All that we want now is a strong government, that will put all things to rights. If the poor king had lived—'

'He would have sent these men to the right-abouts;' said Egremont, a young politician, proud of his secret intelligence.

'Ah! the poor king!' said Sir Vavasour, shaking his head.

'He was entirely with us,' said Egremont.

'Poor man!' said Sir Vavasour.

'You think it was too late, then?' said his companion.

'You are a young man entering political life,' said the baronet, taking Egremont kindly by the arm, and leading him to a sofa; 'everything depends on the first step. You have a great opportunity. Nothing can be done by a mere individual. The most powerful body in this country wants a champion.'

'But you can depend on Peel?' said Egremont.

'He is one of us;* we ought to be able to depend on him. But I have spoken to him for an hour, and could get nothing out of him.'

'He is cautious; but depend upon it, he will stand or fall by the land.'

'I am not thinking of the land,' said Sir Vavasour; 'of something much more important; with all the influence of the land, and a great deal more besides; of an order of men who are ready to rally round the throne, and are, indeed, if justice were done to them, its natural and hereditary champions (Egremont looked perplexity); I am speaking,' added Sir Vavasour, in a solemn voice, 'I am speaking of the baronets!'

'The baronets! And what do they want?'

'Their rights; their long withheld rights. The poor king was with us. He has frequently expressed to me and other deputies, his determination to do us justice; but he was not a strong-minded man,' said Sir Vavasour, with a sigh; 'and in these revolutionary and levelling times, he had a hard task perhaps. And the peers, who are our brethren, they were, I fear, against us. But in spite of the ministers, and in spite of the peers, had the poor king lived, we should at least have had the badge,'* added Sir Vavasour mournfully.

'The badge!'

'It would have satisfied Sir Grosvenor le Draughte,' said Sir Vavasour; 'and he had a strong party with him; he was for compromise, but d— him, his father was only an accoucheur.'

'And you wanted more?' inquired Egremont, with a demure look.

'All, or nothing,' said Sir Vavasour; 'principle is ever my motto—no expediency. I made a speech to the order at the Clarendon; there were four hundred of us; the feeling was very strong.'

'A powerful party,' said Egremont.

'And a military order, sir, if properly understood. What could stand against us? The Reform Bill could never have passed if the baronets had been organized.'

'I have no doubt you could bring us in now,' said Egremont.

'That is exactly what I told Sir Robert. I want him to be brought in by his own order. It would be a grand thing.'

'There is nothing like esprit de corps,' said Egremont.

'And such a body!' exclaimed Sir Vavasour, with animation. 'Picture us for a moment, to yourself going down in procession to Westminster for example to hold a chapter. Five or six hundred baronets in dark green costume,—the appropriate dress of equites aurati;* each not only with his badge, but with his collar of S.S.; belted and scarfed; his star glittering; his pennon flying; his hat white with a plume of white feathers; of course the sword and the gilt spurs. In our hand, the thumb ring and signet not forgotten, we hold our coronet of two balls!'

Egremont stared with irrepressible astonishment at the excited being, who unconsciously pressed his companion's arm, as he drew this rapid sketch of the glories so unconstitutionally withheld from him.

'A magnificent spectacle!' said Egremont.

'Evidently the body destined to save this country,' eagerly continued Sir Vavasour. 'Blending all sympathies: the crown of which they are the peculiar champions; the nobles of whom they are the popular branch; the people who recognize in them their natural leaders. But the picture is not complete. We should be accompanied by an equal number of gallant knights, our elder sons, who, the moment they come of age, have the right to claim knighthood* of their sovereign, while their mothers and wives, no longer degraded to the nomenclature of a sheriff's lady, but resuming their legal or analogical dignities, and styled the 'honourable baronetess,' with her coronet and robe, or the 'honourable knightess,' with her golden collar of S.S., and chaplet or cap of dignity, may either accompany the procession, or ranged in galleries in a becoming situation, reign influence from above.'

'I am all for their going in the procession,' said Egremont.

'The point is not so clear,' said Sir Vavasour solemnly; 'and indeed, although we have been firm in defining our rightful claims in our petitions, as for 'honorary epithets, secondary titles, personal decorations, and augmented heraldic bearings,' I am not clear if the government evinced a disposition for a liberal settlement of the question, I would not urge a too stringent adherence to every point. For instance, I am prepared myself, great as would be the sacrifice, even to renounce the claim of secondary titles for our eldest sons, if for instance they would secure us our coronet.'

'Fie, fie, Sir Vavasour,' said Egremont very seriously, 'remember principle: no expediency, no compromise.'

'You are right,' said the baronet, colouring a little; 'and do you know, Mr. Egremont, you are the only individual I have yet met out of the Order, who has taken a sensible view of this great question, which, after all, is the question of the day.'

CHAPTER III.

THE situation of the rural town of Marney* was one of the most delightful easily to be imagined. In a spreading dale, contiguous to the margin of a clear and lively stream, surrounded by meadows and gardens, and backed by lofty hills, undulating and richly wooded, the traveller on the opposite heights of the dale would often stop to admire the merry prospect, that recalled to him the traditional epithet of his country.

Beautiful illusion! For behind that laughing landscape, penury and disease fed upon the vitals of a miserable population!

The contrast between the interior of the town and its external aspect, was as striking as it was full of pain. With the exception of the dull high street, which had the usual characteristics of a small agricultural market town, some sombre mansions, a dingy inn, and a petty bourse,* Marney mainly consisted of a variety of narrow and crowded lanes formed by cottages built of rubble, or unhewn stones without cement, and from age, or badness of the material, looking as if they could scarcely hold together. The gaping chinks admitted every blast; the leaning chimneys had lost half their original height; the rotten rafters were evidently misplaced; while in many instances the thatch, yawning in some parts to admit the wind and wet, and in all utterly unfit for its original purpose of giving protection from the weather, looked more like the top of a dunghill than a cottage.* Before the doors of these dwellings, and often surrounding them, ran open drains full of animal and vegetable refuse, decomposing into disease, or sometimes in their imperfect course filling foul pits or spreading into stagnant pools, while a concentrated solution of every species of dissolving filth was allowed to soak through and thoroughly impregnate the walls and ground adjoining.

These wretched tenements seldom consisted of more than two rooms, in one of which the whole family, however numerous, were obliged to sleep, without distinction of age, or sex, or suffering. With the water streaming down the walls, the light distinguished through the roof, with no hearth even in winter, the virtuous mother in the sacred pangs of childbirth, gives forth another victim to our thoughtless civilization; surrounded by three generations whose inevitable presence is more painful

than her sufferings in that hour of travail; while the father of her coming child, in another corner of the sordid chamber, lies stricken by that
typhus which his contaminating dwelling has breathed into his veins,
and for whose next prey is perhaps destined, his new-born child. These
swarming walls had neither windows nor doors sufficient to keep out
the weather, or admit the sun or supply the means of ventilation; the
humid and putrid roof of thatch exhaling malaria like all other decaying
vegetable matter. The dwelling rooms were neither boarded nor paved;
and whether it were that some were situate in low and damp places,
occasionally flooded by the river, and usually much below the level of
the road; or that the springs, as was often the case, would burst through
the mud floor; the ground was at no time better than so much clay, while
sometimes you might see little channels cut from the centre under the
doorways to carry off the water, the door itself removed from its hinges:
a resting place for infancy in its deluged home. These hovels were in
many instances not provided with the commonest conveniences of the
rudest police;* contiguous to every door might be observed the dungheap on which every kind of filth was accumulated, for the purpose of
being disposed of for manure, so that, when the poor man opened his
narrow habitation in the hope of refreshing it with the breeze of summer,
he was met with a mixture of gases from reeking dunghills.

This town of Marney was a metropolis of agricultural labour, for the
proprietors of the neighbourhood having for the last half century acted
on the system of destroying the cottages on their estates, in order to
become exempted from the maintenance of the population, the expelled
people had flocked to Marney, where, during the war,* a manufactory
had afforded them some relief, though its wheels had long ceased to
disturb the waters of the Mar.

Deprived of this resource, they had again gradually spread themselves over that land which had as it were rejected them; and obtained
from its churlish breast a niggardly subsistence. Their re-entrance into
the surrounding parishes was viewed with great suspicion; their renewed
settlement opposed by every ingenious contrivance; those who availed
themselves of their labour were careful that they should not become
dwellers on the soil; and though, from the excessive competition, there
were few districts in the kingdom where the rate of wages was more
depressed, those who were fortunate enough to obtain the scant remuneration, had, in addition to their toil, to endure each morn and even
a weary journey before they could reach the scene of their labour, or
return to the squalid hovel which profaned the name of home. To that
home, over which Malaria hovered, and round whose shivering hearth

were clustered other guests besides the exhausted family of toil—Fever, in every form, pale Consumption, exhausting Synochus,* and trembling Ague,—returned after cultivating the broad fields of merry England* the bold British peasant, returned to encounter the worst of diseases with a frame the least qualified to oppose them; a frame that subdued by toil was never sustained by animal food; drenched by the tempest could not change its dripping rags: and was indebted for its scanty fuel to the windfalls of the woods.

The eyes of this unhappy race might have been raised to the solitary spire that sprang up in the midst of them, the bearer of present consolation, the harbinger of future equality; but Holy Church at Marney had forgotten her sacred mission. We have introduced the reader to the vicar, an orderly man who deemed he did his duty if he preached each week two sermons, and enforced humility on his congregation and gratitude for the blessings of this life. The high street and some neighbouring gentry were the staple of his hearers. Lord and Lady Marney came, attended by Captain Grouse, every Sunday morning with commendable regularity, and were ushered into the invisible interior of a vast pew, that occupied half of the gallery, was lined with crimson damask, and furnished with easy chairs, and, for those who chose them, well-padded stools of prayer. The people of Marney took refuge in conventicles, which abounded; little plain buildings of pale brick with the names painted on them, of Sion, Bethel, Bethesda; names of a distant land,* and the language of a persecuted and ancient race; yet, such is the mysterious power of their divine quality, breathing consolation in the nineteenth century to the harassed forms and the harrowed souls of a Saxon peasantry.

But however devoted to his flock might have been the Vicar of Marney, his exertions for their well-being, under any circumstances, must have been mainly limited to spiritual consolation. Married and a father he received for his labours the small tithes of the parish, which secured to him an income by no means equal to that of a superior banker's clerk, or the cook of a great loanmonger. The great tithes* of Marney, which might be counted by thousands, swelled the vast rental which was drawn from this district by the fortunate earls that bore its name.

The morning after the arrival of Egremont at the Abbey, an unusual stir might have been observed in the high street of the town. Round the portico of the Green Dragon hotel and commercial inn, a knot of principal personages, the chief lawyer, the brewer, the vicar himself, and several of those easy quidnuncs who abound in country towns, and who rank under the designation of retired gentlemen, were in close and very earnest converse. In a short time a servant on horseback in the Abbey livery galloped up to the portico, and delivered a letter to the vicar. The excitement apparently had now greatly increased. On the opposite side of the way to the important group, a knot, larger in numbers but very deficient in quality, had formed themselves, and remained transfixed with gaping mouths and a curious not to say alarmed air. The head constable walked up to the door of the Green Dragon, and though he did not presume to join the principal group, was evidently in attendance, if required. The clock struck eleven; a cart had stopped to watch events, and a gentleman's coachman riding home with a led horse.

'Here they are!' said the brewer.

'Lord Marney himself,' said the lawyer.

'And Sir Vavasour Firebrace, I declare. I wonder how he came here,' said a retired gentleman, who had been a tallow-chandler on Holborn Hill.

The vicar took off his hat, and all uncovered. Lord Marney and his brother magistrate rode briskly up to the inn and rapidly dismounted.

'Well, Snigford,' said his lordship, in a peremptory tone, 'this is a pretty business; I'll have this stopped directly.'

Fortunate man if he succeed in doing so! The torch of the incendiary had for the first time been introduced into the parish of Marney; and last night the primest stacks of the Abbey farm had blazed* a beacon to the agitated neighbourhood.

CHAPTER IV.

'It is not so much the fire, sir,' said Mr. Bingley of the Abbey farm to Egremont, 'but the temper of the people that alarms me. Do you know, sir, there were two or three score of them here, and, except my own farm servants, not one of them would lend a helping hand to put out the flames, though, with water so near, they might have been of great service.'

'You told my brother, Lord Marney, this?'

'Oh! it's Mr. Charles I'm speaking to! My service to you, sir; I'm glad to see you in these parts again. It's a long time that we have had that pleasure, sir. Travelling in foreign parts, as I have heard say?'

'Something of that; but very glad to find myself at home once more, Mr. Bingley, though very sorry to have such a welcome as a blazing rick at the Abbey farm.'

'Well, do you know, Mr. Charles, between ourselves,' and Mr. Bingley lowered his tone, and looked around him, 'things is very bad here; I can't make out, for my part, what has become of the country. Tayn't the same land to live in as it was when you used to come to our moor coursing, with the old lord; you remember that, I be sure, Mr. Charles?'

' 'Tis not easy to forget good sport, Mr. Bingley. With your permission, I will put my horse up here for half an hour. I have a fancy to stroll to the ruins.'

'You wunna find them much changed,' said the farmer, smiling. 'They have seen a deal of different things in their time! But you will taste our ale, Mr. Charles?'

'When I return.'

But the hospitable Bingley would take no denial, and as his companion waived on the present occasion entering his house, for the sun had been some time declining, the farmer, calling one of his labourers to take Egremont's horse, hastened into the house to fill the brimming cup.

'And what do you think of this fire?' said Egremont to the hind.

'I think 'tis hard times for the poor, sir.'

'But rick-burning will not make the times easier, my good man.'

The man made no reply, but with a dogged look led away the horse to his stable.

About half a mile from Marney, the dale narrowed, and the river took a winding course. It ran through meads, soft and vivid with luxuriant vegetation, bounded on either side by rich hanging woods, save where occasionally a quarry broke the verdant bosom of the heights with its rugged and tawny form. Fair stone and plenteous timber, and the current of fresh waters, combined, with the silent and secluded scene screened from every harsh and angry wind, to form the sacred spot that in old days Holy Church loved to hallow with its beauteous and enduring structures. Even the stranger therefore when he had left the town about two miles behind him, and had heard the farm and mill which he had since passed, called the Abbey farm and the Abbey mill, might have been prepared for the grateful vision of some monastic remains. As for Egremont, he had been almost born amid the ruins of Marney Abbey; its solemn relics were associated with his first and freshest fancies; every footstep was as familiar to him as it could have been to one of the old monks; yet never without emotion could he behold these unrivalled remains of one of the greatest of the great religious houses of the North.

Over a space of not less than ten acres might still be observed the fragments of the great abbey: these were, towards their limit, in general moss-grown and mouldering memorials that told where once rose the offices and spread the terraced gardens of the old proprietors; here might still be traced the dwelling of the lord abbot; and there, still more distinctly, because built on a greater scale and of materials still more intended for perpetuity, the capacious hospital, a name that did not then denote the dwelling of disease, but a place where all the rights of hospitality were practised; where the traveller from the proud baron to the lonely pilgrim asked the shelter and the succour that never were denied, and at whose gate, called the Portal of the Poor,* the peasants on the Abbey lands, if in want, might appeal each morn and night for raiment and for food.

But it was in the centre of this tract of ruins, occupying a space of not less than two acres, that, with a strength that had defied time, and with a beauty that had at last turned away the wrath of man, still rose if not in perfect, yet admirable, form and state, one of the noblest achievements of Christian art,—the Abbey church. The summer vault was now its only roof, and all that remained of its gorgeous windows was the vastness of their arched symmetry, and some wreathed relics of their fantastic frame-work, but the rest was uninjured.

From the west window, looking over the transept chapel of the Virgin, still adorned with pillars of marble and alabaster, the eye wandered down the nave to the great orient light, a length of nearly three hundred feet, through a gorgeous avenue of unshaken walls and columns that clustered to the skies. On each side of the Lady's chapel rose a tower. One which was of great antiquity, being of that style which is commonly called Norman, short and very thick and square, did not mount much above the height of the western front; but the other tower was of a character very different. It was tall and light, and of a Gothic* style most pure and graceful; the stone of which it was built, of a bright and even sparkling colour, and looking as if it were hewn but yesterday. At first, its turretted crest seemed injured; but the truth is, it was unfinished; the workmen were busied on this very tower the day that old Baldwin Greymount came as the king's commissioner to inquire into the conduct of this religious house. The abbots loved to memorise their reigns by some public work, which should add to the beauty of their buildings or the convenience of their subjects; and the last of the ecclesiastical lords of Marney, a man of fine taste and a skilful architect, was raising this new belfry for his brethren when the stern decree arrived that the bells should no more sound. And the hymn was no more to be chaunted in the Lady's chapel; and the candles were no more to be lit on the high altar; and the gate of the poor was to be closed for ever; and the wanderer was no more to find a home.

The body of the church was in many parts overgrown with brambles and in all covered with a rank vegetation. It had been a very sultry day, and the blaze of the meridian heat still inflamed the air; the kine for shelter, rather than for sustenance, had wandered through some broken arches, and were lying in the shadow of the nave. This desecration of a spot, once sacred, still beautiful and solemn, jarred on the feelings of Egremont. He sighed and turning away, followed a path that after a few paces led him into the cloister garden. This was a considerable quadrangle, once surrounding the garden of the monks, but all that remained of that fair pleasaunce was a solitary cedar* in its centre, that seemed the oldest tree that could well live, and was, according to tradition, more ancient than the most venerable walls of the Abbey. Round this quadrangle was the refectory, the library and the kitchen, and above them the cells and dormitory of the brethren. An imperfect staircase, not without danger, led to these unroofed chambers; but Egremont familiar with the way did not hesitate to pursue it, so that he soon found himself on an elevation overlooking the garden, while further on extended the vast cloisters of the monks, and adjoining was a cemetery, that had once been enclosed, and communicated with the cloister garden.

It was one of those summer days that are so still, that they seem as it were a holiday of nature. The weary wind was sleeping in some grateful cavern, and the sunbeams basking on some fervent knoll; the river floated with a drowsy unconscious course; there was no wave in the grass, no stir in the branches.

A silence so profound amid these solemn ruins, offered the perfection of solitude; and there was that stirring in the mind of Egremont which rendered him far from indisposed for this loneliness.

The slight words that he had exchanged with the farmer and the hind had left him musing. Why was England not the same land as in the days of his light-hearted youth? Why were these hard times for the poor? He stood among the ruins that, as the farmer had well observed, had seen many changes: changes of creeds, of dynasties, of laws, of manners. New orders of men had arisen in the country, new sources of wealth had opened, new dispositions of power to which that wealth had necessarily led. His own house, his own order, had established themselves on the ruins of that great body, the emblems of whose ancient magnificence and strength surrounded him. And now his order* was in turn menaced. And the People—the millions of Toil, on whose unconscious energies during these changeful centuries all rested—what changes had these centuries brought to them? Had their advance in the national scale borne a due relation to that progress of their rulers, which had accumulated in the treasuries of a limited class the riches of the world; and made their possessors boast that they were the first of nations; the most powerful and the most free, the most enlightened, the most moral, and the most religious? Were there any rick-burners in the times of the lord abbots? And if not, why not? And why should the stacks of the Earls of Marney be destroyed, and those of the Abbots of Marney spared?

Brooding over these suggestions, some voices disturbed him, and looking round, he observed in the cemetery two men: one was standing beside a tomb which his companion was apparently examining.

The first was of lofty stature, and though dressed with simplicity, had nothing sordid in his appearance. His garments gave no clue to his position in life: they might have been worn by a squire or by his game-keeper; a dark velveteen dress and leathern gaiters. As Egremont caught his form, he threw his broad-brimmed country hat upon the ground and showed a frank and manly countenance. His complexion might in youth have been ruddy, but time and time's attendants, thought and passion, had paled it; his chesnut hair, faded, but not grey, still clustered over a noble brow; his features were regular and handsome, a well-formed nose, the square mouth and its white teeth, and the clear grey eye which befitted such an idiosyncracy. His time of vigorous man-hood, for he was much nearer forty than fifty years of age, perhaps better suited his athletic form, than the more supple and graceful season of youth.

Stretching his powerful arms in the air, and delivering himself of an exclamation which denoted his weariness, and which had broken the silence, he expressed to his companion his determination to rest him-self under the shade of the cedar in the contiguous garden, and inviting his friend to follow him, he took up his hat and moved away.

There was something in the appearance of the stranger that inter-ested Egremont; and waiting till he had established himself in his pleas-ant resting place, Egremont descended into the cloister garden and determined to address him.

CHAPTER V.

'YOU lean against an ancient trunk,' said Egremont, carelessly advancing to the stranger, who looked up at him without any expression of surprise, and then replied. 'They say 'tis the trunk beneath whose branches the monks encamped when they came to this valley to raise their building. It was their house, till with the wood and stone around them, their labour and their fine art, they piled up their abbey. And then they were driven out of it, and it came to this. Poor men! poor men!'

'They would hardly have forfeited their resting-place had they deserved to retain it,' said Egremont.

'They were rich. I thought it was poverty that was a crime,' replied the stranger in a tone of simplicity.

'But they had committed other crimes.'

'It may be so; we are very frail. But their history has been written by their enemies; they were condemned without a hearing; the people rose oftentimes in their behalf; and their property was divided with those on whose reports it was forfeited.'

'At any rate, it was a forfeiture which gave life to the community,' said Egremont; 'the lands are held by active men and not by drones.'

'A drone is one who does not labour,' said the stranger; 'whether he wear a cowl or a coronet, 'tis the same to me. Somebody I suppose must own the land; though I have heard say that this individual tenure* is not a necessity; but however this may be, I am not one who would object to the lord, provided he were a gentle one. All agree the Monastics were easy landlords; their rents were low; they granted leases in those days. Their tenants too might renew their term before their tenure ran out: so they were men of spirit and property. There were yeomen* then, sir: the country was not divided into two classes, masters and slaves; there was some resting-place between luxury and misery. Comfort was an English habit then, not merely an English word.'

'And do you really think they were easier landlords than our present ones?' said Egremont, inquiringly.

'Human nature would tell us that, even if history did not confess it. The Monastics could possess no private property; they could save no money; they could bequeath nothing. They lived, received, and expended in common. The monastery too was a proprietor that never died and never wasted. The farmer had a deathless landlord then; not a harsh guardian, or a grinding mortgagee, or a dilatory master in chancery;* all was certain; the manor had not to dread a change of lords, or the oaks to tremble at the axe of the squandering heir. How proud we are still in England of an old family, though, God knows, 'tis rare to see one now. Yet the people like to say, We held under him, and his father and his grandfather before him: they know that such a tenure is a benefit. The abbot was ever the same. The monks were in short in every district a point of refuge for all who needed succour, counsel, and protection; a body of individuals having no cares of their own, with wisdom to guide the inexperienced, with wealth to relieve the suffering, and often with power to protect the oppressed.'

'You plead their cause with feeling,' said Egremont, not unmoved.

'It is my own; they were the sons of the People, like myself.'

'I had thought rather these monasteries were the resort of the younger branches of the aristocracy?' said Egremont.

'Instead of the pension list;'* replied his companion, smiling, but not with bitterness. 'Well, if we must have an aristocracy, I would sooner that its younger branches should be monks and nuns, than colonels without regiments, or housekeepers of royal palaces that exist only in name. Besides see what advantage to a minister if the unendowed aristocracy were thus provided for now. He need not, like a minister in these days, entrust the conduct of public affairs to individuals notoriously incompetent, appoint to the command of expeditions generals who never saw a field, make governors of colonies out of men who never could govern themselves, or find an ambassador in a broken dandy or a blasted favourite. It is true that many of the monks and nuns were persons of noble birth. Why should they not have been? The aristocracy had their share; no more. They, like all other classes, were benefitted by the monasteries: but the list of the mitred abbots when they were suppressed, shows that the great majority of the heads of houses were of the people.'

'Well, whatever difference of opinion may exist on these points,' said Egremont, 'there is one on which there can be no controversy: the monks were great architects.'

'Ah! there it is,' said the stranger, in a tone of plaintiveness; 'if the world but only knew what they had lost! I am sure that not the faintest idea is generally prevalent of the appearance of England before and since the dissolution. Why, sir, in England and Wales alone, there were of these institutions of different sizes, I mean monasteries, and chantries and chapels, and great hospitals, considerably upwards of three thousand; all of them fair buildings, many of them of exquisite beauty. There were on an average in every shire at least twenty structures such as this was; in this great county double that number: establishments that were as vast and as magnificent and as beautiful as your Belvoirs and your Chatsworths, your Wentworths and your Stowes.* Try to imagine the effect of thirty or forty Chatsworths in this county the proprietors of which were never absent. You complain enough now of absentees. The monks were never non-resident. They expended their revenue among those whose labour had produced it. These holy men too built and planted as they did everything else for posterity: their churches were cathedrals; their schools colleges; their halls and libraries the muniment rooms of kingdoms; their woods and waters, their farms and gardens, were laid out and disposed on a scale and in a spirit that are now extinct; they made the country beautiful, and the people proud of their country.'

'Yet if the monks were such public benefactors, why did not the people rise in their favour?'

'They did, but too late. They struggled for a century, but they struggled against property and they were beat. As long as the monks existed, the people, when aggrieved, had property on their side. And now 'tis all over,' said the stranger; 'and travellers come and stare at these ruins, and think themselves very wise to moralize over time. They are the children of violence, not of time. It is war that created these ruins, civil war, of all our civil wars the most inhuman, for it was waged with the unresisting. The monasteries were taken by storm, they were sacked, gutted, battered with warlike instruments, blown up with gunpowder; you may see the marks of the blast against the new tower here. Never was such a plunder. The whole face of the country for a century was that of a land recently invaded by a ruthless enemy; it was worse than the Norman conquest; nor has England ever lost this character of ravage. I don't know whether the union workhouses will remove it. They are building something for the people at last. After an experiment of three centuries, your gaols being full, and your treadmills losing something of their virtue, you have given us a substitute for the monasteries.'

'You lament the old faith,' said Egremont, in a tone of respect.

'I am not viewing the question as one of faith,' said the stranger. 'It is not as a matter of religion, but as a matter of right, that I am considering it: as a matter, I should say, of private right and public happiness. You might have changed if you thought fit the religion of the abbots as you changed the religion of the bishops: but you had no right to deprive men of their property, and property moreover which under their administration so mainly contributed to the welfare of the community.'

'As for community,' said a voice which proceeded neither from Egremont nor the stranger, 'with the monasteries expired the only type that we ever had in England of such an intercourse. There is no community in England; there is aggregation, but aggregation* under circumstances which make it rather a dissociating, than an uniting, principle.'

It was a still voice that uttered these words, yet one of a peculiar character; one of those voices that instantly arrest attention: gentle and yet solemn, earnest yet unimpassioned. With a step as whispering as his tone, the man who had been kneeling by the tomb, had unobserved joined his associate and Egremont. He hardly reached the middle height; his form slender, but well proportioned; his pale countenance, slightly marked with the small pox, was redeemed from absolute ugliness by a highly-intellectual brow, and large dark eyes that indicated deep sensibility and great quickness of apprehension. Though young, he was already a little bald; he was dressed entirely in black; the fairness of his linen, the neatness of his beard, his gloves much worn, yet carefully mended, intimated that his very faded garments were the result of necessity rather than of negligence.

'You also lament the dissolution of these bodies,' said Egremont.

'There is so much to lament in the world in which we live,' said the younger of the strangers, 'that I can spare no pang for the past.'

'Yet you approve of the principle of their society; you prefer it, you say, to our existing life.'

'Yes; I prefer association to gregariousness.'

'That is a distinction,' said Egremont, musingly.

'It is a community of purpose that constitutes society,' continued the younger stranger; 'without that, men may be drawn into contiguity, but they still continue virtually isolated.'

'And is that their condition in cities?'

'It is their condition everywhere; but in cities that condition is aggravated. A density of population implies a severer struggle for existence, and a consequent repulsion of elements brought into too close contact. In great cities men are brought together by the desire of gain. They are not in a state of cooperation, but of isolation, as to the making of fortunes; and for all the rest they are careless of neighbours. Christianity teaches us to love our neighbour as ourself; modern society acknowledges no neighbour.'

'Well, we live in strange times,' said Egremont, struck by the observation of his companion, and relieving a perplexed spirit by an ordinary exclamation, which often denotes that the mind is more stirring than it cares to acknowledge, or at the moment is capable to express.

'When the infant begins to walk, it also thinks that it lives in strange times,' said his companion.

'Your inference?' asked Egremont.

'That society, still in its infancy, is beginning to feel its way.'

'This is a new reign,' said Egremont, 'perhaps it is a new era.'

'I think so,' said the younger stranger.

'I hope so,' said the elder one.

'Well, society may be in its infancy,' said Egremont slightly smiling; 'but, say what you like, our Queen reigns over the greatest nation that ever existed.'

'Which nation?' asked the younger stranger, 'for she reigns over two.'

The stranger paused; Egremont was silent, but looked inquiringly.

'Yes,' resumed the younger stranger after a moment's interval. 'Two nations; between whom there is no intercourse and no sympathy; who are as ignorant of each other's habits, thoughts, and feelings, as if they were dwellers in different zones, or inhabitants of different planets; who are formed by a different breeding, are fed by a different food, are ordered by different manners, and are not governed by the same laws.'

'You speak of—' said Egremont, hesitatingly.

'THE RICH AND THE POOR.'

At this moment a sudden flush of rosy light, suffusing the grey ruins, indicated that the sun had just fallen; and through a vacant arch that overlooked them, alone in the resplendent sky, glittered the twilight star. The hour, the scene, the solemn stillness and the softening beauty, repressed controversy, induced even silence. The last words of the stranger lingered in the ear of Egremont; his musing spirit was teeming with many thoughts, many emotions; when from the Lady's Chapel there rose the evening hymn to the Virgin.* A single voice; but tones of almost supernatural sweetness; tender and solemn, yet flexible and thrilling.

Egremont started from his reverie. He would have spoken, but he perceived that the elder of the strangers had risen from his resting-place, and, with downcast eyes and crossed arms, was on his knees. The other remained standing in his former posture.

The divine melody ceased; the elder stranger rose; the words were on the lips of Egremont, that would have asked some explanation of this sweet and holy mystery, when in the vacant and star-lit arch on which his glance was fixed, he beheld a female form. She was apparently in the habit of a Religious, yet scarcely could be a nun, for her veil, if indeed it were a veil, had fallen on her shoulders, and revealed her thick tresses of long fair hair. The blush of deep emotion lingered on a countenance, which though extremely young, was impressed with a character of almost divine majesty; while her dark eyes and long dark lashes, contrasting with the brightness of her complexion and the lux-uriance of her radiant locks, combined to produce a beauty as rare as it is choice; and so strange, that Egremont might for a moment have been pardoned for believing her a seraph, that had lighted on this sphere, or the fair phantom of some saint haunting the sacred ruins of her desecrated fane.

CHAPTER VI.

'I UNDERSTAND, then,' said Lord Marney to his brother, as on the evening of the same day they were seated together in the drawing-room, in close converse. 'I understand then, that you have in fact paid nothing, and that my mother will give you a thousand pounds. That won't go very far.'

'It will hardly pay for the chairing,' said Egremont; 'the restoration of the family influence was celebrated on so great a scale.'

'The family influence must be supported,' said Lord Marney, 'and my mother will give you a thousand pounds; as I said, that will not do much for you, but I like her spirit. Contests are very expensive things, yet I quite approve of what you have done, especially as you won. It is a great thing in these ten pound days* to win your first contest, and shows powers of calculation which I respect. Everything in this world is calculation; there is no such thing as luck, depend upon it; and if you go on calculating with equal exactness, you must succeed in life. Now the question is, what is to be done with your election bills?'

'Exactly.'

'You want to know what I will do for you, or rather what I can do for you; that is the point. My inclination of course is to do everything for you; but when I calculate my resources, I may find that they are not equal to my inclination.'

'I am sure, George, you will do everything, and more than everything you ought.'

'I am extremely pleased about this thousand pounds of my mother, Charles.'

'Most admirable of her! But she always is so generous!'

'Her jointure has been most regularly paid,' continued Lord Marney. 'Always be exact in your payments, Charles. There is no end to the good it produces. Now if I had not been so regular in paying my mother her jointure, she would not in all probability have been able to have given you this thousand pounds; and, therefore, to a certain extent, you are indebted for this thousand pounds to me.'

Egremont drew up a little, but said nothing.

'I am obliged to pay my mother her jointure, whether ricks are burnt or not,' said Lord Marney. 'It's very hard, don't you think so?'

'But these ricks were Bingley's?'

'But he was not insured, and he will want some reduction in his rent, and if I do not see fit to allow it him, which I probably shall not, for he

ought to have calculated on these things, I have ricks of my own, and
they may be burnt any night.'

'But you, of course, are insured?'

'No, I am not; I calculate 'tis better to run the risk.'

'I wonder why ricks are burnt now, and were not in old days,' said
Egremont.

'Because there is a surplus population in the kingdom,' said Lord
Marney, 'and no rural police* in the county.'

'You were speaking of the election, George,' said Egremont, not
without reluctance, yet anxious, as the ice had been broken, to bring the
matter to a result. Lord Marney, before the election, had written, in
reply to his mother consulting him on the step a letter with which she
was delighted, but which Egremont at the time could have wished to
have been more explicit. However in the excitement attendant on a first
contest, and influenced by the person whose judgment always swayed,
and, in the present case, was peculiarly entitled to sway him, he stifled
his scruples, and persuaded himself that he was a candidate not only
with the sanction, but at the instance, of his brother. 'You were speaking
of the election, George,' said Egremont.

'About the election, Charles. Well, the long and short of it is this:
that I wish to see you comfortable. To be harassed about money is one
of the most disagreeable incidents of life. It ruffles the temper, lowers
the spirits, disturbs the rest, and finally breaks up one's health. Always,
if you possibly can, keep square. And if by any chance you do find yourself
in a scrape, come to me. There is nothing under those circumstances
like the advice of a cool-headed friend.'

'As valuable as the assistance of a cold-hearted one,' thought Egremont,
who did not fancy too much the tone of this conversation.

'But there is one thing of which you must particularly beware,' continued Lord Marney, 'there is one thing worse even than getting into
difficulties—patching them up. The patching-up system is fatal; it is
sure to break down; you never get clear. Now, what I want to do for you,
Charles, is to put you right altogether. I want to see you square and
more than square, in a position which will for ever guarantee you from
any annoyance of this kind.'

'He is a good fellow after all,' thought Egremont.

'That thousand pounds of my mother was very à propos,' said Lord
Marney; 'I suppose it was a sop that will keep them all right till we have
made our arrangements.'

'Oh! there is no pressure of that kind,' said Egremont; 'if I see my
way, and write to them, of course they will be quite satisfied.'

'Excellent,' said Lord Marney; 'and nothing could be more convenient to me, for, between ourselves, my balances are very low at this moment. The awful expenditure of keeping up this place! And then such terrible incumbrances as I came to!'

'Incumbrances, George! Why, I thought you had not any. There was not a single mortgage.'

'No mortgages; they are nothing; you find them, you get used to them, and you calculate accordingly. You quite forget the portions for younger children.'

'Yes; but you had plenty of ready money for them.'

'I had to pay them though,' said Lord Marney. 'Had I not, I might have bought Grimblethorpe with the money; such an opportunity will never occur again.'

'But you talked of incumbrances,' said Egremont.

'Ah! my dear fellow,' said Lord Marney, 'you don't know what it is to have to keep up an estate like this; and very lucky for you. It is not the easy life you dream of. There's buildings—I am ruined in buildings— our poor dear father thought he left me Marney without an incumbrance; why, there was not a barn on the whole estate that was weather-proof; not a farm-house that was not half in ruins. What I have spent in buildings! And draining! Though I make my own tiles, draining, my dear fellow, is a something of which you have not the least idea!'

'Well,' said Egremont, anxious to bring his brother back to the point, 'you think, then, I had better write to them and say—'

'Ah! now for your business,' said Lord Marney. 'Now, I will tell you what I can do for you. I was speaking to Arabella about it last night; she quite approves my idea. You remember the De Mowbrays? Well, we are going to stay at Mowbray Castle, and you are to go with us. It is the first time they have received company since their great loss. Ah! you were abroad at the time, and so you are behind hand. Lord Mowbray's only son, Fitz-Warene, you remember him, a deuced clever fellow, he died about a year ago, in Greece, of a fever. Never was such a blow! His two sisters, Lady Joan and Lady Maud, are looked upon as the greatest heir-esses in the kingdom; but I know Mowbray well; he will make an eldest son of his eldest daughter. She will have it all; she is one of Arabella's dearest friends; and you are to marry her.'

Egremont stared at his brother, who patted him on the back with an expression of unusual kindness, and adding, 'You have no idea what a load this has taken off my mind, my dear Charles; so great has my anxiety always been about you, particularly of late. To see you lord of Mowbray Castle will realize my fondest hopes. That is a position fit

for a man, and I know none more worthy of it than yourself, though
I am your brother who says so. Now let us come and speak to Arabella
about it.'

So saying, Lord Marney, followed somewhat reluctantly by his brother,
advanced to the other end of the drawing-room, where his wife was
employed with her embroidery-frame, and seated next to her young
friend, Miss Poinsett, who was playing chess with Captain Grouse,
a member of the chess club,* and one of the most capital performers
extant.

'Well, Arabella,' said Lord Marney, 'it is all settled; Charles agrees
with me about going to Mowbray Castle, and I think the sooner we go
the better. What do you think of the day after to-morrow? That will suit
me exactly, and therefore I think we had better fix on it. We will consider
it settled.'

Lady Marney looked embarrassed, and a little distressed. Nothing
could be more unexpected by her than this proposition; nothing more
inconvenient than the arrangement. It was very true that Lady Joan
Fitz-Warene had invited them to Mowbray, and she had some vague
intention, some day or other, of deliberating whether they should avail
themselves of this kindness; but to decide upon going, and upon going
instantly, without the least consultation, the least inquiry as to the suit-
ableness of the arrangement, the visit of Miss Poinsett abruptly and
ungraciously terminated, for example—all this was vexatious, distressing:
a mode of management which out of the simplest incidents of domestic
life contrived to extract some degree of perplexity and annoyance.

'Do not you think, George,' said Lady Marney, 'that we had better
talk it over a little?'

'Not at all,' said Lord Marney; 'Charles will go, and it quite suits me,
and therefore what necessity for any consultation?'

'Oh! if you and Charles like to go, certainly,' said Lady Marney in
a hesitating tone; 'only I shall be very sorry to lose your society.'

'How do you mean lose our society Arabella? Of course you must go
with us. I particularly want you to go. You are Lady Joan's most intimate
friend; I believe there is no one she likes so much.'

'I cannot go the day after to-morrow,' said Lady Marney, speaking in
a whisper, and looking volumes of deprecation.

'I cannot help it,' said Lord Marney; 'you should have told me this
before. I wrote to Mowbray to-day, that we should be with him the day
after to-morrow, and stay a week.'

'But you never mentioned it to me,' said Lady Marney, slightly
blushing and speaking in a tone of gentle reproach.

'I should like to know when I am to find time to mention the contents of every letter I write,' said Lord Marney; 'particularly with all the vexatious business I have had on my hands to-day. But so it is; the more one tries to save you trouble, the more discontented you get.'

'No, not discontented, George.'

'I do not know what you call discontented; but when a man has made every possible arrangement to please you and every body, and all his plans are to be set aside merely because the day he has fixed on does not exactly suit your fancy, if that be not discontent, I should like very much to know what is, Arabella.'

Lady Marney did not reply. Always sacrificed, always yielding, the moment she attempted to express an opinion, she ever seemed to assume the position not of the injured but the injurer.

Arabella was a woman of abilities, which she had cultivated. She had excellent sense, and possessed many admirable qualities; she was far from being devoid of sensibility; but her sweet temper shrank from contro-versy, and Nature had not endowed her with a spirit which could direct and control. She yielded without a struggle to the arbitrary will and unreasonable caprice of a husband, who was scarcely her equal in intel-lect, and far her inferior in all the genial qualities of our nature, but who governed her by his iron selfishness.

Lady Marney absolutely had no will of her own. A hard, exact, lit-eral, bustling, acute being environed her existence; directed, planned, settled everything. Her life was a series of petty sacrifices and baulked enjoyments. If her carriage were at the door, she was never certain that she would not have to send it away; if she had asked some friends to her house, the chances were she would have to put them off; if she were reading a novel, Lord Marney asked her to copy a letter; if she were going to the opera, she found that Lord Marney had got seats for her and some friend in the House of Lords, and seemed expecting the strongest expressions of delight and gratitude from her for his unasked and incon-venient kindness. Lady Marney had struggled against this tyranny in the earlier days of their union. Innocent, inexperienced Lady Marney! As if it were possible for a wife to contend against a selfish husband, at once sharp-witted and blunt-hearted! She had appealed to him, she had even reproached him; she had wept, once she had knelt. But Lord Marney looked upon these demonstrations as the disordered sensibility of a girl unused to the marriage state, and ignorant of the wise authority of husbands, of which he deemed himself a model. And so, after a due course of initiation, Lady Marney invisible for days, plunged in remorse-ful reveries in the mysteries of her boudoir, and her lord dining at his club and going to the minor theatres; the countess was broken in, and became the perfect wife of a perfect husband.

Lord Marney, who was fond of chess, turned out Captain Grouse, and very gallantly proposed to finish his game with Miss Poinsett, which Miss Poinsett, who understood Lord Marney as well as he understood chess, took care speedily to lose, so that his lordship might encounter a champion worthy of him. Egremont seated by his sister-in-law, and anxious by kind words to soothe the irritation which he had observed with pain his brother create, entered into easy talk, and after some time, said, 'I find you have been good enough to mould my destiny.'

Lady Marney looked a little surprised, and then said, 'How so?'

'You have decided on, I hear, the most important step of my life.'

'Indeed you perplex me.'

'Lady Joan Fitz-Warene, your friend—'

The countess blushed; the name was a clue which she could follow, but Egremont nevertheless suspected that the idea had never previously occurred to her. Lady Joan she described as not beautiful; certainly not beautiful; nobody would consider her beautiful, many would indeed think her quite the reverse; and yet she had a look, one particular look when according to Lady Marney, she was more than beautiful. But she was very clever, very indeed, something quite extraordinary.

'Accomplished?'

'Oh! far beyond that; I have heard even men say that no one knew so much.'

'A regular blue?'*

'Oh! no; not at all a blue; not that kind of knowledge. But languages and learned books; Arabic, and Hebrew, and old manuscripts. And then she has an observatory, and was the first person who discovered the comet. Dr. Buckland swears by her; and she corresponds with Arago.'*

'And her sister, is she the same?'

'Lady Maud: she is very religious. I do not know her so well.'

'Is she pretty?'

'Some people admire her very much.'

'I never was at Mowbray.* What sort of a place is it?'

'Oh! it is very grand,' said Lady Marney; 'but like all places in the manufacturing districts, very disagreeable. You never have a clear sky. Your toilette table is covered with blacks; the deer in the park seem as if they had bathed in a lake of Indian ink; and as for the sheep, you expect to see chimney-sweeps for the shepherds.'

'And do you really mean to go on Thursday?' said Egremont: 'I think we had better put it off.'

'We must go,' said Lady Marney, with a sort of sigh, and shaking her head.

'Let me speak to Marney.'

'Oh! no. We must go. I am annoyed about this dear little Poinsett: she has been to stay with me so very often, and she has only been here three days. When she comes in again, I wish you would ask her to sing, Charles.'

Soon the dear little Poinsett was singing, much gratified by being invited to the instrument by Mr. Egremont, who for a few minutes hung over her, and then evidently under the influence of her tones, walked up and down the room, and only speaking to beg that she would continue her charming performances. Lady Marney was engrossed with her embroidery; her lord and the captain with their game.

And what was Egremont thinking of? Of Mowbray be you sure. And of Lady Joan or Lady Maud? Not exactly. Mowbray was the name of the town to which the strangers he had met with in the Abbey were bound. It was the only piece of information that he had been able to obtain of them; and that casually.

When the fair vision of the starlit arch, about to descend to her two companions, perceived that they were in conversation with a stranger, she hesitated, and in a moment withdrew. Then the elder of the travellers, exchanging a glance with his friend, bid good even to Egremont.

'Our way perhaps lies the same,' said Egremont.

'I should deem not,' said the stranger, 'nor are we alone.'

'And we must be stirring, for we have far to go,' said he who was dressed in black.

'My journey is very brief,' said Egremont, making a desperate effort to invite communication; 'and I am on horseback!'

'And we on foot,' said the elder; 'nor shall we stop till we reach Mowbray;' and with a slight salute, they left Egremont alone. There was something in the manner of the elder stranger which repressed the possibility of Egremont following him. Leaving then the cloister garden in another direction, he speculated on meeting them outside the abbey. He passed through the Lady's chapel. The beautiful Religious was not there. He gained the west front; no one was visible. He took a rapid survey of each side of the abbey; not a being to be recognized. He fancied they must have advanced towards the Abbey Farm; yet they might have proceeded further on in the dale. Perplexed, he lost time. Finally he proceeded towards the farm, but did not overtake them; reached it, but learned nothing of them; and arrived at his brother's full of a strange yet sweet perplexity.

CHAPTER VII.

IN a commercial country like England, every half century develops some new and vast source of public wealth, which brings into national notice a new and powerful class. A couple of centuries ago, a Turkey merchant was the great creator of wealth; the West Indian Planter followed him. In the middle of the last century appeared the Nabob.* These characters in their zenith in turn merged in the land, and became English aristocrats; while the Levant decaying, the West Indies exhausted, and Hindostan plundered, the breeds died away, and now exist only in our English comedies from Wycherly and Congreve to Cumberland and Morton.* The expenditure of the revolutionary war produced the Loanmonger,* who succeeded the Nabob; and the application of science to industry developed the Manufacturer, who in turn aspires to be 'large-acred,' and always will, as long as we have a territorial constitution; a better security for the preponderance of the landed interest than any corn law, fixed or fluctuating.

Of all these characters, the one that on the whole made the largest fortunes in the most rapid manner,—and we do not forget the marvels of the Waterloo loan, or the miracles of Manchester during the continental blockade,—was the Anglo-East Indian about the time that Hastings* was first appointed to the great viceroyalty. It was not unusual for men in positions so obscure that their names had never reached the public in this country, and who yet had not been absent from their native land for a longer period than the siege of Troy, to return with their million.

One of the most fortunate of this class of obscure adventurers was a certain John Warren. A very few years before the breaking out of the American war, he was a waiter at a celebrated club* in St. James's Street: a quick yet steady young fellow; assiduous, discreet, and very civil. In this capacity, he pleased a gentleman who was just appointed to the government of Madras, and who wanted a valet. Warren, though prudent, was adventurous; and accepted the opening which he believed fortune offered him. He was prescient. The voyage in those days was an affair of six months. During this period, Warren still more ingratiated himself with his master. He wrote a good hand, and his master a very bad one. He had a natural talent for accounts; a kind of information which was useful to his employer. He arrived at Madras, no longer a valet, but a private secretary.

His master went out to make a fortune; but he was indolent, and had indeed none of the qualities for success, except his great position. Warren had every quality but that. The basis of the confederacy therefore was intelligible; it was founded on mutual interests and cemented by reciprocal assistance. The governor granted monopolies to the secretary, who apportioned a due share to his sleeping partner. There appeared one of those dearths not unusual in Hindostan; the population of the famished province cried out for rice;* the stores of which, diminished by nature, had for months mysteriously disappeared. A provident administration it seems had invested the public revenue in its benevolent purchase; the misery was so excessive that even pestilence was anticipated, when the great forestallers came to the rescue of the people over whose destinies they presided; and at the same time fed and pocketed millions.

This was the great stroke of the financial genius of Warren. He was satisfied. He longed once more to see St. James's Street, and to become a member of the club, where he had once been a waiter. But he was the spoiled child of fortune, who would not so easily spare him. The governor died, and had appointed his secretary his sole executor. Not that his excellency particularly trusted his agent, but he dared not confide the knowledge of his affairs to any other individual. The estate was so complicated, that Warren offered the heirs a good round sum for his quittance, and to take the settlement upon himself. India so distant, and Chancery so near—the heirs accepted the proposition. Winding up this estate, Warren avenged the cause of plundered provinces; and the House of Commons itself, with Burke and Francis* at its head, could scarcely have mulcted the late governor more severely.

A Mr. Warren, of whom no one had ever heard except that he was a nabob, had recently returned from India and purchased a large estate in the north of England, was returned to Parliament one of the representatives of a close borough* which he had purchased: a quiet, gentlemanlike, middle-aged man, with no decided political opinions; and, as parties were then getting very equal, of course very much courted. The throes of Lord North's administration* were commencing. The minister asked the new member to dine with him, and found the new member singularly free from all party prejudices. Mr. Warren was one of those members who announced their determination to listen to the debates and to be governed by the arguments. All complimented him, all spoke to him. Mr. Fox declared that he was a most superior man; Mr. Burke said that these were the men who could alone save the country. Mrs. Crewe* asked him to supper; he was caressed by the most brilliant of duchesses.

At length there arrived one of those fierce trials of strength, which precede the fall of a minister, but which sometimes from peculiar circumstances, as in the instances of Walpole and Lord North, are not immediate in their results. How would Warren vote? was the great question. He would listen to the arguments. Burke was full of confidence that he should catch Warren. The day before the debate there was a levee, which Mr. Warren attended. The sovereign stopped him, spoke to him, smiled on him, asked him many questions: about himself, the House of Commons, how he liked it, how he liked England. There was a flutter in the circle; a new favourite at court.

The debate came off, the division took place. Mr. Warren voted for the minister. Burke denounced him; the king made him a baronet.

Sir John Warren made a great alliance, at least for him; he married the daughter of an Irish earl; became one of the king's friends; supported Lord Shelburne, threw over Lord Shelburne, had the tact early to discover that Mr. Pitt was the man to stick to, stuck to him. Sir John Warren bought another estate, and picked up another borough. He was fast becoming a personage. Throughout the Indian debates he kept himself extremely quiet; once indeed in vindication of Mr. Hastings, whom he greatly admired, he ventured to correct Mr. Francis* on a point of fact with which he was personally acquainted. He thought that it was safe, but he never spoke again. He knew not the resources of vindictive genius or the powers of a malignant imagination. Burke owed the Nabob a turn for the vote which had gained him a baronetcy. The orator seized the opportunity and alarmed the secret conscience of the Indian adventurer by his dark allusions, and his fatal familiarity with the subject.

Another estate however and another borough were some consolation for this little misadventure; and in time the French Revolution, to Sir John's great relief, turned the public attention for ever from Indian affairs. The Nabob from the faithful adherent of Mr. Pitt had become even his personal friend. The wits indeed had discovered that he had been a waiter; and endless were the epigrams of Fitzpatrick and the jokes of Hare;* but Mr. Pitt cared nothing about the origin of his supporters. On the contrary, Sir John was exactly the individual from whom the minister meant to carve out his plebeian aristocracy; and using his friend as a feeler before he ventured on his greater operations, the Nabob one morning was transformed into an Irish baron.*

The new Baron figured in his patent as Lord Fitz-Warene, his Norman origin and descent from the old barons of this name* having been discovered at Herald's college. This was a rich harvest for Fitzpatrick and Hare; but the public gets accustomed to everything, and has an easy habit of faith. The new Baron cared nothing for ridicule, for he was working for posterity. He was compensated for every annoyance by the remembrance that the St. James's Street waiter was ennobled, and by his determination that his children should rank still higher in the proud peerage of his country. So he obtained the royal permission to resume the surname and arms of his ancestors, as well as their title.

There was an ill-natured story set afloat, that Sir John owed this promotion to having lent money to the minister; but this was a calumny. Mr. Pitt never borrowed money of his friends. Once indeed, to save his library, he took a thousand pounds from an individual on whom he had conferred high rank and immense promotion: and this individual, who had the minister's bond when Mr. Pitt died, insisted on his right, and actually extracted the 1,000*l.* from the insolvent estate of his magnificent patron. But Mr. Pitt always preferred an usurer to a friend; and to the last day of his life borrowed money at fifty per cent.

The Nabob departed this life before the Minister, but he lived long enough to realize his most aspiring dream. Two years before his death the Irish baron was quietly converted into an English peer; and without exciting any attention, all the squibs of Fitzpatrick, all the jokes of Hare, quite forgotten, the waiter of the St. James's Street club took his seat in the most natural manner possible in the House of Lords.

The great estate of the late Lord Fitz-Warene was situated at Mowbray, a village which principally belonged to him, and near which he had raised a gothic castle, worthy of his Norman name and ancestry. Mowbray was one of those places which during the long war had expanded from an almost unknown village to a large and flourishing manufacturing town; a circumstance, which, as Lady Marney observed, might have somewhat deteriorated the atmosphere of the splendid castle, but which had nevertheless doubled the vast rental of its lord. He who had succeeded to his father was Altamont Belvidere (named after his mother's family) Fitz-Warene, Lord Fitz-Warene. He was not deficient in abilities, though he had not his father's talents, but he was over-educated for his intellect; a common misfortune. The new Lord Fitz-Warene was the most aristocratic of breathing beings. He most fully, entirely, and absolutely believed in his pedigree; his coat of arms was emblazoned on every window, embroidered on every chair, carved in every corner. Shortly after his father's death he was united to the daughter of a ducal house, by whom he had a son and two daughters, christened by names which the ancient records of the Fitz-Warenes authorised. His son, who gave promise of abilities which might have rendered the family really distinguished, was Valence; his daughters, Joan and Maud. All that seemed wanting to the glory of the house was a great distinction of which a rich peer, with six seats in the House of Commons, could not ultimately

despair. Lord Fitz-Warene aspired to rank among the earls of England.
But the successors of Mr. Pitt were strong; they thought the Fitz-Warenes
had already been too rapidly advanced; it was whispered that the king
did not like the new man; that his majesty thought him pompous, full
of pretence, in short, a fool. But though the successors of Mr. Pitt managed to govern the country for twenty years and were generally very
strong, in such an interval of time however good their management or
great their luck, there were inevitably occasions when they found themselves in difficulties, when it was necessary to conciliate the lukewarm
or to reward the devoted. Lord Fitz-Warene well understood how to
avail himself of these occasions; it was astonishing how conscientious
and scrupulous he became during Walcheren expeditions, Manchester
massacres, Queen's trials.* Every scrape of the government was a step
in the ladder to the great borough-monger. The old king too had disappeared from the stage; and the tawdry grandeur of the great Norman
peer rather suited George the Fourth. He was rather a favourite at the
Cottage; they wanted his six votes for Canning* he made his terms; and
one of the means by which we got a man of genius for a minister, was
elevating Lord Fitz-Warene in the peerage, by the style and title of Earl
de Mowbray of Mowbray Castle.

CHAPTER VIII.

WE must now for a while return to the strangers of the Abbey ruins.
When the two men had joined the beautiful Religious, whose appar-
ition had so startled Egremont, they all three quitted the Abbey by
a way which led them by the back of the cloister garden, and so on by
the bank of the river for about a hundred yards, when they turned up
the winding glen of a dried-up tributary stream. At the head of the
glen, at which they soon arrived, was a beer-shop, screened by some
huge elms from the winds that blew over the vast moor, which, except
in the direction of Mardale, now extended as far as the eye could reach.
Here the companions stopped, the beautiful Religious seated herself on
a stone bench beneath the trees, while the elder stranger calling out to
the inmate of the house to apprise him of his return, himself proceeded
to a neighbouring shed, whence he brought forth a very small rough
pony with a rude saddle, but one evidently intended for a female rider.

'It is well,' said the taller of the men, 'that I am not a member of
a temperance society like you, Stephen, or it would be difficult to reward
this good man for his care of our steed. I will take a cup of the drink of

Saxon kings.'* Then leading up the pony to the Religious, he placed her on its back with gentleness and much natural grace, saying at the same time in a subdued tone, 'And you—shall I bring you a glass of nature's wine?'

'I have drank of the spring of the Holy Abbey,' said the Religious, 'and none other must touch my lips this eve.'

'Come, our course must be brisk,' said the elder of the men as he gave up his glass to their host and led off the pony, Stephen walking on its other side.

Though the sun had fallen, the twilight was still glowing, and even on this wide expanse the air was still. The vast and undulating surface of the brown and purple moor, varied occasionally by some fantastic rocks, gleamed in the shifting light. Hesperus* was the only star that yet was visible, and seemed to move before them and lead them on their journey.

'I hope,' said the Religious, turning to the elder stranger, 'that if ever we regain our right, my father, and that we ever can, save by the inter-position of divine will, seems to me clearly impossible, that you will never forget how bitter it is to be driven from the soil; and that you will bring back the people to the land.'

'I would pursue our right for no other cause,' said the father. 'After centuries of sorrow and degradation, it should never be said, that we had no sympathy with the sad and the oppressed.'

'After centuries of sorrow and degradation,' said Stephen, 'let it not be said that you acquired your right only to create a baron or a squire.'

'Nay, thou shalt have thy way, Stephen,' said his companion, smiling, 'if ever the good hour come. As many acres as thou choosest for thy new Jerusalem.'

'Call it what you will, Walter,' replied Stephen; 'but if I ever gain the opportunity of fully carrying the principle of association into practice, I will sing "Nunc me dimittas." '*

' "Nunc me dimittas," ' burst forth the Religious in a voice of thrilling melody, and she pursued for some minutes the divine canticle. Her companions gazed on her with an air of affectionate reverence as she sang; each instant the stars becoming brighter, the wide moor assuming a darker hue.

'Now, tell me, Stephen,' said the Religious, turning her head and looking round with a smile, 'think you not it would be a fairer lot to bide this night at some kind monastery, than to be hastening now to that least picturesque of all creations, a railway station.'

'The railways will do as much for mankind as the monasteries did,' said Stephen.

'Had it not been for the railway, we should never have made our visit to Marney Abbey,' said the elder of the travellers.

'Nor seen its last abbot's tomb,' said the Religious. 'When I marked your name upon the stone, my father;—woe is me, but I felt sad indeed, that it was reserved for our blood to surrender to ruthless men that holy trust.'

'He never surrendered,' said her father. 'He was tortured and hanged.'

'He is with the communion of saints,' said the Religious.

'I would I could see a communion of Men,' said Stephen, 'and then there would be no more violence, for there would be no more plunder.'

'You must regain our lands for us, Stephen,' said the Religious; 'promise me my father that I shall raise a holy house for pious women, if that ever hap.'

'We will not forget our ancient faith,' said her father, 'the only old thing that has not left us.'

'I cannot understand,' said Stephen, 'why you should ever have lost sight of these papers, Walter.'

'You see, friend, they were never in my possession; they were never mine when I saw them. They were my father's; and he was jealous of all interference. He was a small yeoman, who had risen in the war time, well to do in the world, but always hankering after the old tradition that the lands were ours. This Hatton got hold of him; he did his work well, I have heard;—certain it is my father spared nothing. It is twenty-five years come Martinmas* since he brought his writ of right; and though baffled, he was not beaten. But then he died; his affairs were in great confusion; he had mortgaged his land for his writ, and the war prices were gone. There were debts that could not be paid. I had no capital for a farm. I would not sink to be a labourer on the soil that had once been our own, I had just married; it was needful to make a great exertion. I had heard much of the high wages of this new industry; I left the land.'

'And the papers?'

'I never thought of them, or thought of them with disgust, as the cause of my ruin. Then when you came the other day, and showed me in the book that the last abbot of Marney was a Walter Gerard, the old feeling stirred again; and I could not help telling you that my fathers fought at Azincourt, though I was only the overlooker at Mr. Trafford's mill.'

'A good old name of the good old faith,'* said the Religious; 'and a blessing be on it.'

'We have cause to bless it,' said Gerard. 'I thought it then something to serve a gentleman; and as for my daughter, she, by their goodness, was brought up in holy walls, which have made her what she is.'

'Nature made her what she is,' said Stephen in a low voice, and speaking not without emotion. Then he continued, in a louder and brisker tone, 'But this Hatton—you know nothing of his whereabouts?'

'Never heard of him since. I had indeed about a year after my father's death, cause to enquire after him; but he had quitted Mowbray, and none could give me tidings of him. He had lived I believe on our law-suit, and vanished with our hopes.'

After this, there was silence; each was occupied with his thoughts, while the influence of the soft night and starry hour induced to contemplation.

'I hear the murmur of the train,' said the Religious.

' 'Tis the up-train,' said her father. 'We have yet a quarter of an hour; we shall be in good time.'

So saying, he guided the pony to where some lights indicated the station of the railway, which here crossed the moor. There was just time to return the pony to the person at the station from whom it had been borrowed, and obtain their tickets, when the bell of the down-train sounded, and in a few minutes the Religious and her companions were on their way to Mowbray, whither a course of two hours carried them.

It was two hours to midnight when they arrived at Mowbray station, which was about a quarter of a mile from the town. Labour had long ceased; a beautiful heaven, clear and serene, canopied the city of smoke and toil; in all directions rose the columns of the factories, dark and defined in the purple sky; a glittering star sometimes hovering by the crest of their tall and tapering forms.

The travellers proceeded in the direction of a suburb and approached the very high wall of an extensive garden. The moon rose as they reached it, tipped the trees with light, and revealed a lofty and centre portal, by the side of it a wicket at which Gerard rang. The wicket was quickly opened.

'I fear, holy sister,'* said the Religious, 'that I am even later than I promised.'

'Those that come in our lady's name are ever welcome,' was the reply.

'Sister Marion,' said Gerard to the porteress, 'we have been to visit a holy place.'

'All places are holy with holy thoughts, my brother.'

'Dear father, good night,' said the Religious; 'the blessings of all the saints be on thee,—and on thee, Stephen, though thou dost not kneel to them.'

'Good night, mine own child,' said Gerard.

'I could believe in saints when I am with thee,' murmured Stephen; 'Good night,—SYBIL.'

CHAPTER IX.

WHEN Gerard and his friend quitted the convent they proceeded at a brisk pace, into the heart of the town. The streets were nearly empty; and with the exception of some occasional burst of brawl or merriment from a beer-shop, all was still. The chief street of Mowbray, called Castle Street after the ruins of the old baronial stronghold in its neighbour-hood, was as significant of the present civilization of this community as the haughty keep had been of its ancient dependence. The dimensions of Castle Street were not unworthy of the metropolis: it traversed a great portion of the town, and was proportionately wide; its broad pavements and its blazing gas-lights indicated its modern order and prosperity; while on each side of the street rose huge warehouses, not as beautiful as the palaces of Venice, but in their way not less remarkable; magnifi-cent shops; and here and there, though rarely, some ancient factory built among the fields in the infancy of Mowbray by some mill-owner not sufficiently prophetic of the future, or sufficiently confident in the energy and enterprise of his fellow-citizens, to foresee that the scene of his labours would be the future eye-sore of a flourishing posterity.

Pursuing their course along Castle Street for about a quarter of a mile, Gerard and Stephen turned down a street which intersected it, and so on, through a variety of ways and winding lanes, till they arrived at an open portion of the town, a district where streets and squares and even rows, disappeared, and where the tall chimneys and bulky barrack-looking buildings that rose in all directions, clustering yet isolated, announced that they were in the principal scene of the industry of Mowbray. Crossing this open ground they gained a suburb, but one of a very different description to that in which was situate the convent where they had parted with Sybil. This one was populous, noisy, and lighted. It was Saturday night; the streets were thronged; an infinite population kept swarming to and fro the close courts and pestilential cul-de-sacs that continually communicated with the streets by narrow archways, like the entrance of hives, so low that you were obliged to stoop for admission: while ascending to these same streets, from their dank and dismal dwellings by narrow flights of steps the subterraneous nation of the cellars poured forth to enjoy the coolness of the summer night, and market for the day of rest. The bright and lively shops were crowded; and groups of purchasers were gathered round the stalls, that by the aid of glaring lamps and flaunting lanthorns, displayed their wares.

'Come, come, it's a prime piece,' said a jolly looking woman, who was presiding at a stall which, though considerably thinned by previous purchasers, still offered many temptations to many who could not purchase.

'And so it is widow,' said a little pale man, wistfully.

'Come, come, it's getting late, and your wife's ill; you're a good soul, we'll say fi'pence a pound, and I'll throw you the scrag end in for love.'

'No butcher's meat to-morrow for us, widow,' said the man.

'And why not, neighbour? With your wages, you ought to live like a prize-fighter, or the mayor of Mowbray at least.'

'Wages!' said the man, 'I wish you may get 'em. Those villains, Shuffle and Screw, have sarved me with another bate ticket: and a pretty figure too.'

'Oh! the carnal monsters!' exclaimed the widow. 'If their day don't come, the bloody-minded knaves!'

'And for small cops, too! Small cops be hanged! Am I the man to send up a bad-bottomed cop, Widow Carey?'

'You sent up for snicks!* I have known you man and boy John Hill these twenty summers, and never heard a word against you till you got into Shuffle and Screw's mill. Oh! they are a bad yarn, John.'

'They do us all, widow. They pretends to give the same wages as the rest, and works it out in fines. You can't come, and you can't go, but there's a fine; you're never paid wages, but there's a bate ticket. I've heard they keep their whole establishment on factory fines.'

'Soul alive, but those Shuffle and Screw are rotten, snickey, bad yarns,'* said Mistress Carey. 'Now ma'am, if you please; fi'pence ha'penny; no, ma'am, we've no weal left. Weal, indeed! you look very like a soul as feeds on weal,' continued Mrs. Carey in an under tone as her declining customer moved away. 'Well, it gets late,' said the widow, 'and if you like to take this scrag end home to your wife neighbour Hill, we can talk of the rest next Saturday. And what's your will, sir?' said the widow with a stern expression to a youth who now stopped at her stall.

He was about sixteen, with a lithe figure, and a handsome, faded, impudent face. His long, loose, white trousers gave him height; he had no waistcoat, but a pink silk handkerchief was twisted carelessly round his neck, and fastened with a very large pin, which, whatever were its materials, had unquestionably a very gorgeous appearance. A loose frock-coat of a coarse white cloth, and fastened by one button round his waist, completed his habiliments, with the addition of the covering to his head, a high-crowned dark-brown hat, which relieved his complexion, and heightened the effect of his mischievous blue eye.

'Well, you need not be so fierce, Mother Carey,' said the youth with an affected air of deprecation.

'Don't mother me,' said the jolly widow with a kindling eye; 'go to your own mother, who is dying in a back cellar without a winder, while you've got lodgings in a two pair.'

'Dying; she's only drunk,' said the youth.

'And if she is only drunk,' rejoined Mrs. Carey in a passion, 'what makes her drink but toil; working from five o'clock in the morning to seven o'clock at night, and for the like of such as you.'

'That's a good one,' said the youth; 'I should like to know what my mother ever did for me, but give me treacle and laudanum* when I was a babby to stop my tongue and fill my stomach; by the token of which, as my gal says, she stunted the growth of the prettiest figure in all Mowbray.' And here the youth drew himself up, and thrust his hands in the side pockets of his pea-jacket.

'Well, I never,' said Mrs. Carey. 'No; I never heard a thing like that!'

'What, not when you cut up the jackass and sold it for veal cutlets, mother.'

'Hold your tongue, Mr. Imperence,'* said the widow. 'It's very well known you're no Christian, and who'll believe what you say?'

'It's very well known that I'm a man what pays his way,' said the boy, 'and don't keep a huckster's stall to sell carrion by star-light; but live in a two pair, if you please, and has a wife and family, or as good.'

'O! you aggravating imp!' exclaimed the widow in despair, unable to wreak her vengeance on one who kept in a secure position, and whose movements were as nimble as his words.

'Why, Madam Carey, what has Dandy Mick done to thee?' said a good-humoured voice. It came from one of two factory girls who were passing her stall and stopped. They were gaily dressed, a light handkerchief tied under the chin, their hair scrupulously arranged; they wore coral neck-laces and ear-rings of gold.

'Ah! is it you, my child,' said the widow, who was a good-hearted creature. 'The dandy has been giving me some of his imperence.'

'But I meant nothing, dame,' said Mick. 'It was a joke,—only a joke.'

'Well, let it pass,' said Mrs. Carey. 'And where have you been this long time, my child; and who's your friend?' she added in a lower tone.

'Well, I have left Mr. Trafford's mill,' said the girl.

'That's a bad job,' said Mrs. Carey; 'for those Traffords are kind to their people. It's a great thing for a young person to be in their mill.'

'So it is,' said the girl, 'but then it was so dull. I can't stand a country life, Mrs. Carey. I must have company.'

'Well, I do love a bit of gossip myself,' said Mrs. Carey, with great frankness.

'And then I'm no scholar,' said the girl, 'and never could take to learning. And those Traffords had so many schools.'

'Learning is better than house and land,' said Mrs. Carey; 'though I'm no scholar myself; but then, in my time, things was different. But young persons—'

'Yes,' said Mick; 'I don't think I could get through the day, if it wurno' for our Institute.'

'And what's that?' asked Mrs. Carey with a sneer.

'The Shoddy-Court Literary and Scientific, to be sure,' said Mick; 'we have got fifty members, and take in three London papers; one 'Northern Star' and two "Moral Worlds." '*

'And where are you now, child?' continued the widow to the girl.

'I am at Wiggins and Webster's,' said the girl; 'and this is my partner. We keep house together; we have a very nice room in Arbour Court, No. 7, high up; it's very airy. If you will take a dish of tea with us to-morrow, we expect some friends.'

'I take it kindly,' said Mrs. Carey; 'and so you keep house together! All the children keep house in these days. Times is changed indeed!'

'And we shall be happy to see you, Mick; and Julia, if you are not engaged;' continued the girl; and she looked at her friend, a pretty demure girl, who immediately said, but in a somewhat faltering tone, 'Oh! that we shall.'

'And what are you going to do now, Caroline?' said Mick.

'Well, we had no thoughts; but I said to Harriet, as it is a fine night, let us walk about as long as we can and then to-morrow we will lie in bed till afternoon.'

'That's all well eno' in winter time with plenty of baccy,' said Mick, 'but at this season of the year I must have life. The moment I came out I bathed in the river, and then went home and dressed,' he added in a satisfied tone; 'and now I am going to the Temple. I'll tell you what, Julia has been pricked to-day with a shuttle; 'tis not much, but she can't go out; I'll stand treat, and take you and your friend to the Temple.'

'Well, that's delight,' said Caroline. 'There's no one does the handsome thing like you, Dandy Mick, and I always say so. Oh! I love the
Temple! 'Tis so genteel! I was speaking of it to Harriet last night; she
never was there. I proposed to go with her—but two girls alone,—you
understand me. One does not like to be seen in these places, as if one
kept no company.'

'Very true,' said Mick; 'and now we'll be off. Good night, widow.'

'You'll remember us to-morrow evening,' said Caroline.

'To-morrow evening! The Temple!' murmured Mrs. Carey to herself.
'I think the world is turned upside downwards in these parts. A brat like
Mick Radley to live in a two pair, with a wife and family, or as good as
he says; and this girl asks me to take a dish of tea with her and keeps
house! Fathers and mothers goes for nothing,' continued Mrs. Carey,
as she took a very long pinch of snuff and deeply mused. ''Tis the
children gets the wages,' she added after a profound pause, 'and there
it is.'

CHAPTER X.

IN the meantime Gerard and Stephen stopped before a tall, thin, stuc-
coed house, ballustraded and friezed, very much lighted both within
and without, and, from the sounds that issued from it, and the persons
who retired and entered, evidently a locality of great resort and bustle.
A sign, bearing the title of the Cat and Fiddle, indicated that it was
a place of public entertainment, and kept by one who owned the legal
name of John Trottman, though that was but a vulgar appellation, lost
in his well-earned and far-famed title of Chaffing Jack.

The companions entered the spacious premises; and making their
way to the crowded bar, Stephen, with a glance serious but which indicated intimacy, caught the eye of a comely lady, who presided over the
mysteries, and said in a low voice, 'Is he here?'

'In the Temple, Mr. Morley, asking for you and your friend more
than once. I think you had better go up. I know he wishes to see you.'

Stephen whispered to Gerard and after a moment's pause, he asked
the fair president for a couple of tickets for each of which he paid threepence; a sum however, according to the printed declaration of the voucher,
convertible into potential liquid refreshments, no great compensation to
a very strict member of the Temperance Society of Mowbray.

A handsome staircase with bright brass bannisters led them to an
ample landing-place, on which opened a door, now closed and by which

sate a boy who collected the tickets of those who would enter it. The portal was of considerable dimensions and of architectural pretension; it was painted of a bright green colour, the panels gilt. Within the pediment, described in letters of flaming gas, you read, 'THE TEMPLE OF THE MUSES.'*

Gerard and Morley entered an apartment very long and sufficiently lofty, though rather narrow for such proportions. The ceiling was even richly decorated; the walls were painted, and by a brush of considerable power. Each panel represented some well-known scene from Shakespeare, Byron, or Scott: King Richard, Mazeppa, the Lady of the Lake were easily recognized: in one panel, Hubert menaced Arthur; here Haidee rescued Juan; and there Jeanie Deans* curtsied before the Queen. The room was very full; some three or four hundred persons were seated in different groups at different tables, eating, drinking, talking, laughing, and even smoking, for notwithstanding the pictures and the gilding it was found impossible to forbid, though there were efforts to discourage, this practice, in the Temple of the Muses. Nothing however could be more decorous than the general conduct of the company, though they consisted principally of factory people. The waiters flew about with as much agility as if they were serving nobles. In general the noise was great, though not disagreeable; sometimes a bell rang and there was comparative silence, while a curtain drew up at the further end of the room, opposite to the entrance, and where there was a theatre, the stage raised at a due elevation, and adorned with side scenes from which issued a lady in a fancy dress who sang a favourite ballad; or a gentleman elaborately habited in a farmer's costume of the old comedy, a bob-wig, silver buttons and buckles, and blue stockings, and who favoured the company with that melancholy effusion called a comic song. Some nights there was music on the stage; a young lady in a white robe with a golden harp, and attended by a gentleman in black mustachios. This was when the principal harpiste of the King of Saxony* and his first fiddler happened to be passing through Mowbray, merely by accident, or on a tour of pleasure and instruction, to witness the famous scenes of British industry. Otherwise the audience of the Cat and Fiddle, we mean the Temple of the Muses, were fain to be content with four Bohemian brothers, or an equal number of Swiss sisters. The most popular amusements however were the 'Thespian recitations' by amateurs, or novices who wished to become professional. They tried their metal on an audience which could be critical.

A sharp waiter, with a keen eye on the entering guests, immediately saluted Gerard and his friend, with profuse offers of hospitality: insisting that they wanted much refreshment; that they were both very hungry and very thirsty; that, if not hungry, they should order something to drink that would give them an appetite; if not inclined to quaff, something to eat that would make them athirst. In the midst of these embarrassing attentions, he was pushed aside by his master with, 'There, go; hands wanted at the upper end; two American gentlemen from Lowell singing out for Sherry Cobler;* don't know what it is; give them our bar mixture; if they complain, say it's the Mowbray slap-bang, and no mistake. Must have a name, Mr. Morley; name's everything; made the fortune of the Temple; if I had called it the Saloon, it never would have filled, and perhaps the magistrates never have granted a licence.'

The speaker was a very portly man who had passed the maturity of manhood, but active as Harlequin.* He had a well-favoured countenance; fair, good-humoured, but very sly. He was dressed like the head butler of the London Tavern,* and was particular as to his white waistcoats and black silk stockings, punctilious as to his knee-buckles, proud of his diamond pin; that is to say when he officiated at the Temple.

'Your mistress told us we should find you here,' said Stephen, 'and that you wished to see us.'

'Plenty to tell you,' said their host putting his finger to his nose. 'If information *is* wanted in this part of the world, I flatter myself— Come, Master Gerard, here's a table; what shall I call for? glass of the Mowbray slap-bang? No better; the receipt has been in our family these fifty years. Mr. Morley I know won't join us. Did you say a cup of tea, Mr. Morley? Water, only water; well, that's strange. Boy alive there, do you hear me call? Water wanted, glass of water for the Secretary of the Mowbray Temperance and Teetotal. Sing it out. I like titled company. Brush!'

'And so you can give us some information about this—'

'Be back directly,' exclaimed their host; and darting off with a swift precision, that carried him through a labyrinth of tables without the slightest inconvenience to their occupiers. 'Beg pardon, Mr. Morley,' he said, sliding again into his chair; 'but saw one of the American gentlemen brandishing his bowie-knife against one of my waiters; called him Colonel; quieted him directly; a man of his rank brawling with a help; oh! no; not to be thought of; no squabbling here; licence in danger.'

'You were saying—' resumed Morley.

'Ah! yes, about that man Hatton; remember him perfectly well; a matter of twenty or it may be nineteen years since he bolted. Queer fellow; lived upon nothing; only drank water; no temperance and teetotal then,* so no excuse. Beg pardon, Mr. Morley; no offence I hope; can't bear whims; but respectable societies, if they don't drink, they make speeches, hire your rooms, leads to business.'

'And this Hatton—' said Gerard.

'Ah! a queer fellow; lent him a one-pound note—never saw it again— always remember it—last one-pound note* I had. He offered me an old book instead; not in my way; took a china jar for my wife. He kept a curiosity shop; always prowling about the country, picking up old books and hunting after old monuments; called himself an antiquarian; queer fellow, that Hatton.'

'And you have heard of him since?' said Gerard rather impatiently.

'Not a word,' said their host; 'never knew any one who had.'

'I thought you had something to tell us about him,' said Stephen.

'So I have; I can put you in the way of getting hold of him and any-thing else. I havn't lived in Mowbray man and boy for fifty years; seen it a village, and now a great town full of first-rate institutions and estab-lishments like this,' added their host surveying the Temple with a glance of admiring complacency; 'I say I havn't lived here all this time and talked to the people for nothing.'

'Well, we are all attention,' said Gerard with something of a sneer.

'Hush!' said their host as a bell sounded, and he jumped up. 'Now ladies, now gentlemen, if you please; silence if you please for a song from a Polish lady. The Signora sings English like a new-born babe;' and the curtain drew up amid the hushed voices of the company and the restrained clatter of their knives and forks and glasses.

The Polish lady sang 'Cherry Ripe' to the infinite satisfaction of her audience. Young Mowbray indeed, in the shape of Dandy Mick and some of his followers and admirers, insisted on an encore. The lady as she retired curtseyed like a Prima Donna; but the host continued on his legs for some time, throwing open his coat and bowing to his guests, who expressed by their applause how much they approved his enterprise. At length he resumed his seat; 'It's almost too much,' he exclaimed; 'the enthusiasm of these people. I believe they look upon me as a father.'

'And you think you have some clue to this Hatton?' resumed Stephen.

'They say he has no relations,' said their host.

'I have heard as much.'

'Another glass of the bar mixture, Master Gerard. What did we call it? Oh! the bricks and beans—the Mowbray bricks and beans; known by that name in the time of my grandfather. No more! No use asking Mr. Morley I know. Water! well, I must say—and yet, in an official capacity, drinking water is not so unnatural.'

'And Hatton,' said Gerard; 'they say he has no relations, eh?'

'They do, and they say wrong. He has a relation; he has a brother; and I can put you in the way of finding him.'

'Well, that looks like business,' said Gerard; 'and where may he be?'

'Not here,' said their host; 'he never put his foot in the Temple to my knowledge; and lives in a place where they have as much idea of popular institutions as any Turks or heathen you ever heard of.'

'And where might we find him?' said Stephen.

'What's that?' said their host jumping up and looking around him. 'Here boys, brush about. The American gentleman is a whittling his name on that new mahogany table. Take him the printed list of rules, stuck up in a public place, under a great coat, and fine him five shillings for damaging the furniture. If he resists (he has paid for his liquor), call in the police; X. Z. No. 5 is in the bar, taking tea with your mistress. Now brush.'

'And this place is—'

'In the land of mines and minerals,' said their host; 'about ten miles from—. He works in metals on his own account. You have heard of a place called Hell-house Yard; well, he lives there; and his name is Simon.'

'And does he keep up any communication with his brother, think you?' said Gerard.

'Nay, I know no more; at least at present,' said their host. 'The secretary asked me about a person absent without leave for twenty years and who was said to have no relations, I found you one and a very near one. You are at the station and you have got your ticket. The American gentleman's wiolent. Here's the police. I must take a high tone.' And with these words Chaffing Jack quitted them.

In the meantime, we must not forget Dandy Mick and his two young friends whom he had so generously offered to treat to the Temple.

'Well, what do you think of it?' asked Caroline of Harriet in a whisper as they entered the splendid apartment.

'It's just what I thought the Queen lived in,' said Harriet; 'but indeed I'm all of a flutter.'

'Well, don't look as if you were,' said her friend.

'Come along gals,' said Mick; 'who's afraid? Here, we'll sit down at this table. Now, what shall we have? Here waiter; I say waiter!'

'Yes, sir, yes, sir.'

'Well, why don't you come when I call,' said Mick with a consequential air. 'I have been hallooing these ten minutes. Couple of glasses of bar mixture for these ladies and a go of gin for myself. And I say waiter, stop, stop, don't be in such a deuced hurry; do you think folks can drink without eating;—sausages for three; and damme, take care they are not burnt.'

'Yes, sir, directly, directly.'

'That's the way to talk to these fellows,' said Mick with a self-satisfied air, and perfectly repaid by the admiring gaze of his companions.

'It's pretty, Miss Harriet,' said Mick looking up at the ceiling with a careless nil admirari* glance.

'Oh! it is beautiful,' said Harriet.

'You never were here before; it's the only place. That's the Lady of the Lake,' he added, pointing to a picture; 'I've seen her at the Circus, with real water.'

The hissing sausages crowning a pile of mashed potatoes were placed before them; the delicate rummers* of the Mowbray slap-bang, for the girls; the more masculine pewter measure for their friend.

'Are the plates very hot?' said Mick.

'Very sir.'

'Hot plates half the battle,' said Mick.

'Now, Caroline; here, Miss Harriet; don't take away your plate, wait for the mash; they mash their taters here very elegant.'

It was a very happy and very merry party. Mick delighted to help his guests, and to drink their healths.

'Well,' said he when the waiter had cleared away their plates, and left them to their less substantial luxuries. 'Well,' said Mick, sipping a renewed glass of gin twist and leaning back in his chair, 'say what they please, there's nothing like life.'

'At the Traffords',' said Caroline, 'the greatest fun we ever had was a singing class.'

'I pity them poor devils in the country,' said Mick; 'we got some of them at Collinson's—come from Suffolk they say; what they call hagricultural labourers, a very queer lot, indeed.'

'Ah! them's the himmigrants,' said Caroline; 'they're sold out of slavery, and sent down by Pickford's van* into the labour market to bring down our wages.'

'We'll teach them a trick or two before they do that,' urged Mick. 'Where are you, Miss Harriet?'

'I'm at Wiggins and Webster's, sir.'

'Where they clean machinery during mealtime;* that won't do,' said Mick. 'I see one of your partners coming in,' said Mick, making many signals to a person who very soon joined them. 'Well, Devilsdust,* how are you?'

This was the familiar appellation of a young gentleman, who really had no other, baptismal or patrimonial. About a fortnight after his mother had introduced him into the world, she returned to her factory and put her infant out to nurse, that is to say, paid threepence a week to an old woman who takes charge of these new-born babes for the day, and gives them back at night to their mothers as they hurriedly return from the scene of their labour to the dungeon or the den, which is still by courtesy called 'home.' The expense is not great: laudanum and treacle, administered in the shape of some popular elixir, affords these innocents a brief taste of the sweets of existence, and keeping them quiet, prepares them for the silence of their impending grave. Infanticide is practised as extensively and as legally in England, as it is on the banks of the Ganges: a circumstance which apparently has not yet engaged the attention of the Society for the Propagation of the Gospel in Foreign Parts.* But the vital principle is an impulse from an immortal artist, and sometimes baffles, even in its tenderest phasis, the machinations of society for its extinction. There are infants that will defy even starvation and poison, unnatural mothers and demon nurses. Such was the nameless one of whom we speak. We cannot say he thrived; but he would not die. So at two years of age, his mother being lost sight of, and the weekly payment having ceased, he was sent out in the street to 'play,' in order to be run over. Even this expedient failed. The youngest and the feeblest of the band of victims, Juggernaut spared him to Moloch.* All his companions were disposed of. Three months' 'play' in the streets got rid of this tender company,—shoeless, half-naked, and uncombed,— whose age varied from two to five years. Some were crushed, some were lost, some caught cold and fevers, crept back to their garret or their cellars, were dosed with Godfrey's cordial,* and died in peace. The nameless one would not disappear. He always got out of the way of the carts and horses, and never lost his own. They gave him no food: he foraged for himself, and shared with the dogs the garbage of the streets. But still he lived; stunted and pale, he defied even the fatal fever which was the only habitant of his cellar that never quitted it. And slumbering at night on a bed of mouldering straw, his only protection against the plashy surface of his den, with a dungheap at his head and a cesspool at his feet, he still clung to the only roof which shielded him from the tempest.

At length when the nameless one had completed his fifth year, the pest which never quitted the nest of cellars of which he was a citizen, raged in the quarter with such intensity, that the extinction of its swarming population was menaced. The haunt of this child was peculiarly visited. All the children gradually sickened except himself; and one night when he returned home he found the old woman herself dead, and surrounded only by corpses. The child before this had slept on the same bed of straw with a corpse, but then there were also breathing beings for his companions. A night passed only with corpses seemed to him in itself a kind of death. He stole out of the cellar, quitted the quarter of pestilence, and after much wandering laid down near the door of a factory. Fortune had guided him. Soon after break of day, he was woke by the sound of the factory bell, and found assembled a crowd of men, women, and children. The door opened, they entered, the child accompanied them. The roll was called; his unauthorized appearance noticed; he was questioned; his acuteness excited attention. A child was wanted in the Wadding Hole, a place for the manufacture of waste and damaged cotton, the refuse of the mills, which is here worked up into counterpanes and coverlids. The nameless one was prefered to the vacant post, received even a salary, more than that, a name; for as he had none, he was christened on the spot—DEVILSDUST.

Devilsdust had entered life so early that at seventeen he combined the experience of manhood with the divine energy of youth. He was a first-rate workman and received high wages; he had availed himself of the advantages of the factory school; he soon learnt to read and write with facility, and at the moment of our history, was the leading spirit of the Shoddy-Court Literary and Scientific Institute. His great friend, his only intimate, was Dandy Mick. The apparent contrariety of their qualities and structure perhaps led to this. It is indeed the most assured basis of friendship. Devilsdust was dark and melancholy; ambitious and discontented; full of thought, and with powers of patience and perseverance that alone amounted to genius. Mick was as brilliant as his complexion; gay, irritable, evanescent, and unstable. Mick enjoyed life; his friend only endured it; yet Mick was always complaining of the lowness of his wages and the greatness of his toil; while Devilsdust never murmured, but read and pondered on the rights of labour, and sighed to vindicate his order.

'I have some thoughts of joining the Total Abstinence,' said Devilsdust; 'ever since I read Stephen Morley's address it has been in my mind. We shall never get our rights till we leave off consuming exciseable articles; and the best thing to begin with is liquors.'

'Well, I could do without liquors myself,' said Caroline. 'If I was a lady, I would never drink anything except fresh milk from the cow.'

'Tea for my money,' said Harriet; 'I must say there's nothing I grudge for good tea. Now I keep house, I mean always to drink the best.'

'Well, you have not yet taken the pledge, Dusty,' said Mick; 'and so suppose we order a go of gin and talk this matter of temperance over.'

Devilsdust was manageable in little things, especially by Mick; he acceded, and seated himself at their table.

'I suppose you have heard this last dodge of Shuffle and Screw, Dusty,' said Mick.

'What's that?'

'Every man had his key given him this evening—half-a-crown a week round deducted from wages for rent. Jim Plastow told them he lodged with his father and didn't want a house; upon which they said he must let it.'

'Their day will come,' said Devilsdust, thoughtfully. 'I really think that those Shuffle and Screws are worse even than Truck and Trett. You knew where you were with those fellows; it was five-and-twenty per cent off wages and very bad stuff for your money. But as for Shuffle and Screw, what with their fines and their keys, a man never knows what he has to spend. Come,' he added filling his glass, 'let's have a toast— Confusion to Capital.'

'That's your sort,' said Mick. 'Come, Caroline; drink to your partner's toast, Miss Harriet. Money's the root of all evil, which nobody can deny. We'll have the rights of labour yet; the ten-hour bill,* no fines, and no individuals admitted to any work who have not completed their sixteenth year.'

'No, fifteen,' said Caroline eagerly.

'The people won't bear their grievances much longer,' said Devilsdust.

'I think one of the greatest grievances the people have,' said Caroline, 'is the beaks serving notice on Chaffing Jack to shut up the Temple on Sunday nights.'

'It is infamous,' said Mick; 'ayn't we to have no recreation? One might as well live in Suffolk, where the immigrants come from, and where they are obliged to burn ricks to pass the time.'

'As for the rights of labour,' said Harriet, 'the people goes for nothing with this machinery.'

'And you have opened your mouth to say a very sensible thing Miss Harriet,' said Mick; 'but if I were Lord Paramount for eight-and-forty hours, I'd soon settle that question. Wouldn't I fire a broadside into their 'double deckers?' The battle of Navarino* at Mowbray fair with fourteen squibs from the admiral's ship going off at the same time, should be nothing to it.'

'Labour may be weak, but Capital is weaker,' said Devilsdust. 'Their capital is all paper.'

'I tell you what,' said Mick, with a knowing look, and in a lowered tone, 'The only thing, my hearties, that can save this here nation, is—a—good strike.'*

CHAPTER XI.

'YOUR lordship's dinner is served,' announced the groom of the chambers to Lord de Mowbray; and the noble lord led out Lady Marney. The rest followed. Egremont found himself seated next to Lady Maud Fitz-Warene, the younger daughter of the earl. Nearly opposite to him was Lady Joan.

The ladies Fitz-Warene were sandy girls, somewhat tall, with rather good figures and a grand air; the eldest very ugly, the second rather pretty; and yet both very much alike. They had both great conversational powers, though in different ways. Lady Joan was doctrinal; Lady Maud inquisitive: the first often imparted information which you did not previously possess; the other suggested ideas which were often before in your own mind, but lay tranquil and unobserved, till called into life and notice by her fanciful and vivacious tongue. Both of them were endowed with a very remarkable self-possession; but Lady Joan wanted softness, and Lady Maud repose.

This was the result of the rapid observation of Egremont, who was however experienced in the world and quick in his detection of manner and of character.

The dinner was stately, as becomes the high nobility. There were many guests, yet the table seemed only a gorgeous spot in the capacious chamber. The side tables were laden with silver vases and golden shields arranged on shelves of crimson velvet. The walls were covered with Fitz-Warenes, De Mowbrays, and De Veres. The attendants glided about without noise, and with the precision of military discipline. They watched your wants, they anticipated your wishes, and they supplied all you desired with a lofty air of pompous devotion.

'You came by the railroad?' enquired Lord de Mowbray mournfully, of Lady Marney.

'From Marham; about ten miles from us,' replied her ladyship.

'A great revolution!'

'Isn't it?'

'I fear it has a very dangerous tendency to equality,' said his lordship shaking his head; 'I suppose Lord Marney gives them all the opposition in his power.'

'There is nobody so violent against railroads as George,' said Lady Marney; 'I cannot tell you what he does not do! He organized the whole of our division against the Marham line!'

'I rather counted on him,' said Lord de Mowbray, 'to assist me in resisting this joint branch here; but I was surprised to learn he had consented.'

'Not until the compensation was settled,' innocently remarked Lady Marney; 'George never opposes them after that. He gave up all opposition to the Marham line when they agreed to his terms.'

'And yet,' said Lord de Mowbray, 'I think if Lord Marney would take a different view of the case and look to the moral consequences, he would hesitate. Equality, Lady Marney, equality is not our métier. If we nobles do not make a stand against the levelling spirit of the age, I am at a loss to know who will fight the battle. You may depend upon it that these railroads are very dangerous things.'

'I have no doubt of it. I suppose you have heard of Lady Vanilla's trip from Birmingham? Have you not, indeed! She came up with Lady Laura, and two of the most gentlemanlike men sitting opposite her; never met, she says, two more intelligent men. She begged one of them at Wolverhampton to change seats with her, and he was most politely willing to comply with her wishes, only it was necessary that his companion should move at the same time, for they were chained together! Two of the swell mob, sent to town for picking a pocket at Shrewsbury races.'

'A countess and a felon! So much for public conveyances,' said Lord Mowbray. 'But Lady Vanilla is one of those who will talk with everybody.'

'She is very amusing though,' said Lady Marney.

'I dare say she is,' said Lord de Mowbray; 'but believe me, my dear Lady Marney, in these times especially, a countess has something else to do than be amusing.'

'You think as property has its duties as well as its rights, rank has its bores as well as its pleasures.'

Lord Mowbray mused.

'How do you do, Mr. Jermyn?' said a lively little lady with sparkling beady black eyes, and a very yellow complexion, though with good features; 'when did you arrive in the North? I have been fighting your battles finely since I saw you,' she added shaking her head, rather with an expression of admonition than of sympathy.

'You are always fighting one's battles Lady Firebrace; it is very kind of you. If it were not for you, we should none of us know how much we are all abused,' replied Mr. Jermyn, a young M.P.

'They say you gave the most radical pledges,' said Lady Firebrace eagerly, and not without malice. 'I heard Lord Muddlebrains say that if he had had the least idea of your principles, you would not have had his influence.'

'Muddlebrains can't command a single vote,' said Mr. Jermyn. 'He is a political humbug, the greatest of all humbugs; a man who swaggers about London clubs and consults solemnly about his influence, and in the country is a nonentity.'

'Well, that can't be said of Lord Clarinel,' rejoined Lady Firebrace.

'And have you been defending me against Lord Clarinel's attacks?' inquired Mr Jermyn.

'No; but I am going to Wemsbury, and then I have no doubt I shall have the opportunity.'

'I am going to Wemsbury myself,' said Mr. Jermyn.

'And what does Lord Clarinel think of your pledge about the pension list?' said Lady Firebrace daunted but malignant.

'He never told me,' said Mr. Jermyn.

'I believe you did not pledge yourself to the ballot?' inquired Lady Firebrace with an affected air of inquisitiveness.

'It is a subject that requires some reflection,' said Mr. Jermyn. 'I must consult some profound politician like Lady Firebrace. By the bye, you told my mother that the Conservatives would have a majority of fifteen. Do you think they will have as much?' said Mr. Jermyn with an innocent air, it now being notorious that the Whig administration had a majority* of double that amount.

'I said Mr. Tadpole gave us a majority of fifteen,' said Lady Firebrace. 'I knew he was in error; because I had happened to see Lord Melbourne's own list, made up to the last hour; and which gave the government a majority of sixty. It was only shown to three members of the cabinet,' she added in a tone of triumphant mystery.

Lady Firebrace, a great stateswoman among the Tories, was proud of an admirer who was a member of the Whig cabinet. She was rather an agreeable guest in a country-house, with her extensive correspondence, and her bulletins from both sides. Tadpole, flattered by her notice, and charmed with female society that talked his own slang, and entered with affected enthusiasm into all his dirty plots and barren machinations, was vigilant in his communications; while her Whig cavalier, an easy individual who always made love by talking or writing politics, abandoned himself without reserve, and instructed Lady Firebrace regularly after every council. Taper looked grave at this connection between Tadpole and Lady Firebrace; and whenever an election was lost, or a division stuck in the mud, he gave the cue with a nod and a monosyllable, and the Conservative pack that infests clubs, chattering on subjects of which it is impossible they can know anything, instantly began barking and yelping, denouncing traitors, and wondering how the leaders could be so led by the nose, and not see that which was flagrant to the whole world. If, on the other hand, the advantage seemed to go with the Carlton Club,* or the opposition benches, then it was the Whig and Liberal hounds who howled and moaned, explaining everything by the indiscretion, infatuation, treason, of Lord Viscount Masque, and appealing to the initiated world of idiots around them, whether any party could ever succeed, hampered by such men, and influenced by such means.

The best of the joke was, that all this time Lord Masque and Tadpole were two old foxes, neither of whom conveyed to Lady Firebrace a single circumstance but with the wish, intention, and malice aforethought, that it should be communicated to his rival.

'I must get you to interest Lord de Mowbray in our cause,' said Sir Vavasour Firebrace, in an insinuating voice to his neighbour, Lady Joan; 'I have sent him a large packet of documents. You know, he is one of us; still one of us. Once a baronet, always a baronet. The dignity merges, but does not cease; and happy as I am to see one covered with high honours, who is in every way so worthy of them, still I confess to you it is not so much as Earl de Mowbray that your worthy father interests me, as in his undoubted character and capacity of Sir Altamont Fitz-Warene, baronet.'

'You have the data on which you move, I suppose, well digested,' said Lady Joan, attentive but not interested.

'The case is clear; as far as equity is concerned, irresistible; indeed the late king pledged himself to a certain point. But if you would do me the favour of reading our memorial.'

'The proposition is not one adapted to our present civilisation,' said Lady Joan. 'A baronetcy has become the distinction of the middle class; a physician, our physician for example, is a baronet; and I dare say some of our tradesmen; brewers, or people of that class. An attempt to elevate them into an order of nobility, however inferior, would partake in some degree of the ridiculous.'

'And has the duke escaped his gout this year?' enquired Lord Marney of Lady de Mowbray.

'A very slight touch; I never knew my father so well. I expect you will meet him here. We look for him daily.'

'I shall be delighted; I hope he will come to Marney in October. I keep the blue ribbon cover* for him.'

'What you suggest is very just,' said Egremont to Lady Maud. 'If we only in our own spheres made the exertion, the general effect would be great. Marney Abbey, for instance, I believe one of the finest of our monastic remains,—that indeed is not disputed—diminished yearly to repair barns; the cattle browsing in the nave; all this might be prevented. If my brother would not consent to preserve or to restore, still any member of the family, even I, without expense, only with a little zeal as you say, might prevent mischief, might stop at least demolition.'

'If this movement in the church had only revived a taste for Christian architecture,'* said Lady Maud, 'it would not have been barren, and it has done so much more! But I am surprised that old families can be so dead to our national art; so full of our ancestors, their exploits, their mind. Indeed you and I have no excuse for such indifference, Mr. Egremont.'

'And I do not think I shall ever again be justly accused of it,' replied Egremont, 'you plead its cause so effectively. But to tell you the truth, I have been thinking of late about these things; monasteries and so on; the influence of the old church system on the happiness and comfort of the People.'

'And on the tone of the Nobles—do not you think so?' said Lady Maud. 'I know it is the fashion to deride the crusades, but do not you think they had their origin in a great impulse, and in a certain sense, led to great results? Pardon me, if I speak with emphasis, but I never can forget I am a daughter of the first crusaders.'

'The tone of society is certainly lower than of yore,' said Egremont. 'It is easy to say we view the past through a fallacious medium. We have however ample evidence that men feel less deeply than of old and act with less devotion. But how far is this occasioned by the modern position of our church? That is the question.'

'You must speak to Mr. St. Lys about that,' said Lady Maud. 'Do you know him?' she added in a lowered tone.

'No; is he here?'

'Next to mamma.'

And looking in that direction, on the left hand of Lady Mowbray, Egremont beheld a gentleman in the last year of his youth, if youth according to the scale of Hippocrates* cease at thirty-five. He was distinguished by that beauty of the noble English blood, of which in these days few types remain; the Norman tempered by the Saxon; the fire of conquest softened by integrity; and a serene, though inflexible habit of mind. The chains of convention, an external life grown out of all proportion with that of the heart and mind, have destroyed this dignified beauty. There is no longer in fact an aristocracy in England, for the superiority of the animal man is an essential quality of aristocracy. But that it once existed, any collection of portraits from the sixteenth century will show.

Aubrey St. Lys was a younger son of the most ancient Norman family in England. The Conqueror had given them the moderate estate on which they now lived, and which, in spite of so many civil conflicts and religious changes, they had handed down to each other, from generation to generation, for eight centuries. Aubrey St. Lys was the vicar of Mowbray. He had been the college tutor of the late Lord Fitz-Warene, whose mind he had formed, whose bright abilities he had cultivated, who adored him. To that connection he owed the slight preferment which he possessed, but which was all he desired. A bishopric would not have tempted him from his peculiar charge.

In the centre of the town of Mowbray, teeming with its toiling thousands, there rose a building which might vie with many of the cathedrals of our land. Beautiful its solemn towers, its sculptured western front; beautiful its columned aisles and lofty nave; its sparkling shrine and delicate chantry; most beautiful the streaming glories of its vast orient light!

This magnificent temple, built by the monks of Mowbray, and once connected with their famous house of which not a trace now remained, had in time become the parish church of an obscure village, whose population could not have filled one of its side chapels. These strange vicissitudes of ecclesiastical buildings are not singular in the north of England.

Mowbray Church* remained for centuries the wonder of passing peasants, and the glory of county histories. But there is a magic in beautiful buildings which exercises an irresistible influence over the mind of man. One of the reasons urged for the destruction of the monasteries after the dispersion of their inhabitants, was the pernicious influence of their solemn and stately forms on the memories and imagination of those that beheld them. It was impossible to connect systematic crime with the creators of such divine fabrics. And so it was with Mowbray Church. When manufactures were introduced into this district, which abounded with all the qualities which were necessary for their successful pursuit, Mowbray offering equal though not superior advantages to other positions, was accorded the preference, 'because it possessed such a beautiful church.' The lingering genius of the monks of Mowbray hovered round the spot which they had adorned, and sanctified, and loved; and thus they had indirectly become the authors of its present greatness and prosperity.

Unhappily, for a long season the vicars of Mowbray had been little conscious of their mission. An immense population gathered round the sacred citadel and gradually spread on all sides of it for miles. But the parish church for a long time remained the only one at Mowbray when the population of the town exceeded that of some European capitals. And even in the parish church the frigid spell of Erastian self-complacency fatally prevailed. A scanty congregation gathered together for form, and as much influenced by party as higher sentiments. Going to church was held more genteel than going to meeting. The principal tradesmen of the neighbouring great houses deemed it more 'aristocratic;' using a favourite and hackneyed epithet which only expressed their own servility. About the time the Church Commission* issued, the congregation of Mowbray was approaching zero. There was an idea afloat for a time of making it the seat of a new bishopric; the cathedral was ready; another instance of the influence of fine art. But there was no residence for the projected prelate, and a jobbing bishop on the commission was afraid that he might have to contribute to building one. So the idea died away; and the living having become vacant at this moment, instead of a bishop, Mowbray received a humble vicar in the shape of Aubrey St. Lys, who came among a hundred thousand heathens to preach 'the Unknown God.'

CHAPTER XII.

'AND how do you find the people about you, Marney?' said Lord de Mowbray, seating himself on a sofa by his guest.

'All very well, my lord,' replied the earl, who ever treated Lord de Mowbray with a certain degree of ceremony, especially when the descendant of the crusaders affected the familiar. There was something of a Puck-like* malignity in the temperament of Lord Marney, which exhibited itself in a remarkable talent for mortifying persons in a small way; by a gesture, an expression, a look, cloaked too very often with all the character of profound deference. The old nobility of Spain delighted to address each other only by their names, when in the presence of a spick-and-span grandee; calling each other, 'Infantado,' 'Sidonia,' 'Ossuna,' and then turning round with the most distinguished consideration, and appealing to the Most Noble Marquis of Ensenada.

'They begin to get a little uneasy here,' said Lord de Mowbray.

'We have nothing to complain of,' said Lord Marney. 'We continue reducing the rates,* and as long as we do that the country must improve.

The workhouse test tells. We had the other day a case of incendiarism, which frightened some people: but I inquired into it, and am quite satisfied it originated in purely accidental circumstances; at least nothing to do with wages. I ought to be a judge, for it was on my own property.'

'And what is the rate of wages, in your part of the world, Lord Marney?' inquired Mr. St. Lys who was standing by.

'Oh! good enough: not like your manufacturing districts; but people who work in the open air, instead of a furnace, can't expect, and don't require such. They get their eight shillings a-week; at least generally.'

'Eight shillings a-week!' said Mr. St. Lys. 'Can a labouring man with a family, perhaps of eight children, live on eight shillings a week!'

'Oh! as for that,' said Lord Marney; 'they get more than that, because there is beer-money allowed, at least to a great extent among us, though I for one do not approve of the practice, and that makes nearly a shilling per week additional; and then some of them have potato grounds, though I am entirely opposed to that system.'

'And yet,' said Mr. St. Lys, 'how they contrive to live is to me marvellous.'

'Oh! as for that,' said Lord Marney, 'I have generally found the higher the wages the worse the workman. They only spend their money in the beer-shops. *They* are the curse of this country.'

'But what is a poor man to do,' said Mr. St. Lys; 'after his day's work if he returns to his own roof and finds no home: his fire extinguished, his food unprepared; the partner of his life, wearied with labour in the field or the factory, still absent, or perhaps in bed from exhaustion, or because she has returned wet to the skin, and has no change of raiment for her relief. We have removed woman from her sphere; we may have reduced wages by her introduction into the market of labour; but under these circumstances what we call domestic life is a condition impossible to be realized for the people of this country; and we must not therefore be surprised that they seek solace or rather refuge in the beer-shop.'

Lord Marney looked up at Mr. St. Lys, with a stare of high-bred impertinence, and then carelessly observed, without directing his words to him, 'They may say what they like, but it is all an affair of population.'*

'I would rather believe that it is an affair of resources,' said Mr. St. Lys; 'not what is the amount of our population, but what is the amount of our resources for their maintenance.'

'It comes to the same thing,' said Lord Marney. 'Nothing can put this country right but emigration on a great scale; and as the government do not choose to undertake it, I have commenced it for my own defence on a small scale. I will take care that the population of my parishes is not increased. I build no cottages* and I destroy all I can; and I am not ashamed or afraid to say so.'

'You have declared war to the cottage, then,' said Mr. St. Lys, smiling. 'It is not at the first sound so startling a cry as war to the castle.'

'But you think it may lead to it?' said Lord Mowbray.

'I love not to be a prophet of evil,' said Mr. St. Lys.

Lord Marney rose from his seat and addressed Lady Firebrace, whose husband in another part of the room had caught Mr. Jermyn, and was opening his mind on 'the question of the day;' Lady Maud, followed by Egremont, approached Mr. St. Lys, and said, 'Mr. Egremont has a great feeling for Christian architecture, Mr. St. Lys, and wishes particularly to visit our church of which we are so proud.' And in a few moments they were seated together and engaged in conversation.

Lord Mowbray placed himself by the side of Lady Marney, who was seated by his countess.

'Oh! how I envy you at Marney,' he exclaimed. 'No manufactures, no smoke; living in the midst of a beautiful park and surrounded by a contented peasantry!'

'It is very delightful,' said Lady Marney, 'but then we are so very dull; we have really no neighbourhood.'

'I think that such a great advantage,' said Lady Mowbray; 'I must say I like my friends from London. I never know what to say to the people here. Excellent people, the very best people in the world; the way they behaved to poor dear Fitz-Warene, when they wanted him to stand for the county, I never can forget; but then they do not know the people we know, or do the things we do; and when you have gone through the routine of county questions, and exhausted the weather and all the winds, I am positively, my dear Lady Marney, aux abois,* and then they think you are proud, when really one is only stupid.'

'I am very fond of work,' said Lady Marney, 'and I talk to them always about it.'

'Ah! you are fortunate, I never could work; and Joan and Maud, they neither of them work. Maud did embroider a banner once for her brother; it is in the hall. I think it beautiful; but somehow or other she never cultivated her talent.'

'For all that has occurred or may occur,' said Mr. St. Lys to Egremont, 'I blame only the Church. The church deserted the people; and from that moment the church has been in danger and the people degraded. Formerly religion undertook to satisfy the noble wants of human nature, and by its festivals relieved the painful weariness of toil. The day of rest was consecrated, if not always to elevated thought, at least to sweet and noble sentiments. The church convened to its solemnities, under its splendid and almost celestial roofs amid the finest monuments of art that human hands have raised, the whole Christian population; for there, in the presence of God, all were brethren. It shared equally among all its prayer, its incense, and its music; its sacred instructions, and the highest enjoyments that the arts could afford.'

'You believe then in the efficacy of forms and ceremonies?'*

'What you call forms and ceremonies represent the divinest instincts of our nature. Push your aversion to forms and ceremonies to a legitimate conclusion, and you would prefer kneeling in a barn rather than in a cathedral. Your tenets would strike at the very existence of all art, which is essentially spiritual.'

'I am not speaking abstractedly,' said Egremont, 'but rather with reference to the indirect connection of these forms and ceremonies with another church. The people of this country associate them with an enthralling superstition and a foreign dominion.'

'With Rome,' said Mr. St. Lys; 'yet forms and ceremonies existed before Rome.'

'But practically,' said Egremont, 'has not their revival in our service at the present day a tendency to restore the Romish system in this country?'

'It is difficult to ascertain what may be the practical effect of certain circumstances among the uninformed,' said Mr. St. Lys. 'The church of Rome is to be respected as the only Hebræo–christian church extant; all other churches established by the Hebrew apostles have disappeared, but Rome remains; and we must never permit the exaggerated position which it assumed in the middle centuries to make us forget its early and apostolical character, when it was fresh from Palestine and as it were fragrant from Paradise. The church of Rome is sustained by apostolical succession;* but apostolical succession is not an institution complete in itself; it is a part of a whole; if it be not part of a whole it has no foundation. The apostles succeeded the prophets. Our Master announced himself as the last of the prophets. They in their turn were the heirs of the patriarchs: men who were in direct communication with the Most High. To men not less favoured than the apostles, the revelation of the priestly character was made, and those forms and ceremonies ordained, which the church of Rome has never relinquished. But Rome did not invent them: upon their practice, the duty of all congregations, we cannot consent to her founding a claim to supremacy. For would you maintain then that the church did not exist in the time of the prophets?

Was Moses then not a churchman? And Aaron, was he not a high priest? Ay! greater than any pope or prelate, whether he be at Rome or at Lambeth.*

'In all these church discussions, we are apt to forget that the second Testament is avowedly only a supplement. Jehovah-Jesus came to complete the 'law and the prophets.' Christianity is completed Judaism,* or it is nothing. Christianity is incomprehensible without Judaism, as Judaism is incomplete without Christianity. What has Rome to do with its completion; what with its commencement? The law was not thundered forth from the Capitolian mount; the divine atonement was not fulfilled upon Mons Sacer.* No; the order of our priesthood comes directly from Jehovah; and the forms and ceremonies of His church are the regulations of His supreme intelligence. Rome indeed boasts that the authenticity of the second Testament depends upon the recognition of her infallibility. The authenticity of the second Testament depends upon its congruity with the first. Did Rome preserve that? I recognize in the church an institution thoroughly, sincerely, catholic: adapted to all climes and to all ages. I do not bow to the necessity of a visible head in a defined locality; but were I to seek for such, it would not be at Rome. I cannot discover in its history, however memorable, any testimony of a mission so sublime. When Omnipotence deigned to be incarnate, the Ineffable Word did not select a Roman frame. The prophets were not Romans; the apostles were not Romans; she, who was blessed above all women, I never heard she was a Roman maiden. No, I should look to a land more distant than Italy, to a city more sacred even than Rome.'

CHAPTER XIII.

IT was a cloudy, glimmering dawn. A cold withering east wind blew through the silent streets of Mowbray. The sounds of the night had died away, the voices of the day had not commenced. There reigned a stillness complete and absorbing.

Suddenly there is a voice, there is movement. The first footstep of the new week of toil is heard. A man muffled up in a thick coat, and bearing in his hand what would seem at the first glance to be a shepherd's crook, only its handle is much longer, appears upon the pavement. He touches a number of windows with great quickness as he moves rapidly along. A rattling noise sounds upon each pane. The use of the long handle of his instrument becomes apparent as he proceeds, enabling him as it does to reach the upper windows of the dwellings whose inmates he has to rouse. Those inmates are the factory girls, who sub-scribe in districts to engage these heralds of the dawn; and by a strict observance of whose citation they can alone escape the dreaded fine that awaits those who have not arrived at the door of the factory before the bell ceases to sound.

The sentry in question, quitting the streets, and stooping through one of the small archways that we have before noticed, entered a court. Here lodged a multitude of his employers; and the long crook as it were by some sleight of hand seemed sounding on both sides and at many windows at the same moment. Arrived at the end of the court, he was about to touch the window of the upper story of the last tenement, when that window opened, and a man, pale and care-worn and in a melancholy voice spoke to him.

'Simmons,' said the man, 'you need not rouse this story any more; my daughter has left us.'

'Has she left Webster's?'

'No; but she has left us. She has long murmured at her hard lot; working like a slave and not for herself. And she has gone, as they all go, to keep house for herself.'

'That's a bad business,' said the watchman, in a tone not devoid of sympathy.

'Almost as bad as for parents to live on their children's wages,' replied the man mournfully.

'And how is your good woman?'

'As poorly as needs be. Harriet has never been home since Friday night. She owes you nothing?'

'Not a halfpenny. She was as regular as a little bee and always paid every Monday morning. I am sorry she has left you, neighbour.'

'The Lord's will be done. It's hard times for such as us,' said the man; and leaving the window open, he retired into his room.

It was a single chamber of which he was the tenant. In the centre, placed so as to gain the best light which the gloomy situation could afford, was a loom.* In two corners of the room were mattresses placed on the floor, a check curtain hung upon a string, if necessary concealing them. In one was his sick wife; in the other, three young children: two girls, the eldest about eight years of age; between them their baby brother. An iron kettle was by the hearth, and on the mantel-piece, some can-dles, a few lucifer matches, two tin mugs, a paper of salt, and an iron spoon. In a farther part, close to the wall, was a heavy table or dresser; this was a fixture, as well as the form which was fastened by it.

The man seated himself at his loom; he commenced his daily task.

'Twelve hours of daily labour at the rate of one penny each hour; and even this labour is mortgaged! How is this to end? Is it rather not ended?' And he looked around him at his chamber without resources: no food, no fuel, no furniture, and four human beings dependent on him, and lying in their wretched beds because they had no clothes. 'I cannot sell my loom,' he continued, 'at the price of old firewood, and it cost me gold. It is not vice that has brought me to this, nor indolence, nor imprudence. I was born to labour, and I was ready to labour. I loved my loom and my loom loved me. It gave me a cottage in my native village, surrounded by a garden of whose claims on my solicitude it was not jealous. There was time for both. It gave me for a wife the maiden that I had ever loved; and it gathered my children round my hearth with plenteousness and peace. I was content: I sought no other lot. It is not adversity that makes me look back upon the past with tenderness.

'Then why am I here? Why am I, and six hundred thousand subjects of the Queen, honest, loyal, and industrious, why are we, after manfully struggling for years, and each year sinking lower in the scale, why are we driven from our innocent and happy homes, our country cottages that we loved, first to hide in close towns without comforts, and gradually to crouch into cellars, or find a squalid lair like this, without even the common necessaries of existence; first the ordinary conveniences of life, then raiment, and, at length, food, vanishing from us.

'It is that the Capitalist has found a slave that has supplanted the labour and ingenuity of man. Once he was an artizan: at the best, he now only watches machines; and even that occupation slips from his grasp, to the woman and the child. The capitalist flourishes, he amasses immense wealth; we sink, lower and lower; lower than the beasts of burthen; for they are fed better than we are, cared for more. And it is just, for according to the present system they are more precious. And yet they tell us that the interests of Capital and of Labour are identical.

'If a society that has been created by labour suddenly becomes independent of it, that society is bound to maintain the race whose only property is labour, from the proceeds of that other property, which has not ceased to be productive.

'When the class of the Nobility were supplanted in France, they did not amount in number to one-third of us Hand-Loom weavers; yet all Europe went to war to avenge their wrongs, every state subscribed to maintain them in their adversity, and when they were restored to their own country, their own land supplied them with an immense indemnity. Who cares for us? Yet we have lost our estates. Who raises a voice for us? Yet we are at least as innocent as the nobility of France. We sink among no sighs except our own. And if they give us sympathy—what then? Sympathy is the solace of the Poor; but for the Rich, there is Compensation.'

'Is that Harriet?' said his wife, moving in her bed.

The Hand-Loom weaver was recalled from his reverie to the urgent misery that surrounded him.

'No!' he replied in a quick hoarse voice, 'it is not Harriet.'

'Why does not Harriet come?'

'She will come no more!' replied the weaver; 'I told you so last night: she can bear this place no longer; and I am not surprised.'

'How are we to get food then?' rejoined his wife; 'you ought not to have let her leave us. You do nothing, Warner. You get no wages yourself; and you have let the girl escape.'

'I will escape myself if you say that again,' said the weaver: 'I have been up these three hours finishing this piece which ought to have been taken home on Saturday night.'

'But you have been paid for it beforehand. You get nothing for your work. A penny an hour! What sort of work is it, that brings a penny an hour?'

'Work that you have often admired, Mary; and has before this gained a prize. But if you don't like the work,' said the man quitting his loom, 'let it alone. There was enough yet owing on this piece to have allowed us to break our fast. However, no matter; we must starve sooner or later. Let us begin at once.'

'No, no, Philip! work. Let us break our fast come what may.'

'Twit me no more then,' said the weaver resuming his seat, 'or I throw the shuttle for the last time.'

'I will not taunt you,' said his wife in a kinder tone. 'I was wrong; I am sorry; but I am very ill. It is not for myself I speak; I want not to eat; I have no appetite; my lips are so very parched. But the children, the children went supperless to bed, and they will wake soon.'

'Mother, we ayn't asleep,' said the elder girl.

'No, we ayn't asleep, mother,' said her sister; 'we heard all that you said to father.'

'And baby?'

'He sleeps still.'

'I shiver very much!' said the mother. 'It's a cold day. Pray shut the window Warner. I see the drops upon the pane; it is raining. I wonder if the persons below would lend us one block of coal.'

'We have borrowed too often,' said Warner.

'I wish there were no such thing as coal in the land,' said his wife, 'and then the engines would not be able to work; and we should have our rights again.'

'Amen!' said Warner.

'Don't you think, Warner,' said his wife, 'that you could sell that piece to some other person, and owe Barber for the money he advanced?'

'No!' said her husband shaking his head. 'I'll go straight.'

'And let your children starve,' said his wife, 'when you could get five or six shillings at once. But so it always was with you! Why did not you go to the machines years ago like other men and so get used to them?'

'I should have been supplanted by this time,' said Warner, 'by a girl or a woman! It would have been just as bad!'

'Why there was your friend Walter Gerard; he was the same as you, and yet now he gets two pound a-week; at least I have often heard you say so.'

'Walter Gerard is a man of great parts,' said Warner, 'and might have been a master himself by this time had he cared.'

'And why did he not?'

'He had no wife and children,' said Warner; 'he was not so blessed.'

The baby woke and began to cry.

'Ah! my child!' exclaimed the mother. 'That wicked Harriet! Here Amelia, I have a morsel of crust here. I saved it yesterday for baby; moisten it in water, and tie it up in this piece of calico: he will suck it; it will keep him quiet; I can bear anything but his cry.'

'I shall have finished my job by noon,' said Warner; 'and then, please God, we shall break our fast.'

'It is yet two hours to noon,' said his wife. 'And Barber always keeps you so long! I cannot bear that Barber: I dare say he will not advance you money again as you did not bring the job home on Saturday night. If I were you, Philip, I would go and sell the piece unfinished at once to one of the cheap shops.'

'I have gone straight all my life,' said Warner.

'And much good it has done you,' said his wife.

'My poor Amelia! How she shivers! I think the sun never touches this house. It is indeed a most wretched place!'

'It will not annoy you long, Mary,' said her husband: 'I can pay no more rent; and I only wonder they have not been here already to take the week.'

'And where are we to go?' said the wife.

'To a place which certainly the sun never touches,' said her husband, with a kind of malice in his misery,—'to a cellar!'

'Oh! why was I ever born!' exclaimed his wife. 'And yet I was so happy once! And it is not our fault. I cannot make it out Warner, why you should not get two pounds a-week like Walter Gerard?'

'Bah!' said the husband.

'You said he had no family,' continued his wife. 'I thought he had a daughter.'

'But she is no burthen to him. The sister of Mr. Trafford is the Superior of the convent here, and she took Sybil when her mother died, and brought her up.'

'Oh! then she is a nun?'

'Not yet; but I dare say it will end in it.'

'Well, I think I would even sooner starve,' said his wife, 'than my children should be nuns.'

At this moment there was a knocking at the door. Warner descended from his loom and opened it.

'Lives Philip Warner here?' enquired a clear voice of peculiar sweetness.

'My name is Warner.'

'I come from Walter Gerard,' continued the voice. 'Your letter reached him only last night. The girl at whose house your daughter left it has quitted this week past Mr. Trafford's factory.'

'Pray enter.'

And there entered SYBIL.

CHAPTER XIV.

'YOUR wife is ill?' said Sybil.

'Very!' replied Warner's wife. 'Our daughter has behaved infamously to us. She has quitted us without saying by your leave or with your leave. And her wages were almost the only thing left to us; for Philip is not like Walter Gerard you see: he cannot earn two pounds a-week, though why he cannot I never could understand.'

'Hush, hush, wife!' said Warner. 'I speak I apprehend to Gerard's daughter?'

'Just so.'

'Ah! this is good and kind; this is like old times, for Walter Gerard was my friend, when I was not exactly as I am now.'

'He tells me so: he sent a messenger to me last night to visit you this morning. Your letter reached him only yesterday.'

'Harriet was to give it to Caroline,' said the wife. 'That's the girl who has done all the mischief and inveigled her away. And she has left Trafford's works, has she? Then I will be bound she and Harriet are keeping house together.'

'You suffer?' said Sybil, moving to the bed-side of the woman; 'give me your hand,' she added in a soft sweet tone. ''Tis hot.'

'I feel very cold,' said the woman. 'Warner would have the window open, till the rain came in.'

'And you, I fear, are wet,' said Warner, addressing Sybil, and inter-rupting his wife.

'Very slightly. And you have no fire. Ah! I have brought some things for you, but not fuel.'

'If he would only ask the person down stairs,' said his wife, 'for a block of coal; I tell him, neighbours could hardly refuse; but he never will do anything; he says he has asked too often.'

'I will ask,' said Sybil. 'But first, I have a companion without,' she added, 'who bears a basket for you. Come in, Harold.'

The baby began to cry the moment a large dog entered the room; a young bloodhound of the ancient breed, such as are now found but in a few old halls and granges in the north of England. Sybil untied the basket, and gave a piece of sugar to the screaming infant. Her glance was sweeter even than her remedy; the infant stared at her with his large blue eyes, for an instant astonished, and then he smiled.

'Oh! beautiful child!' exclaimed Sybil; and she took the babe up from the mattress and embraced it.

'You are an angel from heaven,' exclaimed the mother, 'and you may well say beautiful. And only to think of that infamous girl, Harriet, to desert us all in this way.'

Sybil drew forth the contents of the convent basket, and called Warner's attention to them. 'Now,' she said, 'arrange all this as I tell you, and I will go down stairs and speak to them below as you wish. Harold, rest there;' and the dog laid himself down in the remotest corner.

'And is that Gerard's daughter?' said the weaver's wife. 'Only think what it is to gain two pounds a-week, and bring up your daughters in that way—instead of such shameless husseys as our Harriet! But with such wages one can do anything. What have you there, Warner? Is that tea? Oh! I should like some tea. I do think tea would do me some good. I have quite a longing for it. Run down, Warner, and ask them to let us have a kettle of hot water. It is better than all the fire in the world. Amelia, my dear, do you see what they have sent us. Plenty to eat. Tell

Maria all about it. You are good girls; you will never be like that infamous Harriet. When you earn wages you will give them to your poor mother and baby, won't you?'

'Yes, mother,' said Amelia.

'And father, too,' said Maria.

'And father, too,' said the wife. 'He has been a very good father to you all; and I never can understand why one who works so hard should earn so little; but I believe it is the fault of those machines. The police ought to put them down, and then every body would be comfortable.'

Sybil and Warner re-entered; the fire was lit, the tea made, the meal partaken. An air of comfort, even of enjoyment, was diffused over this chamber, but a few minutes back so desolate and unhappy.

'Well,' said the wife, raising herself a little up in her bed, 'I feel as if that dish of tea had saved my life. Amelia, have you had any tea? And Maria? You see what it is to be good girls; the Lord will never desert you. The day is fast coming when that Harriet will know what the want of a dish of tea is, with all her fine wages. And I am sure,' she added, addressing Sybil, 'what we all owe to you is not to be told. Your father well deserves his good fortune, with such a daughter.'

'My father's fortunes are not much better than his neighbours,' said Sybil, 'but his wants are few; and who should sympathise with the poor, but the poor? Alas! none else can. Besides, it is the Superior of our convent that has sent you this meal. What my father can do for you, I have told your husband. 'Tis little; but with the favour of heaven, it may avail. When the people support the people, the divine blessing will not be wanting.'

'I am sure the divine blessing will never be wanting to you,' said Warner in a voice of great emotion.

There was silence; the querulous spirit of the wife was subdued by the tone of Sybil; she revolved in her mind the present and the past; the children pursued their ungrudged and unusual meal; the daughter of Gerard, that she might not interfere with their occupation, walked to the window and surveyed the clink of troubled sky, which was visible in the court. The wind blew in gusts; the rain beat against the glass. Soon after this, there was another knock at the door. Harold started from his repose, and growled. Warner rose, and saying, 'They have come for the rent. Thank God, I am ready,' advanced and opened the door. Two men offered with courtesy to enter.

'We are strangers,' said he who took the lead, 'but would not be such. I speak to Warner?'

'My name.'

'And I am your spiritual pastor, if to be the vicar of Mowbray entitles me to that description.'

'Mr. St. Lys.'

'The same. One of the most valued of my flock, and the most influential person in this district, has been speaking much of you to me this morning. You are working for him. He did not hear of you on Saturday night; he feared you were ill. Mr. Barber spoke to me of your distress, as well as of your good character. I came to express to you my respect and my sympathy, and to offer you my assistance.'

'You are most good, sir, and Mr. Barber too, and indeed, an hour ago, we were in as great straits—.'

'And are now, sir,' exclaimed his wife interrupting him. 'I have been in this bed a-week, and may never rise from it again; the children have no clothes; they are pawned; everything is pawned; this morning we had neither fuel, nor food. And we thought you had come for the rent which we cannot pay. If it had not been for a dish of tea which was charitably given me this morning by a person almost as poor as ourselves, that is to say, they live by labour, though their wages are much higher, as high as two pounds a-week, though how that can be I never shall understand, when my husband is working twelve hours a day, and gaining only a penny an hour—if it had not been for this I should have been a corpse; and yet he says we were in straits, merely because Walter Gerard's daughter, who I willingly grant is an angel from heaven for all the good she has done us, has stepped into our aid. But the poor supporting the poor, as she well says, what good can come from that!'

During this ebullition, Mr. St. Lys had surveyed the apartment and recognised Sybil.

'Sister,' he said when the wife of Warner had ceased, 'this is not the first time we have met under the roof of sorrow.'

Sybil bent in silence, and moved as if she were about to retire; the wind and rain came dashing against the window. The companion of Mr. St. Lys, who was clad in a rough great coat, and was shaking the wet off an oilskin hat known by the name of a 'south-wester,' advanced and said to her, 'It is but a squall, but a very severe one; I would recommend you to stay for a few minutes.'

She received this remark with courtesy but did not reply.

'I think,' continued the companion of Mr. St. Lys, 'that this is not the first time also that we have met?'

'I cannot recall our meeting before,' said Sybil.

'And yet it was not many days past; though the sky was so very different, that it would almost make one believe it was in another land and another clime.'

Sybil looked at him as if for explanation.

'It was at Marney Abbey,' said the companion of Mr. St. Lys.

'I was there; and I remember, when about to rejoin my companions, they were not alone.'

'And you disappeared; very suddenly I thought; for I left the ruins almost at the same moment as your friends, yet I never saw any of you again.'

'We took our course; a very rugged one; you perhaps pursued a more even way.'

'Was it your first visit to Marney?'

'My first and my last. There was no place I more desired to see; no place of which the vision made me so sad.'

'The glory has departed,' said Egremont mournfully.

'It is not that,' said Sybil; 'I was prepared for decay, but not for such absolute desecration. The Abbey seems a quarry for materials to repair farm-houses; and the nave a cattle gate. What people they must be—that family of sacrilege who hold these lands!'

'Hem!' said Egremont. 'They certainly do not appear to have much feeling for ecclesiastical art.'

'And for little else, as we were told,' said Sybil. 'There was a fire at the Abbey farm the day we were there, and from all that reached us, it would appear the people were as little tendered as the Abbey walls.'

'They have some difficulty perhaps in employing their population in those parts.'

'You know the country?'

'Not at all; I was travelling in the neighbourhood, and made a diversion for the sake of seeing an abbey of which I had heard so much.'

'Yes; it was the greatest of the Northern Houses. But they told me the people were most wretched round the Abbey; nor do I think there is any other cause for their misery, than the hard hearts of the family that have got the lands.'

'You feel deeply for the people!' said Egremont, looking at her earnestly.

Sybil returned him a glance expressive of some astonishment, and then said, 'And do not you? Your presence here assures me of it.'

'I humbly follow one who would comfort the unhappy.'

'The charity of Mr. St. Lys is known to all.'

'And you—you too are a ministering angel.'

'There is no merit in my conduct, for there is no sacrifice. When I remember what this English people once was; the truest, the freest, and the bravest, the best-natured and the best-looking, the happiest and most religious race upon the surface of this globe; and think of them now, with all their crimes and all their slavish sufferings, their soured spirits and their stunted forms; their lives without enjoyment and their deaths without hope; I may well feel for them, even if I were not the daughter of their blood.'

And that blood mantled to her cheek as she ceased to speak, and her dark eye gleamed with emotion, and an expression of pride and courage hovered on her brow. Egremont caught her glance and withdrew his own; his heart was troubled.

St. Lys, who had been in conference with the weaver, left him and went to the bedside of his wife. Warner advanced to Sybil, and expressed his feelings for her father, his sense of her goodness. She, observing that the squall seemed to have ceased, bade him farewell, and calling Harold, quitted the chamber.

CHAPTER XV.

'WHERE have you been all the morning, Charles?' said Lord Marney, coming into his brother's dressing-room a few minutes before dinner; 'Arabella had made the nicest little riding party for you and Lady Joan, and you were to be found nowhere. If you go on in this way, there is no use of having affectionate relations, or anything else.'

'I have been walking about Mowbray. One should see a factory once in one's life.'

'I don't see the necessity,' said Lord Marney; 'I never saw one, and never intend. Though to be sure, when I hear the rents that Mowbray gets for his land in this neighbourhood, I must say I wish the worsted works had answered at Marney. And if it had not been for our poor dear father, they would.'

'Our family have always been against manufactories, railroads—everything,' said Egremont.

'Railroads are very good things, with high compensation,' said Lord Marney; 'and manufactories not so bad, with high rents; but, after all, these are enterprises for the canaille,* and I hate them in my heart.'

'But they employ the people, George.'

'The people do not want employment; it is the greatest mistake in the world; all this employment is a stimulus to population. Never mind

that; what I came in for, is to tell you that both Arabella and myself
think you talk too much to Lady Maud.'

'I like her the best.'

'What has that to do with it my dear fellow? Business is business. Old
Mowbray will make an elder son out of his elder daughter. The affair is
settled; I know it from the best authority. Talking to Lady Maud is
insanity. It is all the same for her as if Fitz-Warene had never died. And
then that great event, which ought to be the foundation of your fortune,
would be perfectly thrown away. Lady Maud, at the best, is nothing
more than twenty thousand pounds and a fat living. Besides, she is
engaged to that parson fellow, St. Lys.'

'St. Lys told me to-day that nothing would ever induce him to marry.
He would practise celibacy, though he would not enjoin it.'

'Enjoin fiddle-stick! How came you to be talking to such a sanctified
impostor; and, I believe, with all his fine phrases, a complete radical.
I tell you what, Charles, you must really make way with Lady Joan. The
grandfather has come to-day, the old Duke. Quite a family party. It looks
so well. Never was such a golden opportunity. And you must be sharp
too. That little Jermyn, with his brown eyes and his white hands, has
not come down here, in the month of August, with no sport of any kind,
for nothing.'

'I shall set Lady Firebrace at him.'

'She is quite your friend, and a very sensible woman too, Charles,
and an ally not to be despised. Lady Joan has a very high opinion of her.
There's the bell. Well, I shall tell Arabella that you mean to put up the
steam, and Lady Firebrace shall keep Jermyn off. And perhaps it is as
well you did not seem too eager at first. Mowbray Castle, my dear fellow, in spite of its manufactories, is not to be despised. And with a little
firmness, you could keep the people out of your park. Mowbray could
do it, only he has no pluck. He is afraid people would say he was the son
of a footman.'

The Duke, who was the father of the Countess de Mowbray, was
also Lord Lieutenant of the county. Although advanced in years, he
was still extremely handsome; with the most winning manners; full
of amenity and grace. He had been a roué in his youth, but seemed
now the perfect representative of a benignant and virtuous old age.
He was universally popular; admired by young men, adored by young
ladies. Lord de Mowbray paid him the most distinguished consideration. It was genuine. However maliciously the origin of his own father
might be represented, nobody could deprive him of that great fact, his
father-in-law; a duke, a duke of a great house who had intermarried for

generations with great houses, one of the old nobility, and something even loftier.

The county of which his grace was Lord Lieutenant was very proud of its nobility; and certainly with Marney Abbey at one end, and Mowbray Castle at the other, it had just cause; but both these illustrious houses yielded in importance, though not in possessions, to the great peer who was the governor of the province.

A French actress,* clever as French actresses always are, had persuaded, once upon a time, an easy-tempered monarch of this realm, that the paternity of her coming babe was a distinction of which his majesty might be proud. His majesty did not much believe her; but he was a sensible man, and never disputed a point with a woman; so when the babe was born, and proved a boy, he christened him with his name; and elevated him to the peerage in his cradle by the title of Duke of Fitz-Aquitaine and Marquis of Gascony.

An estate the royal father could not endow him with, for he had spent all his money, mortgaged all his resources, and was obliged to run in debt himself for the jewels of the rest of his mistresses; but he did his best for the young peer, as became an affectionate father or a fond lover. His majesty made him when he arrived at man's estate the hereditary keeper of a palace which he possessed in the north of England; and this secured his grace a castle and a park. He could wave his flag and kill his deer; and if he had only possessed an estate, he would have been as well off as if he had helped conquer the realm with King William, or plundered the church for King Harry. A revenue must however be found for the Duke of Fitz-Aquitaine, and it was furnished without the interference of Parliament, but with a financial dexterity worthy of that assembly—to whom and not to our sovereigns we are obliged for the public debt. The king granted the duke and his heirs for ever, a pension on the post-office, a light tax upon coals shipped to London, and a tithe of all the shrimps caught on the southern coast. This last source of revenue became in time, with the development of watering places, extremely prolific. And so, what with the foreign courts and colonies for the younger sons, it was thus contrived very respectably to maintain the hereditary dignity of this great peer.

The present Duke of Fitz-Aquitaine had supported the Reform Bill, but had been shocked by the Appropriation clause; very much admired Lord Stanley,* and was apt to observe, that if that nobleman had been the leader of the Conservative party, he hardly knew what he might not have done himself. But the duke was an old Whig, had lived with old Whigs all his life, feared revolution, but still more the necessity of taking his name out of Brookes',* where he had looked in every day or night since he came of age. So, not approving of what was going on, yet not caring to desert his friends, he withdrew, as the phrase runs, from public life; that is to say, was rarely in his seat; did not continue to Lord Melbourne the proxy* that had been entrusted to Lord Grey; and made Tory magistrates in his county though a Whig lord lieutenant.

When forces were numbered, and speculations on the future indulged in by the Tadpoles and Tapers, the name of the Duke of Fitz-Aquitaine was mentioned with a knowing look and in a mysterious tone. Nothing more was necessary between Tadpole and Taper; but, if some hack in statu pupillari happened to be present at the conference, and the gentle novice greedy for party tattle, and full of admiring reverence for the two great hierophants of petty mysteries before him, ventured to intimate his anxiety for initiation, the secret was entrusted to him, 'that all was right there; that his grace only watched his opportunity; that he was heartily sick of the present men; indeed, would have gone over with Lord Stanley in 1835, had he not had a fit of the gout, which prevented him from coming up from the north; and though to be sure his son and brother did vote against the Speaker,* still that was a mistake; if a letter had been sent, which was not written, they would have voted the other way, and perhaps Sir Robert might have been in at the present moment.'

The Duke of Fitz-Aquitaine was the great staple of Lady Firebrace's correspondence with Mr. Tadpole. 'Woman's mission' took the shape to her intelligence of getting over his grace to the Conservatives. She was much assisted in these endeavours by the information which she so dexterously acquired from the innocent and incautious Lord Masque.

Egremont was seated at dinner to-day by the side of Lady Joan. Unconsciously to himself this had been arranged by Lady Marney. The action of woman on our destiny is unceasing. Egremont was scarcely in a happy mood for conversation. He was pensive, inclined to be absent; his thoughts indeed were of other things and persons than those around him. Lady Joan however only required a listener. She did not make enquiries like Lady Maud, or impart her own impressions by suggesting them as your own. Lady Joan gave Egremont an account of the Aztec cities, of which she had been reading that morning, and of the several historical theories which their discovery had suggested; then she imparted her own, which differed from all, but which seemed clearly the right one. Mexico led to Egypt. Lady Joan was as familiar with the Pharaohs as with the Caciques of the new world. The phonetic system was despatched by the way. Then came Champollion;* then Paris; then all its celebrities, literary and especially scientific; then came the letter from Arago received that morning; and the letter from Dr. Buckland expected to-morrow. She was delighted that one had written; wondered why the other had not. Finally, before the ladies had retired, she had invited Egremont to join Lady Marney in a visit to her observatory, where they were to behold a comet which she had been the first to detect.

Lady Firebrace, next to the duke, indulged in mysterious fiddle-faddle as to the state of parties. She too had her correspondents, and her letters received or awaited. Tadpole said this; Lord Masque, on the contrary, said that: the truth lay perhaps between them: some result developed by the clear intelligence of Lady Firebrace acting on the data with which they supplied her. The duke listened with calm excitement to the transcendental revelations of his Egeria.* Nothing appeared to be concealed from her; the inmost mind of the sovereign; there was not a royal prejudice that was not mapped in her secret inventory; the cabinets of the Whigs and the clubs of the Tories, she had the 'open sesame' to all of them. Sir Somebody did not want office, though he pretended to; and Lord Nobody did want office, though he pretended he did not. One great man thought the pear was not ripe; another that it was quite rotten; but then the first was coming on the stage, and the other was going off. In estimating the accuracy of a political opinion, one should take into consideration the standing of the opinionist.

At the right moment, and when she was sure she was not overheard, Lady Firebrace played her trump card, the pack having been previously cut by Mr. Tadpole.

'And who do you think Sir Robert would send to Ireland?' and she looked up in the face of the Duke of Fitz-Aquitaine.

'I suppose the person he sent before,' said his grace.

Lady Firebrace shook her head.

'Lord Haddington* will not go to Ireland again,' replied her lady-ship, mysteriously; 'mark me. And Lord De Grey does not like to go; and if he did, there are objections. And the Duke of Northumberland, he will not go. And who else is there? We must have a nobleman of the highest rank for Ireland; one who has not mixed himself up with Irish questions; who has always been in old days for emancipation; a Conservative, not an Orangeman. You understand. That is the person Sir Robert will send, and whom Sir Robert wants.'

'He will have some difficulty in finding such a person,' said the duke. 'If, indeed, the blundering affair of 1834 had not occurred, and things had taken their legitimate course, and we had seen a man like Lord Stanley for instance at the head of affairs, or leading a great party, why then indeed your friends the Conservatives,—for every sensible man must be a conservative, in the right sense of the word,—would have stood in a very different position; but now—,' and his grace shook his head.

'Sir Robert will never consent to form a government again without Lord Stanley,' said Lady Firebrace.

'Perhaps not,' said the duke.

'Do you know whose name I have heard mentioned in a certain quarter as the person Sir Robert would wish to see in Ireland?' continued Lady Firebrace.

His grace leant his ear.

'The Duke of Fitz-Aquitaine,' said Lady Firebrace.

'Quite impossible,' said the duke. 'I am no party man; if I be anything, I am a supporter of the government. True it is I do not like the way they are going on, and I disapprove of all their measures; but we must stand by our friends, Lady Firebrace. To be sure, if the country were in danger, and the Queen personally appealed to one, and the Conservative party were really a Conservative party, and not an old crazy faction vamped up and whitewashed into decency—one might pause and consider. But I am free to confess I must see things in a very different condition to what they are at present before I could be called upon to take that step. I must see men like Lord Stanley—'

'I know what you are going to say, my dear Duke of Fitz-Aquitaine. I tell you again Lord Stanley is with us, heart and soul; and before long I feel persuaded I shall see your grace in the Castle of Dublin.'

'I am too old; at least, I am afraid so,' said the Duke of Fitz-Aquitaine, with a relenting smile.

CHAPTER XVI.

ABOUT three miles before it reaches the town, the river Mowe undulates through a plain. The scene, though not very picturesque, has a glad and sparkling character. A stone bridge unites the opposite banks by three arches of good proportion; the land about consists of meads of a vivid colour, or vegetable gardens to supply the neighbouring population, and whose various hues give life and lightness to the level ground. The immediate boundaries of the plain on either side are chiefly woods; above the crest of which in one direction expands the brown bosom of a moor. The few cottages which are sprinkled about this scene being built of stone, and on an ample scale, contribute to the idea of comfort and plenty which, with a serene sky and on a soft summer day, the traveller willingly associates with it.

Such was the sky and season in which Egremont emerged on this scene a few days after the incidents recorded in our last chapter. He had been fishing in the park of Mowbray, and had followed the rivulet through many windings until, quitting the enclosed domain it had forced its way through some craggy underwood at the bottom of the hilly moors we have noticed, and finally entering the plain, lost itself in the waters of the greater stream.

Good sport had not awaited Egremont. Truth to say, his rod had played in a very careless hand. He had taken it, though an adept in the craft when in the mood, rather as an excuse to be alone, than a means to be amused. There are seasons in life when solitude is a necessity; and such a one had now descended on the spirit of the brother of Lord Marney.

The form of Sybil Gerard was stamped upon his brain. It blended with all thoughts; it haunted every object. Who was this girl, unlike all women whom he had yet encountered, who spoke with such sweet seriousness of things of such vast import, but which had never crossed his mind, and with a kind of mournful majesty bewailed the degradation of her race? The daughter of the lowly, yet proud of her birth. Not a noble lady in the land who could boast a mien more complete, and none of them thus gifted, who possessed withal the fascinating simplicity that pervaded every gesture and accent of the daughter of Gerard.

Yes! the daughter of Gerard; the daughter of a workman at a manufactory. It had not been difficult, after the departure of Sybil, to extract this information from the garrulous wife of the weaver. And that father,— he was not unknown to Egremont. His proud form and generous countenance were still fresh in the mind's eye of our friend. Not less so his thoughtful speech; full of knowledge and meditation and earnest feeling! How much that he had spoken still echoed in the heart, and rung in the brooding ear of Egremont. And his friend, too, that pale man with those glittering eyes, who without affectation, without pedantry, with artlessness on the contrary and a degree of earnest singleness, had glanced like a master of philosophy at the loftiest principles of political science,—was he too a workman? And are these then THE PEOPLE? If so, thought Egremont, would that I lived more among them! Compared with their converse, the tattle of our saloons has in it something humiliating. It is not merely that it is deficient in warmth, and depth, and breadth; that it is always discussing persons instead of principles, and cloaking its want of thought in mimetic dogmas and its want of feeling in superficial raillery; it is not merely that it has neither imagination, nor fancy, nor sentiment, nor feeling, nor knowledge to recommend it; but it appears to me, even as regards manner and expression, inferior in refinement and phraseology; in short, trivial, uninteresting, stupid, really vulgar.

It seemed to Egremont that, from the day he met these persons in the Abbey ruins, the horizon of his experience had insensibly expanded; more than that, there were streaks of light breaking in the distance, which already gave a new aspect to much that was known, and which perhaps was ultimately destined to reveal much that was now utterly obscure. He could not resist the conviction that from the time in question, his sympathies had become more lively and more extended; that a masculine impulse had been given to his mind; that he was inclined to view public questions in a tone very different to that in which he had surveyed them a few weeks back, when on the hustings of his borough.

Revolving these things, he emerged, as we have stated, into the plain of the Mowe, and guiding his path by the course of the river, he arrived at the bridge which a fancy tempted him to cross. In its centre, was a man gazing on the waters below and leaning over the parapet. His footstep roused the loiterer, who looked round; and Egremont saw that it was Walter Gerard.

Gerard returned his salute, and said, 'Early hours on Saturday afternoon* make us all saunterers;' and then, as their way was the same, they walked on together. It seemed that Gerard's cottage was near at hand, and having inquired after Egremont's sport, and receiving for a reply a present of a brace of trout,—the only one, by the bye, that was in Egremont's basket,—he could scarcely do less than invite his companion to rest himself.

'There is my home,' said Gerard, pointing to a cottage recently built, and in a pleasing style. Its materials were of a fawn-coloured stone, common in the Mowbray quarries. A scarlet creeper clustered round one side of its ample porch; its windows were large, mullioned,* and neatly latticed; it stood in the midst of a garden of no mean dimensions, but every bed and nook of which teemed with cultivation; flowers and vegetables both abounded, while an orchard rich with promise of many fruits, ripe pears and famous pippins of the north and plums of every shape and hue, screened the dwelling from that wind against which the woods that formed its background were no protection.

'And you are well lodged! Your garden does you honour.'

'I'll be honest enough to own I have no claim to the credit,' said Gerard. 'I am but a lazy chiel.'

They entered the cottage, where a hale old woman greeted them.

'She is too old to be my wife, and too young to be my mother,' said Gerard smiling; 'but she is a good creature, and has looked after me many a long day. Come, dame,' he said, 'thou'lt bring us a cup of tea; 'tis a good evening beverage,' he added, turning to Egremont, 'and what I ever take at this time. And if you care to light a pipe, you will find a companion.'

'I have renounced tobacco,' said Egremont; 'tobacco is the tomb of love,' and they entered a neatly-furnished chamber, that had that habitable look which the best room of a farm-house too often wants. Instead of the cast-off furniture of other establishments, at the same time dingy and tawdry, mock rosewood chairs and tarnished mahogany tables, there was an oaken table, some cottage chairs made of beech wood, and a Dutch clock. But what surprised Egremont was the appearance of several shelves well lined with volumes. Their contents too on closer inspection were very remarkable. They indicated a student of a high order. Egremont read the titles of works which he only knew by fame, but which treated of the loftiest and most subtle questions of social and political philosophy. As he was throwing his eye over them, his companion said, 'Ah! I see you think me as great a scholar as I am a gardener: but with as little justice; these books are not mine.'

'To whomsoever they belong,' said Egremont, 'if we are to judge from his collection, he has a tolerably strong head.'

'Ay, ay,' said Gerard, 'the world will hear of him yet, though he was only a workman, and the son of a workman. He has not been at your schools and your colleges, but he can write his mother tongue, as Shakespeare and Cobbett* wrote it; and you must do that, if you wish to influence the people.'

'And might I ask his name,' said Egremont.

'Stephen Morley, my friend.'

'The person I saw with you at Marney Abbey?'

'The same.'

'And he lives with you?'

'Why, we kept house together, if you could call it so. Stephen does not give much trouble in that way. He only drinks water and only eats herbs and fruits. He is the gardener,' added Gerard, smiling. 'I don't know how we shall fare when he leaves me.'

'And is he going to leave you?'

'Why, in a manner he has gone. He has taken a cottage about a quarter of a mile up the dale; and only left his books here, because he is going into —shire in a day or two, on some business, that may be will take him a week or so. The books are safer here you see for the present, for Stephen lives alone, and is a good deal away, for he edits a paper at Mowbray, and that must be looked after. He is to be my gardener still. I promised him that. Well done, dame,' said Gerard, as the old woman entered; 'I hope for the honour of the house a good brew. Now comrade sit down: it will do you good after your long stroll. You should eat your own trout if you would wait?'

'By no means. You will miss your friend, I should think?'

'We shall see a good deal of him, I doubt not, what with the garden and neighbourhood and so on; besides, in a manner, he is master of his own time. His work is not like ours; and though the pull on the brain is sometimes great, I have often wished I had a talent that way. It's a drear life to do the same thing every day at the same hour. But I never could express my ideas except with my tongue; and there I feel tolerably at home.'

'It will be a pity to see this room without these books,' said Egremont, encouraging conversation on domestic subjects.

'So it will,' said Gerard. 'I have got very few of my own. But my daughter will be able to fill the shelves in time, I warrant.'

'Your daughter—she is coming to live with you?'

'Yes; that is the reason why Stephen quits us. He only remained here until Sybil could keep my house, and that happy day is at hand.'

'That is a great compensation for the loss of your friend,' said Egremont.

'And yet she talks of flitting,' said Gerard, in a rather melancholy tone. 'She hankers after the cloister. She has passed a still, sweet life in the convent here; the Superior is the sister of my employer and a very saint on earth; and Sybil knows nothing of the real world except its sufferings. No matter,' he added more cheerfully; 'I would not have her take the veil rashly, but if I lose her it may be for the best. For the married life of a woman of our class in the present condition of our country is a lease of woe,' he added shaking his head, 'slaves, and the slaves of slaves! Even woman's spirit cannot stand against it; and it can bear against more than we can, master.'

'Your daughter is not made for the common cares of life,' said Egremont.

'We'll not talk of them,' said Gerard. 'Sybil has an English heart, and that's not easily broken. And you, comrade, you are a traveller in these parts, eh?'

'A kind of traveller; something in the way of your friend Morley—connected with the press.'

'Indeed! a reporter, eh? I thought you had something about you a little more knowing than we provincials.'

'Yes; a reporter; they want information in London as to the real state of the country, and this time of the year, Parliament not sitting—'

'Ah; I understand, a flying commission and a summer tour. Well, I often wish I were a penman; but I never could do it. I'll read any day as long as you like, but that writing, I could never manage. My friend Morley is a powerful hand at it. His journal circulates a good deal about here; and if as I often tell him he would only sink his high-flying philosophy and stick to old English politics, he might make a property of it. You'll like to know him?'

'Much.'

'And what first took you to the press, if I may ask!'

'Why—my father was a gentleman—' said Egremont in a hesitating tone, 'and I was a younger son.'

'Ah!' said Gerard, 'that is as bad as being a woman.'

'I had no patrimony,' continued Egremont, 'and I was obliged to work; I had no head I believe for the law; the church was not exactly in my way; and as for the army, how was I to advance without money or connexions! I had had some education, and so I thought I would turn it to account.'

'Wisely done! you are one of the working classes, and will enlist I hope in the great struggle against the drones. The natural friends of the people are younger sons, though they are generally enlisted against us. The more fools they; to devote their energies to the maintenance of a system which is founded on selfishness and which leads to fraud; and of which they are the first victims. But every man thinks he will be an exception.'

'And yet,' said Egremont, 'a great family rooted in the land, has been deemed to be an element of political strength.'

'I'll tell you what,' said Gerard, 'there is a great family in this country and rooted in it, of which we have heard much less than they deserved, but of which I suspect we shall hear very soon enough to make us all think a bit.'

'In this county?'

'Ay; in this county and every other one; I mean the PEOPLE.'

'Ah!' said Egremont, 'that family has existed for a long time.'

'But it has taken to increase rapidly of late, my friend—how may I call you?'

'They call me Franklin.'*

'A good English name of a good English class that has disappeared. Well, Mr. Franklin, be sure of this, that the Population Returns of this country are very instructive reading.'

'I can conceive so.'

'I became a man when the bad times were beginning,' said Gerard;
'I have passed through many doleful years. I was a Franklin's son myself,
and we had lived on this island at least no worse for a longer time than
I care to recollect, as little as what I am now. But that's nothing; I am
not thinking of myself. I am prosperous in a fashion; it is the serfs I live
among of whom I am thinking. Well, I have heard, in the course of years,
of some specifics for this constant degradation of the people; some thing
or some person that was to put all right; and for my part, I was not
unready to support any proposal or follow any leader. There was reform,
and there was paper money and no machinery, and a thousand other remedies; and there were demagogues of all kinds, some as base as myself,
and some with blood in their veins almost as costly as flows in those of
our great neighbour here, Earl de Mowbray, and I have always heard
that was very choice: but I will frankly own to you, I never had much
faith in any of these proposals or proposers; but they were a change, and
that is something. But I have been persuaded of late that there is something going on in this country of more efficacy; a remedial power, as
I believe, and irresistible; but whether remedial or not, at any rate
a power that will mar all or cure all. You apprehend me? I speak of the
annual arrival of more than three hundred thousand strangers* in this
island. How will you feed them? How will you clothe them? How will
you house them? They have given up butcher's meat; must they give
up bread? And as for raiment and shelter, the rags of the kingdom are
exhausted and your sinks and cellars already swarm like rabbit warrens.'

''Tis an awful consideration,' said Egremont musing.

'Awful,' said Gerard; ''tis the most solemn thing since the deluge.
What kingdom can stand against it? Why go to your history—you're
a scholar,—and see the fall of the great Roman empire—what was that?
Every now and then, there came two or three hundred thousand strangers
out of the forests and crossed the mountains and rivers. They come to
us every year and in greater numbers. What are your invasions of the
barbarous nations, your Goths and Visigoths, your Lombards and Huns,
to our Population Returns!'

END OF VOLUME THE FIRST.

VOLUME II

BOOK III.

CHAPTER I.

THE last rays of the sun, contending with clouds of smoke that drifted across the country, partially illumined a peculiar landscape. Far as the eye could reach, and the region was level, except where a range of limestone hills formed its distant limit, a wilderness of cottages or tenements that were hardly entitled to a higher name, were scattered for many miles over the land; some detached, some connected in little rows, some clustering in groups, yet rarely forming continuous streets, but interspersed with blazing furnaces, heaps of burning coal, and piles of smouldering ironstone; while forges and engine chimneys roared and puffed in all directions, and indicated the frequent presence of the mouth of the mine and the bank of the coal-pit. Notwithstanding the whole country might be compared to a vast rabbit warren, it was nevertheless intersected with canals crossing each other at various levels, and though the subterranean operations were prosecuted with so much avidity that it was not uncommon to observe whole rows of houses awry, from the shifting and hollow nature of the land, still, intermingled with heaps of mineral refuse or of metallic dross, patches of the surface might here and there be recognised, covered, as if in mockery, with grass and corn, looking very much like those gentlemen's sons that we used to read of in our youth, stolen by the chimneysweeps* and giving some intimations of their breeding beneath their grimy livery. But a tree or a shrub—such an existence was unknown in this dingy rather than dreary region.

It was the twilight hour; the hour at which in southern climes the peasant kneels before the sunset image of the blessed Hebrew maiden; when caravans halt in their long course over vast deserts, and the turbaned traveller bending in the sand, pays his homage to the sacred stone and the sacred city; the hour, not less holy, that announces the cessation of English toil, and sends forth the miner and the collier to breathe the air of earth, and gaze on the light of heaven.

They come forth: the mine delivers its gang and the pit its bondsmen; the forge is silent and the engine is still. The plain is covered with the swarming multitude: bands of stalwart men, broad-chested and muscular, wet with toil, and black as the children of the tropics; troops of youth—alas! of both sexes,—though neither their raiment nor their language indicates the difference; all are clad in male attire; and oaths that men might shudder at, issue from lips born to breathe words of sweetness. Yet these are to be—some are—the mothers of England! But can we wonder at the hideous coarseness of their language when we remember the savage rudeness of their lives? Naked to the waist, an iron chain fastened to a belt of leather runs between their legs clad in canvas trousers, while on hands and feet an English girl, for twelve, sometimes for sixteen hours a-day, hauls and hurries tubs of coals up subterranean roads, dark, precipitous, and plashy: circumstances that seem to have escaped the notice of the Society for the Abolition of Negro Slavery.* Those worthy gentlemen too appear to have been singularly unconscious of the sufferings of the little Trappers, which was remarkable, as many of them were in their own employ.

See, too, these emerge from the bowels of the earth! Infants of four and five years of age, many of them girls, pretty and still soft and timid; entrusted with the fulfilment of most responsible duties, and the nature of which entails on them the necessity of being the earliest to enter the mine and the latest to leave it. Their labour indeed is not severe, for that would be impossible, but it is passed in darkness and in solitude. They endure that punishment which philosophical philanthropy has invented for the direst criminals,* and which those criminals deem more terrible than the death for which it is substituted. Hour after hour elapses, and all that reminds the infant Trappers of the world they have quitted and that which they have joined, is the passage of the coal-waggons for which they open the air-doors of the galleries, and on keeping which doors constantly closed, except at this moment of passage, the safety of the mine and the lives of the persons employed in it entirely depend.

Sir Joshua, a man of genius and a courtly artist, struck by the seraphic countenance of Lady Alice Gordon, when a child of very tender years, painted the celestial visage in various attitudes on the same canvass, and styled the group of heavenly faces—guardian angels!*

We would say to some great master of the pencil, Mr. Landseer or Mr. Etty,* go thou to the little trappers and do likewise!

A small party of miners approached a house of more pretension than the generality of the dwellings, and announcing its character by a very flagrant sign of the Rising Sun. They entered it as men accustomed, and were greeted with smiles and many civil words from the lady at the bar, who inquired very cheerfully what the gentlemen would have. They soon found themselves seated in the tap, and, though it was not entirely unoccupied, in their accustomed places, for there seemed a general understanding that they enjoyed a prescriptive right.

With hunches of white bread in their black hands, and grinning with their sable countenances and ivory teeth, they really looked like a gang of negros at a revel.

The cups of ale circulated, the pipes were lighted, the preliminary puffs achieved. There was at length silence, when he who seemed their leader and who filled a sort of president's seat, took his pipe from his mouth, and then uttering the first complete sentence that had yet been expressed aloud, thus delivered himself.

'The fact is we are tommied* to death.'

'You never spoke a truer word, Master Nixon,' said one of his companions.

'It's gospel, every word of it,' said another.

'And the point is,' continued Master Nixon, 'what are we for to do?'

'Ay, surely,' said a collier; 'that's the marrow.'

'Ay, ay,' agreed several; 'there it is.'

'The question is,' said Nixon, looking round with a magisterial air, 'what *is* wages? I say, tayn't sugar, tayn't tea, tayn't bacon. I don't think it's candles; but of this I be sure, tayn't waistcoats.'

Here there was a general groan.

'Comrades,' continued Nixon, 'you know what has happened; you know as how Juggins applied for his balance after his tommy-book was paid up, and that incarnate nigger Diggs has made him take two waistcoats. Now the question rises, what is a collier to do with waistcoats? Pawn 'em I s'pose to Diggs' son-in-law, next door to his father's shop, and sell the ticket for sixpence. Now there's the question; keep to the question; the question is waistcoats and tommy; first waistcoats and then tommy.'

'I have been making a pound a-week these two months past,' said another, 'but as I'm a sinner saved, I have never seen the young queen's picture* yet.'

- 'And I have been obliged to pay the doctor for my poor wife in tommy,' said another. 'Doctor,' I said, says I, 'I blush to do it, but all I have got is tommy, and what shall it be, bacon or cheese?' "Cheese at tenpence a pound," says he, "which I buy for my servants at sixpence. Never mind," says he, for he is a thorough Christian, "I'll take the tommy as I find it."

'Juggins has got his rent to pay and is afeard of the bums,'* said Nixon; 'and he has got two waistcoats!'

'Besides,' said another, 'Diggs' tommy is only open once a-week, and if you're not there in time, you go over for another seven days. And it's such a distance, and he keeps a body there such a time—it's always a day's work for my poor woman; she can't do nothing after it, what with the waiting and the standing and the cussing of Master Joseph Diggs,—for he do swear at the women, when they rush in for the first turn, most fearful.'

'They do say he's a shocking little dog.'

'Master Joseph is wery wiolent, but there is no one like old Diggs for grabbing a bit of one's wages. He do so love it! And then he says you never need be at no loss for nothing; you can find everything under my roof. I should like to know who is to mend our shoes. Has Gaffer Diggs a cobbler's stall?'

'Or sell us a penn'orth of potatoes,' said another. 'Or a ha'porth of milk.'

'No; and so to get them one is obliged to go and sell some tommy, and much one gets for it. Bacon at ninepence a-pound at Diggs', which you may get at a huckster's for sixpence, and therefore the huckster can't be expected to give you more than fourpence halfpenny, by which token the tommy in our field just cuts our wages atween the navel.'

'And that's as true as if you heard it in church, Master Waghorn.'

'This Diggs seems to be an oppressor of the people,' said a voice from a distant corner of the room.

Master Nixon looked around, smoked, puffed, and then said, 'I should think he wor; as bloody-a-hearted butty as ever jingled.'

'But what business has a butty to keep a shop?' inquired the stranger. 'The law touches him.'*

'I should like to know who would touch the law,' said Nixon; 'not I for one. Them tommy shops is very delicate things; they won't stand no handling, I can tell you that.'

'But he cannot force you to take goods,' said the stranger; 'he must pay you in current coin of the realm, if you demand it.'

'They only pay us once in five weeks,' said a collier; 'and how is a man to live meanwhile. And suppose we were to make shift for a month or five weeks, and have all our money coming, and have no tommy out of the shop, what would the butty say to me? He would say, 'do you want e'er a note this time' and if I was to say 'no,' then he would say, 'you've no call to go down to work any more here.' And that's what I call forsation.'

'Ay, ay,' said another collier; 'ask for the young queen's picture, and you would soon have to put your shirt on, and go up the shaft.'

'It's them long reckonings that force us to the tommy shops,' said another collier; 'and if a butty turns you away because you won't take no tommy, you're a marked man in every field about.'[†]

'There's wus things as tommy,' said a collier who had hitherto been silent, 'and that's these here butties. What's going on in the pit is known only to God Almighty and the colliers. I have been a consistent methodist for many years, strived to do well, and all the harm I have ever done to the butties was to tell them that their deeds would not stand on the day of judgment.'

'They are deeds of darkness surely; for many's the morn we work for nothing, by one excuse or another, and many's the good stint that they undermeasure. And many's the cup of their ale that you must drink before they will give you any work. If the queen would do something for us poor men, it would be a blessed job.'

'There ayn't no black tyrant on this earth like a butty, surely,' said a collier; 'and there's no redress for poor men.'

'But why do not you state your grievances to the landlords and lessees,' said the stranger.

'I take it you be a stranger in these parts, sir,' said Master Nixon, following up this remark by a most enormous puff. He was the oracle of his circle, and there was silence whenever he was inclined to address them, which was not too often, though when he spoke, his words, as his followers often observed, were a regular ten-yard coal.*

'I take it you be a stranger in these parts, sir, or else you would know that it's as easy for a miner to speak to a main-master, as it is for me to pick coal with this here clay.* Sir, there's a gulf atween 'em. I went into the pit when I was five year old, and I count forty year in the service come Martinmas, and a very good age, sir, for a man what does his work, and I knows what I'm speaking about. In forty year, sir, a man sees a pretty deal, 'specially when he don't move out of the same spot and keeps his 'tention. I've been at play, sir, several times in forty year, and have seen as great stick-outs as ever happened in this country. I've seen the people at play for weeks together, and so clammed* that I never tasted nothing but a potato and a little salt for more than a fortnight. Talk of tommy, that was hard fare, but we were holding out for our

---

[†] A Butty in the mining districts is a middleman: a Doggy is his manager. The Butty generally keeps a Tommy or Truck shop and pays the wages of his labourers in goods. When miners and colliers strike they term it, 'going to play.'

rights, and that's sauce for any gander. And I'll tell you what, sir, that I never knew the people play yet, but if a word had passed atween them and the main-masters aforehand, it might not have been settled; but you can't get at them any way. Atween the poor man and the gentleman there never was no connection, and that's the wital mischief of this country.'

'It's a very true word, Master Nixon, and by this token that when we went to play in—28, and the masters said they would meet us; what did they do but walk about the ground and speak to the butties. The butties has their ear.'

'We never want no soldiers here if the masters would speak with the men; but the sight of a pitman is pison to a gentleman, and if we go up to speak with 'em, they always run away.'

'It's the butties,' said Nixon; 'they're wusser nor tommy.'

'The people will never have their rights,' said the stranger, 'until they learn their power. Suppose instead of sticking out and playing, fifty of your families were to live under one roof. You would live better than you live now; you would feed more fully, and be lodged and clothed more comfortably, and you might save half the amount of your wages; you would become capitalists; you might yourselves hire your mines and pits from the owners, and pay them a better rent than they now obtain, and yet yourselves gain more and work less.'

'Sir,' said Mr. Nixon, taking his pipe from his mouth, and sending forth a volume of smoke, 'you speak like a book.'

'It is the principle of association,' said the stranger; 'the want of the age.'

'Sir,' said Mr. Nixon, 'this here age wants a great deal, but what it principally wants is to have its wages paid in the current coin of the realm.'

Soon after this there were symptoms of empty mugs and exhausted pipes, and the party began to stir. The stranger addressing Nixon, enquired of him what was their present distance from Wodgate.*

'Wodgate!' exclaimed Mr. Nixon with an unconscious air.

'The gentleman means Hell-house Yard,' said one of his companions.

'I'm at home,' said Mr. Nixon, 'but 'tis the first time I ever heard Hell-house Yard called Wodgate.'

'It's called so in joggraphy,' said Juggins.

'But you bay'nt going to Hell-house Yard this time of night!' said Mr. Nixon. 'I'd as soon think of going down the pit with the windlass turned by lushy* Bob.'

'Tayn't a journey for Christians,' said Juggins.

'They're a very queer lot even in sunshine,' said another.

'And how far is it?' asked the stranger.

'I walked there once in three hours,' said a collier, 'but that was to the wake. If you want to see divils carnal, there's your time of day. They're no less than heathens, I be sure. I'd be sorry to see even our butty among them, for he is a sort of a Christian when he has taken a glass of ale.'

CHAPTER II.

Two days after the visit of Egremont to the cottage of Walter Gerard, the visit of the Marney family to Mowbray terminated, and they returned to the Abbey.

There is something mournful in the breaking up of an agreeable party, and few are the roofs in which one has sojourned, which are quitted without some feeling of depression. The sudden cessation of all those sources of excitement which pervade a gay and well arranged mansion in the country, unstrings the nervous system. For a week or so, we have done nothing which was not agreeable, and heard nothing which was not pleasant. Our self-love has been respected; there has been a total cessation of petty cares; all the enjoyment of an establishment without any of its solicitude. We have beheld civilization only in its favoured aspect, and tasted only the sunny side of the fruit. Sometimes there are associations with our visit of a still sweeter and softer character, but on these we need not dwell: glances that cannot be forgotten, and tones that linger in the ear; sentiment that subdues the soul, and flirtation that agitates the fancy. No matter, whatever may be the cause, one too often drives away from a country-house, rather hipped. The specific would be immediately to drive to another, and it is a favourite remedy. But sometimes it is not in our power; sometimes for instance we must return to our household gods in the shape of a nursery; and though this was not the form assumed by the penates* of Lord Marney, his presence, the presence of an individual so important and so indefatigable, was still required. His Lordship had passed his time at Mowbray to his satisfaction. He had had his own way in everything. His selfishness had not received a single shock. He had lain down the law and it had not been questioned. He had dogmatised and impugned, and his assertions had passed current, and his doctrines been accepted as orthodox. Lord Mowbray suited him; he liked the consideration of so great a personage. Lord Marney also really liked pomp; a curious table and a luxurious life; but he liked them under any roof rather than his own. Not that he was what is commonly called a Screw;* that is to say he was not a mere screw; but he was acute and malicious; saw everybody's worth and position at a glance; could not bear to expend his choice wines and costly viands on hangers-on and toad-eaters, though at the same time no man encouraged and required hangers-on and toad-eaters more. Lord Marney had all the petty social vices, and none of those petty social weaknesses which soften their harshness or their hideousness. To receive a prince of the blood or a great peer he would spare nothing. Had he to fulfil any of the public duties of his station, his performance would baffle criticism. But he enjoyed making the Vicar of Marney or Captain Grouse drink some claret that was on the wane, or praise a bottle of Burgundy that he knew was pricked.*

Little things affect little minds. Lord Marney rose in no very good humour; he was kept at the station, which aggravated his spleen. During his journey on the railroad he spoke little, and though he more than once laboured to get up a controversy he was unable, for Lady Marney, who rather dreaded her dull home, and was not yet in a tone of mind that could hail the presence of the little Poinsett as full compensation for the brilliant circle of Mowbray, replied in amiable monosyllables, and Egremont himself in austere ones, for he was musing over Sybil Gerard and a thousand things as wild and sweet.

Everything went wrong this day. Even Captain Grouse was not at the Abbey to welcome them back. He was playing in a cricket match, Marney against Marham. Nothing else would have induced him to be absent. So it happened that the three fellow-travellers had to dine together, utterly weary of themselves and of each other. Captain Grouse was never more wanted; he would have amused Lord Marney, relieved his wife and brother, reported all that had been said and done in their neighbourhood during their absence, introduced a new tone, and effected a happy diversion. Leaving Mowbray, detained at the station, Grouse away, some disagreeable letters, or letters which an ill-humoured man chooses to esteem disagreeable, seemed to announce a climax. Lord Marney ordered the dinner to be served in the small dining-room, which was contiguous to a saloon in which Lady Marney, when they were alone, generally passed the evening.

The dinner was silent and sombre; happily it was also short. Lord Marney tasted several dishes, ate of none; found fault with his own claret, though the butler had given him a choice bottle; praised Lord Mowbray's, wondered where he got it, 'all the wines at Mowbray were good;' then for the twentieth time wondered what could have induced Grouse to fix the cricket match the day he returned home, though he chose to forget that he had never communicated to Grouse even the probable day on which he might be expected.

As for Egremont it must be admitted that he was scarcely in a more contented mood than his brother, though he had not such insufficient cause for his dark humours. In quitting Mowbray, he had quitted something else than merely an agreeable circle: enough had happened in that visit to stir up the deep recesses of his heart, and to prompt him to investigate in an unusual spirit the cause and attributes of his position. He had found a letter on his return to the Abbey, not calculated to dispel these somewhat morbid feelings; a letter from his agent, urging the settlement of his election accounts, the primary cause of his visit to his brother.

Lady Marney left the dining room; the brothers were alone. Lord Marney filled a bumper, which he drank off rapidly, pushed the bottle to his brother, and then said again, 'What a cursed bore it is that Grouse is not here.'

'Well, I cannot say, George, that I particularly miss the presence of Captain Grouse,' said his brother.

Lord Marney looked at Egremont pugnaciously, and then observed, 'Grouse is a capital fellow; one is never dull when Grouse is here.'

'Well, for my part,' said Egremont, 'I do not much admire that amusement which is dependent on the efforts of hangers-on.'

'Grouse is no more a hanger-on than any one else,' said Lord Marney, rather fiercely.

'Perhaps not,' said Egremont quietly; 'I am no judge of such sort of people.'

'I should like to know what you are a judge of; certainly not of making yourself agreeable to young ladies. Arabella cannot be particularly charmed with the result of your visit to Mowbray, as far as Lady Joan is concerned, Arabella's most intimate friend by the bye. If for no other reason, you ought to have paid her more attention.'

'I cannot pay attention unless I am attracted,' said Egremont; 'I have not the ever-ready talent of your friend, Captain Grouse.'

'I do not know what you mean by my friend Captain Grouse. Captain Grouse is no more my friend than your friend. One must have people about the house to do a thousand things which one cannot do oneself, and which one cannot trust to servants, and Grouse does all this capitally.'

'Exactly; he is just what I said, a capital hanger-on if you like, but still a hanger-on.'

'Well, and what then! Suppose he is a hanger-on; may I not have hangers-on as well as any other man?'

'Of course you may; but I am not bound to regret their absence.'

'Who said you were? But I will regret their absence, if I choose. And I regret the absence of Grouse, regret it very much; and if he did happen to be inextricably engaged in this unfortunate match, I say, and you may contradict me if you please, that he ought to have taken care that Slimsey dined here, to tell me all that had happened.'

'I am very glad he omitted to do so,' said Egremont; 'I prefer Grouse to Slimsey.'

'I dare say you do,' said Lord Marney, filling his glass and looking very black; 'you would like, I have no doubt, to see a fine gentleman-saint, like your friend Mr. St. Lys, at Marney, preaching in cottages, filling the people with discontent, lecturing me about low wages, soliciting plots of grounds for new churches, and inveigling Arabella into subscriptions to painted windows.'

'I certainly should like to see a man like Aubrey St. Lys at Marney,' said Egremont quietly, but rather doggedly.

'And if he were here, I would soon see who should be master,' said Lord Marney; 'I would not succumb like Mowbray. One might as well have a Jesuit in the house at once.'

'I dare say St. Lys would care very little about entering your house,' said Egremont. 'I know it was with great reluctance that he ever came to Mowbray Castle.'

'I dare say; very great reluctance indeed. And very reluctant he was, I make no doubt, to sit next to Lady Maud. I wonder he does not fly higher, and preach to Lady Joan; but she is too sensible a woman for such fanatical tricks.'

'St. Lys thinks it his duty to enter all societies. That is the reason why he goes to Mowbray Castle, as well as to the squalid courts and cellars of the town. He takes care that those who are clad in purple and fine linen shall know the state of their neighbours. They cannot at least plead ignorance for the non-fulfilment of their duty. Before St. Lys's time, the family at Mowbray Castle might as well have not existed, as far as benefiting their miserable vicinage. It would be well perhaps for other districts not less wretched, and for other families as high and favoured as the Mowbrays, if there were a Mr. St Lys on the spot instead of a Mr. Slimsey.'

'I suppose that is meant for a cut,' said Lord Marney; 'but I wish the people were as well off in every part of the country as they are on my estate. They get here their eight shillings a week, always at least seven, and every hand is at this moment in employ, except a parcel of scoundrels who prefer wood-stealing and poaching and who would prefer wood-stealing and poaching if you gave them double the wages. The rate of wages is nothing: certainty is the thing; and every man at Marney may be sure of his seven shillings a-week for at least nine months in the year; and for the other three, they can go to the House,* and a very proper place for them; it is heated with hot air, and has every comfort. Even Marney Abbey is not heated with hot air. I have often thought of it; it makes me mad sometimes to think of those lazy, pampered menials passing their lives with their backs to a great roaring fire; but I am afraid of the flues.'

'I wonder, talking of fires, that you are not more afraid of burning ricks,' said Egremont.

'It's an infernal lie,' said Lord Marney, very violently.

'What is?' said Egremont.

'That there is any incendiarism in this neighbourhood.'

'Why, there was a fire the day after I came.'

'That had nothing to do with wages; it was an accident. I examined into it myself; so did Grouse, so did Slimsey; I sent them about everywhere. I told them I was sure the fire was purely accidental, and to go and see about it; and they came back and agreed that it was purely accidental.'

'I dare say they did,' said Egremont; 'but no one has discovered the accident.'

'For my part, I believe it was spontaneous combustion,'* said Lord Marney.

'That is a satisfactory solution,' said Egremont, 'but for my part, the fire being a fact, and it being painfully notorious that the people of Marney—'

'Well, sir, the people of Marney'—said his lordship fiercely.

'Are without question the most miserable population in the county.'

'Did Mr. St. Lys tell you that?' interrupted Lord Marney, white with rage.

'No, not Mr. Lys, but one better acquainted with the neighbourhood.'

'I'll know your informant's name,' said Lord Marney with energy.

'My informant was a woman,' said Egremont.

'Lady Maud, I suppose; second-hand from Mr. St. Lys.'

'My informant was a woman, and one of the people,' said Egremont.

'Some poacher's drab! I don't care what women say, high or low, they always exaggerate.'

'The misery of a family who live upon seven or even eight shillings a-week can scarcely be exaggerated.'

'What should you know about it? Did you ever live on seven or eight shillings a-week? What can you know about the people who pass your time at London clubs or in fine country houses? I suppose you want the people to live as they do at a house dinner at Boodle's. I say that a family can live very well on seven shillings a-week, and on eight shillings very well indeed. The poor are very well off, at least the agricultural poor, very well off indeed. Their incomes are certain, that is a great point, and they have no cares, no anxieties; they always have a resource, they always have the House. People without cares do not require as much food as those whose life entails anxieties. See how long they live! Compare the rate of mortality among them with that of the manufacturing districts. Incendiarism indeed! If there had been a proper rural police, such a thing as incendiarism would never have been heard of!'

There was a pause. Lord Marney dashed off another bumper; Egremont sipped his wine. At length he said, 'This argument made me forget the principal reason, George, why I am glad that we are alone together today. I am sorry to bore you, but I am bored myself deucedly. I find a letter from my agent. These election accounts must be settled.'

'Why, I thought they were settled.'

'How do you mean?'

'I thought my mother had given you a thousand pounds.'

'No doubt of that, but that was long ago disposed of.'

'In my opinion quite enough for a seat in these times. Instead of paying to get into Parliament, a man ought to be paid for entering it.'

'There may be a good deal in what you say,' said Egremont; 'but it is too late to take that view of the business. The expense has been incurred and must be met.'

'I don't see that,' said Lord Marney, 'we have paid one thousand pounds and there is a balance unsettled. When was there ever a contest without a balance being unsettled? I remember hearing my father often say that when he stood for this county, our grandfather paid more than a hundred thousand pounds, and yet I know to this day there are accounts unsettled. Regularly every year I receive anonymous letters threatening me with fearful punishment if I don't pay one hundred and fifty pounds for a breakfast at the Jolly Tinkers.'

'You jest: the matter indeed requires a serious vein. I wish these accounts to be settled at once.'

'And I should like to know where the funds are to come from! I have none. The quantity of barns I am building now is something tremendous!

Then this rage for draining; it would dry up any purse. What think you of two million tiles this year? And rents,—to keep up which we are making these awful sacrifices—they are merely nominal, or soon will be. They never will be satisfied till they have touched the land. That is clear to me. I am prepared for a reduction of five-and-twenty per cent.; if the corn laws* are touched, it can't be less than that. My mother ought to take it into consideration and reduce her jointure accordingly. But I dare say she will not; people are so selfish; particularly as she has given you this thousand pounds, which in fact after all comes out of my pocket.'

'All this you have said to me before. What does it mean? I fought this battle at the instigation of the family, from no feeling of my own. You are the head of the family and you were consulted on the step. Unless I had concluded that it was with your sanction, I certainly should not have made my appearance on the hustings.'

'I am very glad you did though,' said Lord Marney; 'Parliament is a great point for our class; in these days especially, more even than in the old time. I was truly rejoiced at your success, and it mortified the Whigs about us most confoundedly. Some people thought there was only one family in the world to have their Richmond or their Malton.* Getting you in for the old borough was really a coup.'

'Well now, to retain our interest,' said Egremont, 'quick payment of our expenses is the most efficient way, believe me.'

'You have got six years, perhaps seven,' said Lord Marney, 'and long before that I hope to find you the husband of Lady Joan Fitz-Warene.'

'I do not wish to connect the two contingencies,' said Egremont firmly.

'They are inseparable,' said Lord Marney.

'What do you mean?'

'I mean that I think this pedantic acquittance of an electioneering account is in the highest degree ridiculous, and that I cannot interfere in it. The legal expenses are you say paid; and if they were not, I should feel myself bound, as the head of the family, to defray them, but I can go no further, I cannot bring myself to sanction an expenditure for certainly very unnecessary, perhaps, and I much fear it, for illegal and very immoral purposes.'

'That really is your determination?'

'After the most mature reflection, prompted by a sincere solicitude for your benefit.'

'Well, George, I have often suspected it, but now I feel quite persuaded, that you are really the greatest humbug that ever existed.'

'Abuse is not argument, Mr. Egremont.'

'You are beneath abuse, as you are beneath every sentiment but one, which I most entirely feel,' and Egremont rose from the table.

'You may thank your own obstinacy and conceit,' said Lord Marney. 'I took you to Mowbray Castle, and the cards were in your own hands if you chose to play them.'

'You have interfered with me once before on such a subject, Lord Marney,' said Egremont, with a kindling eye and a cheek pallid with rage.

'You had better not say that again,' said Lord Marney in a tone of menace.

'Why not?' asked Egremont fiercely. 'Who and what are you to dare to address me thus?'

'I am your elder brother, sir, whose relationship to you is your only claim to the consideration of society.'

'A curse on the society that has fashioned such claims,' said Egremont in an heightened tone—'claims founded in selfishness, cruelty, and fraud, and leading to demoralization, misery, and crime.'

'Claims which I will make you respect, at least in this house, sir,' said Lord Marney, springing from his chair.

'Touch me at your peril!' exclaimed Egremont, 'or I will forget you are my mother's son, and cleave you to the ground. You have been the blight of my life; you stole from me my bride, and now you would rob me of my honour.'

'Liar and villain!' exclaimed Lord Marney, darting forward; but at this moment his wife rushed into the apartment and clung to him. 'For heaven's sake,' she exclaimed, 'What is all this? George, Charles, dearest George!'

'Let me go, Arabella.'

'Let him come on.'

But Lady Marney gave a piercing shriek, and held out her arms to keep the brothers apart. A sound was heard at the other door; there was nothing in the world that Lord Marney dreaded so much as that his servants should witness a domestic scene. He sprang forward to the door to prevent any one entering; partially opening it, he said Lady Marney was unwell and desired her maid; returning, he found Arabella insensible on the ground, and Egremont vanished!

CHAPTER III.

IT was a wet morning; there had been a heavy rain since dawn, which impelled by a gusty south-wester came driving on a crowd of women and girls who were assembled before the door of a still unclosed shop. Some protected themselves with umbrellas; some sought shelter beneath a row of old elms that grew alongside the canal that fronted the house. Notwithstanding the weather, the clack of tongues was incessant.

'I thought I saw the wicket of the yard gates open,' said a woman.

'So did I,' said her neighbour; 'but it was shut again immediately.'

'It was only Master Joseph,' said a third. 'He likes to see us getting wet through.'

'If they would only let us into the yard and get under one of the workshop sheds, as they do at Simmon's,' said another.

'You may well say Simmon's, Mrs. Page; I only wish my master served in his field.'

'I have been here since half-past four, Mrs. Grigsby, with this chilt at my breast all the time. It's three miles for me here, and the same back, and unless I get the first turn, how are my poor boys to find their dinner ready when they come out of the pit?'

'A very true word, Mrs. Page; and by this token, that last Thursday I was here by half-past eleven, certainly afore noon, having only called at my mother-in-law's in the way, and it was eight o'clock before I got home. Ah! it's cruel work, is the tommy shop.'

'How d'ye do neighbour Prance?' said a comely dame with a large white basket. 'And how's your good man? They was saying at Belfy's he had changed his service. I hear there's a new butty in Mr. Parker's field; but the old doggy kept on; so I always thought, he was always a favourite, and they do say measured the stints* very fair. And what do you hear bacon is in town? They do tell me only sixpence and real home-cured. I wonder Diggs has the face to be selling still at ninepence, and so very green! I think I see Dame Toddles; how wonderful she do wear! What are you doing here, little dear; very young to fetch tommy; keeping place for mother, eh! that's a good girl; she'd do well to be here soon, for I think the strike's on eight. Diggs is sticking it on yellow soap very terrible. What do you think—Ah! the doors are going to open. No—a false alarm.'

'How fare you neighbour?' said a pale young woman carrying an infant to the comely dame. 'Here's an awful crowd, surely. The women will be fighting and tearing to get in, I guess. I be much afeard.'

'Well, 'first come, first served,' all the world over,' said the comely dame. 'And you must put a good heart on the business and tie your bonnet. I dare guess there are not much less than two hundred here. It's grand tommy day you know. And for my part I don't care so much for a good squeedge; one sees so many faces one knows.'

'The cheese here at sixpence is pretty tidy,' said a crone to her companion; 'but you may get as good in town for fourpence.'

'What I complain is the weights,' replied her companion. 'I weighed my pound of butter bought last tommy day, and it was two penny pieces too light. Indeed! I have been, in my time, to all the shops about here, for the lads or their father, but never knew tommy so bad as this. I have two children at home ill from their flour; I have been very poorly myself; one is used to a little white clay, but when they lay it on thick, it's very grave.'

'Are your girls in the pit?'

'No; we strive to keep them out, and my man has gone scores of days on bread and water for that purpose; and if we were not forced to take so much tommy, one might manage—but tommy will beat anything; health first, and honesty afterwards, that's my say.'

'Well, for my part,' said the crone, 'meat's my grievance: all the best bits go to the butties, and the pieces with bone in are chopped off for the colliers' wives.'

'Dame, when will the door open?' asked a very little pale-faced boy. 'I have been here all this morn, and never broke my fast.'

'And what do you want, chilt?'

'I want a loaf for mother; but I don't feel I shall ever get home again, I'm all in a way so dizzy.'

'Liza Gray,' said a woman with black beady eyes and a red nose, speaking in a sharp voice and rushing up to a pretty slatternly woman in a straw bonnet with a dirty fine ribbon, and a babe at her breast; 'you know the person I'm looking for.'

'Well, Mrs. Mullins, and how do you do?' she replied, in a sweet sawney* tone.

'How do you do, indeed! How are people to do in these bad times?'

'They is indeed hard Mrs. Mullins. If you could see my tommy-book! How I wish I knew figures! Made up as of last Thursday night by that little divil, Master Joe Diggs. He has stuck it in here and stuck it in there, till it makes one all of a-maze. I'm sure I never had the things; and my man is out of all patience, and says I can no more keep house than a natural born.'

'My man is a-wanting to see your man,' said Mrs. Mullins, with a flashing eye; 'and you know what about.'

'And very natural, too,' said Liza Gray; 'but how are we to pay the money we owe him, with such a tommy-book as this, good neighbour Mullins?'

'We're as poor as our neighbours Mrs. Gray; and if we are not paid, we must borrow. It's a scarlet shame to go to the spout* because money lent to a friend is not to be found. You had it in your need, Liza Gray, and we want it in our need; and have it I will, Liza Gray.'

'Hush, hush!' said Liza Gray; 'don't wake the little'un, for she is very fretful.'

'I will have the five shillings, or I will have as good,' said Mrs. Mullins.

'Hush, hush, neighbour; now, I'll tell you—you shall have it; but yet a little time. This is great tommy-day, and settles our reckoning for five weeks; but my man may have a draw after to-morrow, and he shall draw five shillings, and give you half.'

'And the other half?' said Mrs. Mullins.

'Ah! the other half,' said Liza Gray, with a sigh. 'Well, then—we shall have a death in our family soon—this poor babe can't struggle on much longer; it belongs to two burial clubs—that will be three pounds from each, and after the drink and the funeral, there will be enough to pay all our debts and put us all square.'

The doors of Mr. Diggs' tommy-shop opened. The rush was like the advance into the pit of a theatre when the drama existed; pushing, squeezing, fighting, tearing, shrieking. On a high seat, guarded by rails from all contact, sate Mr. Diggs senior, with a bland smile on his sanctified countenance, a pen behind his ear, and recommending his constrained customers in honeyed tones to be patient and orderly. Behind the substantial counter which was an impregnable fortification, was his popular son, Master Joseph; a short, ill-favoured cur, with a spirit of vulgar oppression and malicious mischief stamped on his visage. His black, greasy lank hair, his pug nose, his coarse red face, and his projecting tusks, contrasted with the mild and lengthened countenance of his father, who looked very much like a wolf in sheep's clothing.

For the first five minutes Master Joseph Diggs did nothing but blaspheme and swear at his customers, occasionally leaning over the counter and cuffing the women in the van or lugging some girl by the hair.

'I was first, Master Joseph,' said a woman eagerly.

'No; I was,' said another.

'I was here,' said the first, 'as the clock struck four, and seated myself on the steps, because I must be home early; my husband is hurt in the knee.'

'If you were first, you shall be helped last,' said Master Joseph, 'to reward you for your pains;' and he began taking the orders of the other woman.

'O! Lord have mercy on me!' said the disappointed woman; 'and I got up in the middle of the night for this!'

'More fool you! And what you came for I am sure I don't know,' said Master Joseph; 'for you have a pretty long figure against you, I can tell you that.'

'I declare most solemnly—' said the woman.

'Don't make a brawling here,' said Master Joseph, 'or I'll jump over this here counter and knock you down, like nothing. What did you say, woman? are you deaf? what did you say? how much best tea do you want?'

'I don't want any, sir.'

'You never want best tea; you must take three ounces of best tea, or you shan't have nothing. If you say another word, I'll put you down four. You tall gal, what's your name, you keep back there, or I'll fetch you such a cut as'll keep you at home till next reckoning. Cuss you, you old fool, do you think I am to be kept all day while you are mumbling here? Who's pushing on there? I see you, Mrs. Page. Won't there be a black mark against you? Oh! it's Mrs. Prance, is it? Father, put down Mrs. Prance for a peck of flour. I'll have order here. You think the last bacon a little too fat: oh! you do, ma'am, do you? I'll take care you shan't complain in future; I likes to please my customers. There's a very nice flitch hanging up in the engine-room; the men wanted some rust* for the machinery; you shall have a slice of that; and we'll say tenpence a pound, high-dried, and wery lean—will that satisfy you?

'Order there, order; you cussed women, order, or I'll be among you. And if I just do jump over this here counter, won't I let fly right and left? Speak out, you idiot! do you think I can hear your muttering in this Babel? Cuss them; I'll keep them quiet,' and so he took up a yard measure, and leaning over the counter, hit right and left.

'Oh! you little monster!' exclaimed a woman, 'you have put out my babby's eye.'

There was a murmur; almost a groan. 'Whose baby's hurt?' asked Master Joseph in a softened tone.

'Mine, sir,' said an indignant voice; 'Mary Church.'

'Oh! Mary Church, is it!' said the malicious imp, 'then I'll put Mary Church down for half a pound of best arrow-root; that's the finest thing in the world for babbies, and will cure you of bringing your cussed monkeys here, as if you all thought our shop was a hinfant school.

'Where's your book, Susan Travers? Left at home! Then you may go and fetch it. No books, no tommy. You are Jones's wife, are you? Ticket for three and sixpence out of eighteen shillings wages. Is this the only ticket you have brought? There's your money; and you may tell your husband he need not take his coat off again to go down our shaft. He must think us cussed fools! Tell him I hope he has got plenty of money to travel into Wales, for he won't have no work in England again, or my name ayn't Diggs. Who's pushing there? I'll be among you; I'll close the shop. If I do get hold of some of you cussed women, you shan't forget it. If anybody will tell me who is pushing there, they shall have their bacon for seven-pence. Will nobody have bacon for seven-pence? Leagued together, eh! Then everybody shall have their bacon for ten-pence. Two can play at that. Push again, and I'll be among you,' said the infuriated little tyrant. But the waving of the multitude, impatient, and annoyed by the weather, was not to be stilled; the movement could not be regulated; the shop was in commotion; and Master Joseph Diggs, losing all patience, jumped on the counter, and amid the shrieks of the women, sprang into the crowd. Two women fainted; others cried for their bonnets; others bemoaned their aprons; nothing however deterred Diggs, who kicked and cuffed and cursed in every quarter, and gave none. At last there was a general scream of horror, and a cry of 'a boy killed.'

The senior Diggs, who, from his eminence, had hitherto viewed the scene with unruffled complacency; who, in fact, derived from these not unusual exhibitions the same agreeable excitement which a Roman emperor might have received from the combats of the circus; began to think that affairs were growing serious, and rose to counsel order and enforce amiable dispositions. Even Master Joseph was quelled by that mild voice which would have become Augustus. It appeared to be quite true that a boy was dead. It was the little boy who, sent to get a loaf for his mother, had complained before the shop was opened of his fainting energies. He had fallen in the fray, and it was thought, to use the phrase of the comely dame who tried to rescue him, 'that he was quite smothered.'

They carried him out of the shop; the perspiration poured off him; he had no pulse. He had no friends there. 'I'll stand by the body,' said the comely dame, 'though I lose my turn.'

At this moment, Stephen Morley, for the reader has doubtless discovered that the stranger who held colloquy with the colliers was the friend of Walter Gerard, arrived at the tommy-shop, which was about half-way between the house where he had passed the night and Wodgate. He stopped, inquired, and being a man of science and some skill, decided, after examining the poor boy, that life was not extinct. Taking the elder Diggs aside, he said, 'I am the editor of the *Mowbray Phalanx*; I will not speak to you before these people; but I tell you fairly you and your son have been represented to me as oppressors of the people. Will it be my lot to report this death and comment on it? I trust not. There is yet time and hope.'

'What is to be done, sir,' inquired the alarmed Mr. Diggs; 'a fellow-creature in this condition—'

'Don't talk but act,' said Morley. 'There is no time to be lost. The boy must be taken up stairs and put to bed; a warm bed, in one of your best rooms, with every comfort. I am pressed for business, but I will wait and watch over him till the crisis is passed. Come, let you and I take him in our arms, and carry him up stairs through your private door. Every minute is precious.' And so saying, Morley and the elder Diggs entered the house.

CHAPTER IV.

WODGATE, or Wogate, as it was called on the map, was a district that in old days had been consecrated to Woden, and which appeared destined through successive ages to retain its heathen character. At the beginning of the revolutionary war, Wodgate was a sort of squatting district of the great mining region to which it was contiguous, a place where adventurers in the industry which was rapidly developing, settled themselves; for though the great veins of coal and ironstone cropped up, as they phrase it, before they reached this bare and barren land, and it was thus deficient in those mineral and metallic treasures which had enriched its neighbourhood, Wodgate had advantages of its own, and of a kind which touch the fancy of the lawless. It was land without an owner; no one claimed any manorial right over it: they could build cottages without paying rent. It was a district recognized by no parish; so there were no tithes, and no meddlesome supervision. It abounded in fuel which cost nothing, for though the veins were not worth working as a source of mining profit, the soil of Wodgate was similar in its superficial character to that of the country around. So a population gathered, and rapidly increased, in the ugliest spot in England, to which neither Nature nor art had contributed a single charm; where a tree could not be seen, a flower was unknown, where there was neither belfry nor steeple, nor a single sight or sound that could soften the heart or humanise the mind.

Whatever may have been the cause, whether, as not unlikely, the original squatters brought with them some traditionary skill, or whether their isolated and unchequered existence concentrated their energies on their craft, the fact is certain, that the inhabitants of Wodgate early acquired a celebrity as skilful workmen. This reputation so much increased, and in time spread so far, that for more than a quarter of a century, both in their skill and the economy of their labour, they have been unmatched throughout the country. As manufacturers of iron-mongery, they carry the palm from the whole district; as founders of brass and workers of steel, they fear none; while as nailers and lock-smiths,* their fame has spread even to the European markets, whither their most skilful workmen have frequently been invited.

Invited in vain! No wages can tempt the Wodgate man from his native home, that squatters' seat which soon assumed the form of a large village, and then in turn soon expanded into a town, and at the present moment numbers its population by swarming thousands, lodged in the most miserable tenements in the most hideous burgh in the ugliest country in the world.

But it has its enduring spell. Notwithstanding the spread of its civic prosperity, it has lost none of the characteristics of its original society; on the contrary it has zealously preserved them. There are no land-lords, head-lessees, main-masters, or butties in Wodgate. No church there has yet raised its spire; and as if the jealous spirit of Woden still haunted his ancient temple, even the conventicle scarcely dares show its humble front in some obscure corner. There is no municipality, no magistrate, no local acts, no vestries, no schools of any kind. The streets are never cleaned; every man lights his own house; nor does any one know anything except his business.

More than this, at Wodgate a factory or large establishment of any kind is unknown. Here Labour reigns supreme. Its division indeed is favoured by their manners, but the interference or influence of mere capital is instantly resisted. The business of Wodgate is carried on by master workmen in their own houses, each of whom possesses an unlimited number of what they call apprentices, by whom their affairs are principally conducted, and whom they treat as the Mamlouks* treated the Egyptians.

These master workmen indeed form a powerful aristocracy, nor is it possible to conceive one apparently more oppressive. They are ruthless tyrants; they habitually inflict upon their subjects punishments more grievous than the slave population of our colonies were ever visited with; not content with beating them with sticks or flogging them with knotted ropes, they are in the habit of felling them with hammers, or cutting their heads open with a file or lock. The most usual punishment however, or rather stimulus to increase exertion, is to pull an appren-tice's ears till they run with blood. These youths too are worked for sixteen and even twenty hours a day; they are often sold by one master to another; they are fed on carrion, and they sleep in lofts or cellars: yet whether it be that they are hardened by brutality, and really unconscious of their degradation and unusual sufferings, or whether they are supported by the belief that their day to be masters and oppressors will surely arrive, the aristocracy of Wodgate is by no means so unpopular as the aristocracy of most other places.

In the first place it is a real aristocracy; it is privileged, but it does something for its privileges. It is distinguished from the main body not merely by name. It is the most knowing class at Wodgate; it possesses indeed in its way complete knowledge; and it imparts in its manner a certain quantity of it to those whom it guides. Thus it is an aristocracy that leads,* and therefore a fact. Moreover the social system of Wodgate is not an unvarying course of infinite toil. Their plan is to work hard, but not always. They seldom exceed four days of labour in the week. On Sunday the masters begin to drink; for the apprentices there is dog-fighting without any stint. On Monday and Tuesday the whole population of Wodgate is drunk; of all stations, ages, and sexes; even babes, who should be at the breast; for they are drammed with Godfrey's cordial. Here is relaxation, excitement; if less vice otherwise than might be at first anticipated, we must remember that excesses are checked by poverty of blood and constant exhaustion. Scanty food and hard labour are in their way, if not exactly moralists, a tolerably good police.

There are no others at Wodgate to preach or to control. It is not that the people are immoral, for immorality implies some fore-thought; or ignorant, for ignorance is relative; but they are animals; unconscious; their minds a blank; and their worst actions only the impulse of a gross or savage instinct. There are many in this town who are ignorant of their very names; very few who can spell them. It is rare that you meet with a young person who knows his own age; rarer to find the boy who has seen a book, or the girl who has seen a flower. Ask them the name of their sovereign, and they will give you an unmeaning stare; ask them the name of their religion, and they will laugh: who rules them on earth, or who can save them in heaven, are alike mysteries to them.

Such was the population with whom Morley was about to mingle. Wodgate had the appearance of a vast squalid suburb. As you advanced, leaving behind you long lines of little dingy tenements, with infants lying about the road, you expected every moment to emerge into some streets and encounter buildings bearing some correspondence in their size and comfort to the considerable population swarming and busied around you. Nothing of the kind. There were no public buildings of any sort; no churches, chapels, town-hall, institute, theatre; and the principal streets in the heart of the town in which were situate the coarse and grimy shops, though formed by houses of a greater elevation than the preceding, were equally narrow and if possible more dirty. At every fourth or fifth house, alleys seldom above a yard wide and streaming with filth, opened out of the street. These were crowded with dwellings of various size, while from the principal court often branched out a number of smaller alleys or rather narrow passages, than which nothing can be conceived more close and squalid and obscure. Here during the days of business, the sound of the hammer and the file never ceased, amid gutters of abomination and piles of foulness and stagnant pools of filth; reservoirs of leprosy and plague, whose exhalations were sufficient to taint the atmosphere of the whole kingdom and fill the country with fever and pestilence.

A lank and haggard youth, ricketty and smoke-dried, and black with his craft, was sitting on the threshold of a miserable hovel and working at the file. Behind him stood a stunted and meagre girl, with a back like a grasshopper; a deformity occasioned by the displacement of the bladebone, and prevalent among the girls of Wodgate from the cramping posture of their usual toil. Her long melancholy visage and vacant stare at Morley as he passed, attracted his notice, and it occurring to him that the opportunity was convenient to enquire something of the individual of whom he was in search, he stopped and addressed the workman:

'Do you happen to know, friend, a person here or hereabouts by name Hatton?'

'Hatton!' said the youth looking up with a grin, yet still continuing his labour, 'I should think I did!'

'Well, that's fortunate; you can tell me something about him?'

'Do you see this here?' said the youth still grinning, and letting the file drop from his distorted and knotty hand, he pointed to a deep scar that crossed his forehead, 'he did that.'

'An accident?'

'Very like. An accident that often happened. I should like to have a crown for every time he has cut my head open. He cut it open once with a key and twice with a lock; he knocked the corner of a lock into my head twice, once with a bolt and once with a shut; you know what that is; the thing what runs into the staple. He hit me on the head with a hammer once. That was a blow! I fell away that time. When I came to, master had stopped the blood with some fur off his hat. I had to go on with my work immediately; master said I should do my stint if I worked till twelve o'clock at night. Many's the ash stick he has broken on my body; sometimes the weals remained on me for a-week; he cut my eye-lid open once with a nutstick; cut a regular hole in it, and it bled all over the files I was working at. He has pulled my ears sometimes that I thought they must come off in his hand. But all this was a mere nothin to this here cut; that was serious; and if I hadn't got thro' that they do say there must have been a crowner's quest;* though I think that gam-mon, for old Tugsford did for one of his prentices, and the body was never found. And now you ask me if I know Hatton? I should think I did!' And the lank, haggard youth laughed merrily, as if he had been recounting a series of the happiest adventures.

'But is there no redress for such iniquitous oppression,' said Morley, who had listened with astonishment to this complacent statement, 'Is there no magistrate to apply to?'

'No no,' said the filer with an air of obvious pride, 'we don't have no magistrates at Wodgate. We've got a constable, and there was a prentice who coz his master laid it on, only with a seat rod, went over to Ramborough and got a warrant. He fetched the summons himself and giv it to the constable, but he never served it. That's why they has a constable here.'

'I am sorry,' said Morley, 'that I have affairs with such a wretch as this Hatton.'

'You'll find him a wery hearty sort of man,' said the filer, 'if he don't hap to be in drink. He's a little robustious then, but take him all in all for a master, you may go further and fare worse.'

'What! this monster!'

'Lord bless you, it's his way, that's all, we be a queer set here; but he has his pints. Give him a lock to make, and you won't have your box picked; he's wery lib'ral too in the wittals. Never had horse-flesh the whole time I was with him; they has nothin' else at Tugsford's; never had no sick cow except when meat was very dear. He always put his face agin still-born calves; he used to say he liked his boys to have meat what was born alive and killed alive. By which token there never was any sheep what had bust in the head sold in our court. And then sometimes he would give us a treat of fish, when it had been four or five days in town and not sold. No, give the devil his due, say I. There never was no want for anything at meals with the Bishop, except time to eat them in.'

'And why do you call him the Bishop?'

'That's his name and authority; for he's the governor here over all of us. And it has always been so that Wodgate has been governed by a bishop; because as we have no church, we will have as good. And by this token that this day sen'night, the day my time was up, he married me to this here young lady. She is of the Baptist school religion, and wanted us to be tied by her clergyman, but all the lads that served their time with me were married by the Bishop, and many a more, and I saw no call to do no otherwise. So he sprinkled some salt over a gridiron, read 'Our Father' backwards, and wrote our name in a book: and we were spliced; but I didn't do it rashly, did I, Suky, by the token that we had kept company for two years, and there isn't a gal in all Wodgate what handles a file, like Sue.'

'And what is your name, my good fellow?'

'They call me Tummas, but I ayn't got no second name; but now I am married I mean to take my wife's, for she has been baptised, and so has got two.'

'Yes sir,' said the girl with the vacant face and the back like a grasshopper; 'I be a reg'lar born Christian and my mother afore me, and that's what few gals in the Yard can say. Thomas will take to it himself when work is slack; and he believes now in our Lord and Saviour Pontius Pilate who was crucified to save our sins; and in Moses, Goliath, and the rest of the Apostles.'

'Ah! me,' thought Morley, 'and could not they spare one Missionary from Tahiti* for their fellow countrymen at Wodgate!'

CHAPTER V.

THE summer twilight had faded into sweet night; the young and star-attended moon glittered like a sickle in the deep purple sky; of all the luminous host, Hesperus alone was visible; and a breeze, that bore the last embrace of the flowers by the sun, moved languidly and fitfully over the still and odorous earth.

The moonbeam fell upon the roof and garden of Gerard. It suffused the cottage with its brilliant light, except where the dark depth of the embowered porch defied its entry. All around the beds of flowers and herbs spread sparkling and defined. You could trace the minutest walk; almost distinguish every leaf. Now and then there came a breath, and the sweet-peas murmured in their sleep; or the roses rustled, as if they were afraid they were about to be roused from their lightsome dreams. Farther on the fruit trees caught the splendour of the night; and looked like a troop of sultanas taking their gardened air, when the eye of man could not profane them, and laden with jewels. There were apples that rivalled rubies; pears of topaz tint; a whole paraphernalia of plums some purple as the amethyst, others blue and brilliant as the sapphire; an emerald here, and now a golden drop that gleamed like the yellow diamond of Gengis Khan.*

Within—was the scene less fair? A single lamp shed over the chamber a soft and sufficient light. The library of Stephen Morley had been removed, but the place of his volumes had been partly supplied, for the shelves were far from being empty. Their contents were of no ordinary character: many volumes of devotion, some of church history, one or two on ecclesiastical art, several works of our elder dramatists, some good reprints of our chronicles, and many folios of church music, which last indeed amounted to a remarkable collection. There was no musical instrument however in the room of any kind, and the only change in its furniture, since we last visited the room of Gerard, was the presence of a long-backed chair of antique form, most beautifully embroidered, and a portrait of a female saint over the mantel-piece. As for Gerard himself he sat with his head leaning on his arm, which rested on the table, while he listened with great interest to a book which was read to him by his daughter, at whose feet lay the fiery and faithful bloodhound.

'So you see, my father,' said Sybil with animation, and dropping her book which however her hand did not relinquish, 'even then all was not lost. The stout earl retired beyond the Trent, and years and reigns elapsed before this part of the island accepted their laws and customs.'

'I see,' said her father, 'and yet I cannot help wishing that Harold—'* Here the hound, hearing his name, suddenly rose and looked at Gerard, who smiling, patted him and said, 'We were not talking of thee, good sir, but of thy great namesake; but ne'er mind, a live dog they say is worth a dead king.'

'Ah! why have we not such a man now,' said Sybil, 'to protect the people! Were I a prince I know no career that I should deem so great.'

'But Stephen says no,' said Gerard: 'he says that these great men have never made use of us but as tools; and that the people never can have their rights until they produce competent champions from their own order.'

'But then Stephen does not want to recall the past,' said Sybil with a kind of sigh; 'he wishes to create the future.'

'The past is a dream,' said Gerard.

'And what is the future?' enquired Sybil.

'Alack! I know not; but I often wish the battle of Hastings were to be fought over again and I was going to have a hand in it.'

'Ah! my father,' said Sybil with a mournful smile, 'there is ever your fatal specific of physical force. Even Stephen is against physical force, with all his odd fancies.'

'All very true,' said Gerard smiling with good nature; 'but all the same when I was coming home a few days ago, and stopped awhile on the bridge and chanced to see myself in the stream, I could not help fancying that my Maker had fashioned these limbs rather to hold a lance or draw a bow, than to supervise a shuttle or a spindle.'

'Yet with the shuttle and the spindle we may redeem our race,' said Sybil with animation, 'if we could only form the minds that move those peaceful weapons. Oh! my father, I will believe that moral power* is irresistible, or where are we to look for hope?'

Gerard shook his head with his habitual sweet good-tempered smile. 'Ah!' said he, 'what can we do; they have got the land, and the land governs the people. The Norman knew that, Sybil, as you just read. If indeed we had our rights, one might do something; but I don't know; I dare say if I had our land again, I should be as bad as the rest.'

'Oh! no, my father,' exclaimed Sybil with energy, 'never, never! Your thoughts would be as princely as your lot. What a leader of the people you would make!'

Harold sprang up suddenly and growled.

'Hush!' said Gerard; 'some one knocks:' and he rose and left the room. Sybil heard voices and broken sentences: 'You'll excuse me'— 'I take it kindly'—'So we are neighbours.' And then her father returned, ushering in a person and saying, 'Here is my friend Mr. Franklin that I was speaking of, Sybil, who is going to be our neighbour; down Harold, down!' and he presented to his daughter the companion of Mr. St. Lys in that visit to the hand-loom weaver when she had herself met the vicar of Mowbray.

Sybil rose, and letting her book drop gently on the table, received Egremont with composure and native grace. It is civilization that makes us awkward, for it gives us an uncertain position. Perplexed, we take refuge in pretence; and embarrassed, we seek a resource in affectation. The Bedouin and the Red Indian never lose their presence of mind; and the wife of a peasant, when you enter her cottage, often greets you with a propriety of mien which favourably contrasts with your reception by some grand dame in some grand assembly, meeting her guests alternately with a caricature of courtesy or an exaggeration of supercilious self-control.

'I dare say,' said Egremont bowing to Sybil, 'you have seen our poor friend the weaver since we met there.'

'The day I quitted Mowbray,' said Sybil. 'They are not without friends.'

'Ah! you have met my daughter before.'

'On a mission of grace,' said Egremont.

'And I suppose you found the town not very pleasant, Mr. Franklin,' continued Gerard.

'No; I could not stand it, the nights were so close. Besides I have a great accumulation of notes, and I fancied I could reduce them into a report more efficiently in comparative seclusion. So I have got a room near here, with a little garden, not so pretty as yours; but still a garden is something; and if I want any additional information, why, after all, Mowbray is only a walk.'

'You say well and have done wisely. Besides you have such late hours in London, and hard work. Some country air will do you all the good in the world. That gallery* must be tiresome. Do you use shorthand?'

'A sort of shorthand of my own,' said Egremont. 'I trust a good deal to my memory.'

'Ah! you are young. My daughter also has a wonderful memory. For my own part, there are many things which I am not sorry to forget.'

'You see I took you at your word, neighbour,' said Egremont. 'When one has been at work the whole day one feels a little lonely towards night.'

'Very true; and I dare say you find desk work sometimes very dull; I never could make anything of it myself. I can manage a book well enough, if it be well written, and on points I care for; but I would sooner listen than read any time,' said Gerard. 'Indeed I should be right glad to see the minstrel and the storyteller going their rounds again. It would be easy after a day's work, when one has not, as I have now, a good child to read to me.'

'This volume?' said Egremont drawing his chair to the table and looking at Sybil, who intimated assent by a nod.

'Ah! it's a fine book,' said Gerard, 'though on a sad subject.'

'The History of the Conquest of England by the Normans,' said Egremont, reading the title page on which also was written 'Ursula Trafford to Sybil Gerard.'

'You know it?' said Sybil.

'Only by fame.'

'Perhaps the subject may not interest you so much as it does us,' said Sybil.

'It must interest all and all alike,' said her father; 'for we are divided between the conquerors and the conquered.'*

'But do not you think,' said Egremont, 'that such a distinction has long ceased to exist?'

'In what degree?' asked Gerard. 'Many circumstances of oppression have doubtless gradually disappeared; but that has arisen from the change of manners, not from any political recognition of their injustice. The same course of time which has removed many enormities, more shocking however to our modern feelings than to those who devised and endured them, has simultaneously removed many alleviating circumstances. If the mere baron's grasp be not so ruthless, the champion we found in the church is no longer so ready. The spirit of Conquest has adapted itself to the changing circumstances of ages, and however its results vary in form, in degree they are much the same.'

'But how do they show themselves?'

'In many circumstances, which concern many classes; but I speak of those which touch my own order; and therefore I say at once—in the degradation of the people.'

'But are the people so degraded?'

'There is more serfdom in England now than at any time since the Conquest. I speak of what passes under my daily eyes when I say, that those who labour can as little choose or change their masters now, as when they were born thralls. There are great bodies of the working classes of this country nearer the condition of brutes, than they have been at any time since the Conquest. Indeed I see nothing to distinguish them from brutes, except that their morals are inferior. Incest and infanticide are as common among them as among the lower animals. The domestic principle waxes weaker and weaker every year in England; nor can we wonder at it, when there is no comfort to cheer and no sentiment to hallow the Home.'

'I was reading a work the other day,' said Egremont, 'that statistically proved that the general condition of the people was much better at this moment than it had been at any known period of history.'

'Ah! yes, I know that style of speculation,' said Gerard; 'your gentleman who reminds you that a working man now has a pair of cotton stockings, and that Harry the Eighth himself was not as well off. At any rate, the condition of classes must be judged of by the age, and by their relation with each other. One need not dwell on that. I deny the premises. I deny that the condition of the main body is better now than at any other period of our history: that it is as good as it has been at several. I say, for instance, the people were better clothed, better lodged, and better fed just before the War of the Roses* than they are at this moment. We know how an English peasant lived in those times: he ate flesh every day, he never drank water, was well housed, and clothed in stout woollens. Nor are the Chronicles necessary to tell us this. The acts of Parliament from the Plantagenets to the Tudors teach us alike the price of provisions and the rate of wages; and we see in a moment that the wages of those days brought as much sustenance and comfort as a reasonable man could desire.'

'I know how deeply you feel upon this subject,' said Egremont turning to Sybil.

'Indeed it is the only subject that ever engages my thought,' she replied, 'except one.'

'And that one?'

'Is to see the people once more kneel before our blessed Lady,' replied Sybil.

'Look at the average term of life,' said Gerard, coming unintentionally to the relief of Egremont, who was a little embarrassed. 'The average term of life in this district among the working classes is seventeen. What think you of that? Of the infants born in Mowbray, more than a moiety die before the age of five.'

'And yet,' said Egremont, 'in old days they had terrible pestilences.'

'But they touched all alike,' said Gerard. 'We have more pestilence now in England than we ever had, but it only reaches the poor. You never hear of it. Why Typhus alone takes every year from the dwellings of the artisan and peasant a population equal to that of the whole county of Westmoreland. This goes on every year, but the representatives of the conquerors are not touched: it is the descendants of the conquered alone who are the victims.'

'It sometimes seems to me,' said Sybil despondingly, 'that nothing short of the descent of angels can save the people of this kingdom.'

'I sometimes think I hear a little bird,' said Gerard, 'who sings that the long frost may yet break up. I have a friend, him of whom I was speaking to you the other day, who has his remedies.'

'But Stephen Morley does not believe in angels,' said Sybil with a sigh; 'and I have no faith in his plan.'

'He believes that God will help those who help themselves,' said Gerard.

'And I believe,' said Sybil, 'that those only can help themselves whom God helps.'

All this time Egremont was sitting at the table, with the book in his hand, gazing fitfully and occasionally with an air of absence on its title-page, whereon was written the name of its owner. Suddenly he said 'Sybil.'

'Yes,' said the daughter of Gerard, with an air of some astonishment.

'I beg your pardon,' said Egremont blushing; 'I was reading your name. I thought I was reading it to myself. Sybil Gerard! What a beautiful name is Sybil!'

'My mother's name,' said Gerard; 'and my grandame's name, and a name I believe that has been about our hearth as long as our race; and that's a very long time indeed,' he added smiling, 'for we were tall men in King John's reign,* as I have heard say.'

'Yours is indeed an old family.'

'Ay, we have some English blood in our veins, though peasants and the sons of peasants. But there was one of us who drew a bow at Azincourt;* and I have heard greater things, but I believe they are old wives' tales.'

'At least we have nothing left,' said Sybil, 'but our old faith; and that we have clung to through good report and evil report.'

'And now,' said Gerard, 'I rise with the lark, good neighbour Franklin; but before you go, Sybil will sing to us a requiem that I love: it stills the spirit before we sink into the slumber which may this night be death, and which one day must be.'

CHAPTER VI.

A BLOOM was spread over the morning sky. A soft golden light bathed with its fresh beam the bosom of the valley, except where a delicate haze, rather than a mist, still partially lingered over the river, which yet occasionally gleamed and sparkled in the sunshine. A sort of shadowy lustre suffused the landscape, which, though distinct, was mitigated in all its features—the distant woods, the clumps of tall trees that rose about the old grey bridge, the cottage chimneys that sent their smoke into the blue still air, amid their clustering orchards and gardens of flowers and herbs.

Ah! what is there so fresh and joyous as a summer morn! That spring time of the day, when the brain is bright, and the heart is brave; the season of daring and of hope; the renovating hour!

Came forth from his cottage room the brother of Lord Marney, to feel the vigorous bliss of life amid sunshiny gardens and the voices of bees and birds.

'Ah! this is delicious!' he felt. 'This is existence! Thank God I am here; that I have quitted for ever that formal and heartless Marney. Were it not for my mother, I would remain Mr. Franklin for ever. Would

I were indeed a journalist; provided I always had a mission to the vale of Mowbray. Or anything, so that I were ever here. As companions, independent of everything else, they are superior to any that I have been used to. Why do these persons interest me? They feel and they think: two habits that have quite gone out of fashion, if ever they existed, among my friends. And that polish of manners, that studied and factitious refinement, which is to compensate for the heartlessness or the stupidity we are doomed to—is my host of last night deficient in that refinement? If he do want our conventional discipline, he has a native breeding which far excels it. I observe no word or action which is not prompted by that fine feeling which is the sure source of good taste. This Gerard appears to me a real genuine man; full of knowledge worked out by his own head; with large yet wholesome sympathies; and a deuced deal better educated than Lord de Mowbray or my brother—and they do occasionally turn over a book, which is not the habit of our set.

'And his daughter—ay, his daughter! There is something almost sublime about that young girl, yet strangely sweet withal; a tone so lofty combined with such simplicity is very rare. For there is no affectation of enthusiasm about her; nothing exaggerated; nothing rhapsodical. Her dark eyes and lustrous face, and the solemn sweetness of her thrilling voice—they haunt me; they have haunted me from the first moment I encountered her like a spirit amid the ruins of our abbey. And I am one of 'the family of sacrilege.' If she knew that! And I am one of the conquering class she denounces. If also she knew that! Ah! there is much to know! Above all—the future. Away! the tree of knowledge is the tree of death. I will have no thought that is not as bright and lovely as this morn.'

He went forth from his little garden, and strolled along the road in the direction of the cottage of Gerard, which was about three quarters of a mile distant. You might see almost as far; the sunshiny road a little winding and rising a very slight ascent. The cottage itself was hid by its trees. While Egremont was still musing of one who lived under that roof, he beheld in the distance Sybil.

She was springing along with a quick and airy step. Her black dress displayed her undulating and elastic figure. Her little foot bounded from the earth with a merry air. A long rosary hung at her side; and her head was partly covered with a hood which descended just over her shoulders. She seemed gay, for Harold kept running before her with a frolicsome air, and then returning to his mistress, danced about her, and almost overpowered her with his gambols.

'I salute thee, holy sister,' said Egremont.

'Oh! is not this a merry morn!' she exclaimed with a bright and happy face.

'I feel it as you. And whither do you go?'

'I go to the convent; I pay my first visit to our Superior since I left them.'

'Not very long ago,' said Egremont, with a smile, and turning with her.

'It seems so,' said Sybil.

They walked on together; Sybil glad as the hour; noticing a thousand cheerful sights, speaking to her dog in her ringing voice, as he gambolled before them, or seized her garments in his mouth, and ever and anon bounded away and then returned, looking up in his mistress' face to inquire whether he had been wanted in his absence.

'What a pity it is that your father's way each morning lies up the valley,' said Egremont; 'he would be your companion to Mowbray.'

'Ah! but I am so happy that he has not to work in a town,' said Sybil. 'He is not made to be cooped up in a hot factory in a smoky street. At least he labours among the woods and waters. And the Traffords are such good people! So kind to him and to all.'

'You love your father very much.'

She looked at him a little surprised; and then her sweet serious face broke into a smile and she said, 'And is that strange?'

'I think not,' said Egremont; 'I am inclined to love him myself.'

'Ah! you win my heart,' said Sybil, 'when you praise him. I think that is the real reason why I like Stephen; for otherwise he is always saying something with which I cannot agree, which I disapprove; and yet he is so good to my father!'

'You speak of Mr. Morley—'

'Oh! we don't call him 'Mr.',' said Sybil slightly laughing.

'I mean Stephen Morley,' said Egremont recalling his position, 'whom I met in Marney Abbey. He is very clever, is he not?'

'He is a great writer and a great student; and what he is he has made himself. I hear too that you follow the same pursuit,' said Sybil.

'But I am not a great writer or a great student,' said Egremont.

'Whatever you be, I trust', said Sybil, in a more serious tone, 'that you will never employ the talents that God has given you against the People.'

'I have come here to learn something of their condition,' said Egremont. 'That is not to be done in a great city like London. We all of us live too much in a circle. You will assist me, I am sure,' added Egremont; 'your spirit will animate me. You told me last night that there was no other subject, except one, which ever occupied your thoughts.'

'Yes,' said Sybil, 'I have lived under two roofs, only two roofs; and each has given me a great idea; the Convent and the Cottage. One has taught me the degradation of my faith, the other of my race. You should not wonder, therefore, that my heart is concentrated on the Church and the People.'

'But there are other ideas,' said Egremont, 'that might equally be entitled to your thought.'

'I feel these are enough,' said Sybil; 'too great, as it is, for my brain.'

CHAPTER VII.

AT the end of a court in Wodgate, of rather larger dimensions than usual in that town, was a high and many-windowed house, of several stories in height, which had been added to it at intervals. It was in a most dilapidated state; the principal part occupied as a nail-workshop, where a great number of heavy iron machines were working in every room on each floor; the building itself in so shattered a condition that every part of it creaked and vibrated with their motion. The flooring was so broken that in many places one could look down through the gaping and rotten planks, while the upper floors from time to time had been shored up with props.

This was the Palace of the Bishop of Wodgate, and here with his arms bare and black, he worked at those locks, which defied any skeleton key that was not made by himself. He was a short, thickset man, powerfully made, with brawny arms disproportionately short even for his height, and with a countenance, as far as one could judge of a face so disfigured by his grimy toil, rather brutal than savage. His choice apprentices, full of admiration and terror, worked about him; lank and haggard youths, who never for an instant dared to raise their dingy faces and lack-lustre eyes from their ceaseless labour. On each side of their master, seated on a stool higher than the rest, was an urchin of not more than four or five years of age, serious and demure, and as if proud of his eminent position, and working incessantly at his little file;—these were two sons of the bishop.

'Now boys,' said the bishop, in a hoarse, harsh voice, 'steady, there; steady. There's a file what don't sing; can't deceive my ear; I know all their voices. Don't let me find that 'un out, or I won't walk into him, won't I? Ayn't you lucky boys, to have reg'lar work like this, and the best of prog! It worn't my lot, I can tell you that. Give me that shut,* you there, Scrubbynose, can't you move? Look sharp, or I won't move you, won't I? Steady, steady! All right! That's music. Where will you hear music like twenty files all working at once! You ought to be happy boys, oughtn't you? Won't there be a treat of fish after this, that's all! Hulloa, there, you red-haired varmint, what are you looking after? Three boys looking about them; what's all this? won't I be among you?' and he sprang forward and seized the luckless ears of the first apprentice he could get hold off, and wrung them till the blood spouted forth.

'Please, bishop,' sang out the boy, 'it worn't my fault. Here's a man what wants you.'

'Who wants me?' said the bishop, looking round, and he caught the figure of Morley who had just entered the shop.

'Well, what's your will? Locks or nails?'

'Neither,' said Morley; 'I wish to see a man named Hatton.'

'Well, you see a man named Hatton,' said the bishop; 'and now what do you want of him?'

'I should like to say a word to you alone,' said Morley.

'Hem! I should like to know who is to finish this lock, and to look after my boys! If it's an order, let us have it at once.'

'It is not an order,' said Morley.

'Then I don't want to hear nothing about it,' said the bishop.

'It's about family matters,' said Morley.

'Ah!' said Hatton, eagerly, 'what, do you come from him?'

'It may be,' said Morley.

Upon this the bishop, looking up to the ceiling of the room in which there were several large chinks, began calling out lustily to some unseen person above, and immediately was replied to in a shrill voice of objurgation, demanding in peremptory words, interlarded with many oaths, what he wanted. His reply called down his unseen correspondent, who soon entered his workshop. It was the awful presence of Mrs. Hatton; a tall, bearded virago, with a file in her hand, for that seemed the distinctive arm of the house, and eyes flashing with unbridled power.

'Look after the boys,' said Hatton, 'for I have business.'

'Won't I?' said Mrs. Hatton; and a thrill of terror pervaded the assembly. All the files moved in regular melody; no one dared to raise his face; even her two young children looked still more serious and demure. Not that any being present flattered himself for an instant that the most sedulous attention on his part could prevent an outbreak; all that each aspired to, and wildly hoped, was that he might not be the victim singled out to have his head cut open, or his eye knocked out, or his ears half pulled off by the being who was the terror not only of the workshop, but of Wodgate itself,—their bishop's gentle wife.

In the meantime, that worthy, taking Morley into a room where there were no machines at work except those made of iron, said, 'Well, what have you brought me?'

'In the first place,' said Morley, 'I would speak to you of your brother.'

'I concluded that,' said Hatton, 'when you spoke of family matters bringing you here; he is the only relation I have in this world, and therefore it must be of him.'

'It is of him,' said Morley.

'Has he sent anything?'

'Hem!' said Morley, who was by nature a diplomatist, and instantly comprehended his position, being himself pumped when he came to pump; but he resolved not to precipitate the affair. 'How late is it since you heard from him?' he asked.

'Why, I suppose you know,' said Hatton, 'I heard as usual.'

'From his usual place?' inquired Morley.

'I wish you would tell me where that is,' said Hatton, eagerly.

'Why, he writes to you?'

'Blank letters; never had a line except once, and that is more than twelve year ago. He sends me a twenty-pound note every Christmas; and that is all I know about him.'

'Then he is rich, and well to do in the world?' said Morley.

'Why, don't you know?' said Hatton; 'I thought you came from him!'

'I came about him. I wished to know whether he were alive, and that you have been able to inform me: and where he was; and that you have not been able to inform me.'

'Why, you're a regular muff!' said the bishop.

CHAPTER VIII.

A FEW days after his morning walk with Sybil, it was agreed that Egremont should visit Mr. Trafford's factory, which he had expressed a great desire to inspect. Gerard always left his cottage at break of dawn, and as Sybil had not yet paid her accustomed visit to her friend and patron, who was the employer of her father, it was arranged that Egremont should accompany her at a later and more convenient hour in the morning, and then that they should all return together.

The factory was about a mile distant from their cottage, which belonged indeed to Mr. Trafford, and had been built by him. He was the younger son of a family that had for centuries been planted in the land, but who, not satisfied with the factitious consideration with which society compensates the junior members of a territorial house for their entailed poverty, had availed himself of some opportunities that offered themselves, and had devoted his energies to those new sources of wealth that were unknown to his ancestors. His operations at first had been extremely limited, like his fortunes; but with a small capital, though his profits were not considerable, he at least gained experience. With gentle blood in his veins, and old English feelings, he imbibed, at an early period of his career, a correct conception of the relations which should subsist between the employer and the employed. He felt that between them there should be other ties* than the payment and the receipt of wages.

A distant and childless relative, who made him a visit, pleased with his energy and enterprise, and touched by the development of his social views, left him a considerable sum, at a moment too when a great opening was offered to manufacturing capital and skill. Trafford, schooled in rigid fortunes, and formed by struggle, if not by adversity, was ripe for the occasion, and equal to it. He became very opulent, and he lost no time in carrying into life and being the plans which he had brooded over in the years when his good thoughts were limited to dreams. On the banks of his native Mowe he had built a factory which was now one of the marvels of the district;* one might almost say, of the country: a single room, spreading over nearly two acres, and holding more than two thousand work-people. The roof of groined arches, lighted by ventilating domes at the height of eighteen feet, was supported by hollow cast-iron columns, through which the drainage of the roof was effected. The height of the ordinary rooms in which the work-people in manufactories are engaged is not more than from nine to eleven feet; and these are built in stories, the heat and effluvia of the lower rooms communicated to those above, and the difficulty of ventilation insurmountable. At Mr. Trafford's, by an ingenious process, not unlike that which is practised in the House of Commons,* the ventilation was also carried on from below, so that the whole building was kept at a steady temperature, and little susceptible to atmospheric influence. The physical advantages of thus carrying on the whole work in one chamber are great: in the improved health of the people, the security against dangerous accidents for women and youth, and the reduced fatigue resulting from not having to ascend and descend and carry materials to the higher rooms. But the moral advantages resulting from superior inspection and general observation are not less important: the child works under the eye of the parent, the parent under that of the superior workman; the inspector or employer at a glance can behold all.

When the work-people of Mr. Trafford left his factory they were not forgotten. Deeply had he pondered on the influence of the employer on the health and content of his work-people. He knew well that the domestic virtues are dependent on the existence of a home, and one of his first efforts had been to build a village where every family might be well lodged. Though he was the principal proprietor, and proud of that character, he nevertheless encouraged his workmen to purchase the fee:* there were some who had saved sufficient money to effect this; proud of their house and their little garden, and of the horticultural society, where its produce permitted them to be annual competitors. In every street there was a well: behind the factory were the public baths; the schools were under the direction of the perpetual curate of the church, which Mr. Trafford, though a Roman Catholic, had raised and endowed. In the midst of this village, surrounded by beautiful gardens, which gave an impulse to the horticulture of the community, was the house of Trafford himself who comprehended his position too well to withdraw himself with vulgar exclusiveness from his real dependents, but recognized the baronial principle reviving in a new form, and adapted to the softer manners and more ingenious circumstances of the times.

And what was the influence of such an employer and such a system of employment on the morals and manners of the employed? Great; infinitely beneficial. The connexion of a labourer with his place of work, whether agricultural or manufacturing, is itself a vast advantage. Proximity to the employer brings cleanliness and order, because it brings observation and encouragement. In the settlement of Trafford crime was positively unknown: and offences were very slight. There was not a single person in the village of a reprobate character. The men were well clad; the women had a blooming cheek; drunkenness was unknown; while the moral condition of the softer sex was proportionately elevated.

The vast form of the spreading factory, the roofs and gardens of the village, the Tudor chimneys of the house of Trafford, the spire of the gothic church, with the sparkling river and the sylvan back-ground, came rather suddenly on the sight of Egremont. They were indeed in the pretty village-street before he was aware he was about to enter it. Some beautiful children rushed out of a cottage and flew to Sybil, crying out, 'the queen, the queen;' one clinging to her dress, another seizing her arm, and a third, too small to struggle, pouting out its lips to be embraced.

'My subjects,' said Sybil laughing, as she greeted them all; and then they ran away to announce to others that their queen had arrived.

Others came; beautiful and young. As Sybil and Egremont walked along, the race too tender for labour, seemed to spring out of every cottage to greet 'their queen.' Her visits had been very rare of late, but they were never forgotten; they formed epochs in the village annals of the children, some of whom knew only by tradition the golden age when Sybil Gerard lived at the great house, and daily glanced like a spirit among their homes, smiling and met with smiles, blessing and ever blessed.

'And here,' she said to Egremont, 'I must bid you good bye; and this little boy,' touching gently on his head a very serious urchin who had never left her side for a moment, proud of his position, and holding tight her hand with all his strength, 'this little boy shall be your guide. It is not a hundred yards. Now, Pierce, you must take Mr. Franklin to the factory, and ask for Mr. Gerard.' And she went her way.

They had not separated five minutes when the sound of whirling wheels caught the ear of Egremont, and, looking round, he saw a cavalcade of great pretension rapidly approaching; dames and cavaliers on horseback; a brilliant equipage, postilions and four horses: a crowd of grooms. Egremont stood aside. The horsemen and horsewomen caracoled gaily by him; proudly swept on the sparkling barouche; the saucy grooms pranced in his face. Their masters and mistresses were not strangers to him: he recognized with some dismay the liveries, and then the arms of Lord de Mowbray, and caught the cold, proud countenance of Lady Joan, and the flexible visage of Lady Maud, both on horseback, and surrounded by admiring cavaliers.

Egremont flattered himself that he had not been recognised, and dismissing his little guide, instead of proceeding to the factory he sauntered away in an opposite direction, and made a visit to the church.

The wife of Trafford embraced Sybil, and then embraced her again. She seemed as happy as the children of the village, that the joy of her roof, as of so many others, had returned to them, though only for a few hours. Her husband she said had just quitted the house; he was obliged to go to the factory to receive a great and distinguished party who were expected this morning, having written to him several days before for permission to view the works. 'We expect them to lunch here afterwards,' said Mrs. Trafford, a very refined woman, but unused to society, and who rather trembled at the ceremony; 'Oh! do stay with me, Sybil, to receive them.'

This intimation so much alarmed Sybil that she rose as soon as was practicable; and saying that she had some visits to make in the village, she promised to return when Mrs. Trafford was less engaged.

An hour elapsed; there was a loud ring at the hall-door, the great and distinguished party had arrived. Mrs. Trafford prepared for the interview, and tried to look very composed as the doors opened, and her husband ushered in and presented to her Lord and Lady de Mowbray, their daughters, Lady Firebrace, Mr. Jermyn, who still lingered at the castle, and Mr. Alfred Mountchesney and Lord Milford, who were mere passing guests, on their way to Scotland, but reconnoitering the heiresses in their course.

Lord de Mowbray was profuse of praise and compliments. His lordship was apt to be too civil. The breed would come out sometimes. To-day he was quite the coffee-house waiter. He praised everything: the machinery, the workmen, the cotton* manufactured and the cotton raw, even the smoke. But Mrs. Trafford would not have the smoke defended, and his lordship gave the smoke up, but only to please her. As for Lady de Mowbray, she was as usual courteous and condescending, with a kind of smouldering smile on her fair aquiline face, that seemed half pleasure and half surprise at the strange people she was among. Lady Joan was haughty and scientific, approved of much, but principally of the system of ventilation, of which she asked several questions which greatly perplexed Mrs. Trafford, who slightly blushed, and looked at her husband for relief, but he was engaged with Lady Maud, who was full of enthusiasm, entered into everything with the zest of sympathy, identified herself with the factory system almost as much as she had done with the crusades, and longed to teach in singing schools, found public gardens, and bid fountains flow and sparkle for the people.

'I think the works were very wonderful,' said Lord Milford, as he was cutting a pasty; 'and indeed, Mrs. Trafford, everything here is quite charming; but what I have most admired at your place is a young girl we met—the most beautiful I think I ever saw.'

'With the most beautiful dog,' said Mr. Mountchesney.

'Oh! that must have been Sybil!' exclaimed Mrs. Trafford.

'And who is Sybil?' asked Lady Maud. 'That is one of our family names. We all thought her quite beautiful.'

'She is a child of the house,' said Mrs. Trafford, 'or rather was, for I am sorry to say she has long quitted us.'

'Is she a nun?' asked Lord Milford, 'for her vestments had a conventual air.'

'She has just left your convent at Mowbray,' said Mr. Trafford, addressing his answer to Lady Maud, 'and rather against her will. She clings to the dress she was accustomed to there.'

'And now she resides with you?'

'No; I should be very happy if she did. I might almost say she was brought up under this roof. She lives now with her father.'

'And who is so fortunate as to be her father?' enquired Mr. Mountchesney.

'Her father is the inspector of my works; the person who accompanied us over them this morning.'

'What! that handsome man I so much admired,' said Lady Maud, 'so very aristocratic-looking. Papa,' she said, addressing herself to Lord de Mowbray, 'the inspector of Mr. Trafford's works we are speaking of, that aristocratic-looking person that I observed to you, he is the father of the beautiful girl.'

'He seemed a very intelligent person,' said Lord de Mowbray with many smiles.

'Yes,' said Mr. Trafford; 'he has great talents and great integrity. I would trust him with anything and to any amount. All I wish,' he added, with a smile and in a lower tone to Lady de Mowbray, 'all I wish is, that he was not quite so fond of politics.'

'Is he very violent?' enquired her ladyship in a sugary tone.

'Too violent,' said Mr. Trafford, 'and wild in his ideas.'

'And yet I suppose,' said Lord Milford, 'he must be very well off?'

'Why I must say for him it is not selfishness that makes him a malcontent,' said Mr. Trafford; 'he bemoans the condition of the people.'

'If we are to judge of the condition of the people by what we see here,' said Lord de Mowbray, 'there is little to lament in it. But I fear these are instances not so common as we could wish. You must have been at a great outlay, Mr. Trafford?'

'Why,' said Mr. Trafford, 'for my part, I have always considered that there was nothing so expensive as a vicious population. I hope I had other objects in view in what I have done than a pecuniary compensation. They say we all have our hobbies; and it was ever mine to improve the condition of my work-people, to see what good tenements and good schools and just wages paid in a fair manner, and the encouragement of civilizing pursuits, would do to elevate their character. I should find an ample reward in the moral tone and material happiness of this community; but really viewing it in a pecuniary point of view, the investment of capital has been one of the most profitable I ever made; and I would not, I assure you, for double its amount, exchange my work-people for the promiscuous assemblage engaged in other factories.'

'The influence of the atmosphere on the condition of the labourer is a subject which deserves investigation,' said Lady Joan to Mr. Jermyn, who stared and bowed.

'And you do not feel alarmed at having a person of such violent opinions as your inspector at the head of your establishment?' said Lady Firebrace to Mr. Trafford, who smiled a negative.

'What is the name of the intelligent individual who accompanied us?' enquired Lord de Mowbray.

'His name is Gerard,' said Mr. Trafford.

'I believe a common name in these parts,' said Lord de Mowbray looking a little confused.

'Not very,' said Mr. Trafford; ''tis an old name and the stock has spread; but all Gerards claim a common lineage I believe, and my inspector has gentle blood, they say, in his veins.'

'He looks as if he had,' said Lady Maud.

'All persons with good names affect good blood,' said Lord de Mowbray; and then turning to Mrs. Trafford he overwhelmed her with elaborate courtesies of phrase; praised everything again; first generally and then in detail; the factory, which he seemed to prefer to his castle—the house, which he seemed to prefer even to the factory—the gardens, from which he anticipated even greater gratification than from the house. And this led to an expression of a hope that he would visit them. And so in due time the luncheon was achieved. Mrs. Trafford looked at her guests, there was a rustling and a stir, and everybody was to go and see the gardens that Lord de Mowbray had so much praised.

'I am all for looking after the beautiful Nun,' said Mr. Mountchesney to Lord Milford.

'I think I shall ask the respectable manufacturer to introduce me to her,' replied his lordship.

In the meantime Egremont had joined Gerard at the factory.

'You should have come sooner,' said Gerard, 'and then you might have gone round with the fine folks. We have had a grand party here from the castle.'

'So I perceived,' said Egremont, 'and withdrew.'

'Ah! they were not in your way, eh?' he said in a mocking smile. 'Well, they were very condescending—at least for such great people. An earl! Earl de Mowbray,—I suppose he came over with William the Conqueror. Mr. Trafford makes a show of the place, and it amuses their visitors I dare say, like anything else that's strange. There were some young gentlemen with them, who did not seem to know much about anything. I thought I had a right to be amused too; and I must say I liked very much to see one of them looking at the machinery through his eye-glass. There was one very venturesome chap: I thought he was going to catch hold of the fly-wheel, but I gave him a spin which I believed saved his life, though he did rather stare. He was a lord.'

'They are great heiresses, his daughters, they say at Mowbray,' said Egremont.

'I dare say,' said Gerard. 'A year ago this earl had a son—an only son, and then his daughters were not great heiresses. But the son died and now it's their turn. And perhaps some day it will be somebody else's turn. If you want to understand the ups and downs of life, there's nothing like the parchments of an estate. Now master, now man! He who served in the hall now lords in it; and very often the baseborn change their liveries for coronets, while gentle blood has nothing left but—dreams; eh, master Franklin?'

'It seems you know the history of this Lord de Mowbray?'

'Why a man learns a good many things in his time; and living in these parts, there are few secrets of the notables. He has had the title to his broad acres questioned before this time, my friend.'

'Indeed!'

'Yes; I could not help thinking of that today,' said Gerard, 'when he questioned me with his mincing voice and pulled the wool with his cursed white hands and showed it to his dame, who touched it with her little finger; and his daughters who tossed their heads like pea-hens—Lady Joan and Lady Maud. Lady Joan and Lady Maud!' repeated Gerard in a voice of bitter sarcasm. 'I did not care for the rest; but I could not stand that Lady Joan and that Lady Maud. I wonder if my Sybil saw them.'

In the meantime, Sybil had been sent for by Mrs. Trafford. She had inferred from the message that the guests had departed, and her animated cheek showed the eagerness with which she had responded to the call. Bounding along with a gladness of the heart which lent additional lustre to her transcendent brightness, she suddenly found herself surrounded in the garden by Lady Maud and her friends. The daughter of Lord de Mowbray, who could conceive nothing but humility as the cause of her alarmed look, attempted to re-assure her by condescending volubility, turning often to her friends and praising in admiring interrogatories Sybil's beauty.

'And we took advantage of your absence,' said Lady Maud in a tone of amiable artlessness, 'to find out all about you. And what a pity we did not know you when you were at the convent, because then you might have been constantly at the castle; indeed I should have insisted on it. But still I hear we are neighbours; you must promise to pay me a visit, you must indeed. Is not she beautiful?' she added in a lower but still distinct voice to her friend. 'Do you know I think there is so much beauty among the lower order.'

Mr. Mountchesney and Lord Milford poured forth several insipid compliments, accompanied with some speaking looks which they flattered themselves could not be misconstrued. Sybil said not a word, but answered each flood of phrases with a cold reverence.

Undeterred by her somewhat haughty demeanour, which Lady Maud only attributed to the novelty of her situation, her ignorance of the world, and her embarrassment under this overpowering condescension, the good-tempered and fussy daughter of Lord de Mowbray proceeded to re-assure Sybil, and to enforce on her that this perhaps unprecedented descent from superiority was not a mere transient courtliness of the moment, and that she really might rely on her patronage and favourable feeling.

'You really must come and see me,' said Lady Maud, 'I shall never be happy till you have made me a visit. Where do you live? I will come and fetch you myself in the carriage. Now let us fix a day at once. Let me see; this is Saturday. What say you to next Monday?'

'I thank you,' said Sybil, very gravely, 'but I never quit my home.'

'What a darling!' exclaimed Lady Maud looking round at her friends. 'Is not she? I know exactly what you feel. But really you shall not be the least embarrassed. It may feel strange at first, to be sure, but then I shall be there; and do you know I look upon you quite as my protégée.'

'Protégée,' said Sybil. 'I live with my father.'

'What a dear!' said Lady Maud looking round to Lord Milford. 'Is not she naive?'

'And are you the guardian of these beautiful flowers?' said Mr. Mountchesney.

Sybil signified a negative, and added, 'Mrs. Trafford is very proud of them.'

'You must see the flowers at Mowbray Castle,' said Lady Maud. 'They are unprecedented, are they not, Lord Milford? You know you said the other day that they were almost equal to Mrs. Lawrence's.* I am charmed to find you are fond of flowers,' continued Lady Maud; 'you will be so delighted with Mowbray. Ah! mama is calling us. Now fix—shall it be Monday?'

'Indeed,' said Sybil, 'I never leave my home. I am one of the lower order, and live only among the lower order. I am here to-day merely for a few hours to pay an act of homage to a benefactor.'

'Well I shall come and fetch you,' said Maud, covering her surprise and mortification by a jaunty air that would not confess defeat.

'And so shall I,' said Mr. Mountchesney.

'And so shall I,' whispered Lord Milford lingering a little behind.

The great and distinguished party had disappeared; their glittering barouche, their prancing horses, their gay grooms, all had vanished; the sound of their wheels was no longer heard. Time flew on; the bell announced that the labour of the week had closed. There was a half holiday always on the last day of the week at Mr. Trafford's settlement; and every man, woman, and child, were paid their wages in the great room before they left the mill. Thus the expensive and evil habits which result from wages being paid in public houses were prevented. There was also in this system another great advantage for the workpeople. They received their wages early enough to repair to the neighbouring markets and make their purchases for the morrow. This added greatly to their comfort, and rendering it unnecessary for them to run in debt to the shopkeepers, added really to their wealth. Mr. Trafford thought that next to the amount of wages, the most important consideration was the method in which wages are paid; and those of our readers who may have read or can recall the sketches, neither coloured nor exaggerated, which we have given in the early part of this volume of the very different manner in which the working classes may receive the remuneration for their toil, will probably agree with the sensible and virtuous master of Walter Gerard.

He, accompanied by his daughter and Egremont, is now on his way home. A soft summer afternoon; the mild beam still gilding the tranquil scene; a river, green meads full of kine, woods vocal with the joyous song of the thrush and the blackbird; and in the distance, the lofty breast of the purple moor, still blazing in the sun: fair sights and renovating sounds after a day of labour passed in walls and amid the ceaseless and monotonous clang of the spindle and the loom. So Gerard felt it, as he stretched his great limbs in the air and inhaled its perfumed volume.

'Ah! I was made for this, Sybil,' he exclaimed; 'but never mind, my child, never mind; tell me more of your fine visitors.'

Egremont found the walk too short; fortunately from the undulation of the vale, they could not see the cottage until within a hundred yards of it. When they were in sight, a man came forth from the garden to greet them; Sybil gave an exclamation of pleasure; it was MORLEY.

CHAPTER IX.

Morley greeted Gerard and his daughter with great warmth, and then looked at Egremont. 'Our companion in the ruins of Marney Abbey,' said Gerard; 'you and our friend Franklin here should become acquainted, Stephen, for you both follow the same craft. He is a journalist like yourself, and is our neighbour for a time, and yours.'

'What journal are you on, may I ask?' enquired Morley.

Egremont reddened, was confused, and then replied, 'I have no claim to the distinguished title of a journalist. I am but a reporter; and have some special duties here.'

'Hem!' said Morley, and then taking Gerard by the arm, he walked away with him, leaving Egremont and Sybil to follow them.

'Well I have found him, Walter.'

'What, Hatton?'

'No, no; the brother.'

'And what knows he?'

'Little enough; yet something. Our man lives and prospers; these are facts, but where he is, or what he is—not a clue.'

'And this brother cannot help us?'

'On the contrary, he sought information from me; he is a savage, beneath even our worst ideas of popular degradation. All that is ascertained is that our man exists and is well to do in the world. There comes an annual and anonymous contribution, and not a light one, to his brother. I examined the post-marks of the letters, but they all varied, and were evidently arranged to mislead. I fear you will deem I have not done much; yet it was wearisome enough I can tell you.'

'I doubt it not; and I am sure Stephen, you have done all that man could. I was fancying that I should hear from you to-day; for what think you has happened? My Lord himself, his family and train, have all been in state to visit the works, and I had to show them. Queer that, wasn't it? He offered me money when it was over. How much I know not, I would not look at it. Though to be sure, they were perhaps my own rents, eh? But I pointed to the sick box and his own dainty hand deposited the sum there.'

''Tis very strange. And you were with him face to face?'

'Face to face. Had you brought me news of the papers, I should have thought that providence had rather a hand in it—but now, we are still at sea.'

'Still at sea,' said Morley musingly, 'but he lives and prospers. He will turn up yet, Walter.'

'Amen! Since you have taken up this thing, Stephen, it is strange how my mind has hankered after the old business, and yet it ruined my father, and mayhap may do as bad for his son.'

'We will not think that,' said Morley. 'At present we will think of other things. You may guess I am a bit wearied; I think I'll say good night; you have strangers with you.'

'Nay, nay, man; nay. This Franklin is a likely lad enough; I think you will take to him. Prithee come in. Sybil will not take it kindly if you go, after so long an absence; and I am sure I shall not.'

So they entered together.

The evening passed in various conversation, though it led frequently to the staple subject of talk beneath the roof of Gerard—the Condition of the People. What Morley had seen in his recent excursion afforded materials for many comments.

'The domestic feeling is fast vanishing among the working classes of this country,' said Gerard; 'nor is it wonderful—the Home no longer exists.'

'But there are means of reviving it,' said Egremont; 'we have witnessed them to-day. Give men homes, and they will have soft and homely notions. If all men acted like Mr. Trafford, the condition of the people would be changed.'

'But all men will not act like Mr. Trafford,' said Morley. 'It requires a sacrifice of self which cannot be expected, which is unnatural. It is not individual influence that can renovate society; it is some new principle that must reconstruct it. You lament the expiring idea of Home. It would not be expiring, if it were worth retaining. The domestic principle has fulfilled its purpose. The irresistible law of progress demands that another should be developed. It will come; you may advance or retard, but you cannot prevent it. It will work out like the development of organic nature. In the present state of civilization and with the scientific means of happiness at our command, the notion of home should be obsolete. Home is a barbarous idea; the method of a rude age; home is isolation; therefore anti-social. What we want is Community.'*

'It is all very fine,' said Gerard, 'and I dare say you are right, Stephen; but I like stretching my feet on my own hearth.'

CHAPTER X.

TIME passes with a measured and memorable wing during the first period of a sojourn in a new place, among new characters and new manners. Every person, every incident, every feeling, touches and stirs the imagination. The restless mind creates and observes at the same time. Indeed there is scarcely any popular tenet more erroneous than that which holds that when time is slow, life is dull. It is very often and very much the reverse. If we look back on those passages of our life which dwell most, upon the memory, they are brief periods full of action and novel sensation. Egremont found this so during the first days of his now residence in Mowedale. The first week, an epoch in his life, seemed an age; at the end of the first month, he began to deplore the swiftness of time and almost to moralize over the brevity of existence. He found that he was leading a life of perfect happiness, but of remarkable simplicity; he wished it might never end, but felt difficulty in comprehending how in the first days of his experience of it, it had seemed so strange; almost as strange as it was sweet. The day that commenced early, was passed in reading—books lent him often too by Sybil Gerard—sometimes in a ramble with her and Morley, who had time much at his command, to some memorable spot in the neighbourhood, or in the sport which the river and the rod secured Egremont. In the evening, he invariably repaired to the cottage of Gerard, beneath whose humble roof he found every female charm that can fascinate, and conversation that stimulated his intelligence. Gerard was ever the same; hearty, simple, with a depth of feeling and native thought on the subjects on which they touched, and with a certain grandeur of sentiment and conception which contrasted with his social position, but which became his idiosyncracy. Sybil spoke little, but hung upon the accents of her father; yet ever and anon her rich tones conveyed to the charmed ear of Egremont some deep conviction, the earnestness of her intellect as remarkable as the almost sacred repose of her mien and manner. Of Morley, at first Egremont saw a great deal: he lent our friend books, opened with unreserve and with great richness of speculative and illustrative power, on the questions which ever engaged him, and which were new and highly interesting to his companion. But as time advanced, whether it were that the occupations of Morley increased, and the calls on his hours left him fewer occasions for the indulgence of social intercourse, Egremont saw him seldom, except at Gerard's cottage, where generally he might be found in the course of the week, and their rambles together had entirely ceased.

Alone, Egremont mused much over the daughter of Gerard, but shrinking from the precise and the definite, his dreams were delightful, but vague. All that he asked was, that his present life should go on for ever; he wished for no change, and at length almost persuaded himself that no change could arrive; as men who are basking in a summer sun, surrounded by bright and beautiful objects, cannot comprehend how the seasons can ever alter; that the sparkling foliage should shrivel and fall away, the foaming waters become icebound, and the blue serene, a dark and howling space.

In this train of mind, the early days of October having already stolen on him, an incident occurred which startled him in his retirement, and rendered it necessary that he should instantly quit it. Egremont had entrusted the secret of his residence to a faithful servant who communicated with him when necessary, under his assumed name. Through these means he received a letter from his mother, written from London, where she had unexpectedly arrived, entreating him, in urgent terms, to repair to her without a moment's delay, on a matter of equal interest and importance to herself and him. Such an appeal from such a quarter, from the parent that had ever been kind, and the friend that had been ever faithful, was not for a moment to be neglected. Already a period had elapsed since its transmission, which Egremont regretted. He resolved at once to quit Mowedale, nor could he console himself with the prospect of an immediate return. Parliament was to assemble in the ensuing month, and independent of the unknown cause which summoned him immediately to town, he was well aware that much disagreeable business awaited him which could no longer be postponed. He had determined not to take his seat unless the expenses of his contest were previously discharged, and despairing of his brother's aid, and shrinking from trespassing any further on his mother's resources, the future looked gloomy enough: indeed nothing but the frequent presence and the constant influence of Sybil had driven from his mind the ignoble melancholy which, relieved by no pensive fancy, is the invariable attendant of pecuniary embarrassment.

And now he was to leave her. The event, rather the catastrophe, which under any circumstances, could not be long postponed, was to be precipitated. He strolled up to the cottage to bid her farewell and to leave kind words for her father. Sybil was not there. The old dame who kept their home informed him that Sybil was at the convent, but would return in the evening. It was impossible to quit Mowedale without seeing Sybil; equally impossible to postpone his departure. But by travelling through the night, the lost hours might be regained. And Egremont made his arrangements, and awaited with anxiety and impatience the last evening.

The evening, like his heart, was not serene. The soft air that had lingered so long with them, a summer visitant in an autumnal sky and loth to part, was no more present. A cold harsh wind, gradually rising, chilled the system and grated on the nerves. There was misery in its blast and depression in its moan. Egremont felt infinitely dispirited. The landscape around him that he had so often looked upon with love and joy, was dull and hard; the trees dingy, the leaden waters motionless, the distant hills rough and austere. Where was that translucent sky, once brilliant as his enamoured fancy: those bowery groves of aromatic fervor wherein he had loved to roam and muse; that river of swift and sparkling light that flowed and flashed like the current of his enchanted hours? All vanished—as his dreams.

He stood before the cottage of Gerard; he recalled the eve that he had first gazed upon its moonlit garden. What wild and delicious thoughts were then his! They were gone like the illumined hour. Nature and fortune had alike changed. Prescient of sorrow, almost prophetic of evil, he opened the cottage door, and the first person his eye encountered was Morley.

Egremont had not met him for some time, and his cordial greeting of Egremont to-night contrasted with the coldness, not to say estrangement, which to the regret and sometimes the perplexity of Egremont had gradually grown up between them. Yet on no occasion was his presence less desired by our friend. Morley was talking as Egremont entered with great animation; in his hand a newspaper, on a paragraph contained in which he was commenting. The name of Marney caught the ear of Egremont who turned rather pale at the sound, and hesitated on the threshold. The unembarrassed welcome of his friends however re-assured him, and in a moment he even ventured to enquire the subject of their conversation. Morley immediately referring to the newspaper said, 'This is what I have just read—

'EXTRAORDINARY SPORT AT THE EARL OF MARNEY'S. On Wednesday, in a small cover called the Horns, near Marney Abbey, his grace the Duke of Fitz-Aquitaine, the Earl of Marney, Colonel Rippe and Captain Grouse, with only four hours shooting, bagged the extraordinary number of seven hundred and thirty head of game, namely hares three hundred and thirty-nine; pheasants two hundred and twenty-one; partridges thirty-four; rabbits eighty-seven; and the following day upwards of fifty hares, pheasants, &c., (wounded the previous day) were picked up. Out of the four hours' shooting two of the party were absent an hour and a-half, namely the Earl of Marney and Captain Grouse, attending an agricultural meeting in the neighbourhood; the noble earl with his usual considerate condescension having kindly consented personally to distribute the various prizes to the labourers whose good conduct entitled them to the distinction.'

'What do you think of that, Franklin?' said Morley. 'That is our worthy friend of Marney Abbey, where we first met. You do not know this part of the country, or you would smile at the considerate condescension of the worst landlord in England; and who was, it seems, thus employed the day or so after his battue, as they call it.' And Morley turning the paper read another paragraph:—

'At a Petty Sessions holden at the Green Dragon Inn, Marney, Friday, October —, 1837.

'Magistrates present: The Earl of Marney, the Rev. Felix Flimsey, and Captain Grouse.

'Information against Robert Hind* for a trespass in pursuit of game in Blackrock Wood, the property of Sir Vavasour Firebrace, Bart. The case was distinctly proved; several wires being found in the pocket of the defendant. Defendant was fined in the full penalty of forty shillings and costs twenty-seven; the Bench being of opinion there was no excuse for him, Hind being in regular employ as a farm labourer and gaining his seven shillings a-week. Defendant being unable to pay the penalty, was sent for two months to Marham Gaol.'

'What a pity,' said Morley, 'that Robert Hind, instead of meditating the snaring of a hare, had not been fortunate enough to pick up a maimed one crawling about the fields the day after the battue. It would certainly have been better for himself; and if he has a wife and family, better for the parish.'

'Oh!' said Gerard, 'I doubt not they were all picked up by the poulterer who has the contract: even the Normans did not sell their game.'

'The question is,' said Morley, 'would you rather be barbarous or mean; that is the alternative presented by the real and the pseudo Norman nobility of England. Where I have been lately, there is a Bishopsgate Street merchant who has been made for no conceiveable public reason a baron bold. Bigod and Bohun could not enforce the forest laws* with such severity as this dealer in cotton and indigo.'

'It is a difficult question to deal with—this affair of the game laws,' said Egremont; 'how will you reach the evil? Would you do away with the offence of trespass? And if so, what is your protection for property?'

'It comes to a simple point though,' said Morley, 'the Territorialists must at length understand that they cannot at the same time have the profits of a farm and the pleasures of a chase.'

At this moment entered Sybil. At the sight of her, the remembrance that they were about to part, nearly overwhelmed Egremont. Her supremacy over his spirit was revealed to him, and nothing but the presence of other persons could have prevented him avowing his entire subjection. His hand trembled as he touched her's, and his eye, search-ing yet agitated, would have penetrated her serene soul. Gerard and Morley, somewhat withdrawn, pursued their conversation; while Egre-mont, hanging over Sybil, attempted to summon courage to express to her his sad adieu. It was in vain. Alone, perhaps he might have poured forth a passionate farewell. But constrained he became embarrassed; and his conduct was at the same time tender and perplexing. He asked and repeated questions which had already been answered. His thoughts wandered from their conversation but not from her with whom he should have conversed. Once their eyes met, and Sybil observed his suffused with tears. Once he looked round and caught the glance of Morley, instantly withdrawn, but not easy to be forgotten.

Shortly after this and earlier than his wont, Morley rose and wished them good night. He shook hands with Egremont and bade him fare-well with unusual kindness. Harold, who seemed half asleep, suddenly sprang from the side of his mistress and gave an agitated bark. Harold was never very friendly to Morley, who now tried to soothe him, but in vain. The dog looked fiercely at him and barked again, but the moment Morley had disappeared, Harold resumed his usual air of proud high-bred gentleness, and thrust his nose into the hand of Egremont, who patted him with fondness.

The departure of Morley was a great relief to Egremont, though the task that was left was still a painful effort. He rose and walked for a moment up and down the room, commenced an unfinished sentence, approached the hearth and leant over the mantel; and then at length extending his hand to Gerard he exclaimed, in a trembling voice, 'Best of friends, I must leave Mowedale.'

'I am very sorry,' said Gerard; 'and when?'

'Now,' said Egremont.

'Now!' said Sybil.

'Yes; this instant. My summons is urgent. I ought to have left this morning. I came here then to bid you farewell,' he said looking at Sybil, 'to express to you how deeply I was indebted to you for all your good-ness—how dearly I shall cherish the memory of these happy days—the happiest I have ever known;' and his voice faltered. 'I came also to leave a kind message for you, my friend, a hope that we might meet again and soon—but your daughter was absent, and I could not leave Mowedale without seeing either of you. So I must contrive to get on through the night.'

'Well, we lose a very pleasant neighbour,' said Gerard; 'we shall miss you, I doubt not, eh, Sybil?'

But Sybil had turned away her head; she was leaning over and seemed to be caressing Harold and was silent.

How much Egremont would have liked to have offered or invited correspondence; to have proffered his services when the occasion permitted; to have said or proposed many things that might have cherished their acquaintance or friendship; but embarrassed by his incognito and all its consequent deception, he could do nothing but tenderly express his regret at parting, and speak vaguely and almost mysteriously of their soon again meeting. He held out again his hand to Gerard who shook it heartily: then approaching Sybil, Egremont said, 'You have shewn me a thousand kindnesses, which I cherish,' he added in a lower tone, 'above all human circumstances. Would you deign to let this volume lie upon your table,' and he offered Sybil an English translation of Thomas à Kempis,* illustrated by some masterpieces. In its first page was written 'Sybil, from a faithful friend.'

'I accept it,' said Sybil with a trembling voice and rather pale, 'in remembrance of a friend.' She held forth her hand to Egremont, who retained it for an instant, and then bending very low, pressed it to his lips. As with an agitated heart, he hastily crossed the threshold of the cottage, something seemed to hold him back. He turned round. The bloodhound had seized him by the coat and looked up to him with an expression of affectionate remonstrance against his departure. Egremont bent down, caressed Harold and released himself from his grasp.

When Egremont left the cottage, he found the country enveloped in a thick white mist, so that had it not been for some huge black shadows which he recognized as the crests of trees, it would have been very difficult to discriminate the earth from the sky, and the mist thickening as he advanced, even these fallacious landmarks threatened to disappear. He had to walk to Mowbray to catch a night train for London. Every moment was valuable, but the unexpected and increasing obscurity rendered his progress slow and even perilous. The contiguity to the river made every step important. He had according to his calculations proceeded nearly as far as his old residence, and notwithstanding the careless courage of youth and the annoyance of relinquishing a project, intolerable at that season of life, was meditating the expediency of renouncing that night the attempt on Mowbray and of gaining his former quarters for shelter. He stopped, as he had stopped several times before, to calculate rather than to observe. The mist was so thick that he could not see his own extended hand. It was not the first time that it had occurred to him that some one or something was hovering about his course.

'Who is there?' exclaimed Egremont. But no one answered.

He moved on a little, but very slowly. He felt assured that his ear caught a contiguous step. He repeated his interrogatory in a louder tone, but it obtained no response. Again he stopped. Suddenly he was seized; an iron grasp assailed his throat, a hand of steel gripped his arm. The unexpected onset hurried him on. The sound of waters assured him that he was approaching the precipitous bank of that part of the river which, from a ledge of pointed rocks, here formed rapids. Vigorous and desperate, Egremont plunged like some strong animal on whom a beast of prey had made a fatal spring. His feet clung to the earth as if they were held by some magnetic power. With his disengaged arm he grappled with his mysterious and unseen foe.

At this moment he heard the deep bay of a hound.

'Harold!' he exclaimed. The dog, invisible, sprang forward and seized upon his assailant. So violent was the impulse that Egremont staggered and fell, but he fell freed from his dark enemy. Stunned and exhausted, some moments elapsed before he was entirely himself. The wind had suddenly changed; a violent gust had partially dispelled the mist; the outline of the landscape was in many places visible. Beneath him were the rapids of the Mowe, over which a watery moon threw a faint, flickering light. Egremont was lying on its precipitous bank; and Harold panting was leaning over him and looking in his face, and sometimes licking him with that tongue which, though not gifted with speech, had spoken so seasonably in the moment of danger.

END OF THE THIRD BOOK.

BOOK IV.

CHAPTER I.

'ARE you going down to the house, Egerton?' enquired Mr. Berners at Brookes' of a brother M. P., about four o'clock in the early part of the spring of 1839.

'The moment I have sealed this letter; we will walk down together, if you like;' and in a few minutes they left the club.

'Our fellows are in a sort of fright about this Jamaica bill,'* said Mr. Egerton in an undertone, as if he were afraid a passer-by might overhear him. 'Don't say anything about it, but there's a screw loose.'

'The deuce! But how do you mean?'

'They say the Rads* are going to throw us over.'

'Talk, talk. They have threatened this half-a-dozen times. Smoke, sir; it will end in smoke.'

'I hope it may; but I know, in great confidence mind you, that Lord John* was saying something about it yesterday.'

'That may be; I believe our fellows are heartily sick of the business, and perhaps would be glad of an excuse to break up the government: but we must not have Peel in; nothing could prevent a dissolution.'

'Their fellows go about and say that Peel would not dissolve if he came in.'

'Trust him!'

'He has had enough of dissolutions they say.'

'Why, after all they have not done him much harm. Even—34 was a hit.'

'Whoever dissolves,' said Mr. Egerton, 'I don't think there will be much of a majority either way in our time.'

'We have seen strange things,' said Mr. Berners.

'They never would think of breaking up the government without making their peers,' said Mr. Egerton.

'The Queen is not over partial to making more peers; and when parties are in the present state of equality, the Sovereign is no longer a mere pageant.'

'They say her Majesty is more touched about these affairs of the Chartists* than anything else,' said Mr. Egerton.

'They are rather queer; but for my part I have no serious fears of a Jacquerie.'*

'Not if it comes to an outbreak; but a passive resistance Jacquerie is altogether a different thing. When we see a regular Convention assembled in London and holding its daily meetings in Palace Yard; and a general inclination evinced throughout the country to refrain from the consumption of exciseable articles, I cannot help thinking that affairs are more serious than you imagine. I know the government are all on the "qui vive." '*

'Just the fellows we wanted!' exclaimed Lord Fitzheron, who was leaning on the arm of Lord Milford, and who met Mr. Egerton and his friend in Pall Mall.

'We want a brace of pairs,' said Lord Milford. 'Will you two fellows pair?'*

'I must go down,' said Mr. Egerton; 'but I will pair from half-past seven to eleven.'

'I just paired with Ormsby at White's,' said Berners; 'not half an hour ago. We are both going to dine at Eskdale's,* and so it was arranged. Have you any news to-day?'

'Nothing; except that they say that Alfred Mountchesney is going to marry Lady Joan Fitz-Warene,' said Lord Milford.

'She has been given to so many,' said Mr. Egerton.

'It is always so with these great heiresses,' said his companion. 'They never marry. They cannot bear the thought of sharing their money. I bet Lady Joan will turn out another specimen of the TABITHA CROESUS.'*

'Well, put down our pair, Egerton,' said Lord Fitzheron. 'You do not dine at Sidonia's* by any chance?'

'Would that I did! You will have the best dishes and the best guests. I feed at old Malton's; perhaps a tête à tête: Scotch broth, and to tell him the news!'

'There is nothing like being a dutiful nephew, particularly when one's uncle is a bachelor and has twenty thousand a-year,' said Lord Milford. 'Au revoir! I suppose there will be no division to-night.'

'No chance.'

Egerton and Berners walked on a little further. As they came to the Golden Ball,* a lady quitting the shop was just about to get into her carriage; she stopped as she recognized them. It was Lady Firebrace.

'Ah! Mr. Berners, how d'ye do? You were just the person I wanted to see! How is Lady Augusta, Mr. Egerton? You have no idea Mr. Berners, how I have been fighting your battles!'

'Really, Lady Firebrace,' said Mr. Berners rather uneasy, for he had perhaps like most of us a peculiar dislike to being attacked or cheapened. 'You are too good.'

'Oh! I don't care what a person's politics are!' exclaimed Lady Firebrace with an air of affectionate devotion. 'I should be very glad indeed to see you one of us. You know your father was! But if any one is my friend I never will hear him attacked behind his back without fighting his battles; and I certainly did fight yours last night.'

'Pray tell me where it was?'

'Lady Crumbleford—'

'Confound Lady Crumbleford!' said Mr. Berners indignant but a little relieved.

'No, no; Lady Crumbleford told Lady Alicia Severn.'

'Yes, yes,' said Berners, a little pale, for he was touched.

'But I cannot stop,' said Lady Firebrace. 'I must be with Lady St. Julians exactly at a quarter past four;' and she sprang into her carriage.

'I would sooner meet any woman in London than Lady Firebrace,' said Mr. Berners; 'she makes me uneasy for the day: she contrives to convince me that the whole world are employed behind my back in abusing or ridiculing me.'

'It is her way,' said Egerton; 'she proves her zeal by showing you that you are odious. It is very successful with people of weak nerves. Scared at their general unpopularity, they seek refuge with the very person who at the same time assures them of their odium and alone believes it unjust. She rules that poor old goose, Lady Gramshawe, who feels that Lady Firebrace makes her life miserable, but is convinced that if she break with the torturer, she loses her only friend.'

'There goes a man who is as much altered as any fellow of our time.'

'Not in his looks; I was thinking the other night that he was better-looking than ever.'

'Oh! no; not in his looks; but in his life. I was at Christ Church with him, and we entered the world about the same time. I was rather before him. He did everything; and did it well. And now one never sees him, except at the House. He goes nowhere; and they tell me he is a regular reading man.'

'Do you think he looks to office?'

'He does not put himself forward.'

'He attends; and his brother will always be able to get anything for him,' said Egerton.

'Oh! he and Marney never speak; they hate each other.'

'By Jove! However there is his mother; with this marriage of hers and Deloraine House, she will be their grandest dame.'

'She is the only good woman the Tories have: I think their others do them harm, from Lady St. Julians down to your friend Lady Firebrace. I wish Lady Deloraine were with us. She keeps their men together wonderfully; makes her house agreeable; and then her manner—it certainly is perfect; natural, and yet refined.'

'Lady Mina Blake has an idea that far from looking to office, Egremont's heart is faintly with his party; and that if it were not for the Marchioness—'

'We might gain him, eh?'

'Hem; I hardly know that: he has got crotchets about the people I am told.'

'What, the ballot and household suffrage?'

'Gad, I believe it is quite a different sort of a thing. I do not know what it is exactly; but I understand he is crotchetty.'

'Well, that will not do for Peel. He does not like crotchetty men. Do you see that, Egerton?'

At this moment, Mr. Egerton and his friend were about to step over from Trafalgar square to Charing Cross. They observed the carriages of Lady St. Julians and the Marchioness of Deloraine drawn up side by side in the middle of the street, and those two eminent states-women in earnest conversation. Egerton and Berners bowed and smiled, but could not hear the brief but not uninteresting words that have nevertheless reached us.

'I give them eleven,' said Lady St. Julians.

'Well, Charles tells me,' said Lady Deloraine, 'that Sir Thomas says so, and he certainly is generally right; but it is not Charles' own opinion.'

'Sir Thomas, I know, gives them eleven,' said Lady St. Julians; 'and that would satisfy me; and we will say eleven. But I have a list here,' and she slightly elevated her brow, and then glanced at Lady Deloraine with a piquant air, 'which proves that they cannot have more than nine; but this is in the greatest confidence: of course between us there can be no secrets. It is Mr. Tadpole's list; nobody has seen it but me; not even Sir Robert. Lord Grubminster has had a stroke; they are concealing it, but Mr. Tadpole has found it out. They wanted to pair him off with Colonel Fantomme, who they think is dying; but Mr. Tadpole has got a Mesmerist* who has done wonders for him, and who has guaranteed that he shall vote. Well, that makes a difference of one.'

'And then Sir Henry Churton—'

'Oh! you know it,' said Lady St. Julians, looking slightly mortified. 'Yes; he votes with us.'

Lady Deloraine shook her head. 'I think,' she said, 'I know the origin of that report. Quite a mistake. He is in a bad humour, has been so the whole session, and he was at Lady Alice Fermyne's, and did say all sorts of thing. All that is true. But he told Charles this morning on a committee, that he should vote with the Government.'

'Stupid man!' exclaimed Lady St. Julians; 'I never could bear him. And I have sent his vulgar wife and great staring daughter a card for next Wednesday! Well, I hope affairs will soon be brought to a crisis, for I do not think I can bear much longer this life of perpetual sacrifice,' added Lady St. Julians a little out of temper, both because she had lost a vote and found her friend and rival better informed than herself.

'There is no chance of a division to-night,' said Lady Deloraine.

'That is settled,' said Lady St. Julians.

'Adieu, my dear friend. We meet, I believe, at dinner?'

'Plotting,' said Mr. Egerton to Mr. Berners, as they passed the great ladies.

'The only consolation one has,' said Berners, 'is, that if they do turn us out, Lady Deloraine and Lady St. Julians must quarrel, for they both want the same thing.'

'Lady Deloraine will have it,' said Egerton.

Here they picked up Mr. Jermyn, a young Tory M.P., who perhaps the reader may remember at Mowbray Castle; and they walked on together, Egerton and Berners trying to pump him as to the expectations of his friends.

'How will Trodgits go?' said Egerton.

'I think Trodgits will stay away,' said Jermyn.

'Who do you give that new man to—that north-country borough fellow;—what's his name?' said Berners.

'Blugsby! oh, Blugsby dined with Peel,' said Jermyn.

'Our fellows say dinners are no good,' said Egerton; 'and they certainly are a cursed bore: but you may depend upon it they do for the burgesses.* We don't dine our men half enough. Now Blugsby was just the sort of fellow to be caught by dining with Peel; and I dare say they made Peel remember to take wine with him. We got Melbourne to give a grand feed the other day to some of our men who want attention they say, and he did not take wine with a single guest. He forgot. I wonder what they are doing at the House! Here's Spencer May, he will tell us. Well, what is going on?'

'WISHY is up, and WASHY follows.'

'No division, of course?'

'Not a chance; a regular covey ready on both sides.'

CHAPTER II.

ON the morning of the same day that Mr. Egerton and his friend Mr. Berners walked down together to the House of Commons, as appears in our last chapter, Egremont had made a visit to his mother, who had married since the commencement of this history the Marquis of Deloraine, a great noble who had always been her admirer. The family had been established by a lawyer, and recently in our history. The present Lord Deloraine, though he was gartered and had been a viceroy,* was only the grandson of an attorney, but one who, conscious of his powers, had been called to the bar and died an ex-chancellor. A certain talent was hereditary in the family. The attorney's son had been a successful courtier, and had planted himself in the cabinet for a quarter of a century. It was a maxim in this family to make great alliances; so the blood progressively refined, and the connections were always distinguished by power and fashion. It was a great hit, in the second generation of an earldom, to convert the coronet into that of a marquis; but the son of the old chancellor lived in stirring times, and cruised for his object with the same devoted patience with which Lord Anson* watched for the galleon. It came at last, as everything does if men are firm and calm. The present marquis, through his ancestry and his first wife, was allied with the highest houses of the realm and looked their peer. He might have been selected as the personification of aristocracy: so noble was his appearance, so distinguished his manner; his bow gained every eye, his smile every heart. He was also very accomplished, and not ill-informed; had read a little, and thought a little, and was in every respect a most superior man; alike famed for his favour by the fair, and the constancy of his homage to the charming Lady Marney.

Lord Deloraine was not very rich; but he was not embarrassed, and had the appearance of princely wealth; a splendid family mansion with a courtyard; a noble country-seat with a magnificent park, including a quite celebrated lake, but with very few farms attached to it. He however held a good patent place* which had been conferred on his descendants by the old chancellor, and this brought in annually some thousands. His marriage with Lady Marney was quite an affair of the heart; her considerable jointure however did not diminish the lustre of his position.

It was this impending marriage, and the anxiety of Lady Marney to
see Egremont's affairs settled before it took place, which about a year
and a half ago had induced her to summon him so urgently from
Mowedale, which the reader perhaps may have not forgotten. And now
Egremont is paying one of his almost daily visits to his mother at
Deloraine House.

'A truce to politics, my dear Charles,' said Lady Marney; 'you must
be wearied with my inquiries. Besides, I do not take the sanguine view
of affairs in which some of our friends indulge. I am one of those who
think the pear is not ripe. These men will totter on, and longer perhaps
than even themselves imagine. I want to speak of something very different. To-morrow, my dear son, is your birth-day. Now I should grieve
were it to pass without your receiving something which showed that its
recollection was cherished by your mother. But of all silly things in the
world, the silliest is a present that is not wanted. It destroys the sentiment a little perhaps but it enhances the gift, if I ask you in the most
literal manner to assist me in giving you something that really would
please you?'

'But how can I, my dear mother?' said Egremont, 'You have ever
been so kind and so generous that I literally want nothing.'

'Oh! you cannot be such a fortunate man as to want nothing, Charles,'
said Lady Marney with a smile. 'A dressing-case you have; your rooms
are furnished enough: all this is in my way; but there are such things
as horses and guns of which I know nothing, but which men always
require. You must want a horse or a gun, Charles. Well, I should like
you to get either; the finest, the most valuable that money can purchase.
Or a brougham,* Charles; what do you think of a new brougham? Would
you like that Barker should build you a brougham?'

'You are too good, my dear mother. I have horses and guns enough;
and my present carriage is all I can desire.'

'You will not assist me, then? You are resolved that I shall do something very stupid. For to give you something I am determined.'

'Well my dear mother,' said Egremont smiling and looking round,
'give me something that is here.'

'Choose then,' said Lady Marney, and she looked round the blue
satin walls of her apartment, covered with cabinet pictures of exquisite
art, and then at her tables crowded with precious and fantastic toys.

'It would be plunder, my dear mother,' said Egremont.

'No, no; you have said it; you shall choose something. Will you have
those vases?' and she pointed to an almost matchless specimen of old
Sevres porcelain.

'They are in too becoming a position to be disturbed,' said Egremont, 'and would ill suit my quiet chambers, where a bronze or a marble is my greatest ornament. If you would permit me, I would rather choose a picture?'

'Then select one at once,' said Lady Marney; 'I make no reservation, except that Watteau, for it was given me by your father before we were married. Shall it be this Cuyp?'*

'I would rather choose this,' said Egremont, and he pointed to the portrait of a saint by Allori:* the face of a beautiful young girl, radiant and yet solemn, with rich tresses of golden brown hair, and large eyes dark as night, fringed with ebon lashes that hung upon the glowing cheek.

'Ah! you choose that! Well, that was a great favourite of poor Sir Thomas Lawrence. But for my part I have never seen any one in the least like it, and I think I am sure that you have not.'

'It reminds me—' said Egremont musingly.

'Of what you have dreamed,' said Lady Marney.

'Perhaps so,' said Egremont; 'indeed I think it must have been a dream.'

'Well, the vision shall still hover before you,' said his mother; 'and you shall find this portrait to-morrow over your chimney in the Albany.'*

CHAPTER III.

'STRANGERS must withdraw.'

'Division: clear the gallery. Withdraw.'

'Nonsense; no; it's quite ridiculous; quite absurd. Some fellow must get up. Send to the Carlton; send to the Reform;* send to Brookes's. Are your men ready? No; are your's? I am sure I can't say. What does it mean? Most absurd! Are there many fellows in the library? The smoking-room is quite full. All our men are paired till half-past eleven. It wants five minutes to the half-hour. What do you think of Trenchard's speech?* I don't care for ourselves; I am sorry for him. Well that is very charitable. Withdraw, withdraw; you must withdraw.'

'Where are you going, Fitzheron?' said a Conservative whipling.

'I must go; I am paired till half-past eleven, and it wants some minutes, and my man is not here.'

'Confound it!'

'How will it go?'

'Gad, I don't know.'

'Fishy eh?'

'Deuced!' said the under-whip in an undertone, pale and speaking behind his teeth.

The division bell was still ringing; peers and diplomatists and strangers were turned out; members came rushing in from library and smoking-room; some desperate cabs just arrived in time to land their passengers in the waiting-room. The doors were locked.

The mysteries of the Lobby are only for the initiated. Three quarters of an hour after the division was called, the result was known to the exoteric world. Majority for Ministers thirty-seven! Never had the opposition made such a bad division, and this too on their trial of strength for the session. Everything went wrong. Lord Milford was away without a pair. Mr. Ormsby, who had paired with Mr. Berners, never came, and let his man poll; for which he was infinitely accursed, particularly by the expectant twelve hundred a-yearers,* but not wanting anything himself, and having an income of forty thousand pounds paid quarterly, Mr. Ormsby bore their reported indignation like a lamb.

There were several other similar or analogous mischances; the Whigs contrived to poll Lord Grubminster in a wheeled chair; he was unconscious but had heard as much of the debate as a good many. Colonel Fantomme on the other hand could not come to time; the Mesmerist had thrown him into a trance from which it was fated he should never awake: but the crash of the night was a speech made against the opposition by one of their own men, Mr. Trenchard, who voted with the government.

'The rest may be accounted for,' said Lady St. Julians to Lady Deloraine the morning after; 'it is simply vexatious; it was a surprise and will be a lesson: but this affair of this Mr. Trenchard—and they tell me that William Loraine was absolutely cheering him the whole time—what does it mean? Do you know the man?'

'I have heard Charles speak of him, and I think much in his favour,' said Lady Deloraine; 'if he were here, he would tell us more about it. I wonder he does not come: he never misses looking in after a great division and giving me all the news.'

'Do you know, my dear friend,' said Lady St. Julians with an air of some solemnity, 'I am half meditating a great stroke? This is not a time for trifling. It is all very well for these people to boast of their division of last night, but it was a surprise, and as great to them as to us. I know there is dissension in the camp; ever since that Finality speech of Lord John, there has been a smouldering sedition. Mr. Tadpole knows all about it; he has liaisons with the frondeurs.* This affair of Trenchard may do us the greatest possible injury. When it comes to a fair fight, the government have not more than twelve or so. If this Mr. Trenchard and three or four others choose to make themselves of importance—you see? The danger is imminent, it must be met with decision.'

'And what do you propose doing?'

'Has he a wife?'

'I really do not know. I wish Charles would come, perhaps he could tell us.'

'I have no doubt he has,' said Lady St. Julians. 'One would have met him, somehow or other in the course of two years, if he had not been married. Well, married or unmarried, with his wife,—or without his wife, I shall send him a card for Wednesday.' And Lady St. Julians paused, overwhelmed as it were by the commensurate vastness of her idea and her sacrifice.

'Do not you think it would be rather sudden?' said Lady Deloraine.

'What does that signify? He will understand it; he will have gained his object; and all will be right.'

'But are you sure it is his object? We do not know the man.'

'What else can be his object?' said Lady St. Julians. 'People get into Parliament to get on; their aims are indefinite. If they have indulged in hallucinations about place before they enter the House, they are soon freed from such distempered fancies; they find they have no more talent than other people, and if they had, they learn that power, patronage and pay are reserved for us and our friends. Well then like practical men, they look to some result, and they get it. They are asked out to dinner more than they would be; they move rigmarole resolutions at non-sensical public meetings; and they get invited with their women to assemblies at their leader's where they see stars and blue ribbons,* and above all, us, whom they little think in appearing on such occasions, make the greatest conceivable sacrifice. Well then, of course such people are entirely in one's power, if one only had time and inclination to notice them. You can do anything with them. Ask them to a ball, and they will give you their votes; invite them to dinner and if necessary they will rescind them; but cultivate them, remember their wives at assemblies and call their daughters, if possible, by their right names; and they will not only change their principles or desert their party for you; but subscribe their fortunes if necessary and lay down their desert lives in your service.'

'You paint them to the life, my dear Lady St Julians,' said Lady Deloraine laughing; 'but with such knowledge and such powers, why did you not save our boroughs?'*

'We had lost our heads, then, I must confess,' said Lady St. Julians. 'What with the dear King and the dear Duke, we really had brought ourselves to believe that we lived in the days of Versailles or nearly; and I must admit I think we had become a little too exclusive. Out of the cottage circle,* there was really no world, and after all we were lost not by insulting the people, but by snubbing the aristocracy.'

The servant announced Lady Firebrace. 'Oh! my dear Lady Deloraine. Oh! my dear Lady St Julians!' and she shook her head.

'You have no news, I suppose,' said Lady St. Julians.

'Only about that dreadful Mr. Trenchard; you know the reason why he ratted?'

'No, indeed,' said Lady St. Julians with a sigh.

'An invitation to Lansdowne House,* for himself and his wife!'

'Oh! he is married then?'

'Yes; she is at the bottom of it all. Terms regularly settled beforehand. I have a note here—all the facts.' And Lady Firebrace twirled in her hand a bulletin from Mr. Tadpole.

'Lansdowne House is destined to cross me,' said Lady St. Julians with bitterness.

'Well it is very provoking,' said Lady Deloraine, 'when you had made up your mind to ask them for Wednesday.'

'Yes, that alone is a sacrifice,' said Lady St. Julians.

'Talking over the division I suppose,' said Egremont as he entered.

'Ah! Mr. Egremont,' said Lady St. Julians. 'What a hachis* you made of it!'

Lady Firebrace shook her head, as it were reproachfully.

'Charles,' said Lady Deloraine, 'we were talking of this Mr. Trenchard. Did I not once hear you say you knew something of him?'

'Why, he is one of my intimate acquaintance.'

'Heavens! what a man for a friend!' said Lady St. Julians.

'Heavens!' echoed Lady Firebrace raising her hands.

'And why did you not present him to me, Charles,' said Lady Deloraine.

'I did; at Lady Peel's.'

'And why did you not ask him here?'

'I did several times; but he would not come.'

'He is going to Lansdowne House, though,' said Lady Firebrace.

'I suppose you wrote the leading article in the *Standard** which I have just read,' said Egremont smiling. 'It announces in large type the secret reasons of Mr. Trenchard's vote.'

'It is a fact,' said Lady Firebrace.

'That Trenchard is going to Lansdowne House to-night; very likely. I have met him at Lansdowne House half-a-dozen times. He is very intimate with the family and lives in the same county.'

'But his wife,' said Lady Firebrace; 'that's the point: he never could get his wife there before.'

'He has none,' said Egremont very quietly.

'Then we may regain him,' said Lady St. Julians with energy. 'You shall make a little dinner to Greenwich, Mr. Egremont, and I will sit next to him.'

'Fortunate Trenchard!' said Egremont. 'But do you know I fear he is hardly worthy of his lot. He has a horror of fine ladies; and there is nothing in the world he more avoids than what you call society. At home, as this morning when I breakfasted with him, or in a circle of his intimates, he is the best company in the world; no one so well informed, fuller of rich humour, and more sincerely amiable. He is popular with all who know him—except Taper, Lady St. Julians, and Tadpole, Lady Firebrace.'

'Well, I think I will ask him still for Wednesday,' said Lady St. Julians; 'and I will write him a little note. If society is not his object, what is?'

'Ay!' said Egremont, 'there is a great question for you and Lady Firebrace to ponder over. This is a lesson for you fine ladies, who think you can govern the world by what you call your social influences: asking people once or twice a-year to an inconvenient crowd in your house; now haughtily smirking, and now impertinently staring, at them; and flattering yourselves all this time, that to have the occasional privilege of entering your saloons and the periodical experience of your insolent recognition, is to be a reward for great exertions, or if necessary an inducement to infamous tergiversation.'

CHAPTER IV.

It was night: clear and serene, though the moon had not risen; and a vast concourse of persons were assembling on Mowbray Moor. The chief gathering collected in the vicinity of some huge rocks, one of which, pre-eminent above its fellows, and having a broad flat head, on which some twenty persons might easily stand at the same time, was called the Druid's Altar.* The ground about was strewn with stony fragments, covered to-night with human beings, who found a conveni-ent resting-place amid these ruins of some ancient temple or relics of some ancient world. The shadowy concourse increased, the dim circle of the nocturnal assemblage each moment spread and widened; there was the hum and stir of many thousands. Suddenly in the distance the sound of martial music: and instantly, quick as the lightning and far more wild, each person present brandished a flaming torch, amid a chorus of cheers, that, renewed and resounding, floated far away over the broad bosom of the dusk wilderness.

The music and the banners denoted the arrival of the leaders of the people. They mounted the craggy ascent that led to the summit of the Druid's Altar, and there, surrounded by his companions, amid the enthusiastic shouts of the multitude, Walter Gerard came forth to address a TORCH-LIGHT MEETING.

His tall form seemed colossal in the uncertain and flickering light, his rich and powerful voice reached almost to the utmost limit of his vast audience, now still with expectation and silent with excitement. Their fixed and eager glance, the mouth compressed with fierce resolution or distended by novel sympathy, as they listened to the exposition of their wrongs, and the vindication of the sacred rights of labour—the shouts and waving of the torches as some bright or bold phrase touched them to the quick—the cause, the hour, the scene—all combined to render the assemblage in a high degree exciting.

'I wonder if Warner will speak to-night,' said Dandy Mick to Devilsdust.

'He can't pitch it in like Gerard,' replied his companion.

'But he is a trump in the tender,'* said the Dandy. 'The Hand-looms looks to him as their man, and that's a powerful section.'

'If you come to the depth of a question, there's nothing like Stephen Morley,' said Devilsdust. ''Twould take six clergymen any day to settle him. He knows the principles of society by heart. But Gerard gets hold of the passions.'

'And that's the way to do the trick,' said Dandy Mick. 'I wish he would say march, and no mistake.'

'There is a great deal to do before saying that,' said Devilsdust. 'We must have discussion, because when it comes to reasoning, the oligarchs have not got a leg to stand on; and we must stop the consumption of exciseable articles, and when they have no tin to pay the bayonets and their b—y police, they are dished.'

'You have a long head, Dusty,' said Mick.

'Why I have been thinking of it ever since I knew two and two made four,' said his friend. 'I was not ten years old when I said to myself—It's a pretty go this, that I should be toiling in a shoddy-hole to pay the taxes for a gentleman what drinks his port wine and stretches his legs on a Turkey carpet. Hear, hear,' he suddenly exclaimed, as Gerard threw off a stinging sentence. 'Ah! that's the man for the people. You will see, Mick, whatever happens, Gerard is the man who will always lead.'

Gerard had ceased amid enthusiastic plaudits, and Warner—that hand-loom weaver whom the reader may recollect, and who had since become a popular leader and one of the principal followers of Gerard— had also addressed the multitude. They had cheered and shouted, and voted resolutions, and the business of the night was over. Now they were enjoined to disperse in order and depart in peace. The band sounded a triumphant retreat; the leaders had descended from the Druid's Altar; the multitude were melting away, bearing back to the town their high resolves and panting thoughts, and echoing in many quarters the suggestive appeals of those who had addressed them. Dandy Mick and Devilsdust departed together; the business of their night had not yet commenced, and it was an important one.

They took their way to that suburb whither Gerard and Morley repaired the evening of their return from Marney Abbey; but it was not on this occasion to pay a visit to Chaffing Jack and his brilliant saloon. Winding through many obscure lanes, Mick and his friend at length turned into a passage which ended in a square court of a not inconsiderable size, and which was surrounded by high buildings that had the appearance of warehouses. Entering one of these, and taking up a dim lamp that was placed on the stone of an empty hearth, Devilsdust led his friend through several unoccupied and unfurnished rooms, until he came to one in which there were some signs of occupation.

'Now, Mick,' said he, in a very earnest, almost solemn tone, 'are you firm?'

'All right, my hearty,' replied his friend, though not without some affectation of ease.

'There is a good deal to go through,' said Devilsdust. 'It tries a man.'

'You don't mean that?'

'But if you are firm, all's right. Now I must leave you.'

'No, no, Dusty,' said Mick.

'I must go,' said Devilsdust; 'and you must rest here till you are sent for. Now mind—whatever is bid you, obey; and whatever you see, be quiet. There,' and Devilsdust taking a flask out of his pocket, held it forth to his friend, 'give a good pull, man, I can't leave it you, for though your heart must be warm, your head must be cool,' and so saying he vanished.

Notwithstanding the animating draught, the heart of Mick Radley trembled. There are some moments when the nervous system defies even brandy. Mick was on the eve of a great and solemn incident, round which for years his imagination had gathered and brooded. Often in that imagination he had conceived the scene, and successfully confronted its perils or its trials. Often had the occasion been the drama of many a triumphant reverie, but the stern presence of reality had dispelled all his fancy and all his courage. He recalled the warning of Julia, who had often dissuaded him from the impending step; that warning received with so much scorn and treated with so much levity. He began to think that women were always right; that Devilsdust was after all a dangerous counsellor; he even meditated over the possibility of a retreat. He looked around him: the glimmering lamp scarcely indicated the outline of the obscure chamber. It was lofty, nor in the obscurity was it possible for the eye to reach the ceiling, which several huge beams seemed to cross transversally, looming in the darkness. There was apparently no windows, and the door by which they had entered was not easily to be recognised. Mick had just taken up the lamp and was surveying his position, when a slight noise startled him, and looking round he beheld at some little distance two forms which he hoped were human.

Enveloped in dark cloaks and wearing black masks, a conical cap of the same colour adding to their considerable height, each held a torch. They stood in silence—two awful sentries.

Their appearance appalled, their stillness terrified Mick: he remained with his mouth open and the lamp in his extended arm. At length, unable any longer to sustain the solemn mystery, and plucking up his natural audacity, he exclaimed, 'I say, what do you want?'

All was silent.

'Come, come,' said Mick much alarmed; 'none of this sort of thing. I say, you must speak though.'

The figures advanced: they stuck their torches in a niche that was by; and then they placed each of them a hand on the shoulder of Mick.

'No, no; none of that,' said Mick, trying to disembarrass himself.

But, notwithstanding this fresh appeal, one of the silent masks pinioned his arms; and in a moment the eyes of the helpless friend of Devilsdust were bandaged.

Conducted by these guides, it seemed to Mick that he was traversing interminable rooms, or rather galleries, for once stretching out his arm, while one of his supporters had momentarily quitted him to open some gate or door, Mick touched a wall. At length one of the masks spoke, and said, 'In five minutes you will be in the presence of the SEVEN—prepare.'

At this moment rose the sound of distant voices singing in concert, and gradually increasing in volume as Mick and the masks advanced.

One of these attendants now notifying to their charge that he must kneel down, Mick found he rested on a cushion, while at the same time his arms still pinioned, he seemed to be left alone.

The voices became louder and louder; Mick could distinguish the words and burthen of the hymn; he was sensible that many persons were entering the apartment; he could distinguish the measured tread of some solemn procession. Round the chamber, more than once, they moved with slow and awful step. Suddenly that movement ceased; there was a pause of a few minutes; at length a voice spoke. 'I denounce John Briars.'

'Why?' said another.

'He offers to take nothing but piece-work; the man who does piece-work is guilty of less defensible conduct than a drunkard. The worst passions of our nature are enlisted in support of piece-work. Avarice, meanness, cunning, hypocrisy, all excite and feed upon the miserable votary who works by the task and not by the hour. A man who earns by piece-work forty shillings per week, the usual wages for day-work being twenty, robs his fellows of a week's employment; therefore I denounce John Briars.'

'Let it go forth,' said the other voice; 'John Briars is denounced. If he receive another week's wages by the piece, he shall not have the option of working the week after for time. No. 87, see to John Briars.'

'I denounce Claughton and Hicks,' said another voice.

'Why?'

'They have removed Gregory Ray from being a superintendent, because he belonged to this lodge.'

'Brethren, is it your pleasure that there shall be a turn out for ten days at Claughton and Hicks?'

'It is our pleasure,' cried several voices.

'No. 34, give orders to-morrow that the works at Claughton and Hicks stop till further orders.'

'Brethren,' said another voice, 'I propose the expulsion from this Union, of any member who shall be known to boast of his superior ability, as to either the quantity or quality of work he can do, either in public or private company. Is it your pleasure?'

'It is our pleasure.'

'Brethren,' said a voice that seemed a presiding one, 'before we proceed to the receipt of the revenue from the different districts of this lodge, there is I am informed a stranger present, who prays to be admitted into our fraternity. Are all robed in the mystic robe? Are all masked in the secret mask?'

'All!'

'Then let us pray!' And thereupon after a movement which intimated that all present were kneeling, the presiding voice offered up an extemporary prayer of great power and even eloquence. This was succeeded by the Hymn of Labour, and at its conclusion the arms of the neophyte were unpinioned, and then his eyes were unbandaged.

Mick found himself in a lofty and spacious room lighted with many tapers. Its walls were hung with black cloth; at a table covered with the same material, were seated seven persons in surplices and masked, the president on a loftier seat; above which on a pedestal was a skeleton complete. On each side of the skeleton was a man robed and masked, holding a drawn sword; and on each side of Mick was a man in the same garb holding a battle-axe. On the table was the sacred volume open, and at a distance, ranged in order on each side of the room, was a row of persons in white robes and white masks, and holding torches.

'Michael Radley,' said the President. 'Do you voluntarily swear in the presence of Almighty God and before these witnesses, that you will execute with zeal and alacrity, as far as in you lies, every task and injunction that the majority of your brethren testified by the mandate of this grand committee, shall impose upon you, in furtherance of our common welfare, of which they are the sole judges; such as the chastisement of Nobs,* the assassination of oppressive and tyrannical masters, or the demolition of all mills, works and shops that shall be deemed by us incorrigible. Do you swear this in the presence of Almighty God and before these witnesses?'

'I do swear it,' replied a tremulous voice.

'Then rise and kiss that book.'

Mick slowly rose from his kneeling position, advanced with a trembling step, and bending, embraced with reverence the open volume.

Immediately every one unmasked; Devilsdust came forward, and taking Mick by the hand led him to the President, who received him pronouncing some mystic rhymes. He was covered with a robe and presented with a torch, and then ranged in order with his companions. Thus terminated the initiation of Dandy Mick into a TRADES UNION.

CHAPTER V.

'His lordship has not yet rung his bell, gentlemen.'

It was the valet of Lord Milford that spoke, addressing from the door of a house in Belgrave Square, about noon, a deputation from the National Convention,* consisting of two of its delegates, who waited on the young viscount in common with other members of the legislature, in order to call his particular attention to the National Petition which the Convention had prepared, and which in the course of the session was to be presented by one of the members for Birmingham.

'I fear we are too early for these fine birds,' said one delegate to the other. 'Who is next on our list?'

'No. 27,—Street close by; Mr. THOROUGH BASE: he ought to be with the people, for his father was only a fiddler; but I understand he is quite an aristocrat and has married a widow of quality.'

'Well, knock.'

Mr. Thorough Base was not at home; had received the card of the delegates apprising him of the honour of their intended visit, but had made up his mind on the subject.

No. 18 in the same street received them more courteously. Here resided Mr. KREMLIN, who after listening with patience if not with interest, to their statement, apprised them that forms of government were of no consequence, and domestic policy of no interest; that there was only one subject which should engage the attention of public men, because everything depended on it,—that was our external system; and that the only specific for a revival of trade and the contentment of the people, was a general settlement of the boundary questions.* Finally, Mr. Kremlin urged upon the National Convention to recast their petition with this view, assuring them that on foreign policy they would have the public with them.

The deputation in reply might have referred as an evidence of the general interest excited by questions of foreign policy, to the impossibility even of a leader making a house on one; and to the fact that there are not three men in the House of Commons who even pretend to have any acquaintance with the external circumstances of the country; they might have added, that even in such an assembly Mr. Kremlin himself was distinguished for ignorance, for he had only one idea,—and that was wrong.

Their next visit was to WRIGGLE, a member for a metropolitan district, a disciple of Progress, who went with the times, but who took particular good care to ascertain their complexion; and whose movements if expedient could partake of a regressive character. As the Charter might some day turn up trumps as well as so many other unexpected cards and colours, Wriggle gave his adhesion to it, but of course only provisionally; provided that is to say, he might vote against it at present. But he saw no harm in it—not he, and should be prepared to support it when circumstances, that is to say the temper of the times, would permit him. More could hardly be expected from a gentleman in the delicate position in which Wriggle found himself at this moment, for he had solicited a baronetcy of the Whigs, and had secretly pledged himself to Taper to vote against them on the impending Jamaica division.*

BOMBASTES RIP snubbed them, which was hard, for he had been one of themselves, had written confidential letters in 1831 to the secretary of the Treasury, and 'provided his expenses were paid,' offered to come up from the manufacturing town he now represented, at the head of a hundred thousand men, and burn down Apsley House. But now Bombastes Rip talked of the great middle class; of public order and public credit. He would have said more to them, but had an appointment in the city, being a most active member of the committee for raising a statue to the Duke of Wellington.*

FLOATWELL received them in the politest manner, though he did not agree with them. What he did agree with was difficult to say. Clever, brisk, and bustling, with an university reputation and without patrimony, Floatwell shrunk from the toils of a profession, and in the hurry skurry of reform found himself to his astonishment a parliament man. There he had remained, but why, the Fates alone knew. The fun of such a thing must have evaporated with the novelty. Floatwell had entered public life in complete ignorance of every subject which could possibly engage the attention of a public man. He knew nothing of history, national or constitutional law, had indeed none but puerile acquirements, and had seen nothing of life. Assiduous at committees he gained those superficial habits of business which are competent to the conduct of ordinary affairs, and picked up in time some of the slang of economical questions. Floatwell began at once with a little success, and he kept his little success; nobody envied him it; he hoarded his sixpences without exciting any evil emulation. He was one of those characters who above all things shrink from isolation, and who imagine they are getting on if they are keeping company with some who stick like themselves. He was always an idolater of some great personage who was on the shelf, and who he was convinced, because the great personage assured him of it after dinner, would sooner or later turn out *the* man. At present, Floatwell swore by Lord Dunderhead; and the game of this little coterie, who dined together and thought they were a party, was to be courteous to the Convention.

After the endurance of an almost interminable lecture on the currency from Mr. KITE, who would pledge himself to the charter if the charter would pledge itself to one-pound notes,* the two delegates had arrived in Piccadilly, and the next member upon their list was Lord Valentine.

'It is two o'clock,' said one of the delegates, 'I think we may venture;' so they knocked at the portal of the court yard, and found they were awaited.

A private staircase led to the suite of rooms of Lord Valentine, who lived in the family mansion. The delegates were ushered through an ante-chamber into a saloon which opened into a very fanciful conservatory, where amid tall tropical plants played a fountain. The saloon was hung with blue satin, and adorned with brilliant mirrors; its coved ceiling was richly painted, and its furniture became the rest of its decorations. On one sofa were a number of portfolios, some open, full of drawings of costumes; a table of pietra dura* was covered with richly bound volumes that appeared to have been recently referred to; several ancient swords of extreme beauty were lying on a couch; in a corner of the room was a figure in complete armour, black and gold richly inlaid, and grasping in its gauntlet the ancient standard of England.

The two delegates of the National Convention stared at each other, as if to express their surprise that a dweller in such an abode should ever have permitted them to enter it; but ere either of them could venture to speak, Lord Valentine made his appearance.

He was a young man, above the middle height, slender, broad-shouldered, small-waisted, of a graceful presence; he was very fair, with dark blue eyes, bright and intelligent, and features of classic precision; a small Greek cap crowned his long light-brown hair, and he was enveloped in a morning robe of Indian shawls.

'Well, gentlemen,' said his lordship, as he invited them to be seated, in a clear and cheerful voice, and with an unaffected tone of frankness which put his guests at their ease; 'I promised to see you; well, what have you got to say?'

The delegates made their accustomed statement; they wished to pledge no one; all that the people desired was a respectful discussion of their claims; the national petition, signed by nearly a million and a half of the flower of the working classes, was shortly to be presented to the House of Commons, praying the House to take into consideration the five points in which the working classes deemed their best interests involved; to wit, universal suffrage, vote by ballot, annual parliaments, salaried members, and the abolition of the property qualification.

'And supposing these five points conceded,' said Lord Valentine, 'what do you mean to do?'

'The people then being at length really represented,' replied one of the delegates, 'they would decide upon the measures which the interests of the great majority require.'

'I am not so clear about that,' said Lord Valentine; 'that is the very point at issue. I do not think the great majority are the best judges of their own interests. At all events, gentlemen, the respective advantages of aristocracy and democracy are a moot point. Well then, finding the question practically settled in this country, you will excuse me for not wishing to agitate it. I give you complete credit for the sincerity of your convictions; extend the same confidence to me. You are democrats; I am an aristocrat. My family has been ennobled for nearly three centuries; they bore a knightly name before their elevation. They have mainly and materially assisted in making England what it is. They have shed their blood in many battles; I have had two ancestors killed in the command of our fleets. You will not underrate such services, even if you do not appreciate their conduct as statesmen, though that has often been laborious, and sometimes distinguished. The finest trees in England were planted by my family; they raised several of your most beautiful churches; they have built bridges, made roads, dug mines, and constructed canals, and drained a marsh of a million of acres which bears our name to this day, and is now one of the most flourishing portions of the country. You talk of our taxation and our wars; and of your inventions and your industry. Our wars converted an island into an empire, and at any rate developed that industry and stimulated those inventions of which you boast. You tell me that you are the delegates of the unrepresented working classes of Mowbray. Why, what would Mowbray have been if it had not been for your aristocracy and their wars? Your town would not have existed; there would have been no working classes there to send up delegates. In fact you owe your very existence to us. I have told you what my ancestors have done; I am prepared, if the occasion requires it, not to disgrace them; I have inherited their great position, and I tell you fairly, gentlemen, I will not relinquish it without a struggle.'

'Will you combat the people in that suit of armour, my lord?' said one of the delegates smiling, but in a tone of kindness and respect.

'That suit of armour has combated for the people before this,' said Lord Valentine, 'for it stood by Simon de Montfort on the field of Evesham.'*

'My lord,' said the other delegate, 'it is well known that you come from a great and honoured race; and we have seen enough to-day to show that in intelligence and spirit you are not unworthy of your ancestry. But the great question, which your lordship has introduced, not us, is not to be decided by a happy instance. Your ancestors may have done great things. What wonder! They were members of a very limited class which had the monopoly of action. And the people, have not they shed their blood in battle, though they may have commanded fleets less often than your lordship's relatives? And these mines and canals that you have excavated and constructed, these woods you have planted, these waters you have drained—had the people no hand in these creations? What share in these great works had that faculty of Labour whose sacred claims we now urge, but which for centuries have been passed over in contemptuous silence? No, my lord, we call upon you to decide this question by the result. The Aristocracy of England have had for three centuries the exercise of power; for the last century and a half that exercise has been uncontrolled; they form at this moment the most prosperous class that the history of the world can furnish: as rich as the Roman senators, with sources of convenience and enjoyment which modern science could alone supply. All this is not denied. Your order stands before Europe the most gorgeous of existing spectacles; though you have of late years dexterously thrown some of the odium of your polity upon that middle class which you despise, and who are despicable only because they imitate you, your tenure of power is not in reality impaired. You govern us still with absolute authority,—and you govern the most miserable people on the face of the globe.'

'And is this a fair description of the people of England?' said Lord Valentine. 'A flash of rhetoric, I presume, that would place them lower than the Portuguese or the Poles, the serfs of Russia or the Lazzaroni* of Naples.'

'Infinitely lower,' said the delegate, 'for they are not only degraded, but conscious of their degradation. They no longer believe in any innate difference between the governing and the governed classes of this country. They are sufficiently enlightened to feel they are victims. Compared with the privileged classes of their own land, they are in a lower state than any other population compared with its privileged classes. All is relative, my lord, and believe me, the relations of the working classes of England to its privileged orders are relations of enmity, and therefore of peril.'

'The people must have leaders,' said Lord Valentine.

'And they have found them,' said the delegate.

'When it comes to a push they will follow their nobility,' said Lord Valentine.

'Will their nobility lead them?' said the other delegate. 'For my part I do not pretend to be a philosopher, and if I saw a Simon de Montfort again I should be content to fight under his banner.'

'We have an aristocracy of wealth,' said the delegate who had chiefly spoken. 'In a progressive civilization wealth is the only means of class distinction: but a new disposition of wealth may remove even this.'

'Ah! you want to get at our estates,' said Lord Valentine smiling; 'but the effort on your part may resolve society into its original elements, and the old sources of distinction may again develope themselves.'

'Tall barons will not stand against Paixhan's rockets,'* said the delegate. 'Modern science has vindicated the natural equality of man.'

'And I must say I am very sorry for it,' said the other delegate; 'for human strength always seems to me the natural process of settling affairs.'

'I am not surprised at your opinion,' said Lord Valentine, turning to the delegate and smiling. 'I should not be over-glad to meet you in a fray. You stand some inches above six feet, or I am mistaken.'

'I was six feet two inches when I stopped growing,' said the delegate; 'and age has not stolen any of my height yet.'

'That suit of armour would fit you,' said Lord Valentine, as they all rose.

'And might I ask your lordship,' said the tall delegate, 'why it is here?'

'I am to represent Richard Cœur de Lion at the Queen's ball,'* said Lord Valentine; 'and before my sovereign I will not doff a Drury-Lane cuirass, so I got this up from my father's castle.'

'Ah! I almost wish the good old times of Cœur de Lion were here again,' said the tall delegate.

'And we should be serfs,' said his companion.

'I am not sure of that,' said the tall delegate. 'At any rate there was the free forest.'

'I like that young fellow,' said the tall delegate to his companion, as they descended the staircase.

'He has awful prejudices,' said his friend.

'Well, well; he has his opinions and we have ours. But he is a man; with clear, straightforward ideas, a frank, noble, presence; and as good-looking a fellow as I ever set eyes on. Where are we now?'

'We have only one more name on our list to-day, and it is at hand. Letter K, No. 1, Albany. Another member of the aristocracy, the Honourable Charles Egremont.'

'Well, I prefer them, as far as I can judge, to Wriggle, and Rip, and Thorough Base,' said the tall delegate laughing. 'I dare say we should have found Lord Milford a very jolly fellow, if he had only been up.'

'Here we are,' said his companion, as he knocked. 'Mr. Egremont, is he at home?'

'The gentlemen of the deputation? Yes, my master gave particular orders that he was at home to you. Will you walk in, gentlemen?'

'There you see,' said the tall delegate. 'This would be a lesson to Thorough Base.'

They sat down in an antechamber; the servant opened a mahogany folding-door which he shut after him and announced to his master the arrival of the delegates. Egremont was seated in his library, at a round table covered with writing materials, books, and letters. On another table were arranged his parliamentary papers, and piles of blue books. The room was classically furnished. On the mantel-piece were some ancient vases, which he had brought with him from Italy, standing on each side of that picture of Allori of which we have spoken.

The servant returned to the ante-room, and announcing to the delegates that his master was ready to receive them, ushered into the presence of Egremont—WALTER GERARD and STEPHEN MORLEY.

CHAPTER VI.

IT is much to be deplored that our sacred buildings are generally closed* except at the stated periods of public resort. It is still more to be regretted that when with difficulty entered, there is so much in their arrangements to offend the taste and outrage the feelings. In the tumult of life, a few minutes occasionally passed in the solemn shadow of some lofty and ancient aisle, exercise very often a salutary influence: they purify the heart and elevate the mind; dispel many haunting fancies, and prevent many an act which otherwise might be repented. The church would in this light still afford us a sanctuary; not against the power of the law but against the violence of our own will; not against the passions of man but against our own.

The Abbey of Westminster rises amid the strife of factions. Around its consecrated precinct some of the boldest and some of the worst deeds have been achieved or perpetrated: sacrilege, rapine, murder, and treason. Here robbery has been practised on the greatest scale known in modern ages: here ten thousand manors belonging to the order of the Templars,* without any proof, scarcely with a pretext, were forfeited in one day and divided among the monarch and his chief nobles; here the great estate of the church, which, whatever its articles of faith, belonged and still belongs to the people, was seized at various times, under various pretences, by an assembly that continually changed the religion of their country* and their own by a parliamentary majority, but which never refunded the booty. Here too was brought forth that monstrous conception which even patrician Rome in its most ruthless period never equalled—the mortgaging of the industry of the country* to enrich and to protect property; an act which is now bringing its retributive consequences in a degraded and alienated population. Here too have the innocent been impeached and hunted to death; and a virtuous and able monarch martyred, because, among other benefits projected for his people, he was of opinion that it was more for their advantage that the economic service of the state should be supplied by direct taxation levied by an individual known to all, than by indirect taxation, raised by an irresponsible and fluctuating assembly. But thanks to parliamentary patriotism, the people of England were saved from ship-money,* which money the wealthy paid, and only got in its stead the customs and excise, which the poor mainly supply. Rightly was King Charles surnamed the Martyr; for he was the holocaust of direct taxation. Never yet did man lay down his heroic life for so great a cause: the cause of the Church and the cause of the Poor.

Even now in the quiet times in which we live, when public robbery is out of fashion and takes the milder title of a commission of inquiry, and when there is no treason except voting against a Minister, who, though he may have changed all the policy which you have been elected to support, expects your vote and confidence all the same; even in this age of mean passions and petty risks, it is something to step aside from Palace Yard and instead of listening to a dull debate, where the facts are only a repetition of the blue books you have already read, and the fancy an ingenious appeal to the recrimination of Hansard,* to enter the old abbey and listen to an anthem!

This was a favourite habit of Egremont, and though the mean discipline and sordid arrangements of the ecclesiastical body to which the guardianship of the beautiful edifice is intrusted, have certainly done all that could injure and impair the holy genius of the place, it still was a habit often full of charm and consolation.

There is not perhaps another metropolitan population in the world that would tolerate such conduct as is pursued to 'that great lubber, the public' by the Dean and Chapter of Westminster, and submit in silence to be shut out from the only building in the two cities which is worthy of the name of a cathedral. But the British public will bear anything; they are so busy in speculating in railroad shares.*

When Egremont had entered on his first visit to the Abbey by the south transept, and beheld the boards and the spikes with which he seemed to be environed as if the Abbey were in a state of siege; iron gates shutting him out from the solemn nave and the shadowy aisles; scarcely a glimpse to be caught of a single window; while on a dirty form, some noisy vergers sate like ticket-porters or babbled like tapsters at their ease,—the visions of abbatial perfection in which he had early and often indulged among the ruins of Marney rose on his outraged sense, and he was then about hastily to retire from the scene he had so long purposed to visit, when suddenly the organ burst forth, a celestial symphony floated in the lofty roof, and voices of plaintive melody blended with the swelling sounds. He was fixed to the spot.

Perhaps it was some similar feeling that influenced another individual on the day after the visit of the deputation to Egremont. The sun, though in his summer heaven he had still a long course, had passed his meridian by many hours, the service was performing in the choir, and a few persons entering by the door into that part of the Abbey Church which is so well known by the name of Poet's Corner, proceeded through the unseemly stockade which the chapter have erected, and took their seats. One only, a female, declined to pass, notwithstanding the officious admonitions of the vergers that she had better move on, but approaching the iron grating that shut her out from the body of the church, looked wistfully down the long dim perspective of the beautiful southern aisle. And thus motionless she remained in contemplation, or it might be prayer, while the solemn peals of the organ and the sweet voices of the choir enjoyed that holy liberty for which she sighed, and seemed to wander at their will in every sacred recess and consecrated corner.

The sounds—those mystical and thrilling sounds that at once elevate the soul and touch the heart—ceased, the chaunting of the service recommenced; the motionless form moved; and as she moved Egremont came forth from the choir, and his eye was at once caught by the symmetry of her shape and the picturesque position which she gracefully occupied; still gazing through that grate, while the light pouring through the western window, suffused the body of the church with a soft radiance, just touching the head of the unknown with a kind of halo. Egremont approached the transept door with a lingering pace, so that the stranger, who he observed was preparing to leave the church, might overtake him. As he reached the door, anxious to assure himself that he was not mistaken, he turned round and his eye at once caught the face of Sybil. He started, he trembled; she was not two yards distant, she evidently recognised him; he held open the swinging postern of the Abbey that she might pass, which she did and then stopped on the outside, and said 'Mr. Franklin!'

It was therefore clear that her father had not thought fit, or had not yet had an opportunity, to communicate to Sybil the interview of yesterday. Egremont was still Mr. Franklin. This was perplexing. Egremont would like to have been saved the pain and awkwardness of the avowal, yet it must be made, though not with unnecessary crudeness. And so at present he only expressed his delight, the unexpected delight he experienced at their meeting. And then he walked on by her side.

'Indeed,' said Sybil, 'I can easily imagine you must have been surprised at seeing me in this great city. But many things, strange and unforeseen, have happened to us since you were at Mowedale. You know, of course you with your pursuits must know, that the People have at length resolved to summon their own parliament in Westminster. The people of Mowbray had to send up two delegates to the Convention, and they chose my father for one of them. For so great is their confidence in him none other would content them.'

'He must have made a great sacrifice in coming?' said Egremont.

'Oh! what are sacrifices in such a cause!' said Sybil. 'Yes; he made great sacrifices,' she continued earnestly; 'great sacrifices, and I am proud of them. Our home, which was a happy home, is gone; he has quitted the Traffords to whom we were knit by many, many ties,' and her voice faltered—'and for whom, I know well he would have perilled his life. And now we are parted,' said Sybil, with a sigh, 'perhaps for ever. They offered to receive me under their roof,' she continued, with emotion. 'Had I needed shelter there was another roof which has long awaited me; but I could not leave my father at such a moment. He appealed to me; and I am here. All I desire, all I live for, is to soothe and support him in his great struggle; and I should die content if the People were only free, and a Gerard had freed them.'

Egremont mused: he must disclose all, yet how embarrassing to enter into such explanations in a public thoroughfare! Should he bid her after a-while farewell, and then make his confession in writing? Should he at once accompany her home, and there offer his perplexing explanations? Or should he acknowledge his interview of yesterday with Gerard, and then leave the rest to the natural consequences of that acknowledgment when Sybil met her father! Thus pondering, Egremont and Sybil, quitting the court of the Abbey, entered Abingdon Street.*

'Let me walk home with you,' said Egremont, as Sybil seemed to intimate her intention here to separate.

'My father is not there,' said Sybil; 'but I will not fail to tell him that I have met his old companion.'

'Would he had been as frank!' thought Egremont. And must he quit her in this way? Never! 'You must indeed let me attend you!' he said aloud.

'It is not far,' said Sybil. 'We live almost in the Precinct—in an old house with some kind old people, the brother of one of the nuns of Mowbray. The nearest way to it is straight along this street, but that is too bustling for me. I have discovered,' she added with a smile, 'a more tranquil path.' And guided by her they turned up College Street.

'And how long have you been in London?'

'A fortnight. 'Tis a great prison. How strange it is that, in a vast city like this, one can scarcely walk alone!'

'You want Harold,' said Egremont. 'How is that most faithful of friends?'

'Poor Harold! To part with him too was a pang.'

'I fear your hours must be heavy,' said Egremont.

'Oh! no,' said Sybil, 'there is so much as stake; so much to hear the moment my father returns. I take so much interest too in their discussions; and sometimes I go to hear him speak. None of them can compare with him. It seems to me that it would be impossible to resist our claims if our rulers only heard them from his lips.'

Egremont smiled. 'Your Convention is in its bloom, or rather its bud,' he said; 'all is fresh and pure now; but a little while and it will find the fate of all popular assemblies. You will have factions.'

'But why?' said Sybil. 'They are the real representatives of the people, and all that the people want is justice; that Labour should be as much respected by law and society as Property.'

While they thus conversed they passed through several clean, still streets that had rather the appearance of streets in a very quiet country town than of abodes in the greatest city in the world, and in the vicinity of palaces and parliaments. Rarely was a shop to be remarked among the neat little tenements, many of them built of curious old brick, and all of them raised without any regard to symmetry or proportion. Not the sound of a single wheel was heard; sometimes not a single individual was visible or stirring. Making a circuitous course through this tranquil and orderly district, they at last found themselves in an open place in the centre of which rose a church of vast proportions, and built of hewn stone in that stately, not to say ponderous, style which Vanbrugh* introduced. The area round it, which was sufficiently ample, was formed by buildings, generally of a very mean character: the long back premises of a carpenter, the straggling yard of a hackney-man; sometimes a small, narrow isolated private residence, like a waterspout in which a rat might reside; sometimes a group of houses of more pretension. In the extreme corner of this area, which was dignified by the name of Smith's Square, instead of taking a more appropriate title from the church of St. John which it encircled, was a large old house, that had been masked at the beginning of the century with a modern front of pale-coloured bricks, but which still stood in its courtyard surrounded by its iron railings, withdrawn as it were from the vulgar gaze like an individual who had known higher fortunes, and blending with his humility something of the reserve which is prompted by the memory of vanished greatness.

'This is my home,' said Sybil. 'We lodge here with some kind people that we were recommended to by the good priest at Mowbray. It is a still place and suits us well.'

Near the house was a narrow passage which was a thoroughfare into the most populous quarter of the neighbourhood. As Egremont was opening the gate of the courtyard, Gerard ascended the steps of this passage and approached them.

CHAPTER VII.

WHEN Gerard and Morley quitted the Albany after their visit to Egremont, they separated, and Stephen, whom we will accompany, proceeded in the direction of the Temple, in the vicinity of which he himself lodged, and where he was about to visit a brother journalist, who occupied chambers in that famous inn of court. As he passed under Temple Bar* his eye caught a portly gentleman stepping out of a public cab with a bundle of papers in his hand, and immediately disappearing through that well-known archway which Morley was on the point of reaching. The gentleman indeed was still in sight, descending the way, when Morley entered, who observed him drop a letter. Morley hailed him, but in vain; and fearing the stranger might disappear in one of the many inextricable courts, and so lose his letter, he ran forward, picked up the paper, and then pushed on to the person who dropped it, calling out so frequently that the stranger at length began to suspect that he himself might be the object of the salute, and stopped and looked round. Morley almost mechanically glanced at the outside of the letter, the seal of which was broken, and which was however addressed to a name that immediately fixed his interest. The direction was to 'Baptist Hatton, Esq., Inner Temple.'

'This letter is I believe addressed to you, Sir,' said Morley, looking very intently upon the person to whom he spoke—a portly man and a comely; florid, gentleman-like, but with as little of the expression which Morley in imagination had associated with that Hatton over whom he once pondered, as can easily be imagined.

'Sir, I am extremely obliged to you,' said the strange gentleman; 'the letter belongs to me, though it is not addressed to me. I must have this moment dropped it. My name, Sir, is Firebrace—Sir Vavasour Firebrace, and this letter is addressed to a—a—not exactly my lawyer, but a gentleman—a professional gentleman—whom I am in the habit of frequently seeing; daily, I may say. He is employed in a great question in which I am deeply interested. Sir, I am vastly obliged to you, and I trust that you are satisfied.'

'Oh! perfectly, Sir Vavasour;' and Morley bowed; and going in different directions, they separated.

'Do you happen to know a lawyer by name Hatton in this Inn?' inquired Morley of his friend the journalist, when, having transacted their business, the occasion served.

'No lawyer of that name; but the famous Hatton lives here,' was the reply.

'The famous Hatton! And what is he famous for? You forget I am a provincial.'

'He has made more peers of the realm than our gracious Sovereign,' said the journalist. 'And since the reform of parliament the only chance of a Tory becoming a peer is the favour of Baptist Hatton; though who he is no one knows, and what he is no one can describe.'

'You speak in conundrums,' said Morley; 'I wish I could guess them. Try to adapt yourself to my somewhat simple capacity.'

'In a word, then,' said his friend, 'if you must have a definition, Hatton may rank under the genus 'antiquary,' though his species is more difficult to describe. He is a heraldic antiquary; a discoverer, inventor, framer, arranger of pedigrees; profound in the mysteries of genealogies; an authority I believe unrivalled in everything that concerns the constitution and elements of the House of Lords; consulted by lawyers, though not professing the law; and startling and alarming the noblest families in the country by claiming the ancient baronies which they have often assumed without authority, for obscure pretenders, many of whom he has succeeded in seating in the parliament of his country.'

'And what part of the country did he come from; do you happen to know?' inquired Morley, evidently much interested, though he attempted to conceal his emotion.

'He may be a veritable subject of the kingdom of Cockaigne,* for aught I know,' replied his friend. 'He has been buried in this inn I believe for years; for very many before I settled here; and for a long time I apprehend was sufficiently obscure, though doing they say a great deal in a small way; but the Mallory case made his fortune about ten years ago. That was a barony by writ of summons which had been claimed a century before, and failed. Hatton seated his man, and the precedent enabled three or four more gentlemen under his auspices to follow that example. They were Roman Catholics, which probably brought him the Mallory case, for Hatton is of the old church; better than that, they were all gentlemen of great estate, and there is no doubt their champion was well rewarded for his successful service. They say he is very rich. At present all the business of the country connected with descents flows into his chambers. Not a pedigree in dispute, not a peerage in abeyance,* which is not submitted to his consideration. I don't know him personally; but you can now form some idea of his character; and if you want to claim a peerage,' the journalist added laughingly, 'he is your man.'

A strong impression was on the mind of Morley that this was his man; he resolved to inquire of Gerard, whom he should see in the evening, as to the fact of their Hatton being a Catholic, and if so, to call on the antiquary on the morrow.

In the meantime we must not forget one who is already making that visit. Sir Vavasour Firebrace is seated in a spacious library that looks upon the Thames and the gardens of the Temple. Though piles of parchments and papers cover the numerous tables, and in many parts intrude upon the Turkey carpet, an air of order, of comfort, and of taste, pervades the chamber. The hangings of crimson damask silk blend with the antique furniture of oak; the upper panes of the windows are tinted by the brilliant pencil of feudal Germany, while the choice volumes that line the shelves are clothed in bindings which become their rare contents. The master of this apartment was a man of ordinary height, inclined to corpulency, and in the wane of middle life, though his unwrinkled cheek, his undimmed blue eye, and his brown hair, very apparent, though he wore a cap of black velvet, did not betray his age, or the midnight studies by which he had in a great degree acquired that learning for which he was celebrated. The general expression of his countenance was pleasing, though dashed with a trait of the sinister. He was seated in an easy chair, before a kidney table* at which he was writing. Near at hand was a long tall oaken desk, on which were several folio volumes open, and some manuscripts which denoted that he had recently been engaged with them. At present Mr. Hatton, with his pen still in his hand and himself in a chamber-robe of the same material as his cap, leant back in his chair, while he listened to his client, Sir Vavasour. Several most beautiful black and tan spaniels of the breed of King Charles the Second were reposing near him on velvet cushions, with a haughty luxuriousness which would have become the beauties of the merry monarch; and a white Persian cat* with blue eyes and a very long tail, with a visage not altogether unlike that of its master, was resting with great gravity on the writing-table, and assisting at the conference.

Sir Vavasour had evidently been delivering himself of a long narrative, to which Mr. Hatton had listened with that imperturbable patience which characterised him, and which was unquestionably one of the elements of his success. He never gave up anything, and he never interrupted anybody. And now in a silvery voice he replied to his visitor:

'What you tell me, Sir Vavasour, is what I foresaw, but which, as my influence could not affect it, I dismissed from my thoughts. You came to me for a specific object. I accomplished it. I undertook to ascertain the rights and revive the claims of the baronets of England. That was what you required of me; I fulfilled your wish. Those rights are ascertained; those claims are revived. A great majority of the Order have given in their adhesion to the organized movement. The nation is acquainted with your demands, accustomed to them, and the monarch once favourably received them. I can do no more; I do not pretend to make baronets, still less can I confer on those already made the right to wear stars and coronets, the dark green dress of equites aurati, or white hats with white plumes of feathers. These distinctions, even if their previous usage were established, must flow from the gracious permission of the Crown, and no one could expect in an age hostile to personal distinctions, that any ministry would recommend the sovereign to a step which with vulgar minds would be odious, and by malignant ones might be rendered ridiculous.'

'Ridiculous!' said Sir Vavasour.

'All the world,' said Mr. Hatton, 'do not take upon these questions the same enlightened view as ourselves, Sir Vavasour. I never could for a moment believe that the Sovereign would consent to invest such a numerous body of men with such privileges.'

'But you never expressed this opinion,' said Sir Vavasour.

'You never asked for my opinion,' said Mr. Hatton; 'and if I had given it, you and your friends would not have been influenced by it. The point was one on which you might with reason hold yourselves as competent judges as I am. All you asked of me was to make out your case, and I made it out. I will venture to say a better case never left these chambers; I do not believe there is a person in the kingdom who could answer it except myself. They have refused the Order their honours, Sir Vavasour, but it is some consolation that they have never answered their case.'

'I think it only aggravates the oppression,' said Sir Vavasour, shaking his head; 'but cannot you advise any new step, Mr. Hatton? After so many years of suspense, after so much anxiety and such a vast expenditure, it really is too bad that I and Lady Firebrace should be announced at court in the same style as our fishmonger, if he happens to be a sheriff.'*

'I can make a Peer,' said Mr. Hatton, leaning back in his chair and playing with his seals, 'but I do not pretend to make Baronets. I can place a coronet with four balls on a man's brow; but a coronet with two balls* is an exercise of the prerogative with which I do not presume to interfere.'

'I mention it in the utmost confidence,' said Sir Vavasour in a whisper; 'but Lady Firebrace has a sort of promise that in the event of a change of government, we shall be in the first batch of peers.'

Mr. Hatton shook his head with a slight smile of contemptuous incredulity.

'Sir Robert,' he said, 'will make no peers; take my word for that. The Whigs and I have so deluged the House of Lords, that you may rely upon it as a secret of state, that if the Tories come in, there will be no peers made. I know the Queen is sensitively alive to the cheapening of all honours of late years. If the Whigs go out to-morrow, mark me, they will disappoint all their friends. Their underlings have promised so many, that treachery is inevitable, and if they deceive some they may as well deceive all. Perhaps they may distribute a coronet or two among themselves; and I shall this year make three;* and those are the only additions to the peerage which will occur for many years. You may rely on that. For the Tories will make none, and I have some thoughts of retiring from business.'

It is difficult to express the astonishment, the perplexity, the agitation, that pervaded the countenance of Sir Vavasour while his companion thus coolly delivered himself. High hopes extinguished and excited at the same moment; cherished promises vanishing, mysterious expectations rising up; revelations of astounding state secrets; chief ministers voluntarily renouncing their highest means of influence, and an obscure private individual distributing those distinctions which sovereigns were obliged to hoard, and to obtain which the first men in the country were ready to injure their estates and to sacrifice their honour! At length

Sir Vavasour said, 'You amaze me Mr. Hatton. I could mention to you twenty members of Boodle's,* at least, who believe they will be made peers the moment the Tories come in!'

'Not a man of them,' said Hatton peremptorily. 'Tell me one of their names, and I will tell you whether they will be made peers.'

'Well then there is Mr. Tubbe Sweete, a county member, and his son in parliament too—I know he has a promise.'

'I repeat to you, Sir Vavasour, the Tories will not make a single peer; the candidates must come to me; and I ask you what can I do for a Tubbe Sweete, the son of a Jamaica cooper? Are there any old families among your twenty members of Boodle's?'

'Why I can hardly say,' said Sir Vavasour; 'there is Sir Charles Featherly, an old baronet.'

'The founder a lord mayor in James the First's reign. That is not the sort of old family that I mean,' said Mr. Hatton.

'Well there is Colonel Cockawhoop,' said Sir Vavasour. 'The Cockawhoops are a very good family I have always heard.'

'Contractors of Queen Anne; partners with Marlborough and Solomon Medina;* a very good family indeed: but I do not make peers out of good families, Sir Vavasour; old families are the blocks out of which I cut my Mercurys.'

'But what do you call an old family?' said Sir Vavasour.

'Yours,' said Mr. Hatton, and he threw a full glance on the countenance on which the light rested.

'We were in the first batch of baronets,' said Sir Vavasour.

'Forget the baronets for a while,' said Hatton, 'Tell me, what was your family before James the First?'

'They always lived on their lands,' said Sir Vavasour. 'I have a room full of papers that would perhaps tell us something about them. Would you like to see them?'

'By all means; bring them all here. Not that I want them to inform me of your rights; I am fully acquainted with them. You would like to be a peer, sir. Well, you are really Lord Vavasour, but there is a difficulty in establishing your undoubted right from the single writ of summons* difficulty. I will not trouble you with technicalities, Sir Vavasour; sufficient that the difficulty is great though perhaps not unmanageable. But we have no need of management. Your claim on the barony of Lovel is very good: I could recommend your pursuing it, did not another more inviting still present itself. In a word, if you wish to be Lord Bardolf,* I will undertake to make you so, before, in all probability, Sir Robert Peel obtains office; and that I should think would gratify Lady Firebrace.'

'Indeed it would,' said Sir Vavasour, 'for if it had not been for this sort of a promise of a peerage made—I speak in great confidence Mr. Hatton—made by Mr. Taper, my tenants would have voted for the Whigs the other day at the ———shire election, and the Conservative candidate would have been beaten. Lord Masque had almost arranged it, but Lady Firebrace would have a written promise from a high quarter, and so it fell to the ground.'

'Well we are independent of all these petty arrangements now,' said Mr. Hatton.

'It is very wonderful,' said Sir Vavasour, rising from his chair and speaking as it were to himself. 'And what do you think our expenses will be in this claim?' he inquired.

'Bagatelle!' said Mr. Hatton. 'Why a dozen years ago I have known men lay out nearly half a million in land and not get two per cent. for their money, in order to obtain a borough influence which might ultimately obtain them a spick and span coronet; and now you are going to put one on your head, which will give you precedence over every peer on the roll, except three (and I made those), and it will not cost you a paltry twenty or thirty thousand pounds. Why I know men who would give that for the precedence alone.—Here!' and he rose and took up some papers from a table: 'Here is a case; a man you know, I dare say; an earl, and of a decent date as earls go; George the First. The first baron was a Dutch valet of William the Third. Well I am to terminate an abeyance in his favour through his mother, and give him one of the baronies of the Herberts. He buys off the other claimant who is already ennobled with a larger sum than you will expend on your ancient coronet. Nor is that all. The other claimant is of French descent and name; came over at the revocation of the Edict of Nantes.* Well, besides the hush money, my client is to defray all the expense of attempting to transform the descendant of the silkweaver of Lyons into the heir of a Norman conqueror. So you see, Sir Vavasour, I am not unreasonable. Pah! I would sooner gain five thousand pounds by restoring you to your rights, than fifty thousand in establishing any of these pretenders in their base assumptions. I must work in my craft, Sir Vavasour, but I love the old English blood, and have it in my veins.'

'I am satisfied, Mr. Hatton,' said Sir Vavasour; 'let no time be lost. All I regret is, that you did not mention all this to me before; and then we might have saved a great deal of trouble and expence.'

'You never consulted me,' said Mr. Hatton. 'You gave me your instructions, and I obeyed them. I was sorry to see you in that mind, for to speak frankly, and I am sure now you will not be offended, my lord, for such is your real dignity, there is no title in the world for which I have such a contempt as that of a baronet.'

Sir Vavasour winced, but the future was full of glory and the present of excitement; and he wished Mr. Hatton good morning, with a promise that he would himself bring the papers on the morrow.

Mr. Hatton was buried for a few moments in a reverie, during which he played with the tail of the Persian cat.

CHAPTER VIII.

WE left Sybil and Egremont just at the moment that Gerard arrived at the very threshold which they had themselves reached.

'Ah! my father,' exclaimed Sybil, and then with a faint blush of which she was perhaps unconscious, she added, as if apprehensive Gerard would not recall his old companion, 'you remember Mr. Franklin?'

'This gentleman and myself had the pleasure of meeting yesterday,' said Gerard, embarrassed, while Egremont himself changed colour and was infinitely confused. Sybil felt surprised that her father should have met Mr. Franklin and not have mentioned a circumstance natur-ally interesting to her. Egremont was about to speak when the street-door was opened. And were they to part again, and no explanation? And was Sybil to be left with her father, who was evidently in no haste, per-haps had no great tendency, to give that explanation? Every feeling of an ingenuous spirit urged Egremont personally to terminate this prolonged misconception.

'You will permit me, I hope,' he said, appealing as much to Gerard as to his daughter, 'to enter with you for a few moments.'

It was not possible to resist such a request, yet it was conceded on the part of Gerard with no cordiality. So they entered the large gloomy hall of the house, and towards the end of a long passage Gerard opened a door, and they all went into a spacious melancholy room, situate at the back of the house, and looking upon a small square plot of dank grass, in the midst of which rose a very weather-stained Cupid, with one arm broken, and the other raised in the air with a long shell to its mouth. It seemed that in old days it might have been a fountain. At the end of the plot the blind side of a house offered a high wall which had once been painted in fresco. Though much of the coloured plaster had cracked and peeled away, and all that remained was stained and faded, still some traces of the original design might yet be detected: festive wreaths, the colonnades and perspective of a palace.

The walls of the room itself were wainscotted in panels of dark-stained wood; the window-curtains were of coarse green worsted, and encrusted with dust so ancient and irremovable, that it presented almost a lava-like appearance; the carpet, that had once been bright and showy, was entirely threadbare, and had become grey with age. There were several heavy mahogany arm-chairs in the room, a Pembroke table, and an immense unwieldy sideboard, garnished with a few wine-glasses of a deep blue colour. Over the lofty uncouth mantel was a por-trait of the Marquis of Granby, which might have been a sign, and opposite to him, over the sideboard, was a large tawdry-coloured print, by Bunbury, of Ranelagh* in its most festive hour. The general appear-ance of the room, however, though dingy, was not squalid; and what with its spaciousness, its extreme repose, and the associations raised by such few images as it did suggest, the impression on the mind of the spectator was far from unpleasing, partaking indeed of that vague mel-ancholy which springs from the contemplation of the past, and which at all times softens the spirit.

Gerard walked to the window and looked at the grass-plot; Sybil seating herself invited their guest to follow her example; Egremont, not without agitation, seemed suddenly to make an effort to collect himself, and then, in a voice not distinguished by its accustomed clearness, he said, 'I explained yesterday to one who I hope I may still call my friend, why I assumed a name to which I have no right.'

Sybil started a little, slightly stared, but did not speak.

'I should be happy if you also would give me credit, in taking that step, at least for motives of which I need not be ashamed; even,' he added in a hesitating voice, 'even if you deemed my conduct indiscreet.'

Their eyes met: astonishment was imprinted on the countenance of Sybil, but she uttered not a word; and her father, whose back was turned to them, did not move.

'I was told,' continued Egremont, 'that an impassable gulf divided the Rich from the Poor; I was told that the Privileged and the People formed Two Nations, governed by different laws, influenced by differ-ent manners, with no thoughts or sympathies in common; with an innate inability of mutual comprehension. I believed that if this were indeed the case, the ruin of our common country was at hand; I would have endeavoured, feebly perchance, but not without zeal, to resist such a catastrophe; I possessed a station which entailed on me some portion of its responsibility; to obtain that knowledge which could alone qualify me for beneficial action, I resolved to live without suspi-cion among my fellow-subjects who were estranged from me; even void of all celebrity as I am, I could not have done that without suspicion, had I been known; they would have recoiled from my class and my name, as you yourself recoiled, Sybil, when they were once accidentally mentioned before you. These are the reasons, these the feelings, which impelled, I will not say justified, me to pass your threshold under a feigned name. I entreat you to judge kindly of my conduct; to pardon me; and not to make me feel the bitterness that I have forfeited the good opinion of one for whom, under all circumstances and in all situations, I must ever feel the highest conceivable respect,—I would say a reverential regard.'

His tones of passionate emotion ceased. Sybil, with a countenance beautiful and disturbed, gazed at him for an instant, and seemed about to speak, but her trembling lips refused the office; then with an effort, turning to Gerard, she said, 'My father, I am amazed; tell me, then, who is this gentleman who addresses me?'

'The brother of Lord Marney, Sybil,' said Gerard, turning to her.

'The brother of Lord Marney!' repeated Sybil, with an air almost of stupor.

'Yes,' said Egremont; 'a member of that family of sacrilege, of those oppressors of the people, whom you have denounced to me with such withering scorn.'

The elbow of Sybil rested on the arm of her chair, and her cheek upon her hand; as Egremont said these words she shaded her face, which was thus entirely unseen: for some moments there was silence. Then looking up with an expression grave but serene, and as if she had just emerged from some deep thinking, Sybil said, 'I am sorry for my words; sorry for the pain I unconsciously gave you; sorry indeed for all that has past; and that my father has lost a pleasant friend.'

'And why should he be lost?' said Egremont mournfully, and yet with tenderness. 'Why should we not still be friends?'

'Oh, sir!' said Sybil, haughtily; 'I am one of those who believe the gulf is impassable. Yes,' she added, slightly but with singular grace waving her hands, and somewhat turning away her head, 'utterly impassable.'

There are tumults of the mind when like the great convulsions of nature all seems anarchy and returning chaos, yet often in those moments of vast disturbance, as in the material strife itself, some new principle of order, or some new impulse of conduct, develops itself, and controls and regulates and brings to an harmonious consequence, passions and elements which seemed only to threaten despair and subversion. So it was with Egremont. He looked for a moment in despair upon this maiden walled out from sympathy by prejudices and convictions more impassable than all the mere consequences of class. He looked for a moment, but only for a moment, in despair. He found in his tortured spirit energies that responded to the exigency of the occasion. Even the otherwise embarrassing presence of Gerard would not have prevented—but just at this moment the door opened, and Morley and another person entered the room.

CHAPTER IX.

MORLEY paused as he recognised Egremont; then advancing to Gerard, followed by his companion, he said, 'This is Mr. Hatton of whom we were speaking last night, and who claims to be an ancient acquaintance of yours.'

'Perhaps I should rather say of your poor dear father,' said Hatton, scanning Gerard with his clear blue eye, and then he added, 'He was of great service to me in my youth, and one is not apt to forget such things.'

'One ought not,' said Gerard; 'but it is a sort of memory, as I have understood, that is rather rare. For my part I remember you very well, Baptist Hatton,' said Gerard, examining his guest with almost as complete a scrutiny as he had himself experienced. 'The world has gone well with you, I am glad to hear and see.'

'Qui laborat, orat,'* said Hatton in a silvery voice, 'is the gracious maxim of our Holy Church; and I venture to believe my prayers and vigils have been accepted, for I have laboured in my time,' and as he was speaking these words, he turned and addressed them to Sybil.

She beheld him with no little interest; this mysterious name that had sounded so often in her young ears, and was associated with so many strange and high hopes, and some dark blending of doubt and apprehension and discordant thoughts. Hatton in his appearance realised little of the fancies in which Sybil had sometimes indulged with regard to him. That appearance was prepossessing: a frank and even benevolent expression played upon his intelligent and handsome countenance; his once rich brown hair, still long though very thin, was so arranged as naturally to conceal his baldness; he was dressed with great simplicity, but with remarkable taste and care; nor did the repose and suavity of his manner and the hushed tone of his voice detract from the favourable effect that he always at once produced.

'Qui laborat, orat,' said Sybil with a smile, 'is the privilege of the people.'

'Of whom I am one,' said Hatton bowing, well recollecting that he was addressing the daughter of a Chartist delegate.

'But is your labour, their labour,' said Sybil. 'Is yours that life of uncomplaining toil wherein there is so much of beauty and of goodness, that by the fine maxim of our Church, it is held to include the force and efficacy of prayer?'

'I am sure that I should complain of no toil that would benefit you,' said Hatton; and then addressing himself again to Gerard, he led him to a distant part of the room where they were soon engaged in earnest converse. Morley at the same moment approached Sybil, and spoke to her in a subdued tone. Egremont feeling embarrassed advanced, and bade her farewell. She rose and returned his salute with some ceremony; then hesitating while a soft expression came over her countenance, she held forth her hand, which he retained for a moment, and withdrew.

'I was with him more than an hour,' continued Morley. 'At first he recollected nothing; even the name of Gerard, though he received it as familiar to him, seemed to produce little impression; he recollected nothing of any papers; was clear that they must have been quite insignificant; whatever they were, he doubtless had them now, as he never destroyed papers; would order a search to be made for them, and so on. I was about to withdraw, when he asked me carelessly a question about your father; what he was doing, and whether he were married and had children. This led to a very long conversation in which he suddenly seemed to take great interest. At first he talked of writing to see your father, and I offered that Gerard should call upon him. He took down your direction in order that he might write to your father and give him an appointment; when observing that it was Westminster, he said that his carriage was ordered to go to the House of Lords in a quarter of an hour, and that if not inconvenient to me, he would propose that I should at once accompany him. I thought, whatever might be the result, it must be a satisfaction to Gerard at last to see this man of whom he has talked and thought so much—and so we are here.'

'You did well, good Stephen, as you always do,' said Sybil with a musing and abstracted air; 'no one has so much forethought and so much energy as you.'

He threw a glance at her; and immediately withdrew it. Their eyes had met: hers were kind and calm.

'And this Egremont,' said Morley rather hurriedly and abruptly, and looking on the ground, 'how came he here? When we discovered him yesterday your father and myself agreed that we should not mention to you the—the mystification of which we had been dupes.'

'And you did wrong,' said Sybil. 'There is no wisdom like frankness. Had you told me, he would not have been here to-day. He met and addressed me, and I only recognised an acquaintance who had once contributed so much to the pleasantness of our life. Had he not accompanied me to this door and met my father, which precipitated an explanation on his part which he found had not been given by others, I might have remained in an ignorance which hereafter might have produced inconvenience.'

'You are right,' said Morley, looking at her rather keenly. 'We have all of us opened ourselves too unreservedly before this aristocrat.'

'I should hope that none of us have said to him a word that we wish to be forgotten,' said Sybil. 'He chose to wear a disguise, and can hardly quarrel with the frankness with which we spoke of his order or his family. And for the rest, he has not been injured from learning something of the feelings of the people by living among them.'

'And yet if anything were to happen to-morrow,' said Morley, 'rest assured this man has his eye on us. He can walk into the government offices like themselves and tell his tale, for though one of the pseudo-opposition, the moment the people move, the factions become united.'

Sybil turned and looked at him, and then said, 'And what could happen to-morrow, that we should care for the government being acquainted with it or us? Do not they know everything? Do not you meet in their very sight? You pursue an avowed and legal aim by legal means—do you not? What then is there to fear? And why should anything happen that should make us apprehensive?'

'All is very well at this moment,' said Morley, 'and all may continue well; but popular assemblies breed turbulent spirits, Sybil. Your father takes a leading part; he is a great orator, and is in his element in this clamorous and fiery life. It does not much suit me; I am a man of the closet. This Convention, as you well know, was never much to my taste. Their Charter is a coarse specific for our social evils. The spirit that would cure our ills must be of a deeper and finer mood.'

'Then why are you here?' said Sybil.

Morley shrugged his shoulders, and then said, 'An easy question. Questions are always easy. The fact is, in active life one cannot afford to refine. I could have wished the movement to have taken a different shape and to have worked for a different end; but it has not done this. But it is still a movement and a great one, and I must work it for my end and try to shape it to my form. If I had refused to be a leader, I should not have prevented the movement; I should only have secured my own insignificance.'

'But my father has not these fears; he is full of hope and exultation,' said Sybil. 'And surely it is a great thing that the people should have their Parliament lawfully meeting in open day, and their delegates from the whole realm declaring their grievances in language which would not disgrace the conquering race which has in vain endeavoured to degrade them. When I heard my father speak the other night, my heart glowed with emotion; my eyes were suffused with tears; I was proud to be his daughter; and I gloried in a race of forefathers who belonged to the oppressed and not to the oppressors.'

Morley watched the deep splendour of her eye and the mantling of her radiant cheek, as she spoke these latter words with not merely animation but fervour. Her bright hair, that hung on either side her face in long tresses of luxuriant richness, was drawn off a forehead that was the very throne of thought and majesty, while her rich lip still quivered with the sensibility which expressed its impassioned truth.

'But your father, Sybil, stands alone,' at length Morley replied; 'surrounded by votaries who have nothing but enthusiasm to recommend them; and by emulous and intriguing rivals, who watch every word and action, in order that they may discredit his conduct, and ultimately secure his downfall.'

'My father's downfall!' said Sybil. 'Is he not one of themselves! And is it possible, that among the delegates of the People there can be other than one and the same object?'

'A thousand,' said Morley; 'we have already as many parties as in St. Stephen's* itself.'

'You terrify me,' said Sybil. 'I knew we had fearful odds to combat against. My visit to this city alone has taught me how strong are our enemies. But I believed that we had on our side God and Truth.'

'They know neither of them in the National Convention,' said Morley. 'Our career will be a vulgar caricature of the bad passions and the low intrigues, the factions and the failures, of our oppressors.'

At this moment Gerard and Hatton who were sitting in the remote part of the room rose together and advanced forward; and this movement interrupted the conversation of Sybil and Morley. Before however her father and his new friend could reach them, Hatton as if some point on which he had not been sufficiently explicit, had occurred to him, stopped and placing his hand on Gerard's arm, withdrew him again, saying in a voice which could only be heard by the individual whom he addressed, 'You understand—I have not the slightest doubt myself of your moral right: I believe on every principle of justice, that Mowbray Castle is as much yours as the house that is built by the tenant on the lord's land: but can we prove it? We never had the legal evidence. You are in error in supposing that these papers were of any vital consequence; mere memoranda; very useful no doubt; I hope I shall find them; but of no validity. If money were the only difficulty, trust me, it should not be wanting; I owe much to the memory of your father, my good Gerard; I would fain serve you—and your daughter. I'll not tell you what I would do for you, my good Gerard. You would think me foolish; but I am alone in the world, and seeing you again, and talking of old times—I really am scarcely fit for business. Go, however, I must; I have an appointment at the House of Lords. Good bye. I must say farewell to the Lady Sybil.'

CHAPTER X.

'YOU can't have that table, sir, it is engaged,' said a waiter at the Athenæum* to a member of the club who seemed unmindful of the type of appropriation which in the shape of an inverted plate, ought to have warned him off the coveted premises.

'It is always engaged,' grumbled the member. 'Who has taken it?'

'Mr. Hatton, sir.'

And indeed at this very moment, it being about eight o'clock of the same day on which the meeting detailed in the last chapter had occurred, a very handsome dark brougham with a beautiful horse was stopping in Waterloo Place before the portico of the Athenæum Clubhouse, from which equipage immediately emerged the prosperous person of Baptist Hatton.

This club was Hatton's only relaxation. He had never entered society; and now his habits were so formed, the effort would have been a painful one; though with a first-rate reputation in his calling and supposed to be rich, the openings were numerous to a familiar intercourse with those middle-aged nameless gentlemen of easy circumstances who haunt clubs, and dine a great deal at each others' houses and chambers; men who travel regularly a little, and gossip regularly a great deal; who lead a sort of facile, slipshod existence, doing nothing, yet mightily interested in what others do; great critics of little things; profuse in minor luxuries and inclined to the respectable practice of a decorous profligacy; peering through the window of a club-house as if they were discovering a planet; and usually much excited about things with which they have no concern, and personages who never heard of them.

All this was not in Hatton's way, who was free from all pretension, and who had acquired, from his severe habits of historical research, a respect only for what was authentic. These nonentities flitted about him, and he shrunk from an existence that seemed to him at once dull and trifling. He had a few literary acquaintances that he had made at the Antiquarian Society,* of which he was a distinguished member; a vice-president of that body had introduced him to the Athenæum. It was the first and only club that Hatton had ever belonged to, and he delighted in it. He liked splendour and the light and bustle of a great establishment. They saved him from that melancholy which after a day of action is the doom of energetic celibacy. A luxurious dinner without trouble, suited him after his exhaustion; sipping his claret, he revolved his plans. Above all, he revelled in the magnificent library, and perhaps was never happier, than when after a stimulating repast he adjourned up stairs, and buried himself in an easy chair with Dugdale or Selden, or an erudite treatise on forfeiture or abeyance.*

To-day however Hatton was not in this mood. He came in exhausted and excited; ate rapidly and rather ravenously; despatched a pint of champagne; and then called for a bottle of Lafitte. His table cleared; a devilled biscuit* placed before him, a cool bottle and a fresh glass, he indulged in that reverie, which the tumult of his feelings and the physical requirements of existence had hitherto combined to prevent.

'A strange day,' he thought, as with an abstracted air he filled his glass, and sipping the wine, leant back in his chair. 'The son of Walter Gerard! A Chartist delegate! The best blood in England! What would I not be, were it mine.

'Those infernal papers! They made my fortune—and yet, I know not how it is, the deed has cost me many a pang. Yet it seemed innoxious! the old man dead—insolvent; myself starving; his son ignorant of all, to whom too they could be of no use, for it required thousands to work them, and even with thousands they could only be worked by myself. Had I not done it, I should ere this probably have been swept from the surface of the earth, worn out with penury, disease, and heart-ache. And now I am Baptist Hatton with a fortune almost large enough to buy Mowbray itself, and with knowledge that can make the proudest tremble.

'And for what object all this wealth and power? What memory shall I leave? What family shall I found? Not a relative in the world, except a solitary barbarian, from whom when, years ago, I visited him as a stranger I recoiled with unutterable loathing.

'Ah! had I a child—a child like the beautiful daughter of Gerard!'

And here mechanically Hatton filled his glass, and quaffed at once a bumper.

'And I have deprived her of a principality! That seraphic being whose lustre even now haunts my vision; the ring of whose silver tone even now lingers in my ear. He must be a fiend who could injure her. I am that fiend. Let me see—let me see!'

And now he seemed wrapt in the very paradise of some creative vision; still he filled the glass, but this time he only sipped it, as if he were afraid to disturb the clustering images around him.

'Let me see—let me see. I could make her a baroness. Gerard is as much Baron Valence as Shrewsbury is a Talbot. Her name is Sybil.* Curious how, even when peasants, the good blood keeps the good old family names! The Valences were ever Sybils.

'I could make her a baroness. Yes! and I could give her wherewith to endow her state. I could compensate for the broad lands which should be hers, and which perhaps through me she has forfeited.

'Could I do more? Could I restore her to the rank she would honour, assuage these sharp pangs of conscience, and achieve the secret ambition of my life? What if my son were to be Lord Valence?

'Is it too bold? A Chartist delegate—a peasant's daughter. With all that shining beauty that I witnessed, with all the marvellous gifts that their friend Morley so descanted on,—would she shrink from me? I'm not a crook-backed Richard.*

'I could proffer much: I feel I could urge it plausibly. She must be very wretched. With such a form, such high imaginings, such thoughts of power and pomp as I could breathe in her,—I think she'd melt. And to one of her own faith, too! To build up a great Catholic house again; of the old blood, and the old names, and the old faith,—by holy Mary it is a glorious vision!'

CHAPTER XI.

On the evening of the day that Egremont had met Sybil in the Abbey of Westminster, and subsequently parted from her under circumstances so distressing, the Countess of Marney held a great assembly at the family mansion in St. James' Square, which Lord Marney had intended to have let to a new club, and himself and his family to have taken refuge for a short season at an hotel, but he drove so hard a bargain that before the lease was signed, the new club, which mainly consisted of an ingenious individual who had created himself secretary, had vanished Then it was agreed that the family mansion should be inhabited for the season by the family; and to-night Arabella was receiving all that great world of which she herself was a distinguished ornament.

'We come to you as early as possible my dear Arabella,' said Lady Deloraine to her daughter-in-law.

'You are always so good! Have you seen Charles? I was in hopes he would have come,' Lady Marney added in a somewhat mournful tone.

'He is at the House; otherwise I am sure he would have been here,' said Lady Deloraine, glad that she had so good a reason for an absence, which under any circumstances she well knew would have occurred.

'I fear you will be sadly in want of beaus this evening, my love. We dined at the Duke of Fitz-Aquitaine's, and all our cavaliers vanished. They talk of an early division.'

'I really wish all these divisions were over,' said Lady Marney. 'They are very anti-social. Ah! here is Lady de Mowbray.'

Alfred Mountchesney hovered round Lady Joan Fitz-Warene, who was gratified by the devotion of the Cupid of May Fair. He uttered inconceivable nothings, and she replied to him in incomprehensible somethings. Her learned profundity and his vapid lightness effectively contrasted. Occasionally he caught her eye and conveyed to her the anguish of his soul in a glance of self-complacent softness.

Lady St. Julians, leaning on the arm of the Duke of Fitz-Aquitaine, stopped to speak to Lady Joan. Lady St. Julians was determined that the heiress of Mowbray should marry one of her sons. She watched therefore with a restless eye all those who attempted to monopolize Lady Joan's attention, and contrived perpetually to interfere with their manoeuvres. In the midst of a delightful conversation that seemed to approach a crisis, Lady St. Julians was sure to advance, and interfere with some affectionate appeal to Lady Joan, whom she called her 'dear child' and 'sweetest love,' while she did not deign even to notice the unhappy cavalier whom she had thus as it were unhorsed.

'My sweet child!' said Lady St. Julians to Lady Joan, 'you have no idea how unhappy Frederick is this evening, but he cannot leave the House, and I fear it will be a late affair.'

Lady Joan looked as if the absence or presence of Frederick was to her a matter of great indifference, and then she added, 'I do not think the division so important as is generally imagined. A defeat upon a question of colonial government does not appear to me of sufficient weight to dissolve a cabinet.'

'Any defeat will do that now,' said Lady St. Julians, 'but to tell you the truth I am not very sanguine. Lady Deloraine says they will be beat:

she says the Radicals will desert them; but I am not so sure. Why should the Radicals desert them? And what have we done for the Radicals? Had we indeed foreseen this Jamaica business, and asked some of them to dinner, or given a ball or two to their wives and daughters! I am sure if I had had the least idea that we had so good a chance of coming in, I should not have cared myself to have done something; even to have invited their women.'

'But you are such a capital partisan, Lady St. Julians,' said the Duke of Fitz-Aquitaine, who with the viceroyalty of Ireland dexterously dangled before his eyes for the last two years, had become a thorough Conservative and had almost as much confidence in Sir Robert as in Lord Stanley.*

'I have made great sacrifices,' said Lady St. Julians. 'I went once and stayed a week at Lady Jenny Spinner's to gain her looby of a son and his eighty thousand a-year, and Lord St. Julians proposed him at White's; and then after all the Whigs made him a peer! They certainly make more of their social influences than we do. That affair of that Mr. Trenchard was a blow. Losing a vote at such a critical time, when if I had had only a remote idea of what was passing through his mind, I would have even asked him to Barrowley for a couple of days.'

A foreign diplomatist of distinction had pinned Lord Marney, and was dexterously pumping him as to the probable future.

'But is the pear ripe?' said the diplomatist.

'The pear is ripe if we have courage to pluck it,' said Lord Marney; 'but our fellows have no pluck.'

'But do you think that the Duke of Wellington—' and here the diplomatist stopped and looked up in Lord Marney's face, as if he would convey something that he would not venture to express.

'Here he is,' said Lord Marney, 'he will answer the question himself.'

Lord Deloraine and Mr. Ormsby passed by; the diplomatist addressed them: 'You have not been to the Chamber?'

'No,' said Lord Deloraine; 'but I hear there is hot work. It will be late.'

'Do you think—,' said the diplomatist, and he looked up in the face of Lord Deloraine.

'I think that in the long run everything will have an end,' said Lord Deloraine.

'Ah!' said the diplomatist.

'Bah!' said Lord Deloraine as he walked away with Mr. Ormsby, 'I remember that fellow—a sort of equivocal attaché at Paris, when we were there with Monmouth at the peace:* and now he is a quasi ambassador, and ribboned and starred to the chin.'

'The only stars I have got,' said Mr. Ormsby demurely, 'are four stars in India stock.'*

Lady Firebrace and Lady Maud Fitz-Warene were announced: they had just come from the Commons; a dame and damsel full of political enthusiasm. Lady Firebrace gave critical reports and disseminated many contradictory estimates of the result; Lady Maud talked only of a speech made by Lord Milford, which from the elaborate noise she made about it, you would have supposed to have been the oration of the evening; on the contrary, it had lasted only a few minutes and in a thin house had been nearly inaudible; but then, as Lady Maud added, 'it was in such good taste!'

Alfred Mountchesney and Lady Joan Fitz-Warene passed Lady Marney who was speaking to Lord Deloraine. 'Do you think,' said Lady Marney, 'that Mr. Mountchesney will bear away the prize?'

Lord Deloraine shook his head. 'These great heiresses can never make up their minds. The bitter drop rises in all their reveries.'

'And yet,' said Lady Marney, 'I would just as soon be married for my money as my face.'

Soon after this there was a stir in the saloons; a murmur, the ingress of many gentlemen: among others Lord Valentine, Lord Milford, Mr. Egerton, Mr. Berners, Lord Fitzheron, Mr. Jermyn. The House was up; the great Jamaica division was announced; the Radicals had thrown over the government, who left in a majority of only five, had already intimated their sense of the unequivocal feeling of the House with respect to them. It was known that on the morrow the government would resign.

Lady Deloraine, prepared for the great result, was calm: Lady St. Julians, who had not anticipated it, was in a wild flutter of distracted triumph. A vague yet dreadful sensation came over her in the midst of her joy that Lady Deloraine had been beforehand with her; had made her combinations with the new Minister; perhaps even sounded the Court. At the same time that, in this agitating vision, the great offices of the palace which she had apportioned to herself and her husband seemed to elude her grasp, the claims and hopes and interests of her various children haunted her perplexed consciousness. What if Charles Egremont were to get the place which she had projected for Frederick or Augustus? What if Lord Marney became master of the horse? Or Lord Deloraine went again to Ireland? In her nervous excitement she credited all these catastrophes: seized upon 'the Duke' in order that

Lady Deloraine might not gain his ear, and resolved to get home as
soon as possible, in order that she might write without a moment's loss
of time to Sir Robert.

'They will hardly go out without making some peers,' said Sir
Vavasour Firebrace to Mr. Jermyn.

'Why they have made enough.'

'Hem! I know Tubbe Sweete has a promise, and so has Cockawhoop.
I don't think Cockawhoop could show again at Boodle's without
a coronet.'

'I don't see why these fellows should go out,' said Mr. Ormsby.
'What does it signify whether ministers have a majority of five, or ten
or twenty? In my time, a proper majority was a third of the House. That
was Lord Liverpool's majority. Lord Monmouth used to say that there
were ten families in this country who, if they could only agree, could
always share the government. Ah! those were the good old times! We
never had adjourned debates then; but sate it out like gentlemen who
had been used all their lives to be up all night, and then supped at
Watier's* afterwards.'

'Ah! my dear Ormsby,' said Mr. Berners, 'do not mention Watier's;
you make my mouth water.'

'Shall you stand for Birmingham, Ormsby, if there be a dissolution?'
said Lord Fitzheron.

'I have been asked,' said Mr. Ormsby; 'but the House of Commons
is not the House of Commons of my time, and I have no wish to re-
enter it. If I had a taste for business, I might be a member of the
Marylebone vestry.'*

'All I repeat,' said Lord Marney to his mother, as he rose from the
sofa where he had been some time in conversation with her, 'is that if
there be any idea that I wish Lady Marney should be a lady in waiting,
it is an error, Lady Deloraine. I wish that to be understood. I am
a domestic man, and I wish Lady Marney to be always with me; and
what I want I want for myself. I hope in arranging the household the
domestic character of every member of it will be considered. After all
that has occurred the country expects that.'

'But my dear George, I think it is really premature—'

'I dare say it is; but I recommend you, my dear mother, to be alive.
I heard Lady St. Julians just now in the supper room asking the Duke
to promise her that her Augustus should be a Lord of the Admiralty.
She said the Treasury would not do, as there was no house, and that
with such a fortune as his wife brought him he could not hire a house
under a thousand a-year.'

'He will not have the Admiralty,' said Lady Deloraine.

'She looks herself to the Robes.'

'Poor woman!' said Lady Deloraine.

'Is it quite true?' said a great Whig dame to Mr. Egerton, one of her own party.

'Quite,' he said.

'I can endure anything except Lady St Julian's glance of triumph,' said the Whig dame. 'I really think if it were only to ease her Majesty from such an infliction, they ought to have held on.'

'And must the household be changed?' said Mr. Egerton.

'Do not look so serious,' said the Whig dame smiling with fascination; 'we are surrounded by the enemy.'

'Will you be at home to-morrow early?' said Mr. Egerton.

'As early as you please.'

'Very well, we will talk then. Lady Charlotte has heard something: nous verrons.'*

'Courage; we have the Court with us, and the Country cares for nothing.'

CHAPTER XII.

'It is all right,' said Mr. Tadpole. 'They are out. Lord Melbourne has been with the Queen and recommended her Majesty to send for the Duke, and the Duke has recommended her Majesty to send for Sir Robert.'

'Are you sure?' said Mr. Taper.

'I tell you Sir Robert is on his road to the palace at this moment; I saw him pass, full-dressed.'

'It is too much,' said Mr. Taper.

'Now what are we to do?' said Mr. Tadpole.

'We must not dissolve,' said Mr. Taper. 'We have no cry.'

'As much cry as the other fellows,' said Mr. Tadpole; 'but no one of course would think of dissolution before the next registration. No, no; this is a very manageable Parliament, depend upon it. The malcontent radicals who have turned them out are not going to bring them in. That makes us equal. Then we have an important section to work upon—the Sneaks, the men who are afraid of a dissolution. I will be bound we make a good working Conservative majority of five-and-twenty out of the Sneaks.'

'With the Treasury patronage,' said Mr. Taper; 'fear and favour combined. An impending dissolution, and all the places we refuse our own men, we may count on the Sneaks.'

'Then there are several religious men who have wanted an excuse for a long time to rat,' said Mr. Tadpole. 'We must get Sir Robert to make some kind of a religious move, and that will secure Sir Litany Lax and young Mr. Salem.'

'It will never do to throw over the Church Commission,'* said Mr. Taper. 'Commissions and committees ought always to be supported.'

'Besides it will frighten the saints,' said Mr. Tadpole. 'If we could get him to speak at Exeter Hall—were it only a slavery meeting—that would do.'

'It is difficult,' said Taper; 'he must be pledged to nothing—not even to the right of search. Yet if we could get up something with a good deal of sentiment and no principle involved; referring only to the past, but with his practised powers touching the present. What do you think of a monument to Wilberforce or a commemoration of Clarkson?'*

'There is a good deal in that,' said Mr. Tadpole. 'At present go about and keep our fellows in good humour. Whisper nothings that sound like something. But be discreet; do not let there be more than half a hundred fellows who believe they are going to be Under Secretaries of State. And be cautious about titles. If they push you, give a wink and press your finger to your lip. I must call here,' continued Mr. Tadpole as he stopped before the house of the Duke of Fitz-Aquitaine. 'This gentleman is my particular charge. I have been cooking him these three years. I had two notes from him yesterday, and can delay a visit no longer. The worst of it is, he expects that I shall bear him the non-official announcement of his being sent to Ireland, of which he has about as much chance as I have of being Governor-General of India. It must be confessed ours is critical work sometimes, friend Taper; but never mind—what we have to do to individuals Peel has to do with a nation, and therefore we ought not to complain.'

The Duke of Fitz-Aquitaine wanted Ireland and Lord de Mowbray wanted the Garter. Lord Marney, who wanted the Buck-hounds,* was convinced that neither of his friends had the slightest chance of obtaining their respective objects, but believed that he had a very good one of securing his own if he used them for his purpose, and persuaded them to combine together for the common good. So at his suggestion they had all met together at the duke's, and were in full conference on the present state of affairs, while Tadpole and Taper were engaged in that interesting and instructive conversation of which we have snatched a passage.

'You may depend upon it,' said Lord Marney, 'that nothing is to be done by delicacy. It is not delicacy that rules the House of Lords. What has kept us silent for years? Threats; and threats used in the most downright manner. We were told that if we did not conform absolutely and without appeal to the will and pleasure of one individual, the cards would be thrown up. We gave in; the game has been played, and won. I am not at all clear that it has been won by those tactics—but gained it is; and now what shall we do? In my opinion it is high time to get rid of the dictatorship. The new ruse now for the palace is to persuade her Majesty that Peel is the only man who can manage the House of Lords. Well, then it is exactly the time to make certain persons understand that the House of Lords are not going to be tools any longer merely for other people. Rely upon it a bold united front at this moment would be a spoke in the wheel. We three form the nucleus; there are plenty to gather round. I have written to Marisforde; he is quite ripe. Lord Hounslow will be here to-morrow. The thing is to be done; and if we are not firm the grand Conservative triumph will only end in securing the best posts both at home and abroad for one too powerful family.'

'Who had never been heard of in the time of my father,' said the duke.

'Nor in the time of mine,' said Lord de Mowbray.

'Royal and Norman blood like ours,' said Lord Marney, 'is not to be thrown over in that way.'

It was just at this moment that a servant entered with a card, which the duke looking at said, 'It is Tadpole; shall we have him in? I dare say he will tell us something.' And notwithstanding the important character of their conference, political curiosity and perhaps some private feeling which not one of them cared to acknowledge, made them unanimously agree that Mr. Tadpole should be admitted.

'Lord Marney and Lord de Mowbray with the Duke of Fitz-Aquitaine,' thought Mr. Tadpole, as he was ushered into the library and his eye, practised in machinations and prophetic in manœuvres surveyed the three nobles. 'This looks like business and perhaps means mischief. Very lucky I called!' With an honest smile he saluted them all.

'What news from the palace, Tadpole?' inquired the duke.

'Sir Robert is there,' replied Tadpole.

'That's good news,' exclaimed his grace, echoed by Lord de Mowbray, and backed up with a faint bravo from Lord Marney.

Then arose a conversation in which all affected much interest respecting the Jamaica debate; whether the Whigs had originally intended to resign; whether it were Lord Melbourne or Lord John* who had insisted on the step; whether if postponed they could have tided over the session; and so on. Tadpole, who was somewhat earnest in his talk, seemed to have pinned the Duke of Fitz-Aquitaine; Lord Marney who wanted to say a word alone to Lord de Mowbray had dexterously drawn that personage aside on the pretence of looking at a picture. Tadpole, who with a most frank and unsophisticated mien had an eye for every corner of a room, seized the opportunity for which he had been long cruising. 'I don't pretend to be behind the scenes, duke; but it was said to me to-day, "Tadpole, if you do chance to see the Duke of Fitz-Aquitaine you may say that positively Lord Killcroppy will not go to Ireland."'

A smile of satisfaction played over the handsome face of the duke—instantly suppressed lest it might excite suspicion; and then, with a friendly and very significant nod that intimated to Tadpole not to dwell on the subject at the present moment, the duke with a rather uninterested air recurred to the Jamaica debate, and soon after appealed on some domestic point to his son-in-law. This broke up the conversation between Lord de Mowbray and Lord Marney. Lord de Mowbray advancing was met accidentally on purpose by Mr. Tadpole, who seemed anxious to push forward to Lord Marney.

'You have heard of Lord Ribbonville?' said Tadpole in a suppressed tone.

'No; what?'

'Can't live the day out. How fortunate Sir Robert is! Two garters to begin with!'

Tadpole had now succeeded in tackling Lord Marney alone; the other peers were far out of ear-shot. 'I don't pretend to be behind the scenes, my Lord,' said the honest gentleman in a peculiarly confidential tone, and with a glance that spoke volumes of state secrecy; 'but it was said to me to-day, "Tadpole, if you do chance to meet Lord Marney, you may say that positively Lord Rambrooke will not have the Buck-hounds."'

'All I want,' said Lord Marney, 'is to see men of character about her Majesty. This is a domestic country, and the country expects that no nobleman should take household office whose private character is not inexpugnable. Now that fellow Rambrooke keeps a French woman. It is not much known, but it is a fact.'

'Dreadful!' exclaimed Mr. Tadpole. 'I have no doubt of it. But he has no chance of the Buck-hounds, you may rely on that. Private character is to be the basis of the new government. Since the Reform Act that is a qualification much more esteemed by the constituency than public services. We must go with the times, my Lord. A virtuous middle class shrink with horror from French actresses; and the Wesleyans—the Wesleyans must be considered, Lord Marney.'

'I always subscribe to them,' said his Lordship.

'Ah!' said Mr. Tadpole mysteriously, 'I am glad to hear that. Nothing I have heard to-day has given me so much pleasure as those few words. One may hardly jest on such a subject,' he added with a sanctimonious air; 'but I think I may say'—and here he broke into a horse smile— 'I think I may say that those subscriptions will not be without their fruit.' And with a bow honest Tadpole disappeared, saying to himself as he left the house, 'If you were ready to be conspirators when I entered the room, my Lords, you were at least prepared to be traitors when I quitted it.'

In the meantime Lord Marney in the best possible humour said to Lord de Mowbray, 'You are going to White's are you? If so take me.'

'I am sorry, my dear Lord, but I have an appointment in the city. I have got to go to the Temple, and I am already behind my time.'

CHAPTER XIII.

AND why was Lord de Mowbray going to the Temple? He had received the day before when he came home to dress a very disagreeable letter from some lawyers, apprising him that they were instructed by their client Mr. Walter Gerard to commence proceedings against his lordship on a writ of right with respect to his manors of Mowbray, Valence, Mowedale, Mowbray Valence, and several others carefully enumerated in their precise epistle, and the catalogue of which read like an extract from Domesday Book.

More than twenty years had elapsed since the question had been mooted; and though the discussion had left upon Lord de Mowbray an impression from which at times he had never entirely recovered, still circumstances had occurred since the last proceedings which gave him a moral if not a legal conviction that he should be disturbed no more. And these were the circumstances: Lord de Mowbray after the death of the father of Walter Gerard had found himself in communication with the agent who had developed and pursued the claim for the yeoman, and had purchased for a good round sum the documents on which that claim was founded, and by which apparently that claim could only be sustained.

The vendor of these muniments was Baptist Hatton, and the sum which he obtained for them, by allowing him to settle in the metropolis, pursue his studies, purchase his library and collections, and otherwise give himself that fair field which brains without capital can seldom command, was in fact the foundation of his fortune. Many years afterwards

Lord de Mowbray had recognised Hatton in the prosperous parliamentary agent who often appeared at the bar of the House of Lords and before committees of privileges, and who gradually obtained an unrivalled reputation and employment in peerage cases. Lord de Mowbray renewed his acquaintance with a man who was successful; bowed to Hatton whenever they met; and finally consulted him respecting the barony of Valence which had been in the old Fitz-Warene and Mowbray families and to which it was thought the present earl might prefer some hocus-pocus claim through his deceased mother; so that however recent was his date as an English earl, he might figure on the roll as a Plantagenet baron, which in the course of another century would complete the grand mystification of high nobility. The death of his son dexterously christened Valence had a little damped his ardour in this respect; but still there was a sufficiently intimate connection kept up between him and Hatton; so that before he placed the letter he had received in the hands of his lawyers he thought it desirable to consult his ancient ally.

This was the reason that Lord de Mowbray was at the present moment seated in the same chair in the same library as was a few days back that worthy baronet, Sir Vavasour Firebrace. Mr. Hatton was at the same table similarly employed; his Persian cat on his right hand, and his choice spaniels reposing on their cushions at his feet.

Mr. Hatton held forward his hand to receive the letter of which Lord de Mowbray had been speaking to him, and which he read with great attention, weighing as it were each word. Singular! as the letter had been written by himself, and the firm who signed it were only his instruments, obeying the spring of the master hand.

'Very remarkable!' said Mr. Hatton.

'Is it not!' said Lord de Mowbray.

'And your Lordship received this yesterday?'

'Yesterday. I lost no time in communicating with you.'

'Jubb and Jinks,' continued Mr. Hatton, musingly, surveying the signature of the letter. 'A very respectable firm.'

'That makes it more strange,' said his Lordship.

'It does,' said Mr. Hatton.

'A respectable firm would hardly embark in such a proceeding without some show of pretext,' said Lord de Mowbray.

'Hardly,' said Mr. Hatton.

'But what can they have?' urged his Lordship.

'What indeed!' said Mr. Hatton. 'Mr. Walter Gerard without his pedigree is a mere flash in the pan; and I defy him to prove anything without the deed of '77.'

'Well, he has not got that,' said Lord de Mowbray.

'Safe, of course?' said Mr. Hatton.

'Certain. I almost wish I had burnt it as well as the whole box-full.'

'Destroy that deed and the other muniments, and the Earl de Mowbray will never be Baron Valence,' said Mr. Hatton.

'But what use are these deeds now?' said his lordship. 'If we produce them, we may give a colour to this fellow's claim.'

'Time will settle his claim,' said Mr. Hatton; 'it will mature yours. You can wait.'

'Alas! since the death of my poor boy—'

'It has become doubly important. Substantiate the barony, it will descend to your eldest daughter, who, even if married, will retain your name. Your family will live, and ennobled. The Fitz-Warenes Lords Valence will yield to none in antiquity; and as to rank, as long as Mowbray Castle belongs to them, the revival of the earldom is safe at the first coronation, or the first ministry that exists with a balanced state of parties.'

'That is the right view of the case,' said Lord de Mowbray; 'and what do you advise?'

'Be calm, and you have nothing to fear. This is the mere revival of an old claim, too vast to be allowed to lapse from desuetude. Your documents you say are all secure?'

'Be sure of that. They are at this moment in the muniment room of the great tower of Mowbray Castle; in the same iron box and in the same cabinet they were deposited—'

'When, by placing them in your hands,' said Mr. Hatton finishing a sentence which might have been awkward, 'I had the extreme satisfaction of confirming the rights and calming the anxieties of one of our ancient houses. I would recommend your lordship to instruct your lawyers to appear to this writ as a matter of course. But enter into no details, no unnecessary confidence with them. They are needless. Treat the matter lightly, especially to them. You will hear no more of it.'

'You feel confidence?'

'Perfect. Walter Gerard has no documents of any kind. Whatever his claim might be, good or bad, the only evidence that can prove his pedigree is in your possession and the only use to which it ever will be put, will be in due time to seat your grandson in the House of Lords.'

'I am glad I called upon you,' said Lord Mowbray.

'To be sure. Your lordship can speak to me without reserve, and I am used to these start-ups. It is part of the trade; but an old soldier is not to be deceived by such feints.'

'Clearly a feint, you think?'

'A feint! a feint.'

'Good morning. I am glad I have called. How goes on my friend Sir Vavasour?'

'Oh! I shall land him at last.'

'Well, he is an excellent, neighbourly, man. I have a great respect for Sir Vavasour. Would you dine with me, Mr. Hatton, on Thursday? It would give me and Lady de Mowbray great pleasure.'

'Your lordship is extremely kind,' said Mr. Hatton bowing with a slight sarcastic smile, 'but I am an hermit.'

'But your friends should see you sometimes,' said Lord de Mowbray.

'Your lordship is too good, but I am a mere man of business and know my position. I feel I am not at home in ladies' society.'

'Well then come to-morrow: I am alone, and I will ask some persons to meet you whom you know and like,—Sir Vavasour and Lord Shaftesbury and a most learned Frenchman who is over here—a Vicomte de Narbonne, who is very anxious to make your acquaintance. Your name is current, I can tell you, at Paris.'

'Your lordship is too good; another day: I have a great pressure of affairs at present.'

'Well, well; so be it. Good morning, Mr. Hatton.'

Hatton bowed lowly. The moment the door was shut, rubbing his hands, he said, 'In the same box and in the same cabinet: the muniment room in the great tower of Mowbray Castle! They exist and I know their whereabouts. I'll have 'em.'

CHAPTER XIV.

TWO and even three days had rolled over since Mr. Tadpole had reported Sir Robert on his way to the palace, and marvellously little had transpired. It was of course known that a cabinet was in formation, and the daily papers reported to the public the diurnal visits of certain noble lords and right honourable gentlemen to the new first minister. But the world of high politics had suddenly become so cautious that nothing leaked out. Even gossip was at fault. Lord Marney had not received the Buck-hounds, though he never quitted his house for ride or lounge without leaving precise instructions with Captain Grouse as to the identical time he should return home, so that his acceptance should not be delayed. Ireland was not yet governed by the Duke of Fitz-Aquitaine, and the Earl de Mowbray was still ungartered. These three distinguished noblemen were all of them anxious—a little fidg-etty; but at the same time it was not even whispered that Lord Rambrooke or any other lord had received the post which Lord Marney had appropriated to himself; nor had Lord Killcroppy had a suspicious interview with the prime minister, which kept the Duke of Fitz-Aquitaine quiet though not easy; while not a shadow of coming events had glanced over the vacant stall of Lord Ribbonville in St. George's Chapel, and this made Lord de Mowbray tranquil, though scarcely content. In the meantime, daily and hourly they all pumped Mr. Tadpole, who did not find it difficult to keep up his reputation for dis-cretion; for knowing nothing, and beginning himself to be perplexed at the protracted silence, he took refuge in oracular mystery, and delivered himself of certain Delphic sentences which adroitly satisfied those who consulted him while they never committed himself.

At length one morning there was an odd whisper in the circle of first initiation. The blood mantled on the cheek of Lady St. Julians; Lady Deloraine turned pale. Lady Firebrace wrote confidential notes with the same pen to Mr. Tadpole and Lord Masque. Lord Marney called early in the morning on the Duke of Fitz-Aquitaine, and already found Lord de Mowbray there. The clubs were crowded even at noon. Everywhere a mysterious bustle and an awful stir.

What could be the matter? What has happened?

'It is true,' said Mr. Egerton to Mr. Berners at Brookes'.

'Is it true?' asked Mr. Jermyn of Lord Valentine at the Carlton.

'I heard it last night at Crockford's,' said Mr. Ormsby; 'one always hears things there four-and-twenty hours before other places.'

The world was employed the whole of the morning in asking and answering this important question 'Is it true?' Towards dinner time, it was settled universally in the affirmative, and then the world went out to dine and to ascertain why it was true and how it was true.

And now what really had happened? What had happened was what is commonly called a 'hitch.' There was undoubtedly a hitch somewhere and somehow; a hitch in the construction of the new cabinet. Who could have thought it? The Whig ministers it seems had resigned, but somehow or other had not entirely and completely gone out. What a constitutional dilemma! The Houses must evidently meet, address the throne, and impeach its obstinate counsellors. Clearly the right course, and party feeling ran so high, that it was not impossible that something might be done. At any rate, it was a capital opportunity for the House of Lords to pluck up a little courage and take what is called, in high political jargon, the initiative. Lord Marney at the suggestion of

Mr. Tadpole was quite ready to do this; and so was the Duke of Fitz-Aquitaine, and almost the Earl de Mowbray.

But then when all seemed ripe and ready, and there appeared a probability of the 'Independence of the House of Lords' being again the favourite toast of Conservative dinners, the oddest rumour in the world got about, which threw such a ridicule on these great constitutional movements in petto,* that even with the Buck-hounds in the distance and Tadpole at his elbow, Lord Marney hesitated. It seemed, though of course no one could for a moment credit it, that these wrong-headed, rebellious ministers who would not go out, wore—petticoats!*

And the great Jamaica debate that had been cooked so long, and the anxiously expected, yet almost despaired of, defection of the independent radical section, and the full-dressed visit to the palace that had gladdened the heart of Tadpole—were they all to end in this? Was Conservatism, that mighty mystery of the nineteenth century—was it after all to be brained by a fan!

Since the farce of the 'Invincibles'* nothing had ever been so ludicrously successful.

Lady Deloraine consoled herself for the 'Bedchamber Plot' by declaring that Lady St. Julians was indirectly the cause of it, and that had it not been for the anticipation of her official entrance into the royal apartments the conspiracy would not have been more real than the Meal-tub plot* or any other of the many imaginary machinations that still haunt the page of history, and occasionally flit about the prejudiced memory of nations. Lady St. Julians on the contrary wrung her hands over the unhappy fate of her enthralled sovereign, deprived of her faithful presence and obliged to put up with the society of personages of whom she knew nothing and who called themselves the friends of her youth. The ministers who had missed, especially those who had received their appointments, looked as all men do when they are jilted—embarrassed and affecting an awkward ease; as if they knew something which, if they told, would free them from the supreme ridicule of their situation, but which, as men of delicacy and honour, they refrained from revealing. All those who had been in fluttering hopes, however faint, of receiving preferment, took courage now that the occasion had passed, and loudly complained of their cruel and undeniable deprivation. The constitution was wounded in their persons. Some fifty gentlemen who had not been appointed under secretaries of state, moaned over the martyrdom of young ambition.

'Peel ought to have taken office,' said Lord Marney. 'What are the women to us?'

'Peel ought to have taken office,' said the Duke of Fitz-Aquitaine. 'He should have remembered how much he owed to Ireland.'

'Peel ought to have taken office,' said Lord de Mowbray. 'The garter will become now a mere party badge.'

Perhaps it may be allowed to the impartial pen* that traces these memoirs of our times to agree, though for a different reason, with these distinguished followers of Sir Robert Peel. One may be permitted to think that, under all circumstances, he should have taken office in 1839. His withdrawal seems to have been a mistake. In the great heat of parliamentary faction which had prevailed since 1831, the royal prerogative, which, unfortunately for the rights and liberties and social welfare of the people, had since 1688 been more or less oppressed, had waned fainter and fainter. A youthful princess on the throne, whose appearance touched the imagination, and to whom her people were generally inclined to ascribe something of that decision of character which becomes those born to command, offered a favourable opportunity to restore the exercise of that regal authority, the usurpation of whose functions has entailed on the people of England so much suffering and so much degradation. It was unfortunate that one who, if any, should have occupied the proud and national position of the leader of the Tory party, the chief of the people and the champion of the throne, should have commenced his career as minister under Victoria by an unseemly contrariety to the personal wishes of the Queen. The reaction of public opinion, disgusted with years of parliamentary tumult and the incoherence of party legislation, the balanced state in the kingdom of political parties themselves, the personal character of the sovereign—these were all causes which intimated that a movement in favour of prerogative was at hand. The leader of the Tory party should have vindicated his natural position, and availed himself of the gracious occasion: he missed it; and as the occasion was inevitable, the Whigs enjoyed its occurrence. And thus England witnessed for the first time the portentous anomaly of the oligarchical or Venetian party, which had in the old days destroyed the free monarchy of England, retaining power merely by the favour of the Court.

But we forget, Sir Robert Peel is not the leader of the Tory party: the party that resisted the ruinous mystification that metamorphosed direct taxation by the Crown into indirect taxation by the Commons; that denounced the system that mortgaged industry to protect property; the party that ruled Ireland by a scheme which reconciled both churches, and by a series of parliaments which counted among them lords and commons of both religions; that has maintained at all times the territorial constitution of England as the only basis and security for local government, and which nevertheless once laid on the table of the House of Commons a commercial tariff negotiated at Utrecht, which is the most rational that was ever devised by statesmen; a party that has prevented the Church from being the salaried agent of the state, and has supported through many struggles the parochial polity of the country which secures to every labourer a home.*

In a parliamentary sense, that great party has ceased to exist; but I will believe it still lives in the thought and sentiment and consecrated memory of the English nation. It has its origin in great principles and in noble instincts; it sympathises with the lowly, it looks up to the Most High; it can count its heroes and its martyrs; they have met in its behalf plunder, proscription, and death. Nor when it finally yielded to the iron progress of oligarchical supremacy, was its catastrophe inglorious. Its genius was vindicated in golden sentences and with fervent arguments of impassioned logic by St. John; and breathed in the intrepid eloquence and patriot soul of William Wyndham.* Even now it is not dead, but sleepeth; and in an age of political materialism, of confused purposes and perplexed intelligence, that aspires only to wealth because it has faith in no other accomplishment, as men rifle cargoes on the verge of shipwreck, Toryism will yet rise from the tomb over which Bolingbroke shed his last tear, to bring back strength to the Crown, liberty to the Subject, and to announce that power has only one duty—to secure the social welfare of the PEOPLE.

CHAPTER XV.

DURING the week of political agitation which terminated with the inglorious catastrophe of the Bedchamber plot, Sybil remained tranquil, and would have been scarcely conscious of what was disturbing so many right honourable hearts, had it not been for the incidental notice of their transactions by her father and his friends. To the Chartists indeed the factious embroilment at first was of no great moment, except as the breaking up and formation of cabinets might delay the presentation of the National Petition. They had long ceased to distinguish between the two parties who then and now contend for power. And they were right. Between the noble lord who goes out and the right honourable gentleman who comes in, where is the distinctive principle? A shadowy difference may be simulated in opposition, to serve a cry and stimulate the hustings; but the mask is not even worn in Downing

Street; and the conscientious Conservative seeks in the pigeon-holes of a Whig bureau for the measures against which for ten years he has been sanctioning by the speaking silence of an approving nod, a general wail of frenzied alarm.

Once it was otherwise; once the people recognised a party in the state whose principles identified them with the rights and privileges of the multitude: but when they found the parochial constitution of the country sacrificed* without a struggle, and a rude assault made on all local influences in order to establish a severely organised centralisation, a blow was given to the influence of the priest and of the gentleman, the ancient champions of the people against arbitrary courts and rapacious parliaments, from which they will find that it requires no ordinary courage and wisdom to recover.

The unexpected termination of the events of May, 1839, in the re-establishment in power of a party confessedly too weak to carry on the parliamentary government of the country, was viewed however by the Chartists in a very different spirit to that with which they had witnessed the outbreak of these transactions. It had unquestionably a tendency to animate their efforts, and imparted a bolder tone to their future plans and movements. They were encouraged to try a fall with a feeble administration. Gerard from this moment became engrossed in affairs; his correspondence greatly increased; and he was so much occupied that Sybil saw daily less and less of her father.

It was on the morning after the day that Hatton had made his first and unlooked-for visit in Smith's Square, some of the delegates who had caught the rumour of the resignation of the Whigs had called early on Gerard, and he had soon after left the house in their company; and Sybil was alone. The strange incidents of the preceding day were revolving in her mind, as her eye wandered vaguely over her book.

The presence of that Hatton who had so often and in such different scenes occupied their conversation; the re-appearance of that stranger, whose unexpected entrance into their little world had eighteen months ago so often lent interest and pleasure to their life—these were materials for pensive sentiment. Mr. Franklin had left some gracious memories with Sybil; the natural legacy of one so refined, intelligent, and gentle, whose temper seemed never ruffled, and who evidently so sincerely relished their society. Mowedale rose before her in all the golden beauty of its autumnal hour; their wild rambles and hearty greetings and earnest converse, when her father returned from his daily duties and his eye kindled with pleasure as the accustomed knock announced the arrival of his almost daily companion. In spite of the excitement of the passing moment, its high hopes and glorious aspirations, and visions perchance of greatness and of power, the eye of Sybil was dimmed with emotion as she recalled that innocent and tranquil dream.

Her father had heard from Franklin after his departure more than once; but his letters, though abounding in frank expressions of deep interest in the welfare of Gerard and his daughter, were in some degree constrained; a kind of reserve seemed to envelope him; they never learnt anything of his life and duties; he seemed sometimes as it were meditating a departure from his country. There was undoubtedly about him something mysterious and unsatisfactory. Morley was of opinion that he was a spy; Gerard, less suspicious, ultimately concluded that he was harassed by his creditors, and when at Mowedale was probably hiding from them.

And now the mystery was at length dissolved. And what an explanation! A Norman, a noble, an oppressor of the people, a plunderer of the church—all the characters and capacities that Sybil had been bred up to look upon with fear and aversion, and to recognise as the authors of the degradation of her race.

Sybil sighed; the door opened and Egrement stood before her. The blood rose to her cheek, her heart trembled; for the first time in his presence she felt embarrassed and constrained. His countenance on the contrary was collected; serious and pale.

'I am an intruder,' he said advancing, 'but I wish much to speak to you,' and he seated himself near her. There was a momentary pause. 'You seemed to treat with scorn yesterday,' resumed Egremont in accents less sustained, 'the belief that sympathy was independent of the mere accidents of position. Pardon me, Sybil, but even you may be prejudiced.' He paused.

'I should be sorry to treat anything you said with scorn,' replied Sybil in a subdued tone. 'Many things happened yesterday,' she added, 'which might be offered as some excuse for an unguarded word.'

'Would that it had been unguarded!' said Egremont in a voice of melancholy. 'I could have endured it with less repining. No, Sybil, I have known you, I have had the happiness and the sorrow of knowing you too well to doubt the convictions of your mind, or to believe that they can be lightly removed, and yet I would strive to remove them. You look upon me as an enemy, as a natural foe, because I am born among the privileged. I am a man, Sybil, as well as a noble.' Again he paused; she looked down, but did not speak.

'And can I not feel for men, my fellows, whatever be their lot? I know you will deny it; but you are in error, Sybil; you have formed your opinions upon tradition, not upon experience. The world that exists is not the

world of which you have read; the class that calls itself your superior is
not the same class as ruled in the time of your fathers. There is a change
in them as in all other things, and I participate that change. I shared it
before I knew you, Sybil; and if it touched me then, at least believe it
does not influence me less now.'

'If there be a change,' said Sybil, 'it is because in some degree the
People have learnt their strength.'

'Ah! dismiss from your mind those fallacious fancies,' said Egremont.
'The People are not strong; the People never can be strong. Their
attempts at self-vindication will end only in their suffering and confusion. It is civilisation that has effected, that is effecting this change. It is
that increased knowledge of themselves that teaches the educated their
social duties. There is a dayspring in the history of this nation which
those who are on the mountain tops can as yet perhaps only recognize.
You deem you are in darkness, and I see a dawn. The new generation*
of the aristocracy of England are not tyrants, not oppressors, Sybil, as
you persist in believing. Their intelligence, better than that, their hearts
are open to the responsibility of their position. But the work that is
before them is no holiday-work. It is not the fever of superficial impulse
that can remove the deep-fixed barriers of centuries of ignorance and
crime. Enough that their sympathies are awakened; time and thought
will bring the rest. They are the natural leaders of the People, Sybil;
believe me they are the only ones.'

'The leaders of the People are those whom the People trust,' said
Sybil rather haughtily.

'And who may betray them,' said Egremont.

'Betray them!' exclaimed Sybil. 'And can you believe that my
father—'

'No, no; you can feel, Sybil, though I cannot express, how much
I honour your father. But he stands alone in the singleness and purity
of his heart. Who surround him?'

'Those whom the People have also chosen; and from a like confidence in their virtues and abilities. They are a senate supported by the
sympathy of millions, with only one object in view—the emancipation
of their race. It is a sublime spectacle, these delegates of labour advo-
cating the sacred cause in a manner which might shame your haughty
factions. What can resist a demonstration so truly national! What can
withstand the supremacy of its moral power!'

Her eye met the glance of Egremont. That brow full of thought and
majesty was fixed on his. He encountered that face radiant as a seraph's; those dark eyes flashing with the inspiration of the martyr.

Egremont rose, moved slowly to the window, gazed in abstraction for a few moments on the little garden with its dank turf that no foot ever trod, its mutilated statue and its mouldering frescoes. What a silence; how profound! What a prospect; how drear! Suddenly he turned, and advancing with a more rapid pace, he approached Sybil. Her head was averted, and leaning on her left arm she seemed lost in reverie. Egremont fell upon his knee and gently taking her hand he pressed it to his lips. She started, she looked round, agitated, alarmed, while he breathed forth in tremulous accents, 'Let me express to you my adoration!

'Ah! not now for the first time, but for ever; from the moment I first beheld you in the starlit arch of Marney has your spirit ruled my being and softened every spring of my affections. I followed you to your home, and lived for a time content in the silent worship of your nature. When I came the last morning to the cottage, it was to tell, and to ask, all. Since then for a moment your image has never been absent from my consciousness; your picture consecrates my hearth and your approval has been the spur of my career. Do not reject my love; it is deep as your nature, and fervent as my own. Banish those prejudices that have embittered your existence, and if persisted in may wither mine. Deign to retain this hand! If I be a noble I have none of the accidents of nobility: I cannot offer you wealth, splendour, or power; but I can offer you the devotion of an entranced being—aspirations that you shall guide—an ambition that you shall govern!'

'These words are mystical and wild,' said Sybil with an amazed air; 'they come upon me with convulsive suddenness.' And she paused for an instant, collecting as it were her mind with an expression almost of pain upon her countenance. 'These changes of life are so strange and rapid that it seems to me I can scarcely meet them. You are Lord Marney's brother; it was but yesterday—only but yesterday—I learnt it. I thought then I had lost your friendship, and now you speak of—love! Love of me! Retain your hand and share your life and fortunes! You forget what I am. But though I learnt only yesterday what you are, I will not be so remiss. Once you wrote upon a page you were my faithful friend; and I have pondered over that line with kindness often. I will be your faithful friend; I will recall you to yourself. I will at least not bring you shame and degradation.'

'O! Sybil, beloved, beautiful Sybil—not such bitter words; no, no!'

'No bitterness to you! that would indeed be harsh,' and she covered with her hand her streaming eyes.

'Why what is this?' after a pause and with an effort she exclaimed. 'An union between the child and brother of nobles and a daughter of the people! Estrangement from your family, and with cause, their hopes destroyed, their pride outraged; alienation from your order, and justly, all their prejudices insulted. You will forfeit every source of worldly content and cast off every spring of social success. Society for you will become a great confederation to deprive you of self-complacency. And rightly. Will you not be a traitor to the cause? No, no, kind friend, for such I'll call you. Your opinion of me, too good and great as I feel it, touches me deeply. I am not used to such passages in life; I have read of such. Pardon me, feel for me, if I receive them with some disorder. They sound to me for the first time—and for the last. Perhaps they ought never to have reached my ear. No matter now—I have a life of penitence before me, and I trust I shall be pardoned.' And she wept.

'You have indeed punished me for the fatal accident of birth, if it deprives me of you.'

'Not so,' she added weeping; 'I shall never be the bride of earth; and but for one whose claims though earthly are to me irresistible, I should have ere this forgotten my hereditary sorrows in the cloister.'

All this time Egremont had retained her hand, which she had not attempted to withdraw. He had bent his head over it as she spoke—it was touched with his tears. For some moments there was silence; then looking up and in a smothered voice Egremont made one more effort to induce Sybil to consider his suit. He combated her views as to the importance to him of the sympathies of his family and of society; he detailed to her his hopes and plans for their future welfare; he dwelt with passionate eloquence on his abounding love. But with a solemn sweetness, and as it were a tender inflexibility, the tears trickling down her beautiful cheek, and pressing his hand in both of hers, she subdued and put aside all his efforts.

'Believe me,' she said, 'the gulf is impassable.'

END OF VOLUME THE SECOND.

VOLUME III

BOOK V.

CHAPTER I.

'TERRIBLE news from Birmingham,'* said Mr. Egerton at Brookes'. 'They have massacred the police, beat off the military, and sacked the town. News just arrived.'

'I have known it these two hours,' said a grey-headed gentleman, speaking without taking his eyes off the newspaper. 'There is a cabinet sitting now.'

'Well I always said so,' said Mr. Egerton 'our fellows ought to have put down that Convention.'

'It is deuced lucky,' said Mr. Berners, 'that the Bedchamber business is over, and we are all right. This affair in the midst of the Jamaica hitch would have been fatal to us.'

'These Chartists evidently act upon a system,' said Mr. Egerton. 'You see they were perfectly quiet till the National Petition was presented and debated; and now, almost simultaneously with our refusing to consider their petition, we have news of this outbreak.'

'I hope they will not spread,' said the grey-headed gentleman. 'There are not troops enough in the country if there be anything like a general movement. I hear they have sent the guards down by a special train, and a hundred more of the police. London is not over-garrisoned.'

'They are always ready for a riot at Birmingham,' said a Warwickshire peer. 'Trade is very bad there and they suffer a good deal. But I should think it would not go farther.'

'I am told,' said the grey-headed gentleman, 'that business is getting slack in all the districts.'

'It might be better,' said Mr. Egerton, 'but they have got work.'

Here several gentlemen entered, enquiring whether the evening papers were in and what was the news from Birmingham.

'I am told,' said one of them, 'that the police were regularly smashed.'

'Is it true that the military were really beat off?'

'Quite untrue: the fact is there were no proper preparations; the town was taken by surprise, the magistrates lost their heads; the people were masters of the place; and when the police did act, they were met by a triumphant populace, who two hours before would have fled before them. They say they have burnt down above forty houses.'

'It is a bad thing—this beating the police,' said the grey-headed gentleman.

'But what is the present state of affairs?' enquired Mr. Berners. 'Are the rioters put down?'

'Not in the least,' said Mr. Egerton, 'as I hear. They are encamped in the Bull Ring* amid smoking ruins, and breathe nothing but havoc.'

'Well, I voted for taking the National Petition into consideration,' said Mr. Berners. 'It could do us no harm, and would have kept things quiet.'

'So did every fellow on our side,' said Mr. Egerton, 'who was not in office or about to be. Well, Heaven knows what may come next. The Charter may some day be as popular in this club as the Reform Act.'

'The oddest thing in that debate,' said Mr. Berners, 'was Egremont's move.'

'I saw Marney last night at Lady St. Julians,' said Mr. Egerton, 'and congratulated him on his brother's speech. He looked daggers, and grinned like a ghoul.'

'It was a very remarkable speech—that of Egremont,' said the grey-headed gentleman. 'I wonder what he wants.'

'I think he must be going to turn Radical,' said the Warwickshire peer.

'Why the whole speech was against radicalism,' said Mr. Egerton.

'Ah, then he is going to turn Whig, I suppose.'

'He is ultra anti-Whig,' said Egerton.

'Then what the deuce is he?' said Mr. Berners.

'Not a Conservative certainly, for Lady St. Julians does nothing but abuse him.'

'I suppose he is crotchetty,' suggested the Warwickshire noble.

'That speech of Egremont was the most really democratic speech that I ever read,' said the grey-headed gentleman. 'How was it listened to?'

'Oh! capitally,' said Mr. Egerton. 'He has very seldom spoken before and always slightly though well. He was listened to with mute attention; never was a better house. I should say made a great impression, though no one knew exactly what he was after.'

'What does he mean by obtaining the results of the Charter without the intervention of its machinery?'* enquired Lord Loraine, a mild, middle-aged, lounging, languid man, who passed his life in crossing from Brookes' to Boodle's and from Boodle's to Brookes', and testing the comparative intelligence of these two celebrated bodies; himself gifted with no ordinary abilities cultivated with no ordinary care, but the victim of sauntering, his sultana queen, as it was, according to Lord Halifax,* of the second Charles Stuart.

'He spoke throughout in an exoteric vein,' said the grey-headed gentleman, 'and I apprehend was not very sure of his audience; but I took him to mean, indeed it was the gist of the speech, that if you wished for a time to retain your political power, you could only effect your purpose by securing for the people greater social felicity.'

'Well, that is sheer radicalism,' said the Warwickshire peer; 'pretending that the People can be better off than they are, is radicalism and nothing else.'

'I fear, if that be radicalism,' said Lord Loraine, 'we must all take a leaf out of the same book. Sloane was saying at Boodle's just now that he looked forward to the winter in his country with horror.'

'And they have no manufactures there,' said Mr. Egerton.

'Sloane was always a croaker,' said the Warwickshire peer. 'He always said the New Poor Law would not act, and there is no part of the country where it works so well as his own.'

'They say at Boodle's there is to be an increase to the army,' said Lord Loraine, 'ten thousand men immediately; decided on by the cabinet this afternoon.'

'It could hardly have leaked out by this time,' said the grey-headed gentleman. 'The cabinet were sitting less than an hour ago.'

'They have been up a good hour,' said Lord Loraine, 'quite long enough for their decisions to be known in St. James's Street. In the good old times, George Farnley used always to walk from Downing Street to this place the moment the council was up and tell us everything.'

'Ah! those were the good old gentlemanlike times,' said Mr. Berners, 'when members of Parliament had nobody to please and ministers of State nothing to do.'

The riots of Birmingham occurred two months after the events that closed our last volume. That period, as far as the obvious movements of the Chartists were concerned, had been passed in preparations for the presentation and discussion of the National Petition, which the parliamentary embroilments of the spring of that year had hitherto procrastinated and prevented. The petition was ultimately carried down to Westminster on a triumphal car accompanied by all the delegates of the Convention in solemn procession. It was necessary to construct a machine in order to introduce the huge bulk of parchment signed by a million and a half of persons, into the House of Commons, and thus supported, its vast form remained on the floor of the House during the discussion. The House after a debate which was not deemed by the people commensurate with the importance of the occasion, decided on rejecting the prayer* of the Petition, and from that moment the party in the Convention who advocated a recourse to physical force in order to obtain their purpose, was in the ascendant. The National Petition and the belief that although its objects would not at present be obtained, still that a solemn and prolonged debate on its prayer would at least hold out to the working classes the hope that their rights might from that date rank among the acknowledged subjects of parliamentary discussion and ultimately by the force of discussion be recognized, as other rights of other portions of the people once equally disputed, had been the means by which the party in the Convention who upheld on all occasions the supremacy of moral power had been able to curb the energetic and reckless minority, who derided from the first all other methods but terror and violence as effective of their end. The hopes of all, the vanity of many, were frustrated and shocked by finding that the exertions and expenditure of long months were not only fruitless, but had not even attracted as numerous an assembly or excited as much interest, as an ordinary party struggle on some petty point of factitious interest forgotten as soon as fought. The attention of the working classes was especially called by their leaders to the contrast between the interest occasioned by the endangered constitution of Jamaica, a petty and exhausted colony, and the claims for the same constitutional rights by the working millions of England. In the first instance, not a member was absent from his place; men were brought indeed from distant capitals to participate in the struggle and to decide it; the debate lasted for days, almost for weeks; not a public man of light and leading* in the country withheld the expression of his opinion; the fate of governments was involved in it; cabinets were overthrown and reconstructed in the throes and tumult of the strife, and for the first time for a long period the Sovereign personally interposed in public transactions with a significance of character, which made the working classes almost believe that the privileged had at last found a master, and the unfranchised regained their natural chief. The mean position which the Saxon multitude occupied as distinguished from the Jamaica planters sunk deep into their hearts. From that moment all hope of relief from the demonstration of a high moral conduct in the millions, and the exhibition of that well-regulated order of public life which would intimate their fitness for the possession and fulfilment of public rights, vanished. The party of violence, a small minority as is usually the case, but consisting of men of determined character, triumphed; and the outbreak at Birmingham was the first consequence of those reckless councils that were destined in the course of the ensuing years to inflict on the working classes of this country so much suffering and disaster.

It was about this time, a balmy morning of July, that Sybil, tempted by the soft sunshine, and a longing for the sight of flowers and turf and the spread of winding waters, went forth from her gloomy domicile to those beautiful gardens* that bloom in that once melancholy region of marsh, celebrated in old days only for its Dutch canal and its Chinese bridge, and now not unworthy of the royal park that incloses them. Except here and there a pretty nursery-maid with her interesting charge, some beautiful child with nodding plume, immense bow, and gorgeous sash, the gardens were vacant. Indeed it was only at this early hour, that Sybil found from experience, that it was agreeable in London for a woman unaccompanied to venture abroad. There is no European city where our fair sisters are so little independent as in our metropolis; to our shame.

Something of the renovating influence of a beautiful nature was needed by the daughter of Gerard. She was at this moment anxious and dispirited. The outbreak at Birmingham, the conviction that such proceedings must ultimately prove fatal to the cause to which she was devoted, the dark apprehension that her father was in some manner implicated in this movement, that had commenced with so much public disaster, and which menaced consequences still more awful, all these events, and fears, and sad forebodings, acted with immense influence on a temperament which, though gifted with even a sublime courage, was singularly sensitive. The quick and teeming imagination of Sybil conjured up a thousand fears which were in some degree unfounded, in a great degree exaggerated, but this is the inevitable lot of the creative mind practising on the inexperienced.

The shock too had been sudden. The two months that had elapsed since she had parted, as she supposed for ever, from Egremont, while they had not less abounded than the preceding time in that pleasing public excitement which her father's career, in her estimation alike useful, honourable, and distinguished, occasioned her, had been fruitful in some sources of satisfaction of a softer and more domestic character. The acquaintance of Hatton, of whom they saw a great deal, had very much contributed to the increased amenity of her life. He was a most agreeable, instructive, and obliging companion; who seemed peculiarly to possess the art of making life pleasant by the adroit management of

unobtrusive resources. He lent Sybil books; and all that he recommended
to her notice were of a kind that harmonized with her sentiment and
taste. He furnished her from his library with splendid works of art,
illustrative of those periods of our history and those choice and costly
edifices which were associated with her fondest thought and fancy. He
placed in her room the best periodical literature of the day, which for
her was a new world; he furnished her with newspapers whose columns
of discussion taught her, that the opinions she had embraced were not
unquestioned: as she had never seen a journal in her life before, except
a stray number of the *Mowbray Phalanx*, or the metropolitan publication
which was devoted to the cause of the National Convention, and reported
her father's speeches, the effect of this reading on her intelligence was,
to say the least, suggestive.

Many a morning too when Gerard was disengaged, Hatton would
propose that they should show Sybil something of the splendour or the
rarities of the metropolis; its public buildings, museums, and galleries
of art. Sybil, though uninstructed in painting, had that native taste
which requires only observation to arrive at true results. She was much
interested with all she saw and all that occurred, and her gratification
was heightened by the society of an individual who not only sympa-
thised with all she felt, but who, if she made an inquiry, was ever ready
with an instructive reply. Hatton poured forth the taste and treasures of
a well-stored and refined intelligence. And then too, always easy, bland,
and considerate; and though with luxuries and conveniences at his command, to participate in which, under any other circumstances, might
have been embarrassing to his companions, with so much tact, that
either by an allusion to early days, happy days when he owed so much
to Gerard's father, or some other mode equally felicitous, he contrived
completely to maintain among them the spirit of social equality. In the
evening, Hatton generally looked in when Gerard was at home, and on
Sundays they were always together. Their common faith was a bond of
union which led them to the same altar, and on that day Hatton had
obtained their promise always to dine with him. He was careful to
ascertain each holy day at what chapel the music was most exquisite,
that the most passionate taste of Sybil might be gratified. Indeed,
during this residence in London, the opportunity it afforded of making
her acquainted with some of the great masters of the human voice was
perhaps to Sybil a source of pleasure not the least important. For
though it was not deemed consistent with the future discipline which
she contemplated to enter a theatre, there were yet occasions which
permitted her, under every advantage, to listen to the performance

of the master-pieces of sacred melody. Alone, with Hatton and her father, she often poured forth those tones of celestial sweetness and etherial power that had melted the soul of Egremont amid the ruins of Marney Abbey.

More intimately acquainted with Sybil Gerard, Hatton had shrunk from the project that he had at first so crudely formed. There was something about her that awed, while it fascinated him. He did not relinquish his purpose, for it was a rule of his life never to do that; but he postponed the plans of its fulfilment. Hatton was not, what is commonly understood by the phrase, in love with Sybil: certainly not passionately in love with her. With all his daring and talents and fine taste, there was in Hatton such a vein of thorough good sense, that it was impossible for him to act or even to think anything that was ridiculous. He wished still to marry Sybil for the great object that we have stated; he had a mind quite equal to appreciate her admirable qualities, but sense enough to wish that she were a less dazzling creature, because then he would have a better chance of accomplishing his end. He perceived when he had had a due opportunity to study her character, that the cloister was the natural catastrophe impending over a woman who, with an exalted mind, great abilities, a fine and profound education and almost supernatural charms, found herself born and rooted in the ranks of a degraded population. All this Hatton understood; it was a conclusion he had gradually arrived at by a gradual process of induction and by a vigilant observation that in its study of character had rarely been deceived; and when one evening with an art that could not be suspected, he sounded Gerard on the future of his daughter, he found that the clear intellect and straightforward sagacity of the father had arrived at the same result. 'She wishes,' said Gerard, 'to take the veil, and I only oppose it for a time, that she may have some knowledge of life and a clear conception of what she is about to do. I wish not that she should hereafter reproach her father. But, to my mind, Sybil is right. She cannot look to marriage: no man that she could marry would be worthy of her.'

During these two months, and especially during the last, Morley was rarely in London, though ever much with Gerard, and often with his daughter during his visits. The necessary impulse had been given to the affairs of the Convention, the delegates had visited the members, the preparations for the presentation of the National Petition had been completed; the overthrow of the Whig government, the abortive effort of Sir Robert Peel, the return of the Whig administration, and the consequent measures, had occasioned a delay of two months in the presentation of the great document: it was well for Gerard to remain, who was a leader in debate, and whose absence for a week would have endangered his position as the head of a party, but these considerations did not influence Morley, who had already found great inconvenience in managing his journal at a distance; so, about the middle of May, he had returned to Mowbray, coming up occasionally by the train if anything important were stirring, or his vote could be of service to his friend and colleague. The affair of Birmingham however had alarmed Morley and he had written up to Gerard that he should instantly repair to town. Indeed he was expected the very morning that Sybil, her father having gone to the Convention where there were at this very moment very fiery debates, went forth to take the morning air of summer in the gardens of St. James' Park.

It was a real summer day; large, round, glossy, fleecy clouds, as white and shining as glaciers, studded with their immense and immoveable forms the deep blue sky. There was not even a summer breeze, though the air was mellow, balmy, and exhilarating. There was a bloom upon the trees, the waters glittered, the prismatic wild-fowl dived, breathed again, and again disappeared. Beautiful children, fresh and sweet as the new-born rose, glanced about with the gestures and sometimes the voices of Paradise. And in the distance rose the sacred towers of the great Western Minster.*

How fair is a garden amid the toils and passions of existence! A curse upon those who vulgarize and desecrate these holy haunts; breaking the hearts of nursery maids, and smoking tobacco in the palace of the rose!

The mental clouds dispelled as Sybil felt the freshness and fragrance of nature. The colour came to her cheek; the deep brightness returned to her eye; her step that at first had been languid and if not melancholy, at least contemplative, became active and animated. She forgot the cares of life and was touched by all the sense of its enjoyment. To move, to breathe, to feel the sunbeam, were sensible and surpassing pleasures. Cheerful by nature, notwithstanding her stately thoughts and solemn life, a brilliant smile played on her seraphic face, as she marked the wild passage of the daring birds, or watched the thoughtless grace of infancy.

She rested herself on a bench beneath a branching elm, and her eye, that for some time had followed the various objects that had attracted it, was now fixed in abstraction on the sunny waters. The visions of past life rose before her. It was one of those reveries when the incidents of our existence are mapped before us, when each is considered with relation to the rest, and assumes in our knowledge its distinct and absolute position; when, as it were, we take stock of our experience, and ascertain how rich sorrow and pleasure, feeling and thought, intercourse with our fellow creatures and the fortuitous mysteries of life, have made us in wisdom.

The quick intelligence and the ardent imagination of Sybil had made her comprehend with fervor the two ideas that had been impressed on her young mind; the oppression of her church and the degradation of her people. Educated in solitude and exchanging thoughts only with individuals of the same sympathies, these impressions had resolved themselves into one profound and gloomy conviction, that the world was divided only between the oppressors and the oppressed. With her, to be one of the people, was to be miserable and innocent; one of the privileged, a luxurious tyrant. In the cloister, in her garden, amid the scenes of suffering which she often visited and always solaced, she had raised up two phantoms which with her represented human nature.

But the experience of the last few months had operated a great change in these impressions. She had seen enough to suspect that the world was a more complicated system than she had preconceived. There was not that strong and rude simplicity in its organization she had supposed. The characters were more various, the motives more mixed, the classes more blended, the elements of each more subtle and diversified, than she had imagined. The People she found was not that pure embodiment of unity of feeling, of interest, and of purpose, which she had pictured in her abstractions. The people had enemies among the people: their own passions; which made them often sympathize, often combine, with the privileged. Her father, with all his virtues, all his abilities, singleness of purpose and simplicity of aim, encountered rivals in their own Convention, and was beset by open or, still worse, secret foes.

Sybil, whose mind had been nurtured with great thoughts, and with whom success or failure alike partook of the heroic, who had hoped for triumph, but who was prepared for sacrifice, found to her surprise that great thoughts have very little to do with the business of the world; that human affairs, even in an age of revolution, are the subject of compromise; and that the essence of compromise is littleness. She thought that the People, calm and collected, conscious at last of their strength and confident in their holy cause, had but to express their pure and noble convictions by the delegates of their choice, and that an antique and decrepit authority must bow before the irresistible influence of their moral power. These delegates of their choice turned out to be a plebeian senate of wild ambitions and sinister and selfish ends, while the decrepit authority that she had been taught existed only by the sufferance of the millions was compact and organized, with every element of physical power at its command, and supported by the interests, the sympathies, the honest convictions, and the strong prejudices of classes influential not merely from their wealth but even by their numbers.

Nor could she resist the belief that the feeling of the rich towards the poor was not that sentiment of unmingled hate and scorn which she associated with Norman conquerors and feudal laws. She would ascribe rather the want of sympathy that unquestionably exists between Wealth and Work in England, to mutual ignorance between the classes which possess these two great elements of national prosperity; and though the source of that ignorance was to be sought in antecedent circumstances of violence and oppression, the consequences perhaps had outlived the causes, as customs survive opinions.

Sybil looked towards Westminster, to those proud and passionate halls where assembles the Parliament of England; that rapacious, violent, and haughty body, that had brought kings and prelates to the block; spoiled churches and then seized the sacred manors for their personal prey; invested their own possessions with infinite privileges, and then mortgaged for their state and empire the labour of countless generations. Could the voice of solace sound from such a quarter?

Sybil unfolded a journal which she had brought; not now to be read for the first time; but now for the first time to be read alone, undisturbed, in a scene of softness and serenity. It contained a report of the debate in the House of Commons on the presentation of the National Petition; that important document which had been the means of drawing forth Sybil from her solitude, and of teaching her something of that world of which she had often pondered, and yet which she had so inaccurately preconceived.

Yes! there was one voice that had sounded in that proud Parliament, that free from the slang of faction, had dared to express immortal truths: the voice of a noble, who without being a demagogue, had upheld the popular cause; had pronounced his conviction that the rights of labour were as sacred as those of property; that if a difference were to be established, the interests of the living wealth ought to be preferred; who had declared that the social happiness of the millions should be the first object of a statesman, and that if that were not achieved, thrones and dominions, the pomp and power of courts and empires, were alike worthless.

With a heart not without emotion; with a kindling cheek, and eyes suffused with tears, Sybil read the speech of Egremont. She ceased; still holding the paper with one hand, she laid on it the other with tenderness, and looked up to breathe as it were for relief. Before her stood the orator himself.

CHAPTER II.

EGREMONT had recognized Sybil as she entered the garden. He was himself crossing the park to attend a committee of the House of Commons which had sat for the first time that morning. The meeting had been formal and brief; the committee soon adjourned, and Egremont repaired to the spot where he was in the hope of still finding Sybil.

He approached her not without some restraint; with reserve and yet with tenderness. 'This is a great, an unexpected pleasure indeed,' he said in a faltering tone. She had looked up; the expression of an agitation, not distressful, on her beautiful countenance could not be concealed. She smiled through a gushing vision; and with a flushed cheek, impelled perhaps by her native frankness, perhaps by some softer and irresistible feeling of gratitude, respect, regard, she said in a low voice, 'I was reading your beautiful speech.'

'Indeed,' said Egremont much moved, 'that is an honour,—a pleasure,—a reward, I never could have even hoped to have attained.'

'By all,' continued Sybil with more self-possession, 'it must be read with pleasure, with advantage, but by me—oh! with what deep interest.'

'If anything that I said finds an echo in your breast,' and here he hesitated, '—it will give me confidence for the future,' he hurriedly added.

'Ah! why do not others feel like you!' said Sybil, 'all would not then be hopeless.'

'But you are not hopeless,' said Egremont, and he seated himself on the bench, but at some distance from her.

Sybil shook her head.

'But when we spoke last,' said Egremont, 'you were full of confidence—in your cause, and in your means.'

'It is not very long ago,' said Sybil, 'since we thus spoke, and yet time in the interval has taught me some bitter truths.'

'Truth is very precious,' said Egremont, 'to us all; and yet I fear I could not sufficiently appreciate the cause that deprived you of your sanguine faith.'

'Alas!' said Sybil mournfully, 'I was but a dreamer of dreams: I wake from my hallucination as others have done I suppose before me. Like them too I feel the glory of life has gone;* but my content at least,' and she bent her head meekly, 'has never rested I hope too much on this world.'

'You are depressed, dear Sybil?'

'I am unhappy. I am anxious about my father. I fear that he is surrounded by men unworthy of his confidence. These scenes of violence
alarm me. Under any circumstances I should shrink from them, but
I am impressed with the conviction that they can bring us nothing but
disaster and disgrace.'

'I honour your father,' said Egremont, 'I know no man whose character I esteem so truly noble; such a just compound of intelligence and
courage, and gentle and generous impulse. I should deeply grieve were
he to compromise himself. But you have influence over him, the greatest,
as you have over all. Counsel him to return to Mowbray.'

'Can I give counsel?' said Sybil, 'I who have been wrong in all my
judgments? I came up to this city with him, to be his guide, his guardian. What arrogance! What short-sighted pride! I thought the People
all felt as I feel; that I had nothing to do but to sustain and animate him;
to encourage him when he flagged, to uphold him when he wavered.
I thought that moral power must govern the world, and that moral
power was embodied in an assembly whose annals will be a series of
petty intrigues, or, what is worse, of violent machinations.'

'Exert every energy,' said Egremont, 'that your father should leave
London, immediately; to-morrow, to-night if possible. After this business at Birmingham, the government must act. I hear that they will
immediately increase the army and the police; and that there is a circular from the Secretary of State to the Lords Lieutenant of counties.
But the government will strike at the Convention. The members who
remain will be the victims. If your father return to Mowbray and be
quiet, he has a chance of not being disturbed.'

'An ignoble end of many lofty hopes,' said Sybil.

'Let us retain our hopes,' said Egremont, 'and cherish them.'

'I have none,' she replied.

'And I am sanguine,' said Egremont.

'Ah! because you have made a beautiful speech. But they will listen
to you, they will cheer you, but they will never follow you. The dove and
the eagle will not mate; the lion and the lamb will not lie down together;
and the conquerors will never rescue the conquered.'

Egremont shook his head. 'You still will cherish these phantoms,
dear Sybil! and why? They are not visions of delight. Believe me they
are as vain as they are distressing. The mind of England is the mind
ever of the rising race. Trust me it is with the People. And not the less
so, because this feeling is one of which even in a great degree it is
unconscious. Those opinions which you have been educated to dread
and mistrust are opinions that are dying away. Predominant opinions

are generally the opinions of the generation that is vanishing. Let an accident, which speculation could not foresee, the balanced state at this moment of parliamentary parties cease, and in a few years, more or less, cease it must, and you will witness a development of the new mind of England, which will make up by its rapid progress for its retarded action. I live among these men; I know their inmost souls; I watch their instincts and their impulses; I know the principles which they have imbibed, and I know, however hindered by circumstances for the moment, those principles must bear their fruit. It will be a produce hostile to the oligarchical system. The future principle of English politics will not be a levelling principle; not a principle adverse to privileges, but favourable to their extension. It will seek to ensure equality, not by levelling the Few but by elevating the Many.'

Indulging for some little time in the mutual reflections, which the tone of the conversation suggested, Sybil at length rose, and saying that she hoped by this time her father might have returned, bade farewell to Egremont, but he also rising would for a time accompany her. At the gate of the gardens however she paused, and said with a soft sad smile, 'Here we must part,' and extended to him her hand.

'Heaven will guard over you!' said Egremont, 'for you are a celestial charge.'

CHAPTER III.

As Sybil approached her home, she recognized her father in the court before their house, accompanied by several men, with whom he seemed on the point of going forth. She was so anxious to speak to Gerard, that she did not hesitate at once to advance. There was a stir as she entered the gate; the men ceased talking, some stood aloof, all welcomed her with silent respect. With one or two Sybil was not entirely unacquainted; at least by name or person. To them, as she passed, she bent her head; and then going up to her father, who was about to welcome her, she said, in a tone of calmness and with a semblance of composure, 'If you are going out, dear father, I should like to see you for one moment first.'

'A moment, friends,' said Gerard, 'with your leave;' and he accompanied his daughter into the house. He would have stopped in the hall, but she walked on to their room, and Gerard, though pressed for time, was compelled to follow her. When they had entered their chamber, Sybil closed the door with care, and then, Gerard sitting, or rather leaning carelessly, on the edge of the table, she said, 'We are once more together, dear father; we will never again be separated.'

Gerard sprang quickly on his legs, his eye kindled, his cheek flushed. 'Something has happened to you, Sybil!'

'No,' she said, shaking her head mournfully, 'not that; but something may happen to you.'

'How so, my child?' said her father, relapsing into his customary good-tempered placidity, and speaking in an easy, measured, almost drawling tone that was habitual to him.

'You are in danger,' said Sybil, 'great and immediate. No matter at this moment how I am persuaded of this: I wish no mysteries, but there is no time for details. The government will strike at the Convention; they are resolved. This outbreak at Birmingham has brought affairs to a crisis. They have already arrested the leaders there; they will seize those who remain here in avowed correspondence with them.'

'If they arrest all who are in correspondence with the Convention,' said Gerard, 'they will have enough to do.'

'Yes; but you take a leading part,' said Sybil; 'you are the individual they would select.'

'Would you have me hide myself?' said Gerard, 'just because something is going on besides talk.'

'Besides talk!' exclaimed Sybil. 'O! my father, what thoughts are these! It may be that words are vain to save us; but feeble deeds are vainer far than words.'

'I do not see that the deeds, though I have nothing to do with them, are so feeble,' said Gerard; 'their boasted police are beaten, and by the isolated movement of an unorganized mass. What if the outbreak had not been a solitary one? What if the people had been disciplined?'

'What if everything were changed, if everything were contrary to what it is?' said Sybil. 'The people are not disciplined; their action will not be, cannot be, coherent and uniform; these are riots in which you are involved, not revolutions; and you will be a victim, and not a sacrifice.'

Gerard looked thoughtful, but not anxious: after a momentary pause, he said, 'We must not be scared at a few arrests, Sybil. These are haphazard pranks of a government that wants to terrify, but is itself frightened. I have not counselled, none of us have counselled, this stir at Birmingham. It is a casualty. We were none of us prepared for it. But great things spring from casualties. I say the police were beaten and the troops alarmed; and I say this was done without organization and in a single spot. I am as much against feeble deeds as you can be, Sybil; and to prove this to you, our conversation at the moment you arrived, was to take care for the future that there shall be none. Neither vain words nor feeble deeds for the future,' added Gerard, and he moved to depart.

Sybil approached him with gentleness; she took his hand as if to bid him farewell; she retained it for a moment, and looked at him steadfastly in the face, with a glance at the same time serious and soft. Then throwing her arms round his neck and leaning her cheek upon his breast, she murmured, 'Oh! my father, your child is most unhappy.'

'Sybil,' exclaimed Gerard in a tone of tender reproach, 'this is womanish weakness; I love, but must not share it.'

'It may be womanish,' said Sybil, 'but it is wise: for what should make us unhappy if not the sense of impending, yet unknown, danger?'

'And why danger?' said Gerard.

'Why mystery?' said Sybil. 'Why are you ever pre-occupied and involved in dark thoughts, my father? It is not the pressure of business, as you will perhaps tell me, that occasions this change in a disposition so frank and even careless. The pressure of affairs is not nearly as great, cannot be nearly as great, as in the early period of your assembling, when the eyes of the whole country were on you, and you were in communication with all parts of it. How often have you told me that there was no degree of business which you found irksome? Now you are all dispersed and scattered: no discussions, no committees, little correspondence—and you yourself are ever brooding and ever in conclave, with persons too who I know, for Stephen has told me so, are the preachers of violence: violence perhaps that some of them may preach, yet will not practise: both bad; traitors it may be, or, at the best, harebrained men.'

'Stephen is prejudiced,' said Gerard. 'He is a visionary, indulging in impossible dreams, and if possible, little desirable. He knows nothing of the feeling of the country or the character of his countrymen. Englishmen want none of his joint-stock felicity; they want their rights,—rights consistent with the rights of other classes, but without which the rights of other classes cannot, and ought not, to be secure.'

'Stephen is at least your friend, my father; and once you honoured him.'

'And do so now; and love him very dearly. I honour him for his great abilities and knowledge. Stephen is a scholar; I have no pretensions that way; but I can feel the pulse of a people, and can comprehend the signs of the times, Sybil. Stephen was all very well talking in our cottage and garden at Mowbray, when we had nothing to do; but now we must act, or others will act for us. Stephen is not a practical man; he is crotchety, Sybil, and that's just it.'

'But violence and action,' said Sybil, 'are they identical, my father?'

'I did not speak of violence.'

'No; but you looked it. I know the language of your countenance, even to the quiver of your lip. Action, as you and Stephen once taught me, and I think wisely, was to prove to our rulers by an agitation, orderly and intellectual, that we were sensible of our degradation; and that it was neither Christianlike nor prudent, neither good nor wise, to let us remain so. That you did, and you did it well; the respect of the world, even of those who differed from you in interest or opinion, was not withheld from you; and can be withheld from none who exercise the moral power that springs from great talents and a good cause. You have let this great moral power, this pearl of price,' said Sybil with emotion,—'we cannot conceal it from ourselves, my father,—you have let it escape from your hands.'

Gerard looked at her as she spoke with an earnestness unusual with him. As she ceased, he cast his eyes down, and seemed for a moment deep in thought; then looking up, he said, 'The season for words is past. I must be gone, dear Sybil.' And he moved towards the door.

'You shall not leave me,' said Sybil, springing forward, and seizing his arm.

'What would you, what would you?' said Gerard, distressed.

'That we should quit this city to-night.'

'What, quit my post?'

'Why yours? Have not your colleagues dispersed? Is not your assembly formally adjourned to another town?* Is it not known that the great majority of the delegates have returned to their homes? And why not you to yours?'

'I have no home,' said Gerard, almost in a voice of harshness. 'I came here to do the business that was wanting, and, by the blessing of God, I will do it. I am no changeling, nor can I refine and split straws, like your philosophers and Morleys; but if the people will struggle, I will struggle with them; and die, if need be, in the front. Nor will I be deterred from my purpose by the tears of a girl,' and he released himself from the hand of his daughter with abruptness.

Sybil looked up to heaven with streaming eyes, and clasped her hands in unutterable woe. Gerard moved again towards the door, but before he reached it, his step faltered, and he turned again and looked at his daughter with tenderness and anxiety. She remained in the same position, save that her arms that had fallen were crossed before her, and her downward glance seemed fixed in deep abstraction. Her father approached her unnoticed; he took her hand; she started, and looking round with a cold and distressed expression, said, in a smothered tone, 'I thought you had gone.'

'Not in anger, my sweet child,' and Gerard pressed her to his heart.

'But you go,' murmured Sybil.

'These men await me,' said Gerard. 'Our council is of importance. We must take some immediate steps for the aid of our brethren in distress at Birmingham, and to discountenance similar scenes of outbreak as this affair: but the moment this is over, I will come back to you; and for the rest, it shall be as you desire; to-morrow we will return to Mowbray.'

Sybil returned her father's embrace with a warmth which expressed her sense of his kindness and her own soothed feelings, but she said nothing; and bidding her now to be of good cheer, Gerard quitted the apartment.

CHAPTER IV.

THE clock of St. John's church struck three, and the clock of St. John's church struck four; and the fifth hour sounded from St. John's church; and the clock of St. John's was sounding six. And Gerard had not yet returned.

The time for a while after his departure had been comparatively light-hearted and agreeable. Easier in her mind and for a time busied with the preparations for their journey, Sybil sate by the open window more serene and cheerful than for a long period had been her wont. Sometimes she ceased for a moment from her volume and fell into a reverie of the morrow and of Mowbray. Viewed through the magic haze of time and distance, the scene of her youth assumed a character of tenderness and even of peaceful bliss. She sighed for the days of their cottage and their garden, when the discontent of her father was only theoretical, and their political conclaves were limited to a discussion between him and Morley on the rights of the people or the principles of society. The bright waters of the Move and its wooded hills; her matin walks to the convent to visit Ursula Trafford—a pilgrimage of piety and charity and love; the faithful Harold, so devoted and so intelligent; even the crowded haunts of labour and suffering among which she glided like an angel, blessing and blessed; they rose before her—those touching images of the past—and her eyes were suffused with tears, of tenderness, not of gloom.

And blended with them the thought of one who had been for a season the kind and gentle companion of her girlhood—that Mr. Franklin whom she had never quite forgotten, and who, alas! was not Mr. Franklin after all. Ah! that was a wonderful history; a somewhat thrilling chapter in the memory of one so innocent and so young! His voice even now lingered in her ear. She recalled without an effort those tones of the morning, tones of tenderness and yet of wisdom and considerate thought, that had sounded only for her welfare. Never had Egremont appeared to her in a light so subduing. He was what man should be to woman ever—gentle, and yet a guide. A thousand images dazzling and wild rose in her mind; a thousand thoughts, beautiful and quivering as the twilight, clustered round her heart; for a moment she indulged in impossible dreams, and seemed to have entered a newly discovered world. The horizon of her experience expanded like the glittering heaven of a fairy tale. Her eye was fixed in lustrous contemplation, the flush on her cheek was a messenger from her heart, the movement of her mouth would have in an instant become a smile, when the clock of St. John's struck four, and Sybil started from her reverie.

The clock of St. John's struck four, and Sybil became anxious; the clock of St. John's struck five, and Sybil became disquieted; restless and perturbed, she was walking up and down the chamber, her books long since thrown aside, when the clock of St. John's struck six.

She clasped her hands and looked up to heaven. There was a knock at the street door; she herself sprang out to open it. It was not Gerard. It was Morley.

'Ah! Stephen,' said Sybil, with a countenance of undisguised disappointment, 'I thought it was my father.'

'I should have been glad to have found him here,' said Morley. 'However with your permission I will enter.'

'And he will soon arrive,' said Sybil; 'I am sure he will soon arrive. I have been expecting him every minute—'

'For hours,' added Morley, finishing her sentence, as they entered the room. 'The business that he is on,' he continued, throwing himself into a chair with a recklessness very unlike his usual composure and even precision, 'the business that he is on is engrossing.'

'Thank Heaven,' said Sybil, 'we leave this place to-morrow.'

'Hah!' said Morley starting, 'who told you so?'

'My father has so settled it; has indeed promised me that we shall depart.'

'And you were anxious to do so.'

'Most anxious; my mind is prophetic only of mischief to him if we remain.'

'Mine too. Otherwise I should not have come up to-day.'

'You have seen him I hope?' said Sybil.

'I have; I have been hours with him.'

'I am glad. At this conference he talked of?'

'Yes; at this headstrong council; and I have seen him since; alone. Whatever hap to him, my conscience is assoiled.'*

'You terrify me, Stephen,' said Sybil rising from her seat. 'What can happen to him? What would he do, what would you resist? Tell me—tell me, dear friend.'

'Oh! yes,' said Morley, pale and with a slight yet bitter smile. 'Oh! yes; dear friend!'

'I said dear friend for so I deemed you,' said Sybil; 'and so we have ever found you. Why do you stare at me so strangely, Stephen?'

'So you deem me, and so you have ever found me,' said Morley in a slow and measured tone, repeating her words. 'Well; what more would you have? what more should any of us want?' he asked abruptly.

'I want no more,' said Sybil innocently.

'I warrant me, you do not. Well, well; nothing matters. And so,' he added in his ordinary tone, 'you are waiting for your father?'

'Whom you have not long since seen,' said Sybil, 'and whom you expected to find here?'

'No;' said Morley, shaking his head with the same bitter smile; 'no, no, I didn't. I came to find you.'

'You have something to tell me,' said Sybil earnestly. 'Something has happened to my father. Do not break it to me; tell me at once,' and she advanced and laid her hand upon his arm.

Morley trembled; and then in a hurried and agitated voice, said, 'No, no, no; nothing has happened. Much may happen, but nothing has happened. And we may prevent it.'

'We! Tell me what may happen; tell me what to do.'

'Your father,' said Morley, slowly rising from his seat and pacing the room, and speaking in a low calm voice, 'your father—and my friend—is in this position Sybil: he is conspiring against the State.'

'Yes, yes,' said Sybil very pale, speaking, almost in a whisper and with her gaze fixed intently on her companion. 'Tell me all.'

'I will. He is conspiring, I say, against the State. To-night they meet in secret to give the last finish to their plans; and to-night they will be arrested.'

'O God!' said Sybil clasping her hands. 'He told me truth.'

'Who told you truth?' said Morley, springing to her side, in a hoarse voice and with an eye of fire.

'A friend,' said Sybil, dropping her arms and bending her head in woe; 'a kind good friend. I met him but this morn, and he warned me of all this.'

'Hah, hah!' said Morley with a sort of stifled laugh; 'Hah, hah; he told you did he; the kind good friend whom you met this morning? Did I not warn you, Sybil, of the traitor? Did I not tell you to beware of taking this false aristocrat to your hearth; to worm out all the secrets of that home that he once polluted by his espionage, and now would desolate by his treason.'

'Of whom and what do you speak?' said Sybil, throwing herself into a chair.

'I speak of that base spy Egremont.'

'You slander an honourable man,' said Sybil with dignity. 'Mr. Egremont has never entered this house since you met him here for the first time: save once.'

'He needed no entrance to this house to worm out its secrets,' said Morley maliciously. 'That could be more adroitly done by one who had assignations at command with the most charming of its inmates.'

'Unmannerly churl!' exclaimed Sybil starting in her chair, her eye flashing lightning, her distended nostril quivering with scorn.

'Oh! yes, I am a churl,' said Morley; 'I know I am a churl. Were I a noble the daughter of the people would perhaps condescend to treat me with less contempt.'

'The daughter of the people loves truth and manly bearing, Stephen Morley; and will treat with contempt all those who slander women, whether they be nobles or serfs.'

'And where is the slanderer?'

'Ask him who told you I held assignations with Mr. Egremont or with any one.'

'Mine eyes—mine own eyes—were my informant,' said Morley. 'This morn, the very morn I arrived in London, I learnt how your matins were now spent. Yes!' he added in a tone of mournful anguish, 'I passed the gate of the gardens; I witnessed your adieus.'

'We met by hazard,' said Sybil, in a calm tone, and with an expression that denoted she was thinking of other things, 'and in all probability we shall never meet again. Talk not of these trifles, Stephen; my father, how can we save him?'

'Are they trifles?' said Morley, slowly and earnestly, walking to her side, and looking her intently in the face. 'Are they indeed trifles, Sybil? Oh! make me credit that, and then—' he paused.

Sybil returned his gaze: the deep lustre of her dark orb rested on his peering vision; his eye fled from the unequal contest; his heart throbbed, his limbs trembled; he fell upon his knee.

'Pardon me, pardon me,' he said, and he took her hand. 'Pardon the most miserable and the most devoted of men!'

'What need of pardon, dear Stephen?' said Sybil in a soothing tone. 'In the agitated hour wild words escape. If I have used them, I regret; if you, I have forgotten.'

The clock of St. John's told that the sixth hour was more than half-past.

'Ah!' said Sybil, withdrawing her hand, 'you told me how precious was time. What can we do?'

Morley rose from his kneeling position, and again paced the chamber, lost for some moments in deep meditation. Suddenly he seized her arm, and said, 'I can endure no longer the anguish of my life: I love you, and if you will not be mine, I care for no one's fate.'

'I am not born for love,' said Sybil, frightened, yet endeavouring to conceal her alarm.

'We are all born for love,' said Morley. 'It is the principle of existence, and its only end. And love of you, Sybil,' he continued, in a tone of impassioned pathos, 'has been to me for years the hoarded treasure of my life. For this I have haunted your hearth and hovered round your home; for this I have served your father like a slave, and embarked in a cause with which I have little sympathy, and which can meet with no success. It is your image that has stimulated my ambition, developed my powers, sustained me in the hour of humiliation, and secured me that material prosperity which I can now command. Oh! deign to share it; share it with the impassioned heart and the devoted life that now bow before you; and do not shrink from them, because they are the feelings and the fortunes of the People.'

'You astound, you overwhelm me,' said Sybil, agitated. 'You came for another purpose, we were speaking of other feelings; it is the hour of exigency you choose for these strange, these startling words.'

'I also have my hour of exigency,' said Morley, 'and its minutes are now numbering. Upon it all depends.'

'Another time,' said Sybil, in a low and deprecatory voice; 'speak of these things another time!'

'The caverns of my mind* are open,' said Morley, 'and they will not close.'

'Stephen,' said Sybil, 'dear Stephen, I am grateful for your kind feelings; but indeed this is not the time for such passages: cease, my friend!'

'I came to know my fate,' said Morley, doggedly.

'It is a sacrilege of sentiment,' said Sybil, unable any longer to restrain her emotion, 'to obtrude its expression on a daughter at such a moment.'

'You would not deem it so if you loved, or if you could love me, Sybil,' said Morley, mournfully. 'Why it's a moment of deep feeling, and suited for the expression of deep feeling. You would not have answered thus, if he who had been kneeling here had been named Egremont.'

'He would not have adopted a course,' said Sybil, unable any longer to restrain her displeasure, 'so selfish, so indecent.'

'Ah! she loves him!' exclaimed Morley, springing on his legs, and with a demoniac laugh.

There was a pause. Under ordinary circumstances Sybil would have left the room and terminated a distressing interview, but in the present instance that was impossible; for on the continuance of that interview any hope of assisting her father depended. Morley had thrown himself into a chair opposite her, leaning back in silence with his face covered; Sybil was disinclined to revive the conversation about her father, because she had already perceived that Morley was only too much aware of the command which the subject gave him over her feelings and even conduct. Yet time, time now full of terror, time was stealing on. It was evident that Morley would not break the silence. At length, unable any longer to repress her tortured heart, Sybil said, 'Stephen, be generous; speak to me of your friend.'

'I have no friend,' said Morley, without taking his hands from his face.

'The Saints in heaven have mercy on me,' said Sybil, 'for I am very wretched.'

'No, no, no,' said Morley, rising rapidly from his seat, and again kneeling at her side, 'not wretched; not that tone of anguish! What can I do? what say? Sybil, dearest Sybil, I love you so much, so fervently, so devotedly; none can love you as I do; say not you are wretched!'

'Alas! alas!' said Sybil.

'What shall I do? what say?' said Morley.

'You know what I would have you say,' said Sybil. 'Speak of one who is my father, if NO longer your friend: you know what I would have you do—save him: save him from death and me from despair.'

'I am ready,' said Morley; 'I came for that. Listen. There is a meeting to-night at half-past eight o'clock; they meet to arrange a general rising in the country: their intention is known to the government; they will be arrested. Now it is in my power, which it was not when I saw your father this morning, to convince him of the truth of this, and were I to see him before eight o'clock, which I could easily do, I could prevent his attendance, certainly prevent his attendance, and he would be saved; for the government depend much upon the papers, some proclamations, and things of that kind, which will be signed this evening, for their proofs. Well, I am ready to save Gerard, my friend, for so I'll call him as you wish it; one I have served before and long; one whom I came up from Mowbray this day to serve and save; I am ready to do that which you require; you yourself admit it is no light deed; and coming from one you have known so long, and, as you confess, so much regarded, should be doubly cherished; I am ready to do this great service; to save the father from death and the daughter from despair,—if she would but only say to me, "I have but one reward, and it is yours." '

'I have read of something of this sort,' said Sybil, speaking in a murmuring tone, and looking round her with a wild expression, 'this bargaining of blood, and shall I call it love? But that was ever between the oppressors and the oppressed. This is the first time that a child of the people has been so assailed by one of her own class, and who exercises his power from the confidence which the sympathy of their sorrows alone caused. It is bitter; bitter for me and mine—but for you, pollution.'

'Am I answered?' said Morley.

'Yes,' said Sybil, 'in the name of the holy Virgin.'

'Good night, then,' said Morley, and he approached the door. His hand was on it. The voice of Sybil made him turn his head.

'Where do they meet to-night?' she inquired, in a smothered tone.

'I am bound to secrecy,' said Morley.

'There is no softness in your spirit,' said Sybil.

'I am met with none.'

'We have ever been your friends.'

'A blossom that has brought no fruit.'

'This hour will be remembered at the judgment-seat,' said Sybil.

'The holy Virgin will perhaps interpose for me,' said Morley, with a sneer.

'We have merited this,' said Sybil, 'who have taken an infidel to our hearts.'

'If he had only been a heretic, like Egremont!' said Morley.

Sybil burst into tears. Morley sprang to her. 'Swear by the holy Virgin, swear by all the saints, swear by your hope of heaven and by your own sweet name; without equivocation, without reserve, with

fulness and with truth, that you will never give your heart or hand to
Egremont;—and I will save your father.'

As in a low voice, but with a terrible earnestness, Morley dictated
this oath, Sybil, already pale, became white as the marble saint of some
sacred niche. Her large dark eyes seemed fixed; a fleet expression of
agony flitted over her beautiful brow like a cloud; and she said, 'I swear
that I will never give my hand to—'

'And your heart, your heart,' said Morley eagerly. 'Omit not that.
Swear by the holy oaths again you do not love him. She falters! Ah! she
blushes!' For a burning brightness now suffused the cheek of Sybil.
'She loves him,' exclaimed Morley, wildly, and he rushed franticly
from the room.

CHAPTER V.

AGITATED and overcome by these unexpected and passionate appeals,
and these outrageous ebullitions acting on her at a time when she herself was labouring under no ordinary excitement, and was distracted
with disturbing thoughts, the mind of Sybil seemed for a moment to
desert her; neither by sound nor gesture did she signify her sense of
Morley's last words and departure; and it was not until the loud closing
of the street door echoing through the long passage recalled her to herself, that she was aware how much was at stake in that incident. She
darted out of the room to recall him; to make one more effort for her
father; but in vain. By the side of their house was an intricate passage
leading into a labyrinth of small streets. Through this Morley had disappeared; and his name, more than once sounded in a voice of anguish
in that silent and most obsolete Smith's Square, received no echo.

Darkness and terror came over the spirit of Sybil; a sense of confounding and confusing woe, with which it was in vain to cope. The
conviction of her helplessness prostrated her. She sate her down upon
the steps before the door of that dreary house, within the railings of
that gloomy court, and buried her face in her hands: a wild vision
of the past and the future, without thought or feeling, coherence or
consequence: sunset gleams of vanished bliss, and stormy gusts of
impending doom.

The clock of St. John's struck seven.

It was the only thing that spoke in that still and dreary square; it was
the only voice that there seemed ever to sound; but it was a voice from
heaven; it was the voice of St. John.

Sybil looked up; she looked up at the holy building. Sybil listened; she listened to the holy sounds. St. John told her that the danger of her father was yet so much advanced. Oh! why are there saints in heaven if they cannot aid the saintly! The oath that Morley would have enforced came whispering in the ear of Sybil—'Swear by the holy Virgin and by all the saints.'

And shall she not pray to the holy Virgin and all the saints? Sybil prayed; she prayed to the holy Virgin and all the saints; and especially to the beloved St. John: most favoured among Hebrew men, on whose breast reposed the divine Friend.*

Brightness and courage returned to the spirit of Sybil; a sense of animating and exalting faith that could move mountains, and combat without fear a thousand perils. The conviction of celestial aid inspired her. She rose from her sad resting-place and re-entered the house; only, however, to provide herself with her walking attire, and then alone and without a guide, the shades of evening already descending, this child of innocence and divine thoughts, born in a cottage and bred in a cloister, she went forth, on a great enterprise of duty and devotion, into the busiest and the wildest haunts of the greatest of modern cities.

Sybil knew well her way to Palace Yard. This point was soon reached; she desired the cabman to drive her to a street in the Strand in which was a coffee-house,* where during the last weeks of their stay in London the scanty remnants of the National Convention had held their sittings. It was by a mere accident that Sybil had learnt this circumstance, for when she had attended the meetings of the Convention in order to hear her father's speeches, it was in the prime of their gathering and when their numbers were great, and when they met in audacious rivalry opposite that St. Stephen's* which they wished to supersede. This accidental recollection however was her only clue in the urgent adventure on which she had embarked.

She cast an anxious glance at the clock of St. Martin's* as she passed that church; the hand was approaching the half hour of seven. She urged on the driver; they were in the Strand; there was an agitating stoppage; she was about to descend when the obstacle was removed; and in a few minutes they turned down the street which she sought.

'What number, Ma'am?' asked the cabman.

''Tis a coffee-house; I know not the number nor the name of him who keeps it. 'Tis a coffee-house. Can you see one? Look, look, I pray you! I am much pressed.'

'Here's a coffee-house, Ma'am,' said the man in a hoarse voice.

'How good you are! Yes; I will get out. You will wait for me, I am sure?'

'All right,' said the cabman, as Sybil entered the illumined door. 'Poor young thing! she's wery anxious about summut.'

Sybil at once stepped into a rather capacious room, fitted up in the old-fashioned style of coffee-rooms, with mahogany boxes, in several of which were men drinking coffee and reading newspapers by a painful glare of gas. There was a waiter in the middle of the room who was throwing some fresh sand upon the floor, but who stared immensely when looking up he beheld Sybil.

'Now, Ma'am, if you please,' said the waiter inquiringly.

'Is Mr. Gerard here?' said Sybil.

'No, Ma'am; Mr. Gerard has not been here to-day, nor yesterday neither'—and he went on throwing the sand.

'I should like to see the master of the house,' said Sybil very humbly.

'Should you, Ma'am?' said the waiter, but he gave no indication of assisting her in the fulfilment of her wish.

Sybil repeated that wish, and this time the waiter said nothing.

This vulgar and insolent neglect to which she was so little accustomed depressed her spirit. She could have encountered tyranny and oppression, and she would have tried to struggle with them; but this insolence of the insignificant made her feel her insignificance; and the absorption all this time of the guests in their newspapers aggravated her nervous sense of her utter helplessness. All her feminine reserve and modesty came over her; alone in this room among men, she felt overpowered, and she was about to make a precipitate retreat when the clock of the coffee-room sounded the half hour. In a paroxysm of nervous excitement she exclaimed, 'Is there not one among you who will assist me?'

All the newspaper readers put down their journals and stared.

'Hoity-toity,' said the waiter, and he left off throwing the sand.

'Well, what's the matter now?' said one of the guests.

'I wish to see the master of the house on business of urgency,' said Sybil, 'to himself and to one of his friends, and his servant here will not even reply to my inquiries.'

'I say, Saul, why don't you answer the young lady?' said another guest.

'So I did,' said Saul. 'Did you call for coffee, Ma'am?'

'Here's Mr. Tanner, if you want him, my dear,' said the first guest, as a lean black-looking individual, with grizzled hair and a red nose, entered the coffee-room from the interior. 'Tanner, here's a lady wants you.'

'And a very pretty girl too,' whispered one to another.

'What's your pleasure?' said Mr. Tanner abruptly.

'I wish to speak to you alone,' said Sybil; and advancing towards him she said in a low voice, ''Tis about Walter Gerard I would speak to you.'

'Well, you can step in here if you like,' said Tanner very discourteously; 'there's only my wife;' and he led the way to the inner room, a small close parlour adorned with portraits of Tom Paine, Cobbett, Thistlewood, and General Jackson;* with a fire, though it was a hot July, and a very fat woman affording still more heat, and who was drinking shrub* and water and reading the police reports. She stared rudely at Sybil as she entered following Tanner, who himself when the door was closed said, 'Well, now what have you got to say?'

'I wish to see Walter Gerard.'

'Do you indeed!'

'And,' continued Sybil notwithstanding his sneering remark, 'I come here that you may tell me where I may find him.'

'I believe he lives somewhere in Westminster,' said Tanner, 'that's all I know about him; and if this be all you had to say it might have been said in the coffee-room.'

'It is not all that I have to say,' said Sybil; 'and I beseech you, sir, listen to me. I know where Gerard lives; I am his daughter, and the same roof covers our heads. But I wish to know where they meet to-night—you understand me;' and she looked at his wife, who had resumed her police reports; ''tis urgent.'

'I don't know nothing about Gerard,' said Tanner, 'except that he comes here and goes away again.'

'The matter on which I would see him,' said Sybil, 'is as urgent as the imagination can conceive, and it concerns you as well as himself; but if you know not where I can find him'—and she moved as if about to retire—''tis of no use.'

'Stop,' said Tanner, 'you can tell it to me.'

'Why so? You know not where he is; you cannot tell it to him.'

'I don't know that,' said Tanner. 'Come, let's have it out; and if it will do him any good, I'll see if we can't manage to find him.'

'I can impart my news to him and no one else,' said Sybil. 'I am solemnly bound.'

'You can't have a better counseller than Tanner,' urged his wife, getting curious; 'you had better tell us.'

'I want no counsel; I want that which you can give me if you choose—information. My father instructed me that if certain circumstances occurred it was a matter of the last urgency that I should see him this evening and before nine o'clock, I was to call here and obtain from you the direction where to find him; the direction,' she added in a lowered tone, and looking Tanner full in the face, 'where they hold their secret council tonight.'

'Hem!' said Tanner; 'I see you're on the free-list. And pray how am I to know you *are* Gerard's daughter?'

'You do not doubt I am his daughter!' said Sybil proudly.

'Hem!' said Tanner; 'I do not know that I do very much,' and he whispered to his wife. Sybil removed from them as far as she was able.

'And this news is very urgent,' resumed Tanner; 'and concerns me you say?'

'Concerns you all,' said Sybil; 'and every minute is of the last importance.'

'I should like to have gone with you myself, and then there could have been no mistake,' said Tanner; 'but that can't be; we have a meeting here at half-past eight in our great room. I don't much like breaking rules, especially in such a business; and yet, concerning all of us, as you say, and so very urgent, I don't see how it could do harm; and I might—I wish I was quite sure you were the party.'

'How can I satisfy you?' said Sybil, distressed.

'Perhaps the young person have got her mark on her linen,' suggested the wife. 'Have you got a handkerchief Ma'am?' and she took Sybil's handkerchief and looked at it, and examined it at every corner. It had no mark. And this unforeseen circumstance of great suspicion might have destroyed everything, had not the production of the handkerchief by Sybil also brought forth a letter addressed to her from Hatton.

'It seems to be the party,' said the wife.

'Well,' said Tanner, 'you know St. Martin's Lane I suppose? Well, you go up St. Martin's Lane to a certain point, and then you will get into Seven Dials;* and then you'll go on. However it is impossible to direct you; you must find your way. Hunt Street, going out of Silver Street, No. 22. 'Tis what you call a blind street, with no thoroughfare, and then you go down an alley. Can you recollect that?'

'Fear not.'

'No. 22, Hunt Street, going out of Silver Street. Remember the alley. It's an ugly neighbourhood; but you go of your own accord.'

'Yes, yes. Good night.'

CHAPTER VI.

URGED by Sybil's entreaties the cab-driver hurried on. With all the skilled experience of a thorough cockney charioteer he tried to conquer

time and space by his rare knowledge of short cuts and fine acquaintance with unknown thoroughfares. He seemed to avoid every street
which was the customary passage of mankind. The houses, the population, the costume, the manners, the language through which they
whirled their way, were of a different state and nation to those with
which the dwellers in the dainty quarters of this city are acquainted.
Now dark streets of frippery and old stores, now market-places of
entrails and carrion with gutters running gore, sometimes the way was
enveloped in the yeasty fumes of a colossal brewery,* and sometimes
they plunged into a labyrinth of lanes teeming with life, and where the
dog-stealer and the pick-pocket, the burglar and the assassin, found
a sympathetic multitude of all ages; comrades for every enterprise; and
a market for every booty.

The long summer twilight was just expiring; the pale shadows of the
moon were just stealing on; the gas was beginning to glare in the shops
of tripe and bacon, and the paper lanthorns to adorn the stall and the stand.
They crossed a broad street which seemed the metropolis of the district; it flamed with gin-palaces; a multitude were sauntering in the
mild though tainted air; bargaining, blaspheming, drinking, wrangling;
and varying their business and their potations, their fierce strife and
their impious irreverence, with flashes of rich humour, gleams of native
wit, and racy phrases of idiomatic slang.

Absorbed in her great mission Sybil was almost insensible to the
scenes through which she passed, and her innocence was thus spared
many a sight and sound that might have startled her vision or alarmed
her ear. They could not now be very distant from the spot; they were
crossing this broad way, and then were about to enter another series of
small obscure dingy streets, when the cab-driver giving a flank to his
steed to stimulate it to a last effort, the horse sprang forward, and the
wheel of the cab came off.

Sybil extricated herself from the vehicle unhurt; a group immediately formed round the cab, a knot of young thieves, almost young
enough for infant schools, a dustman, a woman nearly naked and very
drunk, and two unshorn ruffians with brutality stamped on every feature, with pipes in their mouths, and their hands in their pockets.

'I can take you no further,' said the cabman: 'my fare is three
shillings.'

'What am I to do?' said Sybil, taking out her purse.

'The best thing the young lady can do,' said the dustman, in a hoarse
voice, 'is to stand something to us all.'

'That's your time o'day,' squeaked a young thief.

'I'll drink your health with very great pleasure my dear,' hiccupped the woman.

'How much have you got there?' said the young thief making a dash at the purse, but he was not quite tall enough, and failed.

'No wiolence,' said one of the ruffians taking his pipe out of his mouth and sending a volume of smoke into Sybil's face, 'we'll take the young lady to Mother Poppy's, and then we'll make a night of it.'

But at this moment appeared a policeman, one of the permanent garrison of the quarter, who seeing one of her Majesty's carriages* in trouble thought he must interfere. 'Hilloa,' he said, 'what's all this?' And the cabman, who was a good fellow though in too much trouble to aid Sybil, explained in the terse and picturesque language of Cockaigne, doing full justice to his late fare, the whole circumstances.

'Oh! that's it,' said the policeman, 'the lady's respectable is she? Then I'd advise you and Hell Fire Dick to stir your chalks, Splinterlegs. Keep moving's the time of day, Madam; you get on. Come;' and taking the woman by her shoulder he gave her a spin that sent her many a good yard. 'And what do you want?' he asked gruffly of the lads.

'We wants a ticket for the Mendicity Society,'* said the captain of the infant band putting his thumb to his nose and running away, followed by his troop.

'And so you want to go to Silver Street?' said her official preserver to Sybil, for she had not thought it wise to confess her ultimate purpose, and indicate under the apprehended circumstances the place of rendezvous to a member of the police.

'Well; that's not very difficult now. Go a-head; take the second turning to your right, and the third to your left, and you're landed.'

Aided by these instructions, Sybil hastened on, avoiding notice as much as was in her power, and assisted in some degree by the advancing gloom of night. She had reached Silver Street; a long, narrow, hilly street; and now she was at fault. There were not many persons about, and there were few shops here; yet one was at last at hand, and she entered to enquire her way. The person at the counter was engaged, and many customers awaited him: time was very precious: Sybil had made the enquiry and received only a supercilious stare from the shopman, who was weighing with precision some article that he was serving. A young man, shabby, but of a very superior appearance to the people of this quarter, good-looking, though with a dissolute air, and who seemed waiting for a customer in attendance, addressed Sybil. 'I am going to Hunt Street,' he said, 'shall I show you the way?'

She accepted this offer most thankfully. 'It is close at hand, I believe?'

'Here it is,' he said; and he turned down a street. 'What is your house?'

'No. 22: a printing-office,' said Sybil; for the street she had entered was so dark she despaired of finding her way, and ventured to trust so far a guide who was not a policeman.

'The very house I am going to,' said the stranger: 'I am a printer.' And they walked on some way, until they at length stopped before a glass and illumined door, covered with a red curtain. Before it was a group of several men and women brawling, but who did not notice Sybil and her companion.

'Here we are,' said the man; and he pushed the door open, inviting Sybil to enter. She hesitated; it did not agree with the description that had been given her by the coffee-house keeper, but she had seen so much since, and felt so much, and gone through so much, that she had not at the moment that clear command of her memory for which she was otherwise remarkable; but while she faltered an inner door was violently thrown open, and Sybil moving aside, two girls, still beautiful in spite of gin and paint, stepped into the street.

'This cannot be the house,' exclaimed Sybil starting back, overwhelmed with shame and terror. 'O! holy Virgin aid me!'

'And that's a blessed word to hear in this heathen land,' exclaimed an Irishman, who was one of the group on the outside.

'If you be of our holy church,' said Sybil appealing to the man who had thus spoken and whom she gently drew aside, 'I beseech you, by everything we hold sacred, to aid me.'

'And will I not?' said the man; 'and I should like to see the arm that would hurt you;' *and* he looked round, but the young man had disappeared. 'You are not a countrywoman I am thinking,' he added.

'No, but a sister in Christ,' said Sybil; 'listen to me, good friend. I hasten to my father,—he is in great danger,—in Hunt Street,—I know not my way,—every moment is precious,—guide me, I beseech you,—honestly and truly guide me!'

'Will I not? Don't you be afraid my dear. And her poor father is ill! I wish I had such a daughter! We have not far to go. You should have taken the next turning. We must walk up this again for 'tis a small street with no thoroughfare. Come on without fear.'

Nor did Sybil fear; for the description of the street which the honest man had incidentally given, tallied with her instructions. Encouraging her with many kind words, and full of rough courtesies, the good Irishman led her to the spot she had so long sought. There was the court she was told to enter. It was well lit, and descending the steps she stopped at the first door on her left, and knocked.

CHAPTER VII.

ON the same night that Sybil was encountering so many dangers, the saloons of Deloraine House blazed with a thousand lights to welcome the world of power and fashion to a festival of almost unprecedented magnificence. Fronting a royal park, its long lines of illumined windows and the bursts of gay and fantastic music that floated from its walls attracted the admiration and curiosity of another party that was assembled in the same fashionable quarter, beneath a canopy not less bright and reclining on a couch scarcely less luxurious, for they were lit by the stars and reposed upon the grass.

'I say, Jim,' said a young genius of fourteen stretching himself upon the turf, 'I pity them ere jarvies a sitting on their boxes all the night and waiting for the nobs what is dancing. They as no repose.'

'But they as porter,' replied his friend, a sedater spirit with the advantage of an additional year or two of experience. 'They takes their pot of half-and-half by turns, and if their name is called, the link* what they subscribe for to pay, sings out 'here;' and that's the way their guvners is done.'

'I think I should like to be a link Jim,' said the young one.

'I wish you may get it,' was the response: 'it's the next best thing to a crossing: it's what every one looks to when he enters public life, but he soon finds 'tain't to be done without a deal of interest. They keeps it to themselves, and never lets any one in unless he makes himself very troublesome and gets up a party agin 'em.'

'I wonder what the nobs has for supper,' said the young one pensively. 'Lots of kidneys I dare say.'

'Oh! no; sweets is the time of day in these here blowouts: syllabubs like blazes, and snapdragon* as makes the flunkys quite pale.'

'I would thank you, sir, not to tread upon this child,' said a widow. She had three others with her, slumbering around, and this was the youngest wrapt in her only shawl.

'Madam,' replied the person whom she addressed, in tolerable English, but with a marked accent, 'I have bivouacked in many lands, but never with so young a comrade: I beg you a thousand pardons.'

'Sir, you are very polite. These warm nights are a great blessing, but I am sure I know not what we shall do in the fall of the leaf.'

'Take no thought of the morrow,' said the foreigner, who was a Pole; had served as a boy beneath the suns of the Peninsula under Soult and fought against Diebitsch* on the banks of the icy Vistula. 'It brings many changes.' And arranging the cloak which he had taken that day out of pawn around him, he delivered himself up to sleep with that facility which is not uncommon among soldiers.

Here broke out a brawl: two girls began fighting and blaspheming; a man immediately came up, chastised and separated them. 'I am the Lord Mayor of the night,' he said, 'and I will have no row here. 'Tis the like of you that makes the beaks threaten to expel us from our lodgings.' His authority seemed generally recognized, the girls were quiet, but they had disturbed a sleeping man, who roused himself, looked around him and said with a scared look, 'Where am I? What's all this?'

'Oh! it's nothin',' said the elder of the two lads we first noticed, 'only a couple of unfortinate gals who've prigged a watch from a cove what was lushy and fell asleep under the trees between this and Kinsington.'*

'I wish they had not waked me,' said the man, 'I walked as far as from Stokenchurch, and that's a matter of forty miles, this morning to see if I could get some work, and went to bed here without any supper. I'm blessed if I worn't dreaming of a roast leg of pork.'

'It has not been a lucky day for me,' rejoined the lad, 'I could not find a single gentleman's horse to hold, so help me, except one what was at the House of Commons and he kept me there two mortal hours and said when he came out, that he would remember me next time. I ain't tasted no wittals to-day except some cat's-meat and a cold potato what was given me by a cabman; but I have got a quid* here, and if you are very low I'll give you half.'

In the meantime Lord Valentine and the Princess Stephanie of Eurasberg with some companions worthy of such a pair, were dancing a new Mazurka* before the admiring assembly at Deloraine House. The ball was in the statue gallery illumined on this night in the Russian fashion,* which while it diffused a brilliant light throughout the beautiful chamber, was peculiarly adapted to develop the contour of the marble forms of grace and loveliness that were ranged around.

'Where is Arabella?' enquired Lord Marney of his mother, 'I want to present young Huntingford to her. He can be of great use to me, but he bores me so, I cannot talk to him. I want to present him to Arabella.'

'Arabella is in the blue drawing-room. I saw her just now with Mr. Jermyn and Charles. Count Soudriaffsky is teaching them some Russian tricks.'

'What are Russian tricks to me; she must talk to young Huntingford; everything depends on his working with me against the Cut-and-Come-again branch-line; they have refused me my compensation, and I am not going to have my estate cut up into ribbons without compensation.'

'My dear Lady Deloraine,' said Lady de Mowbray. 'How beautiful your gallery looks to-night! Certainly there is nothing in London that lights up so well.'

'Its greatest ornaments are its guests. I am charmed to see Lady Joan looking so well.'

'You think so?'

'Indeed.'

'I wish—' and here Lady de Mowbray gave a smiling sigh. 'What do you think of Mr. Mountchesney?'

'He is universally admired.'

'So every one says, and yet—'

'Well what do you think of the Dashville, Fitz?' said Mr. Berners to Lord Fitzheron, 'I saw you dancing with her.'

'I can't bear her: she sets up to be natural and is only rude; mistakes insolence for innocence; says everything which comes first to her lips and thinks she is gay when she is only giddy.'

''Tis brilliant,' said Lady Joan to Mr. Mountchesney.

'When you are here,' he murmured.

'And yet a ball in a gallery of art is not in my opinion in good taste. The associations which are suggested by sculpture are not festive. Repose is the characteristic of sculpture.* Do not you think so?'

'Decidedly,' said Mr. Mountchesney. 'We danced in the gallery at Matfield this Christmas, and I thought all the time that a gallery is not the place for a ball; it is too long and too narrow.'

Lady Joan looked at him, and her lip rather curled.

'I wonder if Valentine has sold that bay cob of his,' said Lord Milford to Lord Eugene de Vere.

'I wonder,' said Lord Eugene.

'I wish you would ask him, Eugene,' said Lord Milford, 'you understand, I don't want him to know I want it.'

''Tis such a bore to ask questions,' said Lord Eugene.

'Shall we carry Chichester?' asked Lady Firebrace of Lady St. Julians.

'Oh! do not speak to me ever again of the House of Commons,' she replied in a tone of affected despair. 'What use is winning our way by units? It may take years. Lord Protocol says that 'one is enough.' That Jamaica affair has really ended by greatly strengthening them.'

'I do not despair,' said Lady Firebrace. 'The unequivocal adhesion of the Duke of Fitz-Aquitaine is a great thing. It gives us the northern division at a dissolution.'

'That is to say in five years, my dear Lady Firebrace. The country will be ruined before that.'

'We shall see. Is it a settled thing between Lady Joan and Mr. Mountchesney?'

'Not the slightest foundation. Lady Joan is a most sensible girl, as well as a most charming person and my dear friend. She is not in a hurry to marry, and quite right. If indeed Frederick were a little more steady—but nothing shall ever induce me to consent to his marrying her, unless I thought he was worthy of her.'

'You are such a good mother,' exclaimed Lady Firebrace, 'and such a good friend! I am glad to hear it is not true about Mr. Mountchesney.'

'If you could only help me, my dear Lady Firebrace, to put an end to that affair between Frederick and Lady Wallington. It is so silly, and getting talked about; and in his heart too he really loves Lady Joan; only he is scarcely aware of it himself.'

'We must manage it,' said Lady Firebrace, with a look of encouraging mystery.

'Do, my dear creature; speak to him; he is very much guided by your opinion. Tell him everybody is laughing at him, and any other little thing that occurs to you.'

'I will come directly,' said Lady Marney to her husband, 'only let me see this.'

'Well, I will bring Huntingford here. Mind you speak to him a great deal; take his arm, and go down to supper with him if you can. He is a very nice sensible young fellow, and you will like him very much I am sure; a little shy at first, but he only wants bringing out.'

A dexterous description of one of the most unlicked and unlickable cubs that ever entered society with forty thousand a year; courted by all, and with just that degree of cunning that made him suspicious of every attention.

'This dreadful Lord Huntingford!' said Lady Marney.

'Jermyn and I will interfere.' said Egremont, 'and help you.'

'No, no,' said Lady Marney shaking her head, 'I must do it.'

At this moment, a groom of the chambers advanced and drew Egremont aside, saying in a low tone, 'Your servant, Mr. Egremont, is here and wishes to see you instantly.'

'My servant! Instantly! What the deuce can be the matter? I hope the Albany is not on fire,' and he quitted the room.

In the outer hall, amid a crowd of footmen, Egremont recognized his valet who immediately came forward.

'A porter has brought this letter, sir, and I thought it best to come on with it at once.'

The letter directed to Egremont, bore also on its superscription these words. 'This letter must be instantly carried by the bearer to Mr. Egremont wherever he may be.'

Egremont with some change of countenance drew aside, and opening the letter read it by a lamp at hand. It must have been very brief; but the face of him to whom it was addressed became, as he perused its lines, greatly agitated. When he had finished reading it, he seemed for a moment lost in profound thought; then looking up he dismissed his servant without instructions, and hastening back to the assembly, he enquired of the groom of the chambers whether Lord John Russell, whom he had observed in the course of the evening, was still present; and he was answered in the affirmative.

About a quarter of an hour after this incident, Lady Firebrace said to Lady St. Julians in a tone of mysterious alarm, 'Do you see that?'

'No! what?'

'Do not look as if you observed them: Lord John and Mr. Egremont, in the furthest window, they have been there these ten minutes in the most earnest conversation. I am afraid we have lost him.'

'I have always been expecting it,' said Lady St. Julians. 'He breakfasts with that Mr. Trenchard and does all those sorts of things. Men who breakfast out are generally Liberals. Have not you observed that? I wonder why?'

'It shows a restless revolutionary mind,' said Lady Firebrace, 'that can settle to nothing; but must be running after gossip the moment they are awake.'

'Yes,' said Lady St. Julians. 'I think those men who breakfast out or who give breakfasts are generally dangerous characters; at least, I would not trust them. The Whigs are very fond of that sort of thing. If Mr. Egremont joins them, I really do not see what shadow of a claim Lady Deloraine can urge to have anything.'

'She only wants one thing,' said Lady Firebrace, 'and we know she cannot have that.'

'Why?'

'Because Lady St. Julians will have it.'

'You are too kind,' with many smiles.

'No, I assure you Lord Masque told me that her Majesty—' and here Lady Firebrace whispered.

'Well,' said Lady St. Julians evidently much gratified, 'I do not think I am one who am likely to forget my friends.'

'That I am sure you are not!' said Lady Firebrace.

CHAPTER VIII.

BEHIND the printing office in the alley at the door of which we left Sybil, was a yard which led to some premises that had once been used as a work-shop, but were now generally unoccupied. In a rather spacious chamber over which was a loft, five men, one of whom was Gerard, were busily engaged. There was no furniture in the room except a few chairs and a deal table, on which was a solitary light and a variety of papers.

'Depend upon it,' said Gerard, 'we must stick to the National Holiday:* we can do nothing effectively, unless the movement is simultaneous. They have not troops to cope with a simultaneous movement, and the Holiday is the only machinery to secure unity of action. No work for six weeks, and the rights of Labour will be acknowledged!'

'We shall never be able to make the people unanimous in a cessation of labour,' said a pale young man, very thin but with a countenance of remarkable energy. 'The selfish instincts will come into play and will baulk our political object, while a great increase of physical suffering must be inevitable.'

'It might be done,' said a middle-aged, thickset man, in a thoughtful tone. 'If the Unions were really to put their shoulder to the wheel, it might be done.'

'And if it is not done,' said Gerard, 'what do you propose? The people ask you to guide them. Shrink at such a conjuncture, and our influence over them is forfeited and justly forfeited.'

'I am for partial but extensive insurrections,' said the young man. 'Sufficient in extent and number to demand all the troops and yet to distract the military movements. We can count on Birmingham again, if we act at once before their new Police Act* is in force; Manchester is ripe; and several of the cotton towns; but above all I have letters that assure me that at this moment we can do anything in Wales.'*

'Glamorganshire is right to a man,' said Wilkins, a Baptist teacher. 'And trade is so bad that the Holiday at all events must take place there, for the masters themselves are extinguishing their furnaces.'

'All the north is seething,' said Gerard.

'We must contrive to agitate the metropolis,' said Maclast, a shrewd carroty-haired paper-stainer. 'We must have weekly meetings at

Kennington and demonstrations at White Conduit House; we cannot do more here I fear than talk, but a few thousand men on Kennington Common* every Saturday and some spicy resolutions will keep the Guards in London.'

'Ay, ay,' said Gerard; 'I wish the woollen and cotton trades were as bad to do as the iron, and we should need no holiday as you say, Wilkins. However it will come. In the meantime the Poor-law pinches and terrifies, and will make even the most spiritless turn.'

'The accounts to-day from the north are very encouraging though,' said the young man. 'Stevens* is producing a great effect, and this plan of our people going in procession and taking possession of the churches very much affects the imagination of the multitude.'

'Ah!' said Gerard, 'if we could only have the Church on our side, as in the good old days, we would soon put an end to the demon tyranny of Capital.'

'And now,' said the pale young man, taking up a manuscript paper, 'to our immediate business. Here is the draft of the projected proclamation of the Convention on the Birmingham outbreak. It enjoins peace and order, and counsels the people to arm themselves in order to secure both. You understand: that they may resist if the troops and the police endeavour to produce disturbance.'

'Ay, ay,' said Gerard. 'Let it be stout. We will settle this at once, and so get it out to-morrow. Then for action.'

'But we must circulate this pamphlet of the Polish Count on the manner of encountering cavalry with pikes,' said Maclast.

'''Tis printed,' said the stout thickset man; 'we have set it up on a broadside.* We have sent ten thousand to the north and five thousand to John Frost.* We shall have another delivery to-morrow. It takes very generally.'

The pale young man read the draft of the proclamation; it was canvassed and criticised sentence by sentence; altered, approved; finally put to the vote, and unanimously carried. On the morrow it was to be posted in every thoroughfare of the metropolis, and circulated in every great city of the provinces and populous district of labour.

'And now,' said Gerard, 'I shall to-morrow to the north, where I am wanted. But before I go I propose, as suggested yesterday, that we five together with Langley, whom I counted on seeing here to-night, now form ourselves into a committee for arming the people. Three of us are permanent in London; Wilkins and myself will aid you in the provinces. Nothing can be decided on this head till we see Langley, who will make a communication from Birmingham that cannot be trusted to writing. The seven o'clock train must have long since arrived. He is now a good hour behind his time.'

'I hear foot-steps,' said Maclast.

'He comes,' said Gerard.

The door of the chamber opened and a woman entered. Pale, agitated, exhausted, she advanced to them in the glimmering light.

'What is this?' said several of the council.

'Sybil!' exclaimed the astonished Gerard, and he rose from his seat.

She caught the arm of her father, and leant on him for a moment in silence. Then looking up with an expression that seemed to indicate she was rallying her last energies, she said, in a voice low yet so distinct that it reached the ear of all present, 'There is not an instant to lose: fly!'

The men rose hastily from their seats; they approached the messenger of danger; Gerard waved them off, for he perceived his daughter was sinking. Gently he placed her in his chair; she was sensible, for she grasped his arm, and she murmured—still she murmured—'fly!'

' 'Tis very strange,' said Maclast.

'I feel queer!' said the thickset man.

'Methinks she looks like a heavenly messenger,' said Wilkins.

'I had no idea that earth had anything so fair,'* said the youthful scribe of proclamations.

'Hush friends!' said Gerard; and then he bent over Sybil and said in a low soothing voice, 'Tell me, my child, what is it?'

She looked up to her father; a glance as it were of devotion and despair; her lips moved, but they refused their office and expressed no words. There was a deep silence in the room.

'She is gone,' said her father.

'Water,' said the young man, and he hurried away to obtain some.

'I feel queer,' said his thickset colleague to Maclast.

'I will answer for Langley as for myself,' said Maclast; 'and there is not another human being aware of our purpose.'

'Except Morley.'

'Yes; except Morley. But I should *as* soon doubt Gerard as Stephen Morley.'

'Certainly.'

'I cannot conceive how she traced me,' said Gerard. 'I have never even breathed to her of our meeting. Would we had some water! Ah! here it comes.'

'I arrest you in the Queen's name,' said a serjeant of police. 'Resistance is vain.' Maclast blew out the light, and then ran up into the loft, followed by the thickset man, who fell down the stairs; Wilkins got up the chimney. The sergeant took a lanthorn from his pocket, and threw a powerful light on the chamber, while his followers entered, seized and secured all the papers, and commenced their search.

The light fell upon a group that did not move; the father holding the hand of his insensible child, while he extended his other arm as if to preserve her from the profanation of the touch of the invaders.

'You are Walter Gerard, I presume,' said the serjeant, 'six foot two without shoes.'

'Whoever I may be,' he replied, 'I presume you will produce your warrant, friend, before you touch me.'

''Tis here. We want five of you, named herein, and all others that may happen to be found in your company.'

'I shall obey the warrant,' said Gerard after he had examined it; 'but this maiden, my daughter, knows nothing of this meeting or its purpose. She has but just arrived, and how she traced me I know not. You will let me recover her, and then permit her to depart.'

'Can't let no one out of my sight found in this room.'

'But she is innocent, even if we were guilty; she could be nothing else but innocent, for she knows nothing of this meeting and its business both of which I am prepared at the right time and place to vindicate. She entered this room a moment only before yourself, entered and swooned.'

'Can't help that; must take her; she can tell the magistrate anything she likes, and he must decide.'

'Why, you are not afraid of a young girl?'

'I am afraid of nothing; but I must do my duty. Come we have no time for talk. I must take you both.'

'By G—d you shall not take her;' and letting go her hand, Gerard advanced before her and assumed a position of defence. 'You know, I find, my height; my strength does not shame my stature! Look to yourself. Advance and touch this maiden, and I will fell you and your minions like oxen at their pasture.'

The inspector took a pistol from his pocket and pointed it at Gerard. 'You see,' he said, 'resistance is quite vain.'

'For slaves and cravens, but not for us. I say you shall not touch her till I am dead at her feet. Now, do your worst.'

At this moment two policemen who had been searching the loft descended with Maclast who had vainly attempted to effect his escape over a neighbouring roof; the thickset man was already secured; and Wilkins had been pulled down the chimney and made his appearance in as grimy a state as such a shelter would naturally have occasioned.

The young man too, their first prisoner who had been captured before they had entered the room, was also brought in; there was now abundance of light; the four prisoners were ranged and well guarded at the end of the apartment; Gerard standing before Sybil still maintained his position of defence, and the serjeant was, a few yards away, in his front with his pistol in his hand.

'Well you are a queer chap,' said the serjeant; 'but I must do my duty. I shall give orders to my men to seize you, and if you resist them, I shall shoot you through the head.'

'Stop!' called out one of the prisoners, the young man who drew proclamations, 'she moves. Do with us as you think fit, but you cannot be so harsh as to seize one that is senseless, and a woman!'

'I must do my duty,' said the serjeant, rather perplexed at the situation. 'Well, if you like, take steps to restore her, and when she has come to herself, she shall be moved in a hackney coach alone with her father.'

The means at hand to recover Sybil were rude, but they assisted a reviving nature. She breathed, she sighed, slowly opened her beautiful dark eyes, and looked around. Her father held her death-cold hand; she returned his pressure; her lips moved, and still she murmured 'fly!'

Gerard looked at the serjeant. 'I am ready,' he said, 'and I will carry her.' The officer nodded assent. Guarded by two policemen the tall delegate of Mowbray bore his precious burthen out of the chamber through the yard, the printing-offices, up the alley, till a hackney coach received them in Hunt Street round which a mob had already collected, though kept at a discreet distance by the police. One officer entered the coach with them; another mounted the box. Two other coaches carried the rest of the prisoners and their guards, and within half an hour from the arrival of Sybil at the scene of the secret meeting, she was on her way to Bow Street* to be examined as a prisoner of state.

Sybil rallied quickly during their progress to the police office. Satisfied to find herself with her father she would have enquired as to all that had happened, but Gerard at first discouraged her; at length he thought it wisest gradually to convey to her that they were prisoners, but he treated the matter lightly, did not doubt that she would immediately be discharged, and added that though he might be detained for a day or so, his offence was at all events bailable and he had friends on whom he could rely. When Sybil clearly comprehended that she was a prisoner, and that her public examination was impending, she became silent, and leaning back in the coach, covered her face with her hands.

The prisoners arrived at Bow Street; they were hurried into a back office, where they remained some time unnoticed, several policemen remaining in the room. At length, about twenty minutes having elapsed, a man dressed in black and of a severe aspect entered the room accompanied by an inspector of police. He first enquired whether these were the prisoners, what were their names and descriptions, which each had to give and which were written down, where they were arrested, why they were arrested: then scrutinising them sharply he said the magistrate was at the Home Office, and he doubted whether they could be examined until the morrow. Upon this Gerard commenced stating the circumstances under which Sybil had unfortunately been arrested, but the gentleman in black with a severe aspect, immediately told him to hold his tongue, and when Gerard persisted, declared that if Gerard did not immediately cease he should be separated from the other prisoners and be ordered into solitary confinement.

Another half hour of painful suspense. The prisoners were not permitted to hold any conversation; Sybil sat half reclining on a form with her back against the wall, and her face covered, silent and motionless. At the end of half an hour the inspector of police who had visited them with the gentleman in black entered and announced that the prisoners could not be brought up for examination that evening, and they must make themselves as comfortable as they could for the night. Gerard made a last appeal to the inspector that Sybil might be allowed a separate chamber and in this he was unexpectedly successful.

The inspector was a kind-hearted man: he lived at the office and his wife was the housekeeper. He had already given her an account, an interesting account, of his female prisoner. The good woman's imagination was touched as well as her heart; she had herself suggested that they ought to soften the rigour of the fair prisoner's lot; and the inspector therefore almost anticipated the request of Gerard. He begged Sybil to accompany him to his better half, and at once promised all the comforts and convenience which they could command. As, attended by the inspector, she took her way to the apartments of his family, they passed through a room in which there were writing materials, and Sybil speaking for the first time and in a faint voice enquired of the inspector whether it were permitted to apprise a friend of her situation. She was answered in the affirmative, on condition that the note was previously perused by him.

'I will write it at once,' she said, and taking up a pen she inscribed these words:—

'I followed your counsel; I entreated him to quit London this night. He pledged himself to do so on the morrow.

'I learnt he was attending a secret meeting; that there was urgent peril. I tracked him through scenes of terror. Alas! I arrived only in time to be myself seized as a conspirator, and I have been arrested and carried a prisoner to Bow Street, where I write this.

'I ask you not to interfere for him; that would be vain; but if I were free, I might at least secure him justice. But I am not free: I am to be brought up for public examination to-morrow, if I survive this night.

'You are powerful; you know all; you know what I say is truth. None else will credit it. Save me!'

'And now,' said Sybil to the inspector in a tone of mournful desolation and of mild sweetness, 'all depends on your faith to me,' and she extended him the letter, which he read.

'Whoever he may be and wherever he may be,' said the inspector with emotion, for the spirit of Sybil had already controlled his nature, 'provided the person to whom this letter is addressed is within possible distance, fear not it shall reach him.'

'I will seal and address it then,' said Sybil, and she addressed the letter to

'THE HON. CHARLES EGREMONT M.P.'
adding that superscription the sight of which had so agitated Egremont at Deloraine House.

CHAPTER IX.

NIGHT waned: and Sybil was at length slumbering. The cold that precedes the dawn had stolen over her senses, and calmed the excitement of her nerves. She was lying on the ground, covered with a cloak of which her kind hostess had prevailed on her to avail herself, and was partly resting on a chair, at which she had been praying when exhausted nature gave way and she slept. Her bonnet had fallen off, and her rich hair, which had broken loose, covered her shoulder like a mantle. Her slumber was brief and disturbed, but it had in a great degree soothed the irritated brain. She woke however in terror from a dream in which she had been dragged through a mob and carried before a tribunal. The coarse jeers, the brutal threats, still echoed in her ear; and when she looked around, she could not for some moments recall or recognise the scene. In one corner of the room, which was sufficiently spacious, was a bed occupied by the still sleeping wife of the inspector; there was a great deal of heavy furniture of dark mahogany; a bureau, several chests of drawers; over the mantel was a piece of faded embroidery framed, that had been executed by the wife of the inspector when she was at school, and opposite to it, on the other side, were portraits of Dick Curtis and Dutch Sam,* who had been the tutors of her husband, and now lived as heroes in his memory.

Slowly came over Sybil the consciousness of the dreadful eve that was past. She remained for some time on her knees in silent prayer: then stepping lightly, she approached the window. It was barred. The room which she inhabited was a high story of the house; it looked down upon one of those half tawdry, half squalid streets that one finds in the vicinities of our theatres; some wretched courts, haunts of misery and crime, blended with gin palaces and slang taverns,* burnished and brazen; not a being was stirring. It was just that single hour of the twenty-four when crime ceases, debauchery is exhausted, and even desolation finds a shelter.

It was dawn, but still grey. For the first time since she had been a prisoner, Sybil was alone. A prisoner, and in a few hours to be examined before a public tribunal! Her heart sank. How far her father had committed himself was entirely a mystery to her; but the language of Morley, and all that she had witnessed, impressed her with the conviction that he was deeply implicated. He had indeed spoken in their progress to the police office with confidence as to the future, but then he had every motive to encourage her in her despair, and to support her under the overwhelming circumstances in which she was so suddenly involved. What a catastrophe to all his high aspirations! It tore her heart to think of him! As for herself, she would still hope that ultimately she might obtain justice, but she could scarcely flatter herself that at the first any distinction would be made between her case and that of the other prisoners. She would probably be committed for trial; and though her innocence on that occasion might be proved, she would have been a prisoner in the interval, instead of devoting all her energies in freedom to the support and assistance of her father. She shrank, too, with all the delicacy of a woman, from the impending examination in open court before the magistrate. Supported by her convictions, vindicating a sacred principle, there was no trial perhaps to which Sybil would not have been superior, and no test of her energy and faith which she would not have triumphantly encountered; but to be hurried like a criminal to the bar of a police office, suspected of the lowest arts of sedition, ignorant even of what she was accused, without a conviction to support her or the ennobling consciousness of having failed at least in a great cause; all these were circumstances which infinitely disheartened and depressed her. She felt sometimes that she should be unable to meet the occasion; had it not been for Gerard she could almost have wished that death might release her from its base perplexities.

Was there any hope? In the agony of her soul she had confided last night in one; with scarcely a bewildering hope that he could save her. He might not have the power, the opportunity, the wish. He might shrink from mixing himself up with such characters and such transactions; he might not have received her hurried appeal in time to act upon it, even if the desire of her soul were practicable. A thousand difficulties, a thousand obstacles now occurred to her; and she felt her hopelessness.

Yet notwithstanding her extreme sorrow, and the absence of all surrounding objects to soothe and to console her, the expanding dawn revived and even encouraged Sybil. In spite of the confined situation, she could still partially behold a sky dappled with rosy hues; a sense of freshness touched her; she could not resist endeavouring to open the window and feel the air, notwithstanding all the bars.* The wife of the inspector stirred, and half slumbering, murmured, 'Are you up? It cannot be more than five o'clock. If you open the window we shall catch cold; but I will rise and help you to dress.'

This woman, like her husband, was naturally kind, and at once influenced by Sybil. They both treated her as a superior being; and if, instead of the daughter of a lowly prisoner and herself a prisoner, she had been the noble child of a captive minister of state, they could not have extended to her a more humble and even delicate solicitude.

It had not yet struck seven, and the wife of the inspector suddenly stopping and listening, said, 'They are stirring early;' and then, after a moment's pause, she opened the door, at which she stood for some time endeavouring to catch the meaning of the mysterious sounds. She looked back at Sybil, and saying, 'Hush, I shall be back directly,' she withdrew, shutting the door.

In little more than two hours, as Sybil had been informed, she would be summoned to her examination. It was a sickening thought. Hope vanished as the catastrophe advanced. She almost accused herself for having without authority sought out her father; it had been as regarded him a fruitless mission, and, by its results on her, had aggravated his present sorrows and perplexities. Her mind again recurred to him whose counsel had indirectly prompted her rash step, and to whose aid in her infinite hopelessness she had appealed. The woman who had all this time been only standing on the landing-place without the door, now re-entered with a puzzled and curious air, saying, 'I cannot make it out; some one has arrived.'

'Some one has arrived.' Simple yet agitating words. 'Is it unusual,' enquired Sybil in a trembling tone, 'for persons to arrive at this hour?'

'Yes,' said the wife of the inspector. 'They never bring them from the stations until the office opens. I cannot make it out. Hush!' and at this moment some one tapped at the door.

The woman returned to the door and reopened it, and some words were spoken which did not reach Sybil, whose heart beat violently as a wild thought rushed over her mind. The suspense was so intolerable, her agitation so great, that she was on the point of advancing and asking if—when the door was shut and she was again left alone. She threw herself on the bed. It seemed to her that she had lost all control over her intelligence. All thought and feeling merged in that deep suspense when the order of our being seems to stop and quiver as it were upon its axis.

The woman returned; her countenance was glad. Perceiving the agitation of Sybil, she said, 'You may dry your eyes my dear. There is nothing like a friend at court; there's a warrant from the Secretary of State* for your release.'

'No, no,' said Sybil springing from her chair. 'Is he here?'

'What, the Secretary of State!' said the woman.

'No, no; I mean is any one here?'

'There is a coach waiting for you at the door with the messenger from the office, and you are to depart forthwith. My husband is here, it was he who knocked at the door. The warrant came before the office was opened.'

'My father! I must see him.'

The inspector at this moment tapped again at the door and then entered. He caught the last request of Sybil, and replied to it in the negative. 'You must not stay,' he said; 'you must be off immediately. I will tell all to your father. And take a hint; this affair may be bailable or it may not be. I can't give an opinion, but it depends on the evidence. If you have any good man you know—I mean a householder long established and well to do in the world—I advise you to lose no time in looking him up. That will do your father much more good than saying good bye and all that sort of thing.'

Bidding farewell to his kind wife, and leaving many weeping messages for her father, Sybil descended the stairs with the inspector. The office was not opened; a couple of policemen only were in the passage, and as she appeared one of them went forth to clear the way for Sybil to the coach that was waiting for her. A milkwoman or two, a stray chimney-sweep, a pieman with his smoking apparatus, and several of those nameless nothings that always congregate and make the nucleus of a mob—probably our young friends who had been passing the night in Hyde Park—had already gathered round the office door. They were dispersed, and returned again and took up their position at a more respectful distance, abusing with many racy execrations that ancient body that from a traditionary habit they still called the New Police.*

A man in a loose white great coat, his countenance concealed by a shawl which was wound round his neck and by his slouched hat, assisted Sybil into the coach, and pressed her hand at the same time with greet tenderness. Then he mounted the box by the driver and ordered him to make the best of his way to Smith's Square.

With a beating heart, Sybil leant back in the coach and clasped her hands. Her brain was too wild to think; the incidents of her life during the last four-and-twenty hours had been so strange and rapid that she seemed almost to resign any quality of intelligent control over her fortunes, and to deliver herself up to the shifting visions of the startling dream. His voice had sounded in her ear as his hand had touched hers. And on those tones her memory lingered, and that pressure had reached her heart. What tender devotion! What earnest fidelity! What brave and romantic faith! Had she breathed on some talisman, and called up some obedient genie to her aid, the spirit could not have been more loyal, nor the completion of her behest more ample and precise.

She passed the towers of the church of St. John; of the saint who had seemed to guard over her in the exigency of her existence. She was approaching her threshold; the blood left her cheek, her heart palpitated. The coach stopped. Trembling and timid she leant upon his arm and yet dared not look upon his face. They entered the house; they were in the room where two months before he had knelt to her in vain, which yesterday had been the scene of so many heart-rending passions.

As in some delicious dream, when the enchanted fancy has traced for a time with coherent bliss the stream of bright adventures and sweet and touching phrase, there comes at last some wild gap in the flow of fascination, and by means which we cannot trace, and by an agency which we cannot pursue, we find ourselves in some enrapturing situation that is as it were the ecstasy of our life; so it happened now, that while in clear and precise order there seemed to flit over the soul of Sybil all that had passed, all that he had done, all that she felt—by some mystical process which memory could not recall, Sybil found herself pressed to the throbbing heart of Egremont, nor shrinking from the embrace which expressed the tenderness of his devoted love!

CHAPTER X.

MOWBRAY was in a state of great excitement. It was Saturday evening; the mills were closed; the news had arrived of the arrest of the Delegate.

'Here's a go!' said Dandy Mick to Devilsdust. 'What do you think of this?'

'It's the beginning of the end,' said Devilsdust.

'The deuce!' said the Dandy, who did not clearly comprehend the bent of the observation of his much pondering and philosophic friend, but was touched by its oracular terseness.

'We must see Warner,' said Devilsdust, 'and call a meeting of the people on the Moor for to-morrow evening. I will draw up some resolutions. We must speak out; we must terrify the Capitalists.'

'I am all for a strike,' said Mick.

''Tisn't ripe,' said Devilsdust.

'But that's what you always say, Dusty,' said Mick.

'I watch events,' said Devilsdust. 'If you want to be a leader of the people you must learn to watch events.'

'But what do you mean by watching events?'

'Do you see Mother Carey's stall?' said Dusty, pointing in the direction of the counter of the good-natured widow.

'I should think I did; and what's more, Julia owes her a tick* for herrings.'

'Right,' said Devilsdust; 'and nothing but herrings are to be seen on her board. Two years ago it was meat.'

'I twig,' said Mick.

'Wait till it's wegetables; when the people can't buy even fish. Then we will talk about strikes. That's what I call watching events.'

Julia, Caroline, and Harriet came up to them.

'Mick,' said Julia, 'we want to go to the Temple.'

'I wish you may get it,' said Mick shaking his head. 'When you have learnt to watch events, Julia, you will understand that under present circumstances the Temple is no go.'

'And why so, Dandy?' said Julia.

'Do you see Mother Carey's stall?' said Mick, pointing in that direction. 'When there's a tick at Madam Carey's there is no tin for Chaffing Jack. That's what I call watching events.'

'Oh! as for the tin,' said Caroline, 'in these half-time days that's quite out of fashion. But they do say it's the last night at the Temple, for Chaffing Jack means to shut up, it does not pay any longer; and we want a lark. I'll stand treat; I'll put my earrings up the spout—they must go at last, and I would sooner at any time go to my uncle's* for frolic than woe.'

'I am sure I should like very much to go to the Temple if any one would pay for me,' said Harriet, 'but I won't pawn nothing.'

'If we only pay and hear them sing,' said Julia in a coaxing tone.

'Very like,' said Mick; 'there's nothing that makes one so thirsty as listening to a song, particularly if it touches the feelings. Don't you remember, Dusty, when we used to encore that German fellow in 'Scots wha ha.' We always had it five times. Hang me if I wasn't blind drunk at the end of it.'

'I tell you what, young ladies,' said Devilsdust, looking very solemn, 'you're dancing on a volcano.'

'Oh! my,' said Caroline, 'I am sure I wish we were; though what you mean exactly I don't quite know.'

'I mean that we shall all soon be slaves,' said Devilsdust.

'Not if we get the Ten-Hour Bill,' said Harriet.

'And no cleaning of machinery in meal time,' said Julia; 'that is a shame.'

'You don't know what you are talking about,' said Devilsdust. 'I tell you, if the Capitalists put down Gerard we're done for another ten years, and by that time we shall be all used up.'

'Lor! Dusty, you quite terrify one,' said Caroline.

'It's a true bill though. Instead of going to the Temple we must meet on the Moor, and in as great numbers as possible. Go you and get all your sweethearts. I must see your father, Harriet; he must preside. We will have the hymn of Labour* sung by a hundred thousand voices in chorus. It will strike terror into the hearts of the Capitalists. This is what we must all be thinking of if we wish Labour to have a chance, not of going to Chaffing Jack's and listening to silly songs. D'ye understand?'

'Don't we!' said Caroline; 'and for my part for a summer eve I prefer Mowbray Moor to all the Temples in the world, particularly if it's a sociable party and we have some good singing.'

This evening it was settled among the principal champions of the cause of Labour, among whom Devilsdust was now included, that on the morrow there should be a monster meeting on the Moor to take into consideration the arrest of the delegate of Mowbray. Such was the complete organisation of this district that by communicating with the various lodges of the Trades Unions fifty thousand persons, or even double that number, could within four-and-twenty hours on a great occasion and on a favourable day be brought into the field. The morrow

being a day of rest was favourable, and the seizure of their cherished
delegate was a stimulating cause. The excitement was great, the enthusiasm earnest and deep. There was enough distress to make people discontented without depressing them. And Devilsdust after attending
a council of the Union, retired to rest and dreamed of strong speeches
and spicy resolutions, bands and banners, the cheers of assembled
thousands, and the eventual triumph of the sacred rights.

The post of the next morning brought great and stirring news to
Mowbray. Gerard had undergone his examination at Bow Street. It was
a long and laborious one; he was committed for trial for a seditious
conspiracy, but he was held to bail. The bail demanded was heavy; but
it was prepared and instantly proffered. His sureties were Morley and
a Mr. Hatton. By this post Morley wrote to his friends, apprising them
that both Gerard and himself intended to leave London instantly, and
that they might be expected to arrive at Mowbray by the evening train.

The monster meeting of the Moor it was instantly resolved should
be converted into a triumphant procession, or rather be preceded by
one. Messengers on horseback were sent to all the neighbouring towns
to announce the great event. Every artisan felt as a Moslemin summoned by the sacred standard.* All went forth with their wives and
their children to hail the return of the patriot and the martyr. The
Trades of Mowbray mustered early in the morning, and in various pro-
cessions took possession of all the churches. Their great pride was
entirely to fill the church of Mr. St. Lys, who not daunted by their
demonstration, and seizing the offered opportunity, suppressed the
sermon with which he had supplied himself and preached to them an
extemporary discourse on 'Fear God and honour the King.' In the dissenting chapels thanksgivings were publicly offered that bail had been
accepted for Walter Gerard. After the evening service, which the Unions
again attended, they formed in the High Street and lined it with their
ranks and banners. Every half hour a procession arrived from some neighbouring town with its music and streaming flags. Each was received by
Warner or some other member of the managing committee, who assigned
to them their appointed position, which they took up without confusion, nor was the general order for a moment disturbed. Sometimes a
large party arrived without music or banners, but singing psalms and
headed by their minister; sometimes the children walked together, the
women following, then the men each with a ribbon of the same colour
in his hat; all hurried, yet spontaneous and certain, indications how
mankind under the influence of high and earnest feelings recur instantly
to ceremony and form; how when the imagination is excited it appeals

to the imagination, and requires for its expression something beyond the routine of daily life.

It was arranged that the moment the train arrived and the presence of Gerard was ascertained, the Trade in position nearest to the station should commence the hymn of Labour, which was instantly to be taken up by its neighbour, and so on in succession, so that by an almost electrical agency the whole population should almost simultaneously be assured of his arrival.

At half past six o'clock the bell announced that the train was in sight; a few minutes afterwards Dandy Mick hurried up to the leader of the nearest Trade, spoke a few words, and instantly the signal was given and the hymn commenced. It was taken up as the steeples of a great city in the silence of the night take up the new hour that has just arrived; one by one the mighty voices rose till they all blended in one vast waving sea of sound. Warner and some others welcomed Gerard and Morley, and ushered them, totally unprepared for such a reception, to an open carriage drawn by four white horses that was awaiting them. Orders were given that there was to be no cheering or any irregular clamour. Alone was heard the hymn. As the carriage passed each Trade, they followed and formed in procession behind it; thus all had the opportunity of beholding their chosen chief and he the proud consolation of looking on the multitude who thus enthusiastically recognised the sovereignty of his services.

The interminable population, the mighty melody, the incredible order, the simple yet awful solemnity, this representation of the great cause to which she was devoted under an aspect that at once satisfied the reason, captivated the imagination, and elevated the heart—her admiration of her father, thus ratified as it were by the sympathy of a nation—added to all the recent passages of her life teeming with such strange and trying interest, overcame Sybil. The tears fell down her cheek as the carriage bore away her father, while she remained under the care of one unknown to the people of Mowbray, but who had accompanied her from London,—this was Hatton.

The last light of the sun was shed over the Moor when Gerard reached it, and the Druid's Altar and its surrounding crags were burnished with its beam.

CHAPTER XI.

IT was the night following the day after the return of Gerard to Mowbray. Morley, who had lent to him and Sybil his cottage in the dale, was at the office of his newspaper, the *Mowbray Phalanx*, where he now resided. He was alone in his room writing, occasionally rising from his seat and pacing the chamber, when some one knocked at his door. Receiving a permission to come in, there entered Hatton.

'I fear I am disturbing an article,' said the guest.

'By no means; the day of labour is not at hand. I am very pleased to see you.'

'My quarters are not very inviting,' continued Hatton. 'It is remarkable what bad accommodation you find in these great trading towns. I should have thought that the mercantile traveller had been a comfortable animal—not to say a luxurious; but I find everything mean and third-rate. The wine execrable. So I thought I would come and bestow my tediousness* on you. 'Tis hardly fair.'

'You could not have pleased me better. I was, rather from distraction than from exigency, throwing some thoughts on paper. But the voice of yesterday still lingers in my ear.'

'What a spectacle!'

'Yes; you see what a multitude presents who have recognised the predominance of Moral Power,' said Morley. 'The spectacle was august; but the results to which such a public mind must lead are sublime.'

'It must have been deeply gratifying to our friend,' said Hatton.

'It will support him in his career,' said Morley.

'And console him in his prison,' added Hatton.

'You think that it will come to that?' said Morley inquiringly.

'It has that aspect; but appearances change.'

'What should change them?'

'Time and accident, which change everything.'

'Time will bring the York Assizes,' said Morley musingly; 'and as for accident I confess the future seems to me dreary. What can happen for Gerard?'

'He might win his writ of right,' said Hatton demurely, stretching out his legs and leaning back in his chair. 'That also may be tried at the York Assizes.'

'His writ of right! I thought that was a feint—a mere affair of tactics to keep the chance of the field.'

'I believe the field may be won,' said Hatton very composedly.

'Won!'

'Ay! the castle and manor of Mowbray and half the lordships round, to say nothing of this good town. The people are prepared to be his subjects; he must give up equality and be content with being a popular sovereign.'

'You jest my friend.'

'Then I speak truth in jest; sometimes, you know, the case.'

'What mean you?' said Morley rising and approaching Hatton; 'for though I have often observed you like a biting phrase, you never speak idly. Tell me what you mean.'

'I mean,' said Hatton, looking Morley earnestly in the face and speaking with great gravity, 'that the documents are in existence which prove the title of Walter Gerard to the proprietorship of this great district; that I know where the documents are to be found; and that it requires nothing but a resolution equal to the occasion to secure them.'

'Should that be wanting?' said Morley.

'I should think not,' said Hatton. 'It would belie our nature to believe so.'

'And where are these documents?'

'In the muniment room of Mowbray castle.'

'Hah!' exclaimed Morley in a prolonged tone.

'Kept closely by one who knows their value, for they are the title deeds not of his right but of his confusion.'

'And how can we obtain them?'

'By means more honest than those they were acquired by.'

'They are not obvious.'

'Two hundred thousand human beings* yesterday acknowledged the supremacy of Gerard,' said Hatton. 'Suppose they had known that within the walls of Mowbray Castle were contained the proofs that Walter Gerard was the lawful possessor of the lands on which they live; I say suppose that had been the case. Do you think they would have contented themselves with singing psalms? What would have become of moral power then? They would have taken Mowbray Castle by storm; they would have sacked and gutted it; they would have appointed a chosen band to rifle the round tower; they would have taken care that every document in it, especially an iron chest painted blue and blazoned with the shield of Valence, should have been delivered to you, to me, to any one that Gerard appointed for the office. And what could be the remedy of the Earl de Mowbray? He could scarcely bring an action against the hundred for the destruction of the castle, which we would prove was not his own. And the most he could do would be to transport some poor wretches who had got drunk in his plundered cellars and then set fire to his golden saloons.'

'You amaze me,' said Morley, looking with an astonished expression on the person who had just delivered himself of these suggestive details with the same coolness and arid accuracy that he would have entered into the details of a pedigree.

' 'Tis a practical view of the case,' remarked Mr. Hatton.

Morley paced the chamber disturbed; Hatton remained silent and watched him with a scrutinizing eye.

'Are you certain of your facts?' at length said Morley, abruptly stopping.

'Quite so; Lord de Mowbray informed me of the circumstances himself before I left London, and I came down here in consequence.'

'You know him?'

'No one better.'

'And these documents—some of them I suppose,' said Morley with a cynical look, 'were once in your own possession then?'

'Possibly. Would they were now! But it is a great thing to know where they may be found.'

'Then they once were the property of Gerard?'

'Hardly that. They were gained by my own pains, and often paid for with my own purse. Claimed by no one, I parted with them to a person to whom they were valuable. It is not merely to serve Gerard that I want them now, though I would willingly serve him. I have need of some of these papers with respect to an ancient title, a claim to which, by a person in whom I am interested, they would substantiate. Now listen, good friend Morley; moral force is a fine thing especially in speculation, and so is a community of goods especially when a man has no property, but when you have lived as long as I have and have tasted of the world's delights, you'll comprehend the rapture of acquisition, and learn that it is generally secured by very coarse means. Come, I have a mind that you should prosper. The public spirit is inflamed here; you are a leader of the people. Let us have another meeting on the Moor, a preconcerted outbreak; you can put your fingers in a trice on the men who will do our work. Mowbray Castle is in their possession; we secure our object. You shall have ten thousand pounds on the nail, and I will take you back to London with me besides and teach you what is fortune.'

'I understand you,' said Morley. 'You have a clear brain and a bold spirit; you have no scruples, which indeed are generally the creatures of perplexity rather than of principle. You ought to succeed.'

'We ought to succeed you mean,' said Hatton, 'for I have long perceived that you only wanted opportunity to mount.'

'Yesterday was a great burst of feeling occasioned by a very peculiar cause,' said Morley musingly; 'but it must not mislead us. The discontent here is not deep. The people are still employed, though not fully. Wages have fallen, but they must drop more. The PEOPLE are not ripe for the movement you intimate. There are thousands who would rush to the rescue of the castle. Besides there is a priest here, one St. Lys, who exercises a most pernicious influence over the people. It will require immense efforts and great distress to root him out. No; it would fail.'

'Then we must wait awhile,' said Hatton, 'or devise some other means.'

' 'Tis a very impracticable case,' said Morley.

'There is a combination for every case,' said Hatton. 'Ponder and it comes. This seemed simple; but you think, you really think it would not answer?'

'At this moment, not; that is my conviction.'

'Well suppose instead of an insurrection we have a burglary. Can you assist me to the right hands here?'

'Not I indeed!'

'What is the use then of this influence over the people of which you and Gerard are always talking? After yesterday I thought here you could do anything.'

'We have not hitherto had the advantage of your worldly knowledge; in future we shall be wiser.'

'Well then,' said Hatton, 'we must now think of Gerard's defence. He shall have the best counsel. I shall retain Kelly* specially. I shall return to town to-morrow morning. You will keep me alive to the state of feeling here, and if things get more mature drop me a line and I will come down.'

'This conversation had better not be mentioned to Gerard.'

'That is obvious; it would only disturb him. I did not preface it by a stipulation of confidence because that is idle. Of course you will keep the secret; it is your interest; it is a great possession. I know very well you will be most jealous of sharing it. I know it is as safe with you as with myself.'

And with these words Hatton wished him a hearty farewell and withdrew.

'He is right,' thought Morley; 'he knows human nature well. The secret is safe. I will not breathe it to Gerard. I will treasure it up. It is knowledge; it is power: great knowledge, great power. And what shall I do with it? Time will teach me.'

END OF THE FIFTH BOOK.

BOOK VI.

CHAPTER I.

'ANOTHER week,' exclaimed a gentleman in Downing Street* on the 5th of August, 1842, 'and we shall be prorogued. You can surely keep the country quiet for another week.'

'I cannot answer for the public peace for another four-and-twenty hours,' replied his companion.

'This business at Manchester must be stopped at once; you have a good force there?'

'Manchester is nothing; these are movements merely to distract. The serious work is not now to be apprehended in the cotton towns. The state of Staffordshire and Warwickshire is infinitely more menacing. Cheshire and Yorkshire alarm me. The accounts from Scotland are as bad as can be. And though I think the sufferings of '39 will keep Birmingham and the Welch collieries in check, we cannot venture to move any of our force from those districts.'

'You must summon a council for four o'clock. I have some deputations to receive which I will throw over; but to Windsor I must go. Nothing has yet occurred to render any notice of the state of the country necessary in the speech from the Throne.'

'Not yet,' said his companion; 'but what will to-morrow bring forth?'

'After all it is only a turn-out. I cannot recast her Majesty's speech and bring in rebellion and closed mills, instead of loyalty and a good harvest.'

'It would be a bore. Well, we will see to-morrow;' and the colleague left the room.

'And now for these deputations,' said the gentleman in Downing Street, 'of all things in the world I dislike a deputation. I do not care how much I labour in the cabinet or the house; that's real work; the machine is advanced. But receiving a deputation is like sham marching: an immense dust and no progress. To listen to their views! As if I did not know what their views were before they stated them! And to put on a countenance of respectful candour while they are developing their exploded or their impracticable systems. Were it not that at a practised crisis, I permit them to see conviction slowly stealing over my conscience, I believe the fellows would never stop. I cannot really receive these deputations. I must leave them to Hoaxem,' and the gentleman in Downing Street rang his bell.

'Well, Mr. Hoaxem,' resumed the gentleman in Downing Street as that faithful functionary entered, 'there are some deputations I understand, to day. You must receive them, as I am going to Windsor. What are they?'

'There are only two, sir, of moment. The rest I could easily manage.'

'And these two?'

'In the first place, there is our friend Colonel Bosky, the members for the county of Calfshire, and a deputation of tenant farmers.'

'Pah!'

'These must be attended to. The members have made a strong representation to me that they really cannot any longer vote with government unless the Treasury assists them in satisfying their constituents.'

'And what do they want?'

'Statement of grievances; high taxes and low prices; mild expostulations and gentle hints that they have been thrown over by their friends; Polish corn, Holstein cattle, and British income tax.'*

'Well you know what to say,' said the gentleman in Downing Street. 'Tell them generally that they are quite mistaken; prove to them particularly that my only object has been to render protection more protective, by making it practical and divesting it of the surplusage of odium; that no foreign corn can come in at fifty-five shillings; that there are not enough cattle in all Holstein to supply the parish of Pancras daily with beef-steaks; and that as for the income tax, they will be amply compensated for it by their diminished cost of living through the agency of that very tariff of which they are so superficially complaining.'

'Their diminished cost of living!' said Mr. Hoaxem a little confused. 'Would not that assurance, I humbly suggest, clash a little with my previous demonstration that we had arranged that no reduction of prices should take place?'

'Not at all; your previous demonstration is of course true, but at the same time you must impress upon them the necessity of general views to form an opinion of particular instances. As for example a gentleman of five thousand pounds per annum pays to the income tax, which by the bye always call property tax, one hundred and fifty pounds a year. Well, I have materially reduced the duties on eight hundred articles.* The consumption of each of those articles by an establishment of five thousand pounds per annum cannot be less than one pound per article. The reduction of price cannot be less than a moiety; therefore a saving of four hundred per annum; which placed against the deduction of the property tax leaves a clear increase of income of two hundred and fifty pounds per annum; by which you see that a property tax in fact increases income.'

'I see,' said Mr. Hoaxem with an admiring glance. 'And what am I to say to the deputation of the manufacturers of Mowbray complaining of the great depression of trade, and the total want of remunerating profits?'

'You must say exactly the reverse,' said the gentleman in Downing Street. 'Show them how much I have done to promote the revival of trade. First of all in making provisions cheaper; cutting off at one blow half the protection on corn, as for example at this moment under the old law the duty on foreign wheat would have been twenty-seven shillings a quarter; under the new law it is thirteen. To be sure no wheat could come in at either price, but that does not alter the principle. Then as to live cattle, show how I have entirely opened the trade with the continent in live cattle. Enlarge upon this, the subject is speculative and admits of expensive estimates. If there be any dissenters on the deputation who having freed the negroes have no subject left for their foreign sympathies, hint at the tortures of the bull-fight and the immense consideration to humanity that instead of being speared at Seville, the Andalusian Toro will probably in future be cut up at Smithfield. This cheapness of provisions will permit them to compete with the foreigner in all neutral markets, in time beat them in their own. It is a complete compensation too for the property tax, which impress upon them is a great experiment and entirely for their interests. Ring the changes on great measures and great experiments till it is time to go down and make a house. Your official duties of course must not be interfered with. They will take the hint. I have no doubt you will get through the business very well, Mr. Hoaxem, particularly if you be 'frank and explicit;' that is the right line to take when you wish to conceal your own mind and to confuse the minds of others. Good morning!'

CHAPTER II.

Two days after this conversation in Downing Street, a special messenger arrived at Marney Abbey from the Lord Lieutenant of the county, the Duke of Fitz-Aquitaine. Immediately after reading the despatch of which he was the bearer, there was a great bustle in the house; Lady Marney was sent for to her husband's library and there enjoined immediately to write various letters which were to prevent certain expected visitors

from arriving; Captain Grouse was in and out the same library every
five minutes, receiving orders and counter orders, and finally mounting
his horse was flying about the neighbourhood with messages and commands. All this stir signified that the Marney regiment of Yeomanry*
were to be called out directly.

Lord Marney, who had succeeded in obtaining a place in the Household*
and was consequently devoted to the institutions of the country, was
full of determination to uphold them; but at the same time with characteristic prudence was equally resolved that the property principally
protected should be his own, and that the order of his own district
should chiefly engage his solicitude.

'I do not know what the Duke means by marching into the disturbed
districts,' said Lord Marney to Captain Grouse. 'These are disturbed
districts. There have been three fires in one week, and I want to know
what disturbance can be worse than that? In my opinion this is a mere
anti-corn-law riot to frighten the government; and suppose they do
stop the mills—what then? I wish they were all stopped, and then one
might live like a gentleman again.'

Egremont, between whom and his brother a sort of bad-tempered
good understanding had of late years to a certain degree flourished,
in spite of Lord Marney remaining childless, which made him hate
Egremont with double distilled virulence, and chiefly by the affectionate
manœuvres of their mother, but whose annual visits to Marney had generally been limited to the yeomanry week, arrived from London the same
day as the letter of the Lord Lieutenant, as he had learnt that his brother's
regiment, in which he commanded a troop, as well as the other yeomanry
corps in the North of England, must immediately take the field.

Five years had elapsed since the commencement of our history, and
they had brought apparently much change to the character of the brother
of Lord Marney. He had become, especially during the last two or three
years, silent and reserved; he rarely entered society; even the company
of those who were once his intimates had ceased to attract him; he was
really a melancholy man. The change in his demeanour was observed
by all; his mother and his sister-in-law were the only persons who
endeavoured to penetrate its cause, and sighed over the failure of their
sagacity. Quit the world and the world forgets you; and Egremont would
have soon been a name no longer mentioned in those brilliant saloons
which he once adorned, had not occasionally a sensation, produced by
an effective speech in the House of Commons, recalled his name to his
old associates, who then remembered the pleasant hours passed in his
society and wondered why he never went anywhere now.

'I suppose he finds society a bore,' said Lord Eugene de Vere; 'I am sure I do: but then what is a fellow to do? I am not in Parliament like Egremont. I believe, after all, that's the thing; for I have tried everything else and everything else is a bore.'

'I think one should marry like Alfred Mountchesney,' said Lord Milford.

'But what is the use of marrying if you do not marry a rich woman—and the heiresses of the present age will not marry. What can be more unnatural! It alone ought to produce a revolution. Why, Alfred is the only fellow who has made a coup; and then he has not got it down.'

'She behaved in a most unprincipled manner to me—that Fitzwarene,' said Lord Milford, 'always took my bouquets and once made me write some verses.'

'By Jove!' said Lord Eugene, 'I should like to see them. What a bore it must have been to write verses.'

'I only copied them out of Mina Blake's album: but I sent them in my own handwriting.'

Baffled sympathy was the cause of Egremont's gloom. It is the secret spring of most melancholy. He loved and loved in vain. The conviction that his passion, though hopeless, was not looked upon with disfavour, only made him the more wretched, for the disappointment is more acute in proportion as the chance is better. He had never seen Sybil since the morning he quitted her in Smith's Square, immediately before her departure for the North. The trial of Gerard had taken place at the assizes of that year: he had been found guilty and sentenced to eighteen months imprisonment in York Castle; the interference of Egremont both in the House of Commons and with the government saved him from the felon confinement* with which he was at first threatened, and from which assuredly state prisoners should be exempt. During this effort some correspondence had taken place between Egremont and Sybil, which he would willingly have encouraged and maintained; but it ceased nevertheless with its subject. Sybil, through the influential interference of Ursula Trafford, lived at the convent at York* during the imprisonment of her father, and visited him daily.

The anxiety to take the veil which had once characterised Sybil had certainly waned. Perhaps her experience of life had impressed her with the importance of fulfilling vital duties. Her father, though he had never opposed her wish, had never encouraged it; and he had now increased and interesting claims on her devotion. He had endured great trials, and had fallen on adverse fortunes. Sybil would look at him, and though his noble frame was still erect and his countenance still displayed that mixture of frankness and decision which had distinguished it of yore, she could not conceal from herself that there were ravages which time could not have produced. A year and a half of imprisonment had shaken to its centre a frame born for action, and shrinking at all times from the resources of sedentary life. The disappointment of high hopes had jarred and tangled even the sweetness of his noble disposition. He needed solicitude and solace: and Sybil resolved that if vigilance and sympathy could soothe an existence that would otherwise be embittered, these guardian angels should at least hover over the life of her father.

When the term of his imprisonment had ceased, Gerard had returned with his daughter to Mowbray. Had he deigned to accept the offers of his friends, he need not have been anxious as to his future. A public subscription for his service had been collected: Morley, who was well to do in the world, for the circulation of the *Mowbray Phalanx* daily increased with the increasing sufferings of the people, offered his friend to share his house and purse: Hatton was munificent; there was no limit either to his offers or his proffered services. But all were declined; Gerard would live by labour. The post he had occupied at Mr. Trafford's was not vacant even if that gentleman had thought fit again to receive him; but his reputation as a first-rate artisan soon obtained him good employment, though on this occasion in the town of Mowbray, which for the sake of his daughter he regretted. He had no pleasant home now for Sybil, but he had the prospect of one, and until he obtained possession of it, Sybil sought a refuge, which had been offered to her from the first, with her kindest and dearest friend; so that at this period of our history, she was again an inmate of the convent at Mowbray, whither her father and Morley had attended her the eve of the day she had first visited the ruins of Marney Abbey.

CHAPTER III.

'I HAVE seen a many things in my time Mrs. Trotman,' said Chaffing Jack as he took the pipe from his mouth in the silent bar room of the Cat and Fiddle; 'but I never see any like this. I think I ought to know Mowbray if any one does, for man and boy I have breathed this air for a matter of half a century. I sucked it in when it tasted of primroses, and this tavern was a cottage covered with honeysuckle in the middle of green fields, where the lads came and drank milk from the cow with their lasses; and I have inhaled what they call the noxious atmosphere, when a hundred chimneys have been smoking like one; and always found myself pretty well. Nothing like business to give one an appetite. But when shall I feel peckish again, Mrs. Trotman?'

'The longest lane has a turning they say, Mr. Trotman.'

'Never knew anything like this before,' replied her husband, 'and I have seen bad times: but I always used to say, 'Mark my words friends, Mowbray will rally.' My words carried weight, Mrs. Trotman, in this quarter, as they naturally should, coming from a man of my experience,—especially when I gave tick. Every man I chalked up was of the same opinion as the landlord of the Cat and Fiddle, and always thought that Mowbray would rally. That's the killing feature of these times, Mrs. Trotman, there's no rallying in the place.'

'I begin to think it's the machines,' said Mrs. Trotman.

'Nonsense,' said Mr. Trotman; 'it's the corn laws. The town of Mowbray ought to clothe the world with our resources. Why Shuffle and Screw can turn out forty mile of calico per day; but where's the returns? That's the point. As the American gentleman said who left his bill unpaid, "Take my breadstuffs and I'll give you a cheque at sight on the Pennsylvanian Bank." '*

'It's very true,' said Mrs. Trotman. 'Who's there?'

'Nothing in my way?' said a woman with a basket of black cherries with a pair of tin scales thrown upon their top.

'Ah! Mrs. Carey,' said Chaffing Jack, 'is that you?'

'My mortal self, Mr. Trotman, tho' I be sure I feel more like a ghost than flesh and blood.'

'You may well say that Mrs. Carey; you and I have known Mowbray as long I should think as any in this quarter—'

'And never see such times as these Mr. Trotman, nor the like of such. But I always thought it would come to this; everything turned topsy-turvy as it were, the children getting all the wages, and decent folk turned adrift to pick up a living as they could. It's something of a judgment in my mind, Mr. Trotman.'

'It's the trade leaving the county, widow, and no mistake.'

'And how shall we bring it back again?' said the widow; 'the police ought to interfere.'

'We must have cheap bread,' said Mr. Trotman.

'So they tell me,' said the widow; 'but whether bread be cheap or dear don't much signify, if we have nothing to buy it with. You don't want anything in my way, neighbour? It's not very tempting I fear,' said the good widow, in a rather mournful tone; 'but a little fresh fruit cools the mouth in this sultry time, and at any rate it takes me into the world. It seems like business, tho' very hard to turn a penny by; but one's neighbours are very kind, and a little chat about the dreadful times always puts me in spirits.'

'Well, we will take a pound for the sake of trade, widow,' said Mrs. Trotman.

'And here's a glass of gin and water, widow,' said Mr. Trotman, 'and when Mowbray rallies you shall come and pay for it.'

'Thank you both very kindly,' said the widow, 'a good neighbour as our minister says, is the pool of Bethesda;* and as you say, Mowbray will rally.'

'I never said so,' exclaimed Chaffing Jack interrupting her. 'Don't go about for to say that I said Mowbray would rally. My words have some weight in this quarter widow; Mowbray rally! Why should it rally? Where's the elements?'

'Where indeed?' said Devilsdust as he entered the Cat and Fiddle with Dandy Mick, 'there is not the spirit of a louse in Mowbray.'

'That's a true bill,' said Mick.

'Is there another white-livered town in the whole realm where the operatives are all working half-time, and thanking the Capitalists for keeping the mills going, and only starving them by inches?' said Devilsdust in a tone of scorn.

'That's your time of day,' said Mick.

'Very glad to see you, gentlemen,' said Mr. Trotman, 'pray be seated. There's a little baccy left yet in Mowbray, and a glass of twist* at your service.'

'Nothing exciseable for me,' said Devilsdust.

'Well it ayn't exactly the right ticket, Mrs. Trotman, I believe,' said Mick, bowing gallantly to the lady; 'but 'pon my soul I am so thirsty, that I'll take Chaffing Jack at his word;' and so saying Mick and Devilsdust ensconced themselves in the bar, while good-hearted Mrs. Carey sipped her glass of gin and water, which she frequently protested was a pool of Bethesda.

'Well Jack,' said Devilsdust, 'I suppose you have heard the news?'

'If it be anything that has happened at Mowbray, especially in this quarter, I should think I had. Times must be very bad indeed that some one does not drop in to tell me anything that has happened and to ask my advice.'

'It's nothing to do with Mowbray.'

'Thank you kindly, Mrs. Trotman,' said Mick, 'and here's your very good health.'

'Then I am in the dark,' said Chaffing Jack, replying to the previous observation of Devilsdust, 'for I never see a newspaper now except a week old, and that lent by a friend, I who used to take my *Sun* regular, to say nothing of the *Dispatch*, and *Bell's Life*.* Times is changed, Mr. Radley.'

'You speak like a book, Mr. Trotman,' said Mick, 'and here's your very good health. But as for newspapers, I'm all in the dark myself, for the Literary and Scientific is shut up, and no subscribers left, except the honorary ones, and not a journal to be had except the *Moral World* and that's gratis.'

'As bad as the Temple,' said Chaffing Jack, 'it's all up with the institutions of the country. And what then is the news?'

'Labour is triumphant in Lancashire,'* said Devilsdust with bitter solemnity.

'The deuce it is,' said Chaffing Jack. 'What, have they raised wages?'

'No,' said Devilsdust, 'but they have stopped the mills.'

'That won't mend matters much,' said Jack with a puff.

'Won't it?'

'The working classes will have less to spend than ever.'

'And what will the Capitalists have to spend?' said Devilsdust.

'Worse and worse,' said Mr. Trotman, 'you will never get institutions like the Temple re-opened on this system.'

'Don't you be afraid Jack,' said Mick, tossing off his tumbler; 'if we only get our rights, won't we have a blow out!'

'We must have a struggle,' said Devilsdust, 'and teach the Capitalists on whom they depend, so that in future they are not to have the lion's share, and then all will be right.'

'A fair day's wage for a fair day's work,' said Mick; 'that's your time of day.'

'It began at Staleybridge,' said Devilsdust, 'and they have stopped them all; and now they have marched into Manchester ten thousand strong. They pelted the police—'

'And cheered the red-coats like blazes,' said Mick.

'The soldiers will fraternise,' said Devilsdust.

'Do what?' said Mrs. Trotman.

'Stick their bayonets into the Capitalists who have hired them to cut the throats of the working classes,' said Devilsdust.

'The Queen is with us,' said Mick. 'It's well known she sets her face against gals working in mills like blazes.'

'Well this is news,' said Mrs. Carey. 'I always thought some good would come of having a woman on the throne;' and repeating her thanks and pinning on her shawl, the widow retired, eager to circulate the intelligence.

'And now that we are alone,' said Devilsdust, 'the question is what are we to do here; and we came to consult you, Jack, as you know Mowbray better than any living man. This thing will spread. It won't stop short. I have had a bird too singing something in *my* ear these two days past. If they do not stop it in Lancashire, and I defy them, there will be a general rising.'

'I have seen a many things in my time,' said Mr. Trotman; 'some risings and some strikes, and as stiff turn-outs as may be. But to my fancy there is nothing like a strike in prosperous times; there's more money spent under those circumstances than you can well suppose, young gentlemen. It's as good as Mowbray Staty* any day.'

'But now to the point,' said Devilsdust. 'The people are regularly sold; they want a leader.'

'Why there's Gerard,' said Chaffing Jack; 'never been a better man in my time. And Warner—the greatest man the Handlooms ever turned out.'

'Ay, ay,' said Devilsdust; 'but they have each of them had a year and a half, and that cools blood.'

'Besides,' said Mick, 'they are too old; and Stephen Morley has got round them, preaching moral force and all that sort of gammon.'

'I never heard that moral force won the battle of Waterloo,' said Devilsdust. 'I wish the Capitalists would try moral force a little, and see whether it would keep the thing going. If the Capitalists will give up their red-coats, I would be a moral force man to-morrow.'

'And the new police,' said Mick. 'A pretty go when a fellow in a blue coat fetches you the Devil's own con on your head and you get moral force for a plaister.'

'Why that's all very well,' said Chaffing Jack; 'but I am against violence—at least much. I don't object to a moderate riot provided it is not in my quarter of the town.'

'Well that's not the ticket now,' said Mick. 'We don't want no violence; all we want is to stop all the mills and hands in the kingdom, and have a regular national holiday for six weeks at least.'

'I have seen a many things in my time,' said Chaffing Jack solemnly, 'but I have always observed that if the people had worked generally for half time for a week they would stand anything.'

'That's a true bill,' said Mick.

'Their spirit is broken,' said Chaffing Jack, 'or else they never would have let the Temple have been shut up.'

'And think of our Institute without a single subscriber!' said Mick. 'The gals is the only thing what has any spirit left. Julia told me just now she would go to the cannon's mouth for the Five Points any summer day.'

'You think the spirit can't be raised, Chaffing Jack,' said Devilsdust very seriously. 'You ought to be a judge.'

'If I don't know Mowbray who does? Trust my word, the house won't draw.'

'Then it is U-P,' said Mick.

'Hush!' said Devilsdust. 'But suppose it spreads?'

'It won't spread,' said Chaffing Jack. 'I've seen a deal of these things. I fancy from what you say it's a cotton squall. It will pass, Sir. Let me see the miners out and then I will talk to you.'

'Stranger things than that have happened,' said Devilsdust.

'Then things get serious,' said Chaffing Jack. 'Them miners is very stubborn, and when they gets excited ayn't it a bear at play, that's all?'

'Well,' said Devilsdust, 'what you say is well worth attention; but all the same I feel we are on the eve of a regular crisis.'

'No, by jingo!'* said Mick, and tossing his cap into the air he snapped his fingers with delight at the anticipated amusement.

CHAPTER IV.

'I DON'T think I can stand this much longer,' said Mr. Mountchesney, the son-in-law of Lord de Mowbray, to his wife, as he stood before the empty fire-place with his back to the mantel-piece and his hands thrust into the pockets of his coat. 'This living in the country in August bores me to extinction. I think we will go to Baden,* Joan.'

'But papa is so anxious, dearest Alfred, that we should remain here at present and see the neighbours a little.'

'I might be induced to remain here to please your father, but as for your neighbours I have seen quite enough of them. They are not a sort of people that I ever met before, or that I wish to meet again. I do not know what to say to them, nor can I annex an idea to what they say to me. Heigho! certainly the country in August is a thing of which no one who has not tried it has the most remote conception.'

'But you always used to say you doted on the country, Alfred,' said Lady Joan in a tone of tender reproach.

'So I do; I never was happier than when I was at Melton,* and even enjoyed the country in August when I was on the Moors.'

'But I cannot well go to Melton,' said Lady Joan.

'I don't see why you can't. Mrs. Shelldrake goes with her husband to Melton, and so does Lady Di with Barham; and a very pleasant life it is.'

'Well, at any rate we cannot go to Melton now,' said Lady Joan mortified; 'and it is impossible for me to go to the Moors.'

'No, but I could go,' said Mr. Mountchesney, 'and leave you here. I might have gone with Eugene de Vere and Milford and Fitzheron. They wanted me very much. What a capital party it would have been, and what capital sport we should have had! And I need not have been away for more than a month or perhaps six weeks, and I could have written to you every day and all that sort of thing.'

Lady Joan sighed and affected to recur to the opened volume which during this conversation she had held in her hand.

'I wonder where Maud is,' said Mr. Mountchesney; 'I shall want her to ride with me to-day. She is a capital horsewoman, and always amuses me. As you cannot ride now, Joan, I wish you would let Maud have Sunbeam.'

'As you please.'

'Well, I am going to the stables and will tell them. Who is this?' Mr. Mountchesney exclaimed, and then walked to the window that looking over the park showed at a distance the advance of a very showy equipage.

Lady Joan looked up.

'Come here, Joan, and tell me who this is,' and Lady Joan was at his side in a moment.

'It is the livery of the Bardolfs,' said Lady Joan.

'I always call them Firebrace; I cannot get out of it,' said Mr. Mountchesney. 'Well, I am glad it is they; I thought it might be an irruption of barbarians. Lady Bardolf will bring us some news.'

Lord and Lady Bardolf were not alone; they were accompanied by a gentleman who had been staying on a visit at Firebrace, and who, being acquainted with Lord de Mowbray, had paid his respects to the castle in his way to London. This gentleman was the individual who had elevated them to the peerage—Mr. Hatton. A considerable intimacy had sprung up between him and his successful clients. Firebrace was an old place rebuilt in the times of the Tudors, but with something of its more ancient portions remaining, and with a storehouse of muniments that had escaped the civil wars. Hatton revelled in them, and in pursuing his researches, had already made discoveries which might perhaps place the coronet of the earldom of Lovel on the brow of the former champion of the baronetage, who now however never mentioned the Order.

Lord de Mowbray was well content to see Mr. Hatton, a gentleman in whom he did not repose the less confidence, because his advice given him three years ago, respecting the writ of right and the claim upon his estate had proved so discreet and correct. Acting on that advice Lord de Mowbray had instructed his lawyers to appear to the action without entering into any unnecessary explanation of the merits of his case. He counted on the accuracy of Mr. Hatton's judgment, that the claim would not be pursued; and he was right; after some fencing and preliminary manœuvring, the claim had not been pursued. Lord de Mowbray therefore, always gracious, was disposed to accord a very distinguished reception to his confidential counsellor. He pressed very much his guests to remain with him some days, and though that was not practicable, Mr. Hatton promised that he would not leave the neighbourhood without paying another visit to the castle.

'And you continue quiet here?' said Mr. Hatton to Lord de Mowbray.

'And I am told we shall keep so,' said Lord de Mowbray. 'The mills are mostly at work, and the men take the reduced wages in a good spirit. The fact is our agitators in this neighbourhood suffered pretty smartly in '39, and the Chartists have lost their influence.'

'I am sorry for poor Lady St. Julians,' said Lady Bardolf to Lady de Mowbray. 'It must be such a disappointment, and she has had so many; but I understand there is nobody to blame but herself. If she had only left the Prince* alone, but she would not be quiet!'

'And where are the Deloraines?'

'They are at Munich; with which they are delighted. And Lady Deloraine writes me that Mr. Egremont has promised to join them there. If he do, they mean to winter at Rome.'

'Somebody said he was going to be married,' said Lady de Mowbray.

'His mother wishes him to marry,' said Lady Bardolf; 'but I have heard nothing.'

Mr. Mountchesney came in and greeted the Bardolfs with some warmth. 'How delightful in the country in August, to meet somebody that you have seen in London in June!' he exclaimed. 'Now, dear Lady Bardolf do tell me something, for you can conceive nothing so triste as we are here. We never get a letter. Joan only corresponds with philosophers and Maud with clergymen; and none of my friends ever write to me.'

'Perhaps you never write to them?'

'Well, I never have been a letter writer; because really I never wanted to write or to be written to. I always knew what was going on because I was on the spot; I was doing the things that people were writing letters about—but now not being in the world any longer, doing nothing, living in the country—and the country in August—I should like to receive letters every day, but I do not know who to fix upon as a correspondent. Eugene de Vere will not write, Milford cannot; and as for Fitzheron he is so very selfish, he always wants his letters answered.'

'That is very unreasonable,' said Lady Bardolf.

'Besides what can they tell me at this moment? They have gone to the Moors and are enjoying themselves. They asked me to go with them, but I could not go, because you see I could not leave Joan; though why I could not leave her, I really cannot understand, because Egerton has got some moors this year, and he leaves Lady Augusta with her father.'

Lady Maud entered the room in her bonnet, returning from an airing. She was all animation—charmed to see everybody; she had been to Mowbray to hear some singing at the Roman Catholic chapel in that town; a service had been performed and a collection made for the suffering workpeople of the place. She had been apprised of it for some days, was told that she would hear the most beautiful voice that she had ever listened to, but it had far exceeded her expectations. A female voice it seemed; no tones could be conceived more tender and yet more thrilling: in short seraphic.

Mr. Mountchesney blamed her for not taking him. He liked music, singing, especially female singing; when there was so little to amuse him, he was surprised that Lady Maud had not been careful that he should have been present. His sister-in-law reminded him that she had particularly requested him to drive her over to Mowbray, and he had declined the honour as a bore.

'Yes,' said Mr. Mountchesney, 'but I thought Joan was going with you, and that you would be shopping.'

'It was a good thing our House was adjourned before these disturbances in Lancashire,' said Lord Bardolf to Lord de Mowbray.

'The best thing we can all do is to be on our estates I believe,' said Lord de Mowbray.

'My neighbour Marney is in a great state of excitement,' said Lord Bardolf; 'all his yeomanry out.'

'But he is quiet at Marney?'

'In a way; but these fires puzzle us. Marney will not believe that the condition of the labourer has anything to do with them; and he certainly is a very acute man. But still I don't know what to say to it. The poor-law is very unpopular in my parish. Marney will have it, that the incendiaries are all strangers hired by the anti-Corn-law League.'*

'Ah! here is Lady Joan,' exclaimed Lady Bardolf, as the wife of Mr. Mountchesney entered the room; 'My dearest Lady Joan!'

'Why Joan,' said Mr. Mountchesney, 'Maud has been to Mowbray, and heard the most delicious singing. Why did we not go?'

'I did mention it to you, Alfred.'

'I remember you said something about going to Mowbray, and that you wanted to go to several places. But there is nothing I hate so much as shopping. It bores me more than anything. And you are so peculiarly long when you are shopping. But singing, and beautiful singing in a Catholic chapel by a woman; perhaps a beautiful woman, that is quite a different thing, and I should have been amused, which nobody seems ever to think of here. I do not know how you find it, Lady Bardolf, but the country to me in August is a something;'—and not finishing his sentence, Mr. Mountchesney gave a look of inexpressible despair.

'And you did not see this singer?' said Mr. Hatton, sidling up to Lady Maud, and speaking in a subdued tone.

'I did not, but they tell me she is most beautiful; something extraordinary; I tried to see her, but it was impossible.'

'Is she a professional singer?'

'I should imagine not; a daughter of one of the Mowbray people I believe.'

'Let us have her over to the Castle, Lady de Mowbray,' said Mr. Mountchesney.

'If you like,' replied Lady de Mowbray, with a languid smile.

'Well at last I have got something to do,' said Mr. Mountchesney. 'I will ride over to Mowbray, find out the beautiful singer, and bring her to the Castle.'

CHAPTER V.

The beam of the declining sun, softened by the stained panes of a small gothic window, suffused the chamber of the Lady Superior of the convent of Mowbray. The vaulted room, of very moderate dimensions, was furnished with great simplicity and opened into a small oratory. On a table were several volumes, an ebon cross was fixed in a niche, and leaning in a high-backed chair, sate Ursula Trafford. Her pale and refined complexion that in her youth had been distinguished for its lustre, became her spiritual office; and indeed her whole countenance, the delicate brow, the serene glance, the small aquiline nose, and the well-shaped mouth, firm and yet benignant, betokened the celestial soul that habited that gracious frame.

The Lady Superior was not alone; on a low seat by her side, holding her hand, and looking up into her face with a glance of reverential sympathy, was a maiden over whose head five summers have revolved since first her girlhood broke upon our sight amid the ruins of Marney Abbey, five summers that have realized the matchless promise of her charms, and while they have added something to her stature have robbed it of nothing of its grace, and have rather steadied the blaze of her beauty than diminished its radiance.

'Yes, I mourn over them,' said Sybil, 'the deep convictions that made me look forward to the cloister as my home. Is it that the world has assoiled my soul? Yet I have not tasted of worldly joys; all that I have known of it has been suffering and tears. They will return, these visions of my sacred youth, dear friend, tell me that they will return!'

'I too have had visions in my youth, Sybil, and not of the cloister, yet am I here.'

'And what should I infer?' said Sybil enquiringly.

'That my visions were of the world, and brought me to the cloister, and that yours were of the cloister and have brought you to the world.'

'My heart is sad,' said Sybil, 'and the sad should seek the shade.'

'It is troubled, my child, rather than sorrowful.'

Sybil shook her head.

'Yes, my child,' said Ursula, 'the world has taught you that there are affections which the cloister can neither satisfy nor supply. Ah! Sybil, I too have loved.'

The blood rose to the cheek of Sybil, and then returned as quickly to the heart; her trembling hand pressed that of Ursula as she sighed and murmured, 'No, no, no.'

'Yes, it is his spirit that hovers over your life, Sybil; and in vain you would forget what haunts your heart. One not less gifted than him; as good, as gentle, as gracious; once too breathed in my ear the accents of joy. He was, like myself, the child of an old house, and Nature had invested him with every quality that can dazzle and can charm. But his heart was as pure, and his soul as lofty, as his intellect and frame were bright,—' and Ursula paused.

Sybil pressed the hand of Ursula to her lips and whispered, 'Speak on.'

'The dreams of by-gone days,' continued Ursula in a voice of emotion, 'the wild sorrows that I can recall, and yet feel that I was wisely chastened. He was stricken in his virtuous pride, the day before he was to have led me to that altar where alone I found the consolation that never fails. And thus closed some years of human love, my Sybil,' said Ursula, bending forward and embracing her. 'The world for a season crossed their fair current, and a power greater than the world forbade their banns; but they are hallowed; memory is my sympathy; it is soft and free, and when he came here to enquire after you, his presence and agitated heart recalled the past.'

'It is too wild a thought,' said Sybil, 'ruin to him, ruin to all. No, we are severed by a fate as uncontrollable as severed you dear friend; ours is a living death.'

'The morrow is unforeseen,' said Ursula. 'Happy indeed would it be for me, my Sybil, that your innocence should be enshrined within these holy walls, and that the pupil of my best years, and the friend of my serene life, should be my successor in this house. But I feel a deep persuasion that the hour has not arrived for you to take the step that never can be recalled.'

So saying, Ursula embraced and dismissed Sybil; for the conversation, the last passages of which we have given, had occurred when Sybil according to her wont on Saturday afternoon had come to request the permission of the Lady Superior to visit her father.

It was in a tolerably spacious and not discomfortable chamber, the first floor over the printing-office of the *Mowbray Phalanx*, that Gerard had found a temporary home. He had not long returned from his factory, and pacing the chamber with a disturbed step, he awaited the expected arrival of his daughter.

She came; the faithful step, the well-known knock; the father and the daughter embraced; he pressed to his heart the child who had clung to him through so many trials, and who had softened so many sorrows, who had been the visiting angel in his cell, and whose devotion had led captivity captive.

Their meetings, though regular, were now comparatively rare. The sacred day united them, and sometimes for a short period the previous afternoon, but otherwise the cheerful hearth and welcome home were no longer for Gerard. And would the future bring them to him? And what was to be the future of his child? His mind vacillated between the convent of which she now seldom spoke, and which with him was never a cherished idea, and those dreams of restored and splendid fortunes which his sanguine temperament still whispered him, in spite of hope so long deferred and expectations so often baulked, might yet be realized. And sometimes between these opposing visions, there rose a third and more practical, though less picturesque result, the idea of her marriage. And with whom? It was impossible that one so rarely gifted and educated with so much daintiness, could ever make a wife of the people. Hatton offered wealth, but Sybil had never seemed to comprehend his hopes, and Gerard felt that their ill-assorted ages was a great barrier. There was of all the men of his own order but one, who from his years, his great qualities, his sympathy, and the nature of his toil and means, seemed not unfitted to be the husband of his daughter; and often had Gerard mused over the possibility of these intimate ties with Morley. Sybil had been, as it were, bred up under his eye; an affection had always subsisted between them, and he knew well that in former days Sybil had appreciated and admired the great talents and acquirements of their friend. At one period he almost suspected that Morley was attached to her. And yet, from causes which he had never attempted to penetrate, probably from a combination of unintentional circumstances, Sybil and Morley had for the last two or three years been thrown little together, and their intimacy had entirely died away. To Gerard it seemed that Morley had ever proved his faithful friend: Morley had originally dissuaded him with energy against that course which had led to his discomfiture and punishment; when arrested, his former colleague was his bail, was his companion and adviser during his trial; had endeavoured to alleviate his imprisonment; and on his release had offered to share his means with Gerard, and when these were refused, he at least supplied Gerard with a roof. And yet with all this, that abandonment of heart and brain, and deep sympathy with every domestic thought that characterized old days, was somehow or other wanting. There was on the part of Morley still devotion, but there was reserve.

'You are troubled, my father,' said Sybil, as Gerard continued to pace the chamber.

'Only a little restless. I am thinking what a mistake it was to have moved in—39.'

Sybil sighed.

'Ah! you were right, Sybil,' continued Gerard; 'affairs were not ripe. We should have waited three years.'

'Three years!' exclaimed Sybil, starting; 'are affairs riper now?'

'The whole of Lancashire is in revolt,' said Gerard. 'There is not a sufficient force to keep them in check. If the miners and colliers rise, and I have cause to believe that it is more than probable they will move before many days are past,—the game is up.'

'You terrify me,' said Sybil.

'On the contrary,' said Gerard, smiling, 'the news is good enough; I'll not say too good to be true, for I had it from one of the old delegates who is over here to see what can be done in our north countree.'

'Yes,' said Sybil inquiringly, and leading on her father.

'He came to the works; we had some talk. There are to be no leaders this time, at least no visible ones. The people will do it themselves. All the children of Labour are to rise on the same day, and to toil no more, till they have their rights. No violence, no bloodshed, but toil halts, and then our oppressors will learn the great economical truth as well as moral lesson, that when Toil plays Wealth ceases.'

'When Toil ceases the People suffer,' said Sybil. 'That is the only truth that we have learnt, and it is a bitter one.'

'Can we be free without suffering,' said Gerard. 'Is the greatest of human blessings to be obtained as a matter of course; to be plucked like fruit, or seized like a running stream? No, no; we must suffer, but we are wiser than of yore,—we will not conspire. Conspiracies are for aristocrats, not for nations.'

'Alas, alas! I see nothing but woe,' said Sybil. 'I cannot believe that after all that has passed, the people here will move: I cannot believe that after all that has passed, all that you, that we, have endured, that you, my father, will counsel them to move.'

'I counsel nothing,' said Gerard 'It must be a great national instinct that does it; but if all England, if Wales, if Scotland won't work, is Mowbray to have a monopoly?'

'Ah! that's a bitter jest,' said Sybil. 'England, Wales, Scotland will be forced to work as they were forced before. How can they subsist without labour? And if they could, there is an organised power that will subdue them.'

'The Benefit Societies, the Sick and Burial Clubs,* have money in the banks that would maintain the whole working classes, with aid in kind that will come, for six weeks, and that will do the business. And as for force, why there are not five soldiers to each town in the kingdom. It's a glittering bugbear this fear of the military: simultaneous strikes would baffle all the armies in Europe.'

'I'll go back and pray that all this is wild talk,' said Sybil earnestly. 'After all that has passed, were it only for your child, you should not speak, much less think, this, my father. What havoc to our hearts and homes has been all this madness! It has separated us; it has destroyed our happy home; it has done more than this—' and here she wept.

'Nay, nay, my child,' said Gerard, coming up and soothing her; 'one cannot weigh one's words before those we love. I can't hear of the people moving with coldness—that's out of nature; but I promise you I'll not stimulate the lads here. I am told they are little inclined to stir. You found me in a moment of what I must call I suppose elation;

but I hear they beat the red-coats and police at Staley Bridge,* and that pricked my blood a bit. I have been ridden down before this when I was a lad, Sybil, by Yeomanry hoofs. You must allow a little for my feelings.'

She extended her lips to the proffered embrace of her father. He blessed her and pressed her to his heart, and soothed her apprehensions with many words of softness. There was a knock at the door.

'Come in,' said Gerard. And there came in Mr. Hatton.

They had not met since Gerard's release from York Castle. There Hatton had visited him, had exercised his influence to remedy his grievances, and had more than once offered him the means of maintenance on receiving his freedom. There were moments of despondency when Gerard had almost wished that the esteem and regard with which Sybil looked upon Hatton might have matured into sentiments of a deeper nature; but on this subject the father had never breathed a word. Nor had Hatton, except to Gerard, ever intimated his wishes, for we could scarcely call them hopes. He was a silent suitor of Sybil, watching opportunities and ready to avail himself of circumstances which he worshipped. His sanguine disposition, fed by a very suggestive and inventive mind, and stimulated by success and a prosperous life, sustained him always to the last. Hatton always believed that everything desirable must happen if a man had energy and watched circumstances. He had confidence too in the influence of his really insinuating manner; his fine taste, his tender tone, his ready sympathy, all which masked his daring courage and absolute recklessness of means.

There were general greetings of the greatest warmth. The eyes of Hatton were suffused with tears as he congratulated Gerard on his restored health, and pressed Sybil's hand with the affection of an old friend between both his own.

'I was down in this part of the world on business,' said Hatton, 'and thought I would come over here for a day to find you all out.' And then after some general conversation he said, 'And where do you think I accidentally paid a visit a day or two back? At Mowbray Castle. I see you are surprised. I saw all your friends, I did not ask his Lordship how the writ of right went on. I dare say he thinks 'tis all hushed. But he is mistaken. I have learnt something which may help us over the stile yet.'

'Well-a-day,' said Gerard, 'I once thought if I could get back the lands the people would at last have a friend; but that's past. I have been a dreamer of dreams often when I was overlooking them at work. And so we all have I suppose. I would willingly give up my claim if I could be sure the Lancashire lads will not come to harm this bout.'

''Tis a more serious business,' said Hatton, 'than any thing of the kind that has yet happened. The government are much alarmed. They talk of sending the Guards down into the north, and bringing over troops from Ireland.'

'Poor Ireland!' said Gerard. 'Well, I think the frieze-coats* might give us a helping hand now, and employ the troops at least.'

'No, my dear father, say not such things.'

'Sybil will not let me think of these matters friend Hatton,' said Gerard smiling. 'Well, I suppose it's not in my way, at least I certainly did not make the best hand of it in—39; but it was London that got me into that scrape. I cannot help fancying that were I on our Moors here a bit with some good lads it might be different, and I must say so, I must indeed, Sybil.'

'But you are very quiet here I hope,' said Hatton.

'Oh! yes,' said Gerard, 'I believe our spirit is sufficiently broken at Mowbray. Wages weekly dropping, and just work enough to hinder sheer idleness; that sort of thing keeps the people in very humble trim. But wait a bit, and when they have reached the starvation point I fancy we shall hear a murmur.'

'I remember our friend Morley in—39, when we returned from London, gave me a very good character of the disposition of the people here,' said Hatton; 'I hope it continues the same. He feared no outbreak then, and the distress in—39 was severe.'

'Well,' said Gerard, 'the wages have been dropping ever since. The people exist, but you can scarcely say they live. But they are cowed I fancy. An empty belly is sometimes as apt to dull the heart as inflame the courage. And then they have lost their leaders, for I was away you see, and have been quiet enough since I came out; and Warner is broken; he has suffered more from his time than I did; which is strange, for he had his pursuits, whereas I was restless enough, and that's the truth, and had it not been for Sybil's daily visit I think, though I may never be allowed to live in a castle,* I should certainly have died in one.'

'And how is Morley?'

'Right well; the same as you left him; I saw not a straw's change when I came out. His paper spreads. He still preaches moral force, and believes that we shall all end in living in communities. But as the only community of which I have personal experience is a gaol, I am not much more inclined to his theory than heretofore.'

CHAPTER VI.

THE reader may not have altogether forgotten Mr. Nixon and his comates, the miners and colliers of that district not very remote from Mowbray, which Morley had visited at the commencement of this history, in order to make fruitless researches after a gentleman whom he subsequently so unexpectedly stumbled upon. Affairs were as little flourishing in that region as at Mowbray itself, and the distress fell upon a population less accustomed to suffering and whose spirit was not daunted by the recent discomfiture and punishment of their leaders.

'It can't last,' said Master Nixon as he took his pipe from his mouth at the Rising Sun.

He was responded to by a general groan. 'It comes to this,' he continued, 'Natur has her laws, and this is one; a fair day's wage for a fair day's work.'

'I wish you may get it,' said Juggins, 'with a harder stint every week and a shilling a day knocked off.'

'And what's to come to-morrow?' said Waghorn. 'The butty has given notice to quit in Parker's field this day se'nnight.* Simmons won't drop wages, but works half time.'

'The boys will be at play afore long,' said a collier.

'Hush!' said Master Nixon with a reproving glance, 'play is a very serious word. The boys are not to go to play as they used to do without by your leave or with your leave. We must appoint a committee to consider the question and we must communicate with the other trades.'

'You're the man, Master Nixon, to choose for churchwarden,' replied the reproved miner with a glance of admiration.

'What is Diggs doing?' said Master Nixon in a solemn tone.

'A-dropping wages and a-raising tommy like fun,' said Master Waghorn.

'There is a great stir in Hell-house yard,' said a miner who entered the tap room at this moment, much excited. 'They say that all the workshops will be shut to-morrow; not an order for a month past. They have got a top-sawyer from London there who addresses them every evening, and says that we have a right to four shillings a day wages, eight hours' work and two pots of ale.'

'A fair day's wage for a fair day's work,' said Master Nixon. 'I would not stickle about hours, but the money and the drink are very just.'

'If Hell-house yard is astir,' said Waghorn, 'there will be a good deal to be seen yet.'

'It's grave,' said Master Nixon. 'What think you of a deputation there? It might come to good.'

'I should like to hear the top-sawyer from London,' said Juggins. 'We had a Chartist here the other day, but he did not understand our case at all.'

'I heard him,' said Master Nixon, 'but what's his Five Points to us? Why he ayn't got tommy among them.'

'Nor long stints,' said Waghorn.

'Nor butties,' said Juggins.

'He's a pretty fellow to come and talk to us,' said a collier. 'He had never been down a pit in all his life.'

The evening passed away in the tap room of the Rising Sun in reflections on the present critical state of affairs and in consultations as to the most expedient course for the future. The rate of wages which for several years in this district had undergone a continuous depression, had just received another downward impulse and was threatened with still further reduction, for the price of iron became every day lower in the market, and the article itself so little in demand that few but the great capitalists who could afford to accumulate their produce were able to maintain their furnaces in action. The little men who still continued their speculations could only do so partially, by diminishing the days of service and increasing their stints or toil and by decreasing the rate of wages as well as paying them entirely in goods, of which they had a great stock and of which they thus relieved themselves at a high profit. Add to all these causes of suffering and discontent among the workmen the apprehension of still greater evils and the tyranny of the butties or middlemen, and it will with little difficulty be felt that the public mind of this district was well-prepared for the excitement of the political agitator, especially if he were discreet enough rather to descant on their physical sufferings and personal injuries than to attempt the propagation of abstract political principles, with which it was impossible for them to sympathise with the impulse and facility of the inhabitants of manufacturing towns, members of literary and scientific institutes, habitual readers *of* political journals and accustomed to habits of discussion of all public questions. It generally happens however that where a mere physical impulse urges the people to insurrection, though it is often an influence of slow growth and movement, the effects are more violent and sometimes more obstinate than when they move under the blended authority of moral and physical necessity, and mix up together the rights and the wants of Man.

However this may be, on the morning after the conversation at the Rising Sun which we have just noticed, the population having as usual gone to their work, having penetrated the pit and descended the shaft, the furnaces all blazing, the chimneys all smoking,—suddenly there rose a rumour even in the bowels of the earth, that the hour and the man had at length arrived; the hour that was to bring them relief and the man that was to bear them redress.

'My missus told it me at the pit-head when she brought me my breakfast,' said a pikeman* to his comrade, and he struck a vigorous blow at the broadseam on which he was working.

'It is not ten mile,' said his companion. 'They'll be here by noon.'

'There is a good deal to do in their way,' said the first pikeman. 'All men at work after notice to be ducked, they say, and every engine to be stopped forthwith.'

'Will the police meet them before they reach this?'

'There is none: my missus says that not a man John of them is to be seen. The Hell-cats as they call themselves halt at every town and offer fifty pounds for a live policeman.'

'I'll tell you what,' said the second pikeman. 'I'll stop my stint and go up the shaft. My heart's all of a flutter, I can't work no more. We'll have a fair day's wage for a fair day's work yet.'

'Come along, I'm your man; if the doggy stop us, we'll knock him down. The People must have their rights; we're driven to this but if one shilling a day is dropped, why not two?'

'Very true; the People must have their rights, and eight hours' work is quite enough.'

In the light of day, the two miners soon learnt in more detail the news which the wife of one of them earlier in the morning had given as a rumour. There seemed now no doubt that the people of Wodgate, commonly called the Hell-cats, headed by their Bishop, had invaded in great force the surrounding district, stopped all the engines, turned all the potters out of the manufactories, met with no resistance from the authorities, and issued a decree that labour was to cease until the Charter was the law of the land.

This last edict was not the least surprising part of the whole affair; for no one could have imagined that the Bishop or any of his subjects had ever even heard of the Charter, much less that they could by any circumstances comprehend its nature, or by any means be induced to believe that its operation would further their interests or redress their grievances. But all this had been brought about, as most of the great events of history, by the unexpected and unobserved influence of individual character.

A Chartist leader had been residing for some time at Wodgate, ever since the distress had become severe, and had obtained great influence and popularity by assuring a suffering and half-starving population, that they were entitled to four shillings a day and two pots of ale, and only eight hours' work. He was a man of abilities and of popular eloquence, and his representations produced an effect; their reception invested him with influence, and as he addressed a population who required excitement, being very slightly employed and with few resources for their vacant hours, the Chartist who was careful never to speak of the Charter became an important personage at Wodgate, and was much patronized by Bishop Hatton and his Lady, whose good offices he was sedulous to conciliate. At the right moment, everything being ripe and well prepared, the Bishop being very drunk and harassed by the complaints of his subjects, the Chartist revealed to him the mysteries of the Charter, and persuaded him not only that the Five Points would cure everything, but that he was the only man who could carry the Five Points. The Bishop had nothing to do; he was making a lock merely for amusement; he required action; he embraced the Charter, without having a definite idea what it meant, but he embraced it fervently, and he determined to march into the country at the head of the population of Wodgate, and establish the faith. Since the conversion of Constantine,* a more important adoption had never occurred. The whole of the north of England, and a great part of the midland counties were in a state of disaffection; the entire country was suffering; hope had deserted the labouring classes; they had no confidence in any future of the existing system. Their organisation, independent of the political system of the Chartists, was complete. Every trade had its union, and every union its lodge in every town, and its central committee in every district. All that was required was the first move, and the Chartist emissary had long fixed upon Wodgate as the spring of the explosion, when the news of the strike in Lancashire determined him to precipitate the event.

The march of Bishop Hatton at the head of the Hell-cats into the mining districts was perhaps the most striking popular movement since the Pilgrimage of Grace.* Mounted on a white mule, wall-eyed and of hideous form, the Bishop brandished a huge hammer with which he had announced he would destroy the enemies of the people: all butties, doggies, dealers in truck and tommy, middle masters and main masters. Some thousand Hell-cats followed him brandishing bludgeons, or armed with bars of iron, pickhandles, and hammers. On each side of the Bishop, on a donkey, was one of his little sons, as demure and earnest as if he were handling his file. A flowing standard of silk inscribed with the

Charter, and which had been presented to him by the delegate, was borne before him like the oriflamme.* Never was such a gaunt, grim crew. As they advanced their numbers continually increased, for they arrested all labour in their progress. Every engine was stopped, the plug was driven out of every boiler, every fire was extinguished, every man was turned out. The decree went forth that labour was to cease until the Charter was the law of the land: the mine and the mill, the foundry and the loom-shop were until that consummation to be idle: nor was the mighty pause to be confined to these great enterprises. Every trade of every kind and description was to be stopped: tailor and cobbler, brushmaker and sweep, tinker and carter, mason and builder, all, all; for all an enormous Sabbath that was to compensate for any incidental suffering that it induced by the increased means and the elevated condition it ultimately would insure—that paradise of artizans, that Utopia of Toil, embalmed in those ringing words, sounds cheerful to the Saxon race—'A fair day's wage for a fair day's work.'

CHAPTER VII.

DURING the strike in Lancashire the people had never plundered, except a few provision shops, chiefly rifled by boys, and their acts of violence had been confined to those with whom they were engaged in what on the whole might be described as fair contest. They solicited sustenance often in great numbers, but even then their language was mild and respectful, and they were easily satisfied and always grateful. A body of two thousand persons, for example—the writer speaks of circumstances within his own experience*—quitted one morning a manufacturing town in Lancashire, when the strike had continued for some time and began to be severely felt, and made a visit to a neighbouring squire of high degree. They entered his park in order—men, women, and children—and then seating themselves in the immediate vicinity of the mansion, they sent a deputation to announce that they were starving and to entreat relief. In the instance in question, the lord of the domain was absent in the fulfilment of those public duties which the disturbed state of the country devolved on him. His wife, who had a spirit equal to the occasion, notwithstanding the presence of her young children who might well have aggravated feminine fears, received the deputation herself; told them that of course she was unprepared to feed so many, but that, if they promised to maintain order and conduct themselves with decorum, she would take measures to satisfy their need. They gave their pledge and remained tranquilly encamped while preparations were making to satisfy them. Carts were sent to a neighbouring town for provisions; the gamekeepers killed what they could, and in a few hours the multitude were fed without the slightest disturbance, or the least breach of their self-organised discipline. When all was over, the deputation waited again on the lady to express to her their gratitude, and the gardens of this house being of celebrity in the neighbourhood, they requested permission that the people might be allowed to walk through them, pledging themselves that no flower should be plucked and no fruit touched. The permission was granted: the multitude in order, each file under a chief and each commander of the files obedient to a superior officer, then made a progress through the beautiful gardens of their beautiful hostess. They even passed through the forcing houses and vineries. Not a border was trampled on, not a grape plucked; and when they quitted the domain, they gave three cheers for the fair castellan.

The Hell-cats and their following were of a different temper to these gentle Lancashire insurgents. They destroyed and ravaged; sacked and gutted houses; plundered cellars; proscribed bakers as enemies of the people; sequestrated the universal stores of all truck and tommy shops; burst open doors, broke windows; destroyed the gas works, that the towns at night might be in darkness; took union workhouses by storm, burned rate-books in the market-place, and ordered public distribution of loaves of bread and flitches of bacon to a mob—cheering and laughing amid flames and rapine. In short they robbed and rioted; the police could make no head against them; there was no military force; the whole district was in their possession; and hearing that a battalion of the Coldstreams were coming down by a train, the Bishop ordered all railroads to be destroyed, and if the Hell-cats had not been too drunk to do his bidding and he too tipsy to repeat it, it is probable that a great destruction of these public ways might have taken place.

Does the reader remember Diggs' tommy shop? And Master Joseph? Well, a terrible scene took place there. The Wodgate girl, with a back like a grasshopper, of the Baptist school religion, who had married Tummas, once a pupil of the Bishop and still his fervent follower, although he had cut open his pupil's head, was the daughter of a man who had worked many years in Diggs' field, had suffered much under his intolerable yoke, and at the present moment was deep in his awful ledger. She had heard from her first years of the oppression of Diggs and had impressed *it* on her husband, who was intolerant of any tyranny except at Wodgate. Tummas and his wife, and a few chosen friends, therefore went out one morning to settle the tommy-book of her father with Mr. Diggs. A whisper of their intention had got about among those interested in the subject. It was a fine summer morning, some three hours from noon, the shop was shut, indeed it had not been opened since the riots, and all the lower windows of the dwelling were closed, barred, and bolted.

A crowd of women had collected. There was Mistress Page and Mistress Prance, old Dame Toddles and Mrs. Mullins, Liza Gray and the comely dame who was so fond of society that she liked even a riot.

'Master Joseph they say has gone to the North,' said the comely dame.

'I wonder if old Diggs is at home?' said Mrs. Mullins.

'He won't show I'll be sworn,' said old Dame Toddles.

'Here are the Hell-cats,' said the comely dame. 'Well I do declare they march like reglars; two, four, six, twelve; a good score at the least.'

The Hell-cats briskly marched up to the elm-trees that shaded the canal before the house, and then formed in line opposite to it. They were armed with bludgeons, crowbars, and hammers. Tummas was at the head and by his side his Wodgate wife. Stepping forth alone, amid the cheering of the crowd of women, the pupil of the Bishop advanced to the door of Diggs' house, gave a loud knock and a louder ring. He waited patiently for several minutes; there was no reply from the interior, and then Tummas knocked and rang again.

'It's very awful,' said the comely dame.

'It's what I always dreamt would come to pass,' said Liza Gray, 'ever since Master Joseph cut my poor baby over the eye with his three foot rule.'

'I think there can be nobody within,' said Mrs. Prance.

'Old Diggs would never leave the tommy without a guard,' said Mrs. Page.

'Now lads,' said Tummas looking round him and making a sign, and immediately some half dozen advanced with their crowbars and were about to strike at the door, when a window in the upper story of the house opened and the muzzle of a blunderbuss was presented at the assailants.

The women all screamed and ran away.

''Twas Master Joseph,' said the comely dame, halting to regain her breath.

''Twas Master Joseph,' sighed Mrs. Page.

''Twas Master Joseph,' moaned Mrs. Prance.

'Sure enough,' said Mrs. Mullins, 'I saw his ugly face.'

'More frightful than the great gun,' said old Dame Toddles.

'I hope the children will get out of the way,' said Liza Gray, 'for he is sure to fire on them.'

In the meantime, while Master Joseph himself was content with his position and said not a word, a benignant countenance exhibited itself at the window and requested in a mild voice to know, 'What his good friends wanted there?'

'We have come to settle Sam Barlow's tommy book,' said their leader.

'Our shop is not open to-day my good friends: the account can stand over; far be it from me to press the poor.'

'Master Diggs,' said a Hell-cat, 'canst thou tell us the price of bacon to-day?'

'Well, good bacon,' said the elder Diggs, willing to humour them, 'may be eightpence a-pound.'

'Thou art wrong Master Diggs,' said the Hell-cat, ''tis fourpence and long credit. Let us see half a dozen good flitches at fourpence, Master Diggs; and be quick.'

There was evidently some controversy in the interior as to the course at this moment to be pursued. Master Joseph remonstrated against the policy of concession, called conciliation, which his father would fain follow, and was for instant coercion; but age and experience carried the day, and in a few minutes some flitches were thrown out of the window to the Hell-cats who received the booty with a cheer.

The women returned.

' 'Tis the tenpence a-pound flitch,' said the comely dame, examining the prize with a sparkling glance.

'I have paid as much for very green stuff,' said Mrs. Mullins.

'And now Master Diggs,' said Tummas, 'what is the price of the best tea a-pound? We be good customers, and mean to treat our wives and sweethearts here. I think we must order half a chest.'

This time there was a greater delay in complying with the gentle hint; but the Hell-cats getting obstreperous, the tea was at length furnished and divided among the women. This gracious office devolved on the wife of Tummas who soon found herself assisted by a spontaneous committee of which the comely dame was the most prominent and active member. Nothing could be more considerate, good-natured, and officious, than the mode and spirit with which she divided the stores. The flitches were cut up and apportioned in like manner. The scene was as gay and bustling as a fair.

'It's as good as a grand tommy day,' said the comely dame with a self-complacent smile as she strutted about smiling and dispensing patronage.

The orders for bacon and tea were followed by a very popular demand for cheese. The female committee received all the plunder and were very active in its distribution. At length a rumour got about that Master Joseph was entering the names of all present in the tommy books, so that eventually the score might be satisfied. The mob had now very much increased. There was a panic among the women, and indignation among the men: a Hell-cat advanced and announced that unless the tommy books were all given up to be burnt, they would pull down the house. There was no reply: some of the Hell-cats advanced; the women cheered; a crowbar fell upon the door; Master Joseph fired, wounded a woman and killed a child.

There rose one of those universal shrieks of wild passion which announce that men have discarded all the trammels of civilization, and found in their licentious rage new and unforeseen sources of power and vengeance. Where it came from, how it was obtained, who prompted the thought, who first accomplished it, were alike impossible to trace; but as it were in a moment, a number of trusses of straw were piled up before the house and set on fire, the gates of the timber-yard were forced, and a quantity of scantlings and battens soon fed the flame. Everything indeed that could stimulate the fire was employed; and every one was occupied in the service. They ran to the water side and plundered the barges, and threw the huge blocks of coal upon the enormous bonfire. Men, women, and children were alike at work with the eagerness and energy of fiends. The roof of the house caught fire: the dwelling burned rapidly; you could see the flames like the tongues of wild beasts, licking the bare and vanishing walls; a single being was observed amid the fiery havoc, shrieking and desperate he clung convulsively to a huge account book. It was Master Joseph. His father had made his escape from the back of the premises and had counselled his son instantly to follow him, but Master Joseph wished to rescue the ledger as well as their lives, and the delay ruined him.

'He has got the tommy book,' cried Liza Gray.

The glare of the clear flame fell for a moment upon his countenance of agony; the mob gave an infernal cheer; then some part of the building falling in, there rose a vast cloud of smoke and rubbish, and he was seen no more.

CHAPTER VIII.

'LIFE'S a tumbleabout thing of ups and downs,' said Widow Carey stirring her tea, 'but I have been down this time longer than I can ever remember.'

'Nor ever will get up, Widow,' said Julia at whose lodgings herself and several of Julia's friends had met, 'unless we have the Five Points.'

'I will never marry any man who is not for the Five Points,' said Caroline.

'I should be ashamed to marry any one who had not the suffrage,' said Harriet.

'He is no better than a slave,' said Julia.

The widow shook her head. 'I don't like these politics,' said the good woman, 'they bayn't in a manner business for our sex.'

'And I should like to know why?' said Julia. 'Ayn't we as much concerned in the cause of good government as the men? And don't we understand as much about it? I am sure the Dandy never does anything without consulting me.'

'It's fine news for a summer day,' said Caroline, 'to say we can't understand politics with a Queen on the throne.'

'She has got her ministers to tell her what to do,' said Mrs. Carey, taking a pinch of snuff. 'Poor innocent young creature, it often makes my heart ache to think how she is beset.'

'Over the left,'* said Julia. 'If the ministers try to come into her bed-chamber, she knows how to turn them to the right about.'

'And as for that,' said Harriet, 'why are we not to interfere with politics as much as the swell ladies in London?'

'Don't you remember, too, at the last election here,' said Caroline, 'how the fine ladies from the Castle came and canvassed for Colonel Rosemary?'

'Ah!' said Julia, 'I must say I wish the Colonel had beat that horrid Muddlefist. If *we* can't have our own man, I am all for the Nobs* against the Middle Class.'

'We'll have our own man soon, I expect,' said Harriet. 'If the people don't work, how are the aristocracy to pay the police?'

'Only think!' said Widow Carey shaking her head. 'Why, at your time of life, my dears, we never even heard of these things, much less talked of them.'

'I should think you didn't, widow, and because why?' said Julia; 'because there was no march of mind* then. But we know the time of day now as well as any of them.'

'Lord, my dear,' said Mrs. Carey; 'what's the use of all that? What we want is, good wages and plenty to do; and as for the rest, I don't grudge the Queen her throne, nor the noblemen and gentlemen their good things. Live and let live say I.'

'Why, you are a regular oligarch, widow,' said Harriet.

'Well, Miss Harriet,' replied Mrs. Carey, a little nettled; ''tisn't calling your neighbours names that settles any question. I'm quite sure that Julia will agree to that, and Caroline too. And perhaps I might call you something if I chose, Miss Harriet; I've heard things said before this, that I should blush to say, and blush to hear too. But I won't demean myself, no I won't. Holly-hock, indeed! Why "holly-hock?"'

At this moment entered the Dandy and Devilsdust.

'Well young ladies,' said the Dandy. 'A-swelling the receipt of customs by the consumption of Congo!* That won't do, Julia; it won't, indeed. Ask Dusty. If you want to beat the enemy, you must knock up the revenue. How d'ye do, widow?'

'The same to you, Dandy Mick. We is deploring the evils of the times here in a neighbourly way.'

'Oh, the times will soon mend,' said the Dandy gaily.

'Well, so I think,' said the widow; 'for when things are at the worst, they always say—'.

'But you always say they cannot mend, Mick,' said Julia, interrupting her.

'Why in a sense, Julia, in a certain sense, you are right; but there are two senses to everything, my girl,' and Mick began singing, and then executed a hornpipe to the gratification of Julia and her guests.

''Tis genteel,' said Mick, receiving their approbation. 'You remember it at the Circus?'

'I wonder when we shall have the Circus again?' said Caroline.

'Not with the present rate of wages,' said Devilsdust.

'It's very hard,' said Caroline, 'that the Middle Class are always dropping our wages. One really has no amusements now. How I do miss the Temple!'

'We'll have the Temple open again before long,' said the Dandy.

'That will be sweet,' exclaimed Caroline. 'I often dream of that foreign nobleman who used to sing, "Oh, no, we never!"'*

'Well, I cannot make out what puts you in such spirits, Mick,' said Julia. 'You told me only this morning that the thing was up, and that we should soon be slaves for life; working sixteen hours a day for no wages, and living on oatmeal porridge and potatoes, served out by the millocrats like a regular Bastile.'*

'But, as Madam Carey says, when things are at the worst—'

'Oh! I did say it,' said the widow, 'surely, because you see, at my years, I have seen so many ups and downs, though I always say—'

'Come, Dusty,' said Julia, 'you are more silent than ever. You won't take a dish I know: but tell us the news, for I am sure you have something to say.'

'I should think we had,' said Dusty.

Here all the girls began talking at the same time, and without waiting for the intelligence, favouring one another with their guesses of its import.

'I am sure it's Shuffle and Screw going to work half time,' said Harriet. 'I always said so.'

'It's something to put down the people,' said Julia: 'I suppose the Nobs have met, and are going to drop wages again.'

'I think Dusty is going to be married,' said Caroline.

'Not at this rate of wages I should hope,' said Mrs. Carey, getting in a word.

'I should think not,' said Devilsdust. 'You are a sensible woman, Mrs. Carey. And I don't know exactly what you mean, Miss Caroline,' he added, a little confused. For Devilsdust was a silent admirer of Caroline, and had been known to say to Mick, who told Julia, who told her friend, that if he ever found time to think of such things, that was the sort of girl he should like to make the partner of his life.

'But Dusty,' said Julia, 'now what is it?'

'Why, I thought you all knew,' said Mick.

'Now, now,' said Julia, 'I hate suspense. I like news to go round like a fly-wheel.'

'Well,' said Devilsdust, dryly, 'this is Saturday, young women, and Mrs. Carey too, you will not deny that.'

'I should think not,' said Mrs. Carey, 'by the token I kept a stall for thirty year in our market, and never gave it up till this summer, which makes me always think that, though I have seen many ups and downs, this—'

'Well, what has Saturday to do with us?' said Caroline; 'for neither Dandy Mick nor you can take us to the Temple, or any other genteel place, since they are all shut from the Corn Laws, or some other cause or other.'

'I believe it's the machines more than the Corn Laws that have shut up the Temple,' said Harriet. 'Machines, indeed! Fancy preferring a piece of iron or wood to your own flesh and blood. And they call that Christianlike!'

'It is Saturday,' said Julia, 'sure enough; and if I don't lie in bed tomorrow till sunset, may I get a bate ticket for every day for a week to come.'

'Well, go it my hearty,' said Mick to Devilsdust. 'It is Saturday, that they have all agreed.'

'And to-morrow is Sunday,' said Devilsdust solemnly.

'And the next day is the blackest day in all the week,' said Julia. 'When I hear the factory bell on Monday morning, I feel just the same as I did when I crossed with my uncle from Liverpool to Seaton* to eat shrimps. Wasn't I sick coming home, that's all!'

'You won't hear that bell sound next Monday,' said Devilsdust solemnly.

'You don't mean that?' said Julia.

'Why, what's the matter?' said Caroline. 'Is the Queen dead?'

'No bell on Monday morning,' said Mrs. Carey, incredulously.

'Not a single ring if all the Capitalists in Mowbray were to pull together at the same rope,' said Devilsdust.

'What can it be?' said Julia. 'Come, Mick; Dusty is always so long telling us anything.'

'Why we are going to have the devil's own strike,' said Mick unable any longer to contain himself and dancing with glee.

'A strike!' said Julia.

'I hope they will destroy the machines,' said Harriet.

'And open the Temple,' said Caroline, 'or else it will be very dull.'

'I have seen a many strikes,' said the widow, 'but as Chaffing Jack was saying to me the other day—'

'Chaffing Jack be hanged,' said Mick. 'Such a slow coach won't do in these high-pressure times. We are going to do the trick and no mistake. There shan't be a capitalist in England who can get a day's work out of us, even if he makes the operatives his junior partners.'

'I never heard of such things,' said Mrs. Carey in amazement.

'It's all booked, though,' said Devilsdust. 'We'll clean out the Savings' Banks; the Benefits and Burials will shell out. I am treasurer of the Ancient Shepherds,* and we passed a resolution yesterday unani-mously, that we would devote all our funds to the sustenance of Labour in this its last and triumphant struggle against Capital.'

'Lor!' said Caroline, 'I think it will be very jolly.'

'As long as you can give us money, I don't care, for my part, how long we stick out,' said Julia.

'Well,' said Mrs. Carey, 'I didn't think there was so much spirit in the place. As Chaffing Jack was saying the other day—'

'There is no spirit in the place,' said Devilsdust; 'but we mean to infuse some. Some of our friends are going to pay you a visit tomorrow.'

'And who may they be?' said Caroline.

'To-morrow is Sunday,' said Devilsdust, 'and the miners mean to say their prayers in Mowbray Church.'

'Well, that will be a shindy!' said Caroline.

'It's a true bill, though,' said Mick. 'This time to-morrow you will have ten thousand of them in this town, and if every mill and work in it and ten mile round is not stopped, my name is not MICK RADLEY!'

CHAPTER IX.

IT was Monday morning. Hatton, enveloped in his chamber robe and wearing his velvet cap, was lounging in the best room of the principal commercial inn of Mowbray, over a breakfast table covered with all the delicacies of which a northern matin meal may justly boast. There were pies of spiced meat and trout fresh from the stream, hams that Westphalia never equalled, pyramids of bread of every form and flavour adapted to the surrounding fruits, some conserved with curious art, and some just gathered from the bed or from the tree.

'It's very odd,' said Hatton to his companion Morley, 'you can't get coffee anywhere.'

Morley, who had supposed that coffee was about the commonest article of consumption in Mowbray, looked a little surprised; but at this moment Hatton's servant entered with a mysterious yet somewhat triumphant air, and ushering in a travelling biggin of their own, fuming like one of the springs of Geyser.*

'Now try that,' said Hatton to Morley, as the servant poured him out a cup; 'you won't find that so bad.'

'Does the town continue pretty quiet?' enquired Morley of the servant as he was leaving the room.

'Quite quiet I believe, Sir; but a great many people in the streets. All the mills are stopped.'

'Well, this is a strange business,' said Hatton when they were once more alone. 'You had no idea of it when I met you on Saturday?'

'None; on the contrary, I felt convinced that there were no elements of general disturbance in this district. I thought from the first that the movement would be confined to Lancashire and would easily be arrested; but the feebleness of the government, the want of decision, perhaps the want of means, have permitted a flame to spread the extinction of which will not soon be witnessed.'

'Do you mean that?'

'Whenever the mining population is disturbed the disorder is obstin-ate. On the whole they endure less physical suffering than most of the working classes, their wages being considerable; and they are so brutal-ized that they are more difficult to operate on than our reading and thinking population of the factories. But when they do stir there is always violence and a determined course. When I heard of their insur-rection on Saturday I was prepared for great disturbances in their dis-trict, but that they should suddenly resolve to invade another country as it were, the seat of another class of labour, and where the hardships however severe are not of their own kind, is to me amazing, and con-vinces me that there is some political head behind the scenes, and that this move, however unintentional on the part of the miners themselves, is part of some comprehensive scheme which, by widening the scene of action and combining several counties and classes of labour in the broil, must inevitably embarrass and perhaps paralyse the Government.'

'There is a good deal in what you say,' said Hatton, taking a straw-berry with a rather absent air, and then he added, 'You remember a conversation we once had, the eve of my departure from Mowbray in—39?'

'I do,' said Morley, reddening.

'The miners were not so ready then,' said Hatton.

'They were not,' said Morley, speaking with some confusion.

'Well they are here now,' said Hatton.

'They are,' said Morley thoughtfully, but more collected.

'You saw them enter yesterday?' said Hatton. 'I was sorry I missed it, but I was taking a walk with the Gerards up Dale to see the cottage where they once lived, and which they used to talk of so much! Was it a strong body?'

'I should say about two thousand men, and as far as bludgeons and iron staves go, armed.'

'A formidable force with no military to encounter them.'

'Irresistible, especially with a favourable population.'

'You think the people were not grieved to see them?'

'Certainly. Left alone they might have remained quiet; but they only wanted the spark. We have a number of young men here who have for a long time been murmuring against our inaction and what they call want of spirit. The Lancashire strike set them all agog; and had any popular leader, Gerard for example or Warner, resolved to move, they were ready.'

'The times are critical,' said Hatton wheeling his arm-chair from the table and resting his feet on the empty fire-place. 'Lord de Mowbray had no idea of all this. I was with him on my way here, and found him quite tranquil. I suppose the invasion of yesterday has opened his eyes a little.'

'What can he do?' said Morley. 'It is useless to apply to the Government. They have no force to spare. Look at Lancashire; a few dragoons and rifles hurried about from place to place and harassed by night service; always arriving too late, and generally attacking the wrong point, some diversion from the main scheme. Now we had a week ago some of the 17th Lancers here. They have been marched into Lancashire. Had they remained the invasion would never have occurred.'

'You haven't a soldier at hand?'

'Not a man; they have actually sent for a party of the 73d* from Ireland to guard us. Mowbray may be burnt before they land.'

'And the castle too,' said Hatton quietly. 'These are indeed critical times Mr. Morley. I was thinking when walking with our friend Gerard yesterday, and hearing him and his charming daughter dilate upon the beauties of the residence which they had forfeited, I was thinking what a strange thing life is, and that the fact of a box of papers belonging to him being in the possession of another person who only lives close by, for we were walking through Mowbray woods—'

At this moment a waiter entered and said there was one without who wished to speak with Mr. Morley.

'Let him come up,' said Hatton, 'he will give us some news perhaps.'

And there was accordingly shown up a young man who had been a member of the Convention in—39 with Morley, afterwards of the Secret Council with Gerard, the same young man who had been the first arrested on the night that Sybil was made a prisoner, having left the scene of their deliberations for a moment in order to fetch her some water. He too had been tried, convicted, and imprisoned, though for a shorter time than Gerard; and he was the Chartist Apostle who had gone and resided at Wodgate, preached the faith to the barbarians, converted them, and was thus the primary cause of the present invasion of Mowbray.

'Ah! Field,' said Morley, 'is it you?'

'You are surprised to see me;' and then the young man looked at Hatton.

'A friend,' said Morley; 'speak as you like.'

'Our great man, the leader and liberator of the people,' said Field with a smile, 'who has carried all before him, and who I verily believe will carry all before him, for Providence has given him those super-human energies which can alone emancipate a race, wishes to confer with you on the state of this town and neighbourhood. It has been represented to him that no one is more knowing and experienced than yourself in this respect; besides as the head of our most influential organ in the Press, it is in every way expedient that you should see him. He is at this moment below giving instructions and receiving reports of the stoppage of all the country works, but if you like I will bring him up here, we shall be less disturbed.'

'By all means,' said Hatton who seemed to apprehend that Morley would make some difficulties. 'By all means.'

'Stop;' said Morley, 'have you seen Gerard?'

'No,' said Field. 'I wrote to him some time back, but his reply was not encouraging. I thought his spirit was perhaps broken.'

'You know that he is here?'

'I concluded so, but we have not seen him; though to be sure, we have seen so many, and done so much since our arrival yesterday, it is not wonderful. By the bye, who is this black-coat you have here, this St. Lys? We took possession of the church yesterday on our arrival, for it's a sort of thing that pleases the miners and colliers wonderfully, and I always humour them. This St. Lys preached us such a sermon that I was almost afraid at one time the game would be spoiled. Our great man was alarmingly taken by it, was saying his prayers all day and had nearly marched back again: had it not been for the excellence of the rum and water at our quarters, the champion of the Charter would have proved a pious recreant.'

'St. Lys will trouble you,' said Morley. 'Alas! for poor human nature, when violence can only be arrested by superstition.'

'Come, don't you preach,' said the Chartist. 'The Charter is a thing the people can understand, especially when they are masters of the country; but as for moral force, I should like to know how I could have marched from Wodgate to Mowbray with that on my banner.'

'Wodgate,' said Morley, 'that's a queer place.'

'Wodgate,' said Hatton, 'what Wodgate is that?'

At this moment a great noise sounded without the room, the door was banged, there seemed a scuffling, some harsh high tones, the deprecatory voices of many waiters. The door was banged again and this time flew open, while exclaiming in an insolent coarse voice, 'Don't tell me of your private rooms; who is master here I should like to know?' there entered a very thickset man, rather under the middle size, with a brutal and grimy countenance, wearing the unbuttoned coat of a *police* serjeant conquered in fight, a cocked hat, with a white plume, which was also a trophy of war, a pair of leather breeches and topped boots, which from their antiquity had the appearance of being his authentic property. This was the leader and liberator of the people of England. He carried in his hand a large hammer which he had never parted with during the whole of the insurrection; and stopping when he had entered the room, and surveying its inmates with an air at once stupid and arrogant, recognizing Field the Chartist, he halloed out, 'I tell you I want him. He's my Lord Chancellor and Prime Minister, my head and principal Doggy; I can't go on without him. Well, what do you think,' he said advancing to Field, 'here's a pretty go! They won't stop the works at the big country mill you were talking of. They won't, won't they? Is my word the law of the land or is it not? Have I given my commands that all labour shall cease till the Queen sends me a message that the Charter is established, and is a man who has a mill, to shut his gates upon my forces, and pump upon my people with engines? There shall be fire for this water;' and so saying the Liberator sent his hammer with such force upon the table, that the plate and porcelain and accumulated luxuries of Mr. Hatton's breakfast perilously vibrated.

'We will enquire into this, Sir,' said Field, 'and we will take the necessary steps.'

'We will enquire into this and we will take the necessary steps,' said the Liberator, looking round with an air of pompous stupidity, and then taking up some peaches, he began devouring them with considerable zest.

'Would the Liberator like to take some breakfast?' said Mr. Hatton.

The Liberator looked at his host with a glance of senseless intimidation, and then as if not condescending to communicate directly with ordinary men, he uttered in a more subdued tone to the Chartist these words, 'Glass of ale.'

Ale was instantly ordered for the Liberator, who after a copious draught assumed a less menacing air, and smacking his lips, pushed aside the dishes, and sate down on the table swinging his legs.

'This is my friend of whom I spoke and whom you wished to see, Sir,' said the Chartist, 'the most distinguished advocate of popular rights we possess, the editor of the *Mowbray Phalanx*, Mr. Morley.'

Morley slightly advanced; he caught the Liberator's eye, who scrutinized him with extreme earnestness, and then jumping from the table shouted, 'Why this is the muff that called on me in Hell-house Yard three years ago.'

'I had that honour,' said Morley quietly.

'Honour be hanged,' said the Bishop, 'you know something about somebody; I couldn't squeeze you then, but by G— I will have it out of you now. Now, cut it short; have you seen him, and where does he live?'

'I came then to gain information, not to give it,' said Morley. 'I had a friend who wished much to see this gentleman—'

'He ayn't no gentleman,' said the Bishop; 'he's my brother: but I tell you what, I'll do something for him now. I'm cock of the walk you see, and that's a sort of thing that don't come twice in a man's life. One should feel for one's flesh and blood, and if I find him out I'll make his fortune, or my name is not Simon Hatton.'

The creator and counsellor of peers started in his chair and turned pale. A look was interchanged between him and Morley which revealed their mutual thoughts, and the great antiquary—looking at the Liberator with a glance of blended terror and disgust—walked away to the window.

'Suppose you put an advertisement in your paper,' continued the Bishop. 'I know a traveller who lost his keys at the Yard and got them back again by those same means. Go on advertising till you find him, and my prime minister and principal doggy here shall give you an order on the town council for your expenses.'

Morley bowed his thanks in silence.

The Bishop continued—'What's the name of the man who has got the big mill here, about three mile off, who won't stop his works and ducked my men this morning with his engines? I'll have fire I say for that water—do you hear that Master Newspaper—I'll have fire for that water before I am many hours older.'

'The Liberator means Trafford,' said the Chartist.

'I'll Trafford him,' said the Liberator and he struck the table with his hammer. 'He ducks my messenger does he? I tell you I'll have fire for that water,' and he looked around him as if he courted some remonstrance in order that he might crush it.

'Trafford is a humane man,' said Morley in a quiet tone, 'and behaves well to his people.'

'A man with a big mill humane!' exclaimed the Bishop; 'with two or three thousand slaves working under the same roof, and he doing nothing but eating their vitals. I'll have no big mills where I'm main master. Let him look to it. Here goes,' and he jumped off the table. 'Before an hour I'll pay this same Trafford a visit and I'll see whether he'll duck me. Come on my prime Doggy,' and nodding to the Chartist to follow him, the Liberator left the room.

Hatton turned his head from the window, and advanced quickly to Morley. 'To business, friend Morley. This savage cannot be quiet for a moment; he exists only in destruction and rapine. If it were not Trafford's mill it would be something else. I am sorry for the Traffords;

they have old blood in their veins. Before sunset their settlement will be razed to the ground. Can we prevent it? And why not attack the castle instead of the mill?'

CHAPTER X.

ABOUT noon of this day there was a great stir in Mowbray. It was generally whispered about that the Liberator at the head of the Hell-cats and all others who chose to accompany them was going to pay a visit to Mr. Trafford's settlement, in order to avenge an insult which his envoys had experienced early in the morning when, accompanied by a rabble of two or three hundred persons, they had repaired to the Mowedale works in order to signify the commands of the Liberator that labour should stop, and if necessary to enforce those commands. The injunctions were disregarded, and when the mob in pursuance of their further instructions began to force the great gates of the premises, in order that they might enter the building, drive the plugs out of the steam-boilers, and free the slaves enclosed, a masqued battery of powerful engines was suddenly opened upon them, and the whole band of patriots were deluged. It was impossible to resist a power which seemed inexhaustible, and wet to the skins and amid the laughter of their adversaries they fled. This ridiculous catastrophe had terribly excited the ire of the Liberator. He vowed vengeance, and as, like all great revolutionary characters and military leaders, the only foundation of his power was constant employment for his troops and constant excitement for the populace, he determined to place himself at the head of the chastising force, and make a great example which should establish his awful reputation and spread terror of his name throughout the district.

Field the Chartist had soon discovered who were the rising spirits of Mowbray, and Devilsdust and Dandy Mick were both sworn on Monday morning of the council of the Liberator, and took their seats at the board accordingly. Devilsdust, used to public business and to the fulfilment of responsible duties, was calm and grave, but equally ready and determined. Mick's head on the contrary was quite turned by the importance of his novel position. He was greatly excited, could devise nothing and would do anything, always followed Devilsdust in council, but when he executed their joint decrees and showed himself about the town, he strutted like a peacock, swore at the men and winked at the girls, and was the idol and admiration of every gaping or huzzaing younker.*

There was a large crowd assembled in the Market Place, in which were the Liberator's lodgings, many of them armed in their rude fashion, and all anxious to march. Devilsdust was with the great man and Field; Mick below was marshalling the men, and swearing like a trooper at all who disobeyed or who misunderstood.

'Come stupid,' said he addressing Tummas, 'what are you staring about? Get your men in order or I'll be among you.'

'Stupid!' said Tummas, staring at Mick with immense astonishment. 'And who are you who says 'Stupid'? A white-livered Handloom as I dare say, or a son of a gun of a factory slave. Stupid indeed! What next, when a Hell-cat is to be called stupid by such a thing as you?'

'I'll give you a piece of advice young man,' said Master Nixon taking his pipe out of his mouth and blowing an immense puff; 'just you go down the shaft for a couple of months, and then you'll learn a little of life, which is wery useful.'

The lively temperament of the Dandy would here probably have involved him in an inconvenient embroilment had not some one at this moment touched him on the shoulder, and looking round he recognised Mr. Morley. Notwithstanding the difference of their political schools Mick had a profound respect for Morley, though why he could not perhaps precisely express. But he had heard Devilsdust for years declare that Stephen Morley was the deepest head in Mowbray, and though he regretted the unfortunate weakness in favour of that imaginary abstraction called Moral Force for which the editor of the *Phalanx* was distinguished, still Devilsdust used to say that if ever the great revolution were to occur by which the rights of labour were to be recognised, though bolder spirits and brawnier arms might consummate the change, there was only one head among them that would be capable when they had gained their power to guide it for the public weal, and as Devilsdust used to add, 'carry out the thing,' and that was Morley.

It was a fine summer day, and Mowedale was as resplendent as when Egremont amid its beauties first began to muse over the beautiful. There was the same bloom over the sky, the same shadowy lustre on the trees, the same sparkling brilliancy on the waters. A herdsman following some kine was crossing the stone bridge, and except their lowing as they stopped and sniffed the current of fresh air in its centre, there was not a sound.

Suddenly the tramp and hum of a multitude broke upon the sunshiny silence. A vast crowd with some assumption of an ill-disciplined order approached from the direction of Mowbray. At their head rode a man on a white mule. Many of his followers were armed with bludgeons and other rude weapons, and moved in files. Behind them spread a more miscellaneous throng, in which women were not wanting and even children. They moved rapidly; they swept by the former cottage of Gerard; they were in sight of the settlement of Trafford.

'All the waters of the river shall not dout* the blaze that I will light up to-day,' said the Liberator.

'He is a most inveterate Capitalist,' said Field, 'and would divert the minds of the people from the Five Points by allotting them gardens and giving them baths.'

'We will have no more gardens in England; everything shall be open,' said the Liberator, 'and baths shall only be used to drown the enemies of the People. I was always against washing; it takes the marrow out of a man.'

'Here we are,' said Field, as the roofs and bowers of the village, the spire and the spreading factory, broke upon them. 'Every door and every window closed! The settlement is deserted. Some one has been before us and apprised them of our arrival.'

'Will they pour water on me?' said the Bishop. 'It must be a stream indeed that shall put out the blaze that I am going to light. What shall we do first? Halt there, you men,' said the Liberator, looking back with that scowl which his apprentices never could forget. 'Will you halt or won't you? or must I be among you?'

There was a tremulous shuffling and then a comparative silence.

The women and children of the village had been gathered into the factory yard, of which the great gates were closed.

'What shall we burn first?' asked the Bishop.

'We may as well parley with them a little,' said Field; 'perhaps we may contrive to gain admission and then we can sack the whole affair, and let the people burn the machinery. It will be a great moral lesson.'

'As long as there is burning,' said the Bishop, 'I don't care what lessons you teach them. I leave them to you; but I will have fire to put out that water.'

'I'll advance,' said Field, and so saying he went forward and rang at the gate; the Bishop, on his mule, with a dozen Hell-cats accompanying him; the great body of the people about twenty yards withdrawn.

'Who rings?' asked a loud voice.

'One who by the order of the Liberator wishes to enter and see whether his commands for a complete cessation of labour have been complied with in this establishment.'

'Very good,' said the Bishop.

'There is no hand at work here,' said the voice; 'and you may take my word for it.'

'Your word be hanged,' said the Bishop. 'I want to know—'

'Hush, hush!' said Field, and then in a louder voice he said, 'It may be so, but as our messengers this morning were not permitted to enter and were treated with great indignity—'

'That's it,' said the Bishop.

'With great indignity,' continued Field, 'we must have ocular experience of the state of affairs, and I beg and recommend you therefore at once to let the Liberator enter.'

'None shall enter here,' replied the unseen guardian of the gate.

'That's enough,' cried the Bishop.

'Beware!' said Field.

'Whether you let us in or not, 'tis all the same,' said the Bishop; 'I will have fire for your water, and I have come for that. Now lads!'

'Stop,' said the voice of the unseen. 'I will speak to you.'

'He is going to let us in,' whispered Field to the Bishop.

And suddenly there appeared on the flat roof of the lodge that was on one side of the gates—Gerard. His air, his figure, his position were alike commanding, and at the sight of him a loud and spontaneous cheer burst from the assembled thousands. It was the sight of one who was after all the most popular leader of the people that had ever figured in these parts, whose eloquence charmed and commanded, whose disinterestedness was acknowledged, whose sufferings had created sympathy, whose courage, manly bearing, and famous feats of strength were a source to them of pride. There was not a Mowbray man whose heart did not throb with emotion, and whose memory did not recall the orations from the Druid's Altar and the famous meetings on the moor. 'Gerard for ever' was the universal shout.

The Bishop who liked no one to be cheered except himself, like many great men, was much disgusted, a little perplexed. 'What does all this mean?' he whispered to Field, 'I came here to burn down the place.'

'Wait awhile,' said Field, 'we must humour the Mowbray men a bit. This is their favourite leader, at least was in old days. I know him well; he is a bold and honest man.'

'Is this the man who ducked my people?' asked the Bishop fiercely.

'Hush!' said Field; 'he is going to speak.'

'My friends,' said Gerard, 'for if we are not friends who should be? (loud cheers and cries of 'Very true'), if you come here to learn whether the Mowedale works are stopped, I give you my word there is not a machine or man that stirs here at this moment (great cheering). I believe you'll take my word (cheers, and cries of 'We will'). I believe I'm known at Mowbray ('Gerard for ever!'), and on Mowbray Moor too (tumultuous cheering). We have met together before this ('That we have'), and shall meet again yet (great cheering). The people haven't so many friends that they should quarrel with well-wishers. The master here has done his best to soften your lots. He is not one of those who deny that Labour has rights (loud cheers). I say that Mr. Trafford has always acknowledged the rights of Labour (prolonged cheers and cries of 'So he has'). Well, is he the man that we should injure? ('No, no'). What if he did give a cold reception to some visitors this morning—(groans)—perhaps they wore faces he was not used to (loud cheers and laughter from the Mowbray people). I dare say they mean as well as we do—no doubt of that—but still a neighbour's a neighbour (immense cheering). Now, my lads, three cheers for the National Holiday,' and Gerard gave the time, and his voice was echoed by the thousands present. 'The master here has no wish to interfere with the National Holiday; all he wants to secure is that all mills and works should alike stop (cries of 'Very just'). And I say *so* too,' continued Gerard. 'It is just; just and manly and like a true-born Englishman as he is, who loves the people and whose father before him loved the people (great cheering). Three cheers for Mr. Trafford I say;' and they were given; 'and three cheers for Mrs. Trafford too, the friend of the poor!' Here the mob became not only enthusiastic but maudlin; all vowing to each other that Trafford was a true-born Englishman and his wife a very angel upon earth. This popular feeling is so contagious that even the Hell-cats shared it—cheering, shaking hands with each other, and almost shedding tears—though it must be confessed that they had some vague idea that it was all to end in something to drink.

Their great leader however remained unmoved, and nothing but his brutal stupidity could have prevented him from endeavouring to arrest the tide of public feeling, but he was quite bewildered by the diversion, and for the first time failed in finding a prompter in Field. The Chartist was cowed by Gerard; his old companion in scenes that the memory lingered over, and whose superior genius had often controlled and often led him, Gerard too had recognized him and had made some personal allusion and appeal to him, which alike touched his conscience and flattered his vanity. The ranks were broken, the spirit of the expedition had dissolved, the great body were talking of returning, some of the stragglers indeed were on their way back, the Bishop silent and confused kept knocking the mane of his mule with his hammer.

'Now,' said Morley who during this scene had stood apart accompanied by Devilsdust and Dandy Mick. 'Now,' said Morley to the latter, 'now is your time.'

'Gentlemen!' sang out Mick.

'A speech, a speech!' cried out several.

'Listen to Mick Radley,' whispered Devilsdust moving swiftly among the mob and addressing every one he met of influence. 'Listen to Mick Radley, he has something important.'

'Radley for ever! Listen to Mick Radley! Go it Dandy! Pitch it into them! Silence for Dandy Mick! Jump up on that ere bank,' and on the bank Mick mounted accordingly.

'Gentlemen,' said Mick.

'Well, you have said that before.'

'I like to hear him say "Gentlemen;" it's respectful.'

'Gentlemen,' said the Dandy, 'the National Holiday has begun—'

'Three cheers for it!'

'Silence; hear the Dandy!'

'The National Holiday has begun,' continued Mick, 'and it seems to me the best thing for the people to do is to take a walk in Lord de Mowbray's park.'

This proposition was received with one of those wild shouts of approbation which indicate the orator has exactly hit his audience between wind and water. The fact is the public mind at this instant wanted to be led, and in Dandy Mick a leader appeared. A leader to be successful should embody in his system the necessities of his followers; express what every one feels, but no one has had the ability or the courage to pronounce.

The courage and adroitness, the influence of Gerard, had reconciled the people to the relinquishment of the great end for which they had congregated; but neither man nor multitude likes to make preparations without obtaining a result. Every one wanted to achieve some object by the movement; and at this critical juncture an object was proposed, and one which promised novelty, amusement, excitement. The Bishop whose consent must be obtained, but who relinquished an idea with the same difficulty with which he had imbibed it, alone murmured, and kept saying to Field, 'I thought we came to burn down this mill! A bloody-minded Capitalist, a man that makes gardens and forces the people to wash themselves: What is all this?'

Field said what he could, while Devilsdust leaning over the mule's shoulder, cajoled the other ear of the Bishop, who at last gave his consent with almost as much reluctance as George the Fourth did to the emancipation of the Roman Catholics;* but he made his terms, and said in a sulky voice he must have a glass of ale.

'Drink a glass of ale with Lord de Mowbray,' said Devilsdust.

CHAPTER XI

WHEN the news had arrived in the morning at Mowbray, that the messengers of the Bishop had met with a somewhat queer reception at the Mowedale works, Gerard prescient that some trouble might in consequence occur there, determined to repair at once to the residence of his late employer. It so happened that Monday was the day on which the cottages up the dale and on the other side of the river were visited by an envoy of Ursula Trafford, and it was the office of Sybil this morning to fulfil the duties of that mission of charity. She had mentioned this to her father on the previous day, and as in consequence of the strike, he was no longer occupied, he had proposed to accompany his daughter on the morrow. Together therefore they had walked until they arrived at the bridge, it being then about two hours to noon, a little above their former residence. Here they were to separate. Gerard embraced his daughter with even more than usual tenderness; and as Sybil crossed the bridge, she looked round at her father, and her glance caught his, turned for the same fond purpose.

Sybil was not alone; Harold, who had ceased to gambol, but who had gained in stature, majesty and weight what he had lost of lithe and frolick grace, was by her side. He no longer danced before his mistress, coursed away and then returned, or vented his exuberant life in a thousand feats of playful vigour; but sedate and observant, he was always at hand, ever sagacious, and seemed to watch her every glance.

The day was beautiful, the scene was fair, the spot indeed was one which rendered the performance of gracious offices to Sybil doubly sweet. She ever begged of the Lady Superior that she might be her minister to the cottages up Dale. They were full of familiar faces. It was a region endeared to Sybil by many memories of content and tenderness. And as she moved along to-day her heart was light, and the natural joyousness of her disposition, which so many adverse circumstances had tended to repress, was visible in her sunny face. She was happy about her father. The invasion of the miners, instead of prompting him as she had feared to some rash conduct, appeared to have filled him only with disgust. Even now he was occupied in a pursuit of order and peace, counselling prudence and protecting the benevolent.

She passed through a copse which skirted those woods of Mowbray wherein she had once so often rambled with one whose image now hovered over her spirit. Ah! what scenes and changes, dazzling and dark, had occurred since the careless though thoughtful days of her early girlhood! Sybil mused: she recalled the moonlit hour when Mr. Franklin first paid a visit to their cottage, their walks and wanderings, the expeditions which she planned and the explanations which she so artlessly gave him. Her memory wandered to their meeting in Westminster, and all the scenes of sorrow and of softness of which it was the herald. Her imagination raised before her in colours of light and life the morning, the terrible morning when he came to her desperate rescue; his voice sounded in her ear; her cheek glowed as she recalled their tender farewell.

It was past noon: Sybil had reached the term of her expedition, had visited her last charge; she was emerging from the hills into the open country, and about to regain the river road that would in time have conducted her to the bridge. On one side of her was the moor, on the other a wood that was the boundary of Mowbray Park. And now a number of women met her, some of whom she recognised, and had indeed visited earlier in the morning. Their movements were disordered, distress and panic were expressed on their countenances. Sybil stopped, she spoke to some, the rest gathered around her. The Hell-cats were coming, they said; they were on the other side of the river, burning mills, destroying all they could put their hands on, man, woman and child.

Sybil, alarmed for her father, put to them some questions, to which they gave incoherent answers. It was however clear that they had seen no one, and knew nothing of their own experience. The rumour had reached them that the mob was advancing up Dale, those who had apprised them had, according to their statement, absolutely witnessed the approach of the multitude, and so they had locked up their cottages, crossed the bridge, and ran away to the woods and moor. Under these circumstances, deeming that there might be much exaggeration, Sybil at length resolved to advance, and in a few minutes those whom she had encountered were out of sight. She patted Harold, who looked up in her face and gave a bark, significant of his approbation of her proceeding, and also of his consciousness that something strange was going on. She had not proceeded very far before two men on horseback, at full gallop, met her. They pulled up directly they observed her, and said, 'You had better go back as fast as you can: the mob is out, and coming up Dale in great force.'

Sybil enquired, with much agitation, whether they had themselves seen the people, and they replied that they had not, but that advices had been received from Mowbray of their approach, and as for themselves they were hurrying at their utmost speed to a town ten miles off, where they understood some yeomanry were stationed, and to whom the Mayor of Mowbray had last night sent a despatch: Sybil would have enquired whether there were time for her to reach the bridge and join her father at the factory of Trafford, but the horsemen were impatient and rode off. Still she determined to proceed. All that she now aimed at was to reach Gerard and share his fate.

A boat put across the river; two men and a crowd of women. The mob had been seen; at least there was positively one person present who had distinguished them in the extreme distance, or rather the cloud of dust which they created; there were dreadful stories of their violence and devastation. It was understood that a body meant to attack Trafford's works, but, as the narrator added, it was very probable that the greater part would cross the bridge and so on to the Moor, where they would hold a meeting.

Sybil would fain have crossed in the boat, but there was no one to assist her. They had escaped, and meant to lose no time in finding a place of refuge for the moment. They were sure if they recrossed now, they must meet the mob. They were about to leave her, Sybil in infinite distress, when a lady driving herself in a pony carriage, with a couple of grooms behind her mounted also on ponies of the same form and colour, came up from the direction of the Moor, and observing the group and Sybil much agitated, pulled up and enquired the cause. One of the men, frequently interrupted by all the women, immediately entered into a narrative of the state of affairs for which the lady was evidently quite unprepared, for her alarm was considerable.

'And this young person will persist in crossing over,' continued the man. 'It's nothing less than madness. I tell her she will meet instant death or worse.'

'It seems to me very rash,' said the lady in a kind tone, and who seemed to recognise her.

'Alas! what am I to do!' exclaimed Sybil. 'I left my father at Mr. Trafford's!'

'Well, we have no time to lose,' said the man, whose companion had now fastened the boat to the bank, and so wishing them good morning, and followed by the whole of his cargo, they went on their way.

But just at this moment a gentleman, mounted on a very knowing little cob, came cantering up, exclaiming, as he reached the pony carriage, 'My dear Joan, I am looking after you. I have been in the greatest alarm for you. There are riots on the other side of the river, and I was afraid you might have crossed the bridge.'

Upon this, Lady Joan related to Mr. Mountchesney how she had just become acquainted with the intelligence, and then they conversed together for a moment or so in a whisper: when turning round to Sybil, she said, 'I think you had really better come home with us till affairs are a little more quiet.'

'You are most kind,' said Sybil, 'but if I could get back to the town through Mowbray Park, I think I might do something for my father!'

'We are going to the Castle through the park at this moment,' said the gentleman. 'You had better come with us. There you will at least be safe, and perhaps we shall be able to do something for the good people in trouble over the water,' and so saying, nodding to a groom who, advancing, held his cob, the gentleman dismounted, and approaching Sybil with great courtesy, said, 'I think we ought all of us to know each other. Lady Joan and myself had once the pleasure of meeting you, I think, at Mr. Trafford's. It is a long time ago, but,' he added in a subdued tone, 'you are not a person to forget.'

Sybil was insensible to Mr. Mountchesney's gallantry, but alarmed and perplexed, she yielded to the representations of himself and Lady Joan, and got into the phaeton. Turning from the river, they pursued a road which entered after a short progress into the park, Mr. Mountchesney cantering on before them, Harold following. They took their way for about a mile through richly-wooded demesne, Lady Joan addressing many observations with great kindness to Sybil and frequently endeavouring, though in vain, to distract her agitated thoughts, till they at length emerged from the more covered parts into extensive lawns, while on a rising ground, which they rapidly approached, rose Mowbray Castle, a modern castellated building, raised in a style not remarkable for its taste or correctness, but vast, grand, and imposing.

'And now,' said Mr. Mountchesney, riding up to them and addressing Sybil, 'I will send off a scout immediately for news of your father. In the mean time let us believe the best!' Sybil thanked him with cordiality, and then she entered—Mowbray Castle.

CHAPTER XII.

LESS than an hour after the arrival of Sybil at Mowbray Castle the scout that Mr. Mountchesney had sent off to gather news returned, and with intelligence of the triumph of Gerard's eloquence, that all had ended happily, and that the people were dispersing and returning to the town.

Kind as was the reception accorded to Sybil by Lady de Mowbray and her daughter on her arrival, the remembrance of the perilous position of her father had totally disqualified her from responding to their advances. Acquainted with the cause of her anxiety and depression and sympathising with womanly softness with her distress, nothing could be more considerate than their behaviour. It touched Sybil much, and she regretted the harsh thoughts that irresistible circumstances had forced her to cherish respecting persons, who, now that she saw them in their domestic and unaffected hour, had apparently many qualities to conciliate and to charm. When the good news arrived of her father's safety, and safety achieved in a manner so flattering to a daughter's pride, it came upon a heart predisposed to warmth and kindness and all her feelings opened. The tears stood in her beautiful eyes, and they were tears not only of tenderness but gratitude. Fortunately Lord de Mowbray was at the moment absent, and as the question of the controverted inheritance was a secret to every member of the family except himself, the name of Gerard excited no invidious sensation in the circle. Sybil was willing to please and to be pleased; every one was captivated by her beauty, her grace, her picturesque expression and sweet simplicity. Lady de Mowbray serenely smiled and frequently when unobserved viewed her through her eyeglass. Lady Joan, much softened by marriage, would show her the castle; Lady Maud was in ecstasies with all that Sybil said or did; while Mr. Mountchesney who had thought of little else but Sybil ever since Lady Maud's report of her seraphic singing, and who had not let four-and-twenty hours go by without discovering, with all the practised art of St James', the name and residence of the unknown fair, flattered himself he was making great play when Sybil, moved by his great kindness, distinguished him by frequent notice. They had viewed the castle, they were in the music-room, Sybil had been prevailed upon, though with reluctance, to sing. Some Spanish church music which she found there called forth all her powers: all was happiness, delight, rapture, Lady Maud in a frenzy of friendship, Mr. Mountchesney convinced that the country in August might be delightful, and Lady Joan almost gay because Alfred was pleased. Lady de Mowbray had been left in her boudoir with the *Morning Post*.* Sybil had just finished a ravishing air, there was a murmur of luncheon—when suddenly Harold, who had persisted in following his mistress and whom Mr. Mountchesney had gallantly introduced into the music-room, rose and coming forward from the corner in which he reposed, barked violently.

'How now!' said Mr. Mountchesney.

'Harold!' said Sybil in a tone of remonstrance and surprise.

But the dog not only continued to bark but even howled. At this moment the groom of the chambers entered the room abruptly and with a face of mystery said that he wished to speak with Mr. Mountchesney. That gentleman immediately withdrew. He was absent some little time, the dog very agitated, Lady Joan becoming disquieted, when he returned. His changed air struck the vigilant eye of his wife.

'What has happened Alfred?' she said.

'Oh! don't be alarmed,' he replied with an obvious affectation of ease. 'There are some troublesome people in the park; stragglers I suppose from the rioters. The gate-keeper ought not to have let them pass. I have given directions to Bentley what to do, if they come to the castle.'

'Let us go to mama,' said Lady Joan.

And they were all about leaving the music-room, when a servant came running in and called out 'Mr. Bentley told me to say, sir, they are in sight.'

'Very well,' said Mr. Mountchesney in a calm tone but changing colour. 'You had better go to your mama, Joan, and take Maud and our friend with you. I will stay below for a while,' and notwithstanding the remonstrances of his wife, Mr. Mountchesney went to the hall.

'I don't know what to do, sir,' said the house steward. 'They are a very strong party.'

'Close all the windows, lock and bar all the doors,' said Mr. Mountchesney. 'I am frightened,' he continued, 'about your lord. I fear he may fall in with these people.'

'My lord is at Mowbray,' said Mr. Bentley. 'He must have heard of this mob there.'

And now emerging from the plantations and entering on the lawns, the force and description of the invading party were easier to distinguish. They were numerous, though consisting of only a section of the original expedition, for Gerard had collected a great portion of the Mowbray men, and they preferred being under his command to following a stranger whom they did not much like on a somewhat licentious adventure of which their natural leader disapproved. The invading section therefore were principally composed of Hell-cats, though, singular enough, Morley of all men in the world accompanied them, attended by Devilsdust, Dandy Mick, and others of that youthful class of which these last were the idols and heroes. There were perhaps eighteen hundred or two thousand persons armed with bars and bludgeons, in general a grimy crew, whose dress and appearance revealed the kind of labour to which they were accustomed. The difference between them and the minority of Mowbray operatives was instantly recognizable.

When they perceived the castle this dreadful band gave a ferocious shout. Lady de Mowbray showed blood; she was composed and courageous. She observed the mob from the window, and re-assuring her daughters and Sybil she said she would go down and speak to them.

She was on the point of leaving the room with this object when Mr. Mountchesney entered and hearing her purpose, dissuaded her from attempting it. 'Leave all to me,' he said; 'and make yourselves quite easy; they will go away, I am certain they will go away,' and he again quitted them.

In the meantime Lady de Mowbray and her friends observed the proceedings below. When the main body had advanced within a few hundred yards of the castle, they halted and seated themselves on the turf. This step re-assured the garrison: it was generally held to indicate that the intentions of the invaders were not of a very settled or hostile character; that they had visited the place probably in a spirit of frolic, and if met with tact and civility might ultimately be induced to retire from it without much annoyance. This was evidently the opinion of Mr. Mountchesney from the first, and when an uncouth being on a white mule, attended by twenty or thirty miners, advanced to the castle and asked for Lord de Mowbray, Mr. Mountchesney met them with kindness, saying that he regretted his father-in-law was absent, expressed his readiness to represent him, and enquired their pleasure. His courteous bearing evidently had an influence on the Bishop, who dropping his usual brutal tone mumbled something about his wish to drink Lord de Mowbray's health.

'You shall all drink his health,' said Mr. Mountchesney humouring him, and he gave directions that a couple of barrels of ale should be broached in the park before the castle. The Bishop was pleased, the people were in good humour, some men began dancing, it seemed that the cloud had blown over, and Mr. Mountchesney sent up a bulletin to Lady de Mowbray that all danger was past and that he hoped in ten minutes they would all have disappeared.

The ten minutes had expired: the Bishop was still drinking ale, and Mr. Mountchesney still making civil speeches and keeping his immediate attendants in humour.

'I wish they would go,' said Lady de Mowbray.

'How wonderfully Alfred has managed them,' said Lady Joan.

'After all,' said Lady Maud, 'it must be confessed that the people—' Her sentence was interrupted; Harold, who had been shut out but who had laid down without quietly, though moaning at intervals, now sprang at the door with so much force that it trembled on its hinges, while the dog again barked with renewed violence. Sybil went to him: he seized her dress with his teeth and would have pulled her away. Suddenly uncouth and mysterious sounds were heard, there was a loud shriek, the gong in the hall thundered, the great alarum-bell of the tower sounded without, and the housekeeper followed by the female domestics rushed into the room.

'O! my lady, my lady,' they all exclaimed at the same time, 'the Hell-cats are breaking into the castle.'

Before any one of the terrified company could reply, the voice of Mr. Mountchesney was heard. He was approaching them; he was no longer calm. He hurried into the room; he was pale, evidently greatly alarmed. 'I have come to you,' he said; 'these fellows have got in below. While there is time and we can manage them, you must leave the place.'

'I am ready for anything,' said Lady de Mowbray.

Lady Joan and Lady Maud wrung their hands in frantic terror. Sybil very pale said, 'Let me go down; I may know some of these men.'

'No, no,' said Mr. Mountchesney. 'They are not Mowbray people. It would not be safe.'

Dreadful sounds were now heard; a blending of shouts and oaths and hideous merriment. Their hearts trembled.

'The mob are in the house, sir,' called out Mr. Bentley, rushing up to them. 'They say they will see everything.'

'Let them see everything,' said Lady de Mowbray, 'but make a condition that they first let us go. Try Alfred, try to manage them before they are utterly ungovernable.'

Mr. Mountchesney again left them on this desperate mission. Lady de Mowbray and all the women remained in the chamber. Not a word was spoken: the silence was complete. Even the maid-servants had ceased to sigh and sob. A feeling something like desperation was stealing over them.

The dreadful sounds continued increased. They seemed to approach nearer. It was impossible to distinguish a word, and yet their import was frightful and ferocious.

'Lord have mercy on us all!' exclaimed the housekeeper, unable to restrain herself. The maids began to cry.

After an absence of about five minutes Mr. Mountchesney again hurried in and leading away Lady de Mowbray, he said, 'You haven't a moment to lose. Follow us!'

There was a general rush, and following Mr. Mountchesney they passed rapidly through several apartments, the fearful noises every moment increasing, until they reached the library which opened on the terrace. The windows were broken, the terrace crowded with people, several of the mob were in the room, even Lady de Mowbray cried out and fell back.

'Come on,' said Mr. Mountchesney. 'The mob have possession of the castle. It is our only chance.'

'But the mob are here,' said Lady de Mowbray much terrified.

'I see some Mowbray faces,' cried Sybil springing forward, with a flashing eye and a glowing cheek. 'Bamford and Samuel Carr: Bamford, if you be my father's friend, aid us now; and Samuel Carr, I was with your mother this morning: did she think I should meet her son thus? No, you shall not enter,' said Sybil advancing. They recognised her, they paused. 'I know you, Couchman; you told us once at the Convent that we might summon you in our need. I summon you now. O, men, men!' she exclaimed, clasping her hands. 'What is this? Are you led away by strangers to such deeds? Why, I know you all! You came here to aid, I am sure, and not to harm. Guard these ladies; save them from these foreigners! There's Butler, he'll go with us, and Godfrey Wells. Shall it be said you let your neighbours be plundered and assailed by strangers and never tried to shield them? Now, my good friends, I entreat, I adjure you, Butler, Wells, Couchman, what would Walter Gerard say, your friend that you have so often followed, if he saw this?'

'Gerard for ever!' shouted Couchman.

'Gerard for ever!' exclaimed a hundred voices.

''Tis his blessed daughter,' said others; ''tis Sybil, our angel Sybil.'

'Stand by Sybil Gerard.'

Sybil had made her way upon the terrace, and had collected around her a knot of stout followers, who, whatever may have been their original motive, were now resolved to do her bidding. The object of Mr. Mountchesney was to descend the side-step of the terrace and gain the flower-garden, from whence there were means of escape. But the throng was still too fierce to permit Lady de Mowbray and her companions to attempt the passage, and all that Sybil and her followers could at present do, was to keep the mob off from entering the library, and to exert themselves to obtain fresh recruits.

At this moment an unexpected aid arrived.

'Keep back there! I call upon you in the name of God to keep back!' exclaimed a voice of one struggling and communing with the rioters, a voice which all immediately recognised. It was that of Mr. St. Lys. 'Charles Gardner, I have been your friend. The aid I gave you was often supplied to me by this house. Why are you here?'

'For no evil purpose, Mr. St. Lys. I came as others did, to see what was going on.'

'Then you see a deed of darkness. Struggle against it. Aid me and Philip Warner in this work; it will support you at the judgment. Tressel,

Tressel, stand by me and Warner. That's good, that's right! And you too, Daventry, and you, and you. I knew you would wash your hands of this fell deed. It is not Mowbray men who would do this. That's right, that's right! Form a band. Good again. There's not a man that joins us now who does not make a friend for life.'

Mr. St. Lys had been in the neighbourhood when the news of the visit of the mob to the castle reached him. He anticipated the perilous consequences. He hastened immediately to the scene of action. He had met Warner the handloom weaver in his way, and enlisted his powerful influence with the people on his side.

The respective bands of Sybil and Mr. St. Lys in time contrived to join. Their numbers were no longer contemptible; they were animated by the words and presence of their leaders: St. Lys struggling in their midst; Sybil maintaining her position on the terrace, and inciting all around her to courage and energy.

The multitude were kept back, the passage to the side-steps of the terrace was clear.

'Now,' said Sybil, and she encouraged Lady de Mowbray, her daughters, and followers to advance. It was a fearful struggle to maintain the communication, but it was a successful one. They proceeded breathless and trembling, until they reached what was commonly called the Grotto, but which was in fact a subterranean way excavated through a hill and leading to the bank of a river where there were boats. The entrance of this tunnel was guarded by an iron gate, and Mr. Mountchesney had secured the key. The gate was opened, Warner and his friends made almost superhuman efforts at this moment to keep back the multitude, Lady de Mowbray and her daughters had passed through, when there came one of those violent undulations usual in mobs, and which was occasioned by a sudden influx of persons attracted by what was occurring, and Sybil and those who immediately surrounded her and were guarding the retreat were carried far away. The gate was closed, the rest of the party had passed, but Sybil was left, and found herself entirely among strangers.

In the meantime the castle was in possession of the mob. The first great rush was to the cellars: the Bishop himself headed this onset, nor did he rest until he was seated among the prime binns of the noble proprietor. This was not a crisis of corkscrews; the heads of the bottles were knocked off with the same promptitude and dexterity as if they were shelling nuts or decapitating shrimps: the choicest wines of Christendom were poured down the thirsty throats that ale and spirits had hitherto only stimulated; Tummas was swallowing Burgundy; Master

Nixon had got hold of a batch of tokay; while the Bishop himself, seated on the ground and leaning against an arch, the long perspective of the cellars full of rapacious figures brandishing bottles and torches, alternately quaffed some very old Port and some Madeira of many voyages, and was making up his mind as to their respective and relative merits.

While the cellars and offices were thus occupied, bands were parading the gorgeous saloons and gazing with wonderment on their decorations and furniture. Some grimy ruffians had thrown themselves with disdainful delight on the satin couches and the state beds: others rifled the cabinets with an idea that they must be full of money, and finding little in their way, had strewn their contents—papers and books and works of art—over the floors of the apartments; sometimes a band who had escaped from below with booty came up to consummate their orgies in the magnificence of the dwelling rooms. Among these were Nixon and his friends, who stared at the pictures and stood before the tall mirrors with still greater astonishment. Indeed many of them had never seen an ordinary looking-glass in their lives.

''Tis Natur!' said Master Nixon surveying himself, and turning to Juggins.

Many of these last grew frantic, and finished their debauch by the destruction of everything around them.

But while these scenes of brutal riot were occurring there was one select but resolute band who shared in none of these excesses. Morley, followed by half a dozen Mowbray lads and two chosen Hell-cats, leaving all the confusion below, had ascended the great staircase, traced his way down a corridor to the winding steps of the Round Tower, and supplied with the necessary instruments had forced his entrance into the muniment room of the castle. It was a circular chamber lined with tall fire-proof cases. These might have presented invincible obstacles to any other than the pupils of Bishop Hatton; as it was, in some instances the locks, in others the hinges, yielded in time, though after prolonged efforts, to the resources of their art; and while Dandy Mick and his friends kept watch at the entrance, Morley and Devilsdust proceeded to examine the contents of the cases: piles of parchment deeds, bundles of papers arranged and docketed, many boxes of various size and materials; but the desired object was not visible. A baffled expression came over the face of Morley; he paused for an instant in his labours. The thought of how much he had sacrificed for this, and only to fail, came upon him—upon him, the votary of Moral Power in the midst of havoc which he had organised and stimulated. He cursed Baptist Hatton in his heart.

'The knaves have destroyed them,' said Devilsdust. 'I thought how it would be. They never would run the chance of a son of Labour being lord of all this.'

Some of the cases were very deep, and they had hitherto in general, in order to save time, proved their contents with an iron rod. Now Morley with a desperate air mounting on some steps that were in the room, commenced formally rifling the cases and throwing their contents on the floor; it was soon strewn with deeds and papers and boxes which he and Devilsdust the moment they had glanced at them hurled away. At length when all hope seemed to have vanished, clearing a case which at first appeared only to contain papers, Morley struck something at its back; he sprang forward with outstretched arm, his body was half hid in the cabinet, and he pulled out with triumphant exultation the box, painted blue and blazoned with the arms of Valence. It was neither large nor heavy; he held it out to Devilsdust without saying a word, and Morley descending the steps sate down for a moment on a pile of deeds and folded his arms.

At this juncture the discharge of musketry was heard.

'Hilloa!' said Devilsdust with a queer expression. Morley started from his seat. Dandy Mick rushed into the room. 'Troops, troops! there are troops here!' he exclaimed.

'Let us descend,' said Morley. 'In the confusion we may escape. I will take the box,' and they left the muniment room.

One of their party whom Mick had sent forward to reconnoitre fell back upon them. 'They are not troops,' he said; 'they are yeomanry;* they are firing away and cutting every one down. They have cleared the ground floor of the castle and are in complete possession below. We cannot escape this way.'

'Those accursed locks!' said Morley clenching the box. 'Time has beat us. Let us see, let us see.' He ran back into the muniment room and examined the egress from the window. It was just possible for any one very lithe and nimble to vault upon the roof of the less elevated part of the castle. Revolving this, another scout rushed in and said, 'Comrades they are here! they are ascending the stairs.'

Morley stamped on the ground with rage and despair. Then seizing Mick by the hand he said, 'You see this window; can you by any means reach that roof?'

'One may as well lose one's neck that way,' said Mick. 'I'll try.'

'Off! If you land I will throw this box after you. Now mind; take it to the convent at Mowbray and deliver it yourself from me to Sybil Gerard. It is light; there are only papers in it; but they will give her her own again, and she will not forget you.'

'Never mind that,' said Mick. 'I only wish I may live to see her.'

The tramp of the ascending troopers was heard.

'Good bye my hearties,' said Mick, and he made the spring. He seemed stunned, but he might recover. Morley watched him and flung the box.

'And now,' he said drawing a pistol, 'we may fight our way yet. I'll shoot the first man who enters, and then you must rush on them with your bludgeons.'

The force that had so unexpectedly arrived at this scene of devastation was a troop of the yeomanry regiment of Lord Marney. The strike in Lancashire and the revolt in the mining districts had so completely drained this county of military, that the lord lieutenant had insisted on Lord Marney quitting his agricultural neighbourhood and quartering himself in the region of factories. Within the last two days he had fixed his head-quarters at a large manufacturing town within ten miles of Mowbray, and a despatch on Sunday evening from the mayor of that town having reached him, apprising him of the invasion of the miners, Egremont had received orders to march with his troop there on the following morning.

Egremont had not departed more than two hours when the horsemen whom Sybil had met arrived at Lord Marney's head-quarters, bringing a most alarming and exaggerated report of the insurrection and of the havoc that was probably impending. Lord Marney being of opinion that Egremont's forces were by no means equal to the occasion resolved therefore at once to set out for Mowbray with his own troop. Crossing Mowbray Moor he encountered a great multitude, now headed for purposes of peace by Walter Gerard. His mind inflamed by the accounts he had received, and hating at all times any popular demonstration, his lordship resolved without inquiry or preparation immediately to disperse them. The Riot Act* was read with the rapidity with which grace is sometimes said at the head of a public table—a ceremony of which none but the performer and his immediate friends are conscious. The people were fired on and sabred. The indignant spirit of Gerard resisted; he struck down a trooper to the earth, and incited those about him not to yield. The father of Sybil was picked out—the real friend and champion of the People—and shot dead. Instantly arose a groan which almost quelled the spirit of Lord Marney, though armed and at the head of armed men. The people who before this were in general scared and dispersing, ready indeed to fly in all directions, no sooner saw their beloved leader fall than a feeling of frenzy came over them. They defied the troopers, though themselves armed only with stones and bludgeons;

they rushed at the horsemen and tore them from their saddles, while a shower of stones rattled on the helmet of Lord Marney and seemed never to cease. In vain the men around him charged the infuriated throng; the people returned to their prey, nor did they rest until Lord Marney fell lifeless on Mowbray Moor, literally stoned to death.

These disastrous events of course occurred at a subsequent period of the day to that on which half-a-dozen troopers were ascending the staircase of the Round Tower of Mowbray Castle. The distracted house-steward of Lord de Mowbray had met and impressed upon them, now that the Castle was once more in their possession, of securing the muniment room, for Mr. Bentley had witnessed the ominous ascent of Morley and his companions to that important chamber.

Morley and his companions had taken up an advantageous position at the head of the staircase.

'Surrender,' said the commander of the yeomanry. 'Resistance is useless.'

Morley presented his pistol, but before he could pull the trigger a shot from a trooper in the rear, and who from his position could well observe the intention of Morley, struck Stephen in the breast; still he fired, but aimless and without effect. The troopers pushed on; Morley fainting fell back with his friends who were frightened, except Devilsdust, who had struck hard and well, and who in turn had been slightly sabred. The yeomanry entered the muniment room almost at the same time as their foes, leaving Devilsdust behind them, who had fallen, and who cursing the Capitalist who had wounded him managed to escape. Morley fell when he had regained the room. The rest surrendered.

'Morley! Stephen Morley!' exclaimed the commander of the yeomanry. 'You, you here!'

'Yes. I am sped,' he said in a faint voice. 'No, no succour. It is useless and I desire none. Why I am here is a mystery; let it remain so. The world will misjudge me; the man of peace they will say was a hypocrite. The world will be wrong, as it always is. Death is bitter,' he said with a deep sigh, and speaking with great difficulty, 'more bitter from you; but just. We have struggled together before, Egremont. I thought I had scotched you then, but you escaped. Our lives have been a struggle since we first met. Your star has controlled mine; and now I feel I have sacrificed life and fame—dying men prophesy—for your profit and honour. O Sybil!' and with this name half sighed upon his lips the votary of Moral Power and the Apostle of Community ceased to exist.

Meanwhile Sybil, separated from her friends who had made their escape through the grotto, was left with only Harold for her protector, for she had lost even Warner in the crush. She looked around in vain for some Mowbray face that she could recognise, but after some fruitless research, a loud shouting in the distance, followed by the firing of musketry, so terrified all around her, that the mob in her immediate neighbourhood dispersed as if by magic, and she remained alone crouching in a corner of the flower-garden, while dreadful shouts and shrieks and yells resounded from the distance, occasionally firing, the smoke floating to her retreat. She could see from where she stood the multitude flying about the park in all directions, and therefore she thought it best to remain in her present position and await the terrible events. She concluded that some military force had arrived, and that if she could maintain her present post, she hoped that the extreme danger might pass. But while she indulged in these hopes, a dark cloud of smoke came descending in the garden. It could not be produced by musket or carbine: its volume was too heavy even for ordnance: and in a moment there were sparks mingled with its black form; and then the shouting and shrieking which had in some degree subsided, suddenly broke out again with increased force and wildness. The Castle was on fire.*

Whether from heedlessness or from insane intention, for the deed sealed their own doom, the drunken Hell-cats brandishing their torches, while they rifled the cellars and examined every closet and corner of the offices, had set fire to the lower part of the building, and the flames that had for some time burnt unseen, had now gained the principal chambers. The Bishop was lying senseless in the main cellar, surrounded by his chief officers in the same state: indeed the whole of the basement was covered with the recumbent figures of Hell-cats, as black and thick as torpid flies during the last days of their career. The funeral pile of the children of Woden was a sumptuous one; it was prepared and lighted by themselves; and the flame that, rising from the keep of Mowbray, announced to the startled country that in a short hour the splendid mimickry of Norman rule would cease to exist, told also the pitiless fate of the ruthless savage, who, with analogous pretension, had presumed to style himself the Liberator of the People.

The clouds of smoke, the tongues of flame, that now began to mingle with them, the multitude whom this new incident and impending catastrophe summoned back to the scene, forced Sybil to leave the garden and enter the park. It was in vain she endeavoured to gain some part less frequented than the rest, and to make her way unobserved. Suddenly a band of drunken ruffians, with shouts and oaths, surrounded her; she shrieked in frantic terror; Harold sprung at the throat of the foremost; another advanced, Harold left his present prey and attacked the new assailant. The brave dog did wonders, but the odds were fearful; and the men had bludgeons, were enraged, and had already wounded him. One ruffian had grasped the arm of Sybil, another had clenched her garments, when an officer covered with dust and gore, sabre in hand, jumped from the terrace, and hurried to the rescue. He cut down one man, thrust away another, and placing his left arm round Sybil, he defended her with his sword, while Harold now become furious, flew from man to man, and protected her on the other side. Her assailants were routed, they made a staggering flight; the officer turned round and pressed Sybil to his heart.

'We will never part again,' said Egremont.

'Never,' murmured Sybil.

CHAPTER XIII.

IT was the Spring of last year,* and Lady Bardolf was making a morning visit to Lady St. Julians.

'I heard they were to be at Lady Palmerston's* last night,' said Lady St. Julians.

'No,' said Lady Bardolf shaking her head, 'they make their first appearance at Deloraine House. We meet there on Thursday I know.'

'Well, I must say,' said Lady St. Julians, 'that I am curious to see her.'

'Lord Valentine met them last year at Naples.'

'And what does he say of her.'

'Oh! he raves!'

'What a romantic history! And what a fortunate man is Lord Marney. If one could only have foreseen events!' exclaimed Lady St. Julians. 'He was always a favourite of mine though. But still I thought his brother was the very last person who ever would die. He was so very hard!'

'I fear Lord Marney is entirely lost to us,' said Lady Bardolf looking very solemn.

'Ah! he always had a twist,' said Lady St. Julians, 'and used to breakfast with that horrid Mr. Trenchard, and do those sort of things. But still with his immense fortune, I should think he would become rational.'

'You may well say immense,' said Lady Bardolf. 'Mr. Ormsby, and there is no better judge of another man's income, says there are not three peers in the kingdom who have so much a year clear.'

'They say the Mowbray estate is forty thousand a year,' said Lady St. Julians. 'Poor Lady de Mowbray! I understand that Mr. Mountchesney has resolved not to appeal* against the verdict.'

'You know he has not a shadow of a chance,' said Lady Bardolf. 'Ah! what changes we have seen in that family! They say the writ of right killed poor Lord de Mowbray, but to my mind he never recovered the burning of the Castle. We went over to them directly, and I never saw a man so cut up. We wanted them to come to us at Firebrace, but he said he should leave the county immediately. I remember Lord Bardolf mentioning to me, that he looked like a dying man.'

'Well I must say,' said Lady St. Julians rallying as it were from a fit of abstraction, 'that I am most curious to see Lady Marney.'

The reader will infer from this conversation that Dandy Mick, in spite of his stunning fall, and all dangers which awaited him on his recovery, had contrived in spite of fire and flame, sabre and carbine, trampling troopers and plundering mobs, to reach the Convent of Mowbray with the box of papers. There he enquired for Sybil, in whose hands, and whose hands alone he was enjoined to deposit them. She was still absent, but faithful to his instructions, Mick would deliver his charge to none other, and exhausted by the fatigues of the terrible day, he remained in the court-yard of the Convent, lying down with the box for his pillow until Sybil under the protection of Egremont herself returned. Then he fulfilled his mission. Sybil was too agitated at the moment to perceive all its import, but she delivered the box into the custody of Egremont, who desiring Mick to follow him to his hotel bade farewell to Sybil, who equally with himself, was then ignorant of the fatal encounter on Mowbray Moor.

We must drop a veil over the anguish which its inevitable and speedy revelation brought to the daughter of Gerard. Her love for her father was one of those profound emotions which seemed to form a constituent part of her existence. She remained for a long period in helpless woe, soothed only by the sacred cares of Ursula. There was another mourner in this season of sorrow who must not be forgotten: and that was Lady Marney. All that tenderness and the most considerate thought could devise to soften sorrow and reconcile her to a change of life which at the first has in it something depressing were extended by Egremont to Arabella. He supplied in an instant every arrangement which had been neglected by his brother, but which could secure her convenience and tend to her happiness. Between Marney Abbey where he insisted for the present that Arabella should reside and Mowbray, Egremont passed his life for many months, until by some management which we need not trace or analyse, Lady Marney came over one day to the Convent at Mowbray and carried back Sybil to Marney Abbey, never again to quit it until on her bridal day, when the Earl and Countess of

Marney departed for Italy where they passed nearly a year, and from which they had just returned at the commencement of this chapter.

During the previous period however many important events had occurred. Lord Marney had placed himself in communication with Mr. Hatton, who had soon become acquainted with all that had occurred in the muniment room of Mowbray Castle. The result was not what he had once anticipated; but for him it was not without some compensatory circumstances. True, another, and an unexpected rival, had stepped on the stage with whom it was vain to cope, but the idea that he had deprived Sybil of her inheritance, had ever, since he had became acquainted with her, been the plague-spot of Hatton's life, and there was nothing that he desired more ardently than to see her restored to her rights, and to be instrumental in that restoration. How successful he was in pursuing her claim, the reader has already learnt.

Dandy Mick was rewarded for all the dangers he had encountered in the service of Sybil, and what he conceived was the vindication of popular rights. Lord Marney established him in business, and Mick took Devilsdust for a partner. Devilsdust having thus obtained a position in society and become a capitalist, thought it but a due homage to the social decencies to assume a decorous appellation, and he called himself by the name of the town where he was born. The firm of Radley, Mowbray, and Co., is a rising one; and will probably furnish in time a crop of members of Parliament and Peers of the realm. Devilsdust married Caroline, and Mrs. Mowbray became a great favorite. She was always perhaps a little too fond of junketting but she had a sweet temper and a gay spirit, and sustained her husband in the agonies of a great speculation, or the despair of glutted markets. Julia became Mrs. Radley, and was much esteemed: no one could behave better. She was more orderly than Caroline, and exactly suited Mick, who wanted a person near him of decision and method. As for Harriet, she is not yet married. Though pretty and clever, she is selfish and a screw. She has saved a good deal and has a considerable sum in the Savings' Bank, but like many heiresses she cannot bring her mind to share her money with another. The great measures of Sir Robert Peel, which produced three good harvests,* have entirely revived trade at Mowbray. The Temple is again open, newly-painted, and re-burnished, and Chaffing Jack has of course 'rallied' while good Mrs. Carey still gossips with her neighbours round her well-stored stall, and tells wonderful stories of the great stick-out and riots of—42.

And thus I conclude the last page of a work, which though its form be light and unpretending, would yet aspire to suggest to its readers some considerations of a very opposite character. A year ago, I presumed to offer to the public some volumes* that aimed to call their attention to the state of our political parties; their origin, their history, their present position. In an age of political infidelity, of mean passions and petty thoughts, I would have impressed upon the rising race not to despair, but to seek in a right understanding of the history of their country and in the energies of heroic youth—the elements of national welfare. The present work advances another step in the same emprise. From the state of Parties it now would draw public thought to the state of the People whom those parties for two centuries have governed. The comprehension and the cure of this greater theme depend upon the same agencies as the first: it is the past alone that can explain the present, and it is youth that alone can mould the remedial future. The written history of our country for the last ten reigns has been a mere phantasma; giving to the origin and consequence of public transactions a character and colour in every respect dissimilar with their natural form and hue. In this mighty mystery all thoughts and things have assumed an aspect and title contrary to their real quality and style: Oligarchy has been called Liberty; an exclusive Priesthood has been christened a National Church; Sovereignty has been the title of something that has had no dominion, while absolute power has been wielded by those who profess themselves the servants of the People. In the selfish strife of factions two great existences have been blotted out of the history of England— the Monarch and the Multitude; as the power of the Crown has diminished, the privileges of the People have disappeared; till at length the sceptre has become a pageant, and its subject has degenerated again into a serf.

It is nearly fourteen years ago,* in the popular frenzy of a mean and selfish revolution which neither emancipated the Crown nor the People, that I first took the occasion to intimate and then to develop to the first assembly of my countrymen that I ever had the honour to address, these convictions. They have been misunderstood as is ever for a season the fate of Truth, and they have obtained for their promulgator much mis-representation as must ever be the lot of those who will not follow the beaten track of a fallacious custom. But Time that brings all things has brought also to the mind of England some suspicion that the idols they have so long worshipped and the oracles that have so long deluded them are not the true ones. There is a whisper rising in this country that Loyalty is not a phrase, Faith not a delusion, and Popular Liberty something more diffusive and substantial than the profane exercise of the sacred rights of sovereignty by political classes.

That we may live to see England once more possess a free Monarchy and a privileged and prosperous People, is my prayer; that these great consequences can only be brought about by the energy and devotion of our Youth is my persuasion. We live in an age when to be young and to be indifferent can be no longer synonymous. We must prepare for the coming hour. The claims of the Future are represented by suffering millions; and the Youth of a Nation are the trustees of Posterity.

THE END.

EXPLANATORY NOTES

TITLE PAGE, DEDICATION, AND ADVERTISEMENT

1 '. . . *so little Gentleness.*'—*BISHOP LATIMER*: the quotation is not, in fact, from Hugh Latimer, Protestant martyr and Bishop of Worcester, but from Bernard Gilpin (1517–83) whose sermon on Luke 2: 41–50 was preached at Greenwich before King Edward VI on the First Sunday After Epiphany, 1552, and published in 1581 ('The mean men, they murmur and grudge, and say the gentlemen have all, and there never were so many gentlemen and so little gentleness'). Disraeli probably derived the mis-attribution from Sharon Turner (1768–1847) who confuses this sentence with material from Latimer's sermon on covetousness (Luke 12: 15; preached before Edward VI in Lent 1550) in his *History of the Reigns of Edward VI, Mary, and Elizabeth* (1829), republished as part of his *Modern History of England* in 1839.

3 *a perfect Wife!*: Disraeli had married Mary Anne Wyndham Lewis (née Evans) in August 1839.

4 *of his own observation*: only partly true: see Introduction.

BOOK I

5 *poneys*: a pony is a slang term for £25; the odds for Caravan (a bay colt, by Camel out of Wings, owned by Lord Suffield) are 7 to 2 against, so Mr Latour is making a bet of £50 (£2,500 in modern money).

the Jockey Club: founded in Pall Mall, London, in 1750, and with premises in Newmarket, Suffolk, from 1752, the Jockey Club was both an exclusive aristocratic club and (until 2006) the governing body of British horse racing.

the Derby of 1837: first run in 1780, the Derby is a flat race for 3-year-old thoroughbred colts and fillies over an undulating course of a mile and four furlongs on Epsom Downs in Surrey: in 1848 Disraeli would describe it to Lord George Bentinck as 'the blue ribbon of the turf'. In 1837 it took place on 25 May and Disraeli's account of the race is, for the most part, historically accurate (see notes to pp. 6–11).

a vast and golden saloon: not named but clearly Crockford's, a gambling house at 50 St James's Street which passed itself off as a conventional gentleman's club from 1828 to 1845, thus eluding the laws against gaming. It was decorated 'in the most florid style of Louis Quatorze' (*Bentley's Miscellany* XVII (1845), p. 253) though the pictures by 'Watteau and Boucher' were actually replicas. Disraeli was first proposed for membership in July 1834 and became a member in 1840.

the grand monarch: King Louis XIV (1638–1715), known as 'Louis le Grand'.

5 *a buhl table . . . Mortemart*: buhl furniture, with brass and tortoiseshell marquetry, was perfected at Versailles by André Charles Boulle (1642–1732); Gabriel de Rochechouart, Duke of Mortemart (1600–75), was a close friend of King Louis XIII and the father of Madame de Montespan (1640–1707), mistress of King Louis XIV.

Egremont: though the family name is really Greymount and was only changed to the similar-sounding Egremont 'at the commencement of the seventeenth century', the adopted Norman name (from Aigremont in Normandy via Egremont in Cumbria) has an allusive link to Wordsworth's poem 'The Horn of Egremont Castle' (1807), in which an honourable brother displaces a greedy and disloyal one after returning from the Crusades. The real Egremont was part of the estates of the Norman knight William de Perci (d. 1096); an earldom of Egremont, created in 1749, was held by his collateral descendants, the Wyndham family, until it became extinct in April 1845.

6 *Badminton*: a drink made from red wine and soda water, sometimes with the addition of ice, cucumber, sugar, and nutmeg.

tennis: not modern lawn tennis but Real, or Royal Tennis, played in a walled court of which there is an example, dating from the 1620s, at Hampton Court Palace.

the Toy: a seventeenth-century inn near Hampton Court Palace, now the Mitre Hotel.

Hybiscus: a brown colt, by Priam out of Diamentina, owned by Lord Exeter.

7 *lustre*: a period of five years, from *lustrum* (Latin).

the little Bertie: in 1833 Disraeli had himself flirted with Lady Charlotte Bertie (1812–95), wealthy daughter of the 9th Earl of Lindsey, though she was a married woman by the time of the 1837 Derby. As Lady Charlotte Guest she would be a sympathizer with the Chartists and the translator of the *Mabinogion* (1838–45).

the Clarendon: the Clarendon Hotel at 169 New Bond Street, famous in the 1830s for the French cuisine served there by Louis Jaquier, a chef formerly employed by Louis XVIII.

Phosphorus: a bay colt, by Lamplighter out of a Rubens mare, bred and owned by Robert Wilson, 9th Baron Berners. Though he won the Rowley Mile at Newmarket in May, he had lost the Newmarket Stakes in April, by a length, to Rat-trap.

8 *John Day*: the jockey 'Young' John Day (1819–83), son of the trainer 'Honest' John Day, who rejected the ride on Phosphorus in favour of Mr Wreford's colt Wisdom.

Seltzer water: William Hazlitt had picked out 'Seltzer Water', along with 'silver forks', as an example of the snobbish product placement which he so disliked in his 'Dandy School' review of Disraeli's *Vivian Grey* (*Examiner*, 18 November 1827).

Chifney: the jockey Samuel Chifney Jnr (b. 1786) who would ride Lord Chesterfield's colt Critic.

tiger: a smartly liveried boy-servant.

9 *Juan*: in Tirso de Molina's play *El burlador de Sevilla* (*c*.1630), set in Andalucia, and Mozart's opera *Don Giovanni* (1787) the serial seducer Don Juan is confronted by the stone statue of the father of one of his victims and carried off to Hell in a clap of thunder; the weather on Derby Day 1837 was actually 'fine . . . but somewhat cold' (*The Times*, 25 May 1837).

Saxon peer, in a white great coat: we are probably meant to recognize this figure as Lord George Bentinck (1802–48): Disraeli would mention the distinctive 'white great-coat' in his *Lord George Bentinck: A Political Biography* (1851). The Bentincks were Dutch, rather than 'Saxon', but not involved in the sixteenth-century dissolution of the monasteries.

Mango: brown colt, by Emilius out of Mustard, owned by Charles 'Punch' Greville; he went on to win the St Leger in September.

the plains of Newmarket: Newmarket, in Suffolk, is not a battlefield but the centre of British horseracing.

Pall Mall . . . Tattersalls: the Jockey Club (see note to p. 5) had London premises both in Pall Mall and at Tattersall's, an auction house for horses, which operated in a yard near Hyde Park Corner from 1766 to 1865 and has since moved to Newmarket.

10 *Benedict . . . Pocket Hercules . . . Dardanelles*: Benedict was a bay colt, by Peter Lely out of Phantasima, owned by Captain Gardnor; the Pocket Hercules was a grey colt, by St Nicholas out of Fickle, owned by 'Squire' Osbaldeston; Dardanelles was a bay colt, by Sultan, owned by Lord Exeter.

square cob: a short-legged, stout horse.

Carnaby market: a meat market opened in the 1720s near Carnaby Street, Soho (on what is now Lowndes Court), but closed in 1820; Disraeli may be confusing it with Newport Market which retained its slaughter house and butchers' shops until Charing Cross Road and Shaftesbury Avenue were built over its site in the 1880s.

Man-trap: there was no horse called Man-trap in the 1837 Derby but Disraeli could not name the real horse, Rat-trap, without accusing its owner (the Duke of Rutland, father of his Young England colleague Lord John Manners) of betting against his own runner.

the Warren: until 1847 the Derby course started behind a wood on Epsom Downs called the Warren; this was changed to make the race more visible from the grandstand.

11 *Hogarth . . . 'Before' and 'After'*: William Hogarth (1697–1764) painted two versions of *Before* and *After* in 1730–1, both showing a couple immediately before and immediately after sexual intercourse. One version (J. Paul Getty Museum, Los Angeles) is set out of doors, the other

(Fitzwilliam Museum, Cambridge) indoors. A third version, also set indoors, was made as a pair of engravings in 1736 and is the image most likely to have been known to Disraeli and his readers.

11 *Pompeius . . . Harold . . . Napoleon*: Gnaeus Pompeius (Pompey the Great) was defeated at the Battle of Pharsalus (48 BC), King Harold II (Harold Godwinson) at the Battle of Hastings (1066), and Napoleon at the Battle of Waterloo (1815).

new world . . . new planet: 'Then felt I like some watcher of the skies | When a new planet swims into his ken; | Or like stout Cortez when with eagle eyes | He stared at the Pacific' (Keats, 'On First Looking into Chapman's Homer', 1816). Though Keats was little known between 1821 and the appearance of Monckton Milnes's *Life, Letters, and Literary Remains, of John Keats* in 1848, Disraeli knew Milnes (he stayed with his family at Fryston in 1844) and might also have encountered the poem in his own father's remarkable library.

Pavis . . . his employer: Arthur Pavis (1806–39), a skilful and famously good-looking jockey but unsuccessful in big races, finishing second in two Derbies, one Oaks, and one St Leger; his employer in 1837 was Lord Suffield.

Phosphorus . . . his forelegs bandaged: Phosphorus sprained a foreleg and went lame while training for the Derby but his owner, Lord Berners, was old, ill (he would die in 1838), and anxious to see the horse run, so told his trainer, John Doe, to enter him anyway.

the Rubbing House: since the Rubbing House is at the end of the course (where horses were rubbed down after their exertions) this seems to be a mistake; Disraeli probably meant Downs House, a training stable a few hundred yards after the start.

the grey: the Pocket Hercules (though his jockey was Sam Rogers, not Chifney).

Tattenham corner . . . the road: Tattenham Corner is a sharp bend in the Derby course between the steep descent from the Downs and the straight run to the finishing post; the Old London Road crosses the track and has to be covered with turf during races.

Edwards . . . in by half a length: George Edwards (1805–51), son of the trainer James 'Tiny' Edwards, and a 'strong' rather than subtle jockey. Phosphorus (40/1) won by half a length from Caravan (7/2), followed by Hybiscus (11/2), Dardanelles (25/1), and Mahometan (40/1).

12 *drag*: a private vehicle resembling a stage coach, drawn by four horses and with seats both inside and on top.

commissioners . . . pix . . . patens: commissioners were appointed to inspect religious institutions in 1534–5; their reports led to the dissolution of smaller monasteries in 1536 and of larger monasteries in 1539. A pyx is the vessel in which the consecrated bread of the sacrament is reserved; a paten is the dish on which the bread is placed during the mass. Disraeli's list echoes Cobbett's *History of the Protestant 'Reformation' in England* (1824–6):

'patens of golde . . . candlesticks, sockets, cruets, cups, pixes, goblets, basons, spoons . . . finger-rings, ear-rings . . . bits of gold and silver torn from the covers of books, or cut and beaten out of the altars' (Book I, Letter 6).

13 *Baron Marney*: the real barony of Marney was created in 1523 for the Tudor politician Henry Marney (whose ancestors had come from Marigny in Normandy) and became extinct on the death of his son, without heirs, in 1525; Disraeli invents a fictitious re-creation of the barony in the early seventeenth century for the Greymount family, at which point they change their surname to Egremont.

Whig lords: the real Whig families of the 1680s, who led the movement for the replacement of the Roman Catholic James II by the Protestant William III, were the Ashley Coopers (earls of Shaftesbury), Russells (dukes of Bedford), Sidneys (earls of Leicester), and Cavendishes (dukes of Devonshire); 'civil and religious liberty' was the slogan of the Whig party which opposed Stuart claims to the divine right of kings. John Hampden (1594–1643) was killed fighting against Charles I's army during the Civil War; William Russell (1639–83) was executed by Charles II after the Rye House Plot. Disraeli adapts his phraseology here from Macaulay's review (*Edinburgh Review*, 1828) of Henry Hallam's *Constitutional History of England* (see note to p. 20).

St. Germains: the court of the deposed King James II (1633–1701) was at the chateau of Saint-Germain-en-Laye, granted to him by Louis XIV. Since William III had no children, James's Anglican daughters Mary and Anne (rather than his Catholic son, also called James) took the throne in 1689 and 1702, and were succeeded in 1714 by their Protestant cousin George, Elector of Hanover. Several English politicians, including John Churchill, Duke of Marlborough, corresponded secretly with James but Disraeli's claim that Whig families had illicit links with France probably reflects a discovery made by Sir John Dalrymple in the French state archives while writing the second volume (1773) of his *Memoirs of Great Britain and Ireland*. This revealed that the Whig martyrs William Russell and Algernon Sidney had had secret contact with the French court in the 1670s and that Sidney had accepted money from Louis XIV. The Stuart court moved to Rome in 1715.

fall of Mr. Fox: the coalition government of Lord North and the Duke of Portland, in which Charles James Fox (1749–1806) was Foreign Secretary, fell in December 1783, sixty-nine years after the accession of George I (October 1714).

garters: the Order of the Garter is the oldest and highest order of knighthood, founded in 1348 and limited to twenty-four members at any one time.

14 *only in America*: presumably a reference to the defeats of Edward Braddock at Monongahela in 1755 and James Abercrombie at Ticonderoga in 1758, or to the campaigns of Thomas Gage (son of Viscount Gage), William Howe

(son of Viscount Howe), and John Burgoyne (said to be the illegitimate son of Lord Bingley) during the American War of Independence, rather than to the victories won by generals such as James Wolfe, William Johnson, and Jeffrey Amherst.

14 *grace of Newcastle*: Thomas Pelham-Holles, 1st Duke of Newcastle (1693–1768), long-serving Whig politician who was Prime Minister in 1754–6 and 1757–62; an adroit political manipulator who is usually seen as an ill-informed and incompetent statesman.

Venetian constitution: though Venice remained a republic until 1797 it was not a democracy but an oligarchy, run by a group of powerful aristocratic families with the Doge as a nominal leader (recent historians have argued that the Doge's presence on key committees made him more powerful than was once assumed). Disraeli equates this with the way in which the British 'Whig lords' (see note to p. 13) had installed first William III and then George I while retaining real power for themselves: the purpose of the Whigs was 'to reduce the King of England to the situation of a Venetian Doge' (*Vindication of the English Constitution*, 1835, p. 168). The Bill of Rights (1689) established a limited or constitutional monarchy; Disraeli claims that the powers of the Crown were then further reduced.

strawberry leaf: peers wear coronets only at coronations; the coronets of dukes and earls have eight silver-gilt strawberry leaves, the coronets of marquesses have four. The coronets of viscounts and barons have silver balls but no strawberry leaves.

half a hundred victories: modern military historians credit Arthur Wellesley (1769–1852) with between thirty and forty victories in battles, sieges, and skirmishes between 1799 and 1815; he was made Duke of Wellington in 1814.

Pratts . . . Robinsons: Charles Pratt (1714–94), lawyer and Whig politician, Baron Camden from 1765, Earl Camden from 1786; Robert Smith (1752–1838), banker and MP, Baron Carrington from 1797; Charles Jenkinson (1729–1808), Tory politician, Baron Hawkesbury from 1786, Earl of Liverpool from 1796; Frederick Robinson (1782–1859), Tory politician, Prime Minister 1827–8, Viscount Goderich from 1827, Earl of Ripon from 1833.

15 *Great Revolution families*: see note to p. 13.

boroughs: originally a walled town, later an urban settlement with the right to elect members of Parliament ('burgesses'); over time some such towns became largely ('closed boroughs') or entirely ('rotten boroughs') depopulated, so that their electoral power passed into the hands of a single landowner, such as the Earl of Marney.

young king: George III became King in 1760 at the age of 22; in May 1762 he replaced the Whig government of the Duke of Newcastle with a Tory ministry led by Lord Bute, a close friend of his mother. The Whigs returned to power in April 1763.

Rockingham: Charles Watson-Wentworth, 2nd Marquess of Rockingham (1730–82), Whig politician, Prime Minister 1765–6 and 1782.

Burke . . . Bolingbroke: Edmund Burke (1729–97), Anglo-Irish politician and philosopher; originally a Whig and private secretary (1765–82) to Rockingham, he supported Pitt's government in 1791, when the Whig party split over the French Revolution, and became an important Tory theorist. Henry St John, Viscount Bolingbroke (1678–1751), Tory politician and political thinker, minister under Queen Anne. He fled to France and joined the Jacobite court in exile in 1715; pardoned in 1725, he returned to England where, though excluded from the House of Lords, he published a series of attacks on Walpole's Whig government and *The Idea of a Patriot King* (1749).

16 *dissolute noble . . . Catiline*: Charles James Fox (1749–1806), younger son of Lord Holland and notorious for his gambling and womanizing, became a Rockingham Whig under the influence of Burke. He went on to be Foreign Secretary in 1782 and 1783 and, from 1794 to 1806, the leader of the 'Foxite' rump of the Whig party. Catiline (Lucius Sergius Catilina) was a Roman patrician, ruined by his dissolute lifestyle, who in 64 BC conspired to overthrow the Senate and loot Rome.

admitted into the Cabinet: when Rockingham became Prime Minister in 1782, Burke was given the junior post of Paymaster of the Forces, unlike his much younger protégé Charles James Fox who joined the cabinet as Foreign Secretary.

Nemesis: in Greek myth a child of the goddess Nyx (or Night) who punished those who were guilty of 'hubris': pride, or arrogance towards the gods.

wild pictures . . . rended in twain the proud oligarchy: Burke's *Reflections on the Revolution in France* (1790) predicted the destructive consequences of the French Revolution and prompted the split in the Whig party (an aristocratic 'oligarchy' in Disraeli's view) between the Foxites, who sympathized with the revolutionaries, and the Portland Whigs who supported Pitt's hostile view of the new French regime.

the ancient serpent: according to Dr Johnson, 'the first Whig was the Devil' (28 April 1778, recorded in Boswell's *Life of Samuel Johnson*, 1791).

Mr. Pitt: William Pitt ('Pitt the Younger', 1759–1806), Prime Minister 1783–1801 and 1804–6; son of 'Pitt the Elder': see note to p. 17.

17 *Niebuhr . . . Republic of Plato . . . Peter Wilkins*: Barthold Georg Niebuhr (1776–1831), Danish-German historian whose stress on institutions rather than individuals and sceptical treatment of legendary source material in his *Roman History* (1812–32) transformed the understanding of ancient history. It is contrasted with the ideal or fantastical qualities of Plato's *Republic* (fourth century BC; a dialogue about justice in which the characteristics of a perfect city-state are suggested), together with Sir Thomas More's *Utopia* (1516), Simon Berington's *The Memoirs of Sigr Gaudentio di Lucca* (1737), and Robert Paltock's *The Life and Adventures of Peter*

Wilkins, a Cornishman (1751) in which imaginary countries are discovered and described.

17 *Major Wildman*: John Wildman (1621–93) supported the Levellers' case for manhood suffrage and the abolition of monarchy in 1647, plotted the overthrow of Cromwell in 1654, was imprisoned for republican plots against Charles II, acted as agent for the Monmouth rebellion in 1685, and became Postmaster General under William III. Though dismissed in 1691 after rumours of intrigues with the Jacobites, he was knighted in 1692. He can be seen either as a consistent republican or as 'a false fellow to everybody'.

Chatterton . . . 'marvellous boy': Thomas Chatterton (1752–70) began to publish his remarkable pseudo-medieval poems (supposedly by a fifteenth-century monk called Thomas Rowley) at the age of 17. He committed suicide a year later but would be celebrated by Wordsworth in 'Resolution and Independence' (1807; l. 43) as 'the marvellous Boy'. Pitt became Prime Minister at the age of 24.

Chatham . . . Lord Shelburne: William Pitt, 1st Earl of Chatham (1708–78; 'Pitt the Elder'), one of the 'Patriot Whigs' who opposed Walpole, Paymaster General 1746–55, effective Prime Minister in 1757–61 and 1766–8; William Petty, 2nd Earl of Shelburne (1737–1805), a minister in Pitt's government 1766–8, Home Secretary 1782, Prime Minister 1782–3 (see notes to pp. 18 and 19).

18 *Carteret . . . married his daughter*: John Carteret (1690–1763), 2nd Earl Granville, was a Whig politician and rival to Walpole. Effectively Prime Minister 1742–3, his close links with the King were helped by his fluent German, acquired while Ambassador to Sweden in the 1720s. Shelburne did indeed marry Carteret's daughter Sophia but in 1765, two years after her father's death, and had met his future father-in-law only once, in 1753.

Bute: John Stuart, 3rd Earl of Bute (1713–92), Prime Minister 1762–3. See note to p. 15. Though Lord Chatham was often at odds with 'the Great Revolution families', he did not invent the phrase.

negotiations of Utrecht: the Congress of Utrecht (1712–13) gradually ended the War of the Spanish Succession, established a balance of power in European affairs, and encouraged international trade. The fact, however, that a Tory government led by Harley and Bolingbroke had signed a separate treaty with France, before hostilities ended for Britain's continental allies, enraged the Whigs. Disraeli suggests a link between the commercial treaties signed at Utrecht and Lord Shelburne's later advocacy (influenced by Adam Smith) of freer trade with France: the Peace of Paris, 1783, made provision for new commercial treaties. In 1842, when he was still supporting Peel's tariff reductions, Disraeli had used this to argue that free trade was, historically, a Tory rather than a Whig policy (*Hansard*, 10 May, 21 July 1842).

19 *Shelburne . . . Coalition*: when Shelburne became Prime Minister in July 1782, Charles James Fox and his supporters resigned and the 23-year-old

William Pitt ('the Younger') became Chancellor of the Exchequer. Fox then formed an improbable coalition with Lord North and forced Shelburne's government from office in April 1783. This coalition of different kinds of Whig lasted only until December, when it was replaced by a government led by Pitt. Shelburne was not given a place in the cabinet and retired from public life.

Jena . . . Austerlitz . . . Canning: Napoleon decisively defeated the Prussians at the Battle of Jena, October 1806, and crushed Russian and Austrian armies at the Battle of Austerlitz in December 1805; George Canning (1770–1827), Tory politician, was the Prime Minister of a coalition government of liberal Tories and conservative Whigs from April 1827 until his sudden death on 8 August.

20 *Lansdowne House . . . Price . . . treaties of '87 . . . a corn-law*: Lansdowne House, Berkeley Square, the London seat of Lord Shelburne. Richard Price (1723–91), Unitarian minister and friend of Shelburne since the 1760s; though best remembered for his address to the Revolution Society in November 1789, his *Appeal to the Public on the Subject of the National Debt* (1771) influenced Pitt's decision, in 1786, to establish a sinking fund to repay the national debt. The Eden Treaty (signed 1786, put into effect 1787) opened the British market to French wines and silks, and the French market to British machine-made goods. The Corn Bounty Act of 1689 subsidized exports and taxed imports of grain but, unlike the controversial Corn Laws of 1815–46, had little effect.

Sir William Petty: William Petty (1623–87; knighted 1661), doctor, statistician, pioneering political economist, and founder member of the Royal Society, was Shelburne's great-grandfather.

counting-houses of Cornhill: not so: it was 'the promotion of Scottish and Irish peers, country gentlemen and cadets of noble families . . . which transformed the Lords from a Whig to a Tory stronghold' (Donald Southgate, *The Passing of the Whigs 1832–1886* (London: Macmillan, 1962), p. 81).

'the cause for which . . . scaffold': Macaulay referred to the Whig creed as 'the cause for which Hampden bled on the field and Sydney on the scaffold' in his review of Henry Hallam's *Constitutional History of England* (*Edinburgh Review*, September 1828); Algernon Sidney (1623–83) was a republican politician and writer who was beheaded after being implicated in the Rye House Plot against Charles II (see notes to p. 13).

French war and Dutch finance: France declared war on Britain on 1 February 1793; Britain joined the coalition against France on the 13th, and Exchequer bills to fund the war were issued on 11 March. The national debt was created in 1694 (during the reign of William III, the Dutch husband of Queen Mary; the first bonds had been issued by the city of Amsterdam in 1517) when a syndicate of London merchants agreed to raise a loan of £1.2m for the English government; the syndicate became the Bank of England and the ability to buy and sell debt removed the danger of government default at times (such as wars) when expenditure exceeded taxation.

20 *Dutch invasion*: William of Orange was invited to England (by the 'great Revolution families'; see note to p. 13) but landed, nonetheless, with an army of 15,000 soldiers.

21 *debt a national habit*: between 1793 and 1816 the British national debt rose from £243 million to £778 million and many middle-class households became used to living on the interest from government bonds. After that, however, the national debt fell steadily until 1913.

Saxon mode . . . Habeas Corpus: the prototype of trial by jury (or 'by our peers') was traditionally found in a legal code enacted in 997 by the Anglo-Saxon King Aethelred II. The German historian Heinrich Brunner would attack this view in 1872, arguing that juries were introduced to England by the Normans and first firmly established during the reign (1154–89) of Henry II. Habeas Corpus was given statutory force in two laws passed under Stuart monarchs (the Habeas Corpus Acts, 1640 and 1679) but in practice dates from the Assize of Clarendon, 1166 (not, as was once thought, from Magna Carta, 1215) and the seventeenth-century laws were checks upon the power of Charles I and Charles II, not measures sought by them.

Bill of Rights: the Bill of Rights (1689) was the statutory enactment of the conditions on which William and Mary had accepted the English throne. Though it claimed to assert 'certain ancient rights and liberties', and had been anticipated in some respects by the Petition of Right (1628), it also reflected the recent thought of John Locke (1632–1704) and was a key statement of the powers of Parliament, the rights of the individual under the rule of law, and the scope of a constitutional monarchy. Disraeli had made this case for the insignificance of the Bill of Rights on a previous occasion: 'The Long Parliament in a few months [in 1641] restored the constitution of the Plantagenets . . . the revolution of 1688 added no important feature to our political system' (*A Vindication of the English Constitution*, 1835, p. 113).

22 *anti-papal*: Plantagenet monarchs ruled England from 1154 to 1399. Disraeli's claim that the English were 'anti-papal' during this period is perhaps based on the quarrels between the Pope and Henry II (about Thomas Becket in the 1160s), King John (excommunicated 1209), and Robert Grosseteste, Bishop of Lincoln (who wrote a letter of 'expostulation and refusal' to the Pope in 1253).

Puritanism in Ireland: since the Plantation of Ulster with English and Scottish Protestants began in 1609, under the Stuart monarch James I, it seems odd to attribute it to the Glorious Revolution. A second wave of Scottish immigration into Ulster had, however, occurred in the late 1690s, after a famine in Scotland, and it was this which made Presbyterians a majority in the province. Disraeli's real point is that the Declaration of Indulgence (1687) of the Catholic James II was more acceptable to the native population of Ireland than the stress on the Protestant identity of Britain found in the Bill of Rights and the Toleration Act (1689).

secret envoy: legal obstacles to diplomatic relations with the Papal States were removed in 1829 but formal relations were not established with the Vatican until 1914. Instead, British envoys to Naples or Florence (Henry Fox 1839–46) conducted negotiations when necessary. Disraeli may, however, have heard gossip about Gladstone's suggestion, in a letter to Peel in July 1844, that he should leave the cabinet and become a special envoy to the Vatican during the dispute over the Maynooth grant. Peel ignored the request.

another work: *Coningsby* (1844), Book II, Chapter I.

exhausted sensualist: George IV (Prince Regent 1811–20, King 1820–30); Leigh Hunt described him (*Examiner*, March 1812) as 'a libertine over head and ears in debt and disgrace'.

23 DUKE OF WELLINGTON: Arthur Wellesley (1769–1852; Duke of Wellington 1814), soldier and Tory politician, commanded British armies in India, the Peninsula, and at Waterloo before becoming a cabinet minister (from 1818) and Prime Minister (1828–30 and November 1834).

Mr. Peel: Sir Robert Peel (1788–1850), Tory politician, Home Secretary 1822–7 and 1828–30, Prime Minister 1834–5 and 1841–6; Disraeli had supported him until 1843 but in the spring of 1845, while writing the later chapters of *Sybil*, would be making savage attacks on him from the Tory back benches.

wrecked his party: Wellington's ministry of 1828–30 first alienated the Canningite Tories by failing to redistribute parliamentary seats to Manchester and Birmingham, then offended the Ultra Tories by granting Catholic Emancipation, thus splitting the party.

Bishop Burnet . . . Lord Shaftesbury: Gilbert Burnet, Bishop of Salisbury (1643–1715), whose *History of my Own Time* (1724–34) remarked of Shaftesbury that, 'His strength lay in the knowledge of England, and of all the considerable men in it . . . And he knew how to apply himself to them so dextrously, that, tho' by his changing sides so often it was very visible how little he was to be depended on, yet he was to the last much trusted by all the discontented party' (Vol. 1, Book 2). Anthony Ashley Cooper (1621–83; Earl of Shaftesbury 1672) fought first on the Royalist then the Parliamentary side in the Civil War, was a member of Cromwell's Council of State, took a leading part in the restoration of Charles II, was Chancellor of the Exchequer 1661–72, supported the Exclusion Bill, was arrested for high treason, and died in exile in 1683.

24 *Lord Goderich*: Frederick Robinson (1782–1859; Viscount Goderich 1827, Earl of Ripon 1833), Tory politician (though Whig 1830–4), Chancellor of the Exchequer 1823–7, briefly Prime Minister 1827–8, President of the Boards of Trade and Control 1841–6.

Paris . . . Vienna: the Duke of Wellington entered Paris as the leader of a victorious army in 1814 and returned from the Congress of Vienna (where he had plenipotentiary powers for the post-war settlement of Europe) to do so again in 1815, after Napoleon's 'Hundred Days' and the Battle of Waterloo.

24 *Lord Liverpool*: Robert Jenkinson (1770–1828; 2nd Earl of Liverpool 1808), Tory politician, Prime Minister 1812–27; though Disraeli called him 'the Arch-Mediocrity' in *Coningsby*, Book II, Chapter I, he united the Tory party in ways which his successors, Canning, Goderich, and Wellington, could not manage.

Lord Castlereagh: Robert Stewart (1769–1822; Viscount Castlereagh 1796), Tory politician, responsible for the Act of Union with Ireland in 1800, Secretary of State for War 1804–6 and 1807–9, and Foreign Secretary from 1812 to 1822 when he committed suicide.

25 *Colonel Joyce*: when Charles I was under house arrest at Holdenby House, Northamptonshire, in 1647, Cornet George Joyce, supposedly ordered by Parliament to guard him there, instead seized him and took him to the Army's headquarters in Cambridgeshire.

second-rate soldiers: Huskisson, Palmerston, Dudley, Grant, and Melbourne left Wellington's cabinet in the summer of 1828 (see note to p. 23). Huskisson was replaced (as Secretary of State for War) by Lieutenant General Sir George Murray, Palmerston (as Secretary at War) by Colonel Sir Henry Hardinge. But both these posts had a security dimension, as did the other positions previously assigned to soldiers: Lord Lieutenant of Ireland (General Sir Henry Paget) and Master-General of the Ordnance (General William Beresford), and some first-rate politicians did stay in the cabinet: Lyndhurst (Lord Chancellor), Peel (Home Secretary), Aberdeen (Foreign Secretary), and Goulburn (Chancellor of the Exchequer).

beer bill: Wellington's government began in January 1828 as a coalition which combined Canningites (both Tory and Whig) who had served in the previous administration with Tories who had not. But the former group resigned that summer (see previous note) and the General Election caused by George IV's death in June 1830 left Wellington with an unreliable majority (310 supporters, 225 opponents, 121 uncertain). He resigned in November 1830 and the Whigs formed a government, despite the nominal Tory predominance. Goulburn's Beerhouse Act (1830) discouraged gin drinking by introducing a cheap licence to brew and sell beer; more than 45,000 'beer houses' had opened by 1841.

revolution: the Reform Act of 1832.

Brennus . . . rival of Sylla: Brennus was the leader of the Gauls who captured Rome (except for the Capitol, alerted by the cackling of its sacred geese) in 390 BC; when taking the ransom paid to redeem the city he remarked 'Vae victis' ('Woe to the conquered'; Livy 5.48). The 'rival of Sylla' was Gaius Marius (157–86 BC) who, during his civil war with Lucius Cornelius Sulla (138–78 BC), was captured in Minturnae where the magistrates sent a soldier ('either a Gaul or a Cimbrian') to execute him; overcome by Marius' gaze, the soldier threw down his weapon and fled (Plutarch, *Life*).

white wand: a white wand or staff is the symbol of office of the Lord Chamberlain, the senior officer of the Royal Household, and of the Lord Great Chamberlain who controls the Palace of Westminster.

26 '*the king is dying*': William IV (1765–1837) was asthmatic and suffered a severe attack in April 1837. But he also had a weak heart which deteriorated rapidly during May (this scene takes place on 26 May). Though a bulletin had been issued stating that it was merely a chest infection, he would die of cardiac failure and bronchopneumonia in the early hours of 20 June. He had (briefly) 'turned out' the Whigs in November 1834 (the last time a British monarch dismissed a government with a parliamentary majority) and the Tory Lady Marney has been hoping that he might do so again.

Mr. Tadpole: Tadpole and Taper are Tory party activists who had previously appeared in *Coningsby*; the review in *Tait's Edinburgh Magazine* (Vol. 11, 1844, p. 452) calls them 'the old displaced functionaries of the Percival and Liverpool periods'.

27 *registration*: before 1832, returning officers (the High Sheriff of a country, the mayor of a borough) used their discretion to determine who could vote. The Reform Act introduced electoral registers and a complicated process to determine who was entitled to appear on them, involving appearances before the Overseers of the Poor (or Assessors of Taxes in boroughs) and a panel of Revising Barristers; political parties employed agents to help their supporters to qualify. Peel's advice to his party in 1837 was 'register, register, register'.

28 *Christchurch . . . minority*: Christ Church is an Oxford college notable for its links with the Church of England and the aristocracy; Charles is 20 ('last year of his minority') at the time of his father's death and appears to have been born in 1810.

fifteen thousand pounds: about one million pounds in modern money.

Eton: public school in Berkshire, founded in 1440; Disraeli had given a rapturous account of the hero's time at Eton in *Coningsby*, using information from one of the masters, William Gifford Cookesley (1802–80). Tancred will also be an Etonian though he is withdrawn by his nervous mother after an outbreak of scarlet fever 'during his first half'. Egremont is there in the 1820s, under John Keate (Headmaster 1809–34, notorious for his use of the birch), and before the arrival in 1840 of the reforming Francis Hodgson.

the great change: the Reform Act, 1832.

29 *Erastianism . . . varied by visits to Windsor*: Erastianism is the doctrine that the Church should be subordinate to the state, fiercely attacked by the Oxford or Tractarian Movement, initially in John Keble's Oxford Assize Sermon of July 1833. Charles's schoolboy ambition is to be an officer in the Guards, based alternately at Wellington Barracks (on land which was officially part of St James's Park) and at Windsor Castle.

29 *crapulence . . . Dukism*: intemperance; 'Dukism' is a Disraelian coinage for the cult of the Duke of Wellington whose prestige as a leader suffered when his government fell in 1830.

one house of Parliament: the House of Lords.

select vestry: a committee, selected from the ratepayers, which managed local government matters, so called because it usually met in the vestry of the parish church. Vestries lost their power over poor relief in 1834, public health in 1848, and all non-ecclesiastical responsibilities in 1894.

30 *Utopia . . . WEALTH and TOIL*: Disraeli is suggesting that British culture, since the Reform Act of 1832, has been dominated by Utilitarians (with their materialist definition of well-being as 'The greatest happiness of the greatest number') and Political Economists (with their stress on gross domestic product and the labour theory of value). Bulwer-Lytton's *England and the English* (1833; partly dedicated to Isaac D'Israeli) had observed that, 'The spirit of the age demands political economy now, as it demanded moral theories before.'

Lady Carlisle: Lucy Hay, Countess of Carlisle (1599–1660), Lady of the Bedchamber to Queen Henrietta Maria, and a political intriguer who appears to have communicated secrets to both sides during the Civil War.

31 *Lord Grey*: Charles Grey (1764–1845, Earl Grey 1807), Whig politician, Prime Minister 1830–4, responsible for the Reform Act of 1832. 'Peace, retrenchment, and reform' was the slogan of the Whig party in the first half of the nineteenth century.

Taper: see note to p. 26. The Reform Bill was blocked by a Tory amendment on 21 March 1831; the Whigs dissolved Parliament on 22 April and called a General Election (see note to p. 35) to reaffirm their mandate, won it in June, and introduced a new Reform Bill which would be passed in June 1832. London shopkeepers, supplying items for Lady Marney's ball in April 1831, would be enfranchised as ten-pound householders.

Carpe diem: 'seize the day' or live for the moment (Latin; Horace, *Odes* I.xi.8).

32 *New Zealand*: the South Australia Colonization Act (15 August 1834) authorized a scheme whereby land in Australia and New Zealand (then officially still part of New South Wales) was to be sold to 'gentleman settlers' and the proceeds used for the travel costs of working-class emigrants (not convicts); Charles is 'four-and-twenty' in 1834.

33 *East India director*: founded in 1600, the East India Company had a monopoly of British trade with India until 1834 and dominated trade between the Far East and Europe in cotton, silk, tea, indigo, and saltpetre (an essential ingredient of gunpowder). Its political control of India, limited by the appointment of a Governor General in 1776, was abolished in 1858 but it continued as a trading company until 1874. The major shareholders (known as the Court of Proprietors) annually elected six directors to a board of twenty-four, technically for four years, in practice for life; the directors were very wealthy men.

a great step to knowledge: a version of the famous remark by Socrates (though nowhere recorded by Plato as such) that he was wiser than other men 'because he knew that he knew nothing'.

34 *the four orders*: the four orders of knighthood are the Garter, the Thistle, St Patrick (now dormant), and the Bath.

Esterhazy ... Grand Cross: Prince Esterhazy (Paul Anton III, 1786–1866) was Austrian Ambassador to London 1815–42; he would be made an Honorary Knight Grand Cross of the Order of the Bath on 12 July 1837.

35 *red tapers*: bureaucrats (so called because lawyers and civil servants tied their papers together with red tape).

hackney coach: the Reform Bill passed its second reading in March 1831 but was defeated by a Conservative amendment in April. When the Whig government announced that it would therefore dissolve Parliament and hold a General Election, the Conservatives proposed an Address in the House of Lords to block dissolution. This was an attack on the royal pre-rogative and Lord Grey told King William that he must immediately go to the House of Lords, prorogue Parliament, and prevent the Address. When informed that his horses could not be ready at such short notice, William replied, 'Then I will go in a hackney cab!', though in fact his own coach was hastily made available.

Sir Robert: Sir Robert Peel (see note to p. 23), Tory Leader of the Opposition. Though the Tories had lost a General Election in 1835, they thought they could win one with the voters enrolled during the 1837 registration exer-cise (see note to p. 27). But the law required an election to be held within six months of the death of a monarch so William IV's death meant that it took place in July 1837, before the new electoral rolls were ready. The Whigs were returned with a reduced majority and (like Charles Egremont) Disraeli won his first seat (Maidstone) as a Tory.

Guelphs: the Guelphs were the Italians who, in the twelfth and thirteenth centuries, opposed the authority of the German Holy Roman Emperor and, instead, saw the Pope as their ruler; the term is here applied to eighteenth-century Tories like Bolingbroke, Carteret, and Shelburne who, in Disraeli's account, tried to save the monarch from the power of the Whig nobles.

Thirty at Athens: after Athens's defeat in the Peloponnesian War in 404 BC, a body of thirty 'tyrants', led by Critias, briefly took control of the state; civil war broke out and democracy was restored in 403.

36 *Venetian conclave*: until 1797 Venice had been an oligarchy (see note to p. 14), ruled nominally by its aristocratic families but in practice by a series of small committees, the most powerful and sinister of which was the Consiglio dei Dieci (Council of Ten).

system of national education: this first government grant for education was made in 1833: £20,000 split between Anglican and Nonconformist schools. Attacked by Radicals as insufficient, and by Tories as an improper extension of the powers of the state, it was carried only after ingenious political manoeuvring by the Whig government.

36 *Whig secretary of the treasury*: the Parliamentary Secretary to the Treasury (or Chief Whip) in 1837 was Francis Baring (1796–1866).

Lord Durham: John Lambton (1792–1840; Baron Durham 1828), Whig politician known as 'Radical Jack' who helped to draft the Reform Bill and in 1834 campaigned for universal household suffrage (a change likely to alienate the wealthier, newly enfranchised ten-pound householders). But he was Ambassador to Russia 1835–7 and would be sent to Canada as Governor General in 1838, so Taper's vision of an unsustainably radical Whig administration was not realized.

the Queen Dowager: Queen Adelaide (1792–1849), widow of William IV and aunt of Queen Victoria, was known to have Tory views but would, in practice, spend her widowhood in pious seclusion.

dined at Kensington: Princess Victoria and her mother, the Duchess of Kent, were living at Kensington Palace; Victoria was 18 on 24 May 1837 (the day of the novel's opening scene), so she was the heir presumptive without any need for a regency.

37 *Croucher . . . the Carlton*: Joseph Croucher was a parliamentary and election agent. The Carlton Club was founded in 1821 as a Tory counterpart to the Whig Reform Club; Disraeli became a member in 1836.

King of Hanover: between 1714 and 1837 the British monarch was also King (or Elector) of Hanover. Under Hanover's Semi-Salic Law, however, a female could not inherit if there was a male descendant, so Victoria's uncle Ernest, Duke of Cumberland (1771–1851), became King after the death of his brother William IV. Frequently involved in scandals, and known for his reactionary views, there were rumours in 1836 that he was plotting with the Protestant Orange Lodges to dispossess Princess Victoria and take the British throne.

Brookes' . . . Swan River!: Brooks's is a Whig club in St James's Street, founded in 1764; for Crockford's see note to p. 5; Sydney, a penal colony 1788–1850, is the capital of New South Wales where marsupials such as kangaroos and wallabies are common; the Swan River Colony, established in 1829, was renamed Western Australia in 1832.

38 *gaugership . . . tidewaiter . . . land-waiter*: salaried posts in the Customs service, necessary when ships were unloaded in mid-stream but redundant after the construction of enclosed docks; Pitt had tried in 1792 to suppress the notorious sinecures in the Customs (sixty-one nominal posts in the Port of London alone) but without success.

last son of George III who probably will ever reign: two sons of George III were still alive when Disraeli was writing: the Duke of Cumberland (1771–1851) and the Duke of Cambridge (1774–1850). Both were younger brothers of Victoria's father, the Duke of Kent (1767–1820), but could have succeeded to the throne had Victoria and her children (four of whom had been born by 1845) died.

palace in a garden: Kensington Palace is set in Kensington Gardens, separated from Hyde Park in 1728 and open (to the 'respectably dressed') only

on Sundays until Victoria moved to Buckingham Palace in 1837. Disraeli
accompanied Lord Lyndhurst to Kensington for the young Queen's first
council and heard his account of it 'as we drove home'.

39 *Macedonian . . . Columbus*: Alexander the Great, King of Macedon, led his
army into Afghanistan but turned back from an invasion of India in 326
BC; Christopher Columbus discovered America but did not know of the
existence of Australia.

beauty of the Saxon . . . Saxon thraldom: though Queen Victoria inherited
the throne by her descent from Norman monarchs, her mother was
Princess Victoria of Saxe-Coburg-Saalfeld, a Saxon Duchy in central
Germany. The 'Saxon thraldom' was the historical theory that the English
had lost their traditional liberties when the 'Norman yoke' was imposed.

BOOK II

40 *MARNEY ABBEY . . . sylvans*: Disraeli based the 'ancient monastery' on
Fountains Abbey, near Ripon in North Yorkshire (*Benjamin Disraeli
Letters*, ed. M. G. Wiebe et al. (Toronto: Toronto University Press, 1982–
present), 4.167–8). The house may therefore have been suggested by
Fountains Hall and Marney by the town of Ripon. But he also says that he
'took' his 'idea' of Mowbray (not Marney) Church 'from Ripon wh: was at
hand', so there is no direct correspondence between the real and imaginary places. Disraeli visited Ripon while staying with Ferrand at Bingley in
October 1844. A sylvan is a faun or god of the woods.

41 *Helvetius*: Claude Adrien Helvétius (1715–71), whose *De l'esprit* (1758),
with its Lockean view of the mind as a tabula rasa and its insistence that all
human action is motivated by rational self-interest, can be seen as an
anticipation of Utilitarianism.

petty sessions: hearings held by Magistrates, or Justices of the Peace, to
consider petty, rather than major, criminal offences; Disraeli had been
a Buckinghamshire JP since 1836.

artificial flies: hooks dressed with feathers to resemble insects, used in fly
fishing.

42 *Mr. Paget's tales*: Francis Edward Paget (1806–82), Rector of Elford,
Staffordshire, was a Tractarian clergyman and prolific writer whose *Tales
of the Village* were published in three series 1840–1 and whose novel *The
Warden of Berkingholt; or, Rich and Poor* had been cited by Lord John
Manners in his *The Monastic and Manufacturing Systems* (1843).

baronet: the modern Order of Baronets dates from 1611, when James
I invited 200 'gentlemen of good birth' to pay £1,095 each to fund the army
in Ireland in return for a title ('Sir'). They were not Peers, so did not sit in
the House of Lords, but, unlike Knights, their titles were hereditary. Further
baronetcies were created from time to time (more than 3,000 in total) until
1991. Sir Vavasour Firebrace is based on Sir Richard Broun (1801–58) who
set up a 'Committee of the Baronetage for Privileges' in 1835 and published

The Dignity of the Honourable Baronettesses of the Realm (1839) and annual editions of *The Baronetage* from 1841; the *Athenaeum* (29 April 1843, p. 406) mocked Broun's claims as an 'absurdity'. Valvasour or Vavasour was a rank equivalent to baronet in medieval England.

43 *new poor law . . . Union*: the 'New Poor Law' of 1834 was technically an amendment to the Elizabethan Poor Law of 1601 but in practice involved fundamental changes: moving the relief of poverty from individual parishes to workhouses run by groups (or 'Unions') of parishes, and seeking to abolish 'out-door relief' (support outside the workhouse). The positive case for it was that it prevented pauperization (the acceptance of life on the dole). Lord Marney, as a rate-paying landowner, thinks it will save him money.

allotments: the Enclosure Act 1773 empowered landowners to privatize 'common' land but in 1809 the King provided 6 acres at Great Somerford, Wiltshire, on which villagers could once again grow their own food. The idea became popular with High Tories and William Busfeild Ferrand introduced an unsuccessful Allotments Bill in 1843. He also created fifteen acres of allotments near Bingley, where Disraeli spoke on 11 October 1844 at a dinner to celebrate them (*The Times*, 14 October 1844).

presented: presentation is the process of appointing a clergyman to a living, or parish. The advowson, or right to present a candidate to the diocesan bishop, had traditionally belonged to the local lord of the manor but could be sold or bequeathed. After the Dissolution of the Monasteries the many livings previously controlled by religious houses also passed to lay patrons. In the twentieth century most advowsons were returned to the Church.

44 *from Canton*: until 1842 Canton (Guangzhou) was the only port through which China traded with the West. The East India Company bought tea from China, paying for it with silver until 1781 when it adopted the Portuguese practice of selling Indian-grown opium to the Chinese. The Jiaquing emperor banned opium in 1796 but it continued to be grown in Bengal, auctioned in Calcutta, and then smuggled into China. The removal of the Company's monopoly in 1834 encouraged individual traders to become directly involved and in 1839 the Daoguang emperor destroyed more than 1,000 tons of opium. The British responded with the First Opium War (1839–42), during which they captured Canton and acquired Hong Kong. McDruggy resembles William Jardine (1784–1843), born in Scotland, based in Canton from 1822, known in China as 'the ring-leader of the opium smugglers', founder of Jardine, Matheson & Co., and Whig MP for Ashburton 1841–3.

'*Peel . . . will support the Poor Law*': the Radical Tories had opposed the Whig New Poor Law and hoped that the Tory government of August 1841 would repeal it. Peel did not speak during the original debates on the New Poor Law but made his support for it clear during the 1837 election campaign and, once in office, proposed only minor amendments. Disraeli opposed the renewal of the New Poor Law legislation, both in February 1841 and in 1847.

45 *they'll stand?*: the Whig government elected in 1837 had only twenty-four seats more than the Tories, with a hostile House of Lords and unreliable support from the Radicals. They were kept in office in 1839 by the 'Bedchamber plot' (see notes to pp. 233 and 234).

46 *one of us*: a baronet: Peel's father, a cotton manufacturer and MP, was made a baronet in 1800 and died in 1830.

the badge: Charles I created a second batch of baronets (see note to p. 42) in 1625 to fund the colonization of Nova Scotia. These wore a badge, showing the arms of Nova Scotia; other baronets did not acquire the right to a badge until 1929.

47 *equites aurati*: golden knights (Latin): the equites were a Roman social order intermediate between the plebeians and the patricians; originally a body of cavalry soldiers, they wore a gold ring (*anulus auratus*); English Knights Bachelor (knighted by the sovereign but not members of one of the four Orders of Knighthood; see note to p. 34) were referred to as *equites aurati* because they had been entitled to gild their armour.

claim knighthood: the royal warrant of 1613 granting the eldest sons of baronets the right of knighthood had been revoked by George IV in 1827; though the wives of baronets are given the courtesy title of 'Lady', they have no more right to it than the wives of sheriffs (today 'High Sheriffs'), the monarch's representatives as chief legal officers of the counties.

48 *Marney*: based in part on Ripon, North Yorkshire (see note to p. 40).

bourse: here a market hall though more usually a stock exchange.

dunghill than a cottage: derived from the Revd Dr W. S. Gilly's *The Peasantry of the Border: An Appeal on their Behalf* (1841) as cited in Edwin Chadwick's *Report on the Sanitary Condition of the Labouring Population of Great Britain, 1842*: 'built of rubble or unhewn stone, loosely cemented; and from age, or from badness of the materials, the walls look as if they would scarcely hold together . . . The chimneys have lost half their original height . . . The rafters are evidently rotten and displaced; and the thatch, yawning to admit the wind and wet in some parts, and in all parts utterly unfit for its original purpose of giving protection from the weather, looks more like the top of a dunghill than of a cottage.' The rest of the description of Marney is similarly taken from the accounts in Chadwick of Truro, Epping, Tiverton, and Cerne.

49 *police*: cleansing or keeping clean (usually of a military camp or garrison).

during the war: the wars with France between 1793 and 1815; the 'manufactory' would have made munitions or uniforms.

50 *Synochus*: Synochus is a continued fever, sometimes linked to typhoid; the account of Cerne, in Chadwick's *Report* (1843), noted the presence of Synochus in 'mud hovels . . . situated in low and damp places'.

merry England: the verse 'Introduction' to Canto 6 of Scott's *Marmion* (1808) had said that 'England was merry England when | Old Christmas brought his sports again' and William Hazlitt's essay 'Merry England' (in his *Lectures on the English Comic Writers*, 1819) extended the phrase 'Merry Sherwood' to celebrate, not just Robin Hood, but the 'freedom' of thirteenth-century life in general. Wordsworth's sonnet 'They called thee MERRY ENGLAND in old time' (*Yarrow Revisited*, 1835) asked whether the phrase was still appropriate when 'rural beauty,' could be, 'a mask | For discontent, and poverty, and crime'.

50 *names of a distant land*: unlike Anglican churches, the chapels built by Protestant Nonconformists were not named after saints. Instead, they took names directly from the Bible, usually Old Testament place names: Ripon had Bethel (Evangelical), Bethesda (Primitive Methodist), and Zion (Baptist) chapels. Disraeli liked this because it endorsed his view of Christianity as 'completed Judaism' (see note to p. 99); the 'language of a persecuted and ancient race' is the (translated) Hebrew of the Old Testament.

small tithes . . . great tithes: tithes were a tax on agricultural produce, paid to support the parish clergyman. Great (or rectorial) tithes were those on major crops, such as wheat; small (or vicarial) tithes were charged on other items. Monasteries had received the great tithes from their estates and, after their dissolution in the sixteenth century, this income passed to the new, secular owners of the land, leaving only the small tithes to support vicars in such areas. A loanmonger is a broker who buys and sells government debt.

51 *stacks . . . had blazed*: the Swing Riots of 1830 were the most conspicuous protest by agricultural workers in this period but arson attacks on haystacks continued, reaching a climax in the winter of 1843–4.

53 *Portal of the Poor*: the account of medieval monasteries as a welfare system for the poor derives from Scott's *Marmion* ('The poor her convent's bounty blessed', *Marmion* (1808), Canto 2, 3.23) and William Cobbett's *History of the Protestant 'Reformation'* (1824–6): the monks 'had large estates, were easy landlords, and . . . wholly provided for all the indigent within miles of their monastery' (Letter 2). Monasteries had, on these grounds, been suggested as a solution to modern social problems in Lord John Manners's *The Monastic and Manufacturing Systems* (1843).

Norman . . . Gothic: though 'Norman', 'Saxon', and 'Gothic' had been used synonymously by early nineteenth-century architectural writers, Thomas Rickman's *Attempt to Discriminate the Styles of English Architecture* (1817) established the distinction between Norman (or Romanesque) and the later Gothic styles which Disraeli uses here. Fountains Abbey (see note to p. 40) has a tower which was built in the early sixteenth century, shortly before the dissolution in 1539.

54 *cedar*: yew (*MS* and *1853*). There were notable yews at Fountains Abbey and there is no evidence for the planting of cedars of Lebanon in Britain before the mid-seventeenth century. Disraeli originally wrote 'yew' (*MS*) but changed it to 'cedar' (manuscript correction and *1845*), probably to suggest a biblical link with the Middle East. A letter from a reader (signed 'JM') on

11 May 1845 pointed out the anachronism so Disraeli (or his sister Sarah) restored 'yew' in the second edition (*1853*); see Thom Braun, 'Mr Disraeli Changes Trees', *Disraeli Newsletter*, 3.1 (Spring 1978), pp. 53–9.

his order: the nobility.

56 *individual tenure*: private ownership (Gerard has been listening to the Utopian Socialist views of his friend Stephen Morley; see note to p. 58).

yeomen: in the late Middle Ages a yeoman was a commoner who cultivated his own land, similar in status to a franklin (see note to p. 119).

dilatory master in chancery: the Court of Chancery administered Equity, the branch of law developed to provide relief for wrongs which the Common Law could not remedy. By the early nineteenth century it was notorious for delay, especially in complicated inheritance cases. Farmers could therefore be without a functional landlord for years or even decades while the will which transferred an estate from its previous owner to his heirs was in dispute.

57 *pension list*: the practice of awarding 'perpetual' or hereditary pensions to favourites, political supporters, or distinguished public servants began during the reign of Charles II; the English, Scottish, and Irish pension lists were consolidated in 1830 and abolished in the 1880s (with the exception of the families of the naval heroes Lord Rodney and Lord Nelson). In a slightly different sense, many military officers had been put onto 'half pay' when the end of the Napoleonic Wars made them redundant.

Belvoirs . . . Chatsworths . . . Wentworths . . . Stowes: Belvoir Castle, Leicestershire, seat of the dukes of Rutland; Chatsworth House, Derbyshire, seat of the dukes of Devonshire; Wentworth Woodhouse, Yorkshire, seat of Lord Rockingham and the Earls Fitzwilliam; Stowe House, Buckinghamshire, seat of the dukes of Buckingham and Chandos. Disraeli attended the royal visit to Stowe in January 1845, while writing *Sybil*.

58 *no community . . . but aggregation*: Morley appears to be an Owenite or Utopian Socialist, drawing ideas from Robert Owen (1771–1858), whose *Report to the County of Lanark* (1821) recommended the creation of 'associations' of working people since 'combination and unity' were more productive than 'individual interest' (pp. 26–9), and from William Thompson (1775–1833), whose *Labor Rewarded* (London: Hunt & Clark, 1827) recommended cooperative organization, the 'substitution of joint for individual possessions' (p. 117), and 'self-supplying unions of the industrious' (p. 116); Walter Gerard refers to Morley's 'joint-stock felicity' in Book V, Chapter III, and, like Morley, Thompson was a vegetarian and a teetotaller. Carlyle's *Past and Present* (1843) argued that, in modern society, 'Cash-payment' was 'the one nexus of man to man' (Book 3, Chapter 6).

60 *evening hymn to the Virgin*: derived from Canto 3 of Scott's poem *The Lady of the Lake* (1810) where, as night falls, Ellen Douglas sings 'Ave Maria! maiden mild!' from the 'Goblin-cave' in which she and her father are sheltering. Scott's lyric was set by Schubert as 'Ellens Gesang III', the sixth of his *Sieber Gesänge aus Walter Scotts 'Fräulein am See'* (1826); the words of

the Latin hymn 'Ave Maria, gratia plena' were later substituted for Scott's text and the music is now better known in that form. Sybil as 'a seraph' echoes Scott's 'What melting voice attends the strings? | 'Tis Ellen, or an angel, sings' (3.711–12); Rebecca sings a Jewish evening hymn in Chapter 39 of Scott's *Ivanhoe*.

61 *ten pound days*: the new voters enfranchised by the 1832 Reform Act were householders in the boroughs (not counties) paying a yearly rent of at least £10.

62 *no rural police*: the 1839 County Police Act allowed local JPs to create a paid police force but it would not be compulsory until 1856 and many counties chose not to do so. There had been a professional police force in London since 1829 and in other towns since 1835.

64 *the chess club*: the London Chess Club was formed in 1810, meeting in a room in Cornhill.

66 *regular blue*: a 'blue' or blue-stocking was a derisive term for a woman with literary tastes, first used in the 1750s of the London salon of Mrs Montague though it was actually one of her male guests, Benjamin Stillingfleet, who wore blue stockings; Lady Joan is learned rather than literary.

the comet., Dr. Buckland . . . Arago: the Great Comet of 1831 (C/1831/A1) was discovered on 7 January 1831 (actually from Hounslow Heath by the physicist John Herapath). William Buckland (1784–1856) was a canon of Christ Church, Oxford, and a pioneering geologist and palaeontologist. Francois Arago (1786–1853) was a French physicist and astronomer whose *Treatise on Comets* was published in 1833.

Mowbray: a composite northern town, chiefly based on Manchester (actually in Lancashire though here set in Yorkshire) with traces of Bingley (Yorkshire) and, latterly, Nottingham (Nottinghamshire); see notes to p. 40 and p. 356. The medieval 'Honour of Mowbray' was a great estate in Yorkshire and Northumberland, originally held jointly with the lordship of Montbrai in Normandy.

68 *Turkey merchant . . . Planter . . . Nabob*: a Turkey merchant was a member of the Levant Company (1592–1825) which traded with Venice and the Middle East. English planters, such as the Beckford family, began to grow sugar in the West Indies in the seventeenth century; by 1750 it was the single most valuable commodity in European trade (Disraeli was pleased to receive an appreciative letter about *Contarini Fleming* in 1832 from William Beckford, novelist and millionaire). Nabob (Hindustani 'Nawab', deputy governor) was the term used of employees of the East India Company (see note to p. 33) who enriched themselves while in India.

Wycherly . . . Congreve . . . Cumberland . . . Morton: William Wycherly (1640–1716), playwright; William Congreve (1670–1729), playwright; Richard Cumberland (1732–1811), playwright, author of *The West Indian* (1771); Thomas Morton (1764–1838), playwright. Though he does not name him, Disraeli is perhaps thinking of Samuel Foote's play *The Nabob* (1772).

Loanmonger: a dealer in government debt (see notes to p. 20 and p. 21) issued to meet the costs of the American War of Independence and the wars which followed the French Revolution.

Waterloo loan . . . continental blockade . . . Hastings: in the 'Hundred Days' before the Battle of Waterloo, the British government made a £30 million issue of 3 per cent bonds, through Baring Brothers, to fund a loan to its continental allies; the persistent legend that Nathan Mayer Rothschild made a fortune by speculating in these bonds on the basis of early information about the outcome of the battle is false. The Continental Blockade, introduced by Napoleon's Berlin Decree of November 1806, was designed to harm the British economy by preventing exports to Europe; in practice British manufacturers, especially in Manchester, developed worldwide markets while their European competitors declined. Warren Hastings (1732–1818) was head of the Supreme Council of Bengal (in effect Governor General of India) 1773–85.

longer period than the siege of Troy . . . American war . . . waiter at a celebrated club: the siege of Troy lasts ten years in Homer's *Iliad*. The American War of Independence began in April 1775. The fictitious John Warren's career may have been suggested by the rumour that Sir Thomas Rumbold (1736–91; Governor of Madras 1777–80) had been a waiter at White's Club; in fact he was the son of an officer in the East India Company's naval service and himself began work as a Company writer (clerk) at the age of 16.

69 *cried out for rice*: the Bengal Famine of 1769–70 caused more than 10 million deaths and there were allegations in British newspapers in 1771 that East India Company officials had been profiteering; Adam Smith in *The Wealth of Nations* (1776) famously argued that it was government interference in the market to prevent speculation ('improper regulations, some injudicious restraints imposed by the servants of the East India Company upon the rice trade'), rather than speculation itself, that had helped 'to turn that dearth into a famine' (Vol. 2, p. 110) and this view would influence responses to the Irish Famine of 1845–9.

Burke and Francis: Sir Philip Francis (1740–1818) was a Whig politician and a member of the Supreme Council of Bengal, where he was a bitter opponent of Warren Hastings (see note to p. 68); in 1787 he encouraged Edmund Burke (see note to p. 15) to launch the impeachment of Hastings in the House of Commons, a process which continued for seven years and financially ruined Hastings (though he was eventually found not guilty and compensated by the East India Company); like Warren's fictitious employer, Hastings had been Governor of Madras (1769–71).

close borough: see note to p. 15.

Lord North's administration: Lord North was Prime Minister 1770–82.

Mrs Crewe: Frances Anne Crewe (née Greville), Lady Crewe (1748–1818), was a wit, a beauty, and a Whig political hostess; much admired by Fox, Burke, and the Prince of Wales, Sheridan 'addressed' his play *The School for Scandal* (1777) to her.

70 *Mr Hastings . . . Mr Francis*: see note to p. 69.

Fitzpatrick . . . Hare: Richard Fitzpatrick (1748–1813), soldier, MP, and close friend of Charles James Fox, was a wit and writer of satirical verse. James Hare (1747–1804) was also valued as a wit in Whig high society, despite his undistinguished record as diplomat and MP.

Irish baron: until the Act of Union in 1801, Irish peers sat in the Irish House of Lords. When that was abolished, they were allowed to elect just twenty-eight representative peers to the Westminster House of Lords. Other Irish peers had no constitutional role (though they could sit, as elected MPs, in the House of Commons) and the creation of non-representative Irish titles was a convenient way of awarding honours.

the old barons of this name: William de Warenne (from Varenne, Normandy) was made Earl of Surrey after the Norman Conquest. The Warenne line died out in 1347 when the 7th Earl died without legitimate heirs, thus creating the opportunity for the Heralds to discover a supposedly over- looked line of descent. The 6th Earl had married Maud, daughter of William Marshal, Earl of Pembroke, and her niece Joan de Munchensi married William de Valence (1225–96). This collateral link makes possible a further (spurious) claim to Valence ancestry, also conveniently extinct in the direct line since 1389, and explains the family's choice of the names 'Valence', 'Joan', and 'Maud' for their three children. An earl stands higher in the ranks of the peerage than a baron but the Warrens' (ficti- tious) earldom is very recent (1827), so adding a vacant Valence barony would establish their status as 'Norman' aristocrats. The character Alfred Mountchesney must be similarly descended (either genuinely or spuri- ously) from the medieval Munchensis, so there is a curious symmetry about the marriage plot in which he is involved.

72 *Walcheren expeditions, Manchester massacres, Queen's trials*: three political crises when the 2nd Baron Fitz-Warene's votes (one in the Lords, six from his closed boroughs in the Commons) were important. The Walcheren expedition was an unsuccessful campaign in the Netherlands in 1809: the Prime Minister, the Duke of Portland, resigned and his successor, Spencer Perceval, narrowly survived a motion of censure. After the Peterloo Massacre in Manchester in August 1819 there was an emergency session of Parliament in November in which the Whig demand for a public inquiry was defeated. When George IV became King in January 1820, his estranged wife Caroline of Brunswick returned from Italy to assert her rights as Queen. The government did not dare to submit its Bill to dissolve the marriage to the Commons, though it had been narrowly passed in the Lords where Caroline's private life was investigated in what was, in effect, a trial; she died in 1821.

the Cottage . . . Canning: the Prince Regent's 'Cottage' in Windsor Great Park (Royal Lodge) was a modest house enlarged into an elaborate *cottage ornée* after the Prince (later George IV) moved into it in 1815. When Lord Liverpool's health failed in April 1827, the King asked George Canning

(1770–August 1827) to become Prime Minister but it was only with the backing of some Whigs and the bribing of some Tories (such as the fictitious Lord Fitz-Warene) that he could take office. Disraeli helped John Murray launch a Canningite daily newspaper, the *Representative*, in January 1826 though it closed six months later.

73 *the drink of Saxon kings*: Anglo-Saxon monarchs feasted in 'Mead' or 'Beer' Halls.

Hesperus: the evening star, actually the planet Venus when seen in the evening.

'Nunc me dimittas': the 'Nunc dimittis' is a Christian hymn, traditionally part of Compline or Evensong, using the words of Simeon in Luke 2: 29–32 in the Vulgate version ('Nunc dimittis servum tuum, Domine, secundum verbum tuum in pace': 'Now let thy servant depart in peace, according to thy word Lord').

74 *Martinmas*: St Martin's Day, 11 November, and the traditional end of the agricultural year.

Azincourt . . . name of the good old faith: the Battle of Agincourt was fought in 1415. Gerard is indeed the name of an old-established Roman Catholic family in Lancashire and Cheshire, whose members included the martyr Miles Gerard (1550–90); if the reference is to Trafford, that too is the name of an old Lancashire Catholic family (see note to p. 157).

75 *holy sister*: Roman Catholic convents, banned from England after the Reformation, had been legal since 1791 (though The Bar Convent in York, where Sybil stays in Book VI, Chapter II, had survived in secret throughout the intervening period). The Presentation Nuns, a teaching order from Clonmel, opened a convent in Livesey Street, Manchester, in 1833.

77 *bate ticket . . . small cops . . . snicks*: a bate ticket is a fine, or deduction from wages; cops are balls of new spun yarn, so 'small cops' are under-measure and 'bad-bottomed' cops have been snagged during the spinning; 'snicks' are cuts or clippings. The vocabulary is directly derived from William Dodd's *The Factory System Illustrated* (1842), pp. 263–4; see Martin Fido, ' "From his Own Observation': Sources of Working Class Passages in Disraeli's *Sybil*', *Modern Languages Review*, 72 (1977), pp. 270–1.

snickey, bad yarns: damaged, imperfect fabric.

78 *laudanum*: a painkiller, first developed by Paracelsus, mixing one part of opium with nine of alcohol (usually sherry), which was freely available without prescription until the early twentieth century.

Imperence: impertinence.

79 *'Northern Star' . . . 'Moral Worlds'*: The Northern Star, published in Leeds from 1837 to 1852, was a Chartist newspaper owned and edited by Feargus O'Connor; Disraeli borrowed a file of its editorial correspondence in August 1844 as he began work on *Sybil*. The New Moral World was an Owenite newspaper published from 1834 to 1845.

81 *'THE TEMPLE OF THE MUSES'*: closely based on the account in William Dodd's *The Factory System Illustrated* (1842) of the 'Thespian Gallery,

and Temple of the Muses' in The Jolly Hatters at Stockport (Dodd, *The Factory System Illustrated*, pp. 182–4) with some further detail from Dodd's description of The Highland Laddie, Stockport (pp. 184–5); see Fido, ' "From his Own Observation" ', pp. 273–3.

81 *King Richard, Mazeppa . . . Jeanie Deans*: King Richard and Hubert menacing Arthur are from Shakespeare's *Richard III* (1592) and *King John* (1596); Mazeppa and Haidee rescuing Juan are from Byron's *Mazeppa* (1819) and *Don Juan* (1819–24); the Lady of the Lake and Jeanie Deans curtseying before Queen Caroline (wife of George II) are from Scott's *The Lady of the Lake* (1810) and *The Heart of Midlothian* (1818).

King of Saxony: though the itinerant musicians are claiming a distinction they do not possess, the King of Saxony in the 1840s was Frederick Augustus II (1797–1854), whose illegitimate son was the viola player, composer, and music critic Theodor Uhlig (1822–53).

82 *Lowell . . . Sherry Cobler*: Lowell, Massachusetts, developed in the 1820s as America's chief cotton spinning and weaving town. Sherry Cobbler is an American cocktail, invented in the 1830s, made with sherry, sugar, orange juice, and crushed ice, and drunk through a straw; it had been praised in Dickens's *Martin Chuzzlewit* (1843–4).

Harlequin: the principal character in the 'transformation scenes' of nineteenth-century pantomimes, known for his balletic runs and leaps.

the London Tavern: the City of London Tavern in Bishopsgate had a large and splendid dining room used for public meetings and formal dinners.

no temperance and teetotal then: the first Temperance Society had been founded in Preston in 1833.

83 *last one-pound note*: the Bank Notes Act of 1826 prohibited the circulation of notes under £5 in England; £1 notes were not reissued until 1914.

85 *nil admirari*: indifferent ('to wonder at nothing', Latin).

rummers: large drinking glasses, originally from the Rhineland.

Pickford's van: Pickford's transport company was founded in Manchester in the 1630s, moving to London in 1756. London parishes had contracted with manufacturers to supply child workers, technically as apprentices, from their orphanages and workhouses since the 1760s and, after the introduction of the New Poor Law, the unemployed could similarly be moved to the new industrial towns from rural districts.

clean machinery during mealtime: requiring workers to clean machinery during their meal breaks was a way in which employers evaded legal limitations on working hours in mills and factories (see note to p. 88).

Devilsdust: usually a cheap fabric made by the dusty process of tearing up woollen rags with a machine called a 'devil', mixing the result with gum, and compressing it into 'shoddy', but here the 'wadding' or padding made in a similar way from cotton waste. Carlyle had referred to both kinds of 'devil's dust' in *Past and Present* (1843) and the name of the hero of his philosophical fiction *Sartor Resartus* (1833–4) is a German version of the term: Teufelsdröckh.

86 *Society for the Propagation of the Gospel in Foreign Parts*: a Church of England society founded in 1701, initially to send missionaries to North America but also to Africa in 1752 and India in 1820; the East India Company was conducting a campaign against female infanticide in the Bombay Presidency in the 1830s.

Juggernaut . . . Moloch: Juggernaut ('world-lord') is one of the names of the Hindu god Krishna; during the annual procession of huge chariots carrying images of gods at the Jagannath Temple in Puri, devotees allowed themselves to be crushed under the wheels. Moloch is a Canaanite deity (Leviticus 18: 21) traditionally represented as a bronze statue, heated with fire, into which child victims were thrown.

Godfrey's cordial: a popular children's medicine, also known as Mother's Friend, which mixed one grain of opium with two ounces of treacle and water.

88 *ten-hour bill*: the Ten Hours Movement, or campaign for a ten-hour working day in cotton mills and wool factories, was launched in 1830 by Richard Oastler. The Tory MPs Michael Sadler and Lord Ashley continued the campaign but the 1833 Factory Act set the limit at twelve hours (for those under 18). The Factory Act of 1844 again set a twelve-hour day and it would be the Factory Act of 1847 ('Fielden's Bill') which would establish, from May 1848, a fifty-eight-hour working week for women and children (ten hours a day from Monday to Friday, with eight hours on Saturday). Since it was difficult for mills to function without female and child labour, such limits were usually effective for men as well. But the Factory Act of 1850 would raise the limit to ten and a half hours (with Disraeli speaking against it) and it would not be until the Factory Act of 1867 (passed when Disraeli was Chancellor of the Exchequer) and the Acts of 1874 and 1878 (passed when Disraeli was Prime Minister) that the cause would finally be won.

Navarino: the naval Battle of Navarino was fought in October 1827 during the Greek War of Independence. British, French, and Russian vessels had been sent to enforce an armistice but, when fired on, responded by using their superior gunnery to sink the entire Turkish fleet.

89 *a—good strike*: the omitted word is 'bloody' in *MS*.

91 *a majority*: the effective Whig majority, after the General Election of 1837, was twenty-four seats.

92 *Carlton Club*: see note to p. 37.

blue ribbon cover: the best place for shooting on the estate; this is clearly the Horns cover about which Morley will read a newspaper report in Book III, Chapter X.

93 *Christian architecture*: unlike Greek or Roman architecture, Gothic was the product of a Christian era and came to be valued for that reason: Pugin's

True Principles of Pointed or Christian Architecture was published in 1841. The founders of the Oxford Movement were more concerned with theology than architecture but their early followers, especially the Cambridge Camden Society (1839; renamed the Ecclesiological Society in 1845), would campaign strenuously for church building in the Early English or Decorated styles of Gothic.

93 *the scale of Hippocrates*: the Greek physician Hippocrates (460–370 BC) originated the notion of the seven ages of man, though 'youth' in his account ended at 28, not 35, and this sounds more like the definition of youth by Galen (AD 129–*c*.200) in his scale of four ages.

94 *Mowbray Church*: based on Ripon church (cathedral since 1836); see note to p. 40. St Peter and St Wilfrid, Ripon, had been a minster, with a college of clergy rather than a monastery of monks, before its dissolution, as had St Mary, St Denys, and St George, Manchester (cathedral since 1847) which also became a parish church but (unlike Ripon) of a smoky industrial town: Mowbray is a version of Manchester set in Yorkshire (see note to p. 66) with a church which blends minsters from the two counties.

95 *Erastian . . . Church Commission*: the Oxford Movement argued that the Erastian subordination of Church to state by eighteenth-century Anglicanism had undermined religious belief; the Ecclesiastical Commissioners were appointed by Parliament in 1836 to reform the finances of the Church of England.

Puck-like: like Puck in Shakespeare's *A Midsummer Night's Dream* (1594–6) who takes a mischievous pleasure in the tricks he plays on other characters.

reducing the rates: the Poor Relief Act 1601 had introduced a tax on property to relieve poverty at a 'rate' determined annually by each parish vestry (see note to p. 29). By the 1820s such taxation had become a heavy burden, especially in rural parishes, and the New Poor Law of 1834 (see note to p. 43) was designed to spread and reduce it.

96 *affair of population*: the economist Thomas Robert Malthus (1766–1834) argued in his *Essay on the Principle of Population* (1798, expanded 1803) that population had a tendency to increase more rapidly than the means of subsistence. Since welfare systems encouraged this process, by removing such 'checks' as the postponement of marriage, he recommended the abolition of poor relief (rather than the limitation of relief enacted by the New Poor Law).

97 *no cottages*: Martin Fido ('The Treatment of Rural Distress in Disraeli's *Sybil*', *Yearbook of English Studies*, 5 (1975), pp. 153–63) argues that Lord Marney is under a misapprehension here, since he remains responsible for the poor relief due to parishioners whether they live in 'cottages' or in houses in the town ('the expelled people had flocked to Marney', Book I, Chapter III). But even under the Poor Law Settlement and Removal Act 1662 (which allowed migrants to establish rights to relief from the poor rates in a new parish after forty days) rural landlords had demolished cottages to prevent people from arriving or returning, and the New Poor Law

of 1834 actively encouraged movement from the land to the new industrial cities.

aux abois: in a fix (literally 'at bay'; French).

98 *forms and ceremonies*: the Oxford Movement reasserted the Catholic identity of the Church of England and recommended ceremonial rather than spontaneous forms of worship.

Hebræo-christian . . . apostolical succession: with the possible exception of the Patriarchate of Antioch, the Roman Catholic Church is the only surviving Christian denomination directly founded by one of the Twelve Apostles of Jesus Christ: Simon Peter (St Peter), a Jewish or Hebrew fisherman from Bethsaida in Galilee who was martyred in Rome in AD 65. The apostolic succession is the process by which authority passed from the apostles to the first bishops, and then from bishop to bishop down the generations; the Oxford Movement used it to counter the Erastian view that the Church should be governed by Parliament. Disraeli, however, gives his own twist to the concept by extending the succession, beyond the Apostles, to the Prophets and Patriarchs of the Old Testament.

99 *Moses . . . Aaron . . . Lambeth*: Moses was the Hebrew prophet who led the Israelites to the Promised Land. Aaron, the elder brother of Moses, was the first High Priest of the Israelites. Lambeth Palace is the London residence of the Archbishop of Canterbury.

completed Judaism: born and initially brought up as a Jew, Disraeli was baptized in 1817, at the age of 12, and remained a member of the Church of England. His view of Christianity, however, placed particular stress on Christ as the Messiah foretold in the Old Testament and on the Jewish identity of Jesus: 'Christianity is Judaism for the multitude' (*Tancred*, Book VI, Chapter IV).

Mons Sacer: the 'Sacred Hill' on the road from Rome to Nomentum (Mentana), where representation by Tribunes of the People was granted to the Plebeians in 494 BC: 'to the Romans what Runnymede is to Englishmen . . . an altar was built on it, and sacrifices offered to Jupiter' (Thomas Arnold, *History of Rome* (1838), 1.149).

100 *a loom*: though machinery for spinning thread was developed in the 1760s, machinery for weaving it into cloth did not become reliable until the 1820s and, in the interval, there was a huge demand for weavers who could make cloth by hand on traditional wooden looms. In the 1830s the new weaving machines made these numerous hand-loom workers redundant.

109 *canaille*: rabble (French).

111 *French actress*: a combination of two mistresses of Charles II: Louise de Kérouaille (French; her son Charles was created Duke of Richmond in 1675) and Nell Gwynn (actress; her son Charles was created Duke of St Albans in 1684).

Appropriation clause . . . Lord Stanley: the 'lay appropriation clause' of the Irish Church Temporalities Bill 1833, which allowed excess revenue of the

Anglican Church in Ireland to be used for educational purposes, proved so controversial that four ministers resigned from the Whig cabinet in May 1834 and the clause had to be dropped from the Act and from subsequent legislation on Irish Tithes. One of the ministers who resigned was Edward Stanley (1799–1869; Lord Stanley from 1834; Baron Stanley from 1844; 14th Earl of Derby 1851), Whig politician 1820–34, Tory politician from 1841, leader of the Protectionist Tory Party from 1846 (with Disraeli as his spokesman in the Commons from 1849), Tory Prime Minister 1852, 1858–9, 1866–8.

112 *Brookes'*: Brooks's Club; see note to p. 37.

proxy: voting by proxy was allowed in the House of Lords until 1867, absent peers nominating their substitutes in a book kept by the Clerk; the Duke of Fitz-Aquitaine has allowed a Whig Prime Minister to use his vote until Melbourne succeeded Grey in July 1834.

in statu pupillari . . . hierophants . . . with Lord Stanley in 1835 . . . vote against the Speaker: 'in statu pupillari' (Latin): with the status of a ward or pupil. 'Hierophants' are priests or expounders of sacred mysteries. Lord Stanley (see note to p. 111) had resigned from the Whig cabinet in 1834 and by 1835 it was thought that he had joined the Tories; in fact he led an independent group known as the 'Derby Dilly' until 1841. Though the re-election of the Speaker of the House of Commons at the beginning of each parliamentary session is usually a formality, when the Whigs returned to office in 1835 they voted against the Tory Charles Manners-Sutton (1780–1845), Speaker since 1817, and elected one of their own MPs.

Caciques . . . Champollion: Caciques were the leaders of the Pre-Colombian tribes found in the Bahamas and Antilles; the Spanish applied the term to the rulers of Mexico during their conquest of the mainland. Jean-Francois Champollion (1790–1832) was a French Orientalist famous for deciphering the Ancient Egyptian hieroglyphic script.

113 *Egeria*: a nymph or minor goddess who supposedly married Numa Pompilius, King of Rome, in the seventh century BC and communicated the laws and religious rituals of Ancient Rome to him.

Lord Haddington: Thomas Hamilton, 9th Earl of Haddington (1780–1858), Lord Lieutenant of Ireland during the brief Conservative government of 1834–5.

116 *Early hours on Saturday afternoon*: though a six-day working week was usual until Henry Ford introduced a five-day week in his factories in 1926, work sometimes ended earlier on Saturdays (see note to p. 88).

mullioned: with stone pillars between the panes.

117 *Cobbett*: William Cobbett (1763–85), journalist and politician, famous for his *Political Register* (1802–35), *Rural Rides* (1830), and the *History of the Protestant 'Reformation'* (1824–6) echoed in Walter Gerard's account of medieval monasteries in Book II, Chapter V.

119 *Franklin*: a freeman, socially intermediate between serfs and nobles, in medieval England; the term is Norman, not Saxon, though in Scott's *Ivanhoe* (1819) 'Cedric the Saxon' is a 'franklin' and franklins are, 'by the

law and spirit of the English constitution . . . entitled to hold themselves independent of feudal tyranny' (Chapter 1).

120 *three hundred thousand strangers*: England and Scotland saw a rapid increase in immigration from Ireland after the famine of 1823 and remained the usual destination until the late 1840s, when Irish emigrants turned to Canada and the USA. Carlyle's *Chartism* (1839) stated that 'Crowds of miserable Irish darken all our towns' (Chapter 4).

BOOK III

121 *stolen by the chimneysweeps*: Dickens's 'The First of May' (*Sketches by 'Boz'*, 1836) mentions the 'legends' of boys from wealthy families who were stolen by sweeps and rediscovered when cleaning chimneys in their own parents' houses.

122 *Society for the Abolition of Negro Slavery*: though the slave trade was abolished in the British Empire in 1807, and slavery in 1833, the practice was continued by other countries and a Society for the Extinction of the Slave Trade and the Civilization of Africa was founded in 1839.

punishment . . . for the direst criminals: solitary confinement was adopted as a policy in prisons in 1837 because it isolated prisoners from the bad influence of their fellow criminals; in practice it often led to nervous breakdowns.

guardian angels!: the painting, *A Child's Portrait in Different Views: 'Angels' Heads'* (1786–7), by Sir Joshua Reynolds (1723–92), showing the head of the 5-year-old Lady Frances Gordon from five different angles, now in the Tate.

Landseer . . . Etty: the painters Edwin Landseer, RA (1802–73; knighted 1850), and William Etty, RA (1787–1849).

123 *tommied*: obliged to take wages in goods ('tommy') rather than cash, under the truck system (see note to p. 124).

the young queen's picture: a coin bearing the image of the Queen's head; the 'young head' designed by William Wyon first appeared on coins in 1839.

124 *bums*: a bum-bailiff was the officer sent to enforce payment or recover debts.

'The law touches him': there had been legislation since 1464 to limit truck systems (whereby workers were forced to take wages in goods rather than cash; from French 'troquer', exchange) but it had often been ignored. William Cobbett described the 'tommy shops' of Wolverhampton in his *Rural Rides* (1830) and the old laws were revised and consolidated in the Truck Act 1831. William Busfeild Ferrand denounced evasions of that Act in a speech in the Commons on 24 February 1842 and a Select Committee published a Truck Report later that year (which noted the 'difficulties in the way of obtaining convictions under it'). Disraeli's source for his tommy shop scenes, however, both here and in subsequent chapters, was *The First Report from the Midland Mining Commissioners, South Staffs* (1843): see Fido, ' "From his Own Observation" ', who comments that Disraeli must have 'worked with the Blue Book open before him' (p. 283).

The law would be reinforced by the Truck Amendment Act 1887 and replaced by the Wages Act 1986.

125 *ten-yard coal*: the 'ten-yard' or 'Dudley' coal was a famously thick band of fourteen coal seams, conveniently close to the surface, near Wolverhampton: the best coal to mine.

clay: a fragile tobacco pipe.

play . . . stick-outs . . . clammed: 'at play' and 'stick-outs' are strikes; 'clammed' means hungry or starving (clemmed; Black Country dialect). The dialogue here is closely, sometimes directly, taken from *The First Report from the Midland Mining Commissioners, South Staffs* (1843): see Fido, ' "From his Own Observation" ', pp. 275–9.

126 *Wodgate*: a fictitious Black Country town named by its Anglo-Saxon founders after their god Woden (or Odin) and closely based on the accounts of Willenhall, Sedgley, and Wolverhampton in the *Second Report of the Children's Employment Commissioners: Trades and Manufactures* (1842). As Sheila Smith shows ('Willenhall and Wodgate: Disraeli's Use of Blue Book Evidence', *Review of English Studies*, 13 (1962)), these towns had churches which Disraeli omitted to make his Wodgate seem more pagan. Willenhall (Anglo-Saxon 'Wilgenhalh') dates from the eighth century and was famous for the manufacture of locks and keys, as was Sedgley (Anglo-Saxon 'Secgleah') for nail making; the real Hellhouse Yard was in Wolverhampton (Anglo-Saxon 'Wulfruneheantun'). Carlyle had discussed Odin in the first of his lectures *On Heroes* (1841), observing that 'traces', of his worship, 'are yet in many ways visible amongst us', and that, 'Many places in our country bear his name.'

lushy: drunk.

127 *hipped . . . penates*: depressed, low-spirited; the penates (Latin) were the household gods of families in Ancient Rome.

128 *a Screw*: a miser.

pricked: a pricked wine is acid or vinegary.

129 *the House*: the Workhouse.

131 *spontaneous combustion*: the self-induced ignition of piles of hay or coal after the internal generation of heat by oxidization; the improbable theory that it could happen to the human body would be taken seriously in Dickens's *Bleak House* (1852–3).

133 *corn-laws*: there had technically been a Corn Law since 1689 (see note to p. 20) but the law introduced in 1815 to protect British agriculture from foreign competition by excluding imports was more significant and controversial. Though the original barrier at 80 shillings a quarter was never reached, the sliding scale introduced in 1828 to impose a duty when domestic corn was 52 shillings a quarter or less was seen to help farmers but penalize consumers and an Anti-Corn-Law League was founded in 1838 (see note to p. 309). Peel reduced the duty in 1842 (see note to p. 297) and would abolish the Law entirely in 1846, with bitter opposition from Disraeli.

Richmond . . . Malton: notorious Whig 'closed boroughs' (see note to p. 15) in Yorkshire, controlled by Baron Dundas and Earl Fitzwilliam respectively.

135 *stints*: allocations of work, here of the amount of coal to be cut.

136 *sawney*: wheedling, ingratiating.

spout: pawnbroker.

138 *rust*: grease (though the usage is either ironic or a mistake by Disraeli).

141 *locksmiths*: Willenhall was famous for making locks and keys; see note to p. 126.

Labour . . . division . . . Mamlouks: Adam Smith's *Inquiry into the Nature and Causes of the Wealth of Nations* (1776) identified the division of labour (into specialized branches) as the key cause of the growth of national wealth, usually requiring capital investment to make it possible. Mamlouks, originally slaves from the Caucasus used as bodyguards by Muslim monarchs, became a powerful military caste which seized the Sultanate of Egypt 1250–1517; their Egyptian subjects were excluded from all military and political posts.

142 *an aristocracy that leads*: Carlyle had noted the 'cry . . . for an 'Aristocracy of Talent,' a Governing Class namely which did govern, not merely which took the wages of governing' in Book 1, Chapter 5 of *Past and Present* (1843).

144 *crowner's quest*: coroner's inquest.

145 *Missionary from Tahiti*: the London Missionary Society sent missionaries to Tahiti in 1797. John Williams, who followed in 1817, was eaten by cannibals in 1839 and in March 1844 the LMS launched a missionary ship, named after him and paid for by donations from children.

146 *golden drop . . . yellow diamond of Gengis Khan*: Coe's Golden Drop is a variety of greengage popular since the eighteenth century. Though now classified as 'colourless', the Koh-i-Noor diamond had a yellow tint until it was recut in 1852 and had probably belonged to the Moghul Emperor Babur (1483–1530), a descendant through his mother of Genghis Khan. In 1845 it was owned by Dulip Singh, ruler of the Punjab.

Harold: Harold Godwinson (1020–66), killed during the Battle of Hastings, was the last Anglo-Saxon king of England.

147 *physical force . . . moral power*: William Lovett, the original leader of the Chartist movement (see note to p. 175), was an advocate of 'moral force', believing that its aims should be achieved by persuasion and 'without commotion or violence'. In 1840 this approach was challenged by Feargus O'Connor and Joseph Rayner Stephens (see notes to p. 79 and p. 278) who argued for the use of 'physical force' or violent protest.

148 *gallery*: in 1803 part of the public gallery in the House of Commons was reserved for reporters; a separate Press Gallery was created in 1835.

'*. . . by the Normans' . . . conquerors and the conquered*: Augustin Thierry's *History of the Conquest of England by the Normans; with its Causes, and*

Consequences to the Present Time (1825, translated by Charles Hamilton, London, 1841) gave an account of the Norman Conquest, much influenced by Scott, which saw it as the suppression of English liberty by tyrannous invaders and described 'two nations, violently united on the same soil' (p. vii) who would eventually recover the lost Saxon rights and achieve parliamentary government. Sybil is summarizing, rather than quoting, when she puts this book down earlier in the chapter, and it is not clear who the 'stout earl' might be, unless he is Robin Hood, seen by Thierry as the leader of a persistent Saxon resistance. Scott's *Ivanhoe* (1819) took a similar view of Robin Hood and describes the 'line of separation between the descendants of the victor Normans and the vanquished Saxons' (Chapter 1).

149 *before the War of the Roses*: the Wars of the Roses began in 1455.

151 *King John's reign*: from 1199 to 1216.

Azincourt: the Battle of Agincourt took place in October 1415; a Henry Gerard did indeed fight in it.

155 *prog . . . shut*: prog is a slang word for food; a shut is a locking bar or bolt.

157 *other ties*: 'Cash-payment the one nexus of man to man' (Carlyle, *Past and Present* (1843), Book 3, Chapter 6); see note to p. 58.

a factory . . . one of the marvels of the district: Trafford's mill, like Millbank's in *Coningsby*, is often said to have been based on the Ashworth mills near Bolton. Disraeli knew Henry Ashworth and describes an event at the Ashworth mills during the 1842 Plug Plot strikes in Book VI, Chapter VII (see note to p. 321). But, though the Ashworths were good employers, their workers' village did not have gardens (Rhodes Boyson, *The Ashworth Cotton Enterprise* (Oxford: Clarendon Press, 1970), pp. 257–9) and they were Quakers, not Roman Catholics—unlike the Trafford family of Manchester. Since Thomas Trafford (1778–1852) was the commander of the Yeomanry at the Peterloo Massacre (1819), however, this too is only a partial source for a picture also based on accounts of Robert Owen's mills at New Lanark. The Yorkshire model villages of Saltaire (1851), Ackroyden (1859), and Ripley Ville (1866) are later in date than *Sybil*.

ventilation . . . in the House of Commons: when the Palace of Westminster was destroyed by fire in 1834, David Boswell Reid (1805–63) designed an innovative heating and 'displacement ventilation' system for the temporary building constructed in New Palace Yard to accommodate the Commons until the new Houses of Parliament were completed. Highly praised at the time, it became controversial in the 1850s when reused in Barry and Pugin's permanent building, probably because Barry altered Reid's plans to suit his own designs.

158 *the fee*: fee simple, the freehold ownership of property.

160 *the cotton*: Mr Trafford's factory here seems to be a cotton mill (appropriate if Mowbray is Manchester or Bolton) but later in the chapter Gerard pulls 'the wool' (which suggests a Yorkshire woollen mill, like those in Bingley).

164 *Mrs Lawrence's*: Louisa Lawrence (1803–55), a celebrated horticulturalist whose garden at Drayton Green was praised by the *Gardener's Magazine* in 1838 as the model suburban plot. She then moved to a larger garden at Ealing Park which Queen Victoria visited, as did the King of Saxony (see note to p. 81) in 1844. She was married to the surgeon Sir William Lawrence (1783–1867), whose *Natural History of Man* (1819) influenced the evolutionary theory of Wallace and Darwin.

167 *Community*: see note to p. 58.

171 *Robert Hind*: changed to 'Thomas Hind' in *1853* though not in the second instance below; see Thom Braun, '*Sybil*: A Misprint', *Notes and Queries* (June 1978), pp. 232–3.

Bigod and Bohun . . . forest laws: Roger Bigod (1245–1306), 5th Earl of Norfolk, and Humphrey Bohun (1249–98), Earl of Hereford, were powerful barons who had a series of quarrels with Edward I, in part about the jurisdiction of the royal forests. One of Scott's own footnotes to *Ivanhoe* (1819) describes the Forest Laws (which reserved to the Crown the right to hunt and to take firewood) as 'oppressive enactments' which 'were the produce of the Norman Conquest' (chapter 1); Magna Carta (1215) diminished their effect.

173 *Thomas à Kempis*: *The Imitation of Christ (De Imitatione Christi)* is a devotional book written 1418–27 at Zwolle (now in the Netherlands) by an Augustinian canon from Kempen, near Cologne, known as Thomas à Kempis. Popular with Protestants as well as Catholics, there were many English translations; this one is expensively illustrated with engravings after religious paintings.

BOOK IV

175 *Jamaica bill*: slavery was abolished in the British Empire in 1834 but in the West Indies slaves were indentured to their former owners as apprentices until 1838, while steps were taken to create a conventional system of law and order. The Jamaica Assembly, dominated by planters, refused to implement this so in 1839 the Whig government in London introduced a Bill to suspend the Assembly and impose direct rule. Radicals and many Whigs found this policy illiberal, the government's majority fell to five, and on 6 May it resigned.

Rads: the Radicals in Parliament were not a party but a miscellany of independent members and small groups with diverse views, including the Manchester School free-traders and the Utilitarian 'Philosophical Radicals'.

Lord John: Lord John Russell (1792–1878), leader of the Whig party in the Commons 1834–41, Home Secretary 1835–9, and later twice Prime Minister.

Chartists: Chartism was a response to the 1832 Reform Act's extension of the franchise to middle-class men but not to the working-class men who had campaigned for it, though it was also (in Disraeli's words) 'something between an economical and a political cause' (*Hansard*, 12 July 1839) and flared up when the economy was depressed. William Lovett founded the London Working Men's Association in 1836 which in June 1837 drew up a 'Charter' of six demands or 'Points': universal male suffrage, annual Parliaments, vote by secret ballot, payment for MPs, abolition of property qualification for MPs, and equal electoral districts (though the last of these was omitted from the 'Five Point' Charter of 1839). The Charter was published in May 1838. A National Convention assembled in London in February 1839 and in June presented a Petition to Parliament, where it was rejected on 12 July (see note to p. 191). There was a riot in Birmingham (see note to p. 241) and a clash between Chartist demonstrators and troops in the Welsh town of Newport on 4 November 1839 (the 'Newport Rising') where more than twenty people were killed. Many Chartist leaders were arrested and either imprisoned or transported in the spring of 1840. During the economic recession of 1842 a second Petition was presented and rejected; this was followed by the Plug Plot strikes and riots (see note to p. 304) in Staffordshire and Lancashire. A third and last Petition would be presented after a mass meeting on Kennington Common in April 1848; the movement had died out by the late 1850s.

176 *Jacquerie*: a peasants' revolt, first used of the French uprising of 1358, supposedly because the nobles assumed all lower-class men to be named 'Jacques'.

'qui vive': on the alert, literally a French sentry's 'Who goes there?'

pair: pairing is an agreement between two MPs of different parties that neither of them will vote in a particular division, thus giving themselves leave of absence from the debate.

Ormsby . . . White's . . . Eskdale's: Mr Ormsby (based on John Irving, 1766–1845, MP for County Antrim) and Lord Eskdale (based on the Tory politician William Lowther, 2nd Earl of Lonsdale, 1787–1872) had both appeared in *Coningsby*; White's is a club in St James's Street, founded in 1693 and Tory since the 1780s.

TABITHA CROESUS: a wealthy and charitable old maid. Tabitha (or Dorcas) was a Christian disciple in Joppa 'full of good works and alms-deeds' who worked with a circle of widows sewing clothes for the poor (Acts of the Apostles 9: 36–42); Croesus was a famously rich king of Lydia (560–546 BC).

Sidonia's: Sidonia is the Jewish multi-millionaire and mastermind who plays a significant role in *Coningsby* and an incidental one in *Tancred*; he is a fantasy of power, wealth, and wisdom based, in part, on Disraeli's friend Lionel Rothschild (1808–79).

the Golden Ball: a gilded time-ball above a clockmaker's shop in Cockspur Street, between Pall Mall and Trafalgar Square, demolished in 1924; the Duke of Wellington supposedly corrected his watch by it every morning on his way from Apsley House to the War Office.

178 *Mesmerist*: the theory of animal magnetism or mesmerism (now usually called hypnosis) formulated by Franz Mesmer (1734–1815) developed

into a therapeutic technique in the 1830s; John Elliotson (1791–1868) of University College Hospital began to use it to treat nervous disorders in 1837.

179 *burgesses*: see note to p. 15. Egerton is distinguishing urban MPs from the 'knights of the shires' who represented county constituencies.

180 *a viceroy*: of Ireland.

Lord Anson: in 1740 George Anson (1697–1762, later Admiral Lord Anson) commanded a squadron sent to harass Spanish ports in South America and capture the galleon which carried silver from Acapulco to Manila. Reduced to a single ship by bad weather, Anson crossed the Pacific, cruised for two months off the Philippines, captured the galleon, and returned to England in 1744. Anson's *Voyage Round the World* was published in 1748.

patent place: patents were royal grants of offices, titles, estates, and pensions (see note to p. 57); the meaning has since narrowed to the grant of an exclusive right to an invention.

181 *brougham*: a one-horse closed carriage; Barker & Co. (1710–1910) were a famous London firm of coachbuilders.

182 *Watteau . . . Cuyp*: Antoine Watteau (1684–1721), French painter; Aelbert Cuyp (1620–91), Dutch landscape painter.

Allori: probably a copy of the head of Judith in Christofano Allori's *Judith with the Head of Holofernes* (*c.* 1613) of which there are several versions and many copies, including those at Buckingham Palace, the Pitti Palace in Florence, and Tabley House, Cheshire. The English painter Sir Thomas Lawrence (1769–1830; 'poor' because he died insolvent) owned drawings by Allori's father Alessandro Allori (1535–1607) and Disraeli may also be conflating Christofano's Judith (who is an Old Testament heroine rather than a 'saint') with Guercino's paintings of sibyls: *The Libyan Sibyl* (1651) is in the Royal Collection. Sybil's hair is 'fair' in Book II, Chapter V; 'golden brown' here.

the Albany: built in 1802 between Piccadilly and Burlington Gardens as a set of chambers, or small apartments, for bachelors; Byron lived there, as had Disraeli's father before his marriage.

Reform: the Reform Club in Pall Mall, founded in 1836 for supporters of the Whig government which had passed the Reform Act in 1832.

Trenchard's speech: Trenchard is often said to be Thomas Milner Gibson (1806–84), Disraeli's schoolfellow at Higham Hill, who became Tory MP for Ipswich in 1837 but developed free-trade views, resigned in 1839, and returned as a Whig MP for Manchester in 1841. But though his views were changing, none of Gibson's speeches in the spring of 1839 was 'against the Opposition' in the manner described here and he did have a wife.

183 *twelve hundred a-yearers*: £1,200 was a customary salary for the more senior public offices to which government ministers had the power of appointment: Edwin Chadwick was paid this as Secretary to the Poor Law Commissioners.

184 *Finality speech of Lord John . . . frondeurs*: on 20 November 1837 the Whig Home Secretary, Lord John Russell, stated in the Commons that the Reform Act of 1832 had been introduced as 'a final measure'; Radicals saw this as a sign that the Whigs had turned Tory, rather as Disraeli, by 1845, would be accusing Peel's Tories of turning Whig. A *frondeur* is a fault-finder or malcontent (French).

stars and blue ribbons: emblems of the orders of knighthood (see note to p. 34); all wear stars, members of the Order of the Garter also wear a blue riband.

our boroughs: under the Reform Act (1832) fifty-six rotten and closed boroughs were abolished and thirty small boroughs lost one member each.

185 *the cottage circle*: the circle of King George IV (see note to p. 72).

Lansdowne House: see note to p. 20.

hachis: hash, literally minced meat (French).

the Standard: a London newspaper founded in 1827 and edited by Stanley Lees Giffard, known for his anti-Catholic and High Tory views.

186 *the Druid's Altar*: a crag overlooking the Aire Valley near Bingley in Yorkshire; Disraeli visited it with his wife and Lord John Manners in October 1844 and wrote to Manners on 12 May 1845: 'I was very pleased that you recognised the moor where we were companions. Do you remember your mounting the Druids altar? Mrs. Di. was frightened at your audacity. I think it gave me the idea of Walter Gerards rostrum' (*Letters*, 4.167). Mowbray Moor, however, is a combination of Yorkshire (Bingley) and Lancashire (Manchester), since the protest meetings held on it, here and in Book V, Chapter X, are clearly based on the two Chartist 'Monster Meetings' held on Kersal Moor, near Manchester, on 24 September 1838 and 25 May 1839. The first was attended by more than 50,000 people (reported as 300,000 by the *Morning Advertiser*), the second by about 30,000.

187 *a trump in the tender*: a hero to the hand-loom workers (weavers were known as 'loom tenders').

191 *Nobs*: the upper classes (as opposed to 'snobs', though this word has since reversed its meaning).

the National Convention: the first Chartist National Convention met in London on 4 February 1839; its National Petition would be presented to the House of Commons on 14 June by Thomas Attwood, MP for Birmingham, and debated on 12 July (see note to p. 175) when it was rejected by 235 to 46.

192 *boundary questions*: the Oregon Question was a long-running dispute between the British and American governments about the boundary between the United States and what is now Canada in the Pacific Northwest, first raised in the 1820s, substantially agreed in 1846, but only finally settled in 1872.

193 *Jamaica division*: see note to p. 175.

statue to the Duke of Wellington: this appears to be the statue by Francis Chantrey outside the Royal Exchange, paid for by the City of London and a public subscription in 1838, and unveiled in June 1844, rather than the statue (now at Aldershot) by Matthew Wyatt, funded by an appeal led by the Duke of Rutland in 1837, and originally placed on the triumphal arch at Hyde Park Corner (at that time set immediately in front of the Duke of Wellington's London home, Apsley House) in 1846.

one-pound notes: see note to p. 83.

194 *pietra dura*: inlay work, using pieces of marble and other stones to create decorative images, developed in Florence in the sixteenth century.

195 *the field of Evesham*: the Battle of Evesham, on 4 August 1265, at which rebel barons led by Simon de Montfort, Earl of Leicester, were defeated by the army of King Henry III.

196 *Lazzaroni*: the *lazzaroni* (Italian) were the poorest class in the Kingdom of Naples, so called from the hospital of St Lazarus which ministered to street people and the destitute; fiercely monarchist in their views, they resisted the French occupation in 1799.

197 *Paixhan's rockets*: Henri-Joseph Paixhan (1783–1854) was a French artillery officer who, in 1823, invented the first flat-trajectory gun firing explosive shells, rather than solid shot, thus revolutionizing naval warfare and ending the era of wooden warships. Disraeli is confusing Paixhan's guns with the military rockets developed by Sir William Congreve (1772–1828) in 1804 and used by the British army and navy until the 1850s.

the Queen's ball: the medieval fancy-dress ball held by Queen Victoria and Prince Albert would not in fact take place for another three years, in May 1842.

198 *sacred buildings are generally closed*: Westminster Abbey was open only between 11 a.m. and 3 p.m. in the 1840s (except for the services at 10 a.m. and 3 p.m.); Poets' Corner was free but there was an entrance charge of 6*d*. for the rest of the building and much of it could only be seen with a guide. In a debate on the report of the Select Committee on National Monuments in 1842, Herbert Curteis (MP for Rye) complained about 'the barricades erected on Sundays in Westminster Abbey for the purpose of preventing the people getting a view of the monuments' and pointed out that at St Paul's such barriers had been removed (*Hansard*, 14 July 1842); the matter would be raised again in Parliament in August 1845, when the Abbey abolished the 6*d*. charge except for the Chapels and the Choir.

the Templars: the Poor Fellow-Soldiers of Christ and of the Temple of Solomon were a religious order of crusading knights (1129–1312) which owned property throughout Europe. When Templars in England were arrested for heresy in 1308 their rural estates were transferred to the similar order of Knights Hospitallers of St John, only to be confiscated by the Crown in 1540; their land in London was given to the Duke of Lancaster and became the Inns of Court of the Middle and Inner Temple.

199 *changed the religion of their country*: the established religion of England had been changed by the Act of Supremacy 1534, making Henry VIII supreme head of the Church, and was altered again under Edward VI, Queen Mary, and Queen Elizabeth. Disraeli, however, is probably referring to more recent changes: disestablishment under the Commonwealth, restoration in 1662, the Act of Toleration in 1689, the Repeal of the Test Acts and Catholic Emancipation in 1828 and 1829, the Irish Church Temporalities Act 1833, and the Established Church Act 1836.

mortgaging the industry of the country: Disraeli sees the national debt (see note to p. 21) as a form of mortgage, since future generations of taxpayers are required to pay the interest on previous government spending; it 'protects property' because it is a substitute for direct taxation of the wealthy at the time of the expenditure.

ship-money: a medieval requirement that coastal towns should provide the King with ships in time of war, this became a tax which, unusually, did not require the consent of Parliament. When Charles I imposed it in 1634, on inland counties and in time of peace, it provoked a fierce constitutional dispute. John Hamden (see note to p. 13) was tried and convicted in 1638 for refusing to pay it; the Bill of Rights (1689; see note to p. 21) prohibited all forms of extra-parliamentary taxation.

Hansard: the published transcripts of British parliamentary debates, named after Thomas Curson Hansard (1776–1833), who printed them from 1809, published them from 1812, and had his name on the title page from 1829. The reference to 'voting against a Minister' who has 'changed all the policy which you have been elected to support' is a defence of Disraeli's own, apparently disloyal campaign against his party leader, Sir Robert Peel, in the months in which he was writing *Sybil*.

railway shares: hundreds of companies were launched to build railway lines in the mid-1840s: shares could be purchased with a 10 per cent deposit, and high dividends were promised. The resulting 'Railway Mania' would collapse in 1847 leaving many investors ruined and many lines unbuilt. Disraeli had shares in the Dyffryn, Llynvi and Porthcawl Railway but this had been founded in 1825 and would operate successfully until the 1960s.

201 *Abingdon Street*: a road between the Palace of Westminster and Millbank; the houses built along it in the 1750s were destroyed in the twentieth century to create the open space of College Green.

202 *Vanbrugh*: Sir John Vanbrugh (1664–1726), dramatist and architect, was a pioneer of the English baroque style; St John's, Smith Square (1728), was designed in that style by Thomas Archer (1688–1743). Smith Square and the elegant streets round it were laid out in the 1720s but the area became shabby and bordered the 'Devil's Acre' slum: Victoria Street (1845–51) and Parliament Square (1868) would be built as slum-clearance measures.

203 *Temple Bar*: a neoclassical arched gateway of 1670–2 which stood in Fleet Street on the site of one of the gates of the walled, medieval City. Long

seen as an inconvenient obstacle to traffic, it would be removed in 1880 but has now returned to the City in the new Paternoster Square.

205 *kingdom of Cockaigne*: a legendary place of idleness and luxury.

claiming the ancient baronies . . . peerage in abeyance: baronies are the lowest of the five ranks of the peerage (Duke, Marquess, Earl, Viscount, Baron) though, like the others, they had (until 1999) the right to vote in the House of Lords and are (with the exception of modern life peers) hereditary. Dating from the twelfth century, when Henry II created the title by summoning the owners of manors to attend the King's Council (later the House of Lords), they could die out or be absorbed into the family titles of dukes and earls. They could, however, be revived from 'abeyance' because 'baronies by writ of summons' were inherited not by 'the heir male' but by 'heirs of the body'—that is, daughters as well as sons. If the daughter of a baron was his only surviving child, she would inherit the barony and pass it on to her own heir. But there was no precedence between daughters so, if there were two or more of them, the title went 'into abeyance' until such time as the heirs of all but one had died out. This meant that professional genealogists, like Baptist Hatton, could sometimes discover legitimate rights to a barony hundreds of years after the families involved had forgotten about them. The Botetourt case in 1764 (reviving a barony in abeyance since 1406) was the first successful recovery of a long-lapsed title and by the early nineteenth century the process had become a flourishing branch of legal practice. Samuel Egerton Bridges, a literary antiquarian and friend of Isaac D'Israeli, had his claim for the barony of Chandos refused in 1803. But others were successful: the Camoys and Braye baronies in 1839, Beaumont in 1840, and Hastings in 1841. By the 1850s the House of Lords was losing patience with the burden placed on its Committee of Privileges by such business and the Mowbray case in 1877 would be the last successful claim in the nineteenth century (ironically, given the use of the name in *Sybil*, though it is a fictitious earldom, rather than the barony, which the Warren family is given in 1827).

kidney table: a curved table, in the shape of a kidney, into which a chair can be fitted.

206 *white Persian cat*: the motif of a villain stroking a white, long-haired cat would be borrowed for the 1963 film version of Ian Fleming's novel *From Russia with Love* (1957), possibly at the suggestion of the novelist Len Deighton, the first of the film's several screenwriters.

207 *sheriff*: see note to p. 47.

coronet with two balls: a marquess's coronet has four silver balls and four strawberry leaves (though Hatton perhaps means the six silver balls of a baron's coronet); Firebrace, like the real Sir Richard Broun, is trying to involve the baronets in coronations and has invented a ceremonial dress, with a coronet of two balls, for them (see Book II, Chapter II).

shall this year make three: in reality two baronies were called out of abeyance in 1839: Camoys (dormant since 1426) and Braye (dormant since 1557).

208 *Boodle's*: a club founded in Pall Mall in 1762 by Lord Shelburne (see note to p. 17); it moved to St James's Street in 1782 and was predominantly Tory. In *1845* Hatton's subsequent reference was to 'twenty members of Brookes' (corrected *1853*).

Solomon Medina: Solomon de Medina (1650–1730), a Jewish financier who came to England with William III, as an army contractor, and served the Duke of Marlborough in the same role during the War of the Spanish Succession; the first Jew to receive an English knighthood, he was a benefactor of the Bevis Marks Synagogue (attended by the Disraeli family until 1817).

Lord Vavasour . . . single writ of summons: the barony of Vavasour was created in 1299 but lapsed when the 3rd Baron (d. 1322) was not summoned to Parliament and became abeyant, even as a nominal title, on the death of the 25th (so-called) Baron in 1826. Baronies were created by a personal summons to attend the King's Council (see note to p. 205). Though Lord Abergavenny's Case (1610) had created a precedent for establishing a barony on the basis of a single writ of summons, in practice the Privileges Committee of the House of Lords required evidence of a long series of writs before a family's claim would be accepted: Blackstone's *Commentaries on the Laws of England* (1765–9) held that there must be at least two writs and evidence of attendance in two separate Parliaments.

Lovel . . . Lord Bardolf: the barony of Lovel had been forfeit since the attainder of Francis Lovel in 1485, and the barony of Bardolf since 1406 when Thomas Bardolf joined the Percy rebellion against Henry IV. Notional rights in both of them had descended through Lovel's sisters to the Barons Beaumont, a title which had itself become abeyant in 1507 but would be revived in 1840 for Miles Thomas Stapleton (1805–54) of Carlton Towers, Yorkshire, a Roman Catholic, minor novelist, and acquaintance of Disraeli.

209 *Edict of Nantes*: the Edict of Nantes (1598) gave French Protestants, or Huguenots, political rights; it was revoked by Louis XIV in 1685 causing an exodus of Protestants, many of them skilled silkweavers.

211 *Marquis of Granby, which might have been a sign . . . Bunbury, of Ranelegh*: there is, in fact, a Marquis of Granby pub in Romney Street (then Vine Street), close to Smith Square. Henry William Bunbury (1750–1811) was a caricaturist who made prints of London society in St James's Park and Carlton House gardens in the 1780s. Ranelagh Gardens in Chelsea (in the grounds of Ranelagh House, originally built by Solomon Rieti, uncle of Disraeli's grandmother) were pleasure gardens opened in 1742 and used for concerts, balls, and parties until their closure in 1803.

213 *'Qui laborat, orat'*: 'He who works, prays', a version of the motto of the Benedictine order of monks, 'Laborare est orare' ('To work is to pray', Latin).

216 *St. Stephen's*: Parliament: St Stephen's Chapel, the chapel of the old Royal Palace of Westminster, was the chamber used by the House of Commons from 1547 until its destruction by fire in 1834.

217 *the Athenæum*: club in Pall Mall, founded in 1824 by J. W. Croker (Disraeli's 'Mr Rigby') and known for its intellectual and artistic membership. Isaac D'Israeli belonged but Benjamin's application was rejected in 1832 and he would not be made a member until 1866. The rejection may have guided his choice of club for the criminal Baptist Hatton.

218 *the Antiquarian Society*: the Society of Antiquaries, founded in London in 1707; Isaac Disraeli became a Fellow in 1821.

Dugdale . . . Selden . . . forfeiture or abeyance: Sir William Dugdale (1605–86), herald and antiquary, protégé of Sir Christopher Hatton (1605–70), and author of *The Baronage of England* (1675–6). John Selden (1584–1654), lawyer and scholar, supporter of the Petition of Right (1628; see note to p. 21), whose writings included *The Privileges of the Baronage of England* (1642). Forfeiture and abeyance are means by which baronies can become extinct or dormant (see note to p. 205).

Lafitte . . . devilled biscuit: Chateau Lafite (Lafite-Rothschild since 1868) is one of the four Bordeaux wines awarded *premier cru* status in 1855; devilled biscuits were buttered, sprinkled with cayenne pepper, and grilled, often with the addition of anchovies and curry paste.

219 *Baron Valence . . . Talbot . . . Sybil*: though the Valence family was real (see note to p. 70), the barony of Valence is fictitious. Unlike the Talbot family, who have been both earls of Shrewsbury and Barons Talbot since 1442, the real Valences were simply earls—a title which (unlike baronies) cannot usually be restored from abeyance (see note to p. 205). Sybil does not seem to have been a name used by the de Valence family themselves, though Joan de Valence (née Munchensi) had an aunt called Sybil Marshal (1201–45) who married William de Ferrers, Earl of Derby, and had daughters called Sybil, Maud, and Joan. The heroine of Bulwer-Lytton's medievalist novel *The Last of the Barons* (1843; set during the Wars of the Roses) is called Sibyll Warner.

crook-backed Richard: King Richard III (1452–85), depicted by Shakespeare as a hunchbacked monster.

221 *Sir Robert . . . Lord Stanley*: Sir Robert Peel (see note to p. 23); Edward Stanley, later Lord Derby (see note to p. 111).

222 *with Monmouth at the peace*: Lord Monmouth appears in *Coningsby* and was probably based on Francis Seymour-Conway, 3rd Marquess of Hertford (1777–1842), who was often in Paris and had acted (as Lord Yarmouth) as a confidential negotiator with the French government in 1806. The first Treaty (or 'Peace') of Paris was signed in May 1814; a second was required in November 1815 after Napoleon's return from Elba and defeat at Waterloo.

'four stars in India stock': shareholders in the East India Company (see note to p. 33) had voting rights in the Court of Proprietors according to the size of their stockholding (shown in lists by asterisks): £1,000 stock one vote; £3,000 stock two votes; £6,000 stock three votes; £10,000 stock

four votes. Mr Ormsby is based on John Irving (see note to p. 176) who was indeed extremely wealthy, having founded the Ballylig Lime Works, ancestor of Blue Circle Cement.

223 *Watier's*: a gambling and dining club in Piccadilly, 1807–19, founded by the Prince Regent, with advice from Jean-Baptiste Watier (his chef at Carlton House) and with Labourie as its cook, in response to the dullness of the food at other gentlemen's clubs.

the Marylebone vestry: the parish vestry (see note to p. 29) of St Marylebone was the administrative authority for this large part of London until 1889 and was known for its radical sympathies and interest in national as well as local politics.

224 *nous verrons*: we shall see (French).

225 *Church Commission*: see note to p. 95.

Exeter Hall . . . Wilberforce . . . Clarkson: Exeter Hall (1829–1907) was a building in the Strand used for public meetings, especially by religious and philanthropic organizations. William Wilberforce (1759–1833) and Thomas Clarkson (1760–1846) were Evangelical Anglicans who had been leaders of the Committee for the Abolition of the Slave Trade. The 'right of search' was the controversial matter, frequently discussed in Parliament, of whether the Royal Navy should stop foreign vessels suspected of carrying slaves (see *Hansard*, 15 August 1839).

the Buck-hounds: the Mastership of the Buckhounds was an office in the Royal Household (see note to p. 299); created in 1536 to manage the King's pack of staghounds, it developed into the role of a junior minister and was abolished in 1901. The real Master of the Buckhounds in Peel's government of 1841–6 was the soldier and former Tory MP James St Clair-Erskine, 3rd Earl of Rosslyn.

226 *Lord Melbourne or Lord John*: William Lamb (1779–1848; Viscount Melbourne 1828) was the Whig Prime Minister and Lord John Russell the Home Secretary at the time of the Jamaica debate in 1839 (see note to p. 175).

233 *in petto*: in private, secret (Italian: 'in the breast').

petticoats!: the Bedchamber plot; see note to p. 234.

the farce of the 'Invincibles': *The Invincibles; or, Les Femmes soldats* was a two-act musical farce by Thomas Morton (see note to p. 68) first produced at Covent Garden in February 1828. It is not an intellectually demanding play: the mistresses of three French military officers disguise themselves as soldiers in order to get into Fort Ravage, where their lovers have been confined during the carnival; wearing tight military uniforms, they are put through a series of military exercises to prove their credentials. Disraeli's point is that the Whig government of 1839 was similarly rescued by the Ladies of the Bedchamber.

the Meal-tub plot: a fabricated 'popish plot' to kill Charles II and Lord Shaftesbury (intended to discredit the future James II), concocted in 1679 by Thomas Dangerfield and so called because the supposedly incriminating documents were hidden in a tub of oatmeal.

234 *the impartial pen*: Disraeli's irony is so elaborate here that his logic becomes hard to follow. In May 1839 the Whig government had lost the confidence of the House of Commons, so resigned. When Peel tried to form a Tory government, Queen Victoria refused to have her Whig Ladies of the Bedchamber replaced by Tory ladies. She thus exercised the royal prerogative to keep the Whigs in office ('the Bedchamber plot'). Disraeli approves of the royal prerogative but paradoxically suggests that Peel should have formed a government. The explanation is that Peel is not really a Tory but a Whiggish 'Conservative' (see Introduction) who could have worked with Whig court officials ('ladies' because the monarch was female) to implement policies which were Whig in all but name. In 1839 Disraeli's views had been rather different: in letters to *The Times* published over the signature 'Laelius' he had rebuked the Queen for her behaviour (13 May 1839) and praised Peel as a man of 'unimpeached integrity' and 'unrivalled Parliamentary talents' (28 May 1839). For a later account of the same matter see *Endymion*, Chapter 58.

235 *tariff negotiated at Utrecht . . . every labourer a home*: the Treaty of Utrecht (1712–13) included an agreement to remove trade barriers between Britain and France (see note to p. 18). The Old Poor Law of 1601 and 1662 (see note to p. 43) gave labourers rights to welfare payments from the poor rate without having to leave their home for a workhouse.

St. John . . . Wyndham: Henry St John, Viscount Bolingbroke (see note to p. 15). Sir William Wyndham (1688–1740), Tory politician, ally of Bolingbroke, and opponent of Walpole; his son would be the 2nd Earl of Egremont (see note to p. 5).

236 *parochial constitution of the country sacrificed*: by the New Poor Law of 1834 (see note to p. 43).

238 *new generation*: 'The New Generation' is the subtitle of Disraeli's *Coningsby* (1844).

BOOK V

241 *news from Birmingham*: the National Convention of Chartists met in London in February 1839; after the presentation of the Charter to Parliament on 14 June the Convention dispersed, reconvening in Birmingham on 1 July. The local magistrates asked for police reinforcements from London who clashed with a gathering in the Bull Ring on 4–5 July. The Riot Act was read, three Chartist leaders were arrested, and the Convention returned to London.

242 *the Bull Ring*: a marketplace in the centre of Birmingham, first established in 1154, rebuilt in 1832, and so called because butchers had once kept live cattle there.

results of the Charter without the intervention of its machinery: a version of Disraeli's own remark in his speech during the debate on the Chartist Petition: 'although they did not approve of the remedy suggested by the

Chartists, it did not follow that they should not attempt to cure the disease complained of' (*Hansard*, 12 July 1839); Disraeli voted to reject the Petition.

243 *his sultana queen . . . Lord Halifax*: the attribution is corrected to 'Sheffield, Duke of Buckingham' in *1853*; Halifax refers to the King's 'predilection for . . . *sauntering*' in his *Character of King Charles II* (1685, first published 1750) but it was John Sheffield, Duke of Buckingham and Normanby, in his *A Character of Charles II, King of England* (1696), who said that this 'Sauntring . . . was the true *Sultana Queen* he delighted in' (*Works*, 1723, 2.61). Disraeli took the phrase and its misattribution from his father's *Curiosities of Literature* (1791); see Daniel Whitmore, 'A Mistaken Allusion in Disraeli's Sybil', *Notes and Queries* (August 1983), pp. 300–1.

244 *the prayer*: a petition to Parliament must contain a 'prayer', or request to the House that is within its competence to grant. In 1842 debates on petitions would be abolished and they have since been sent to the relevant government department, with the House considering only the Minister's reply.

man of light and leading: 'The men of England, the men, I mean, of light and leading in England . . . would be ashamed . . . to profess any religion in name, which by their proceedings, they appear to contemn' (Edmund Burke, *Reflections on the French Revolution* in his *Writings and Speeches* (Oxford: Clarendon Press, 1989), 8.151).

245 *gardens*: St James's Park, originally a marshy field attached to a leper hospital, turned into a garden by James I, and given a 'Dutch canal' by Charles II. A Chinese pagoda and bridge were built in 1814 for a gala to celebrate the anniversary of the Battle of the Nile; the pagoda burnt down during the firework display and the bridge was demolished in 1825, just before the canal was remodelled into its subsequent 'winding' shape.

248 *Western Minster*: Westminster Abbey.

251 *the glory of life has gone*: Eli's 'daughter in law, Phinehas's wife . . . named the child I-chabod . . . And said, The glory is departed from Israel' (1 Samuel 4: 19–22), though Disraeli is also thinking of Wordsworth's 'Whither is fled the visionary gleam? | Where is it now, the glory and the dream?' ('Ode, Intimations of Immortality' (1807), ll. 56–7).

256 *to another town*: Birmingham (see note to p. 241).

259 *assoiled*: absolved, set free.

261 *The caverns of my mind*: the image of the mind or memory as a 'cavern' derives from Chapter 17 of *The Confessions of St Augustine* (AD 397–400).

265 *on whose breast reposed the divine Friend*: corrected to 'who reposed on the breast of the divine Friend' in *1853*: 'Now there was leaning on Jesus' bosom one of his disciples, whom Jesus loved' (John 13: 23). The 'beloved disciple' is usually taken to be St John, the Evangelist and Apostle, a Jewish fisherman from Galilee.

the Strand . . . coffee-house: the Arundel Coffee House, in Arundel Street just off the Strand, was used by the Chartist National Convention in 1839 as a London meeting place when they no longer needed their larger premises at Bolt Court, Fleet Street.

St. Stephen's: see note to p. 216; in 1839 the Convention held debates in the Crown & Anchor Tavern in the Strand (near the Arundel Coffee House) and, on 22 April, had a meeting on Kennington Common (see note to p. 278). The Radical MP Thomas Duncombe said in the Commons that 'in this metropolis two other Parliaments were actually sitting . . . a corn law Parliament . . . and a Chartist Parliament' (*The Times*, 6 February 1839), though it was actually the Anti-Corn-Law delegates who met in a hotel in Palace Yard, Westminster.

clock of St Martin's: St Martin-in-the-Fields church, Trafalgar Square.

267 *Tom Paine, Cobbett, Thistlewood . . . General Jackson*: Tom Paine (1737–1809), author of *The Rights of Man* (1791–2). William Cobbett (see note to p. 117), imprisoned for seditious libel 1810–12. Arthur Thistlewood (1774–1820), member of the Society of Spencean Philanthropists, executed for his part in the Cato Street Conspiracy (1820), a plot to assassinate the cabinet. Andrew Jackson (1767–1845), military commander against the British in 1812, President of the USA 1829–37, and associated with popular or 'Jacksonian', rather than elitist, or Jeffersonian, democracy (though also a slave owner and fierce enemy of Native Americans).

shrub: rum or brandy mixed with sugar and lemon juice.

268 *Seven Dials*: an area near Covent Garden where seven streets converge, developed in the 1690s and a notorious slum by the early nineteenth century.

269 *entrails and carrion . . . colossal brewery*: on the butchers of Newport Market see note to p. 10; the enormous Woodyard Brewery of Combe, Delafield & Co. was in Castle Street (now Shelton Street), Long Acre.

270 *her Majesty's carriages*: the London Hackney Carriages Acts of 1831 and 1843 transferred control of London cabs, or hackney carriages, from a local Board of Commissioners to the Crown (operating through the Home Secretary and the police).

Mendicity Society: the London Mendicity Society was founded in 1818 to discourage begging; it issued tickets, to be given instead of money, which could be exchanged for food or medicine at an office in Red Lion Square.

272 *jarvies . . . link*: jarvies were drivers of hackney carriages; link boys provided torches in the era before street-lighting; here the coachmen seem to be sitting in the pub and paying a link boy to respond and fetch them when they are summoned by a fare.

snapdragon: raisins in a dish of flaming brandy.

273 *Soult . . . Diebitsch*: Marshal Soult (1769–1851) commanded Napoleon's forces in Spain and Portugal during the Peninsular War (1807–14), where the Polish Legion fought as allies of the French. Field Marshal Hans Diebitsch (1785–1831) was a German-born commander of the Russian army who in 1830 invaded Poland to suppress the November Uprising. After a series of inconclusive battles, including the Battle of Grochow on

the 'banks of the Vistula' in February 1831, Diebitsch died of cholera but his successor completed the conquest and the remnants of the Polish army crossed into Prussia in October 1831 to become exiles.

273 *prigged a watch from a cove what was lushy . . . Kinsington*: stolen a watch from a drunk; Kensington is on the other side of Hyde Park from the ficti-tious Deloraine House (probably based on Londonderry House) in Park Lane, Mayfair.

quid: a piece of chewing tobacco.

Mazurka: a traditional Polish dance made fashionable by the pieces writ-ten for it by Frédéric Chopin between 1825 and 1849; ironically there is a Polish veteran sleeping rough in the park outside.

in the Russian fashion: lighting in Russian Orthodox churches is tradition-ally confined to the faces of the icons; here just the statues are lit.

274 *Repose is the characteristic of sculpture*: Lady Joan, the learned bluestocking, is echoing Johann Winckelmann (1717–68), whose *History of Ancient Art* (1764) influentially argued that 'repose' or serenity ('Heiterkeit') was the key quality of Greek sculpture.

277 *National Holiday*: National Strike; William Benbow (1787–1864) had pub-lished a scheme for a general strike in a pamphlet entitled *Grand National Holiday and Congress of the Productive Classes* (1832). The Chartists adopted Benbow's idea of a 'Sacred Month' (without work) in 1839 but dropped it when he was arrested for seditious libel.

new Police Act: though the County Police Act 1839 (see note to p. 62) implemented the recommendations of a Royal Commission set up in 1836, the three Bills in July and August 1839 to transfer control of the police in Birmingham, Manchester, and Bolton to the Home Secretary were a response to recent unrest. Disraeli attacked the Birmingham Bill as 'hos-tile to the liberties of the people' (*Hansard*, 15 August 1839); control would be returned to the local authorities in 1842.

Wales: an anticipation of the Newport Rising (see note to p. 175).

278 *White Conduit House . . . Kennington Common*: White Conduit House (1649–1849) in Pentonville was a tavern and tea-room next to a cricket pitch (the predecessor of Lord's) where open-air meetings could be held; some of the Tolpuddle Martyrs were greeted with a dinner here after their release from Australia in 1838. Kennington Common (surviving, in part, as Kennington Park and The Oval) was an open space in Lambeth, con-veniently close to Westminster for demonstrations; the last big Chartist meeting would be held here in 1848.

Stevens: Joseph Rayner Stephens (1805–79), Methodist preacher, advo-cate of the disestablishment of the Church of England, Tory Radical, and (though he disliked the label) Chartist orator whose speeches drew enor-mous crowds in the north. In the summer of 1839 he was actually under arrest and awaiting trial in Chester Castle.

the Polish count . . . broadside: Count Tadeusz Kosciuszko (1746–1817) formed units of peasants armed with scythes and pikes (*kosynierzy*) for his uprising against Russian rule in Poland in 1794 and they were used again, against the Russian army led by Diebitsch (see note to p. 273), in 1831; the pamphlet is the *Brief Treatise on Scythes and Pikes* (1794) by Kosciuszko's supporter, the architect Chrystian Piotr Aigner (1756–1841). A broadside is a large sheet of paper printed, like a poster, on one side only.

John Frost: Welsh Chartist leader (1784–1877); a prosperous tailor with radical views and formerly Mayor of Newport, arrested for his part in the Newport Rising of November 1839 in which twenty-two people were killed. Convicted of high treason in 1840, and sentenced to be hung, drawn, and quartered (the last time that sentence was imposed), he was instead transported to Tasmania, where he worked as a schoolteacher, returning to Britain in 1856.

279 *earth had anything so fair*: 'Earth has not anything to show more fair', Wordsworth, 'Composed upon Westminster Bridge, September 3, 1802' (1807).

281 *Bow Street*: there was a magistrates' court in Bow Street, Covent Garden, from 1740 to 2006; the Bow Street Runners were based there 1750–1839 and the Metropolitan Police Service, which gradually replaced them, built a station house in Bow Street in 1832.

284 *Dick Curtis . . . Dutch Sam*: Dick Curtis (1802–43) was a boxer, born in Southwark and known as 'The Pet of the Fancy'. Samuel Elias (1775–1816), known as 'Dutch Sam', 'The Terrible Jew', and 'The Man with the Iron Hand', was born in Whitechapel to a family of Jewish émigrés from Holland and was the boxer who invented the right-hand uppercut, though his son 'Young Dutch Sam' (1808–43), welterweight champion in the 1820s, is more likely to have been the inspector's 'tutor'.

gin palaces . . . slang taverns: gin palaces, first opened in the 1820s, were elaborately decorated bars which sold spirits; a slang tavern was a similarly showy wine and beer house. Slums have smart pubs.

285 *the bars*: *1853*; 'her bars' *1845*.

286 *the Secretary of State*: the Home Secretary, Lord John Russell.

287 *the New Police*: the Metropolitan Police Service, founded in 1829, had fully replaced the Bow Street Runners only in 1839, so was still relatively 'new' in 1845.

288 *a tick*: a debt.

289 *my uncle's*: the pawnbroker's.

hymn of Labour: probably 'Uphold those bold Comrades, who suffer for you', the Chartist hymn quoted in the letter of protest written by John Frost (see note to p. 278) to Lord John Russell in 1839, after Frost had been dismissed as a magistrate.

290 *Moslemin summoned by the sacred standard*: 'Moslemin', the Arabic plural of Moslem, here used as a singular; the battle standard of Mohammad, originally attached to the spear of his ally Buraydah ibn al-Khusaib, was

acquired by the Turkish Sultan Selim I (1465–1520), kept in the Topkapi Palace, and displayed whenever a sultan appeared before his army.

292 *bestow my tediousness*: an allusion to Shakespeare's *Much Ado About Nothing* 3.5.18–21.

293 *Two hundred thousand human beings*: there were probably about 30,000 people at the second Kersal Moor Monster Meeting on 25 May 1839 but, as with the first one (see note to p. 186), some newspaper reports gave a higher figure.

295 *Kelly*: Fitzroy Kelly KC (1796–1880; knighted 1845), lawyer and Tory MP; well known at the time of *Sybil's* first appearance for his recent defence of the notorious 'Quaker murderer' John Tawell, he had defended the Welsh Chartist leader John Frost (see note to p. 278) during his trial for High Treason in 1840, after the Newport Rising.

BOOK VI

296 *gentleman in Downing Street*: Sir Robert Peel, Prime Minister since 30 August 1841. His 'companion' is the Home Secretary, Sir James Graham (1792–1861); the second Chartist Petition had been rejected on 3 May 1842; strikes in the Staffordshire mines had begun in July, and the Plug Plot strikes and riots in Lancashire would begin on 8 August, three days after this conversation. As Peel says, Parliament would be prorogued (not sitting again until February 1843) on 12 August 1842.

297 *Polish corn . . . British income tax*: Peel's 1842 Budget changed the sliding scale of the Corn Law to maintain the price of wheat at 50–60 shillings per quarter; this meant that at some points the duty was less than half that previously charged on imported corn. He also cut the tariff on the import of live cattle and reintroduced income tax (abolished in 1816) at a flat rate of 3% on incomes over £150 a year.

eight hundred articles: the 1842 Budget removed or reduced duties on more than 700 articles.

299 *Yeomanry*: see note to p. 353.

the Household: in the Middle Ages the members of the Royal Household were, in effect, the government but the posts have gradually lost their political function and become (with the exception of government whips) ceremonial or domestic. In the 1840s the eighteen lords and one lady (Mistress of the Robes) who formed Her Majesty's Household were technically 'Ministers not in Cabinet'.

300 *felon confinement*: there was a distinction between prisoners, such as debtors and 'prisoners of state', who were merely 'confined' and felons who were 'punished'. Feargus O'Connor, editor of the *Northern Star*, was imprisoned in York Castle in 1840 for publishing a seditious libel; the chairman of magistrates wrote to the Home Office in June 1840 to confirm that 'Mr O'Connor is not subject to any indignities of the person', was not

required to clean his own chamber, had 'animal food' (meat) and wine, clean linen, a chair and a table, and his own clothes. The Home Secretary replied that O'Connor should additionally have newspapers and be allowed to receive visitors. Other, less conspicuous Chartist prisoners were more harshly treated.

the convent at York: see note to p. 75.

302 *Pennsylvanian Bank*: the Bank of Pennsylvania, founded in 1780 to provide funds for the Continental Army during the Revolutionary War, became notorious in 1798 when it was the scene of America's first major bank robbery. The criminal, Isaac Davis, had the effrontery to deposit his ill-gotten gains in the bank from which he had recently stolen them.

303 *pool of Bethesda*: a pool in Jerusalem with healing powers where Jesus cures a crippled man waiting for his turn in the water (John 5:1–15).

twist: a drink which mixes two ingredients, usually gin or brandy and hot water.

304 *Sun . . . Dispatch . . . Bell's Life*: if this is the *Sun* published 1792–1806 by John Heriot (1760–1833) as part of the Pitt government's campaign to counter revolutionary opinion, Chaffing Jack is drawing on a rather distant memory; the *Weekly Dispatch* (1801–1928) was a Sunday newspaper later merged with the *Sunday Express*; *Bells' Life in London and Sporting Chronicle* (1822–86) was a popular broadsheet known for its coverage of racing and boxing.

in Lancashire: the Plug Plot (so called because strikers in Lancashire knocked the plugs out of boilers to shut down mills powered by steam) was a strike which began in July 1842 among the Staffordshire miners and spread to Lancashire, starting in Stalybridge on 8 August (see note to p. 315) before moving to Ashton, Manchester, and Preston, where four strikers were shot by troops on 13 August (see note to p. 332). Many arrests were made, of both Chartists and Union leaders, and the strikes ended gradually in late August and September.

305 *Mowbray Staty*: Mowbray Fair, an annual 'statute fair' at which servants and other workers would be hired.

306 *by jingo!*: a popular exclamation used since the seventeenth century, perhaps originally 'By Gingulph' (St Gangulphus of Burgundy), itself a minced oath to avoid saying 'By Jesus'; in the late 1870s it would become associated with aggressive nationalism or 'jingoism'.

Baden: Baden-Baden is a spa in south-west Germany; a popular high-society resort in the mid-nineteenth century, it became known as 'Europe's summer capital'.

Melton: Melton Mowbray, a town in the Leicestershire fox-hunting country of the Cottesmere, Quorn, and Belvoir Hunts, and supposedly the source of the phrase 'to paint the town red' after a drunken frolic there in 1837.

308 *the Prince*: Prince Albert of Saxe-Coburg (1819–61) married Queen Victoria in February 1840. In Book V, Chapter VII, during the Bedchamber Crisis of

1839 (see note to p. 234), the Tory Lady St Julians was seeking a place as a member of the Royal Household; now, in 1842, with a Tory government actually in office, she has lost her chance by annoying the Prince Consort.

309 *anti-Corn-law League*: founded in 1838 by Richard Cobden (1804–65) and John Bright (1811–89) to campaign for the abolition of the Corn Laws and for free trade rather than protection of British agriculture.

314 *Benefit Societies . . . Sick and Burial Clubs*: savings clubs in which the poor could build up funds for funeral expenses or illness.

315 *Staley Bridge*: Stalybridge, now part of Greater Manchester, was a cotton manufacturing town which contributed 10,000 signatures to the Chartist petition of 1842; the Lancashire phase of the Plug Plot Riots began there that August (see note to p. 304).

316 *frieze-coats*: Irish peasants, from the coarse woollen cloth of which their clothes were made.

a castle: Gerard has been held in York Castle, rebuilt as a prison in 1701.

317 *this day se'nnight*: in a week's (seven nights') time.

319 *pikeman*: a miner who cuts coal with a pickaxe.

320 *conversion of Constantine*: the Roman Emperor Constantine the Great (AD 306–37) saw a cross in the sky with the words 'In this sign you will conquer' at the Battle of the Milvian Bridge in 312; his Edict of Milan in 313 ended the persecution of Christians.

Pilgrimage of Grace: an uprising in Yorkshire in 1536 against the dissolution of the monasteries and Henry VIII's break with Rome. The insurgents occupied York but were dispersed after (false) promises of a reprieve for the abbeys and a general pardon; their leader, Robert Aske, was executed in 1537 at York Castle.

321 *oriflamme*: the sacred banner of the abbey of St Denis, used by the kings of France in the Middle Ages when leading armies to war.

within his own experience: the experience was not direct (Disraeli was in London and Bradenham during the Plug Plot strikes of August 1842) but he appears to have heard about it from his acquaintance Henry Ashworth (see note to p. 157) whose New Eagley and Egerton Mills near Bolton had their boiler plugs drawn on 15 August: 'The crowd then begged politely for food . . . but took none of the ripe fruit from the mill and house gardens' (Boyson, *The Ashworth Cotton Enterprise*, p. 214 and p. 259). The incident had been mentioned in the *Westminster Review*, 38 (1842), p. 395.

326 *'Over the left'*: not so ('over the left shoulder with it').

Nobs: see note to p. 191.

march of mind: 'The March of Mind' is the title of chapter 2 of *Crotchet Castle* (1831) by Thomas Love Peacock (see Introduction) which satirizes the Society for the Diffusion of Useful Knowledge (1826–48), founded by Henry Brougham to provide reading material for newly literate members of the working class.

327 *Congo*: Congou (or kang-hu) is a black Chinese tea. There was a tax on tea in Britain until 1929: the strikers are depriving the government of revenue by not drinking it.

'*Oh, no, we never!*': 'Oh, no! We never mention her', a popular ballad by Thomas Haynes Bayly (1797–1839).

Bastile: the Bastille was a medieval fortress on the east of Paris, used as a state prison; the attack on it (14 July 1789) began the French Revolution. In England the name was satirically applied to the workhouses built for the New Poor Law of 1834 (see note to p. 43): workers 'sit enchanted, by the million, in their Poor-Law Bastille' (Carlyle, *Past and Present* (1843), Book 3, Chapter 6).

329 *Seaton*: Julia means Seacombe, now part of Wallasey, at the mouth of the Mersey estuary and a short ferry trip from Liverpool.

Savings' Banks . . . Ancient Shepherds: savings banks for the poor developed out of 'benefit clubs' and 'friendly societies' in the late eighteenth century; the Loyal Order of Ancient Shepherds is a friendly society founded at Ashton-under-Lyne, Lancashire, in 1826.

330 *biggin . . . Geyser*: a biggin is a coffee pot with an internal strainer; Geysir is the spouting volcanic spring of hot water in south-west Iceland from which other geysers take their name.

332 *the 73d*: the 73rd Regiment of Foot, later known as the Perthshire Regiment. The 17th Lancers were, in fact, still in Yorkshire in August 1842 and were among the troops who opened fire in Halifax on the 15th. It was the 72nd Regiment (later Seaforth Highlanders) who were sent to Lancashire and killed four strikers in Preston. The government used Scots and Irish regiments because they were less likely to identify with English strikers.

336 *younker*: youth, young man.

338 *dout*: douse, extinguish.

341 *emancipation of the Roman Catholics*: penal laws against Roman Catholics began to be removed in 1778 but Catholics could not take seats in the House of Commons until the Catholic Relief Act 1829. George III had refused to accept Catholic emancipation because it violated his Coronation Oath; George IV took a similar view until the fear of civil war in Ireland led the Duke of Wellington to persuade him that it was indispensable. In *The Young Duke* (1831) the hero's speech in the Lords in support of the Relief Act (Book V, Chapter VIII) is what persuades the heroine to like him.

346 *Morning Post*: a daily newspaper founded in London in 1772; originally Whig but Tory by the 1830s, it was taken over by the *Daily Telegraph* in 1937.

353 *not troops . . . yeomanry*: 'troops' are regular soldiers; 'yeomanry' were part-time, volunteer cavalry regiments.

354 *Riot Act*: the Riot Act (1714) authorized magistrates to declare any group of twelve or more people an unlawful assembly and require them to disperse. In practice it was not easy to hear whether the Act had been read out

to a noisy mob and the death penalty implications were reduced to transportation in 1837; the Act was repealed in 1973.

356 *the Castle was on fire*: probably suggested by the burning of Nottingham Castle in October 1831 by a mob protesting against the Duke of Newcastle's opposition to the Reform Bill.

357 *last year*: 1844.

Lady Palmerston's: Emily Lamb (1787–1869) was the sister of one Whig Prime Minister (Lord Melbourne) and the wife of another; she married Lord Palmerston in 1839 and became a famous political hostess, both at Broadlands in Hampshire and at their London house in Carlton Terrace.

Mr Mountchesney has resolved not to appeal: Mr Mountchesney seems to have received poor legal advice (see Introduction) but, despite the loss of the Mowbray estate, he would retain his wife's marriage settlement.

359 *three good harvests*: after a series of poor years, there were good harvests in 1842, 1843, and 1844, though Disraeli is ironically attributing the economic recovery produced by Peel's budget of 1842 to an accident of the weather.

360 *some volumes*: the three volumes of *Coningsby; or, the New Generation* (1844).

nearly fourteen years ago: on 9 June 1832, in his speech from the portico of the Red Lion during the High Wycombe by-election; see W. F. Monypenny and G. E. Buckle, *The Life of Benjamin Disraeli, Earl of Beaconsfield* (rev. edn, 2 vols, London: John Murray, 1929), 1.218.

American Literature

British and Irish Literature

Children's Literature

Classics and Ancient Literature

Colonial Literature

Eastern Literature

European Literature

Gothic Literature

History

Medieval Literature

Oxford English Drama

Philosophy

Poetry

Politics

Religion

The Oxford Shakespeare

A complete list of Oxford World's Classics, including Authors in Context, Oxford English Drama, and the Oxford Shakespeare, is available in the UK from the Marketing Services Department, Oxford University Press, Great Clarendon Street, Oxford OX2 6DP, or visit the website at www.oup.com/uk/worldsclassics.

In the USA, visit www.oup.com/us/owc for a complete title list.

Oxford World's Classics are available from all good bookshops. In case of difficulty, customers in the UK should contact Oxford University Press Bookshop, 116 High Street, Oxford OX1 4BR.